Night Meets the Elf Queen
THE ELF QUEEN SERIES BOOK 4

J.M. KEARL

Night Meets the Elf Queen

By J.M. Kearl
Copyright J.M. Kearl 2025
All rights reserved

The characters and events portrayed in this book are fictitious. Any similarity to real persons, living or dead, is coincidental and not intended by the author.

No part of this book may be reproduced, or stored in a retrieval system, or transmitted in any form or by any means, electronic, mechanical, photocopying, recording, or otherwise, without express written permission of the publisher.

Cover design by: Janie Hannan Kearl

For Travis, the love of my life, and our wonderful kids Jaylee and Titus.

CONTENTS

Content Notice	ix
Name Pronunciation Guide	xi
Book 1 Recap	1
Book 2 Recap	5
Book 3 Recap	9
Prologue	13
Chapter 1	19
Chapter 2	32
Chapter 3	45
Chapter 4	54
Chapter 5	74
Chapter 6	82
Chapter 7	91
Chapter 8	100
Chapter 9	113
Chapter 10	126
Chapter 11	144
Chapter 12	152
Chapter 13	166
Chapter 14	180
Chapter 15	192
Chapter 16	208
Chapter 17	219
Chapter 18	228
Chapter 19	236
Chapter 20	252
Chapter 21	261
Chapter 22	270
Chapter 23	279
Chapter 24	291

Chapter 25	300
Chapter 26	313
Chapter 27	327
Chapter 28	336
Chapter 29	349
Chapter 30	362
Chapter 31	373
Chapter 32	385
Chapter 33	394
Chapter 34	404
Chapter 35	415
Chapter 36	426
Chapter 37	438
Chapter 38	454
Chapter 39	472
Chapter 40	483
Chapter 41	497
Chapter 42	506
Chapter 43	511
Chapter 44	525
Chapter 45	536
Chapter 46	551
Chapter 47	561
Chapter 48	571
Chapter 49	577
Chapter 50	591
Chapter 51	602
Chapter 52	610
Chapter 53	627
Chapter 54	640
Chapter 55	650
Chapter 56	664
Chapter 57	672
Chapter 58	699
Epilogue	720

Acknowledgments	729
About the Author	731
Also by J.M. Kearl	733

CONTENT NOTICE

Please note this book includes content that may not be suitable for all audiences. Content includes violence, death, a villainous love interest, steamy content, mentions of domestic violence (not from the love interest), and profanity.

Name Pronunciation Guide

Layala- Lay- all-uh
Valeen- Vuh-leen
Katana- Kuh-tawn-uh
Evalyn- Ev-uh-lynn
Athayel- Ath-ā-el
Fennan- Fen-en
Mathekis- Math-eh-kiss
Atarah- Uh-tar-uh
Zaurahel- Zar-uh-hel
Ronan- Ro-nan
Orlandia- Or-land-ee-uh
Tifapine- Tif-uh-pine
Balneir- Bal-neer
Katana- Kuh-t-on-uh.
Servante- Serv-on-tay
Presco- Press-co

Palenor- Pal-eh-nor
Calladira- Cal-uh-deer-uh
Svenarum- Sven-are-um

NAME PRONUNCIATION GUIDE

Vessache- Vess-ach
Ryvengaard- Riven-gard
Adalon- Ad-uh-lon

Murlian- Mer-lee-an

Zythara– Z-ith-ar-uh: the name of Valeen's goddess blade

Realms
Runevale
Ryvengaard
Adalon
Underrealm
Serenity

The 7 primordials - the 7 original gods of Runevale
Valeen, goddess of night
Katana, goddess of day
Elora, goddess of wisdom
Creed, god of nature
Atlanta, god of waters
Synick, god of elements
Era, god of time

Drivaar & Primevar—two opposing sides of the gods. Drivaar worship the All Mother as the highest deity. The Primevar worship the Maker. They believe in the existence of both.

Book 1 Recap

Layala trained in hiding her entire life to kill the elf king, Tenebris, and his son, Prince Thane, for executing her parents and the raids in search of her, the last mage. Thane, her magic-bound mate from the time they were children, waited for the day to reunite with Layala but he couldn't do that until his evil father was gone. After Thane thought he killed King Tenebris, he went after Layala in her hometown of Briar Hollow where she lived among the humans. The time limit on their mate spell waned and he had to bring her to his home so she could take her place as Queen of Palenor beside him.

She had other plans, and after trying to take his life, they reached an agreement: if she could break their mate bond spell, they could part. She had eight weeks. During those weeks she learned the enemy wanted to use her to raise the Black Mage, the creator of the pale ones. The twisted, cursed elves were drawn to her magic and sought to take her captive.

She also found that Thane wasn't the wicked king she

believed him to be and with time and much back and forth they began to fall in love.

In the end she found a way to break the bond between them and chose not to.

Instead, she chose Thane.

They planned to marry and finish the mate spell before they would be cursed to turn into pale ones, but Thane's father returned from the "dead" and his lackey, the dragon shifter Varlett, broke the mate bond and abandoned Thane to die in the cursed forest.

After, Layala was taken captive and with a broken heart, left wondering: was Thane alive and if so, could he save her?

Book 2 Recap

Layala was held for weeks by the evil King Tenebris and his minions, Mathekis, and the dragon shifter Varlett. Thane spent weeks recovering from nearly being killed by Varlett with the old mage Vesstan and Tifapine.

After Layala tried to escape, King Tenebris placed her in a prison cart and they moved toward the Void to use her to bring back the Black Mage, the long-gone creator of the Void and the pale one curse. She was always said to be his destroyer or his salvation. All the while, she was being haunted by the Black Mage's voice, calling to her, asking her to go to him.

Thane and the Ravens rescued her before she could be forced into the dangerous Void, and the group went on the run to find a way to destroy the Void and the Black Mage along with it.

But Layala's dreams of the wicked Black Mage grew with intensity and vividness, only pushing her more to find the answers they needed: why she was connected to him and how to stop him. They fought pale ones, sirens, lost a friend, and killed the Lord of Calladira for the All Seeing Stone and then went to the dragon kingdom to find the Scepter of Knowing. There they meet Prince Ronan and the Royal Drakonan dragons, and Layala and Thane fought and bested the dragon prince Yoren to get the Scepter of Knowing.

Once the two pieces were put together, they accessed the goddess of wisdom, and she told them the key to ending the curse of the pale ones was the Black Mage's heart, and to get to him, Layala must wake him. They go to battle at the Void, the Ravens versus King Tenebris and his army. Layala nearly killed Thane's sister Talon to save her Aunt Evalyn and the battle began. In an epic fight, Layala had her chance to end Tenebris but was dragged into the Void by Varlett.

Thane fought him and ended his father's life. Layala was brought to the tower holding the Black Mage's body. When she saw him, she was surprised at how much he resembled Thane and how striking he was. With the intent to kill him and end the curse, she performed the magic to wake him, giving her blood and breath. But her blade broke on his chest, and he came to. His magic took hold of her, rendering her immobile, and with a wicked smile he announced that she was his wife, Valeen, the goddess of night reborn, and he was the god of mischief and magic, and Thane was his cousin, the god of war.

He wants revenge and his wife back.

Book 3 Recap

Hel, the Black Mage, and the god of mischief and magic woke up and wanted his wife and mate, Valeen, back. But Layala had no memory of him or her past life as Valeen, and she didn't want anything to do with it. The one she desired was Thane, the Elf King who she loved and she feared remembering could change that.

Hel was the wicked villain not to be trusted or believed. Despite protests from Thane and Layala, Hel moved into Castle Dredwich. He forced her to train with him so she could defend herself against a powerful enemy from another world. The Council of the Gods.

Every life before this, Layala, Hel, and Thane had been killed by assassins sent by the council who sentenced them to die and be reborn without memories of the reincarnated gods they truly were.

Through her training with Hel, pieces of her old life came back to her, and she began to see Hel as not just a villain responsible for a curse. Thane also started to remember that Hel was his cousin and as close to him as a brother. A brother he loved and couldn't fathom betraying by stealing his wife.

Not wanting to take advantage of her, Thane pushed Layala away. He suspected knowing the past might change how she felt about him... and Hel.

When assassins came close to killing Layala, and she was bitten by and almost turned into a pale one, Thane ended their relationship and told her to leave with Hel somewhere far away.

After going to Ryvengaard and meeting her friend Presco from her past, they planned to steal her journals detailing her life as the goddess of night. They snuck into the Drakonan Dragon Treasury to get them. Once she read the journals, her memory returned fully, and the betrayal by Varlett was revealed.

Knowing who she truly was, Valeen made her choice between Thane and Hel, and chose Hel.

They returned to Palenor and killed the demon prince assassin. Valeen and Thane talked about what their life might have been together, but she confessed she had chosen to be with Hel, and Thane, though heartbroken, accepted her choice.

With peace between Thane, Layala/Valeen, and Hel once more, she opened the portals to Runevale, home of the gods, and there her sister Katana was brought back to life, along with an old enemy, Synick.

PROLOGUE

A bright sun in the azure sky blanketed the fields of wildflowers, each petal shimmering with dew drops on the crisp morning air. With a wicker basket in hand, Katana whistled as she glided along beside the stream that cut through the heart of the meadow. A soft humming made her still for a moment.

A white fox trotted by and said, "Hello."

She waved back with a smile. "Good morning, Mrs. Sander."

She went back to her task of collecting a basket of flowers for the children who played near the fountain —those who were lost too young and waited for their parents to follow them. Seeing the smiles on their faces as she presented them each with a bright bloom was worth it. She plucked a handful of white daisies, a bunch of buttercups, and kept following the winding path of the creek until she came upon a serene grove with graceful willows, their verdant branches swaying in the breeze.

"Good morning, Katana," the largest willow said.

"Good morning to you too, Mr. Willow."

"A beautiful morning it is," he said in his gruff voice.

"Wonderful," she replied with a smile. Shafts of sunlight filtered through the canopy, dappling the ground below with patterns of light and shadow. Birdsong filled the air, a chorus of melodies... and then that humming again.

"Do you hear that, Mr. Willow?"

He twisted, his branches creaking, and a squirrel hopped down carrying an acorn. "I don't hear anything," the fluffy-tailed squirrel said.

"I only heard your whistling as you approached," said Mr. Willow.

She tilted her head, now following the sound of the humming rather than the creek. Her bare feet traipsed lightly over the soft green grass. What could it be?

She suddenly stilled, the hairs on the back of her neck standing on end. A patch of midnight lily blooms were before her... but they did not exist here. They only existed where the goddess of night did. "Valeen?" she whispered, glancing around. Was her sister here now too?

She grinned at the thought of not being alone anymore, and then slowly her smile fell. If Valeen were here that meant she had passed from mortality, that the Council of the Gods had won. It meant the realms were missing a beautiful spirit to protect them.

The humming continued until a split in the air above the lilies opened and soon grew to a large round circle tall and wide enough that she could easily walk through. On the other side the glittering night sky awaited, a place blanketed in ethereal darkness. And there she was, hair black as midnight, a face as lovely as the sunrise, eyes as blue as the midday sky. "Valeen!" she shouted in excitement, but her sister did not turn.

She stretched her fingers toward the shimmering pool, it was cool moist air to the touch. There were others with Valeen too.

"Go," called a soft voice from everywhere but nowhere.

She looked up among the willows and oaks. Could she go back to her old life? The basket in the crook of her elbow was more than just for flowers. It was for little faces who needed her. Of course she wasn't the only one who loved them but...

A tug in her chest almost seemed to jerk her forward toward the portal. How long had it been since she came to this place of peace and love? Leaving would mean pain and suffering, darkness and evil, that didn't exist here. It would mean facing what happened to her all over again. Here in this wonderful place, there was no fear, anger, jealousy, or murder.

She swallowed hard, setting the wicker basket down in the grass. Going back meant seeing her children, her sister, and the realms she missed. It was a chance at life anew. A chance she didn't think she'd ever have.

Mrs. Sander, the fox, appeared and took the basket handle into her mouth. She bobbed her soft furry head as if she knew what she was going to do.

"Thank you," she said with a smile.

Mrs. Sander trotted away with the basket swaying, heading back toward the children at the fountain. Katana took a deep, steadying breath and stepped from the light into darkness.

Chapter 1

VALEEN

Very little surprised a goddess who'd existed through the ages where life changed as often as shifting sands in a high tide. After she discovered the depths people would go to deceive and beguile for power. Mortals lived and died, their names remembered only in the history books if they should be so privileged. Even gods could be lost to the ravages of time, becoming mere remnants talked about over a pint of ale.

That was what she had become.

That was what her sister Katana had become too, a whisper in her memory. It was impossible and yet thousands of years after death had stolen the purest soul she'd ever known from this wretched world, the goddess of day now stood under the shimmering lights of the night sky.

Was she a mirage sent here to torment Valeen? Did

the All Mother wish to punish Valeen further for all her sins? Seeing how achingly beautiful her sister was, Valeen wondered how she ever could have let the image of her fade into the dark recesses of her mind.

Katana's alabaster blonde hair draped around her like a cloak, and the fitted pearl silk gown hung to her ankles. She stood still as a statue, lips parted, staring back at Valeen as if she couldn't trust her own eyes.

"Katana, is it you? Is it truly you?" Valeen's voice was barely above a whisper. It could be deception, a shapeshifter, but somehow deep in her heart, she knew it was her. Something in her soul recognized her as familiar as her own shadow. Her heart started beating faster with excitement.

Katana's face lit up with a beautiful smile. Oh, how she'd missed her sister's smile. It was like coming home. Their bond was the only thing she'd never questioned in all her existence. She was the only person Valeen had ever fully trusted. Katana's sun was the companion to her moon.

"Valeen. My dear sister. It is truly me." Tears welled and Katana put her hands over her heart.

"I'd hate to interrupt this joyous occasion but am I mistaken or are these my nephews with the goddess of night?" The tenor voice was one that had haunted Valeen's nightmares millennia ago, one she had not let bother her in as long.

Valeen tore her gaze away from Katana to the god she'd once driven the immortal killing weapon, Soulender, through. She'd stood over his body as he bled out on the floor of his bedroom and watched the life leave his eyes, watched him choke on the crimson that stained his lips. Some said that revenge never made a person feel better, but the satisfaction of watching that bastard die wasn't revenge, it was justice—and it had felt good.

He turned his head and Valeen gasped, he was no longer the beautiful god he once was. Half his face was grotesque. The white of his skull was visible in places where his skin decayed. His flesh on that half was shriveled and rotted, even oozing around his eye. While the other side was lovely and whole, the opposition made him even more repulsive.

Synick's fingers were stained black, soot smudged his face and sandy hair, his clothes were singed at the edges as if he'd fought his way through fire and ash to get here. The portal he'd come through made her believe he'd somehow crawled out of the underrealm, but he hadn't gotten out whole.

Her mind still reeled at the both of them standing close, standing at all. Immortal weapons were not banishments like what had happened to her, Hel, and War, they killed the immortal soul so they could not return to the realms of the living. Confusion and wonder danced with a slow simmer of cold fury. How was it that they both stood here now? Valeen had killed other gods with Soulender, and they never returned.

Could Valeen's magic have pulled Katana back to the land of the living? She had thought of her sister the moment the portal opened, and how her death was the domino that started everything...

It was Synick's slow perusal down her form that made the hairs on the back of her neck stand on end and goosebumps pebble her flesh. Those same disgusting eyes that longed for her from afar, watched her with lust. The corner of the decayed side of his mouth lifted, reminding her of the vile words he murmured in dark corners.

This was no illusion.

"Well, you're at least half dead." Hel, the god of mischief and magic, her mate, all cool and darkness, gripped her arm and the whisper of his magic coiled around her. "And if you ever look at my wife like that again, Synick, I will carve your fucking eyes out." Hel's voice was low and venomous.

"Wife?" His single brow rose.

"Wife, mate, queen—*Mine*."

"I don't know what's more surprising," he glanced over at Katana, "seeing her alive again after I stuck an immortal sword through her belly or witnessing the betrayal of my most promising protege."

The cool weight of Soulender appeared in Valeen's palm. "Don't look at her!" She wrapped her fingers around the hilt until her hand began to ache. "Look at me. I'm the one you always wanted and could never have."

Katana stepped back slowly, terror widening her eyes, then she whirled and ran.

"Katana! Wait!" Valeen ripped free of Hel's grasp and sprinted after her, boots flying over soft grass until a sizzling bolt of lightning lit up the night. She threw up her shield and was struck by a searing blast that swept her feet out from under her. Her shoulder hit the ground first, shooting pain through her arm, pain that drove her to her feet faster.

Synick glared with hate-filled brown eyes. "You think I'd let you walk away after you killed me and sent me to the underrealm to be tortured for eternity?" Ten creatures materialized from shadow, five on each side of him, men-like with rotting skin falling off their starved muscles, carrying stained bone-handled weapons, edges with a green gooey substance. Poison.

"You sent yourself there," Hel said, and then everything exploded into chaos. The skeleton men charged with guttural war cries. Hel was already inches from Synick, the weight of his magic in the air. Valeen's elven companions, Leif and Piper, clashed with the skeletons. Metal hit metal, roars through gritted teeth filled the night. Presco, her dragon right hand, half-shifted into his beast form, talons every bit as lethal as daggers to shred through bone, and Thane, the elf king she once thought she'd spend her life with, looked to her.

"Find my sister. Protect her. Please." Valeen wanted to go after her, but she couldn't leave Hel. Synick was a primordial god, as old as time, and even if Hel was powerful and feared, she would not risk losing him.

"Then you must make sure that nothing happens to them." He threw a glance at Piper and Leif.

"I will."

Thane pressed his lips together, held her blue eyes for a moment, then disappeared into the dark. She had to trust that he would find her and keep her safe.

Varlett, the dragon shifter she despised, and yet was forced into companionship with, ran in with talons slashing. She cut down three in a matter of moments... but the undead bodies reformed, pieces that had been cut off rolled back together and attached.

The monsters rose again.

Presco adjusted his glasses, taking a step back. "Regenerative like the gargoyles at the Treasury."

Not again, she thought and searched for Hel. Panic shot through her—she couldn't find him or Synick. "HEL!" She sprinted forward to where she last saw them locked in a fight. "Sever their heads and keep them separated!" she commanded the others.

Her mind reached out for him, *Hel, where are you?* Blood rushed in her ears like war drums, terror clawed its way through her. She could not lose him again.

"Hel!" She charged up the hillside and found an ice storm swirling in a tornado around Hel. The shadow of his form could be seen inside. He stood upright as if he were shielded against it, but for some reason he couldn't escape from the cage of the winter maelstrom.

In a drift of shadow, Valeen appeared behind Synick, reforming and swinging her golden blade. He dipped and the blade whooshed over the top of his head.

She hacked down at him. He rolled and sprung back to his feet. A bone-handled sword came up to meet her next strike and they pushed against one another.

"You think it's revenge I want for what you did," Synick said. "But I don't want to kill you. I want your body. I want the child from you I never got."

Valeen dropped her shoulder and sidestepped, letting him stumble forward. She threw her fist and cracked his jaw. The pain in her knuckles was worth the satisfaction of seeing him falter and hearing him groan. Shadows seeped around her ankles and feet and slipped from her hands.

The gale force winter winds around Hel began to

slow. He punched his arm through, cracking a hole through the ice.

"You hit hard, goddess, I'll give you that." He swiped the corner of his mouth. "But it won't be enough. I *will* have you. I don't care about Hel's claim. We primordials were always meant to be together."

"The only thing that is meant to be is my sword through your heart."

He ran at her, wildly swinging his weapon. She dipped and bobbed, easily maneuvering out of range. His feet were unsteady and his body off balance. He roared, getting angrier with each miss. Valeen hooked her ankle around his and he fell forward onto his hands and knees. She smiled.

"I see you learned nothing in the underrealm. You are as dreadful at combat as you were when I killed you last time. It almost makes this less satisfying."

His mouth curled into an unsettling grin. "I could say the same about your sister. The way she screamed when the blood ran down her flesh. The horror in those big eyes. Now that was satisfying." With a snarl, he thrust out his palm, sending a blast of icy wind. Even if combat wasn't his strength, this was. Shards of ice like tiny daggers hit her shield, building a wall of frost before her, impossible to see through.

Moments later, he crashed through it and tackled her to the ground, knocking the wind out of her lungs. His heavy body pressed her into the grass while she bucked and fought his weight. She swung the butt of Soulender, knocking him on the temple. It split his skin and blood oozed down the side of his face, but he wrapped his hands around her neck.

"Now I have you exactly as I've always wanted."

A scream of rage ripped from her, shadows and vines coiling around him like a giant serpent. Blackness seeped into his eyes, his open mouth, and then he was the one screaming. He slapped his hands to the sides of his head, pressing in as if it would ease the fire. She would burn out his insides, until he lost consciousness.

Suddenly he was torn off her, flying backward. Hel had him by the top of his scalp and slammed him on the ground, dropping a knee into his gut, and shoved the point of his sword to his heart.

Valeen yelled, "Wait! We could use him alive."

Hel's arm trembled, his garnet eyes filled with malice she'd rarely seen. He was usually calm, even when killing, but now, he was on the verge of losing himself to fury. His beautiful face was twisted. The shadows around his eyes, and the curl of his lip made him as terrifying as any monster that hunted in the underrealm. A little more pressure and his sword would go straight through Synick, and if he wasn't immortal anymore, he was dead.

"He is the only one who knows where the Sword of Truth is." They could use Synick as leverage against the Council of the Gods. He knew of the *only* other weapon that could kill a god. It also occurred to her that with the portal now open again, the council could get to him in the underrealm... if the demon princes allowed it. In the past, the three princes wouldn't let anyone near him and since it was their realm, not even the gods could find him there.

But since Valeen killed one of the brothers only days before, there was no telling what they might do, what deal they might be willing to make with the council. For all she knew, the princes were the ones who had given him the power to control the undead.

They needed information from him, and they needed to know that when they ended him, he wouldn't be able to come back.

"Do it," Synick hissed. "Don't be a coward, Hel. Mercy is not what I taught you."

Hel leaned in closer, and said through his teeth, "Killing you *would* be a mercy compared to what I'm going to do."

Valeen kicked Synick in the face, snapping his head to the side. He didn't turn back, and for a moment she worried she'd broken his spine, but his chest still moved with breath. Hel flicked his fingers, and a fluorescent green rope appeared in his hands. He quickly bound Synick's wrists and ankles tying an intricate knot. Then slowly, he rose up. "Gods, he is just as powerful as he was. And he knows my tricks, Val." His hard eyes settled on her. "He *knows* me. He trained me *and* War." Hel swore under his breath and turned away.

She swallowed hard and reached for his hand. "He knew who you *were*, not the nightmare you are now. We have the upper hand." Hel was used to always being steps ahead, he had an uncanny ability to outmaneuver his enemies, but Synick's appearance threw a boulder into his carefully thought-out plans. It was rare to see him rattled like this. Synick unsettled them both for different reasons.

Varlett walked up and crossed her arms. "You should kill him now. I think letting him live even to question him would be a mistake. If he gets free..."

Hel's upper lip curled. "Where the fuck were you?"

"Trying not to die," she growled back. "Those monsters aren't easy to put down."

Valeen shook her head. "We need him alive. The Sword of Truth is leverage that could win us this war. They might even surrender if we have both weapons."

"I will not accept a surrender. Not after what they did," Hel said. "We need katagas serum to subdue his magic. This suppressing rope won't be enough to hold him for long."

"Will it work on him?" Valeen asked.

Varlett opened a pouch on the side of her pant leg, taking a clear vial and a barb out.

"It works on you, doesn't it?" He took the barb and dipped it into the vial then jabbed it into Synick's neck.

"I'm in a mortal elven body, it wouldn't work on an immortal. And it doesn't work on you," Valeen argued.

"I made myself immune to it with micro doses. He hasn't. And since he was knocked unconscious by a kick, he has a weakened body like us." Hel grabbed Synick's chin and turned his face. Blood oozed out of the good side of his mouth. "And if that wasn't proof enough, he's half rotten. All immortal gods are without imperfection and have a luminescence about them. He doesn't. He didn't get to come back from the dead the same as before."

"I need to make sure everyone else is alright." Valeen made her way back up to the crest of the hill where she was able to peer down at where the other battle had happened. The undead creatures that came with Synick had their heads and arms cut off, all pinned down by boulders, spare rope, or weapons separately. Each body part wiggled and moved, fighting to reform.

Piper walked over, sheathing her sword. "We have them all restrained for now. But we'll need a more permanent solution. The nasty things are still trying to come back together. One of the heads kept snapping its jaws at me."

"Eww." Valeen shuttered. "We can hold them in the dungeons of my castle... assuming it's still mine. Or drop them into the sea with heavy stones tied to them."

"The second option." Hel walked up behind her. "Even when we have your castle. They can't be near Synick for him to control."

Piper peered out into the darkness over Valeen's shoulder. "There's no sign of Thane yet. Or your sister."

Valeen turned, facing the direction Katana and Thane had gone. Katana must be terrified after coming back from... wherever she was, and Valeen was the only one she'd trust. *Unless,* the hairs on the back of her neck rose, *unless she doesn't remember me. Maybe that's why she ran.*

Piper continued, "I went into your room after you left and found the cards with all the gods. I asked Thane about Katana since it said she was your sister. He told me the story of how she was murdered by Synick and why. I'm surprised you didn't kill him."

"Trust me, I want to, but we need to interrogate him first. We need the other immortal weapon." It took everything in her not to cut off his head right then. She hoped keeping him alive was the right move and it didn't come back to bite them later.

"Good thinking." But Piper frowned down at his unconscious body.

Heavy footsteps trod in. Presco's pearl scales still

covered his body as he joined them. He pushed his round, gold glasses up further on his nose. "I can go look for War and Katana. I'll find them the fastest from the sky."

"Take me with you," Valeen said. "She doesn't know anyone but me and she's scared."

Hel's white wings materialized, and he shook his head. "I'll be taking you."

"Hel, one of us needs to stay with Synick. When he wakes up, he will be able to use persuasion on them until they're trained to resist it." Varlett would likely be able to withstand persuasion, but Leif and Piper wouldn't, and she couldn't trust Varlett to help them.

He didn't look happy when he said, "Go." *But if you're not back soon, I'll come looking, Synick be damned.*

Valeen shifted to shadow while Presco transformed into his dragon. With ease she drifted in her airy form onto Presco's back, settling into place on his hard scales. She thought of the last time she'd rode on a dragon with Hel before she remembered everything. The way she was afraid to desire him but falling fast. How he looked at her like she was a star he wanted to capture but was scared of the burn. He had that same expression on his face now. Fighting between letting her go and wanting her to stay.

"Find Tifapine!" Valeen hollered, as she scanned the grass. She'd likely run to hide during the fight, but she usually didn't go far.

"I'll look for her!" Leif yelled back.

Presco lifted into the night sky with his great wings picking up wind, blowing Piper's red hair loose from its tie.

"We need to hurry." Valeen gripped the spike in

front of her as they soared. "I'm worried Synick wasn't alone coming from the underrealm, and Varlett has the demon prince's ring. They'll be looking for it."

"Hel is formidable on his own," Presco said. "I worry more he will abandon them to come for you. You will always be his first priority."

Chapter 2

THANE

Thane's breaths came even and steadily as he sprinted through the dark landscape. Leaving behind every person he cared about while they were in a fight went against most of his instincts, except one, protecting a maiden who was scared and possibly helpless. From what he knew about the goddess of day, she was kind and wouldn't hurt anyone, maybe not even to defend herself.

She was faster than he anticipated. He'd been running for at least a mile and hadn't caught her yet, but her scent kept him in the right direction. It was unmistakable, like the embodiment of lavender and sunshine.

He picked up his pace, sensing he was drawing closer and caught sight of her silvery dress in the light of the moons. She had stopped under a large weeping willow, the branches offering partial cover. He slowed and glanced down at the weapons in both hands. These would only frighten her more, so he tucked them in the sheaths on his back and walked carefully toward her.

As he came up to the outside of the hanging willow branches, she partially hid herself behind the wide trunk, her fingers clutching the bark. She peeked out, her lavender-colored eyes locking onto his. Something warmed in the gaping hole in his chest that had been there since his mate bond to Layala was broken. He'd grown so accustomed to the emptiness he'd forgotten it was there.

He held up his hands to show he didn't have weapons, and a gesture meant to show no harm. "You're Katana, right?"

"Yes," she said softly, but didn't come out from behind the tree. There was fear in her trembling voice. "Why are you following me?

"Valeen asked me to find you and help you. I'm not here to harm you."

With brows furrowed, she hid herself a little more behind the trunk. "And you are?"

"My name is Thane. I'm a friend of Valeen's. Are you alright?"

"Why did she not come herself?"

"A fight broke out as soon as you ran. She wanted to."

"If she sent you in her place, she trusts you."

He moved the curtain-like branches aside and stepped into the tree's canopy. Tucking her blonde hair behind her ear, she cautiously moved out from the tree trunk, a sign she trusted him enough not to run again. The silhouette of her figure was outlined against the moonlight behind her, the brightness of her hair lit up from the backlighting. She was beautiful. Valeen always said she was the most beautiful of the goddesses and having seen her, he wouldn't argue that. It wasn't just her lovely face, thick hair, or the curves of her body, there was something else about her. Like she radiated goodness.

That warmth in his chest tingled now.

A branch swung in his face and when he lifted his hand to move it out of his way, she flinched and back stepped ready to retreat again. Someone had hit her before... and though he only just met her, it pissed him off.

He froze. "I promise I won't hurt you."

Relaxing some, she forced a smile. "I am..." she trailed off, as if contemplating her existence. "I am in Runevale."

"Yes."

"And so are you."

He smiled. "I am."

"How?"

"I don't know."

She looked around with an almost childlike wonder. "I heard a voice... but I do not remember where I was. Yet, I know in my heart it was lovely and good. It was without evil and malice."

Thane rubbed his chin, wondering if she'd been in what they called Serenity, a place where good souls went after mortality. "Do you remember Valeen?"

"Of course. She is my sister."

He tried to think back to the time when she was alive here, but it was long before he was born as War. She was killed at least a thousand years before his birth. He wouldn't know events and people of that time.

"Why were you all with Synick?" Her beautiful face scrunched in disgust.

"We weren't with him. He appeared at the same time as you."

"What do you mean by appeared?"

"A portal opened."

"From where?"

"I can only make a guess. He was dead, but I don't think he was in the same place you were, if you understand."

"He killed me." She pawed at her long locks then she lifted her eyes again, curious now, not fearful. "If he was dead, who killed him?"

"Valeen. A very long time ago."

"How long has it been?"

He was growing a little uncomfortable talking about her death. She was a complete stranger, and though he knew some facts about what happened through Valeen, it wasn't as if he could offer her comfort. "A few thousand years."

"A few *thousand*?" she repeated and put a hand over her mouth. She slowly dragged her delicate fingers down her chin and over her throat, coming to rest in a balled fist at her chest. "All Mother above," she whispered. "My children, are they well? How is Valeen?"

It was strange she didn't mention her husband Atlanta. "I can't speak of your children because I don't know. Valeen is—well, she's been gone too. Exiled by the Council of the Gods."

The corner of her mouth twitched, and she blinked several times. "I think I knew that. I think I have come to help her. She has not been in House of Night. She needs her home back."

Thane smiled. "Yes. She was reborn as an elf in Adalon, but we're here now."

"Reborn? But she is a goddess."

"When I said the council exiled her, I meant they took her immortality and killed her, forcing her to be reborn over and over, never remembering who she was... until now."

She frowned at that. "My poor sister. She does not deserve that cruelty." Her lavender eyes trailed over him from head to toe. "You are also an elf, but I sense something more."

"I am the god of war, my name was War. The same thing happened to me as Valeen."

"But you said your name is Thane."

He chuckled. "I can see how that would be confusing. Twenty-nine years ago, I was reborn as an elf, the son of an Elf King. I was named Thane Athayel, and I am now the High Elf King in Palenor. I think I prefer that name. War is not all of who I am. The act of war itself is ugly and the more I think about it the more I don't want to be called that anymore."

"Thane," she said and smiled, flashing pretty white teeth. "If you and Valeen were both exiled together—what is your relationship to her? What was your crime?"

Thane rubbed his lips together then let out a long slow breath. "Now, that is a question."

She giggled and it sounded like bells. "I should think it is a fairly simple one."

"It's quite complicated actually."

"A lover?"

"Once," he replied.

"Ah," she said as understanding dawned on her. "A story for another time."

"A story Valeen can tell you." He didn't want to relive it again. It hurt too much. It hurt seeing her with someone else, even if he understood it, even if he'd let her go. All those months after Hel woke up, he'd waited for Layala to remember her past, holding out hope that she'd choose him. He should have known better.

Valeen would always choose Hel, even if when she was simply Layala, she had been his.

"And the crime?"

"For the most part, taking her side when the council found out she stole the weapon Soulender. They want it back."

She bobbed her head. "I think I knew that too. My memory of the place I was in is fuzzy. Like waking up from a dream and the details fade, lost to the aether."

He glanced over his shoulder, back toward the way they'd come. He needed to return to the others, even if he trusted Hel and Valeen to be able to handle it. Something could go wrong. Synick was a primordial and as ruthless as anyone—he would know, Synick had mentored him. Then the moonlight caught something small and white dangling from the branches above. Thane furrowed his brows and realized an insect dropped onto Katana's shoulder, a long-legged spindly thing.

So he wouldn't alarm her, he said as calmly as he could. "There's a spider on you." Would it be rude to bat it off? He didn't want to touch her without permission. It was not like they were friends, barely acquaintances.

Her eyes flashed and she started swatting randomly. "Where? Get it off me."

It crawled over her shoulder. Shit. He quickly closed the distance between them and turned her, pushing her hair aside. It could be poisonous, and the last thing he needed was to carry her back to Valeen with a deadly bite.

Goosebumps peppered her skin with his touch. The spider skittered under the hem of the back of her dress just as he spotted it. Gods, was he going to—"It went under your dress, I—"

"Get it! Get it!" She shook her body and squealed.

He tried not to laugh as he plunged his hand inside her silk gown, swiping for the nuisance critter. If it were Val or Piper, he wouldn't think twice, but this was the goddess of day. A legend. "I can't find it." But he certainly found soft luscious skin.

"It is on the left side! I feel the legs!"

The hem of her silky underwear brushed his fingers, but still no spider. With a jerk on the string that held the back of her dress together, the fabric fell open. She wrapped her arms around herself to hold the front up, and the white spider about the size of the pad of his thumb crawled on the top of her—ass. With a quick swipe he knocked it into the grass and the heel of his boot drove it into its grave.

"Got it," he said triumphantly.

She turned and searched the ground to be certain. Then her eyes lifted to his and she started laughing. "Imagine, a primordial goddess terrified of spiders. Thank you. I feel more vulnerable than before. I do not think I am what I once was."

"Lay—Valeen and I know the feeling. Hel is a little

different. His magic is as strong as it ever was." As an elf, even with a god's healing abilities, speed, strength and magic, Thane wasn't a full god without his immortality. There were vulnerabilities to his body and even magic that weren't there before.

"Hel? And did you say 'Lay'?"

"Oh, right, you don't know him. Zaurahel is Valeen's husband and mate." He shifted anxiously thinking of all that had transpired the past eight months. "Recently reconciled."

"It never ends well when two males love the same goddess. It often results in war. Territorial things, you are."

"We've already been there and done that," Thane said with a chuckle. "In another life. We've moved past it. And Valeen was reborn as Layala, but she doesn't want to be called that anymore."

"But you still want to be known as your elf name," she said with an air of curiosity to her voice.

"Right." His gaze dropped and heat inched up his neck. Breasts. Round, full breasts. The silk dress she held pressed against her chest, barely covered her nipples and he felt like scum for noticing, but they were hard to miss. He was sure she had no idea how much she had exposed and quickly turned his head away. "Your dress is, um, falling."

"Oh, dear, I am sorry. I did not mean to give you a free peek." She grinned like it bothered him more than her and tugged the straps over her shoulders. "Well, now that you have practically gotten me out of my dress, you will have to tie it back up."

His heart skipped a beat, and he pressed his lips together to keep from smiling. Already she was different than he might have guessed. Clearly she wasn't shy. "Of course." He stepped behind her and his fingers trembled as if he were a young lad touching a lady for the first time and pulled the two pieces together and threaded the string through the loop. "We need to get back to the others and I think I'll insist you come with me. It could be dangerous out here."

With the turn of her head, he caught the smile tugging at the corners of her lovely mouth. "You are a protector by nature."

"As a king, it's my duty."

"And as a god. Protector of the realms," she added.

"Yes, that too." He finished tying the bow and stepped back, even tucking his hands behind himself like if he didn't, they'd touch her again of their own volition.

He still felt like both sides of him fought for dominance. He couldn't ignore his past, but he preferred his life as Thane, as High King. Maybe because it was most recent, but he wasn't adapting to this new reality as quickly as Valeen seemed to be. He remembered and accepted it before her, but he longed to be in Palenor. He longed to be at Castle Dredwich. Maybe because he hadn't yet seen his family here, but Runevale, home of the gods, and Ryvengaard, home of the dragons, were distant memories. Bad memories. This place felt like tragedy.

Whooshing wings caught his attention. He turned, pushing her behind him and nudged her up against the tree with his backside, protectively standing in front of her. Metal slid against metal as he tugged a sword free and his magic hummed in his veins.

"What is it?" she whispered.

A great dragon was in the sky above them, from here it looked like a shadow. It was massive, with lighter scales, so it wasn't Varlett—her dragon form was jet-black. *Please don't be an enemy.* The last thing he wanted to fight right now was a dragon. The beast began to lower until pearl scales glimmered in the moons' light. Thane sighed and peeked over his shoulder. "It's Presco."

"You know this dragon?"

"Yes, he's a shifter and Valeen's right-hand man."

She nodded and released the hold around his bicep. He hadn't even realized she'd grabbed him until she let go.

"Come on. It's safe." He led the way out with Katana close behind.

Valeen dropped from Presco's back, boots hitting with a soft thud. She brushed the white streak in her black hair out of her face and sauntered forward. Her steps started slow, until Katana came out from behind Thane. Valeen's broke into a smile, and she ran, throwing her arms around Katana.

Katana embraced her back, and both of them choked on sobs, trying to talk but unable to get words out. Even Thane felt his throat tightening up at their reunion. It was the reunion he wished he could have gotten with Hel, if only things had gone different in the past.

"I can't believe it's you!" Valeen's voice wavered with emotion. She finally pulled back and looked her in the face. "It's really you." She wiped the tears off her cheeks but more flowed.

"It is me, and I hardly believe it myself. How are you?"

Valeen sobbed and hugged her again. "Oh, Katana, I'm fine. What about you? Do you feel well? I don't understand what happened, but it doesn't matter, you're here."

Katana brushed her hand over Valeen's hair like a mother would and wiped her sister's tears but let her own fall. "I do not know either, but I missed you. You are as beautiful as I remember. And what is this?" She picked up the white piece of her hair and then giggled when she touched Valeen's pointed ear then her moon and star crown. "The night elf queen!"

"I know, it's strange, isn't it?" she said, laughing with her. Thane wasn't sure he'd ever seen Valeen so happy. It warmed his chest to see her lit up like this. She turned to him. "Thane introduced himself, I hope. You can trust him. He's one of my closest friends."

"He did." She nodded and they stepped apart. "He is lovely."

"When he wants to be."

"Hey." Thane narrowed his eyes. "I ran after her when you asked. A 'thank you' would be nice." He assumed everyone else was fine based on her behavior. If there were trouble, she'd be dragging him back to fight.

"Thank you, Thane." Valeen grinned, took Katana's hand, and tugged her toward Presco. "Let's go. I want to introduce you to the others. You need to meet Hel."

Katana halted and pulled her hand back.

Valeen's eyes flicked to Thane then back to her sister. "It's alright. Synick can't hurt you. We've... subdued him."

"What if he gets free?" she said, barely more than a whisper. "I am not ready to see him. I cannot."

"We won't let him hurt you," Thane added.

"You don't have to." Valeen's lips formed a hard line, and she shoved her hand into her hair. "Thane, Presco can take you back to the others, and Katana and I will wait here until you hide Synick somewhere."

"I'm not leaving you both here. We don't know who is in control of this territory right now. We don't know if Synick was alone. We don't know if your wall held up after all this time. This place could be crawling with the council's assassins. The new ruler here could see you as a threat. We don't know anything."

"We'll be fine."

"No."

"I suppose it's alright if you stay with her though, *War,* right? I'm done with the double standards. You and Hel both have treated me like I'm a porcelain doll."

Thane rolled his eyes. "*Thane,* and it's not about that, Valeen. The council hunts you first, not me. I'm not the one with Soulender, you are. That is why Hel and I are so protective over you. You should appreciate that we care about you so much."

"I love you both and I do appreciate it but sometimes it's smothering," Valeen said, calmly. "And I don't think you should be saying that I have you-know-what so loudly."

He looked around. "Do you see anyone else here besides us? And I doubt Presco would want to leave you either." Thane clenched his teeth. Maker above, she could be a pain in the ass. The most stubborn person he'd ever met. Always had been. Sometimes he wondered why he ever loved her to begin with. Half of their relationship had been arguing.

"Don't bring me into this," Presco grumbled, laying his head on his huge paws.

"Well, if there's no one around, you should be fine going with Presco while we wait. Maybe Katana and I will just start walking and find my castle. You can meet us there."

"*Valeen.*"

Full of attitude, she folded her arms. "Thane."

"You know what, I think I will go get Hel and maybe your *husband* can get you to listen, because you damn sure never listen to me."

"I don't need a couple of *broody* males telling me what to do but thank you."

"Exactly how long ago were you lovers?" Katana interrupted. "I am getting the feeling that it was… recent."

Too bloody recent, he thought, turning away from Valeen. He couldn't even look at her at the moment. If they didn't need each other to survive, they would be better off with some time apart. *Far* apart too. Things were certainly easier for him when she and Hel were in an entirely different realm in Ryvengaard.

After a long stretch of silence Katana said, "I will go. I will go with you both to find the others, so no one has to stay here with me. Just keep Synick away from me."

Chapter 3

HEL

With magic dragging Synick along behind him, Hel trudged ahead. His memory of this land wasn't as sharp as he thought it would be. The vast open grassy fields with sparse trees and black rocky cliffs jutting out in various places were familiar, but he hadn't the faintest idea where Valeen's old castle was located from here. It could be in any direction. He glanced up at the stars, even they were different from Adalon, the constellations forming in unique shapes. The brightest stars in the sky stood North and the other South, the southernmost star being red.

He stopped and pulled out a civar, the end already lit and bright in the low evening light and brought it to his lips. Where was the damned castle from here? He flicked through his memory for the stars she'd built it beneath. The ones they'd danced and made love under many times. He thought of the time they laid on the balcony that hung off their room, he could see her pointing up and turning to smile at him. He remembered how beautiful she looked, how carefree and light compared to what she was now, while she explained why she built her castle in that specific place... they weren't even married yet and all he could think about was his burning desire to kiss her, to touch her, but was it something to do with horses?

He quietly swore as the specifics eluded him and let out a cloud of smoke. It had been so long ago. Some events of that time were branded into his mind, a scar he could never escape, and others were lost as if the wind carried them away and stored them somewhere else. It was there though, on the tip of his tongue.

Leif, Piper, and Varlett in her dragon form, were taking care of the undead. Varlett carried the two elves in her dragon form to the sea to drop the creatures of the underrealm into a watery grave. The brine of it was faint in the air so he knew it wasn't far. Varlett might remember, but he couldn't even stomach looking at her let alone ask for her help.

There was nothing more he wanted to do than shove his hand into Varlett's chest and rip her heart out. But breaking the link between her and Valeen would be tricky. If he used rune magic to combat Varlett's spell, there would be other consequences; she would have taken precautions. The bitch was clever and had learned much of what she knew from him.

Hel paused and pressed his boot on the back of Synick's head, driving his face into the grass. His former mentor mumbled and bucked, drawing a smile out of Hel. It was only a small payback for the years of torture Hel had endured at his hand, and for what he'd done to his wife and her sister.

Asking Valeen the constellation she'd build her castle directly under was an option, obviously, but he wanted to find it before she did. She held out hope that everything would be as it once was, that her castle would stand strong, that it would have been memorialized and made into a temple they'd keep excellent care of.

He didn't share her sentiments, even if he kept it to himself. Two thousand years was a long time, and she might have been too caught up in the chaos of Katana and Synick's return to notice, but one of the three moons was cracked, pieces of it floated apart from the silver orb. Her magical wall that kept her territory, House of Night, protected from the rest of Runevale's territories was connected to the strength of those moons. He took another deep inhale off his civar, sending a sense of calm through his body, even if it only lasted moments, it aided in keeping his treacherous thoughts at bay.

Given the state of the moon Fennor, Valeen's wall had likely fallen, and he hesitated to even imagine what that meant, what this place had become in their absence. *Fuck.* The council would have done horrible things to Villhara and her people to show everyone what happened to those who stood against them.

A rustle in the grass behind him pulled his attention. Hel finally lifted his boot off Synick's head and turned. The magic in his veins flared ready to seek and kill.

A dull red hat poked out first, then the little gnome named Tifapine parted the tall grass, an inch or two over her head, and stepped up beside him. She adjusted her hat, brushed her stubby hands over her dirty floral-print dress and lifted her big brown eyes. "Um, hello. I hope you don't mind that I've been following you. It's scary out here."

For some irrational reason he had the urge to squat down to her level, but he didn't. "They've been looking for you."

"I heard Leif and Piper calling for me, but those monsters were by them, and I am not cut out to be dealing with monsters. One of the arms, and I mean only the arm, tried to grab me. The fingers pulled it forward in the grass!" she wailed.

That was disturbing, even to him, and for a small gnome, he could only imagine. "If safety is your priority, I'm surprised you didn't wait for Valeen to return before you came out of hiding." He and the gnome weren't well acquainted. If anything, she'd been scared of him in the past.

"Well," she began and tapped her chin with a finger, "since you're her, um, lover now, I suppose you're safe. There isn't anyone scarier than you and you're on our side now. And you wouldn't hurt someone as cute as me, you said so yourself. Even if Thane said I should stay far away from you. He exaggerates sometimes."

He smiled and took another pull from his civar. "I'm her husband and mate, more than a lover. And although your king is probably correct, I wouldn't hurt you."

"I've been meaning to ask but since those creepy things appeared and you had to fight, it didn't seem like the opportune time, but why are there three moons? And why is one of them broken, and one of them is red at the center, it almost looks like it's bleeding."

"There are three because that's the way that it is." He pointed at the one with the crimson center. "That's Luna. They say that Soulender was forged from the heart of it and that's why she bleeds."

Her eyes widened and she clutched her hat on both sides, tugging on it. "Is that true?"

"Might be. Might just be an old tale. The broken one is Fennor... I don't know why it's broken. Perhaps a falling star impacted it." Or the council got to it somehow. "The one with the rings is Nuna."

"I don't see any rings around any of them."

Hel looked again and frowned. The once bright rings were so faint they were barely visible. The gnome probably didn't have the eyesight to catch them. He roughly scrubbed at his chin cursing himself for not realizing it before. Another sign the protective wall had likely fallen.

"Where are you going?" Tifapine asked.

"Looking for Valeen's castle."

"Is it nearby?"

"I believe so. She built it"—the location suddenly came to him—"in the northwest under the constellation of the rearing winged horse Sargentos."

After searching the glittering night sky full of moving colors of amethyst, turquoise, and bright green, he found Sargentos. If he went north about three miles, her castle should be there.

"Should we wait for the others, or can we go look? She was just telling me how beautiful it was last night, made of moonstone so it glowed in the dark and crescent moons and stars adorned the peaks and valleys of it. She said the path leading to the castle entrance was paved with shimmering black stones that reflected the stars above, and it sounds so beautiful. She said the air smelled like ever blooming wisteria and jasmine and her black lilies from her big gardens. I can't wait to see it."

"If you can keep up, you can come."

"My little legs don't go very fast so I might fall behind, but I'll find your trail through the grass," she said, as chipper as ever.

He took one last pull from his civar then pressed his lips together. Why did it bother him to let the tiny creature lag behind? He stooped down and picked her up around her chubby middle and set her on his shoulder.

"Wo," she said with a giggle. "I wasn't expecting to get to ride on the master of darkness's shoulder."

"The master of what?"

"You have a dimple when you smile. It's strange that it gives me tummy butterflies." She blushed furiously, twirling a curl around her finger. "Oh, and I said the master of darkness. It's what you are, isn't it? I like it better than the Black Mage, and I'm not sure if we're on a first name basis quite yet. Unless you prefer I call you Hel."

"I think I like the master of darkness." He chuckled and dropped his civar onto Synick's face and stepped on it with his boot, smashing it in.

"Ahh, that burns!"

"Does it? I never would have guessed." He was tempted to end him now and be rid of the problem. How much of a fight would it be with Valeen? He licked his lower lip, would it be worth the argument? Either way, at some point in the very near future, Synick was dead for touching Valeen. The way he'd put his hands around her neck... Hel stepped on Synick's hand, smashing his fingers, and didn't stop until he heard the bones pop.

Synick cried out once and slammed his jaw shut. Then with a snap of Hel's fingers he floated off the ground a few inches and trailed behind him once more.

After a brisk walk Hel came upon a familiar black rocky ridge. The shiny boulders jutted up above the grass about ten feet, and in the valley below awaited the location of Castle Starcrest.

Quickening his pace, he stepped into a gap between the rocks. The wind picked up, whisking his black hair about, snapping his cloak behind him. Unease twisted his gut and Hel gulped. Tifapine gasped and put a hand over her mouth.

It was indeed Valeen's castle—in ruins. The moonstone had crumbled in on itself with moss and other vegetation growing on top of it. One section where the walls still stood was riddled with holes and weathered stone. Vine-like weeds overtook much of it, and a great oak grew out of what he suspected was once her throne room. Although there were many flowers blooming around it, one couldn't say there was a flower garden as there once was. Grass, weeds, and a few birch and aspen trees grew in between the blooms as the wilds took over.

It was in worse shape than the manor in Ryvengaard they'd stayed at for months while he trained Valeen, where she slowly began to remember her past. This wasn't livable, and certainly not a place fit for his queen. It would be hazardous to even step inside the portion where the walls stood.

A small ache in his chest made him shift uncomfortably. This was where he married Valeen, made love to her, gave her his everything, and it was gone, taken by the enemy, and the cruelty of time, time that was stolen from them. He told her he'd return her to *her* throne, and it didn't appear that he could keep that promise now. But he would make the people responsible for this bow to her and build her a new throne made of their fucking bones.

"Is that supposed to be the castle?" Tif whimpered.

"Yeah," Hel murmured.

"She's going to be devastated."

Where are you? Valeen's voice entered his mind.

He felt like he could finally breathe fully again. If it had been anyone other than Katana, he wasn't sure he would have let her go after them even with Presco to have her back. This place was much more dangerous than Palenor. Immortals lived here. He clenched his hands into fists. *I found your castle. I'm looking at it now,* he replied.

Oh, good. We'll head your way then. He could hear the smile in her voice and

debated on warning her but didn't.

Nothing would prepare her for this.

"Hold on." He reached up and grasped the gnome's little legs and stepped off the cliff with a twenty foot or so drop. Wind whipped by as they plummeted. Tif let out a squeal, and then he hit the soft grass, landing in a crouch.

A moment later a loud thump hit beside him, and

Synick groaned. "Fucking, prick," he wheezed. "You could have softened my landing."

"Why would I do that?" Hel mused.

"That was crazy!" Tif squealed. "You just jumped off a cliff that would have certainly shattered and broken my legs and, let's be honest, in all likelihood I'd be dead. I'd probably look more like a pancake than a nice round roll."

"Silence."

"Sorry," she whispered.

With an inhale through the nose, he picked up the pungent scent of piss and shit. He stood and walked toward the old ruins then froze with his foot midair above a fresh pile of dung. A large animal was near here and likely more than one.

A fresh plume of smoke drifted out of the top of the standing portion of the ruins. "I wonder what's in there."

"Whoever they are, they probably won't be breathing much longer." Tif shook her fist at the ruins.

He smirked. "No, they probably won't."

Chapter 4

VALEEN

Wind whipped through Valeen's hair as Presco took a sharp downturn. Her stomach tickled with the quick descent, and she gripped the powder-blue spike in front of her just a little tighter.

Katana circled her arms around Valeen's waist and let out a laugh. "Wahoo! This is fun! I have never ridden a dragon before!"

Presco's massive, scaled body rumbled with deep laughter. "I'm glad I am the first to escort you."

"Don't turn so fast, Presco," Thane hollered. Valeen sat in front, then Katana, then Thane behind her, but he didn't hold onto her sister for balance. He was gripping the smaller spike his back rested against and his knees were up to his chest. The look of worry on his face made her giggle.

"And I thought you were the one most comfortable

riding dragons," Valeen teased. "Shall I fasten you a safety belt with my vine?"

He sneered at her. "I'm fine. I'm just in an awkward position, that's all."

"You can hold onto me," Katana suggested, patting the spot behind her. Her hair flowed out behind her like a ripped sail on a windy sea. Reaching up, she grabbed hold of her hair, twisted it, and tucked it under the strap of her dress. "Scoot closer. Or if you are more comfortable, you can hold onto Val and I will hold onto you."

His brows shot up. That appeared to scare him more than the potential of falling. "Sit sandwiched between the two of you? I'm good right where I am, thanks."

All it took was one glance at each other and the sisters giggled together. "I think your beauty makes him nervous," Valeen said, quietly.

"I think what makes him nervous is being squished by *two* goddesses."

Valeen laughed. "He would love it, who wouldn't?"

"You are naughty, Val, but I agree. It would be a dream come true for just about any male." Katana giggled. Oh, it was good to have her sister again. The males they had drooling over them back in the day were numerous and how they loved to tease. They fell right back into their friendship like they'd spent no time apart.

"I can hear you, you know," Thane grumbled.

"Then why haven't you accepted the invitation?" Valeen winked at him over her shoulder. It might be too soon for this, but she'd always liked teasing Thane just as he teased her. "You can hold onto me. Don't make it awkward and it won't be."

"It's not *awkward*. But when we land and Hel sees me holding onto you, he'll lose his bloody mind. I'm not up for dealing with his bullshit right now. I've dealt with enough of it the past several months."

That was certainly true. But she kind of liked it when Hel got jealous, she just didn't want it to happen at the expense of Thane and now wasn't a good time to poke the bear so to speak. It was much too soon for that. Hel and Thane had very recently accepted to be friendly again. Although being with Katana was making her feel a little more mischievous.

"So, hold onto *me*." Katana grinned. "You look like you might fall. Come." Katana patted the spot behind her again.

"Yeah, Thane, come on," she razzed.

Finally, his broody glare broke and even though he tried not to smile, he failed. "Fine. Since you both are pestering me." He dropped his boots to the side of Presco and scooted forward, putting himself behind Katana.

"Now, hold my waist." She picked up his hands and put them on her hips. "See, that is not so hard."

"You two are going to cause me problems, aren't you?"

Katana laughed, throwing her head back against his chest. "Only problems you will enjoy. Presco, I dare you to do something wild!"

"Hold on," his deep voice rumbled.

Oh, that was a dare she should not have given Presco. Valeen pressed herself against his spike and held on tight. He tumbled left, turning in a full circle.

Katana screamed, half terror, half glee, right in her ear. And Thane lifted off his seat then slammed back down once Presco leveled out.

"Damn, Presco." Thane's arms were completely circled around Katana now.

He turned his massive head around. "Too much? I never lose my riders. If you fall, I'll catch you."

"That's reassuring," Thane mumbled.

"This is where we left them." Presco dropped into a dive, the ground came up quickly, making her stomach leap until pearl wings shot out with a pop against the wind, slowing their descent. His paws touched down with the gentle landing only an experienced dragon had. In her old life, he'd flown her all around House of Night to meet with lords and ladies who helped her run the territory. In the great war of the realms, he was her battle dragon, the one who rode with her into the bloodiest of conflicts. He may have a brilliant mind better suited for books and libraries, but he was a ferocious warrior especially when it came to protecting his goddess and queen.

"Hel's not even here, so I guess I was worried for nothing. Synick isn't here either." Showing off, it would seem, Thane dropped down to Presco's elbow. With one of his charming smiles, he held his hand up. "Who's first?"

Presco bowed lower to let them off. "Actually, Valeen, may we speak privately?"

A nervous pulse slid up her gut. The briefly carefree fun mood she had gotten from reuniting with her sister vanished. "Of course."

Katana touched her shoulder. "Is something wrong?"

"No, I just need to discuss something with Valeen. There is no danger that I can see." Presco laid on his belly, making it easier for them to get down.

Katana took Thane's waiting hand. "What a gentleman. Thank you." He helped her get to the grass below then she smiled up at Presco and blew him a kiss. "And thank you for the ride. I think I need to travel by dragon more often. How exhilarating."

Beating wings caught her ear. Above, Varlett's sleek black dragon form descended with Piper and Leif on her back. Her scales glistened, reflecting the colorful night sky. If she didn't hate the wench so much, she'd be able to admire her beautiful dragon's form.

Presco gave her no time to ask the others where Hel had gone. His long strides shifted her side to side. A cool breeze brought with it the smell of cherry blossoms. Crickets chirped and an owl hooted in a nearby tree.

"Did you take in the landscape while we flew?"

Brows furrowed, she thought back. For the most part she was having fun and not paying attention to the scenery. From what she did see, it was mostly barren with a few scattered farms. That was what it had always been on the outskirts of the cities. She glanced up at the stars, looking for the constellations to guide her location. Sargento was almost directly above. No cities were allowed to be built within several miles of her castle. Privacy was important to her.

"Be direct, Presco."

"There were no animals at the farms, the homes were very old, ancient..."

"So they are abandoned. What does that matter?"

"Things feel—different. I want you to be prepared for the worst."

Valeen sucked her bottom lip between her teeth. "If the ruler here has abused his or her power, I will fix it. We'll make things right."

"I'm not trying to upset you. I know you're happy with your sister's return, and I don't want to ruin that for you."

"I'm not upset," she said, trying to keep her voice light. He saw right through it though.

"A lot of time has passed. Remember that. People may not even know who you are anymore."

"Take me back to the others, please." Her tone was clipped. He was being a great right-hand advisor, like he always did, but she didn't want to hear it.

Without another word, he ambled over to the group and dropped onto his belly, lightly shaking the ground. Valeen took her shadowy form and quickly settled on the soft grass.

Piper, Leif, and Varlett stared at Katana as she stood awkwardly beside Thane, fidgeting with her hands. He'd probably already introduced her, but Leif and Piper hadn't seen another goddess before. Leif was the first to strut forward, holding out his hand with a goofy grin. Valeen rolled her eyes knowing how this was about to go. Forever a shameless flirt and dreadfully inappropriate.

"I'm Leif, at your service, my lady." He took her hand and kissed the top of it, then stooped into a dramatic bow. His tangled red hair fell forward.

"How do you do?"

He stood straight, adjusted his hair, and wiped the

dirt off his cheek with his sleeve. "Having met you, much better."

Katana giggled and turned to Piper as she approached. Piper went to a knee before her and bowed her head. "Goddess of day, my name is Piper."

"Oh, please do not bother with formalities. I am sure we will be close friends soon."

In certain settings, Katana enjoyed the praise. She knew that others revered her and wouldn't take that from them but with a close-knit group she'd always kept it casual, as if she wasn't a primordial goddess, at least, that was how Valeen knew her to be many, many years before.

With her golden hair tied back into a tight braid and her unsettling reptilian eyes roaming over Katana as if assessing a threat, Varlett tapped her black talons. Her five-inch black horns rose in two curved spikes out of the crown of her head. "It's been a long time since I met a true beauty. You're almost difficult to look at."

Katana beamed at her, not caring about the backhanded compliment. "And you are?"

"Varlett. It's a pleasure, goddess."

Katana was as sweet and lovely as a person came but she was no stranger to the schemes and darkness of this world. It would be surprising if anyone else caught the minute tightening around her eyes, the barely noticeable shift away with her hips. "Varlett, nice to meet you. My, this is a fun group. Elves, dragons, and gods."

"Don't let the bitch fool you, goddess, she's not one of us by choice." Hel's voice tingled down her spine. A moment later his hand slid around the back of her neck, and he hooked his elbow around it. His dimple was pronounced and his dark eyes smoldered. Even if she'd known Hel for a long time, this reconciliation was still new. His simple touch sent heat to her core and a flush to her cheeks. "Hello, love." Teeth nipped her ear, and she had to let her breath out slowly. Her heart was already pounding.

"Hi." She searched his eyes, wondering what he'd done with Synick.

He's contained, don't worry.

It was uncanny the way he could read her even when she didn't intend him to.

Katana's lavender eyes shifted between Hel and Varlett. The backstory of why exactly Varlett wasn't one of them could come at a later time. For now, Katana only needed to know the shifter couldn't be trusted, although instinctually her sister likely already sensed that.

Valeen opened her mouth to introduce Hel when Tif popped through the grass and ran to her, wrapping her small arms halfway around her boot. "I'm so glad you're back. It's scary out here."

"Tif, you had me worried. Where did you go?"

"Well, I ran when those creepy skeleton things popped up. I have become braver but not that brave."

"It's lucky you found Hel. Something could have happened to you."

"Not with the master of darkness to watch over me." The tips of her fingers drummed together like she'd become his tiny henchman.

Master of darkness? Valeen nudged Hel's side.

What? She came up with it, not me.

Lifting her hand to his chest and pressing it flat

against his leather armor plate, she said, "Hel, meet my sister, Katana. Katana, this is my husband, Hel."

Taking hold of the edges of her silvery-white dress, she dipped into a curtsy. "It is wonderful to meet you."

"He's the god of magic, and of course he knows you're the goddess of day."

"Let's not forget the mischief part. The god of *mischief* and magic. It's the most interesting thing about me."

Katana smiled. "You do have an air of mystery about you." She wiggled her brows at Valeen. "Good catch. You always had a thing for the dark broody type, and you certainly found him."

"The sister comes in with the good gossip. Who else was there?" Hel lightly tugged on Valeen's braid. "First and last names will do, Katana. I'm sure I could find them from that. I already know of one and *he's* lucky to be alive." His eyes shifted to Thane.

"Here we go," Thane bemoaned.

"Oh." Katana blinked several times. "Um no one in particular. She didn't—"

"He's teasing." Valeen smacked his arm that was still hooked around her shoulders.

"Am I?" Then he mouthed to Katana. "Tell me later."

"Stop it. She's going to think you're out of your mind." All Mother, she only *thought* of jealous Hel and got it.

"I mean, the assessment wouldn't be far off. She might as well know now." Hel pulled away from Valeen and held out his hand to her. Interestingly, she hesitated but did take it. It could be because something in him frightened her, but she didn't appear to be scared. More uncertain.

When her sister had a puzzled expression, Valeen finally caught onto the reason behind the hesitation and laughed. "To shake hands is a newer but customary greeting."

"Oh." Katana smiled at Hel. "So we hold each other's hands for a moment and squeeze, gently but not too gently. I like it. I thought you were going to kiss my hand, which is not customary for a married male to do, especially in front of his wife. I take it that Leif is unmarried."

"Definitely single but looking," Leif said. "If you're in the market."

Piper elbowed him in the side. "She's a goddess, have some respect."

"It's not wrong to admire her."

"Asking if she's in the market for a husband when you just met her isn't *admiration*."

Hel smiled despite the interruptions. "It's good to meet you, Katana. I am a bit mad, but I do love your sister so no worries there. Valeen has told me all about you." Normally he'd have something to say about people butting into his introduction, he'd find it disrespectful, but something kept his darker side at bay. It had the hairs on the back of her neck rising. A sudden pit in her gut made her queasy.

Something was wrong.

She searched the shadows around them. She found Synick bound with Hel's magic near the black boulders several yards away. There were no signs of another intruder. Presco landed in his half-shifted form, wings protruding from his back. She hadn't even realized he'd left again. The solemn expression on his face caught her attention, turning the conversation between Hel and Katana into background noise.

"All good things I hope," Katana said.

"Is there anything bad to say? I hear from your sister that you're pretty perfect."

"You are much too kind. I am far from perfect."

"Humility is a rare trait in a goddess," Hel mused. He slipped his arm around Valeen again. "This one has a superiority complex."

Valeen's attention was drawn back. Her fingers curled around the soft black fabric of Hel's cloak. "Where is my castle?"

She pulled out from under his arm and started toward the ridge. If the stars were correct, and her memory sharp, the castle waited below this ridge of boulders. Palenor's Castle Dredwich was beautiful, but nothing compared to her Castle Starcrest. To the silver moonstone and the elegance and detail in every room she'd spent years perfecting to her own tastes. If they had to steal it back from someone, she was prepared to do it.

Hel caught her wrist, spun her around, and held her waist in a playful manner. "You just proved my point." But there was something about his face that sent another shot of worry through her. He might be smiling but it didn't reach his eyes, didn't bring out the dimple on his cheek.

"Hel?" she whispered.

He brushed the side of her face with the back of his hand and combed the stray hairs off her cheek. "Look at the moons."

Her stomach plummeted, and she twisted out of

his arms. Thane was looking at her with... pity. If Hel wasn't here, she was sure he would go to her. She didn't want to believe anything was wrong, but it was suddenly difficult to draw breath. Her legs weakened and her heart crashed in her chest like fire waiting to explode. Clouds covered two of the three moons. She didn't understand what he was saying. With a wave of her hand, she pushed the clouds away... No.

Fennor was cracked, a dark line cut across the upper left corner, and chunks of silver detached from it, leaving a giant crevice, and Nuna's rings were almost gone.

How is this possible?

"What are you saying?" Her voice was raw, but in her heart, she knew this meant her protective wall failed. It was the only thing that kept her land and people safe from the other gods' conquests, it would have been the only barrier between the council's vast armies and House of Night... "No." She shook her head, panic clawing its way up her chest. "Who has my castle and this land, Hel? One of the council?"

She started for the cliffside, and Hel appeared in front of her, eyes soft. "It's gone, love."

"Gone?" He may as well have punched her in the chest. "What do you mean? It can't be. It was made with magic... it's like the manor in Ryvengaard, right? We can fix it. It will just take time."

"It's—in complete ruin. I'm sorry." His throat bobbed and he reached for her hand.

"I want to see it."

Reluctantly, he stepped aside, and she ran to the edge of the cliff. Her breath was ripped from her lungs. Her hand flew to her chest trying to hold in the wound spreading like ice. The walls and rooms that once stood were now piles of broken stone covered in years and years of nature reclaiming her home. The flower gardens were scattered with wildness, not a careful hand.

When she stepped through the portal, the glittering night sky greeted her, the vast green hills and the colorful lights above—she thought it was here, her heart wanted to be home... She slowly sunk to her knees and sat back on her heels. Just when she believed the Council of the Gods hadn't taken everything from her, just when she had a small bit of hope that maybe they hadn't tainted and ruined all that she'd ever loved...

Synick's laugh cut through the sorrowful silence like sharp fingernails raking down her back. "Oh, how the mighty have fallen. You have nothing left!" His laughter grew louder. "Serves you right for what you did to me."

A hot tear slid down the cool skin of her cheek. Valeen slowly turned her head. Blood pumped loudly in her ears—the drums of war. Like someone else took hold, her fingers curled around her goddess blade Zythara, and she jerked it from the scabbard. The gold glinted in the moonlights.

"Valeen. I know you're hurt. I know it's terrible." Thane stepped into her peripheral. "But now is not the time—"

"Hurt? I'm more than hurt!" Her head snapped in his direction.

"No castle for a queen!" Synick howled, laughing hysterically now. "You're not even a goddess anymore. Just a pathetic mortal with nothing left. A *peasant*."

Suddenly he started choking and gasping for air. Hel must have cut his breathing off.

"You kept him alive for a reason. Think of it," Thane said. "It's all lies. You are a goddess and queen. No one can take that from you."

But they weren't lies. And they *could* take it from her. The truth hurt worse than any lie. She couldn't stop herself as she flew at him, as her blade arched through the air.

Thane was suddenly in front of her, holding her blade wielding arm. He pushed against her and forced her to step back. "He knows things that could be crucial to us winning this war."

"Let go of me," she growled. She didn't see the male she once loved right now, she only saw the prick who stood in her way. She was tempted to drive her knee into his groin.

"Kill him." Varlett added fuel to the fire.

"Think for a moment. He knows where the Sword of Truth is."

"Kill him," Varlett said again.

Thane snapped his head in her direction. "Shut up! This has nothing to do with you."

"It has everything to do with me."

"Let go of me," Valeen jerked.

Thane gripped her forearm tighter. "When you gain composure, I will."

"Don't tell me what to do. You *will* release me, Thane."

They stared into each other's faces, a battle of wills. Out of the corner of her eye, she caught a dark shadow moving closer—Hel. "You have three seconds before this turns into something more than it needs to be, cousin. Let her go." *All Mother,* if Thane were anyone else Hel would have lost it by now. He would have snapped his neck.

Thane was the first to break eye contact and slowly his fingers uncurled. Valeen jerked away. Without looking at the others, she turned and dropped off the edge of the ravine and onto the ground. Smoke from a fire rolled out of the only walls left standing. It was her former throne room. She recognized the placement of it.

"Valeen, wait!" Presco shouted down at her. With shadow trailing behind her, she ignored him. Midnight lilies popped and blossomed along her path. She had one thing on her mind and nothing would interfere.

Someone had to pay for this.

Something had to take the brunt of the sorrow keeping her from falling to the ground and never getting up.

"Wait for us!" Piper added. "You don't know what's in there!"

Her boots crunched over pebbles and stone, pieces that were once her home. A gentle wind carried the smell of burning wood and... flesh. Whoever was inside those walls roasted meat. A second pair of steps joined hers until a dark cloak appeared in her side view.

"You scared the shit out of your sister." Hel sounded irritated. "She doesn't know who to trust right now and you were about to fight War, someone you told her she *could* trust."

She marched on, gripping Zythara tighter. Why did he have to be right?

"What are you planning to do now? There is nothing to take back. Let it be."

She snarled at him. "It's our *home!*" She took off into a sprint, bounding up the large stones toward the black hole that led inside her old throne room. The cries and hollers of what sounded like wild animals drifted out. Before she could step through the dark threshold, she was grabbed and shoved against the wall.

Hel gripped her arms, keeping her pinned. He was deadly calm and fiercely strong. "Get yourself together right now. There are at least a hundred goblins in there, maybe more and who knows what else. Now, I will go in there with you and kill anything that moves but get your emotions under control. You never go into a fight with blind rage, it leaves you open to danger all around. You know better. That's how you die."

"I am not afraid."

"Like that wasn't obvious, but you should be cautious."

"I don't fear goblins, and I certainly don't fear the dark." Her heart pounded and her breath came sharp and uneven. Sometimes the most serene people snapped when pushed, and she was far from that. She was a night terror, born in darkness before there was ever light.

"Listen, little rabbit."

"*Don't* call me that."

"Little rabbit." He drug his tongue across his lower lip, egging her on.

Oh, she wanted to punch that smug look right off his face. "Say it one more fucking time."

"And you'll do what? I can't wait to hear it." His smirk almost put her over the edge. Then his lips crashed hard on her mouth. She wanted to claw and spit at him, but he knew exactly what to do to get her mind clear. Her breathing slowed, as did her heart rate. The sounds all around them came back into focus, as did his hands on her body, the feel of his lips and tongue on hers. Once he pulled his kiss, he studied her face. "Can I let you go now or are you going to keep up this attitude?"

"You really just know how to rile me up. Let me go."

He did. "What do you gain by going in there and killing these goblins?"

"I want to see what is left. I *have* to go in there. I just..." Hot tears pricked her eyes. A lump rose in her throat. "They've taken everything from me. What is a queen without a throne, without her people? What is a goddess without her immortality? Synick is right, I have nothing." Those tears slipped down her cheeks, spilling on the ruins of her old life. She should have expected this, should have prepared for this outcome but she'd hoped. Hope was one thing that kept her going in perilous times and it was shattered like a stone to a mirror.

What was there to even fight for anymore?

"You have me, and you have people who love you and will do anything for you." He cupped her face. "I will get it all back for you and more. I promise."

"This is my fault. I should have never left you. I should have trusted you. All of House of Night is gone. Your people most certainly are too. Presco pointed out the signs, but I refused to see it. The people of Villhara are probably slaves or dead because of me. All those people... Gods, I let Varlett fool me, and now it's fucked up. It's all gone." Anger turned to panic. She struggled to pull air into her lungs; her throat was closing up.

"Shh." He wiped her tears with his thumbs. "Baby, listen to me. None of that matters anymore. It doesn't, alright. What matters is that we're together now. We can get it back."

"I can't breathe," she gasped, clutching at her chest.

He swept her up into his arms, and they were pulled through a blink of darkness and came out at the base of a large oak tree. He set her on her feet but held her around the waist. His hold was the only thing keeping her from falling. "Breathe in through your nose, out through your mouth. Come on, deep breaths." He sounded muffled and far away, as if she were under water. A ringing in her ears intensified. She gripped the edges of his cloak and focused on his moving lips. "Breathe, love. If our people are slaves, we will free them. It isn't your fault. It's the assholes on the council, not yours. They did this. And they would have come for you for Soulender no matter what Varlett did. None of this is on you."

His voice slowly came back into focus, but she still couldn't breathe. The ground seemed to tip and tilt, it was as if she stood on a ship. "Why did any of this happen?" She sobbed, gripping him harder. He was the only thing keeping her from falling. From lying on the ground and succumbing to a hopeless pit of despair.

"Maybe there isn't a reason, maybe there will never be understanding, but we can't give up. We have been brought back together, love. It is a gift from your All Mother that we are standing here together now. Your sister is *alive*. It is not over."

She focused on his calming voice, on the steady beat of his heart. Air came in easier; her lungs and throat opened back up. She lifted her chin and looked into his garnet eyes. For someone who hated all the world, he had more faith than anyone. "A gift? We have been forgetting each other for thousands of years."

"I'd do it a thousand times and a thousand more after that if it meant I got to be with you even for a moment. Nothing will ever keep you from me." His soft lips met hers. "Anyone who stands in my way should wish they were never born. Our enemies will beg for forgiveness and not get it, and they will ask for mercy and will be shown none. You will get your immortality even if I have to cut theirs out of them to give to you, and you will get your throne and castle if that means I build it from their skulls and broken bones."

His promises were beautiful, poetic even. "We have nothing, Hel. How can we ever beat them?"

"You are underestimating the lengths I would go for you. How can you doubt so much when you are a primordial? Have you forgotten that dragons fall to their knees before you? You were once worshiped by mortals from every facet of the realms. Have you forgotten you turned the god of mischief from your enemy into your lover not once, but twice?"

Valeen coughed out a half-sob, half-laugh.

"You have your sister back, your friends, and we have the god of war on our side, and no one is better at war than him. I wouldn't say we have nothing." He smiled. "And we have an army of cursed elves waiting to be commanded. This is a disappointment, not an ending."

Her chin quivered and more tears welled in her

eyes. "Even with the pale ones we will be outnumbered by thousands. The council has eleven members, that's eleven armies, eleven gods and territories, and they will have other allies. This wall was our only chance of winning and it's gone. We don't even have one stronghold. Who here would side with us when they've been poisoned against us for two thousand years? And if we go back to Palenor they would destroy it. If we go to Ryvengaard, the Drakonans are still looking for us. They're the wealthiest, most influential dragon family in all the realms. They will fight against us for killing Caliban and breaking into their treasury. When I said we have nothing, that is what I meant. We have no one."

He wiped another tear off her cheek. "I see things differently. I haven't been plotting my revenge for so long to be deterred by one setback. It is a tragedy, but I didn't plan for the walls around House of Night to be standing after all this time. We will go back to Palenor where my army waits, where War is king. We will be ready for them when they come." He gripped her chin and raised it. "And you, my love, will show them why you are the queen of the night."

Chapter 5

THANE

Thane stood at the base of what was left of Valeen's castle ruins, watching her and Hel in the distance. Being at odds with her was the last thing he wanted but he couldn't let her kill Synick. Not yet.

Why was he alive? How did he get here? Did the council make a deal with the demon princes to bring him back? They must know these things to plan for future attacks. Because if they didn't make a deal, that meant that Synick got out of the underrealm in a different way and it could mean the door was open and only the Maker knew what else could have crawled out.

He turned to the heap of old stone, wishing he could remember the details of what it once was in all its glory. It had been too long. Wisps of another time flickered at the back of his mind, the jasmine trellises, the ornate celestial sconces on the stone walls, a glossy floor made of moonstone he'd once danced across with Valeen. But the finer details were lost.

Now goblins and monsters had taken over this place. They shouldn't linger here.

Even though this was never his home, it was devastating to know what it once was and what had become of it in her absence. Witnessing the pain in her voice, seeing her face twisted with agony, it cut into him. Part of him wished he was the one wiping her tears away under the oak tree, but seeing them together... He had never been able to console her the way Hel did. She didn't trust him in the same way, he hated admitting that, even to himself.

Synick groaned under Thane's boot. His chest heaved up and down, struggling to breath under his weight. "I can hardly believe your betrayal, War. Zaurahel, I understand, he was never as loyal—rebellious to his core, but how could you betray your own and join forces with one of the Drivaar? Not to mention my killer."

Drivaar, Primevarr... the two sides of the gods were something he hadn't thought about in a long time. Fighting over whether the All Mother or the Maker was superior seemed foolish now.

Thane tilted his chin down. Seeing Synick after so much time brought up strange feelings. This was the god who mentored him and Hel with cruelty and malice, but he was also one of the things that had forged a strong bond between him and his cousin.

"She poisoned you with her lies. Females and their wiles, you can't trust them. Especially a primordial goddess. She will take everything from you with the promise of pleasure."

"Stop talking."

"You understand my animosity with her, do you not? She took my life, War. Sent me to the underrealm. It is only fair—"

"You killed her sister first. Don't act like you're innocent."

Katana sat a few yards off, tucked under a tree, with her arms hooked around her knees. Hopefully she couldn't hear Synick. Her face was paler than before, those lavender eyes almost hollow.

The others gathered on the broken stones, taking seats while they waited for Valeen to compose herself. It was as if they shared an unspoken knowing that she was the one to decide what would happen next.

"There is no, 'innocent or not innocent', there is only power and who has it," Synick retorted.

"Well by that logic, currently we have the power." Thane shook his head at the messed-up worldview his former mentor had. Whether he knew it or not, Hel had picked up on some of his worse traits.

"Just listen to me. Valeen is not going to win. You can't win by choosing her side. Is she humping you both? Is that what's got you so hooked?"

Thane pulled his sword from the sheath on his back and bashed Synick on the head with it. His body went limp with unconsciousness.

With crossed arms, Piper raised her brows at him. "Frustrated?"

"I couldn't take the sound of his voice any longer."

Leif tapped his boots and lowered his voice, "I've never seen her like that."

"She's just realized she lost her home, Leif, and all

the people in it," Piper said, softly. "There is no one left."

"It was lost long ago," Thane said. "She shouldn't have gotten her hopes up."

"I wouldn't say that to her if I were you," Leif drawled. "Might lose your balls."

After the tension earlier, Leif was probably right. It was not a good time to antagonize her. In all the years Thane had known her, he *had* seen her break down worse. After she discovered what she thought was Hel's betrayal. He hadn't known her when she lost Katana, but he imagined it took her down a dark road.

"Thane, can we talk?" Piper stood, crossing her arms.

He gestured for Leif to take over watching Synick and followed Piper away from the others. When they were out of earshot he turned to his second-in-command. "What's going on?"

"You can't look at her like she's yours." Piper rested her hand on her dagger handle, an old habit they all had.

"Katana?" He'd been watching her, wondering what he could do to make her feel better. He knew what trauma looked like in a person and she was riddled with it.

"Are you daft? Valeen, obviously. She's not Layala anymore. I know you spent all your life as Thane wanting her and thinking she was supposed to be yours but that person with Hel is not her. Which only makes sense given in her mind, she's thousands of years old."

Although he didn't feel the same way as Piper, he understood why she thought that Layala and Valeen weren't one and the same. "I'm sure if you just talk to her, you'll see it's still her. You've been avoiding her since she got back from Ryvengaard."

"You said yourself she was a different person," Piper murmured. "It's why you pushed her away." She'd let him taste her wrath the day Layala and Hel left to Ryvengaard. He'd never seen her so upset. She'd sobbed as if she lost her, too. He supposed in a way, she did. She screamed at him for letting her leave without being able to say goodbye to her friend. She didn't know if she'd ever see her again. "And don't try to turn this conversation back on me. She chose *the Black Mage*."

"I'm acutely aware she chose him over me, Piper. No one is more aware of that than me."

"Are you? Because right now, you're staring at her like there is still a chance."

"No, I'm not." His tone turned sharper.

"It's your fault she's with him anyway. You told her to leave."

Thane frowned, the crack in his chest he'd ignored for months began to split and throb. "I had to. She needed to know all of who she is. I was holding her back."

"You lost her, and it was one thing when they weren't with us but now... now she's with him. I don't understand how she can love him. *Him*. After everything he did to Palenor. We had to fight the pale ones for hundreds of years, we lost countless people because of that curse he's responsible for, and let's not forget the way he treated all of us when he first arrived. I can't even fathom how you and her just welcome him with open arms. I'm disgusted every time she touches him and when he calls her his *wife*. He created the pale ones, Thane."

Thane ran a hand over the top of his head. Everything she said was absolutely true and yet she didn't know him the way he and Valeen did and never would. There were no excuses for him either. He couldn't say, "Once you get to know him, he's not so bad"... because well, Hel wasn't a hero. He didn't share Piper's morals. He'd cross every line if it meant saving Valeen.

"I know what he did. You're going to have to accept that he's with us now."

"Why should I? Why are we even here, Thane? This is about them, not us."

"You swore to be her bodyguard, didn't you? To protect her?" A falling pebble from the top of the ruins bounced until it rolled to his foot.

"I swore loyalty to you, and through you, her, as your future queen. She's obviously not that anymore." Piper let out a long breath. "She's—not one of us. She's a goddess from this strange world. And I've only seen a fraction of what she's capable of, but she and Hel will be fine on their own."

"You have no idea what we're up against. And she is still your friend." The sound of the goblins inside the ruins caught his attention and he lowered his voice. If the creatures came out here and found them, it was a fight they didn't need. "You've only ever known me as Thane, but I came from this world, too."

"Let Hel protect her. We can go back home. The gods will leave us alone in Palenor. It's her they're after, right?"

"Wow, you would really leave her alone to die?

You're not who I thought you were. And no, they will *not* leave us alone."

Shaking her head, Piper looked away. "You're doing this because you're still in love with her."

"So what if I was? She is one of the closest people in the world to me. I do love her."

"I bet if the situation was reversed and she chose you and not Hel, he wouldn't be here. You don't owe either of them loyalty."

"He's my family, Piper."

"So is Aldrich and you'd kill him if you had the chance. Wherever that weasel disappeared to."

Thane's jaw began to ache with how hard he clenched his teeth. Piper was almost as stubborn as Valeen and never held back either, even to her king. "Aldrich didn't spend hundreds of years with me. Didn't defend me as a child, didn't take beatings for me, didn't stand by my side whenever I needed him. Hel and I were inseparable until... You'll never understand because you see him as the Black Mage first."

"I want to go home."

He waved a hand at the ruins. "You see this—this is what they will do to Palenor. They will come with armies the likes you have never seen. Creatures from every realm, beasts and monsters, races who know the sword as good as any Raven. I had a thousand dragons on my side, and we still eventually lost. Valeen and I were captured at our full power, so was Hel. And the gods, they cannot be killed except with the blade Valeen has. Even if she and Hel stayed and we went home, they would destroy Palenor to punish me, to punish them."

Her brows furrowed into what seemed to be

turning into a permanent scowl. "I thought—how could they do that to all the innocent people in Palenor? I thought the gods were supposed to be just and fair?"

Thane let out a humorless laugh. "Just? Those are fairy tales for children. The gods of Runevale lost justice and peace keeping long ago. Like Synick said, it's about power and who has it. We are a threat to theirs." Out of the corner of his eye, he caught Valeen and Hel leaving the cover of the oak tree. She appeared to be composed but even from this distance sadness was etched into her face. "I want you to talk to her and see that Layala is still in there."

Rolling her eyes, Piper stubbornly crossed her arms. "I will but I don't know if I'll ever forgive her for choosing to be with Hel. She swore she had no feelings for him, no loyalty at all, then they disappear for a few months and she's his godsdamn *wife*."

A gurgled, throaty call cut through the air; Thane snapped his head toward it. A goblin with gray-black skin and a fanged skull covering the top half of his face stood at the darkened threshold of the old castle ruins. He raised a spear above his head and a trill for battle brought hundreds crawling up over the crest of the wall and scaling down ropes like spiders from webs.

Chapter 6

VALEEN

"Holy All Mother," Valeen breathed. The sheer number of goblins dropping from the walls, spilling out from the cracks in the stone reminded her of ants scattering from a hill under attack. In the dim light of the moons with their dirty, rusted armor and oiled black hair they resembled them too.

"I did warn you how many there were." Hel pulled his electric, blue sword and faced the oncoming invasion. He put a burning civar to his lips, as calm as could be as a black wave swept toward them. The ground rumbled with the stampede. Their trilling calls echoed off the cliff and the ruins. "Do you still want to fight?"

Valeen pulled Zythara from her hip. Shadows pooled around her feet. Her black vines crept up from the ground ready to be commanded. "I don't want to fight them. I want to destroy them."

"So be it." Hel waved his arm, and an arc of blue

flame rose up, cutting across the landscape. With an unnatural speed it circled around the goblins' chance of retreat. Thane already had the others sprinting for the cliff to climb up and out of this valley. Presco picked up Katana and carried her away on his wings, but Varlett stayed. She shifted into her black dragon and roared, sending an arc of fire upward, lighting up the night with red flame.

Valeen ran onto her rolling vine and rode it like a wave.

Hel soared above on white wings, a god of death.

The goblins screeched and roared, raising weapons behind the wall of fire. They wanted to fight. Lesser beasts did not fear dying.

Valeen's vine took her high over the flames and she dove off, cutting her blade across the throat of a goblin. Black blood spewed into the air. She ducked under a blunted sword and shoved her goddess blade into the attacker's chest. She moved on through goblins, slicing, cutting, hacking. It didn't require thought, years and years of honing the sword moved her like a methodical dance. Her magic flared out, shadows surrounding her so the enemy could not see her. Her vines shot from the ground like spears, impaling the monsters who had taken her land for their own.

Suddenly Hel was on her right, his blue sword swung out, hacking off two heads. Black blood ran down his cruelly beautiful face. One moment he was there, the next he was gone. His magic allowed him to defy laws, shifting through space, body vanishing and reforming in milliseconds. Goblins around him crumbled to the ground holding their heads while screaming, leg bones snapped and buckled.

Varlett soared over their heads, claws raking across groups, flinging bodies into the air.

Fire all around made the rising heat close to unbearable, but Valeen kept swinging. Vengeance moved her.

This was for her people.

This was for her home.

Even if it was in shambles, one day she would rebuild it.

She only wished it was the council she fought against now, not the goblins who'd merely taken advantage of their barbarism.

Thane came up on her left, shifting and rolling like the wind, two swords cutting through the enemies as if they were not moving. Limbs severed, hitting the ground in thuds, blood ran in rivers. Even if the bodies piled up, the goblins kept coming. Their numbers seemed endless as they poured out of the ruins.

Valeen ducked under a jagged blade. An icy feeling rushed through her veins. A power filled her blood, a charge before thunder.

Hel slammed his fist into the ground and a crack split the earth before him. Goblins screeched as they fell into the abyss. With a spinning kick, Valeen knocked out the legs of the goblin in front of her, then shoved her sword into its sheath and thrust out her palms. She screamed as power roared through her; a great cloud of shadow flooded out, taking the shape of an ocean wave. Its crest rolled over the goblins, sweeping them into the pit.

Hel grabbed Valeen around the waist and shot into the air. The speed made her grip around his neck and wrap her thighs around his hips, hooking her ankles together as they rose higher. But Thane was still down there in the flames and widening crevice. Panicked, she searched the ground and found him. He sprinted over the dead bodies and fire, as if his feet suddenly sprouted wings he bounded up the cliffside to where the others waited.

Their ascent stilled and Hel's huge white wings slowly beat, keeping them afloat. Blue, red, and orange embers floated into the night sky. Flames caught hold of everything that was. She'd rather what was left of her castle grounds be burned than be home to these creatures. With a clench of Hel's hand, the crevice changed directions and began to close. It had been a long time since she'd seen him in combat. He was certainly the god of magic. And this was exactly why he was widely feared.

Once the split in the ground reformed, Hel snapped his fingers, and the flames doused as if a waterfall had washed over the land. The walls to the ruins had fallen, there was nothing left but a pile of stone and blackened vegetation, with cinder scattered over the area.

When they touched down on the clifftop, Piper and Leif stared as if she were a complete stranger. She strode forward, wiping her sleeve across her face to clear the wetness sticking to her skin.

Leif suddenly fell to his knees. "Goddess," he murmured. "Forgive me, Valeen. I did not—I've treated you as if you are one of us. You are not."

It seemed like it had been forever since she was looked upon with such reverence. The dragons had bowed to her, but this was personal; this was a revelation. A slow smile spread across her lips. "Leif, it's still me."

"You have my sword for all my life." He touched his forehead where his celestial tattoos brandished his skin and then pressed his nose to the ground.

Valeen dropped into a squat and laid a gentle hand on his shoulder. "And you have mine, Leif."

He lifted his head, cheeks wet. "My Nana always said the goddesses of the day and night would one day return." His blue eyes shifted to Katana for a moment. "I never told you this but in my tribe you are the chosen goddesses we prayed to for protection."

"And your tribe will get their wish. We are going home to Palenor. I will not lose the elves the way I have lost House of Night."

PINK AND SALMON stained the horizon as the sun rose. The crisp cool morning air bit against her cheeks. The dew on the blades of grass dampened her boots. Valeen stood just inside the newly finished towering stone wall at the crest of the hill, overlooking the Valley of the Sun. The construction of it had started long before Hel woke up. It was originally to keep out the pale ones. Now they'd need it for their new enemy.

The gold-painted roofs lit up the city at this time of day and would take the breath of even the oldest of elves. It beheld a beauty and splendor rare in the realms. It wasn't simply appearances. There was a feel here that radiated goodness and hope.

Castle Dredwich stood strong, and beautiful. The flag of Palenor flew at the highest peak. The waterfall roared over the seventy-foot drop into the ravine protecting the castle that had become her place of refuge even if it had once been a prison.

They'd only been gone a day, and it somehow felt like a lifetime. She'd lost and yet gained everything in hours. This was what her castle should look like, solid and immovable. Her people should be bustling about as the elves of Palenor did on the streets below. Soft music drifted over the grasses and flowers, the smell of the bakeries and burning of wood from the nearby smithies carried on the breeze—then it hit her.

These were her people too.

She was as much elf as she was goddess and even if the council had taken a part of her, she would not let them take it all.

Hel seemed to have expected this outcome. As if he'd only gone with her through the portal to appease her, so she could see for herself that the great House of the Goddess of Night only existed in their memory now. She'd let hope blind her to what should have been obvious. The council would have never let her territory stand, it was a part of her punishment. They even destroyed one of the moons to show her and everyone that mutiny would not stand. That was how ruthless they were.

There was one good thing in all of this; opening the portal brought her Katana. If all of this had to happen for her sister to return, she would accept the gift from the All Mother and move on from her regrets and from the past.

She would look forward now and hold in her mind her castle restored until it came into reality. This only fueled her more to win this war. To erase the council and anyone else who stood against them.

The smoke from Hel's civar drifted by in a curling wave before her face, bringing her focus back to the here and now. "There is something special about this place, isn't there?"

"We must not let it fall," Valeen whispered. She couldn't see it become ruined. But once the gods realized the portals were open, they would march their armies here to break them.

But as long as they held Synick, it would give them time to prepare. He wouldn't be able to go to them and sound the alarm.

Thane and Presco dragged Synick between them, moving quickly toward the castle. Piper and Tif were close behind. Tif skipped merrily, scattering butterflies into the wind. Piper said something to Leif, and they laughed. She didn't begrudge them their happiness. It wasn't their world that was crushed. It wasn't their hearts that were stamped on and bled out.

Katana stepped up beside her, wrapping a warm hand around hers. "It is beautiful." Her smile was radiant and cheerful, too good for this world. "I have always wanted to return to Palenor and witness the splendor of the high elves once again. You will have to take me through the city sometime."

Valeen nodded absently. Giving her sister's hand a gentle squeeze, mustering up a half smile was the best she could do. She watched Thane as his dark hair wrapped around his back and bounced against his Raven armor. The king returned home. Orlandia and Talon would no doubt want to throw a celebratory dinner, and Valeen wasn't up for that.

"Come on, Val." Katana gave her a gentle tug.

"Go on ahead. I'll catch up in a moment."

She gave her a long look, one of worry and sorrow. Katana was an empath, and no doubt felt her sister's pain, but she let go and with graceful steps, made her way down the hill. Somewhere behind them, she felt Varlett's presence. The dragon knew she wasn't welcome in Thane's home and preferred the outdoors anyway. With all there was to consider, Valeen couldn't worry about her; Varlett had survived this long.

Valeen sank to the ground and wrapped her arms around her legs, resting her chin on her knees. The aftermath of the rage, sorrow, and power tearing through her was numbness.

Hel sat beside her. He didn't speak. But his presence was needed. She felt bad that she'd lost her temper on him and Thane. Though not so bad after he called her "little rabbit" many times.

Hours passed, the sun was high in the sky before she spoke. Her throat was still scratchy from the smoke of the fires and her hair smelled of singed earth and death. "I need to bathe. I need to get this stink and blood off me."

He took her hand, pulling her to her feet. In a flash, they appeared inside Castle Dredwich. She didn't know if she was still welcome in her old room next to Thane's, but it was familiar and that's where she stood now. She quickly stripped her armor and clothes. Hel had already summoned hot water into the golden basin. Rose petals and scented oils floated along the surface. Her leg swung over the edge, and she sank down, fading into the warmth.

Later that evening, she curled up on her side on top of the soft quilt. Guilt clung to the recesses of her mind. She should be with her sister in this new place among people who were strangers to her or at least ensure she was in a comfortable room. She should go into the dungeons to question Synick. She should find Presco and make certain he was also taken care of. He would do it for her, but exhaustion kept her in this bed, damp hair spread across the silk pillows.

Hel lay beside her, stroking his fingertips along her back. He smelled of pine soap and an alluring musk that was unique to him. The heat of his body, and the gentle hum of a song put her into a hypnotic state of relaxation. Maybe he was using his magic to calm her. Maybe it was just having her mate close. Her fingers curled against his chest, and she pulled herself closer to him; she couldn't be close enough.

"Sleep, love. I will watch over you."

Chapter 7

VALEEN

Birds chirping outside the window drew Valeen from sleep. Heavy eyelids barely peeled open as she sat up and ran her hands over her disheveled hair. The sun was out, spilling bright light in through the open curtains. The green vines draping around the bed almost startled her; she'd been dreaming she was still in Ryvengaard at the manor with Hel. The wide fireplace with the white mantel led into Thane's room. A twinge of guilt hit her chest. It felt wrong to be in this room when he'd meant for it to be his wife's, especially when that was supposed to be her. The statues of them reaching toward each other were still on the shelf. The dresses he had made for her still waited in the closet. He hadn't touched this space when she'd gone to Ryvengaard.

The sound of creaking leather made her turn. Dark hair curled against ivory skin. Maroon eyes watched her the way a cat in a window pondered a bird, with primal need and curiosity. "Good morning, love." Hel sat in a brown leather armchair in the corner with his feet propped up on a matching footrest. If he was the first thing she saw every morning for the rest of forever, she'd be happy.

"How long did I sleep?" The sun hadn't even set yet when she drifted off. Was it still the same day? Her head ached and her throat felt dry.

"You slept two full days."

She blinked in disbelief. It felt like she'd shut her eyes not long ago. "Why didn't you wake me?"

He dropped his boots to the floor with a heavy thud and leaned forward. "After everything you went through following the portal opening and even before, with the demon attack, you needed the rest, Val. No one has come. There wasn't any reason for me to wake you."

"Did I miss anything?"

"Not that I know of. I've been in here and no one came knocking in a panic. Everything is fine... for now."

"You stayed here the entire time?" she asked, baffled.

"I did say I would watch over you, did I not? The portals are open. The attempts on your life will only intensify." He tore his gaze from her and scowled at the window. "War came in for a while to discuss Synick. Your sister and Presco both stopped by to check on you. Your gnome and a couple servants brought food, so I didn't have to go anywhere."

She rubbed the sleep from her eyes and swung her feet to the floor; the stone was cool. "Katana..." she stood, stretching her arms overhead. "I'm a terrible sister."

"She was the *most* adamant that we didn't wake you."

"How is she? Does she have a room? If Talon said anything rude to her..." she hurried over to the vanity and plucked a comb out of the drawer and ripped it through her tangles. "Where is Presco?"

Hel appeared suddenly and wrapped her in a hug from behind, putting them both in the frame of the mirror. He rested his chin on her shoulder. "You think War would allow your sister to sleep in the hallway? Of course, Katana has a room. Presco has been in the library most of the past two days as far as I know, looking for a way to break the link between you and Varlett. Relax."

His reassurance lifted the weight off her shoulders some but relaxing wasn't something she did well. She'd been hunted for so long. Someone always wanted to use, hurt, or kill her. She set the comb back on the vanity. "I can't relax when I'm being hunted and the whole of Adalon will suffer simply because I am here. I should try to create another magical barrier around Palenor and connect it to this moon, but I don't know if I have that kind of power anymore, and we'd need an anchor. A powerful one. In House of Night, it was my castle made of moonstone, and of course my own magic. And we'd risk this moon being broken if I do."

"*Can* you create a barrier with a single moon?"

She ran her hands through her black hair, pulling out of Hel's arms, and walked over to the window to peer out over the castle grounds. The trees along the front path bloomed soft pink and white. On a breeze, petals fluttered through the air like snowflakes. "I don't think it would be as strong, but something would be better than nothing. It would at least slow them down and keep out assassins."

"Can you use Castle Dredwich as the anchor?"

"No, its stone is not connected to the moon."

"What is?"

Valeen lifted a shoulder. "Other than me...?"

"I can only assume that would drain you. Find something else."

"So demanding," Valeen said, crossing her arms, and leaning back against the window ledge.

"Yeah, well I'm not going to watch you suffer so you can protect the people who've treated you like shit. The same people who wrote gossip columns about you, who have entire secret societies that have wanted to ensure your death since you were born here, and who believe you're a dark mage, a plague on their people. I don't give a fuck what they think about me, but I do care what they say about you. You create that barrier to protect you, your aunt, your sister, and your friends."

"I'm not you, Hel, I can't ignore that there are plenty of innocent people in Palenor who don't feel that way about me."

"You're innocent."

This wasn't an argument he would relent on, and in the end they both wanted the same thing for different reasons. "I will talk to Presco. He helped me create the first one."

"Are you trying to make me jealous?" he purred. "You can talk with the god of magic."

With a laugh, Valeen sauntered over to him and

wrapped her arms around his neck. "I agree, but three minds are better. Presco is brilliant."

"I know. Too brilliant. It annoys me."

"Stop it," Valeen chuckled. "You like Presco."

"He's not the worst," Hel said, failing to hold back his smile.

A knock on the door startled her. *The servants—I didn't really think about it but—with me and Hel sharing a room...*

"Yes, their king's former betrothed is now sleeping with his cousin. No doubt it's all the gossip." He went quiet for a moment. "I almost feel bad for him."

Valeen let out a slow breath. It was going to be difficult in the coming weeks. They were supposed to be in House of Night, away from anyone who would know her as Layala. "I think he is at peace with my choice. He understands."

Hel put his finger to his temple. "He understands here." Then he dropped his hand to his heart, "But it's this that will take time to understand and move on, and it will be difficult to do with you always around and people gossiping about it. Trust me, I know."

Valeen pulled her bottom lip between her teeth. "I don't even know what Thane told everyone when we left for Ryvengaard. Was the break off of our engagement announced?"

"I think Talon and her dreadful mother were all too eager to leak it to the *Palenor Scroll*."

Another knock. "I have your breakfast, Lord Hel," a feminine voice came from the other side.

Hel waved his hand, the warmth of his magic tingled along her skin then he called out, "Go away. We're busy." Then closed his hand into a fist. She didn't even ask what magic he was using, but guessed there was a silencing spell on this room.

"Lord? And do you have to be rude?"

"I'm direct. And yes, 'Lord'. I'm the king's cousin. Obviously it's not just Hel. It should be most magnificent Lord, most wise and powerful god, Hel, but I let them get away with just 'Lord'."

She rolled her eyes. "Has Synick talked?"

He kissed her cheek and removed his arms from around her middle. "We've been letting him... marinate in the dark of the dungeons. He'll talk when I go down there."

Valeen turned and leaned into him, pressing a hard kiss on his mouth. "Thank you for staying with me."

He smiled against her lips. "There is no place I'd rather be. I missed you. I can't get enough of you. I want more and *more*." His hands slid up the sides of her hips, and slowly to her waist. She tilted her head, exposing her neck to him. His lips brushed her sensitive skin, pulling a moan from her. His magic trickled over her like warm water and the bottom hem of her dress rose up where his hand slipped under, brushing the inside of her thigh. "You are everything to me. Since the moment I saw you, I knew everything would change. Gods, I think even before I met you, I knew."

Valeen pulled herself closer, inhaling his intoxicating scent. She nuzzled her face into his neck and nibbled on his skin. His answering groan and tightening grip around her made her smile. Knowing that all it took was a nibble to get him going was absolutely satisfying. He slowly ushered her toward the bed until the back of her legs bumped into the frame. She pressed her lips to his and pulled him on top of her. His kisses were hard against her throat, her neck, her jaw. His touch sliding over her body promised pleasure. Her fingers dug hard into his back, and he groaned. He pulled away, sliding off the bed and she frowned.

"Are you... leaving?" Her nightgown was bunched up around her waist already and she didn't have any undergarments on.

"Leaving?" His brow rose. "Why would I leave?"

"I just... you got off of me."

He tugged his shirt overhead, revealing his delicious body. His muscles were taut and the sunlight made his skin glisten. Her eyes traveled to the "KING" tattoo below his belly button. "I can't very well love you properly with my clothes on."

She smiled as his belt jingled and hit the floor with a thud.

"Don't think I'll ever leave you unsatisfied, love. You can have me whenever and wherever you want. On the dining room table with everyone sat down for dinner if you asked."

"You're terrible," she teased.

"Not one of your fantasies then?"

"No!"

He threw his head back with a laugh. "I'm not one for onlookers either. But I think I would like to take you over to War's empty room just to make a point."

"Stop."

"I'm joking. Somewhat."

"You don't need to rub it in. You already have me."

"That's right, I do. Open those pretty thighs for me." He crawled back on top of her and her hands slid up his bare chest and around his neck. His lips crashed against hers as he gave her what she wanted.

His magic whispered along her skin, like extra hands kneading and stroking. She rolled her hips with him, gripped by his garnet eyes. He was so beautiful, and even if no one saw it, she did. Somewhere in his darkness was a heart and she felt it in the way he loved her—worshiped her.

His touch, his riveting, absolutely intoxicating touch, made her eyes roll back and she gently bit down on his shoulder, stifling a moan.

"No need to be quiet," he murmured. "There are sound barriers in this room."

So she wasn't. She let every pleasure roll through her, sighing and moaning as he rocked his hips. It was the high she needed from the agony of loss she had felt the days before. Like soaring through the sky, his hands were the wind that whipped through her hair. She drew her tongue across his throat tasting the salt of his skin, and he shuddered. "*Fuck,*" he muttered.

He pulled down the top of her nightdress to see her exposed breasts and his face melted in pleasure. *I could come just by looking.*

Shadows rose along her arms. Her powers were unruly when she was with Hel. He made her lose all control, like he took it for his own. His lips covered her body for what felt like hours. She lost herself in him, in this moment. There was nothing else, no problems, no loss, no one wanting her dead. Right now, there was nothing but Hel.

She hooked her ankles behind his hips. He suddenly lifted her off the bed, and he took her to the wall. He was both gentle with his kisses and like a violent storm. With her nails pressed into his flesh, he slammed his eyes shut. *You're making me lose control.*

Lose it.

His runes started to glow as he kept driving into her until she shimmered like diamonds in sunlight cascading across her skin. She buried her face into his neck.

"Uh, you're good. You're so good." She almost started laughing as her limp arms draped around his shoulders. "I can't believe I've been missing out on this for so long."

He panted in her ear, still holding her tightly against the wall. "It's like nothing else. No one has ever made me feel this way." Then he pressed his forehead against hers. "I'll never get over you."

Chapter 8

HEL

The sour smell of the dungeons filled Hel's nostrils. He flicked his fingertips and a burning civar appeared between them to mask the mildew. With the wave of his hand the torches along the walls lit up, bringing an orange flickering light to the darkness. His boots lightly clapped over the dirty stone steps until he made it to the bottom level and rounded the corner to find Synick sat in a chair against the wall behind bars. Hel stopped directly outside his cell and took a drag.

"Gods, it smells like shit down here."

"It's the dungeons," War said, as if it should be obvious. He'd gotten down here first but by the lack of fresh blood, his cousin hadn't been doing much.

Leave it to Hel to do the dirty work. Not that he minded.

Synick lifted his head. Giving him full view of his putrid face. He was filthy from crown to toe and the bloodstains on his top looked brown and rusted. Katagas serum and chains kept him in his cell.

"You look like you crawled out of a demon's asshole," Hel said and took a puff of the sweet herbs.

Synick rolled his eyes or at least tried to. Only the good one seemed capable of the movement. The decayed eye was cloudy and stared endlessly ahead. "Get me out of these chains."

"Let me get right to that." He gave him the middle finger instead.

War stuck a key into the lock and metal grated on metal, squealing as he tugged the door open. Hel pulled a dirty wooden chair from the wall and twisted it around to sit. He rested his elbow on the back of it and took an inhale of his civar. Something moved in the decaying side of Synick's face, a maggot perhaps. Hel nearly shuddered. "How did you get out of the underrealm?" He blew smoke into his face. "You've been sucking cock and got a favor?"

"Fuck you," Synick growled.

War's fist cracked against the good half of his flesh, and blood sprayed across the floor. He groaned but lifted his chin defiantly.

"You bleed easier than you used to," War said.

"Come on, Syn," Hel drawled. "Confession is good for the soul. Or so I hear."

"How should I know? I saw an opening and I took it."

"You were just sitting there in your misery and suddenly a portal opened? And it really must be misery for a god down there. It's the oldest rivalry time has, demons versus gods." There were some people he might feel sorry for having to endure what he no doubt had, but Synick wasn't one of those people. "Has it been so long you have forgotten I can taste lies?"

Synick stared at him. The cloudy, lidless eye suddenly flicked side to side then forward again. "It's worse than you can imagine."

"I don't need to imagine it. I've been there."

"Not as long as I have."

"Thank the Maker for that. But here's the thing," Hel took another pull on his civar, "no one could have known when Valeen was going to open the portal to Runevale. And it wouldn't explain a doorway into the underrealm."

"I don't know."

War hit him in the face again, knocking him and his chair to the ground. Synick groaned then spit a glob of saliva and blood near Hel's boot. War dragged him and the chair upright once again. "You really have fallen from grace. Rotten, filthy, and can you even see out of that eye?"

"You wouldn't expect after that *bitch* killed me, I'd be exactly the same, would you?"

Hel snarled, leaned forward and snatched a handful of Synick's hair, scraping his nails against his scalp. "I'd cut out your tongue, but I need you to be able to speak. You know what you don't need though?" The burning end of Hel's civar glowed orange in the low light of the dungeon. He rolled it in between his fingers, then shoved it into Synick's good eye. "To see."

"You fucking bastard!" Synick roared, jerking like a fish caught on a line. Hel got up from his chair, kicking it aside, and drove his knee onto Synick's thigh to keep him from tipping back and smiled. There was something poetic about being able to torture the male who had made his life miserable since childhood.

"Let's move on. It doesn't really matter how you got out. You're already here. Where would the council hide our immortality? Where are their most secret hiding places?" He pulled the civar back, keeping it ready for the other eye.

"I've been gone a long time. And I was dead before they did their ritual to take your immortality. You can't expect me to be privy to this."

If Synick knew about the ritual then he had some relationship with the demon princes, which made him wonder if they knew who had the third brother's ring. But he wouldn't ask. It was too dangerous of information to even let Synick wonder about it.

"I didn't ask you where they were, did I?" Hel let go of Synick's greasy hair and wiped his hand on his black coat. Disgusting.

"There is a myriad of places they could hide things. But something as precious and rare as immortality, The Drakonan Treasury in Ryvengaard namely. It's the most secure place in the realms and has never been breached."

Hel smirked. "Well, that's not true anymore, but it can't be there. The portals in and out of Runevale closed once Valeen was executed. They would be hidden in Runevale. Where?"

"I'll start talking when you get me out of these chains."

"That's not going to happen," War said, drumming his fingers along the handle of the dagger at his hip. "Let's not forget you're the one who said that mercy is for fools and females, and we're neither of those."

"You'll start talking because if you don't, I'll make what you did to us look like a child's game."

"Nothing you could do would be worse than what the demons did, I can assure you, Hel. There is no amount of torture that will get anything out of me. Just as Valeen will never give up Soulender, I won't be giving away leverage of any kind. Don't even bother asking about the Sword of Truth. Even the demons couldn't get it out of me."

Hel tapped the toe of his boot. That might be true, but he'd find out for himself.

Synick let out a dark chuckle. "Speaking of your... *wife*, when we made the bet about Valeen you weren't supposed to actually fall in love with her. Did you help her kill me to get rid of your competition?"

Laughter bubbled in Hel's throat, and he couldn't help the grin that spread across his face. "*You* competition for *me*? I know you think highly of yourself, but I didn't believe you were quite so delusional. She's always despised you. I don't think there is a person in all the realms she hates more than you. I might be a dick but at least I still have a pretty face. You on the other hand..." Hel shoved another fresh civar into Synick's rotten eye just to see if it caused pain. He screamed through his teeth and jerked away. "I could use Soulender and make that eye disappear permanently."

"Where would they hide our immortality?" War crossed his arms.

"I said I'm not talking."

Hel summoned his magical crimson snake, Selene, and soon she coiled down his arm. Her black forked tongue flicked out and her yellow eyes glowed in the dim torchlight. "If you don't know anything, there's no reason to keep you alive."

Synick stiffened and pushed back in his chair. "I said I wasn't talking, not that I didn't know anything. I know of several places they would hide your immortality. Places you'd never find without knowing."

"Too late. I'm bored of you now." Hel lifted a shoulder and Selene slithered down to his wrist and onto Synick's lap. "I know you can't see so let me elaborate. My serpent friend here has a bite that is lethal in seconds, but first there is burning, really intense, like your insides are melting. I'm sure the demon princes will be missing you and they might even have a welcome home party. I'm sorry I won't be able to make it. Busy, you see."

War shifted slightly closer to Hel and gave him a wary look. They did need information from him, and no doubt War was unsure if he would actually kill him. But Synick was only one tool in their arsenal. He had never planned for Synick to be alive to question. He'd find their immortality without him. The Sword of Truth was really the only thing worth keeping this prick alive for, but they wouldn't be able to torture it out of him... they'd have to fight him while he used it.

Synick kicked and wiggled, trying to bounce Selene off. She curled her tail around his calf and glided up his chest. "We can go to the council together and settle this. They'll take me back and I can pardon my nephews."

"You think they would take you back looking like that?" War asked. "A grotesque demon-looking thing? No."

"There are problems with your proposal, Synick.

First of all, I made a promise to kill everyone on the council, and I don't go back on my word. Two, you didn't add my wife into the deal even if we could work out a peace treaty. And most importantly, three, you murdered Katana to punish Valeen because she wouldn't fuck a piece of shit like you. And for that, one day I will carve out not simply your eyes but your heart and give your body to the trolls to tear apart, and your soul will spend eternity in the underrealm. I'll pay the demon princes handsomely to make certain you never get peace."

Synick scrunched his face into a sneer. "You're as much of a monster as I am, Hel. You may end up there yourself one day."

Hel took a pull from his civar. "And then there wouldn't be princes of the underrealm there'd be a *king*. Now, I'm going to count to three and then she bites. Because I don't give a fuck whether you live or die. It's no skin off my ass if the rest of your body rots and your soul is tortured endlessly. I'll sleep like a wee babe and still get what I want one way or another." Hel gave War a pointed look to make sure he knew he was telling the truth. He better not try to get in the way either. War's jaw muscles flickered, and he narrowed his eyes, but he stayed silent.

"Actually, let's skip the counting. Three," Hel said.

"Wait!" Synick screeched. "I'll help. Just get this snake off me."

Hel flicked his fingers, and she vanished, reappearing around his own shoulders. "It's a little disappointing how easy that was really," he said to War.

War shook his head but smiled. "So, Synick, where should we start looking?"

"Start with Rogue. One thing the demons deal in is secrets, and Rogue has one that will make him fold."

"That's not a location," War said, raising his fist. "You said you'd give us locations."

"No, it's better than random places where they might hide our immortality." Hel took hold of War's wrist to stop him from delivering the blow. "We could spend months looking, months we don't have, and still not find anything. What's his secret?"

WAR CLOSED the heavy metal door to the wing of the dungeons Synick was located in. A section deep under the castle that few knew existed. "I thought you were going to kill him," War said, locking the door.

"I was. If you want to be feared the way I am, War, you can't bluff. You have to be willing to do it."

"Thane. My name is Thane."

Hel tilted his head. "You're really going with that?"

"Yes."

"So fuck the past, huh?"

He glared at him. "I like Thane better, don't make it more than it is."

"No, you're shedding that part of you. The part that is my brother." He waved his hand up and down his cousin, "You're all elf now."

"You are my brother, Hel, whether my name is Thane or War. But I will stay here as High King when this is over, so it's Thane."

"Fine." Hel didn't like it, he'd called him War for hundreds of years, but it wasn't his choice. He'd already taken the most precious thing in Thane's life—

Layala—so he would give him this. They walked shoulder to shoulder down another dank and musty corridor. "I still think it's best we get rid of Synick so no one can ever know where the Sword of Truth is."

"Except we don't know how he is here. What if he gets let out again?"

"The dead are supposed to stay dead. They can't just let things out. The demon princes can't even leave themselves without the help of a god or goddess, and the gods can't let out the dead, so something else happened."

"What?"

"Maybe Valeen created a momentary rip in every realm. I don't know. We may never know."

Thane stopped and faced him. "How do you think Morv got free?"

"The council sent him to assassinate us. Obviously they used their power to open the gateway. Even if they couldn't leave Runevale themselves, they clearly were able to communicate with people outside Runevale. They have spies and assassins from all over. I'm more than certain they know the portals are open. We need to be prepared for anything they'll throw at us." They came to another door and pushed through. The cells down here were entirely empty. A poor use of space, honestly. There had to be at least a handful of people who needed to be thrown into a cell for a crime. Thane's annoying elven sister and mother for starters. He'd only seen the pair for a few minutes and already wanted to snap their necks. Gods, they'd been gone for a day and Orlandia blubbered like an infant when she saw her son return. "What do we know about the demon prince's power, Thane?"

"You accepted *Thane* quickly." He rubbed his chin. "And their power is fueled by the dead."

"Exactly. Even if they could let him out, they wouldn't. His soul is worth thousands of any mortal and without their third brother and his ring, their power is already weakening. And I can still call you War to be an asshole if you prefer."

Bright sun slipped through the outer edges of the door and then with a flick of Hel's wrist it opened and fresh air burst into the dungeon tunnels. An unknown set of guards waited outside and dipped their chins upon seeing their king and his cousin. He was still waiting to hear what the rumors around the castle staff would be about Hel and the king's former betrothed, *Layala,* clearly sharing a room together.

Hel wasn't going to hide their relationship on anyone's account, least of all peasants and the gossip columns of the *Palenor Scroll*. Though he'd taken care of that problem months ago when he cut off the writer's hands and tongue. He doubted anyone else would dare write about his wife. And if the elves at large figured out he was the Black Mage—well, at least they'd have some fucking respect. He didn't like playing second fiddle to their king.

"Did Katana say how she came to be here?" Hel asked.

Thane shook his head. "She doesn't remember. She mentioned believing she was meant to help Valeen somehow, but that's all."

"She was married to the primordial Atlanta. He might come calling once he learns she is alive, and if my instincts are right, and they always are, he'll be a problem. She would have asked about him by now; shit, she would have wanted to go to him if he wasn't. When you die and come back the first person you want to go to is your lover."

"Maybe she doesn't love him."

"Find out." Hel tapped a finger against his chin. "I wonder what she is capable of. Will she be an asset or a liability?"

"Not everyone is a pawn on a chessboard for you to use."

"No, there are also knights, bishops, rooks, and kings and queens, and then there is the hand moving them. Leif, Piper, even Presco, are pieces, you and I are the hand."

Thane chuckled. "And Valeen?"

"Is the angel on my shoulder. The only thing that keeps me from wiping the board clean. Because if it were only me, I'd take my army and burn through every city I could in Runevale, watching as the pale ones grew in number and let the streets run red."

Thane's deep green eyes flicked over him, no shock or disappointment. He was too used to Hel's antics for that. "You'd be killing thousands of innocent people, and someone would eventually get to you. It wouldn't simply be the council who would see you as a threat. All the gods and goddesses would."

Hel raised a shoulder. "I said if it was *only* me. Now, I can't do that. It risks her life too much, and I have a reason to live. I won't die again only to be reborn and forget it all."

"How long do you think we have before they bring an army? I'm guessing weeks, not months. It will take time for them to gather their forces, but they've been waiting for this."

Hel dragged his tongue over his bottom lip. This question had kept him up most of the last two days. "So have I." He was itching for this battle and to watch the council fall.

The paths around the castle grounds were patrolled with more soldiers than ever before. The guard had been tripled, and so had Hel's wards on this place. With the pale ones locked in the Void, it freed up the elven army to guard the city wall rather than be spread out.

The castle doors were pulled inward as they approached. Thane was quiet as they entered and then stopped under the chandelier in the foyer. His voice was low when he said, "And your plan is just to have your cursed army come up against a force that will outnumber us fifty to one? Can you even control them enough to not attack *us* right alongside the council's forces?"

Hel glared at one of the guards and he quickly shut the front doors, leaving him and Thane alone. There were outliers among the pale ones of course, but the majority of them followed his command. They were drawn to him in a way Hel couldn't even explain. "Of course I'll control them. And that's my plan but what the fuck are you bringing to this fight? Your Ravens won't be enough. We need dragons."

Thane sighed and ran his hand over the top of his hair. He slowly shook his head, and his face twisted into frustration. "If King Zale is still the dragon king in Ryvengaard, which is unlikely, it would be nearly impossible to convince him to fight with me against the council again. He lost more than half his people in that war and then I was captured and never heard from again. If he's still alive, he probably hates me."

"Well, thankfully you have an entire army of dragons up north who have no memory of that time because they weren't there, and one pretty redheaded soldier who I hear has the heart of their prince."

"They won't fight with us because of your curse. They are terrified of becoming infected. It's us and your pale ones."

He started up the wide staircase, leaving Thane behind. "You never used to give up so easily. Use that diplomatic mind and charm I know you have and that handsome mug." He smiled over his shoulder at him. "You really don't want me to do it because I'll start by killing the king and work my way down the royal line until one of the heirs agrees to fight and place a crown on his head."

Chapter 9

KATANA

Sweat covered Katana's brow and dampened her hairline. She gasped, clutching her chest and swung her legs over the edge of the bed. Another terrible dream sent her heart racing. She couldn't shake the image even now as the sun shone through her window. It had been the same nightmare for two days in a row—Katana had been on her knees, pressing her palms over the wound as if it would stop the blood gushing down her body, staining her white silk dress. She was screaming and screaming, her throat raw from it. Synick stood in the corner laughing. Atlanta had sat in his chair watching her suffer, sipping on a drink, no emotion, no movement, as she cried for him to help her. This was her mind reliving the past; the only difference was Atlanta had not been there when she died.

She'd been alone. Synick left her dying, alone.

Trying to catch her breath, Katana rushed to the balcony doors and threw them open for fresh air. They told her she'd been gone thousands of years, but it felt like a lie. To her, it was as if she'd gone to sleep lying in a pool of her own blood and had then woken up when she stood confused in the middle of Valeen's territory. Though she vaguely felt the gap of time and remembered being called to step through a bright portal. It was more a feeling than anything.

But the night of her death she knew vividly and had been forced to relive the sticky blood on her palms, the desperate pleas, begging Synick to help her. Asking why he would do this. They were primordials. They'd been with each other since the beginning... he was supposed to be her friend, to protect her, not harm her.

More than anything that was what plagued her the most—why? Why would he do that to her? Where had he gotten a weapon that even could? It had never existed before.

A strange sensation rose up in her throat like something was coming up and she cupped her hand over her mouth, leaning over the edge of the balcony. Was this what mortals called nausea? Taking deep inhales through the nose, breathing in crisp cool air, made the sensation slowly subside. A set of guards walked by below and she ducked.

Breathe, breathe.

She was told Synick was locked up in a dungeon. He couldn't get to her. She'd said this over and over, but it hadn't helped. Even with the reassurance of him being bound, too loud of a noise would make her jump. A shadow cast from a flickering candle would raise panic.

Worst of all, she was more vulnerable than before. She felt the weakness in the very marrow of her bones.

An immortal body did not tire climbing stairs, did not feel exhaustion from lack of sleep. A goddess slept, but if she didn't, she wouldn't weaken. It was more to clear the mind, not to restore the body. Her hands trembled even now—from what, she didn't know. Her stomach ached and made a strange gurgling sound, an entirely new sensation.

Once, she ate food for pleasure, not to survive, and being in an entirely new place with strangers and the only person she knew asleep for days, she ignored the signs. She wanted to pretend that she was not—mortal. Mortals required food and water, and she hadn't eaten much since she arrived. Maybe subconsciously she hadn't eaten as a test to herself, trying to prove she wasn't in this strange fragile body, that the weakness would go away, and that her strength would return.

She made her way back into the bedroom she'd been given, opened a desk drawer and found a silver letter opener. Gripping the handle, she jabbed the point of it into her palm. The sting sent a shock up her arm. Blood beaded up and she waited for it to close. She shouldn't have even been able to pierce her flesh with such a flimsy thing, and the wound should close instantly, but a crimson trail slid across her skin and plopped onto the floor.

Was this a nightmare? Everything was wrong.

Had she actually come back to the realms? Or had she dreamed it all?

Valeen—she must find her. If she found her sister, she would know it was real. Panic wrapped its horrible hand around her chest, and she dashed out of the room, down the hallway, bare feet slapping against the cold stone. Strangers' portraits on the walls passed by her in a blur. Nothing was familiar here. Not the smells, not the people. Even the sounds of the birds were different. There were no gulls. The sun wasn't as intense.

Where were the ocean waves crashing against black sand to soothe her? Her home was on the cliffs where the sea air made her skin damp, and the salt lingered on her lips.

She bolted around a corner and slammed into someone. Her arms flailed, attempting to catch her balance before tipping backward.

Strong hands caught her around the waist and held her steady. She lifted her chin and found familiar emerald-green eyes staring back at her. Long dark hair framed a handsome but surprised face.

Shaking, she touched his smooth cheek. His skin was supple and warm. Soft breath parted his full lips. His dark brows furrowed in confusion.

She knew him but... "Are you real?" she whispered.

The corner of his mouth lifted into a slight curve. "Yes, I am real."

Slowly, she moved her hand down to his chest and pressed her palm flat above his heart, a steady *thud, thud, thud,* beat there. If it were a dream, she wouldn't find a heartbeat so strong.

"Are you hurt? Did something happen?" His deep voice sent a tremble down to her gut. He sounded real, felt real. As if the hazy worry lifted away, every sense she possessed sharpened.

She was once again in the land of the living.

This was the realm of Adalon, home of the elves,

and she stood before the god of war also known as Thane, the High King of the elves.

She lifted her hand off his chest and turned it over to find the self-inflicted wound on her palm had stopped bleeding, but it was sore and still bright red. Before she could tuck away the wound, he took hold of her wrist and opened her fingers. "How did this happen?"

"I–I did it."

"Why would you hurt yourself?"

She glanced down, recalling she was wearing a short, thin nightgown. Too embarrassed to admit why she stabbed her own hand and was racing through the halls questioning reality. "I am looking for Valeen."

"She's here but do you need to sit down?" His brows furrowed as he inspected her further, seeing deeper. "Can I get you some water?"

Her mouth was dry, and her throat ached from what she suspected was dehydration. "No, I will be fine. I–I had a nightmare and now it seems silly."

She pulled out of his grasp and started back down the corridor to her guest chambers, heat working its way up her neck. Someone had left a pitcher of water on the bedside table and a tray of snacks, and she'd rather eat than burden Thane. Surely, he had better things to do.

"Katana, wait." She hadn't had much interaction with him, or anyone since they'd arrived here a few days ago. "Tell me about it."

"It is nothing."

"You asked me if I was real... I don't think it's nothing."

She took in a sharp breath and came to a slow stop.

Shame worked its way up her throat. Would he think she was losing her mind? She couldn't meet his eyes when she confessed, "I keep having the same dream of Synick killing me, and then I thought maybe all this was also a dream, and I had to see someone else. I had to..."

"You're here in Palenor. It's real."

"I know that now."

"I should have checked on you sooner. I assumed since you didn't come out of your room except to check on Valeen you wanted space." He lifted a hand toward her but then curled his fingers and dropped his arm to his side.

Space away from everyone was likely the reason she felt this way in the first place. "You do not need to apologize."

"Is it because he's here? We can move him somewhere else, but I give you my word he is well guarded. He won't hurt you."

Atlanta would have told her to quit whining about nothing, and yet Thane offered to move Synick somewhere else entirely simply because she was having nightmares.

"I trust you know what you are doing."

His face softened. "Would it help if I moved you into the room next to Valeen? It's my old room. You can be close to her."

Katana's legs seemed to weaken as the rush of panic wore off. She had never felt like this before and reached for the wall to hold herself steady. "I cannot ask you to give up your room."

"I already gave it up. No one sleeps there now."

"Why did you give it up?"

He tilted his head slightly to one side. "Because Valeen and Hel are right next to it."

She had yet to learn the details of what his relationship to Valeen was. A past lover was all she knew. Most of the last two days she'd sat in her room waiting for Valeen to wake up. "Thank you. I will think about it." She was in an entirely different wing than her sister and this castle was vast, easy to get lost in.

"You look a little pale. Have you eaten?"

"Oh, umm, I ate an apple a couple of days ago. I think." The corridor around her started to spin and she closed her eyes, pressing her head back against the cold wall. Warm fingers closed around her wrist.

"I'm a terrible host. Let's get you something to eat."

She wrapped her arm around his, leaning on him more than she would have liked. In the dining hall, Thane pulled out a seat for her and then sat at the head of the table. A male servant with a silver tray in hand entered through a side door. Another came in after and pulled open the velvet blue curtains, allowing in sunshine and a wonderful view of the lush, green castle grounds.

The servant approached the table and his gaze flicked over her nightgown. The thin straps showed more skin than he was likely used to. His face barely gave away his surprise, but he didn't say anything as he set a tray between her and Thane. He lifted the lid and then dipped into a bow.

"Thank you, Cassius," Thane said.

"You're welcome, sire." He gave her one more questioning appraisal before he and the other servant left.

Katana smiled. It was a good quality for a king and a god to be humble enough to thank a servant. Most she knew at his status didn't even acknowledge the existence of servants unless they fell short of a task.

The spread of fruit, nuts, and cheeses made her mouth water. She toyed with the edge of the cream tablecloth, waiting for him to go first. Even if she was starved, it was only appropriate as she was his guest.

He pushed the silver tray toward her. "It's all yours. I've already eaten."

She popped a grape into her mouth and sighed as the sweetness burst over her tongue. It seemed juicier and more flavorful in this body, at least more satisfying. Perhaps because she needed it rather than thought of it as an indulgence. She had consumed more than half of the tray by the time her stomach signaled it was full to the brim, and she drank water to wash down the last remnants of food.

Thane had watched her eat in silence, and she finally looked up to find a small smile. She picked up a napkin, dabbed the corners of her mouth and sat taller. "I seem to have forgotten my manners, Thane. How has your morning been? Anything new?"

"You're hungry. No need to worry about manners." He drummed his fingers on the tabletop. "And considering all that has happened in the past few days, it's been quiet. I don't know if that's a good or bad thing."

"'*It's*', '*that's*'. The way you all speak, it is how the lesser mortals spoke, and you all use Murilian tongue rather than the celestial language of Runevale. Has so much changed since I have been gone?"

His brows rose slightly. "I guess I hadn't considered that even the language would be different since you were alive. We do speak in contractions and Murilian is the primary language of Adalon, but I do know the celestial language." He leaned forward, reaching across the table and turned her hand over so her palm was face up. "You're mortal, aren't you? That's why you did this... to see."

She pulled away and tucked her hand against her chest. "I had to be sure. Hunger pains are something new as well. It felt like my stomach was trying to consume itself and my body was shaky." She picked up a piece of cheese and ate it even though she was full.

"You will need to eat at least twice a day and drink plenty of water."

She nodded absently. "I have been worried about Valeen. Is sleeping so much normal for an elf?"

"No." Thane picked up a silver goblet and took a sip. "She must have been exhausted. But Hel said she's awake and was changing right before I ran into you."

"Thank the All Mother." She ran a hand over her silk nightgown. "Which is exactly what I should be doing. From what I have seen, short thin sleeping gowns are not the fashion among ladies in Palenor."

He chuckled. "Not exactly."

"You do not seem bothered by it, but I think your servant was taken aback by my lack of modesty."

"I think his surprise had less to do with the lack of modesty and more to do with the fact that you're wearing a nightgown and we're having breakfast together."

"Oh dear, it must look like we spent the night together." She giggled and covered her mouth before laughter burst out. "I had not considered that." But a thought hit her, and she gasped. "You do not have a wife, do you? I would feel awful if rumors started and she was hurt. I would never do that."

He settled into his chair, spine less rigid. "No."

"Someone you are promised to?"

"Not anymore. I am completely unattached as of several months ago."

Relieved, Katana brushed her hair behind her ears. She should have spent more time learning the gossip around the castle rather than hiding in her room for the past two days. But he said Valeen was his former lover and there was some talk about a lady named Layala who had recently returned. "Valeen was your betrothed."

"At the time her name was Layala, but yes."

"Right, you said that under the tree back in Runevale. I got the impression it was recent but neither of you said so. It must be difficult to see her with Hel then. I am sorry." She knew what it was like to watch the person you loved be with someone else. Her husband Atlanta had taken several wives and concubines after they were wed. It was more rare for a god to be loyal to one person than not, but even if it was accepted, it didn't hurt any less. She felt like a body to be used for his pleasure, a rotation among many to bear children. As his first wife and a primordial, she had her own home that none of the other females lived at, but it didn't make the nights he was with someone else any less painful. It didn't stop the sting of his backhand when she had something to say about it either.

Thane pressed his lips together and only lifted a shoulder. "It's over. Not much else to say about it." His green eyes sparkled with moisture as he turned his head to look out the window. Her heart sank. She knew the sadness etched into his face and that reaction well.

It was one she had mirrored many times when she went to parties and saw Atlanta with someone else.

"And the staff is probably gossiping about her being with him since they do not know who she truly is, or who he is?" It was a nightmare for him. His former betrothed with someone else under his own roof. It wasn't as if they knew she was married to Hel in a previous life. They were elves here.

"No one has had the balls to say anything around me about what they speculate. Our engagement was publicly called off months ago but now people will know why—because of him. Though the servants are at a minimum, I still need help to keep this place running, and it would raise too many questions if I released all the in-house staff."

The servants' door creaked open and a maid walked in, wearing a black dress with a white apron. Katana had seen her once, whispering to another maid in the hallway about how she swore Thane's cousin was sleeping in the same bed as Layala and what a scandal it was. The other one questioned whether or not that could be true.

She had flashbacks of her own servants whispering about Atlanta's latest fling and how *loud* the pair were making love. Her cheeks flamed, and the chair legs scraped against the floor as Katana pushed back. Before she even thought about the consequences, she dropped onto Thane's lap and wrapped her arms around his neck.

His big hands clamped around her waist and she felt his heartbeat pick up speed.

Leaning in, she whispered, "Well, we can just give them something else to gossip about."

His stiff posture relaxed, and he brushed her blonde hair behind her ear, playing into it. "Only problems I like." His touch tickled and sent a tingle down her spine. The maid had stopped halfway to the table, eyes wide. "Give us the room," he said, keeping his eyes on her. She quickly followed his command.

Katana smiled. "Do you think she will go tell the others the High King is sitting in the dining hall with a new, scantily-clad lady?"

"Certainly."

"I hope that does not bother you."

He let out a low laugh. "I think you might have made my day actually. As much as I care for them, Hel and Val, and know it's right they are together... It was easier when they were gone. Layala was betrothed to me since birth."

"That was your father's arrangement I am guessing."

"Yes."

"And what if you told people you made your own choice, and the relationship was not in either of your best interests?" Katana slowly kicked her feet as they hung over the edge of the chair's armrest. "You could always tell them the truth."

"That she is a goddess reborn, and I was once a god of Runevale? The gods were forgotten here long ago. The elves aren't ready to hear it."

"The council will bring war soon and they will have no choice but to be ready."

He half smiled and let out a long breath, closing his eyes. It was as if he had the weight of the world on his shoulders. He shouldn't have to worry about petty gossip among servants in the castle when his people's lives were at stake.

"They won't believe it," he whispered.

The door burst open, and a beautiful elven maiden glided into the room. Her heels tapped lightly, her lush red gown trailed behind her in an overstated train. Brown curls tumbled down her back in an extravagant style. She paused halfway to the table, hands clasped before her and glared at Katana. "Thane, who is this trollop?"

He sighed and sat back against the chair but kept his hands around Katana's waist. "Hello, Mother."

Chapter 10

THANE

Thane kept hold of Katana as he brought them both to stand. First gossip from the servants and now this. If he didn't have duties and powerful people that wanted him dead, he'd simply go take Phantom out for a long ride and not return for weeks.

His mother, Queen Orlandia, had come back from their manor in Brightheart a few weeks after Valeen and Hel had left to Ryvengaard. She had many questions, and he had answered them as best as he could. His mother accepted that Hel was the Black Mage and Layala had left with him without so much as a flinch. He'd once suspected she knew Tenebris had made a deal with Hel long ago in regard to Valeen, but that confirmed it. She'd known all along and was only too happy they had left. Maybe she never liked Layala because she was looking out for him, maybe she knew it wouldn't end well when the Black Mage returned.

And he hadn't heard the end of her complaints for

the last two days. Sure, she was overjoyed that Thane, Piper, and Leif had returned so soon, but not that Valeen or Hel or the dragons were here. Although Varlett hadn't made an appearance since they returned. As much as he hated her, it would be better for her to remain close so they could keep an eye on her.

"I wouldn't call the goddess of day a trollop, Mother."

Orlandia took a half step back, face pinched in a sour expression. "The what?"

"You heard."

Her cheeks puffed as a slow breath parted her lips. "I swear you're only doing this to get back at me. All this talk of gods and portals to other realms... is it to punish me for not telling you the truth about your father's deal with you know who? I don't understand why"—she looked around and lowered her voice—"*he* is back here. How are we supposed to keep this all under wraps?"

"Hel is my cousin and that's all anyone knows. I kept it under wraps fine while you were in Brightheart."

"Your cousin." She pressed her lips together and her already rouged cheeks reddened. "I carried you in my womb. I birthed you. I held you in my arms and watched you grow and yet you want to have me believe you are the god of war? I know you are special and always have been, but that Layala is a goddess reborn and this maiden you have hanging all over you is... It's too much, dear. It's—"

"I don't know how else to explain it," he snapped. Rehashing this same conversation and her acting like he had lost his rationality was getting old. Thane held out his arm to Katana. She wrapped her hands around his elbow, and they started for the door. "I have to go north."

His mother followed them out into the corridor, and she caught up to his other side. "For what?"

"I have to meet with the dragons to secure an alliance. War is coming, Mother."

"We have been at war for hundreds of years. How is this any different? We should plan a party or a dance to appease the Maker."

Doing a dance to please the Maker who had never once shown any sign of help for the elves seemed silly now. The creator of this world abandoned it long ago and the All Mother had only taken the magic from the elves.

Katana walked silently, her warm fingers curled against his skin, but she pressed her lips together trying not to laugh.

"No parties. No unnecessary people in this castle. Do you understand?"

"Fine," she huffed. "Are you sleeping with this girl now? What are we to say about Layala, er Valeen, then? You called off the engagement only to have her return with someone else..."

"No, I'm not sleeping with her. Katana is Valeen's sister, and a friend." And despite a few flirtations and how devastatingly beautiful she was, that's how it would stay. He would not get attached to another goddess with a vengeful husband and have his life shattered all over again when she chose the other male.

Orlandia scoffed. "Her *sister*. Maker Above, have

you lost your good sense? This girl cannot stay here, and neither can the other two."

"I am not a *girl*. That would imply I am barely more than a child." Katana smiled at Orlandia. "I may not look it, but I am much older than you. I was created before time existed. And you should ask Valeen what she wants said about her. I would not incur the goddess of night's wrath, Queen Mother, or it may be the last thing you ever do."

"Mother, please," Thane said softly, and took her hand. "Just try to be nice for once. Nice to Valeen, nice to Katana, to all the people I care for. I know this is strange but it's necessary. It's not always about you. It's for me."

The corners of her mouth turned down and she let out a sigh. "I am doing what's best for you. I don't want you to get hurt again."

"I'm fine."

"You weren't fine."

"I am now."

"Alright." She threw up her hands. "I love you and want what's best for you, that's all. I will stay out of your business."

He smiled at her. As much as she was a pain in his ass, he loved her. "Thank you."

KATANA EMERGED from her room in a royal-blue dress with gold links across her shoulders and a belt at her waist to match. The color complemented her bright hair and warm skin. The neckline cut into a "V", revealing a demure yet enticing amount of cleavage that made his mind wander to days before when he untied her dress to get the spider. He clenched his jaw and tugged at the collar of his top. *Was it hot in here today?* "I like that color on you, er, what I mean is you look... nice." She was stunning in anything she wore, from short silk nightgowns to something as lavish as this, but he wouldn't allow himself to think anything beyond that. She was beautiful, but there were a lot of females he found beautiful.

She flashed a smile. "Thank you. Perhaps I will not be presumed a trollop now."

"I'm sorry about her. My mother can be difficult and is very territorial."

"I gathered. I take it she does not care for my sister much."

He tilted his head slightly. "They've always clashed. Especially after she almost killed my sister Talon with a throwing star to the neck."

Katana blinked a few times. "She... what?"

"It's a long story." One he didn't want to rehash.

"Alright," Katana said slowly. "I take it she had a reason?"

"In her mind it was justifiable."

"But not in yours?"

"I don't know. It was a move to save her aunt. Valeen has many shades of gray. I see things more in black and white. Right and wrong." To be a gentleman, he offered his arm, and they slipped through the halls on their way to Valeen.

"She did not used to be that way. It hurts my heart."

"Sometimes life changes you." He lifted a shoulder. "I don't blame her after... everything."

She let out a heavy sigh. "I wish I could have been there for her."

"And she wishes she could have been there for you that night."

Katana looked up at him sorrowfully. "I know."

"I have a question that I need to know for security purposes," Thane said.

"This has something to do with me?"

"It does. If Atlanta discovers the portals are open and somehow finds out you're here, will he come to Palenor, and what do you want us to do about it if he does?"

Her lips pressed firmly together, and her grip tightened on his arm. "He will come. As far as what you should do about it... I do not want any of you in harm's way. I will speak to him."

"Can I ask why you don't want to go see him? I can only guess you didn't love him even if he was your husband."

"I did love him." She gulped. "And he loved many."

Thane nodded. The sorrowful change around her eyes flared an angry heat in his cheeks. It was typical for a god to have several lovers. They lived long lives, and among many it was competition to produce as many heirs and powerful offspring as possible.

"I want to start a new life. Katana—Atlanta's first wife—is not who I will be anymore."

"You felt like an extension of him even as a primordial goddess?"

"In many ways, yes. Nothing we had together ever truly felt like mine. It was his. Even *my* palace was modeled after the sea... not the sun. My own bed chambers were the only thing I had complete control over."

What an asshole. "You had separate palaces?"

Typically, it was the females who took charge of the decor. Even here Thane's mother, Orlandia, oversaw that. He might agree to the overall feel or theme, but she did the rest unless there was something specific he wanted done.

"I was not about to watch him parade around with a different female day and night, sometimes several. I raised my children in my home, not in the shared female house. That was one thing I would not budge on."

He had the goddess of day as his wife, and it wasn't enough? "The more I hear, the more I think he shouldn't be a welcome guest. Did you not want to divorce him?" It wasn't common but it was done in Runevale.

The silence was filled with her shoes tapping lightly on the stone as they descended the stairs. "I did ask for one once. He did not like that."

"It doesn't really matter if he liked it, does it?"

There was strange energy coming off her. Almost like she was...afraid. "To keep it simple, divorcing someone powerful like Atlanta when he said 'no' seemed impossible. There was not much I could do about it at the time. And should Atlanta want to come here, I doubt anyone would be able to stop him."

She underestimated what he, Hel, and Valeen were capable of. No more needed to be said for him to decide that Atlanta was indeed a threat. Katana was one of them now. And if they had to fight a battle against her former husband, they would. "So, you don't want to see him?"

"Ideally, he does not find out I am alive."

Just ahead Valeen stood in the foyer and his stomach tumbled. It brought up strange feelings to see her standing in his castle again. He'd avoided one-on-one interaction with her as much as possible since their talk in his room. Their relationship had been over months before that, but that night was the finality of her choice. The mixed emotions whirling inside him made sweat bead on his brow. A flurry of excitement, sadness, and trepidation. The way she teased him while they rode on dragon back made him want her again. Friends or lovers, he'd take either. Now that she knew everything it wasn't like he could take advantage. At the very least he wanted them to be close friends like they had been when he was War but after loving her so deeply, and her sharing those same feelings, it couldn't be the same.

She beamed at them both. "Good morning." In a few quick strides she threw her arms around her sister. "I'm so sorry I slept for two days. I should have been with you."

"Do not trouble yourself over me. You needed the rest, Val."

Valeen tilted her chin toward him and playfully tapped his arm. "Hello, Thane."

"Valeen."

The corner of her mouth turned up. "Wow, I'm reduced to a name as a greeting. Not even a smile."

"Good morning."

"You're so formal today, High King."

"Should I be something other than formal,

Valeen?" He wasn't even sure how to act. He wanted to say that she looked lovely, that he was torn with her here, and to tell her to leave and then ask her to stay. It was confusing.

Valeen folded her arms. "I'm sorry for how I reacted when I saw the ruins. I should have had better control of my emotions. You were right about Synick." She held out her hand. "I don't want to fight with you. Truce?"

He shook her hand trying not to smile. That wasn't why he was feeling the way he did but he appreciated the apology. "I'm sorry for what has become of House of Night, but I will help you get it back. And I don't want to fight with you either."

"Friends?" Valeen smiled sweetly.

"Always."

"I expected to be at my castle and since I'm not, I've thought about going to stay with Aunt Evalyn. I know it's not ideal for me to stay here with Hel." She pushed her hair behind her ears.

That was an understatement. But he wouldn't ask her to leave. He blew out a slow breath. "Look, if Hel can live in this castle when it was you and me to make sure you were safe from assassins, I certainly can, and I'll do it without killing random guards and being an asshole to everyone."

"Good." She arched a brow.

"It's safer if you stay. It's a big castle and that's your room. You just won't find me next door to you anymore."

"It's probably for the best."

"It's *certainly* for the best."

Katana reached out and took her sister's hand,

"Have you eaten breakfast?" It was a welcome change of subject.

"Not yet but I am hungry. Have you?"

"We did but I will sit with you. We can talk and have a good time."

"Just the two of you?" Valeen slipped into a mischievous smile. Katana smiled back as if they had some secret way of communicating. These two together were trouble.

"Just us. But I am sure he would enjoy both of our company for lunch. Or another dragon ride perhaps. Snuggled up between us this time." Katana giggled and playfully nudged his arm.

Valeen laughed. If turning it into a joke worked to ease the tension in the air, then he'd take it.

"Is this going to be a thing now? Just wait until Hel hears about it," Thane grumbled, even though he liked this playful banter more than awkwardness between them.

"He would not get angry with you will he, Val?" She suddenly looked nervous and started pawing at her hair. "Maybe we should not tease Thane anymore. If Hel loses his temper with you..."

Her eyes narrowed slightly. "If either of us has a temper it's me, and he wouldn't hurt me if that's what you're worried about. Hel loves to get a rise out of people more than anyone."

"He's actually fanatical about keeping her safe," Thane added, but he wondered if she heard rumors about things Hel had done or if there was another reason she would think that. His mind drifted to her former husband. Maybe the reason she didn't want Atlanta to know she was alive went deeper.

Out of the corner of his eye, a guard approached with a letter in hand. "Excuse me, ladies." He took a few steps away from Katana and Valeen and held out his hand.

"Sire, a letter from the woodland elves."

He recognized the green seal on the back and tore it open. One thing he had not kept a close eye on were his old rivals. He still hadn't met the new Lord of Calladira and it had been half a year since he killed Lord Brunard in his manor. His spies reported the new ruler was a cousin of Lord Brunard's, but not much else was known about him. They'd kept themselves locked up tightly while the pale ones roamed free. He'd been too preoccupied with Hel, the pale ones, and a demon prince terrorizing his land to bother with the woodland elves.

The last time Calladira was supposedly coming it was only Hel playing a trick.

> High King Thane Athayel,
> The new lord of Calladira, Lord Maelus, requests an audience with the High King of Palenor at Castle Dredwich for your convenience. Please respond with a desired date.
> Lord Maelus

The name sounded familiar though he couldn't remember why. No details in the letter as to why he would request an audience was odd. They usually included a reason—talk of opening trade, or more often than he liked, land boundary discrepancies. Without prior permission, High Elves caught roaming on their land were considered trespassing. But times had changed with the Black Mage awake, and more than likely it was to discuss that particular problem. Their new lord would faint to know he now roamed about Castle Dredwich freely and as an ally.

THANE SHOVED the letter into Hel's chest and then dropped onto his throne. "This better not be you again." The sun shone down from the high windows casting an ethereal light, even making Hel look less sinister. He'd eased up on the black cloaks and kept his rune tattoos covered except for those on his hands but often he wore fingerless gloves to not raise questions. Surprisingly he'd become well-liked among the staff. The males thought he was suave and even funny, while the females whispered about his handsome face and air of mystery.

Hel's brows furrowed and he looked the letter over. "I wouldn't pull the same thing twice. I'm more creative than that. Besides, why would I trick you now? I thought we were friends again. Although, I do sort of miss being the villain around here. I might need to kill a few people just so no one forgets who I really am. Where are those green sash people that formed when Val was born? You know, the ones who think she's a dark mage and should be killed."

"Oh, you're still hated, no need to worry about that. And you have better things to do with your time than worry about them." He pointed at the letter from Lord Maelus. "And I don't know why you do half the things you do, so it wouldn't be far-fetched if you sent this."

"Everything I do is either for her or my vengeance. I'm a simple creature really." Hel crumpled up the paper and tossed it into the air where it vanished. "You seem a little jealous."

"Of you? Far from it."

"We haven't talked about her choice so let's get it out of the way."

"I don't want to talk about it. You're too sensitive."

Hel chuckled and put a hand on his chest. "*I'm* sensitive?"

"We'd end up in a fight."

"You want to fight me?" he mused, curiosity and challenge rising.

"Not at the moment."

"Good, because we already did that in this room once, and we both know how that went. You almost cried."

Thane let out a barking laugh. It stung that Hel had taken on both him and Valeen while barely breaking a sweat. His magic held Thane in place without Hel even moving. The strength he drew from the Void made him more powerful than both him and Valeen for now. Even if Thane was a full immortal, he wouldn't want to fight him. "Gods, you're such an arrogant ass. If you didn't use your magic, there would have been a very different outcome."

"Are we back to measuring cocks? If you want to fist fight, I'm up for it." His red eyes flashed, and he slipped his jacket off and with a snap of his fingers it hung on a hook near the entrance doors. He rolled up his charcoal sleeves and adjusted his black vest.

Thane rested one boot across his knee and drummed his fingers on the onyx armrest of his throne.

He truly was not angry with Hel for what Valeen chose, it was her choice to make, but he did want to punch him for being such an asshole and all the shit he pulled before. "The last time we had a duel you dropped me into an illusion of the underrealm."

"Well, you were an idiot and didn't set any rules." He walked to the base of the steps leading to Thane's throne and tapped his chin. "Hit me. Right here. I know you want to."

"This feels like a trick."

"I will allow you to hit me once, real fucking hard without consequences. I deserve it."

"You know what, you do deserve it." Thane made it down the steps in two strides, and swung hard. His fist cracked against Hel's jaw, snapping his head to the side. Hel stumbled off balance, caught himself before he fell, and held a hand to his mouth.

"Fuck," Hel murmured. "I forgot how hard you hit." He stood tall, and Thane punched him a second time. The sound of his fist hitting flesh echoed off the high rafters above. Blood splattered on the floor, and Hel backed up several steps, wiping his mouth with his sleeve. A wide split had opened on his bottom lip. The playfulness was gone now. "I gave you *one* shot."

"That first one was for the way you treated me when you first woke up. The second was for everything else." He needed several but two would have to do.

He let out a low rumble deep in his throat and then flipped him a middle finger. "Fine. It's done now but if you ever sucker punch me like that again, expect a *very* different reaction." He flicked a dismissive hand then crossed his arms behind his back and started pacing. "I heard gossip this morning. Care to explain?"

"What gossip?"

"Involving you and a pretty blonde. I don't know if I'd step into that arena, cousin."

Thane rolled his eyes. As if Hel was the one to lecture him on morals and what was right and wrong. "I'm sure whatever you heard is gossip and nothing more."

"Really?" His brow rose. "So she wasn't eating breakfast with you in a risqué nightgown on your lap? I mean, do whatever you want as long as you're not pining for my wife anymore."

"It's not what you think."

Hel laughed; the split on his lip was already gone. "Gods, so it did happen. Well, be careful. You break that one's heart and you'll have one very wrathful Valeen on the warpath."

"Yes, she sat on my lap, but nothing happened. Nothing is happening between Katana and I. Nothing *will* happen. It's too—they're sisters and given my past with Valeen…"

"They're not actually related and let's not pretend you don't cross lines when it comes to family. But it's probably best not to dredge up that old tale again."

Thane sneered at him. "Definitely best not to."

"What about the redhead?"

"Piper?"

"No, Leif," Hel said sarcastically and rolled his eyes. "What about Piper?"

"Haven't you ever thought about it? I *know* you've thought about it."

"I have not thought about her that way. She and I have only ever been friends."

Hel laughed. "Don't act like you're some innocent

virgin. I remember the night you had three demigoddesses in your bed at once."

"*That* was a very long time ago and not who I am anymore."

"If you say so. Piper is an angry little thing. She could probably use a good lay if you're up for the challenge. It would be less messy than with Katana."

Thane rubbed his temples. Why was he like this? "You're trying to get under my skin. It's not going to work."

He smiled, dimpling his cheek. "You're too easy to rile up. You might as well sweet-talk Katana and get it out of your system now. If she was sitting on your lap in a scanty nightgown, I *know* you've thought about her even if you aren't interested in Piper."

"Can you not try to play matchmaker? I wouldn't have trouble finding someone to bed if that's what I wanted."

"No denial. Interesting. I hear she's very sweet. She'd be perfect for you. You might have to"—he moved his thumb across his throat—"her husband though. I'll help."

Thane narrowed his eyes at him. Part of Hel must feel guilty for taking back Valeen and breaking his heart even if he'd never admit it.

"She doesn't want to be with Atlanta anymore. He's a prick."

"Is he a threat?"

"Yes."

"Fuck. Well, what's one more enemy in the grand scheme of things? Anyways, while I was roaming around the months before I came back here, I made a quick visit to Calladira. I've met this new Lord Maelus from the letter. I needed to assess the threat level. He isn't much of one. There was, however, something interesting about him. He has magic, and I wondered how that could be. Does the name Aldrich ring any bells?"

Thane's spine went rigid. "Aldrich?"

"You see, when you killed your elven father, my deal passed on to the next in his bloodline, which would ordinarily be you, but you're *you* so it went somewhere else and unfortunately it wasn't your sister. Or fortunately, depending on how you think about it. Talon is already a prissy nightmare; imagine if she had magic."

Heat trickled up Thane's neck and he rose to his feet. "Are you saying that Aldrich is Lord Maelus? In what world would Aldrich become the Lord of Calladira? He isn't from there."

"As it turns out, Tenebris had an affair with the aunt of the previous ruler of Calladira. Looks like he wanted to secure his line for both elven thrones. Can we make this work in our favor? If you can get the woodland elves to fight with us—"

"Aldrich pretended to be my friend and then betrayed me," he growled. "He and Tenebris kept Valeen locked in a tower with no water or food for months."

Hel frowned, and the red of his irises seemed to fall into shadow. Thane could almost see the dark thoughts churning behind his eyes. "He did what?"

"They starved her and kept her locked in a room until she was weak enough they thought they could force her to wake *you*."

"And you allowed him to live? I don't care if he's your brother. This is *Valeen*."

"I know," Thane snapped. He would have hunted him down if he had the time. "He got away, Hel. And if I didn't have a million other things I needed to deal with he'd already be dead."

"It's time the Black Mage made an appearance."

Light footsteps tapped on the floor, drawing their attention. Valeen stopped in the entry to the throne room and leaned against the archway. "Let me negotiate with Aldrich. Katana told me you're heading north, Thane."

"Negotiate?" Hel narrowed his eyes. "There will be no negotiations. He dies."

Chapter 11

VALEEN

"Exactly what Hel said. Aldrich almost killed you, and kept you locked in the tower," Thane said, standing at the base of the stairs leading up to his throne. Hel sat on the bottom step, watching her glide into the room with a mischievous look in his eye.

"I'm less afraid of Aldrich than I am of a lamb." She smirked at him. "Primordial goddess, remember? And even if I wasn't, I'd still beat that little prick's ass."

Thane chuckled. "Do what you want. I won't stop you."

"Of course you won't. You can't."

"She's feisty today," Hel said to Thane and rose to his full height.

"She usually is," he said back. "Quite the temper on that one."

"Like a feral, hungry cat."

"Alright!" Valeen crossed her arms and pressed her lips together to keep from smiling. "A feral cat? I think I liked it better when you hated each other."

NIGHT MEETS THE ELF QUEEN

They laughed and warmth bloomed in her core at the joy between them. As difficult as it was with the three of them together again and the past hurt lingering in Thane's eyes, she had hope that they could all be... happy. The three of them had been inseparable for many years.

"She must need something to eat. She's angry when she hasn't eaten," Hel said, still talking to Thane. "Scones sound good." He winked at her.

"Oh, or woodland elf wine," Thane replied. "She gets nicer when she's had a glass or two. Before you woke up, we had a party, and she wore a flower crown—"

Valeen cut him off with a glare. The last thing she wanted was for him to bring up her straddling him in a chair in front of the elves telling him how she wished she could sleep with him. It was much too soon to bring up anything like that, if there was even enough time in existence for that to be appropriate.

"So we're not teasing now?" Thane purred.

"Not about that."

"Well now I must know, and by the look on your face I'm going to need a smoke." Hel took out a civar and put it to his lips.

Hel would see it as a threat or a jab, not as playful banter. And Thane might even want to take shots at him. It was hard to know what Thane was feeling. Playful, by the smirk, but his brows were tight and there was a tenseness to his shoulders. There must be part of him that was jealous of Hel, and she didn't blame him. Part of her wanted to wrap her arms around him and ask if he was alright. But the friendship between Hel and Thane would be fragile for a while and she wouldn't see it shatter again.

"Trust me, you don't want to know," Valeen snatched the civar and took a puff herself. It immediately calmed her thumping heart and eased her racing thoughts about being in the same room with the two males she loved. No wonder he liked these things. "Unless you want to start rethinking about what life was like before I remembered you, before I ever knew you existed at all."

His brows rose watching her blow out smoke. He looked more shocked she'd taken his civar than anything. "I'll pass, little rabbit."

Thane chuckled. "She must *love* that nickname."

"*She* is going to kick both your asses in a minute." They laughed again, and Hel slipped behind her and hugged her waist. They were as bad as she and Katana together. The nickname instantly flamed her cheeks. She wasn't the little rabbit anymore, but it still pissed her off. "And I swear, Hel if you don't stop saying that—"

"Maybe I missed the way it made you want to attack me. There's just something about that dark side of you that does it for me."

Thane pressed his lips together and his gaze flicked down to Hel's arms curled on her waist.

"You have a bit of blood on your neck, Hel." Thane gestured and sauntered up the stairs to his throne and sat.

Twisting out of his arms she saw the dried blood. "What's that from?"

"He punched me. Twice. Nasty temper."

Valeen looked between them. It was hard to tell if

he was being serious or not. Thane just rested his head nonchalantly on the palm of his hand.

"Did you punch him?" She asked.

"Yep."

"Did he deserve it?"

"You know he did."

She didn't even want to ask why, and it was time for a change of subject. "So are you going north?"

"Yes, to talk to Ronan and the dragons but not for a few days. We need allies."

"Why wait?" Hel asked. "We don't have time for you to twiddle your thumbs."

Looking annoyed, Thane tapped the toe of his boot. "Because Palenor is my responsibility. It was one thing to leave when the danger was in another realm, but now they are coming here. Preparations need to be made. I need to make sure my generals are running necessary training."

"Well hurry up with that and while you're busy, I'll take care of some other business."

"What business would that be? Killing Aldrich?" Thane asked, brow raised.

Valeen heard what he said when she first walked in, but he couldn't mean now. "You can't do that. We might be able to get them on our side," Valeen argued.

"Why did you have to rat me out like that?" Hel glared at Thane then turned to her. "You know, you didn't seem all that upset when I cut out that *Palenor Scroll* writer's tongue and killed Baby Drakonan, so let me do what I need to do."

Valeen ran a hand over her hair and rolled her eyes. She *was* upset about Caliban Drakonan's death, but it needed to be done, or they'd have been caught. "Do you have to call him *baby* Drakonan?" She looked at Thane. "He wasn't a baby."

"You killed a *Drakonan* on Ryvengaard?" Thane groaned and rubbed a hand down his face. "What is wrong with you?"

With a shrug, Hel said, "It had to be done. You weren't there."

"You can't start problems with the woodland elves right now," Valeen snapped.

His tongue slid over his bottom lip as he brushed his fingers across her collarbone then pushed her hair behind her shoulder. "Mmm, I'm not starting problems. I'm taking care of business. There's a difference."

They did not need another enemy. "Hel."

In a few long strides, he was halfway across the room.

"Hel," she said sharply.

"You know he does what he wants. There's no stopping him," Thane murmured, resting his chin on his palm.

Clenching her teeth, she turned to shadow and in a blink, she reformed directly in front of the exit doorways. Hel paused, dragging his gaze down her body, then the corner of his mouth curled upward. "Are you planning to physically restrain me, Mrs. Black?"

"I'm planning on you listening to *reason*."

"No one wants Aldrich dead more than me, but she is right," Thane added, making his way down the steps from his throne. At least he was backing her up.

"You know when I get an idea in my head it doesn't just go away. This elf starved you and kept you isolated in a tower. I don't care what his reasons were. Nobody does that to my wife and gets to live to speak of it. I specifically told his father you were not to be harmed. In fact, I told him you were to be treated as a precious jewel, safeguarded and well cared for. And while we're at it, why don't you tell me who else was involved. Thane said they drugged you with katagas serum and didn't even give you water. Who drugged you? I want names."

All Mother, I should have expected this.

Thane walked up behind them and stood beside her. "Anyone who was involved with my father or what happened to her is already gone."

Eyes narrowed in suspicion, he said, "In the grave? I know they aren't in the prison cells below. It's barren down there. The fact that you allowed the *Palenor Scroll* to write about her and allowed this group who wants her dead to live, makes me think you didn't do what should have been done, so once again, I have to be the bad guy."

Valeen loved and hated that he was this way. Loved that he would do anything and hated that he was so spiteful, he couldn't see how they could use Aldrich in this war. "If Aldrich is the new Lord of Calladira, we could use them as allies. If you *kill* him that isn't going to happen. Aldrich will listen to me."

"I already kept one asshole alive who doesn't deserve to be here because you asked me to, and I even let Thane stop you from killing him. That piece of shit rotting in the dungeons should be dead already and would be. And now you two are going to stand here and stop me again? No. Aldrich doesn't get mercy whether or not he is a Lord."

"It's not mercy, it's strategy. The same reason I asked you to keep Synick alive."

"We don't want Synick here either, Hel," Thane added, "but because he is, we were able to get something useful out of him. I don't think Aldrich would help us, but I don't want to go to battle with the woodland elves right now."

"That information is yet to be determined. Synick could be sending us to a dead end just to get to live longer. And Aldrich could very well join with the council because they both hate you."

Footsteps came from outside the doors, and one side was pulled open. A guard stood there, looked between the three of them and dipped his head. "My apologies for the interruption."

Hel glared at the guard and his magic suddenly brushed past like an icy wind. The guard slowly rose off the ground, grasping at his throat. A heartbeat later he was pulled inside the throne room and to Hel's side. "Is this one of them that drugged you, Val?" He grabbed a handful of his dark hair and jerked his head back. "Was he one of the guards who locked you up?"

Thane let out a low growl, his magic mixed with Hel's in the air. It was a battle of hot and cold. "You think he'd be here if he was? I care about her too."

"You two want to team up against me? Fine then, it's him or Aldrich. Make a choice. It should be easy. You both care about the innocent so much."

"That's not fair. We're not teaming up against you. We just happen to agree." Valeen stepped closer, and Hel's eyes flashed a warning. She knew right then that he'd kill the guard if she didn't stop. The young elf's eyeballs looked like they might pop out of his head.

"Go kill Aldrich then and let him go," Thane snapped.

"I thought so." With a flick of his wrist the guard's boots hit the ground and Hel kicked him in the ass sending him stumbling back out the door. The guard choked and coughed, catching his breath then scurried out of sight. "Remember when I said I'd do what I needed to do and not what was good? Remember when I said I wasn't *him*." He pointed at Thane. "That hasn't changed, Valeen."

"Hel, you can't act like—"

"The Black Mage?" He walked closer. His boots tapped lightly as he backed her up until she hit the wall. Her breaths came faster, her heart started to pound, as much from desire as anger. "Like the serpent you know that I am? I am the Black Mage, love. I *am* the villain." *And you knew exactly who I was when you chose to be with me, Val. You're not afraid of my darkness? Well now you get to see it. And despite that precious bleeding heart of yours, you love it. I can hear it in your heartbeat. I can feel it.* He stared at her mouth like he wanted to claim it but brushed his thumb across her bottom lip. *Now, you can come with me to deal with Aldrich, or you can stay here but those are the only two options. Either way he will be punished for what he did to you.*

She hadn't even realized she was holding her breath. "I'll come with you." She grabbed onto the front of his coat and braced herself for the pull to darkness.

Chapter 12

VALEEN

The last time Valeen was in Calladira, she'd snuck into the lord's Manor where Thane had killed their ruler and Varlett had chased them out of the city by setting it on fire. So much had happened between then and now. She felt like a different person setting foot on the soft green grass below her feet. For a moment she wondered where Varlett was.

The fountain at the town square was surrounded by children laughing and splashing in it. Their sacred tree that had burned the previous year blossomed with white blooms and new green buds, but the char covering the trunk showed the remnants of the fire.

Hel pulled up his black hood and turned to face her. "Wait here."

Did he really think she came here to just watch from afar? "I'm not—"

He vanished before she could finish. *That prick.* She ground her teeth and stepped out from the shadows of the trees she hid amongst, searching for a sign of where he'd gone. The white Lord's manor waited at the end of the busy street. A pair of guards in their green and brown uniforms strolled around the side of the three-tiered fountain.

She quickly slipped back into the shadows. The gown she wore was not fit to blend into this place—a deep purple with thin straps and lace embroidery on the bodice. Other than the ladies inside the Manor, the fashion was simple in earthy tones, greens, ivory, browns, and soft pinks. And most of them were fair-haired.

If she was recognized they'd immediately try to detain her.

A quiet hiss like wind dancing through reeds made her turn. Gray smoke swirled around Hel and beside him stood... a pale one. But not just any pale one, Mathekis.

The hairs on her arms and along her spine immediately prickled and rose. Her magic ignited at the surface of her skin, and she itched to reach for the dagger tucked against her thigh. But she wasn't the elf he hunted anymore. He wasn't there to command her and drag her to the void. That didn't mean she wanted him or any pale one in close proximity. "What is *he* doing here?"

His black lips curled into a sinister smile, stark against his snow-white skin. His all-onyx eyes quickly gave her a once-over.

"He's here so there's no mistaking who I am." Hel's hood shadowed his forehead and brow. All softness vanished from him. That lovely smile she knew was nowhere to be found. The severe set to his jaw reminded her of the dark dreams he chased her in. Reminded her of the vengeful god who thought he'd been betrayed. The only thing that resembled the person she loved right now were his bright garnet eyes sparkling with mischief.

"I doubt you needed him to make that a reality," Valeen sneered.

"You have no reason to fear me, goddess," Mathekis said. "I will not harm you. I never would have."

Valeen glared at him and leaned closer. "Do I look afraid of you?" Her vines materialized and wrapped around his throat.

His white brows shot upward. "No."

"Good. Because it would be that easy to end you." She waved her hand and the vines vanished.

Out of the corner of her eye she caught Hel grinning. He snapped his fingers, and her clothes transformed from the dress to her thick leather pants, a black corset with silver runes along the top and bottom hemlines, and purple bell sleeves. Her dagger was still strapped to the outside of her thigh, and Zythara was now at her hip. The boots were different than anything she'd worn in *this* life... black with silver moon cycles going up to her knees.

On top of her midnight waves she felt the weight of a halo. "Is the crown necessary?"

"Yes, is it necessary for you to argue with me all the time?"

"I don't argue all the time."

He chuckled. "I beg to differ."

"Oh, he smiles and laughs, very un*Black Mage*-like of you."

Hel rolled his eyes, put a hand on her lower back

and guided her out from the woods into the bark-covered path alongside him. It smelled like rain had fallen recently despite the sun shining. Woodland elves bartered and traded with the shop owners. Giggling ladies under a booth with a white canopy were getting their hair braided.

No one seemed to notice them yet.

"Keep up the attitude Mrs. Black. I like it when you're feisty. Start calling me names and you'll give me a stiffy."

"You're unbelievable. And you better not kill these innocent children or their mothers or fathers."

The children at the fountain stopped splashing, laughing, and playing. The rush of the running water seemed louder now. Their mothers snatched them out and that's when the screaming started. The crowd of people ran in all directions. Tables were knocked down. Food spilled. Booths shut their curtains.

He certainly had an effect on people.

"I wouldn't dream of it," he drawled.

"I'm serious."

"When have I ever killed children and their mothers? Why would you even think that? I thought we were past you hating me."

Two guards ran toward them with swords drawn. Hel waved his hand and sent them flying until their backs slammed into the outside wall of a cottage with a sign above that read "apothecary".

They didn't get up.

"I don't hate you," she snapped. "I think this morning was proof of that."

"You can still hate me and fuck me, love."

"Ugh." Her cheeks warmed and she glanced at

Mathekis walking on Hel's other side. He didn't react but he was certainly listening. Did pale ones even have those urges? Valeen shoved her wedding ring in his face. "I don't hate you. I'm wearing this, aren't I? If I hated you, I'd throw it into the aether where no one would find it and tell you to go to the underrealm."

"Like you did last time?" He leaned down and his lips touched her ear. A pleasurable trill rolled down her spine. "Because I found it."

She glared at him. "You didn't go to the underrealm."

He chuckled. "No, I did not. I wouldn't be able to find you there."

"I love you, Zaurahel."

"Good. There's no changing your mind now. You're mine." He lifted her hand to his mouth and kissed the tops of her knuckles. But there was something about his cold expression that sent a shudder through her. What was he planning?

With weapons drawn, a set of three guards ran at them. "Pale ones! The Black Mage! Kill them!" They looked as terrified as they were angry. The screams only got louder with the guards running in. She might have felt bad if these weren't the same people who locked Thane in a cage, tossing rotten food at him all while laughing. They'd taken turns cutting him while he was helpless. "Bring everyone!" More guards came from the woods.

"No, hide!" someone else shouted. There was confusion and chaos among the people running and the guards.

An amber-haired male charged at her, screaming wildly. Valeen quickly pulled her sword but before she could bring it up to block a strike, everyone within a fifteen-foot radius went flying backward.

Bodies rolled and slammed into trees lining the roadway. A canopy toppled. The rest of the guards out of range of Hel's magic stilled.

"I'm here to speak to your Lord. No one needs to die," Hel announced. "Let us pass and you won't."

Most of the civilians were hidden now but those that remained backed off, clearing the way for them. The guards stared now.

"Oh good, you're not all stupid."

With his hand still on her back, they marched up the front steps of the Lord's Manor. With a flick of Hel's fingers, the guards crumpled to the ground, unconscious or dead, she wasn't sure. She didn't think about it, or guilt might start eating at her.

A breeze from Hel's magic threw the doors open, slamming them against the wall with a crack, and they strutted inside.

"Stop right there!" A set of guards stood at the center of the red rug running down the entry to the stairs. They raised their spears and slowly marched forward. A couple of scantily dressed ladies squealed and darted out of sight. She remembered all too well wearing something similar to sneak into this place.

"Where is your Lord?" Hel asked as if he'd just arrived for a dinner party. "He has guests."

Without anyone summoning him, Aldrich emerged from a room under the stairs with an elf wearing scraps of black that barely covered her private parts, hanging on his arm. By their laughter and general lack of acknowledgment, it was obvious he had no idea that she stood in his home with the Black Mage and a pale one. He palmed the elf's breast and shoved his hips against her.

"Is he drunk?" Valeen said, arching a brow.

"Well, now he's ruined my entrance." Hel threw his hand toward him, and Aldrich was ripped away from the maiden, slammed into the stair railing and dragged toward them like he was pulled by an invisible rope around his neck. A vein in his forehead popped out as he struggled to breathe. His arms were splayed out to his sides as he hung a few inches off the ground before them.

Hel stroked the side of Valeen's cheek with the back of his hand. "Do you recognize this beautiful face?"

"Layala?" He panted. Whatever magic Hel used to hold him was cutting into his air supply. He looked at Mathekis and then back to Hel.

"This is my wife. I warned your father what would happen if she was harmed."

"Your... what?"

"I'm sure I didn't stutter."

His wide eyes shifted to Valeen, full of questions and something that looked like guilt. "It's true," she said. "Waking him turned out to be much different than I previously thought. How are you even Lord here? You were a Prince of Palenor."

"Because of my experience as a Raven and Lord Brunard was my cousin."

"And?" It didn't add up.

Hel flicked his fingers and Aldrich sucked in a sharp pained breath. "Alright, I killed anyone else in line of succession with poison."

The guards murmured amongst each other.

"You're one of those cowards. Not that I'd really

care or bother myself with your pitiful affairs, but," Hel lifted her hand with the black diamond ring, "Wife. And I don't allow anyone to hurt her and live to talk about it."

"I—I didn't—hurt her," he wheezed. "I swear."

Valeen let out a short laugh. "You're going to deny it?"

"I was following the order of my father. We were doing it for," he slowly uncurled a finger to point at Hel, "*him*. We did it for you, Lord. To wake you. You are awake because of me. I will swear my allegiance to you here and now."

Just when she thought he couldn't sink any lower. "He is awake because of *me,* not you."

He turned to Mathekis. "Bite him."

"What?" Valeen balked.

Without hesitation, Mathekis sunk his teeth into Aldrich's forearm and a scream tore from his throat. "NO!"

It was a fate worse than death. Valeen's heart clenched in her chest. "You were supposed to kill him," she hissed through her teeth.

"I thought you wanted to use him in this war? What does it matter if he is dead or a pale one loyal to me—to us?"

His head thrashed back and forth, and a low belly roar echoed through the manor's high walls. The guards all slowly backed away. Two of them dropped to their knees and set down their weapons.

Her stomach rolled as Aldrich fell to the ground. His back arched and his arms jerked. The rage that ripped through her, the coldness that seeped into her bones when she was bitten came rushing back to her.

Her heart pounded. The hysteria had been uncontrollable, the rage overwhelming. It started to make her sweat even now. If Hel hadn't intervened for her, she'd have suffered this same fate. The monstrous things she would have been capable of as one of those things scared her.

She gulped and inched back until Hel's hand against her spine stopped her. "We agreed you wouldn't change any more elves. He will tear through Calladira."

"I said the elves of Palenor were safe. We're not in Palenor."

Oh, she hated his trickery sometimes.

Aldrich shook uncontrollably and screamed again. His roar echoed through the high ceiling and halls, and the hairs on the back of her neck rose. His golden-blond hair was already fading and his skin shined with a sickly pallor.

The tattoo on her thigh that kept her from changing began to tingle. "I can't watch this," she whispered and whirled to leave. Hel caught her wrist and turned her back.

"This needs to happen. He betrayed you once. He'd do it again. Traitors can never be trusted, but as a pale one he will be loyal to me."

"It's what you're forcing him to become," she breathed. "Cut off his head, I don't care, but this?"

"Listen, love, it's going to happen on the battlefield, and you need to be indifferent about it. I know you hate them, but we need them against the council."

A tear slid down her cheek. It wasn't just that he was turning, it was that Hel was the reason. Hel was the reason there were pale ones at all. She couldn't seem to tear away from watching the horror. Aldrich slammed the back of his head against the ground and bucked and screeched so loud she pressed her hands to her ears.

Hel released her and his eyes softened. *Go outside.*

She didn't care for Aldrich. She would even kill him herself without a second thought but watching anyone turn into this made her sick. When Aldrich's lips and eyes changed to the color of ink, she had to look away.

She'd somehow separated Hel from the pale ones because she hadn't truly seen him with them. She'd almost forgotten this was who he was here in Adalon, the wicked villain feared by all.

A crease formed between his brows when she looked up at him. She had to find her husband in his eyes, the male she'd loved through the ages and fell for again. She needed to see he wasn't just as much of a monster as the thing Aldrich was changing into.

The harshness in his expression fell and shifted into something close to sadness. *You don't have to see this. It's alright. Go.*

That was her husband. The Hel she knew, the one with his soul still intact. The Black Mage was a persona... but the pale ones were very real.

Valeen, go outside, he said more forcefully.

The fresh air made it easier to breathe. The doors shut behind her, muffling the terrible sounds. Her gaze swept around the town. The children who'd been playing were gone. The people walking and talking had run. Not even guards or soldiers came out into the open. The quiet emptiness was so unnatural for a city.

She sank onto the steps and hugged her knees.

She didn't know how long she sat there before Hel settled beside her.

You're angry with me. He stared ahead with the tips of his fingers drumming together. *Why did you cry for him? He kept you locked up. He treated you in a way you know I'd never tolerate.*

"It wasn't him I was crying for," she whispered, staring at her hands.

He pulled his hood back and looked at her, but her gaze was fixed on the toes of her boots now.

His fingers slid along her jaw, closed around her chin, and turned her face. "Then who?" His brows pinched and his lips parted slightly.

"You."

"Ah." He dropped his hand and the lines in his face smoothed out. He rubbed his thumb over the runes along his knuckles. "Ryvengaard was our sanctuary, and you forgot who I've become."

It was because she knew who he *really* was before the betrayal and the wars and execution. Before he was ever the Black Mage.

He went silent for a few beats.

"I just want this all to be over." She cupped his face. "I just want peace. I want to lay in bed with you all day and not worry that someone will sneak in to kill us. I want to hear you really laugh again and never have to be... cold and cruel."

"If all of Adalon passed away into darkness, if every realm was burned to ash, I would still love you. If I had to become something so little as cold and cruel to save you, Valeen, it's worth it." *This is only the beginning. When the chaos becomes too much, when you doubt everything, and you think the darkness has taken me, remember*

I'm still your Zaurahel, and I always will be. He took her hands and kissed them one at a time. "One last fight, love, and when it's over I'll be your peace." With his thumb, he swiped another tear off her cheek. "But you don't have to fight. I will do it for you. You can go back with your sister and never see a battlefield again."

"You know I won't let you fight this war alone."

He smiled, dimpling his cheek. "It was worth a shot."

The door creaked open and Mathekis peeked out. "He's ready, Lord."

Shiny black eyes followed her steps as she crossed through the Manor's entrance and into the foyer. Aldrich bared little resemblance to who he was before. The only reason she knew it was him was because of the clothes he wore, and his facial structure was the same, but he was as pale as the moon and his golden hair was white and straight. There was nothing about him that would make her call him Sunshine anymore.

Deep down she knew he deserved to die a traitor's death, but this fate was worse than being buried six feet under.

Aldrich bowed his head to Hel. "Master." His voice was rougher than before like he'd breathed in smoke for too long. His black gaze flicked to Valeen. "You belong to him now?"

"You know who I am?"

"Layala Lightbringer. I've wanted to tell you for a long time but I'm sorry for what I did to you and Thane. I'm sorry for," he glanced at Hel, "for my part in this."

She turned to Hel. *How is he so... normal?*

It may be because Mathekis is the one who turned him.

Or because he's still in transition. "What is your name?" Hel asked.

"Aldrich."

He nodded and placed his hands behind his back. "And you are loyal to who?"

"You, Master."

"Good." Hel smiled cruelly. "You will not bite anyone unless I tell you to. You will remain the Lord of Calladira and come with your army when I call. If anyone refuses to follow your command, kill them."

Valeen blew out a slow breath. The elves wouldn't want him to be their ruler now. He was setting Aldrich up to die or fail. Then again, the woodland elves might fear him enough to fall in line.

"Yes, Master. I will come when you call."

"Now get on your knees in front of my wife."

He dropped immediately and stared up at Valeen. Her skin itched the longer he kept those black eyes on her. They used to be... blue, didn't they?

"Beg for her forgiveness."

"Please, Layala, forgive me. I'm truly sorry. I should have never betrayed you and Thane. I wish I never shot you with that arrow. I'm truly sorry I almost killed you. That day in the woods I left you to bleed out... It wasn't supposed to happen that way. I regret joining Tenebris. I do. I should have helped you get free." He probably meant what he said but it didn't change anything. She didn't hate him for it anymore. It seemed so long ago.

Hel cut a glare her way. Fury rippled through the room in an icy chill. "He almost *killed* you? What else have you and Thane kept from me?" He vanished and reappeared behind Aldrich. The bottom of Hel's boot smashed into Aldrich's spine. With a groan, he fell flat to the ground at Valeen's feet. Hel stomped on his fingers and ground them into the wood floor. Then he bent down and grabbed Aldrich by the hair and jerked his head up. "Slit your throat."

Hel put a knife in his hand. Aldrich brought the blade across the center of his neck. Black blood cascaded down his white skin. He stared up at Valeen almost... relieved. He mouthed "I'm sorry" once more. Maybe he was sorry because he thought she was forced to be with the Black Mage. He regretted helping his father and Varlett take her to wake him. Aldrich didn't know who he truly was. He wouldn't know any different than any outsider.

Blood seeped out, pooling near her toes. Her boots scraped against the ground as she took a half step back. Hel dropped his hold and Aldrich's head fell with a thud.

In some ways, it was a mercy. She should have felt remorse, but she only breathed easier with him gone rather than a flesh-eating monster.

The guards still hadn't dared to move. They watched everything happen without even a sound. No protests or gasps as their lord changed or as he bled out and died. For the second time she was present as the Lord of Calladira died.

Hel stepped over Aldrich, took her hand and marched for the open doors. "If I were the woodland elves, I wouldn't even think about retaliation," he said over his shoulder. "Consider this a warning of what happens to those who touch my wife, and a favor that his is the only life taken today."

Chapter 13

KATANA

The first time Katana saw Thane she thought he was handsome, beautiful even, but many gods and elves were. There wasn't anything particular about him that drew her in until they ate breakfast alone together. Seeing someone who hid his brokenness the way she did built a sort of bridge between them.

Now he sat under the shade of an oak in a bed of soft grass; his focus was on the whetstone he ran across the edge of his blade as she approached. The sun filtered through the branches of the tree creating beams of amber across him. The light seemed to brighten his dark hair, revealing strands of gold.

"I do not know if those swords can get any sharper," Katana teased.

He lifted his chin and smiled at her. "Hello, Katana. If you're looking for Valeen, she left with Hel. But I'm sure they'll be back soon."

"Where did they go?"

"Calladira."

That was home of the woodland elves, and a strange place to be when the portals were open and the Council of the Gods wanted them dead. "Why would they go there?"

Thane set the whetstone down beside him. "To kill their new lord, I suppose."

"Did he do something?"

"He starved Valeen and kept her locked in a room for weeks. And pretended to be a close friend of mine and then betrayed me. So yeah, he deserves what's coming."

Katana took a sharp inhale. After seeing what Valeen was capable of it was difficult to imagine anyone keeping her locked up. "How could an elf do that to her?"

"Katagas serum," he said with a shrug. "It takes away your powers temporarily." It was strange he was so nonchalant about it. She'd never heard of a serum capable of quelling a goddess's power... but perhaps it was because she was mortal now. Which meant this serum would likely work on her too. She already felt weak and the thought of losing her magic made her stomach queasy.

"Well, to be honest I am bored, so I came to watch how you all train. I always thought it was fascinating to watch sparring matches even if Atlanta said it was not proper for females." Several groups of soldiers clashed swords or shot arrows in the training grounds nearby. The smell of sweat swirled with blossoming cherry trees in the air.

"He didn't *let* you watch soldiers train?" Thane's

cream shirt was partially unbuttoned revealing hints of his smooth muscular chest.

"I did on occasion without him knowing."

"He sounds like an asshole." His hands came up in a sort of surrender gesture. "Sorry if that offends you."

"No, I agree. He was... an asshole." She giggled having never used that slang word before. It was more freeing to say that than she realized it would be.

"Have you ever trained in any self-defense?"

"I was more into fashion and dancing. And when I was immortal what did I really have to fear until..." she let out a sigh and stopped her mind from wandering to darker things.

"Do you want to learn?"

"Should I?"

"Every female should know the basics of how to defend herself." He hopped to his feet, plucking a small dagger from his belt. Taking it by the blade, he held the handle out to her. Slowly, she reached for it and wrapped her hand around the onyx stone. The only weapon she'd ever wielded was a kitchen knife to cut fruit. This felt heavy in her palm, more than physically. This blade was meant for taking life.

"Now I assume you have powerful magic which should be your first line of defense, but it never hurts to have a weapon if you get cornered or for some reason you can't use your powers."

Her magic warmed under the surface of her skin at the mention of it. She'd never used it to harm.

Thane pointed at his upper left rib cage. "This is where you want to stick someone if you can." He took her wrist and pulled her closer, then brought the dagger point to his chest. "It's the heart. No one survives a dagger to the heart unless they're immortal. The bones protect your vital organs, so you'll have to push hard and try to get between the ribs. Strike fast."

Her arm trembled but she nodded. "Alright." She took a few steps back and practiced thrusting the dagger in the air.

"Harder than that," Thane said.

Piper and Leif left their post of spectating the soldiers and wandered over. Leif had several leaves and small sticks in his wild red hair and a smudge of dirt on his cheek, but his playful grin said he didn't care about his rough appearance. "Have her strike the tree trunk over there," Piper said. She crossed her arms and scrutinized Katana from head to toe.

Suddenly she became self-conscious if she was holding the dagger correctly or if she looked silly. She certainly felt ridiculous stabbing the air. And Piper was a seasoned warrior. They all were.

Leif grabbed Thane's shoulders, turned him, and pointed to a place in his muscular back. "You can stab here to get the kidney. It'll drop even the largest of males or monsters." He took Katana's wrist and tugged her over to Thane's front, putting them toe to toe. She swallowed hard and had to look up to see his green eyes. There was an intensity there she'd never seen before. Almost as if he was afraid to breathe. "Say this big lug has you cornered and you're too close to get a good shot at the heart, reach around and jam it into his kidney. Several times if you can."

Fennan joined in the chorus next, crossing his arms with a grin. "I'd pay to see you do it to Hel."

"Hel?" she whispered. Why would they want that? But she couldn't focus on anything but Thane. She was left breathless with their bodies nearly pressed together, and she angled the blade's point at his back. They were talking about violence and killing, yet this was the opposite of that. A swirl of heat and pheromones wrapped around her. Warmth pooled in her lower belly. She pressed her free hand against his abdomen and lightly scraped the dagger over the thin fabric of his shirt, trying to find the correct spot. "Here?"

Thane took her arm and guided it upward an inch or so. "Here." His voice came out raspy.

She nodded and dropped the dagger to her side. "I think I have it."

"Keep that on you at all times."

"I will."

He was the first to move away. "What are your powers?"

"I harvest my magic from the sun. So light and heat mostly."

Leif chuckled. "You mean you could burn down a city if you wanted to."

She smiled back at him. "Well, I do not know. I have never even thought about that, and I would not dream of such a thing. I can clear a storm or turn night to day. I can light a fire with the snap of my fingers. I float using the sun's energy to push against the ground."

"But you *could* burn someone with your touch?" Thane asked.

She licked her lower lip and nodded. It would be easy. The heat generated in her palms could melt metal, turning it liquid. Flesh would be nothing. "I could."

"That would be my first instruction then. Burn them with one hand and stab with the other."

"Oh, yeah," Leif said. "Go for the eyes, too. Burn them right out of the sockets."

"That's gruesome." Piper scrunched her nose.

"And so is war," Leif argued. "Burn 'em."

"Can we get a demonstration?" Fennan asked.

"Oh, I would rather not." Her cheeks warmed at the thought of it. She did not like violence.

"I agree." The little gnome with her red hat and holey boots seemed to pop up out of nowhere. "Go for the eyes. Then they wouldn't be able to see you and it would be that much easier to kill them. I cut off an elf's ear once."

Katana squatted down to Tif's level. "You did? I can hardly imagine that from one so small."

"I may be small, but I can slice and dice. I won best carver in my gnome colony the year before my mother kicked me out of the hole."

"I didn't know that about you, Tif," Piper said. "You should whittle something."

"I think I will. It's been so long since I have. I doubt I'd be the best in the gnome colony anymore, but I'll work on my skills. What should I carve? A bird or perhaps a fox? One time a fox tried to eat me, and Thane had to save my life. So, I think I'll stick with a bird. I speak tweet, you know." She pulled a berry out of her burlap sack. "Want one? They're perfectly ripe and juicy. I picked the best ones myself. They must be the right color and firmness, soft but not mushy."

Katana learned many things about the gnome in a few sentences and each one surprised her. It would be rude to refuse so Katana took it and popped it into her mouth. "It is very good. Excellent berry picking."

Tifapine twirled a brown curl around her finger and blushed. "My, such a compliment coming from a goddess, I don't know what to say."

"I find it hard to believe *you* are at a loss for words," Thane grumbled.

"Are you saying I talk a lot?"

"That's exactly what I'm saying."

"Well, I'm good at it."

Thane chuckled. "I won't argue that."

"Where is Layala, or er—Valeen. It's been a difficult adjustment for me. She still looks like her, talks like her, but wants to be called something else. Of course, she is with someone else too and maybe it's better if we do call her by a different name now. Then I can make sense of her being with," she lowered her voice to a whisper, "you know who. I call him the master of darkness."

"They're... out," Thane answered.

It was interesting that Thane hadn't told his friends they were in Calladira. He must not want them to know.

Fennan toyed with the sword at his hip. "As much as I hate having the prick around, I have to say I'm glad he's on our side and not against us—even though I'd rather stab out my own eyes with a fork than fight *with* the pale ones."

Katana's brows rose. "I suppose I do not know a lot about Hel. Why would you call him the master of darkness and what are pale ones?" Everyone looked amongst each other in a way that sent a chill down her spine. In the couple days she'd spent with this group,

Hel had never given her a reason to think he was anything but loving to Valeen. Powerful certainly, but the way he looked at her, it was like she was the only thing that mattered in his world. The way she'd always wished Atlanta would look at her. "He has not hurt Valeen, has he?"

"It's not her anyone needs to worry about," Piper said, turning away with a frown.

"You mean he hurts other people?"

"That's the understatement of the year." Fennan's tone was harsh though Katana didn't think he meant to snap at her. "And the pale ones were once elves but now they're monsters who eat people and have no remorse or conscience. He created them."

Katana blinked rapidly trying to picture elves eating people and shook her head to clear that image. "Excuse me? He created them how?"

"Oh, I know!" Tif's hand shot up and she jumped in place then blushed when everyone looked at her. "Well, according to him it was the All Mother's punishment, not entirely his doing. Something about balance and consequences for magical greed. I don't understand it myself, but you might."

"Even you're defending him now?" Fennan groaned.

"The important thing is he's on our side so none of us need to worry about him," Thane said quickly. "Do you want to see more of the grounds, Katana?"

So apparently there was a lot she needed to catch up on, but she'd rather hear it from her sister. "That would be lovely."

They left the others behind and walked side by side on a path toward the gray high cliffs at the back of the castle. It wasn't long before their walk touring the grounds brought them to a hot spring surrounded by a small grove of pink and purple poplar trees. The sunshine brought out the bright blooms and butterflies danced in the air. A quiet wind made the grass and flowers sway and carried a sweet scent.

Thane stopped at the water's edge and dipped his fingers in. "This is called the Casburn Springs. It's named after an elven ancestor of mine. It's hot but not scalding. I used to swim here when I was young, but I don't even remember the last time I went in."

"Should we get in then?" Katana lit up with the idea. She hadn't had a bath since she arrived and had only wiped herself down with a cloth. She had been too timid to ask the servants to fill the tub.

"If you want to, I can keep watch."

"You want to watch me bathe?" She slowly smiled.

His cheeks flushed and he rubbed the back of his neck. "I didn't mean you... the area for—you know what I mean."

"You are cute when you blush." She pushed the sleeves of her dress off her shoulders and let the fabric pool around her feet, leaving her in a bralette and high-cut underwear. "I was teasing by the way."

"Um." His eyes widened as they trailed down her form. He didn't try to look away or pretend like he wasn't inspecting every inch of her flesh. But it wasn't in a way that made her skin crawl or even brought a blush to her cheeks. He was simply taking in what was in front of him.

"So surprised. You already untied my dress once and had me on your lap in something almost as revealing." She winked and dipped her toe in.

"I—what?"

"Have you forgotten already?" She sank down into the water until it reached her throat and sighed. "This was exactly what I needed."

"No, I just didn't expect you to strip down like that I guess."

"I am not ashamed of my body. It is beautiful."

He laughed and the sound of it made her stomach flutter. "Well, I had forgotten that goddesses aren't as modest. In Adalon there is a certain dress code among females. Males don't walk around with their shirts off either unless training on a particularly warm day or in close company." He sat at the edge of the water and tucked his knees toward his chest. "Did Atlanta hit you, Katana?"

Katana's breath stopped and she ran her hands through the warm water. "Why would you think that?"

"The night I found you under the tree, you flinched when I raised my hand. And there's a few other things you've said..."

It wasn't something she liked to talk about. "He did."

"How many times?" His voice had dropped lower.

"Too many to count," she whispered. She didn't know why she felt she could tell him things she didn't confess to others. Lying to him felt wrong.

"And you stayed?" He sounded like he wanted to truly know without judgment.

"It is complicated."

"I understand complicated well."

"Would you understand if I said it was more difficult to leave than to stay? Remember when I told you I wanted a divorce, and he would not allow it? We shared a territory, we have children, and a long history. And it did not happen that often. I learned what I could say and do and what I should not."

"You said it happened more times than you could count."

She sighed. "We were together for a very long time. More time than you have been alive. It is part of my past now. It feels like another life—because it was. I decided that is not who I am anymore." There was no excuse for it. She knew that even then, but it was impossible to part with someone powerful like Atlanta. Where would she have gone to escape him? It terrified her to think of him finding out she was alive now. The thought of facing him was the only thing keeping her from going to Runevale to find her son and two daughters. Eventually she would but she needed to build her courage and learn this new mortal body better. "I will not ever go back to him. I do not even consider him my husband. I died. Should death not set me free?"

His eyes darkened. "I hope I don't ever meet him."

"Why?"

"Because I might kill him."

The corners of her mouth threatened to curl upward. "Why do you care?"

He pinned her with those eyes, like a deep whimsical forest. "Why shouldn't I?"

"You barely know me."

"It doesn't mean I can't care."

"Maybe we should get to know each other better then. Did you prefer your life in Palenor or Runevale?"

"My life in Runevale isn't who I am anymore either," he murmured.

"So, you will stay here then, when you have your

immortality back and the threat of the council is gone?"

"Yes, I will remain in Palenor to be High King."

So, he wanted to be where Valeen wasn't? Or was it duty that called him? Most gods wanted to be in Runevale. It was their homeworld.

The heat of the water was getting to be a bit much, so she rose until it was at her waist. Steam rolled off her skin and the water clung to her white bralette. She noticed his eyes slowly move down. It was only then she realized how see-through the fabric had become. But she was never one to be embarrassed of her body and it seemed silly to dip back under.

"What do you want out of life, Thane?"

His throat bobbed and green eyes flicked back to her face. "I don't know anymore."

"But you did once?"

"Yes," he whispered.

"Well, I want to travel the realms. I want to see the Deserts of Anahar and the woodland elves' tree houses. I want to walk down the infamous Pearl Avenue in Ryvengaard with the dragons and see the ice caves in the Frostlands. I rarely left Runevale. Seeing this place has been a dream. Thank you for showing me around."

"Why didn't you do this before?" His brows knitted.

Cupping water she splashed herself and thought back. "I had responsibilities. I felt chained to my territory in some ways." Admitting that Atlanta didn't like her leaving was hard, but she finally said, "And Atlanta hated when I left. If I did leave the realm, it was with him, and he does not enjoy traveling."

"Because he thought it was dangerous or..."

She frowned. "Partly, but mostly because he was worried I would fall in love with someone else."

"And yet he had other lovers." Thane shook his head. "Well, now you can do whatever you want. How does it feel to be free?"

She spread her arms wide and tilted her chin toward the azure sky. "It feels like when you see a bird flying, riding on the wind simply existing. Without him here I get to be... me."

Thane smiled and she couldn't help but admire his full lips over his perfect teeth, but it slowly faded.

"Is something wrong?" Katana asked. Had she brought up something she shouldn't have?

He simply shook his head and looked up at the blossoms in the trees.

"Do you know how long it has been since I have been kissed?" Katana splashed her chest once more. His head snapped in her direction and looked like she'd struck him across the face. Then his gaze dipped again to her wet bralette and now peaked nipples. Could she get that blush to deepen even further? Get him to smile again? He had such a lovely smile; it was a shame to see him frown.

"And it has been even longer since I have been properly bedded." Yes, those cheeks could get rather rosy. "It has been at least a few thousand years. I am practically a virgin these days."

The bob of his throat and the sudden flare of his pupils were satisfying to watch. "Maker Above, Katana," he murmured, but the corners of his mouth began to curl up. "I'm going to have to go find a cold river to plunge into in a minute."

"Or you could join me, but it is far from cold."

"I better not."

She strode out of the water and past him, brushing her knuckles against his shoulder. She walked out from under the shade of the poplar trees where the sun felt wonderful on her skin. Her magic tingled and relished in the light.

When she turned back around, he was leaned up against a tree trunk with his muscular arms crossed. It was freeing to be away from Atlanta, and to flirt like she never could without worrying he would hurt her. "I think it is almost supper. My stomach is growling." She picked up her dress and draped it over her arm.

He practically stumbled pushing off the tree and was at her side in a flash. "You can't go inside like that."

"Like what?"

His eyes flared. "Like—dripping wet and practically naked. That white bra isn't hiding *anything*."

"I suppose I will just have to stand here until I am dry. I do not want to get my dress wet. It could stain the silk. It is a delicate fabric."

Her brow arched as she watched him tug off his tunic. A moment later, he took the dress from her arm and slipped his too-large shirt over her head. Giggling, she pushed her arms through the sleeves and let the white cotton fabric drape to her mid thighs. The sleeves fell just past her fingertips. "This is sure to cause more gossip than breakfast."

Chapter 14

THANE

Thane anxiously curled and uncurled his fingers. She was correct about the gossip. Maybe he could sneak her inside... No, why did this even bother him? There was no reason to sneak about with her. He was High King and committed to no one. Gods, she looked good. Her round perky ass was even noticeable in his oversized shirt. *It has been even longer since I have been properly bedded...* She was either sweetly naive or knew exactly what she was doing, and she was too old to be naive. Now all he could think about was what bedding her might be like. But it was wrong. He shouldn't be thinking about her this way. They would only ever be friends. He wouldn't let what was left of his heart get tangled up into another mess.

Slamming his eyes shut, he rubbed his forehead as if it could scrub away the thoughts. "We can go in and change first, then dinner."

She playfully patted his arm. "I did not plan to go like this, Thane. Remember when I said I have an affinity for fashion? I like to attend dinner parties properly dressed." They started walking side by side. "How will the seating arrangements be?" she tsked. "I do not think Valeen should be seated anywhere near your mother."

Dread slowly worked its way through him. A dinner party with Valeen, Hel, his mother, and Katana sounded like a nightmare. It was sure to be an interesting evening. "Definitely not. Although I don't think any amount of distance will keep them from arguing."

Katana let out a *ha*. "Oh, so it will be a fun night then. Entertaining at least." She gestured ahead. "There is Valeen and Hel now." She practically bounced on her toes as she waved at them.

Thane groaned. Valeen's face was difficult to read as her bright blue eyes flicked back and forth between them. Hel on the other hand looked like he was about to have the best time of his life.

"Hello, Katana," Hel said with a mischievous smirk. His eyes dragged over her and then he glanced at Thane. "What have we been up to? Something where clothes were optional, I see."

She grinned at him. "We—well, I took a dip in the hot springs. It felt so nice. And I did not want to ruin my dress, so Thane lent me his shirt. We are heading inside for dinner if you would join us. Oh, um, did you do what you needed to in Calladira?" she grimaced at even asking the question.

Valeen stared at Thane, scrutinizing his face. Whether she wanted to smile or tear his head off, he couldn't decide. "Aldrich is dead."

A strange sense of relief washed through him. Aldrich had been on the back of his mind since the battle with his father. Now he didn't have to worry he'd show up to try to kill him and take the throne for his. Or even gather supporters to campaign against him for the rightful heir. "How did they react to another Lord of theirs dying?" He tapped his boot. They were never going to have peace with the woodland elves.

"No one had anything to say about it, if that's what you're asking." Hel rubbed his chin. "I have that effect on people. Didn't someone say something about dinner? I'm famished."

THANE PACED OUTSIDE the dining hall. Piper, Fennan, Leif, Orlandia, Talon, and Katana were already inside. He peeked through the crack in the door and spotted Hel casually drop into the chair on the opposite end of the High King's seat.

"What are you doing with Katana? I know about the whole flirting and teasing thing between you but what was that outside?" Valeen's voice sent a shiver down his spine. He had to take a deep breath before he turned around and faced her. The dying light from sunset peeked through the nearby window and bathed her in amber.

"You're going to have to clarify."

"Don't play dumb." Her face hardened, and shadows flickered around her from the torch on the wall nearby. "Are you doing this to get back at me?"

He ground his teeth together. "I'm not doing *anything*. The only thing I've done is be a good host."

"I find that difficult to believe based on what I saw

earlier. She's not someone to use against me, Thane. I thought you were fine with... us."

"I am," he snapped and tore his gaze away.

"She was wearing *your* clothes, and you didn't have a shirt on."

"Why don't you ask her?"

"I will."

"Why do you care anyway? You got what you wanted. You sound jealous." With everything in him, he wanted her to be. Gods, he didn't think it would be this hard. She left with Hel and he was the one who told her to go.

Part of him was just jealous that they had a soulmate and he was left with nothing. Even if they'd been as close as anyone could be all those years before in their past life, he was still the third wheel. Even when he had Varlett as his fiancée, she wasn't what Valeen was to Hel. It had been an arrangement for political power, and sex. That was all it was.

Hel and Valeen had a special bond that even time and war and heartache couldn't break. They had a love that he desperately craved.

A love that he thought he had with her...

Now he wasn't even sure he knew what love was if it could be taken away, if love could slip right through his fingertips and into the hands of someone else.

She glared at him, and he swore soft shadows began to flutter around her. "You've never seen me jealous, Thane. If I was, believe me, you'd know. But she is my sister."

"And Hel is my cousin."

Her crushing blue eyes bore into him, straight to his soul. It made him a little uneasy. It had been a long time since he'd been on the wrong side of her wrath. "And I was with him before I was ever with you. This is different and you know it."

"Are you saying she's off-limits then?"

"I thought nothing was going on," she retorted and folded her arms, lifting a brow.

"Katana understands what I'm going through, with people gossiping behind my back about my ex-fiancée sleeping with my cousin. She knows what it's like to watch the person you were in love with be with someone else. Compared to how Hel acted, I think I'm doing a remarkably good job. I could be a territorial asshole, couldn't I?"

He realized he talked about their love in the past tense, and that it was true. He'd been drawn to her and loved her here and in his life as War, but those chains were... broken somehow. It was as if he was seeing her for who she truly was, not the love of his life for the first time. He wasn't even sure when it happened.

With a sigh she dropped her arms to her sides. "Look, I'm not saying she's off-limits—"

"Well good because it isn't your place anymore."

Valeen's eyes flashed then she cracked a smile. "No, it's not. Katana is a beautiful person, and I wouldn't blame you if you did develop feelings—"

"There is nothing going on, as I said. I barely know her." She was gorgeous and he did find himself very attracted to her but there wasn't anything beyond that.

"Alright, but you will know her. I've never met anyone else like Katana. She used to be the brightest person in any room, and one could argue she still is, but I can see in her eyes she's traumatized. She needs safety." They both glanced through the crack in the door. He found her sitting at the table, smiling. The sunlight shined on the back of her head making her hair even brighter, illuminating her golden skin. "And I should have anticipated the gossip of the servants. I am sorry."

He lifted a shoulder. "I really don't care all that much about the gossip of servants."

"Just be careful with Katana. I don't know what is going to happen with her and Atlanta. She told me she doesn't want to see him and that she doesn't consider him her husband anymore, but I don't want you to get hurt again."

The last thing he needed was to fall for another goddess and have her go back to her former lover. The main difference between them was that Katana remembered her last life. "You don't need to worry. Shall we?" Thane pulled the door all the way open and gestured for her to go in first.

Wearing her gold crown tonight, Orlandia stared Hel down while he smoked a civar and picked at something beneath his nails. Katana beamed at them both, waved at Valeen and patted the seat between her and Hel. Fennan picked at the food on his plate while Piper and Leif sipped their wine looking anywhere but at the others at the table.

"Well, well, the High King and my wife are late." Hel blew out a cloud of smoke and narrowed his eyes at him. "Busy?"

Thane quickly took his seat. The chair legs scraped loudly on the stone floor as he scooted up to the table. It was set with a mouth-watering spread. Meats and steamed vegetables and colorful fruit with a silver candelabra centered and a royal-blue tablecloth beneath it all. "Nope, just preparing myself for what is sure to be a *lovely* dinner."

Valeen passed behind Hel, ran her hand along his shoulders, then bent down and kissed his cheek. He thought she whispered "play nice" into his ear but he wasn't sure. Once she sat beside him, Hel looked at her, and if Thane had to guess they were having one of their silent conversations. It always bothered him when they did that. Even *before*.

Hel took another inhale from his civar. The smoke cloud hung above the dinner table and Thane's mother looked absolutely unhinged about it. She swatted at the smoke with her napkin and mumbled something under her breath.

"The conversation has been riveting in your absence," Hel drawled. "Orlandia and friends were just saying what a joy I am to have as a guest."

Orlandia raised her chin in defiance and scoffed. "It's incredibly rude to smoke while dining with royalty."

"Oh," Katana said, setting down her glass. "I was going to ask, Orlandia, do I still resemble a trollop or am I more presentable?"

Hel laughed. "Do I even want to know?"

"No," Thane said. "We need to discuss what the council's next move will be. Will they send another assassin before they bring their armies? We need to prepare for that."

Orlandia pressed her bright red lips together and dabbed the corner of her mouth with a napkin. "You actually look quite lovely, Katana."

"Well, thank you," Katana said. "I was going to compliment you on your dress. Red is your color."

Thane blinked at Katana in surprise. Either she was just that nice or she understood that his mother would like compliments. Could it be possible that his mother and Katana would get along?

"Well, look at that," Orlandia crooned. "Someone with manners." Then she sneered at Valeen. "Katana is lovelier than my son's last conquest. Thinner too. I always told the staff Layala needed a few less treats."

Thane choked on his bite of food and fumbled his fork; it clattered loudly onto his dinner plate. Did she truly just say that?

Katana flushed and whispered to Valeen how beautiful she was. Although Valeen didn't seem bothered by the rude comment as she sipped her drink then said, "Orlandia, I really don't want to do this with you tonight."

"And I don't want you at our dinner table. It's disrespectful. This whole affair is. Why, with you breaking my poor son's heart and flaunting your new relationship in front of him, it's disgusting. *You* are disgusting."

"You're on dangerous grounds, Orlandia." Hel flicked his lit civar at her and it bounced off her chest and onto her plate. "You're awfully fucking mouthy for someone that is lucky to be alive. You mate bonded your *son* to my *wife*. If his heart is broken, *you* are to blame. That was never part of the deal. If you say one more godsdamn word of insult to her, I'll stop your heart with a snap of my fingers. Is that understood?"

Leif and Fennan both were half laughing behind their glasses of wine. While Piper's eyes darted back and forth between Hel and Orlandia.

Orlandia shifted in her seat and nervously pawed

at the curl dangling on the side of her face. "I had no idea she was your wife. She was a baby. You do understand that wouldn't have made sense to me or my late husband. All Tenebris said was that we were to expect a child born with a lily mark, to keep her safe, and then take her to the Void when she was of a proper age."

"You're alive because you're his mother." Hel pointed at Thane. "That's it."

She stupidly scowled at Hel. The lack of fear of him was going to get her killed. Did she think because Hel was his cousin that it would stop him? She knew he was the Black Mage. Thane closed his eyes and blew out a slow breath. Maker above. "Mother, enough. I would like to enjoy my dinner."

"Fine but I'm only protecting my son."

"I know," Thane said gently, and in some ways, he did appreciate it. In her eyes, her son's former fiancée was living in their house with a new love. If he had a child in this situation he would probably react the same way.

A male servant came through holding a large bouquet of pink lilies and white roses covered in a sheer cream cloth. "Delivery for the queen."

Orlandia grinned and tossed her napkin onto her plate and adjusted her crown as she got up. Her heels tapped loudly on the way toward the door. "I wonder who they could be from? I have many admirers." She took the vase. The servant lifted the cloth and immediately stepped back into the hall. Now that the flowers weren't covering his face, Thane realized he didn't recognize him. And he knew every servant in his house.

Thane slowly stood, worry gnawing at his gut. "Who are they from?"

NIGHT MEETS THE ELF QUEEN

She lifted the card with a huge grin. "'For the queen of nothing, love Pricilla'. Hmmm I don't know a Pricilla. And that's rather rude. My husband may be dead, but I still hold the title of Queen Mother."

Hel immediately jumped up. Silverware clattered and glasses tipped. Valeen shouted, "Throw the flowers away!"

Thane ran toward her, but she took a deep inhale of the blooms. As if in slow motion, the vase fell from her grasp and shattered on the floor. Then her eyes rolled back, and she was falling. Thane caught her before she hit the ground. "Mother, look at me." Her lips were already turning a deep blue, her skin fading to an awful shade of grayish white. Thane's heart crashed hard. "Mom!"

"Help me," she croaked and clutched at his shirt.

"Hel!" Thane shouted. He didn't have the power to stop this, but Hel did.

"I-I love you." Her head fell to the side, and she breathed out slowly.

The flowers swiftly disintegrated into black muck. Hel dropped to a knee beside them, and with a quick flick of his hand the mess vanished. He pressed his fingers to the side of her neck and shook his head. "Poison," he muttered and turned her face side to side. Blood slowly dripped out of her nose, eyes, and from her ears.

"Do something, Hel!" Thane shouted. "Save her! I don't care if you hate her. This is my mother!"

He touched her neck again then sighed. "I'm sorry. She's already gone."

"Bring her back!" Thane pulled her limp body against his chest. Why did she already feel cold? He began to tremble as memories of her flashed in his mind. Her clapping when he first picked up a sword and swung it. Playing hide and seek with him as a child. There were many times she intervened when Tenebris beat him. She took a blow or two herself by stepping in between them.

"I can't," Hel said, softly. "You know I can't bring people back from death."

Thane gently laid her on the floor, her brown curls spilled out from the pins holding them in place and her crown clattered to the ground. He turned to Hel and shoved a finger into his chest. "If you did this..."

His brows pulled down and he looked truly offended. "Why would you blame me?" He snapped back.

"You threatened to kill her a moment ago and then someone just happens to bring poisonous flowers? This has you written all over it!" He shoved him hard in the chest and Hel fell back.

With a low growl, he stood and glared down at him. "I didn't do this. You wanted to know the council's next move, well now you do. I'm sorry your mother got caught in the crossfire." He vanished in a puff of gray smoke. Thane slammed his fist into the ground, cracking the white tile, and let out a roar.

It was a week later that Thane pressed his palm against the cold gray stone of Orlandia Morningflower's tomb. Her likeness was already being carved into the door. The quiet *tap, tap tap*, mingled with the sounds of birds chirping. The stone carver paused only a moment to watch him then went back to his work. She would have wanted a large celebration for her life and to be honored by their people. Despite not wanting to have any parties he would give her that as a gift. He'd have Talon and the staff plan it for the following weekend. Right now, it seemed the council wanted to play games and not bring a full-scale war.

A quiet rustle caught his ear and Hel appeared beside him, wearing an all-black suit, hair combed back in a way he only wore for ceremonial purposes. He tucked his hands behind himself and carefully inspected Thane. "I am sorry, Thane. I mean that."

He kept his hand on the stone, like if he did so long enough it would bring her back. "I killed my own father and now my mother is also dead because of me."

"You can't blame yourself for Pricilla's wickedness."

"My past is destroying the present," he grumbled.

"I know exactly what you mean." He watched a blue sparrow fly by and cleared his throat. "It's time to retaliate. They took one of ours. We'll take one of theirs."

Thane dropped his hand from his mother's tomb and faced his cousin. There was no more waiting for the council to make a move. They needed reminding who the god of war was. "Whatever it is, I'm in."

Chapter 15

VALEEN

Street vendors shouted at passersby to come enjoy the tastes and styles of the city of Nelfara. Exotic spices and smells of roasting meat drifted out among the large crowds gathered under the light drizzle of rain. A breeze threatened to toss Valeen's hood back, so she gripped the edges of the fabric. It would be improbable odds for anyone to recognize her, but she couldn't be too careful.

"Fresh spices from the hills of the goddess of the harvest! You won't find any better!" shouted a male with a large round hat with a circular brim. Old brown feathers poked out of the left side.

There was a healthy mixture of demigods, humans, elves, dwarves, and shifters of many kinds in this city. Runevale was the melting pot of the realms; before the way was shut, the gods and goddesses had brought many races from every known kingdom and system of the living to thrive in their territories. Most thought of it as a gift to be chosen.

She had yet to spot a full-blooded god or goddess in the streets. They rarely did their own shopping, and things hadn't changed in her absence; most wouldn't be caught doing such a "lowly" task, and would have no reason to be in the commoner markets. Several streets over would be the stretch for the affluent, wealthy, and high-status families.

A street she'd avoid at all costs. Right now, she, Hel, and Thane needed to blend in as commoners.

A dwarf with a large, bushy beard braided into three plaits grinned up at her as she passed. He waved his arm over a precious gold jewelry set on a table display. "The finest gold for a fine lady. Perhaps one of you gents wants to purchase your partner a lovely necklace?" He stared up at Hel, whose face was half covered under his hood, hiding his distinctive rune marks and red eyes. Looking startled he turned to Thane with a half-smile.

The gold pieces were likely fake or stolen at the prices listed and the fact that he wasn't in an area where most people could afford such gaudy pieces. "Another time, dwarf," Hel said in their mother tongue, the commonly spoken language on Runevale.

They walked on until someone gripped her wrist, she broke the hold, twisted the assailant's arm and whirled to find a merchant grimacing with a bottle of bubbling pink liquid in his other hand. "My apologies, lady. I only wanted to show you the finest skin-perfecting potion in the territory."

She squeezed a little harder, digging her nails into the skin of his forearm. "Do I look like I need it?"

His caterpillar-like black brows rose high on his

forehead. "No, lady. I didn't mean it that way. Your beauty is unmatched, lady. I only meant..."

Valeen released him. "It's rude to grab someone to get their attention. Don't do it again. Next time you might lose a hand."

"Of course, lady." He dipped his head and backed toward his stand.

Hel's jaw muscles flickered, and his eyes darkened like a hawk set on diving for a mouse. "This place is testing my patience."

Without him even saying a word she knew he was contemplating killing the merchant. "Don't. We can't afford to draw attention to ourselves right now. In and out, that was the plan."

"If he disappears in the night that won't be a problem."

Thane glared at him too. "No one will know it was us."

"Stop it, both of you." She quickened her pace hoping they'd keep up and leave it alone.

There was a definite mysterious gloom about Rogue, the god of justice and order's, territory. Someone disappearing in the night may not seem all that out of the ordinary, especially in a city of at least half a million. Tall evergreen trees loomed high around their destination outside of the main town. A light drizzle from a heavy coat of gray clouds left the air humid. Rogue, one of the eleven council members lived where high mountain ranges on one side and the sea on the other made for a perfect concoction of being the dreariest and greenest territory in Runevale.

They made their way through the city and followed the road to the beige-stoned castle with an aqua roof that looked to be made of terracotta tiles. A clocktower at the east end was the highest peak but there were several turrets of various heights. A quick scan of the many windows had Valeen guessing there were at least a hundred bedrooms in the four levels.

Standing behind a tall bush with dark blue berries, she inspected the grounds. Several guards walked the black iron fence surrounding the property, more at the entrances. The quiet buzz, almost like a swarm of bees, gave away the magical wards present.

A set of guards with tall metal-tipped spears in hand laughed loudly on top of their silver- and blue-feathered griffin mounts. The large beaks of the creatures could easily tear off a limb, as could their razor-sharp talons on the front. Their hindquarters were that of a large gray feline with a tail tipped with a tuft of black fur.

The guards all wore black domed hats with a wide brim and aqua-blue feathers peeking out on both sides. Although one of the males on a griffin wore white feathers in his hat. *The colors must be of significance in ranking,* Valeen thought.

Hel stepped out of the cover of the bushes, turning nearly transparent and pressed his palm to the invisible barrier. After a moment he glanced back at them, "The magic is weak. I'll be able to teleport us in."

Moments later the three of them stood in the center of a room with wide dramatic wood arches above. Although the wall to the left was lined with many windows, it was dark and dreary enough outside to need more light. The glow stones on the chandeliers were only marginally brighter than firelights and offered a soft ambiance.

Valeen scanned the many shelves filled with precious items—a bronze scepter in a glass case, a golden egg adored in rare rubies and sapphires, gaudy necklaces, and the skeleton of a hand of someone he must have found important. The day her immortality was taken it was siphoned into a hollowed crystal hung on a necklace. None of these items looked like it. Valeen knew she'd feel it if it were near. Like a call to her soul that had been, in some ways, ripped in half.

Hel flicked his fingers, and a shimmering veil trickled down the walls and moved across the ceiling and floor. "Silencing spell."

"You've been in this house before? You knew where to take us," Valeen mused. Rogue was one of the Primevarr, her opposing side and the one Hel and Thane had been loyal to as young gods. She'd only met him at her execution.

"Rogue had the same tutors as us," Thane said, pulling open drawers on the desk. Hel immediately went for the shelves of scrolls.

"Was Synick one of those tutors you shared?"

"Synick was very selective." Hel's fingers lightly passed over the scrolls, as if whatever he was looking for would reveal itself. "Rogue didn't make the cut."

"Your lessons may be the reason that Rogue was the only one to vote against our exile. Which is why I have to ask why we're here if this is a retaliation mission."

Thane and Hel glanced at one another then Thane answered, "Synick gave us something on him that might get him to tell us where our immortality is."

"Something?"

"He has a secret child I doubt he wants anyone to

know about." Hel grinned and pulled a scroll free and unfolded it. "Also, Rogue didn't like me, and I didn't like him. He usually had his face in a book about the law and thought he was smarter than everyone. It's more likely he didn't feel our punishment was justified than he felt any kindness toward us."

"He liked me," Thane rifled through the drawer.

"Yes, Mr. Popular," Hel drawled.

"A secret child he doesn't want his *wife* to know about?"

"Something like that. You'll see."

"What do you mean, I'll see? Do you have to be cryptic?"

"I mean, you'll see. It's a surprise."

She and Thane exchanged a glance, and he just chuckled and shook his head. "Are you in on this too?" she asked.

"You really don't like surprises, do you?" Thane took out a stack of papers and peeled through them.

"No." Valeen gave up and her boots lightly tapped as she hurried across the warm wooden floors to the glass case of precious items. She tugged open the doors and found a drawer at the bottom. Bottles of ink rolled around, feather quills sat on the left, and a black notebook was stuffed in the back. If she knew anything about little black notebooks, it was that they usually held important information.

She lifted it out of the drawer and pried at the cover, but it wouldn't open. Magically sealed, damn. But she was even more certain she could find something useful for blackmail inside. If the All Mother was merciful, it would contain the location of her immortality as well. They wouldn't even need to get him to talk.

"Hel, I need your help getting this open."

He looked over his shoulder. "Are there runes on it?"

She turned it over in her hands to view the edges of the paper. There were three runes she didn't recognize. "Yes."

"These bastards love to hate me but still use my magic."

She tossed it to him, and he caught it. The tip of his fingers brushed down the spine like he was petting a cat and then the book opened with the sound of a cork popping. "All you need to do is give it a little stroke, you know, like something else."

She rolled her eyes and crossed the room, snatching it back. "Always inappropriate."

"You act like you didn't do that just last night."

Valeen's cheeks warmed, and he chuckled. "Can we focus?" she flicked through the pages. It looked to be full names and dates... encounters with females? Not at all what she needed. "And stop staring at me."

"Now I can't look at you?"

"I can't read with you staring at me like that."

He smirked. "Like what, love? Like you're the most extraordinary being to ever exist? Like you're my entire world?"

Thunder clapped outside and lightning streaked, brightening the gray atmosphere for a flash.

"When did you get so mushy?" Thane shoved the papers back on the desk and shut the drawer loudly. "We're not going to find anything useful in here. It's not like he'd have the location just sitting in his office for anyone to find."

Footsteps outside the door made them all freeze. Hel maneuvered Valeen to the desk and pushed her into the seat. *Let's play with him a little first,* he said in her mind. *Thane and I will be hiding over there.*

She smiled and propped her muddy boots up on his desk and took out her dagger. The door creaked open, and Rogue stepped inside, paused for a moment to inspect her with curiosity, then closed it behind him. Like many gods he was attractive with a sharp jaw and straight nose. His short cinnamon-brown hair was combed with a perfect curl on his forehead and a tailored coffee-colored suit.

"Who are you?" His lip curled with distaste at her boots dripping mud all over his paperwork. "Did Seffner send me an early beautiful but ruggish birthday present?"

With the tip of her dagger, she dug a piece of dirt out from underneath her nail, then lifted her chin. "You would like that I'm sure, but why don't you look a little harder."

He scrutinized her face and stepped to the front of his desk, opposite of her. "I know you."

"You do."

"Who are you?"

"It would ruin our little game if I just told you. I'll give you a hint—we met once, the day I died a very, very long time ago."

Recognition flashed and he moved back a step. "Valeen," he said in surprise.

"Don't tell me you didn't know the portal was back open again."

His head snapped in both directions. "You came alone?"

She jammed her dagger into the wooden desk and stood but didn't speak.

"I'm not going to hurt you as long as you're not here to kill me," he said, raising his hands in surrender. "I don't want to fight."

"It's funny you think you could hurt me. But I didn't come to fight. I came for something else."

A slow smile started at one side of his mouth. "You are as lovely as ever, Valeen. It's surreal seeing you here after all this time and with the ways off Runevale being shut for so long. To behold you, someone powerful enough to do that..." He tsked his tongue. "There is something about primordials that just scratches an itch; rare and coveted. It's one of the reasons I voted against your... punishment." His eyes flicked over her once again. "I like the white in your hair. It fits you, moon goddess."

Valeen plastered on a fake smile and was about to reply but Hel materialized in the chair with a civar in hand. The sweet smoke rolled out of the burning tip and curled around him. "She is lovely, and she knows it. Compliments don't do much."

"Hel." He sounded even more surprised than when he realized who she was.

"Let's skip the niceties and the part where you bore us with details about how you've been the last two thousand years after you sentenced us to die over and over."

Once he got over his initial shock, he took two small steps toward the door. "What do you want?"

"My fucking immortality."

Thane sauntered out from behind a bookshelf and Rogue whipped around to face him. He was pale now. "War. Maker have mercy; all of you are here. I always liked you, War." He turned to Hel, "You too. You never pretend to be something you're not. That's a rare trait among the gods." The corner of his mouth curled but it didn't reach his eyes. "I will remind you again that I voted against that punishment. It wasn't just nor did it fit the crime, so there is no reason to fight. I'm on your side."

"You can't talk your way out of this," Hel said, then put the civar to his lips. "Where is our immortality?"

"If I told you, I'd be going against the other members of the council, which I cannot do. I can, however, call a meeting with them which you will be invited to under parley. I think it's been long enough that tensions are down, and we can all have a civil discussion."

"Tensions are down?" Hel rose out of the chair and kicked it so hard it crashed into the shelf behind him. Half the books clattered and spilled to the floor. Dust billowed up making her nose itch. "They're higher than they've ever fucking been. You sent a *demon* prince to Adalon to assassinate my *wife*. Letting one of them out goes against your own fucking rules. None of you deserve to be in your position."

"And you just killed my mother," Thane growled.

He balked and his back hit against the window's ledge. Rain streaked down the glass, and he grimaced. "*I* told Pricilla she was insane for letting one of the princes loose. And if your elf mother is dead, it wasn't on purpose."

"If Pricilla sent the demon and the flowers, then

you did." Valeen jerked her dagger free from the desk. "You are as responsible for what she does as she is. All matters must be agreed upon with a majority vote."

Rogue put his hands up in surrender then nervously ran one of them through his wavy hair. "I have been calling for a stop to this for a thousand years. Neither of those instances received a vote from me."

"If you truly think what they're doing is wrong, then tell us where our immortality is hidden," Thane growled. "If you believed what you're saying, then you would help us."

"I can't. I'd lose my position and possibly my freedom."

Hel flicked his civar at Rogue and it hit him on the tip of the nose. "If you wish to do this the hard way, so be it."

"Wait!" He gulped and tugged on the bottom of his suit coat to straighten it out. He raised his chin and cleared his throat as if trying to regain some confidence. Rogue didn't have any particular power that would be useful in a fight. What he had was an amazing ability to recall facts especially pertaining to law and order. The only reason he wasn't head of the council was because they didn't think he was ruthless enough. "It is against the law for any single god or goddess to possess the immortal weapons, as was decreed during the peace treaty between the Primevarr and Drivaar in section 108. Soulender and the Sword of Truth, if found, are to be safeguarded by the council in the decreed vaults. We are chosen from the gods of all territories to be the rule makers and enforcers, to ensure justice for all on Runevale. I'll arrange an exchange."

"Do you practice that speech in the mirror in the mornings?" Hel jested.

"Section 108 also states the weapons are not to be used again unless there is a unanimous decision among every council member. Now, since you used and killed with Soulender, Valeen, you broke the law, but I can argue you've served enough time as a mortal. I can guarantee they won't get my vote to use Soulender against you. I'll arrange an exchange."

"You'll arrange an ambush." Valeen shook her head. Did he think they were fools? As if they hadn't dealt with these people long enough to know they couldn't be trusted. "No."

"If you give us the weapons we'll *give* you your immortality. It's simple. You can't expect something for nothing, Valeen."

Out of the corner of her eye, she spotted Thane's nod to Hel, and he interjected, "Your daughter, Amelia," Hel began. "I bet your wife and the council don't know about her. The half-breed ogre. I don't know if there's ever been a half-ogre half-god. According to section 234 of the Decree of Eligible and Ineligible Breeding for Gods and Goddesses, she is an abomination. You're not the only one who knows the laws, Rogue."

Rogue's eyes widened and his spine erected. "I have no such child."

"Oh, they definitely don't know about her." Thane looked at Hel with a smirk.

"I don't imagine I'd admit to sticking my cock in a hideous, stupid ogre let alone impregnating one either.

The child must be grotesque. And the council would have you removed and have her destroyed. Reproducing with one of the forbidden creatures is illegal, god of justice. But that was the draw for you, wasn't it? The forbidden."

Valeen got a visual from that description that she never wanted in her mind. Yuck.

Rogue tugged at his collar. "You have no proof. This is a salacious accusation."

"Or was it the size of her? Nine foot tall, moss instead of pubic hair, the strength of ten men? Maybe you liked to be dominated by a swamp beast."

"Shut up."

Valeen's nails bit into her palms as she watched Rogue begin to crumble. This would either end in a fight or a revelation.

"You're a submissive, I see," Hel said. "And poor Amelia has gone her whole life not being claimed by her father. I think it's time, don't you?"

Rogue bared his teeth. "I cannot do that!"

"Pity, I'll just have to tell her and the Dunekor ogre clan. I'm assuming you compelled the mother to forget, she doesn't know you're the father either. Pricilla will find a note with information to lead to the child, along with the others on the council."

"Hel, *please.*"

"I love the groveling stage." Hel's cruel eyes darkened. "It's also the part where we make a deal."

"I can't tell you where your immortality is."

With a flick of his fingers, a circular swirling pool the size of a dinner plate opened above his palm. "Oh, she has red hair. That was unexpected."

The scrying pool revealed a green-skinned ogre with dark red hair, stooping down with a bucket in her hands at the edge of a river. Her face was pretty, goddess like, and she was slighter, smaller framed than a typical ogre. By her size and youthful yet mature features, she must be in her upper teen years. What looked like a burlap sack wrapped around her body for a dress.

"Nobody could look at her and think she was fully ogre," Thane said.

"And she looks oddly like you even being green," Hel added. "Those same brown eyes."

Rogue stared, as if mesmerized by the image.

"Maybe I'll snap my fingers, and a very deadly snake will appear. We can all watch as she suffers and let's face it, she isn't immortal, so she'll die. It's not a good way to go. The slow suffocation isn't pretty. The gasping for breath, it's even bothersome to me. I wonder, would she call out for her mother?"

"Don't!" Rogue cried, reaching forward.

"Where?" Hel snarled.

"I don't know. There was a time they were hidden in a vault, but Pricilla moved them."

"I don't believe you."

"I don't know, Hel, I swear it. But I can find out."

He snapped his fingers and Hel's red serpent appeared on the rocks at the shore of the river beside Amelia. Valeen gulped. *Hel,* she silently pleaded.

Stay out of it, Valeen.

He would kill the girl. Murdering innocents went against everything in her, but this was war. And war made monsters of many.

She is a child, Valeen said in Hel's mind.

"I won't ask again, Rogue," Hel growled. *She is an ogre and a bargaining tool,* he silently argued back.

The snake slithered silently over the rocks, inching closer and closer to the girl.

"I will find them! I will find them and send you the location. Just don't hurt her!"

The snake reared back to bite the unsuspecting ogre and Hel snapped his fingers again, and his serpent vanished. "You have three days. If I don't have a location by then, everyone in Runevale finds out about Amelia and then three days after that, she's dead." He clamped his palm closed and the image of the ogre in the woods vanished.

And just so he didn't forget about this meeting, Valeen would leave him with a reminder. With Soulender in her palm, blade tip pressed to his throat, she gripped his dark hair.

"Wait, wait, don't kill me. I'll find out!"

She gritted her teeth and gently dragged the blade across his throat, lightly piercing his flesh, until blood ran down like a stream of red but wouldn't kill him. With Soulender, the scar would never go away.

"Remember this moment, Rogue. Do you know what it's like to die over and over? Do you know what it's like to be kept from those you love for thousands of years, forced to start over with no memory of them? This will not end peacefully. This will only end in war," Valeen said. "We could have ended you and your daughter today, but showed mercy that you never showed us. You say you didn't vote for what was done to us, but you didn't stand in the way either."

Hel held up three fingers. "Three days, Rogue."

"We want what is rightfully ours," Thane said. He

pulled a burning torch from the wall, walked over to the scrolls and let the flames lick at the paper. Thick gray smoke rolled up the shelves into the high rafters.

"What are you doing?" Rogue howled. "That's my life's work!"

With the paper as fuel, the wooden shelves quickly caught flame. The shadows darkened in Thane's face as the fire burned brightly behind him. "Your life's work for my mother's life."

Hel grabbed them both as the heat sweltered and they were pulled into darkness.

Chapter 16

THANE

The bedroom door creaked open, and Thane rolled over. In the low light he only saw her curvy hourglass frame, her hips swaying side to side as light footsteps tapped on the floor. He sat up with a jolt realizing who it was. Black hair glistened in the pale moonlight cascading in from the sheer curtains. She wore nothing at all.

"Thane," Valeen whispered and stopped at the side of his bed.

"Did something happen?" he asked, dropping his feet to the floor.

She put her fingers to her lips to quiet him. Stepping between his thighs, she pushed her hands into his hair. "No, my love."

His own hands slid up her hips, up bare skin, to her waist then heavy breasts. Her nipples were peaked and begging for his mouth. "I knew you'd come to me. I knew it wasn't over."

She pushed him back on the bed and crawled onto

him. "I still want you," she whispered. "I want all of you right now."

Her lips crashed into his, tongue slipping into his mouth. He closed his eyes and moaned. Teeth bit into his bottom lip hard enough to sting and his eyes shot open... blonde hair draped over him, tickling his bare skin. Valeen was gone and Katana was naked, smiling on top of him. Her bright lavender eyes locked onto his, then her tongue slid up his bare chest.

She curled a lock of his hair between her fingers and tugged. "Kiss me again. Kiss me until you can think of nothing else."

THANE FLEW UP IN BED, and blinked at the bright sunlight filling his room. Birds chirped outside the window and the cool morning air brought goosebumps along his sweaty skin. *Maker above, it was a dream. Just a dream.*

Shaking his head to clear the thought of her naked body on him, he hopped out of bed and stepped into the adjoining bathing room, pouring water from a gold pitcher into his hand and splashing his face and neck.

After burning down Rogue's study and traveling through the realms, he'd crashed out all night. None of them were counting on Rogue to come through with the location of their immortality, but it was enough to show the council they could get to them just as easily as they could send assassins.

He lifted his face to the mirror. His thoughts should be on battle strategy, on gaining the dragons as allies, on what the council might do next... anything but envisioning Katana naked. He needed to go for a run and shake this edge.

Once he was dressed, he slipped out the door. This floor of the castle had once been his fathers, and well, Tenebris didn't need it anymore. His rooms had been the largest and most extravagant and were meant for the High King. Even if the thought of being next to Hel and Valeen was what drove him into a new room, it was time he took it anyway. The paintings he passed on the stone walls were of the elf kings from his family line, all seven of them. Even Tenebris's portrait still hung. Despite Thane's hatred of him, he was still part of their history and kept it there to remind him never to become like him.

He quickly made it down the stairs to the next level where Piper, Fennan, Leif, and Katana all had rooms. If they were up this early, they wouldn't be ready for the day yet. But nonetheless he hurried past Katana's door. The dream was still all too heavy on his mind. He was almost to the end of the hall at the set of stairs when the quiet squeal of door hinges made him slow. The arched windows let in the morning sunlight shining over the red carpet down the center of the corridor. The heat from the sun warmed his already too-hot skin. *Please don't be her.*

"Hey, Thane."

It was Leif.

Breathing a sigh of relief, he turned on his heel and faced him. Leif's hair was still a tangled mess, and he only had on a pair of trousers. "What are you doing up this early?" he asked.

"I'm going on a run. I'll be back shortly."

"As much as I'd love to join you, sire, I'm not

ready." He folded his arms over his bare chest. "I was going to ask if I have your permission to bring a date to your mother's celebration of life this evening."

"Bring whoever you want, Leif." Thane shrugged.

Leif smirked at him. "I was going to ask Katana. She'll need an escort."

A slow heat burned its way up his chest and to his face. His heart started beating harder. He shouldn't be angry at the thought of that. "I already asked her," he lied. "As a friend of course, not a date."

Leif chuckled. "Oh, sure, sire, just as a friend when you're now single and she happens to be single too? Let's not forget to add she's positively stunning. If you only want to be her friend, I'll take my shot."

"Go back to bed, Leif." He shook his head at Leif's laughter chasing him down the hallway.

BOOTS POUNDED the grass in a steady rhythm. He had no direction in mind. He just needed to move. Standing in one place made him feel like water on the edge of boiling. Horses grazed in the field surrounded by a soft brown wooden fence near the stables. A golden mare with a white mane lifted her head and neighed as Thane tore by. He nodded at the guards at the entrance of the bridge. The sprays of water from the falls misted across his skin.

His mind flashed to Katana in the hot pool wearing her white bralette and underwear. She may as well have not been wearing anything at all with how sheer the fabric became when wet. He'd badly wanted to join her. Wanted to pull off what fabric was left on her wet body.

He was used to females throwing themselves at him, as a god and as High King, and typically they didn't get under his skin, didn't burrow themselves into his mind. No one had since Layala. Why should Katana be any different than any of the beautiful elves who'd lusted after him for years? Or the goddesses he'd bedded and felt nothing for long ago. Varlett had hooked him when she was a young dragon princess, but he rarely found himself daydreaming about her. Yet that image of Katana standing in the hot springs was burned into his mind like a brand.

Maybe there was something about primordial goddesses he couldn't resist.

Shit.

He ground his teeth. *Shit shit shit.*

The wind tore through his hair as he pushed himself hard. He didn't want to think about anyone. He couldn't let himself fall again just to be left shattered with nothing. His legs and lungs burned, keeping his focus on his body.

When he reached the wall surrounding the city he found the hidden door and shoved through, then kept going to a small wood a few miles from the castle and finally came to a stop and put his hands on his hips. A flicker of movement caught his eye, and he turned to find nothing, but his skin prickled from the presence of another.

"Hello, dear."

"Varlett," he mumbled before facing her. "What are you doing here?"

She smiled and tilted her head, making her black

horns glisten in the sunlight atop her golden head. "I was out for a morning stroll and saw you. I thought you might be running to something and needed help, but I get the impression you're running away from something or," she arched a brow, "someone."

"I don't need your help."

"If it's any consolation, I'm sorry she hurt you. I'm sorry she didn't choose you." The softness of her amber gaze would say she meant it, but she was apologizing for the wrong thing.

"*She* hurt me?" he growled. "You did this. And you knew as well as I did the moment they left together it was over for both of us."

"It was over the second he woke up. You just didn't know it yet. I did."

"Did you ever even care for me?" Not that it mattered.

Her reptilian eyes lifted to the canopy of the tree branches above her, and her long ebony talons clicked together in a drumming motion. "You were my first love, War. A dragon never truly gets over that." She paused and lowered her voice, shifting her stance nervously. He hadn't seen her nervous—maybe ever. Was this a new act? A new form of manipulation? "It drove me mad to see the way you looked at her, to know you loved her. And I don't mean that as a figure of speech. Do you understand?"

He swallowed hard... madness? Once a dragon made their choice, they typically mated for life. Of course, he knew this but back then the young dragon princess had always been so blasé about her feelings toward him. He believed she was using him to gain status as much as he was, but had he been wrong? Did

Varlett see War as her *mate?* Did she still feel this way? And when she felt betrayed, when she realized his heart belonged to someone else...

"So you orchestrated her falling right into my arms? No, that makes no sense. You're lying."

"I—If I wasn't going to be happy with you, I wanted none of you to be happy. I wanted to see her fall." She ran her long fingers through her golden hair and looked away. "I'm not saying it was rational. I was young."

"What you did was one of the worst things anyone could have done."

"Dragons mate for life," she bit out. "We cannot stop the bond that forms. Don't you see that? Couldn't you see how I loved you?"

His mouth nearly dropped open. "You loved me then with your body but not your heart. It's a bond of the heart, not through sex." He started to walk away, and she gripped his wrist, forcing him to turn.

"I was a young dragon, and you were a god! I was terrified to let you see how much I loved you. I didn't feel like I deserved you, and I was scared you'd leave me—a mortal—like so many other gods do. I didn't want to form a bond to you in my heart, but it happened. Especially when I saw the way you watched *her*. And how could I ever compare to a primordial goddess?"

"So now you're claiming you weren't in control? That madness overwhelmed you? You're unbelievable."

She ran her talon down the fabric on his chest. "You don't have to believe it, but it's true. Why do you think I saved you? If I didn't care, War, I would have let you die. If you meant nothing to me, you wouldn't be here now. The demon hound's venom would have killed you. Your heart had stopped. I had to use the demon prince's ring to pull you back."

"I'm not War anymore." He snatched her wrist then jerked her flush against his body. It didn't matter what her reasons were. They were all probably lies anyway. More lies, more deception like the snake she was. He leaned down to her ear and whispered, "You disgust me." Then he bumped his shoulder into hers as he trudged away.

"I could tell Hel, you know," she called after him. "About your part in all this."

A tingle ran down his spine and he slowly turned. "Tell him what? I didn't know what you were doing."

"Do you know how easy it would be to convince him you did? Maybe I'll say it was you in that bedroom with me with cloaking magic to look exactly like him while Valeen watched from the hall."

His heart skipped a beat. "I wasn't there."

"But weren't you? You were outside when she went running. You scooped her right up into your arms and took her home." Varlett's tongue ran across her pointed canine. "Maybe you did suspect I was up to something and took advantage. Maybe I'm not the only one who's a little mad when they don't get what they want."

Thane's stomach dropped to his toes. He didn't want to lose his brother again. He couldn't. "Don't you dare try to turn this on me." He charged at her and gripped her by the throat until he slammed her back against a tree trunk.

"Careful," she said softly, "don't hurt your precious Valeen... or do. Choke me a little more. I don't mind it if you're the one doing it."

His free hand trembled with rage and curled into a fist, punching the tree trunk beside her head. "If you poison Hel against me with your lies again..."

"You'll kill me? There's a line you'll have to get into first."

He jerked his hand back and took several steps away before he lost control. The edges of his vision had begun to shadow, a sign he was on the verge of giving into his dark side, the wraith who killed without remorse. The reason for his god name.

"You've always had so much potential, Varlett. You could use your gifts to help us, but yet again I have a feeling anything you do that may look like help is for your own gain."

"And even if I did, you'd trust me?" She let out a cackle. "There is no coming back from it. With time, you might forgive me, but Valeen and Hel never will. And so, I did what I had to. I linked my body to Valeen's. It was the only way to save myself for when the truth came out. There is no place I could hide where Hel wouldn't find me. You know this."

"And you know they'll find a way to break the link."

She lifted a shoulder. "Perhaps I have sealed my fate and will die by Hel or Valeen's hand, but I always seem to find a way to survive."

"Like a cockroach."

She rolled her eyes. "Didn't any part of you miss me?"

"Like you said, what you did was unforgivable. You destroyed my relationship with Hel, the closest person in my life. Even if we have reconciled that bond will always be tainted because of *you*."

NIGHT MEETS THE ELF QUEEN

SWIPING his sweaty brow with his sleeve, Thane made his way back up the steps to his room. Varlett was really the most vile person he'd ever known, and he'd known a great many cruel and terrible people in his life.

A couple of guards bowed to him as he passed. "Good morning," Thane greeted them. Three maids carrying fresh linens stopped and stepped against the wall allowing him to pass. "Morning, ladies."

They curtsied. "Morning, sire."

One of them whispered, "Is it just me or has he gotten even more attractive since he and Layala split?"

The others giggled and he couldn't help but smile.

"I'd lay in his bed without a stitch of clothing on if I thought he'd take me," another said.

He hoped she did *not* do that and turned the corner. Blonde hair was the first thing he saw then a clatter of porcelain came next and suddenly the front of his shirt was soaked. Thane jumped at the hot liquid on his already hot sweaty skin. Katana caught her teacup before it fell, and gasped.

"Oh, goodness, I am so sorry, Thane. I did not see you." She quickly set her teacup on the window's ledge but kept the napkin and started wiping at the front of his shirt. "Does it burn? It was still a little hot. Ugh and it is going to stain. I am so clumsy sometimes." Flustered, she continued wiping. "And, *All Mother* help me. It even spilled on your pants."

"It's fine." He stiffened and caught her wrist to stop her from wiping below his belt. "They're only clothes."

Lifting her big, lavender eyes, she let out a sharp

breath. "Oh, sorry," she blushed, "you can clean yourself, ugh, down there." She tucked her hands behind her back. "Now that I am completely embarrassed, I will go to my room and die a little." She whirled on her heel and hurried away.

"Katana," he said, and she froze. Now that he told Leif he had already asked her, he had to now, or he'd get shit for it later. The image from his dream of her sitting naked on top of him came to mind and he started to clam up. But he wasn't going to ask her to be his date. It was just so neither of them would have to go alone.

Right, that was all it was.

He cleared his throat, but the words wouldn't come out.

She finally faced him again. There was still a flush to her cheeks. "Yes?"

"Would you escort me to my mother's memorial tonight?"

She fidgeted with the ends of her long hair. "Are you sure? It is a public event. People may think, well, you know what they will think. When the High King brings someone, it has meaning."

"I know, but you and I know that we are only friends. And if I ask one of the courtiers she will certainly want more than that. At the moment, I'm not looking for a queen."

"Ah yes, what courtier would not want more from their very handsome, very eligible High King." She smiled and winked. "I would love to be of assistance."

Chapter 17

KATANA

The whispers started as soon as Thane offered her his arm. Before they even set foot inside the ballroom. There was arranged seating for three hundred. The sea of people was already seated when they stepped in, arm in arm. By the number of guards throughout the castle and at every entrance and exit, anything that looked suspicious would be spotted. She had a good feeling about tonight and wasn't worried about an attack.

The room was drenched in red and white tapestries and matching roses. Red was apparently the Queen Mother's favorite rose.

While Valeen helped Katana do her hair, she said she wouldn't be going, for one because she didn't like the queen and two, she didn't want to disrespect Thane. Not having her sister there made her nervous but she promised Thane she would go, and she wouldn't let him down.

Talon walked down the center aisle ahead of them with Fennan as her escort.

Smiling, she looked amongst the elves. They were such a lovely people. All statuesque and beauty. Everyone in attendance wore fine pastels and had beautiful silver and gold jewelry.

"Who is that with the High King?" a lady asked.

"Does the High King have a new betrothed?"

"She is... quite lovely."

The whispered and hushed questions continued. It didn't bother Katana. In fact, she was happy to have them all distracted rather than focusing on his breakup with Valeen. She'd even spoken to her sister before this so it wouldn't cause a rift between them in case feelings still lingered on both sides. Valeen assured her that nothing would ever happen between her and Thane again.

Thane leaned close to her ear, and it sent a shiver down her back. "Are you alright?" he whispered.

"I am perfect." And she was. It was exhilarating to be on the arm of the most desired elf king and have everyone talk about it. She hadn't had anything intriguing happen like this in a long time. Even in her previous life, the longer she was married to Atlanta, the more he wanted to keep her locked inside. In the beginning, he was charming, and she enjoyed his possessiveness, but then it turned into abuse when she'd only look at another male. If he heard rumors that she'd spoken to a male, even if it was a simple greeting, he would get angry. After many years, she stopped going out into public unless she needed to. The only place she'd ever been shielded was when she stayed at House of Night. Atlanta didn't want her sister to find out how he was with her and left her alone there.

Thane guided her to a seat in the front row. Music played, elves went up on the dais to sing the king's mother's praises. Her shoulder touched Thane's, and she felt a strange electricity between them. It made her pulse rush in her ears. His knuckles turned white from gripping his thighs.

"We gather together for the great loss of the Queen Mother, Orlandia Morningflower, she was a wonderful..."

Katana started to tune out the speakers too focused on Thane. Through every song and speaker, he didn't relax. There were a few times he glanced over at her but otherwise he stared straight ahead. The talks at the podium became background noise to the intensity between them. It started to affect her own breathing. How was it that sitting next to someone made her feel like she might spontaneously combust? She finally reached over and set her hand on his. His grip finally loosened, and he smiled down at her.

"It's almost over," he whispered. "Sorry it's so long."

"I am content, no need to worry about me. Are you not speaking?"

"I'm not feeling up to it."

Poor Thane. She patted the top of his hand gently. After a moment, he turned his hand and held hers.

"Thank you for joining me."

"Of course."

His sister Talon leaned over to him. "Mother would want to celebrate her life late into the night so don't try to end this early and ruin it with all your paranoia. I want to have a good time."

His jaw muscles feathered, and he took a deep breath. "Her death wasn't an accident. My paranoia is warranted."

"I won't live in a cage."

"Be thankful there is a public celebration at all. It ends at midnight, Talon."

"Maybe for you." She smirked and curled her hands on her lap.

Katana nudged his side. The reaction of a young girl who'd just lost her mother was strange. Perhaps they didn't get along well. "Your sister is...spirited."

"She likes to drink too much wine and act inappropriately with males much older than her. And with our mother's death, she'll fall into it all the more."

THE FORMALITIES ENDED and the chairs were cleared out, opening the room up for dancing. Music started quickly, string music and drums and wind instruments. The lights went low with only candlelight from the chandeliers. Ball gowns swished and the tapping of heels shuffled across the glossy floor.

Talon and her group of friends quickly went to the wine table. The annoyance at that was obvious in Thane's expression but he didn't say anything to his sister. It likely wasn't worth causing a scene.

The focus of the room shifted from his mother's passing to Thane and her. So many people stared and whispered behind their hands as they passed them. Maidens glared at her. One even whispered, "Did you see her round ears? She's not even an elf, or she's at least a half-breed."

"The High King couldn't possibly choose a bride who is not an elf," another said.

Oh, the things young ladies worried about. Katana had been out of the spotlight for so long she forgot that details like this were what people concerned themselves with. "They must think I am human with my rounded ears." She smiled. "We are causing quite a stir."

"Yes," he grumbled. "Will you walk with me? I'm not really in the mood to be here."

"Lead the way, High King." She took his arm, and they quickly left the ballroom and went out a side door to stroll along a path through the gardens. The blossoms were in full bloom perfuming the air. Water trickled from a small fountain ahead. "It was kind of you to host a celebration for your mother even in these troubled times. I know you did not want to."

"Yes, well she's dead because of me so it's the least I could do."

Her heart ached and she squeezed his arm gently. "Do not blame yourself."

"Who else is to blame?"

"The one who did it, Thane." He kept his bright green eyes everywhere but her. Maybe he didn't want to be around her either. "If you would like to be alone, I can find my way to my room."

He came to a sudden stop and finally met her eyes. "I don't want to be alone."

That same charged energy she felt inside the ballroom returned. She'd never felt anything like it before. Was it his magic? She gasped when an idea came to mind. "We should ask Presco to take us for a ride. The sky is clear, and it is warm. It is the perfect evening."

"Now?"

"Why not?"

"I guess there isn't a reason but—"

"Then we shall go." Grinning, she tugged on his hand and dragged him back inside.

They found Presco reading the *Palenor Scroll* in his study in the library. The two headlines of the front page were, **Dragons Back In Palenor Once Again,** and **The Life and Death of the Queen Mother Orlandia Morningflower.**

She briefly wondered what Thane said the cause of her death was. Elves lived long lives, and it wasn't as if she'd been in battle. It wasn't mentioned during her ceremony. They only spoke of the good things she had done.

Presco was all too happy to agree to fly them again and followed them out to the large open grassy area by the horse pasture. When he took his beast form the grazing horses bolted, kicking up dirt clods and bucking.

"Ladies first." Thane gestured.

Presco scooped her up with his massive paw and set her on his back. A moment later Thane plopped down behind her. "Tell me when you're ready," Presco said.

Katana scooted up to the large spike in front of her and wrapped her arms around it. Without the hesitation he had last time, Thane pressed himself against her back. Only now, Valeen wasn't with them to turn it into fun. It was much more intimate. "Oh, my hair. It will whip you in the face." Her long locks hung loosely aside from a few twists pinned back. She reached up to gather it until Thane's hand brushed against her, and she stilled.

"May I braid it for you?" he asked.

With a giggle, she twisted around in surprise. "You know how?"

"All elves know how to braid hair, in case you haven't noticed." He gestured toward his own, with braids in his dark brown hair starting at his temples and tied into a knot at the back of his head.

"I suppose I assumed someone else did it for you."

"You're not questioning my masculinity, are you?"

"Ummm, no." She shook her head and couldn't even say why she suddenly blushed. "You are quite masculine even if you have such a pretty face."

He chuckled and combed his fingers through her hair. It made the skin on her scalp tingle and a warm feeling slide through her body. Once he tied it off at the ends from a thin leather strap he kept in his pocket, she ran her hands over the plaits. "Thank you. I can tell just from feeling that it is perfect."

"It is, rest assured. We're ready, Presco." He wrapped his arms snuggly around her waist, and it made her stomach flip.

"Hold on," Presco said.

His great wings spread out and he trotted forward, gathering a little speed before liftoff. Rising from the ground tickled her belly and she let out a laugh. The city was lit up with torchlight. Elves still walked the main streets. Soft music drifted up even as they rose high above the tallest trees. The stars glittered and the moon was almost full. The warmth of Thane pressed against her warded off the cooler temperature.

"This is amazing!" She grinned. "I love flying!"

"There's nothing else quite like it."

Presco evened out and went into a steady glide. Feeling brave, she let go of the spike and held out her arms. "Wahoo!" Thane's laugh rumbled against her back. It was good to hear him laugh. He'd been rather melancholy since she'd met him. "Try it. Hold out your arms."

Once he let go of her, she glanced back because she had to see his face, and it didn't disappoint. He was lit up with joy, and even if he was beautiful broody, his perfect white smile made her heart flutter.

Tonight was about freedom and taking risks. She tucked her legs up in front of her, then slowly rose to her full height and held her arms out again.

"Katana." Thane sounded worried, and his hand wrapped around one of her ankles. "Please sit down. You could fall."

The last time they rode, Presco said he didn't lose his riders and even if someone fell, he'd catch them. She trusted that. "Oh, but it is so fun!" The little hairs around her face whipped in the wind and she closed her eyes, with her arms spread wide as if she had wings herself. Maybe she'd ask the god of magic to give her a set one day. Would it be hard to learn to fly?

"*Katana.*"

Glancing back at him, he did look a little scared. What would he do if—She pretended to lose her balance and wobbled, waving her arms and gasping. Lightning fast, he was on his feet. His arms caged around her, pinning her back against Presco's spike. He was breathing heavily, and his pulse visibly throbbed in his neck. "*Please*, sit down," he said, all throaty and raspy.

She gripped the front of his suit jacket and started laughing. "I am sorry, that was mean."

His jaw dropped. "You *pretended* to lose your balance?"

"It was just a bit of fun. I will not fall."

He let out a low growl and pulled her down with him to sit. "You scared the shit out of me."

Still smiling, she gripped Presco's spike again. "I will hold on just for you."

"Thank you," he said grumpily. "No more tricks."

She twisted to wink at him. "Promise, as long as you keep holding onto me."

Chapter 18

HEL

Hel tossed Thane's boots at his gut and stood over him. Thane shot up out of sleep, wild-eyed and ready to defend an attack. The sun was already up, and the birds were chirping. The fool should be awake already or at least sleep lighter.

Hel bent over and patted Thane's rosy cheek. "Get up, princess. And how in Maker's name do you sleep like the dead when a vast number of people *want* you dead? Late nights with a certain blonde goddess?"

With a groan, he rubbed his sleepy eyes and dropped his feet to the floor. "Can't I just simply be tired?"

"Better cut that shit out right now. If I'd been an assassin, you'd be dead." With his hands tucked behind him, Hel headed for the door. "We gave Rogue three days. It's been three days."

"*Shit*, and not a word from Rogue?"

Hel paused in the doorway with a grin. Oh, to

finally get some decent revenge. It would be sweet. It was time to take his gloves off. "Nope. Prepare to get those hands bloody."

HEL ADJUSTED the sleeves on his black suit and rolled his neck before stepping through the front doors of Rogue's apartment building in the capital of Runevale, a city not ruled by any one god or goddess but the council in Dramalin. It was a beautiful desert oasis with tropical flowers and distant rolling sand hills. It didn't take a genius to know he wouldn't be at home in his own territory after he, Valeen, and Thane so easily slipped past his defenses.

By making him and Thane invisible, they bypassed the people on the busy streets, where large-brimmed hats and head scarves were standard to combat the hot sun. The feline shifter guards at the entrance to the four-story building kept chatting about the drunk night they had before, unaware that two dangerous assassins walked right by. Up the stairs they strutted, their feet quiet as a mouse. He came upon Rogue's door and touched it with his fingertips. It hummed with magical wards. Other than the Drakonan's treasury and Valeen's magical wall around House of Night, it was rare he met a magic barrier he couldn't get through in minutes if not faster. And Rogue was no Valeen.

A whisper of magic and the wards fell. They quickly slipped through the door and inside. The apartment was open and airy with tall windows to let in the light and a view of the vast city of at least a million people from all over the realms. Hel lifted the invisibility magic off them both and listened. It was silent, not a creak or patter of footsteps.

He wasn't here.

"We'll have to wait." He plopped down on the soft blue sofa and propped his boots up on the glass table in front of him and crossed his ankles. On every wall Rogue had some sort of academic award or shelves of textbooks on the law. The decor was stiff, but he didn't expect more from the prick.

Thane walked into the kitchen with wooden butcher blocks for countertops and red brick along the walls and picked up a glass bottle with a wine label from the goddess of the harvest. A moment later he set it down and moved over to a fruit bowl. "It's fresh. And the wine is unopened. They've been here recently."

"If I didn't already know that I wouldn't have brought us here. He came here thinking we wouldn't know of this apartment."

Leaning up against the honey-wood countertop, Thane crossed his arms. "Why isn't Valeen with us?"

"She's been through a lot recently, and why would I ask her to do what you and I can?"

"You mean, she might have a problem with your methods."

Self-righteous bastard. He chuckled and took out a civar, watching the end light and smoke roll upward before he put it to his lips. He hated and loved the habit. The smoke calmed his nerves and that darkness that often wanted to fight its way to the surface, but he was irritated he relied on it so much. "If she had such a problem with me, I think she'd be in your bed, not mine." Thane's jaw muscles twitched and his eyes hardened. He opened his mouth to speak, and Hel lifted a finger. "I'd rethink whatever it is you're going to say. She's my mate, my wife, and if fate wasn't a cruel bitch, she would have never been with you at all."

"Well, fate is cruel, and she was."

He took a puff off his civar and slowly blew out the smoke. "Save the anger for Rogue. We're on the same side now, cousin. Just like old times."

"You're actually going to kill the ogre girl?" Thane said, smartly changing the subject. It wasn't an argument either of them would come out of unscathed.

Hel lifted a shoulder. "That's what I said I would do. You know, one of the reasons I brought you rather than my wife was so I didn't have to have this discussion."

"She's young, and it's not her fault."

"She's a damn ogre." Since when did everyone get so sentimental? "And we're at war. What did you expect to happen? We'd all sing songs and dance together? Shit, Thane, you're the god of war; you know full well how this works."

He turned to stare out the windows. He knew the horrors of war just as much as Hel did, more even. It must be part of the reason he wanted to be called Thane and not War, he knew *too* well.

"I'm the god of war because no one can best me in combat and I have a mind for battle strategy not because I like war. Besides, I'm not the same person I was."

"Really? I never would have guessed." He flicked the ashes off his civar onto the seat cushion beside him. The little embers burnt tiny holes in the fabric. "You're fucking soft."

He shot him a glare. "Are there even any lines you won't cross?"

"Can't think of any," Hel said, and laughed when Thane rolled his eyes.

"You know, you used to care about more than just revenge."

"That was before I had everything taken from me." He rested his arms on the back of the cushy couch and let his civar dangle between his lips. "Would I kill this half-ogre girl and not ever think about her again? Yes."

Voices and footsteps outside silenced them. Hel signaled Thane to move behind the door while he waited on the sofa with his hands behind his head. A female's laugh came through as it opened, then the *tap tap tap* of heels. She didn't even notice him sitting in her common room before she turned to the kitchen. Rogue, however, stood frozen like he faced his own death.

He did.

Thane shoved the door closed behind Rogue, causing him to jump and twist. He wore a similar dark brown suit to the last time he'd seen him, only this time Hel spotted a shiny piece of chain mail peeking out from under the collar of his shirt. He backed away from Thane and into a side table knocking over an oil lamp that shattered on the floor.

"Who are these people?" the lady asked from the kitchen, sliding behind the countertop as if it could save her. Her fear practically coated the room. At least she had survival instincts.

"What are you doing here? How did you find me?" Rogue demanded.

"Rogue," Hel said with his best, charming smile.

"The clock has run out. The timer is out of sand. Your three days are up. I hope that's clear."

"Get out of my house."

"You thought we wouldn't come. How unfortunate for you."

Rogue's throat bobbed. "I went to the archives and Pricilla followed me. She didn't know why I was there so I made something up, but she was suspicious especially after the fire at my house. She moved the record book."

Hel tsked and wagged his finger. "Don't lie to me."

"Rogue," the lady whimpered. His wife if he assumed correctly. "Tell me what is going on."

"Your husband has made some very bad, very unforgiving enemies." Hel slid his boots to the floor and stood. "Rogue, I'll give you one last chance to tell us the truth."

Rogue looked downright ghostly for one who normally had chestnut skin. "I'm telling you the truth. I could either wait for my turn to be a keeper of the knowledge or look for the records again in a few days, but I need time to not draw suspicion. If she suspects you're blackmailing me, I'll be out, and I won't be able to help you."

"If *my* life was on the line, I'd have gotten the record, Rogue."

Rogue stopped breathing and clutched at the wall behind him. "I tried."

Thane shook his head and something dark flashed across his eyes. Hel hummed, the god of war might come out to play. "You didn't try hard enough," Thane snapped.

"Please, give me another chance. Just one more day."

"For an immortal you're pathetic." Thane's hands were fisted at his sides.

"He always was," Hel added.

"I never wanted Valeen to get hurt—"

Heat flooded Hel's body as he charged him, gripped his throat, and slammed his head into the wall, cracking the stone. "What the fuck are you talking about?"

The wife in the kitchen started blubbering and Hel shot her a glare. "Shut up!" Her chin wobbled and the tears silently flowed but not a sound came from her.

"They have spies," he gasped. "They'll know she's there alone..."

Hel pulled the golden blade from inside his jacket. It hummed with an otherworldly power, a power even immortal gods could not survive. With one quick thrust he shoved it into Rogue's chest, cracking through chainmail, bone, and cartilage. Rogue wheezed out a breath, and gripped onto Hel's shoulders, while fear filled his wide brown eyes.

"Maybe Serenity will be beautiful or maybe you'll find the ugliness of the underrealm."

"Hel, please." Blood slid out of the corners of his mouth. "My wife."

He leaned in close to his ear. "Don't worry, she will follow you into the afterlife and you can be together."

"No," he groaned, then one more ragged breath was all he had left before he slumped forward. Hel jerked Soulender free and let him fall to the floor where a pool of red quickly stained the white floors.

The wife screamed and ran for the balcony. Thane

caught her around the waist before she made it outside. She kicked and fought in his grasp, screaming and clawing at his hands. There was a moment he waited for Thane to take care of the problem. Her screaming like a banshee would draw attention, bring people up here. But Thane hesitated. He always did when it came to the fairer sex. It was up to Hel to do the dirty work, as usual. He crossed the room and stood before the wife, taking in her tears and feeling nothing. He knew he should have the same hesitation Thane did. Somewhere in his black heart he thought it would be better to let her go, but then he thought of Valeen and what was done to *his* wife by these people. She was innocent. She shed tears too and found only savagery.

"I didn't do anything!" she wailed. "Please, have mercy."

Hel took hold of her head with both hands. "Mercy is not something I possess anymore." One quick jerk snapped her neck.

With a frown, Thane gently laid her body to the floor. His fingers brushed over her eyelids, closing them for eternity. She wasn't an immortal, not even a demigoddess but an elf brought to this world of gods and monsters long ago. Too bad she was caught in the crossfire of the worst monster of them all.

"We need to get back now," Thane said as Hel hurried across the room and stopped beside Rogue.

"I know." He quickly checked his pockets and inside his jacket and found a small, folded note. Hel opened it and read: *Their immortality isn't hidden; it's been given.* He set fire to it and tossed it onto the ground while the curling edges turned black.

Chapter 19

VALEEN

Fire crackled in the hearth covering the third-floor balcony of the library in orange light. The place where Presco had taken up residence. It wasn't cold out, he just liked the sound of a fire burning while he studied. Stacks of books covered the edges of the desk while Presco poured over an old scroll laid out before him. The large stained-glass arched window behind him was a mix of swirling blues and violets. He looked right at home with his beakers bubbling in the corner.

He lifted his chin as Valeen and Katana strode off the spiraling metal staircase. Gold-rimmed glasses reflected off the candlelight, hiding reptilian eyes that unsettled many. "Valeen, Katana," he said as a greeting. "How are you both?"

Valeen waited for Katana to answer first. She beamed at Presco and played with the ends of her long hair. "I am quite well. Valeen and I have been walking around the castle and talking. It really is a beautiful place and this library is spectacular. I can see why you have been spending so much time here."

He looked around as if just noticing he was in a fancy library. "It is a nice library... for elves." He winked at Valeen and she and Katana settled into the two cushioned leather seats across from his large wooden desk. "You didn't answer how you are doing, Valeen. It's been three days since you visited Rogue..."

"Yes, Hel and Thane are *visiting* again."

"You didn't wish to go?"

"Not this time." It wasn't that she was against what they were doing. She even gave Hel Soulender to kill Rogue, but she had to find a way to build the wall around The Valley of the Sun, and Hel and Thane needed time alone to bond again. With her in the mix it added tension, and she wanted them to be able to lean on each other. "Have you gotten word to your wife?"

Presco bobbed his head and closed the book in front of him, then placed the cork stopper back on the bottle of ink beside him. "I have. Hel was able to send the letter for me and enchanted it so she would be able to write on the back of the same page, and it returned itself. It's fascinating what he's capable of. He's nice to have around."

"Good. I hope she is doing well. How are things in Ryvengaard since... you know."

Katana turned toward her, curiosity lighting her face. "*I* do not know. Tell me."

She and Presco exchanged a glance. Going through the Drakonan Treasury had been a terrifying experience for both of them. The unkillable gargoyles still gave her the chills. Though Presco probably feared being trapped down there more than them. He hated small spaces. "I had to retrieve my journals from the Drakonan Treasury, and we had to sneak in. Someone died."

"Oh, my, that is terrible."

Part of Valeen's heart still hurt for Caliban Drakonan. He had been young and loyal to his family. An innocent casualty in this war.

"Yes, it was," Presco said nodding, "and you are still a suspect—or should I say, Mr. and Mrs. Black are suspects. The Drakonans don't forgive when it's one of their own."

Katana let out a nervous laugh. "When you said someone died, I thought you meant it was an accident..."

"Unfortunately, no," she answered with a grimace but didn't want to get into the details. Katana didn't believe in taking life and if she heard the details... She turned back to Presco. "I'm not afraid of the Drakonans. If they want to come for us, I'll out them to everyone that we broke into their armory and stole from them. Their reputation will be ruined. They could no longer claim their treasury has never been breached. In fact, why don't you send them a letter for me, and tell them what happened? Tell them exactly who Mr. and Mrs. Black are. Of course, leave out your part in it. I don't want your family targeted."

He smiled and leaned back in his chair, folding his arms over his belly. "It's good to have my queen again."

"Was I so different before?"

He lifted his shoulder. "Yes and no. With your memories restored you are more—how do I put this—

sure of yourself, and you not knowing who I was definitely changed how I could interact with you before."

She pulled her lower lip between her teeth and scanned the books on the shelves around them. It was strange to think only months ago she didn't know Presco at all. He was simply a friendly dragon from her supposed past who stayed with her and Hel in the manor. Now he was one of her longest friends. They made up their own language once just to pass the time. She'd all but forgotten it now. "Have you had any luck with the Varlett situation?"

"Not yet. Can you explain a bit more about this connection with you and Varlett? Can you feel anything from her? Can you hear her thoughts?"

Valeen shook her head. "The only consequence of our connection that I can tell is if she gets injured, so do I, and vice versa. She wanted to ensure we couldn't kill her and when I become immortal again, essentially so will she." She picked up a gold letter opener off Presco's desk. The head of it was a phoenix with wings spread. "When I have my immortal strength, something like this won't be able to penetrate my skin like it can now." She sighed thinking how much easier life had been. Goddesses didn't get sick, they didn't go hungry or get scrapes and bruises. There were weapons that could hurt, and someone strong enough could make her bleed, but it healed almost instantly, and nothing but Soulender or the Sword of Truth could pierce her heart or vital organs.

A quiet rustle somewhere near Presco's desk drew her attention. Like candy wrappers being unraveled.

"Where is she, anyway?" Presco asked, seemingly unaware of whatever was in his desk. His hands were visible, so it wasn't him doing it. "I don't believe it's a good idea to let her wander around unattended. If anyone ever found out about the connection, she'd be a target. We should bring her inside the castle."

Over the last few days that very thing weighed heavily on her. The previous evening, she found Varlett in the woods, lying in a hammock chewing on a bone. She said she'd rather be alone in the woods with the insects than near her and her two lovers. Valeen would rather that too, but the dragon wench was the one who bound them together. "She is a vulnerability that I cannot have. We need to end it."

"Even Hel is puzzled by it. It did not leave a mark like his own magic and if you tried to counteract her magic with his, it could be a disaster. There would be—"

"Consequences. Hel told me Varlett often uses magic derived from what he calls dark matter. He uses runes. They're not the same."

"It's likely the demon's ring she had all along. I'm surprised that Hel didn't sense it before."

"She must have cloaked it."

"It would have been a necessary step to keep it hidden for so long."

"Wait," Katana said, blinking rapidly. "She has a demon prince's ring. Will they not come for her?"

"If they found out," Valeen answered. "They don't know who has it... well, they know I stole it, but they don't know she blackmailed me into doing it. So, if they're coming for anyone, it's me."

Katana's eyes widened. "Valeen," she whispered. "The demon princes will come for you too?"

"I know. I have attracted many enemies since you've been gone."

"Which is why it's imperative that she get her immortality. Varlett, the demon princes, even the council won't matter if we get that first. They won't be able to kill her. She has the only weapon."

That wasn't true though. "You're forgetting who is in the dungeons."

"Oh, right." Presco pushed his round glasses up. "Synick. I think you should kill him. If the demon princes didn't get him to reveal its location, I doubt you or even Hel will get him to confess."

"But if we get that weapon, Presco, no one will dare stand up to us. We will have both of the immortal weapons."

"And if he gets free, you have a massive problem."

All Mother, she didn't even want to consider the possibility of him getting free. Right now, no one but them knew he was even alive again. She turned to Katana, "What do you think?"

She brushed her hair behind her rounded ears. "Well, you know I am not one for killing but in this case, I might make an exception. But I also do not want Synick to be in possession of one of the immortal weapons even in the underrealm. As we have seen there is a chance he could come back. The demons would use torture. There are non-violent ways to get people to talk."

"What are you suggesting?" Presco asked.

"I am not suggesting anything. I am only saying that sometimes you get more bees with honey. If he has been in the underrealm I would wager he has not been shown kindness for a long time."

"Be nice to him?" Valeen scrunched her nose. That prick didn't deserve kindness from any of them, least of all her or Katana.

"Oh," she put a hand to her chest and almost laughed, "Not me or you. His nephews." She gave a sly smile. "That is how he thinks of Hel and Thane. He *wants* to trust them."

"It would probably take months," Valeen mused.

"The time will pass anyway. And keep in mind, he does not want to go back to the underrealm, Valeen."

It was worth a try. Now the question was, which of his nephews would be best to get him to talk?

"Another thing I need your brilliant mind for Presco, is how do you think we can go about placing a wall around Palenor like at House of Night."

"That took us a very long time to create," he bemused. "And with the size of Palenor we would need a powerful anchor, and it would take a significant amount of magic." She could already see his mind flipping through possibilities and his expression grew less hopeful.

"I know. Even if we can't protect the entirety of Palenor, at least the Valley of the Sun. We can shelter most of the elves here and this is where the council would attack."

"I don't wish to doubt you, Valeen, but with only one moon, you being mortal, and without a structure like your moonstone castle it won't be as strong. There would likely be weak points. We need to be prepared for that."

She didn't expect a miracle, but she did have faith in her ability. "Something is better than nothing. The force they will bring will be..." *devastating otherwise.*

Katana sat slightly forward, bouncing one of her legs. "You built a magical wall around your territory? When?"

Tapping her fingers along her thigh, she debated on whether or not she should say. "After you died. I didn't trust anyone. Atlanta didn't believe me and Synick was still alive. I shut everyone out."

Her lavender eyes widened but she nodded. "I see. I am sorry you had to do that."

"The important thing is you're here now. That doesn't matter anymore."

Presco leaned his elbow on the armrest and placed his chin in his palm. "How are you dealing with all this? The council, losing House of Night, and reconciling with Hel?"

The last words ordering her death and punishment came to mind now, *"The council has decided you are henceforth stripped of your immortality, where it will be bound, and you will be mortal. Where you will live and die again and again until we decide enough is enough. May the All Mother and the Maker have mercy on you."*

Enough was never enough for Pricilla, the sly rodent-faced bitch, who made that order. Valeen stared out the window at the branches of a lilac tree swaying in a rainy breeze. Dark storm clouds hung over the city. "I'm fine, Presco."

"You don't have to be strong all the time. It's alright to feel."

Katana reached over and placed her hand on top of Valeen's. "He is right, you know. You have been through so much. We are family. You can tell us anything."

"You have been through just as much and you're

always smiling. You don't let it weigh you down," she argued.

Her sister's radiant smile faltered then as if a crack in her shell opened up. "Well," she started, her voice higher pitched than before, "I am naturally bright, as you know. But it does not mean that what happened does not bother me."

"And you let yourself feel it?"

"Sometimes," she said softly. "If you suppress how you feel, it will only build until you break."

Valeen shook her head. "If I let myself feel this, I *will* break, and I can't do that right now. You saw me at my castle ruins," she whispered, afraid if she spoke louder her voice would falter and tears would flow. Pulling in a deep breath, she said, "So I focus on what I gained, not what I lost. I wish none of it ever happened but what does wishing do?"

"Not much I am afraid." Katana gently squeezed her hand. "And maybe you are right. We focus on now, not what we cannot change." She rose up and walked toward the stained-glass window, running her fingertips along the decorative swirls. Then she turned and sat on the cushioned window seat.

Presco took his glasses off and with the bottom of his white tunic, rubbed the smudges. "I've been meaning to ask, now that you are back here, do you feel you made the correct choice?"

Valeen met his gaze. "Between Hel and Thane?" He nodded and Katana leaned forward as if eager to hear the answer to that. "There was no other choice for me. I loved Thane, and it hurt to let him go. But Hel... I could never move on from him. I would never stop loving him. I don't think I ever did stop." She looked down at her black ring. "Remembering our past made me miss him but it's who he is now that has recaptured my heart and soul. He became what he is. He created that army for *me* because he loves me, because he's my soulmate."

Holding up his glasses at a distance he seemed satisfied and pushed them back on. "As an outsider watching you two at the manor in Ryvengaard pretend you did not care about each other was... interesting. Your chemistry even then was unmistakable. You've never been like that with anyone but him, even if you loved Thane. You can love someone who isn't meant for you."

Romance novels often told the story of falling in love and getting married with a happily ever after, but they rarely told of falling in love with the person who had become your everything and how much it hurt to realize they weren't the happily ever after... "I realize that now."

"I have something to cheer you both right up." The creaking of his large side drawer as he pulled it open interrupted the silence. His brows tugged together. "But it looks like someone else got to them first." In one hand he pulled out a small, round, gold-foil-wrapped chocolate and in the other he lifted a gnome with wild brown curls and a red hat. The reason for the rustling in the desk she'd heard earlier.

Tif's ruddy cheeks grew a shade darker than usual, and she wiped at the chocolate smeared across her lips with the back of her floral print sleeve. "Hi, Val, Katana, and um," she looked up at Presco, "dragon man. There's big rats around here eating the chocolate—and... and other snacks too. Their beady little eyes are too keen. One followed me and tried to steal the bread I found in the cupboard downstairs."

Valeen crossed her arms and eyed the chocolate smear on the corner of her mouth. "Big rats you say."

"Huge." She cupped her mouth and whispered, "I'll find them to get rid of the problem."

"Are we sure a gnome with a red hat isn't eating all the snacks?" Presco mused, and set her on the desk.

Katana giggled and placed her hand over her mouth, slowly shaking her head.

Tif plopped down and crossed her legs on top of a stack of Presco's papers. "I'm sure it's not a gnome." She began wiping her chocolate-covered hands on the parchment, leaving smears, oblivious that Presco was referring to her. "Gnomes do like snacks, but we also contribute to the snack pile. I make a rather delicious cinnamon bun with icing. Rats only eat and leave trails of turds. Gnomes certainly do not do that."

"Have you ever heard of a handkerchief?" Presco pulled one out of his pocket and handed it to her. It was nearly the size of her.

"Why yes, I have. Thank you. My hands are dreadfully dirty." She glanced down at the parchment she'd ruined and flushed. "From, um, trying to stop the rats from eating the chocolate, I mean. But I did have maybe one. And I must say they are spectacular. Very creamy with hints of salt and caramel."

Presco tossed the two remaining chocolates to Valeen and Katana. Valeen peeled off the wrapper and popped it into her mouth. The candy melted on her tongue and was exactly as Tif described. It brought back memories of eating a pile of chocolates with Hel and Presco one evening to see who could eat the most.

Presco won of course. Dragons had a voracious appetite.

Tif twisted her hair around her hand and fluttered her eyes. "Do you happen to have more of them?" Gnomes had a voracious appetite too it would seem.

"I think you ate them all," Presco answered.

"Oh dear." She rubbed her belly. "Sometimes my tummy makes me eat more than I should. It's a gnome thing." Tif shot to her feet and pointed to the corner of the room. "There's one of the bastards now!"

Valeen turned to a brown rat squeaking in the corner. It skittered along the wall and into the crack. She tried not to laugh as Tif slid down Presco's leg and ran toward where the rat disappeared. "You'll not get away next time!" she shouted with a raised fist. "I'll find where you sleep." She turned back around and crossed her arms with a harumph. "Gnomes and rats do not mix. I do not like to share my snacks with rodents."

"Do we need to get a cat?" Valeen wondered.

"Oh, I'll find where they're hiding. Gnomes are good hunters like cats, when it comes to our snacks, that is," Tif said with a raised pointer finger. "Mama used to chase an orange tabby with a broom...."

The hairs on the back of Valeen's neck stood on end and Tif's voice faded to a mumble as her focus shifted. Quiet footsteps pattered close by. Someone's soft breath... no, more than one. She glanced over her shoulder at the railing of the balcony and the entrance of the stairwell; she knew both Thane and Hel's steps like her own. It wasn't them. Then came the familiar sound of a dagger sliding against its sheath as it was pulled free.

She gave Presco a hand signal, one they'd settled on many years before to sign for intruders. His spine went rigid, his pupils narrowed, while Tif kept prattling on about her mother and the gnome colony. Katana was enraptured with their little friend, seemingly unaware of the danger nearby.

Footsteps rumbled up the metal staircase, rattling hard with each step. Whoever it was didn't care for stealth any longer. Valeen shot to her feet, her magic rippled through her veins with a cool fire, and she angled herself in front of the others with her goddess blade in hand.

With soaked blonde hair, black horns curling from the crown of her head, Varlett appeared at the crest, out of breath. The black eyeliner she often wore streaked down her cheeks. Her dark clothes were soaked through. Either it was the low lighting or the smeared makeup, but she appeared almost ill. Her cheeks were more sunken in than the last time she'd seen her, and her clothes were loose, as if she'd lost weight.

"What's wrong?" Valeen demanded. There was no way she would be here otherwise.

"Ten males came through the portal, heavily armored and carrying weapons, headed this way. They must have realized I was following them and split up. I lost track of half the group and rushed here. They might already be—"

The stained-glass window behind Katana shattered. Her scream sliced into Valeen's heart as shards pelted into Katana's back. She fell to her knees and crawled to the corner of the room, with blood blossoms already staining her cream dress.

Valeen became shadow and reformed at Presco's back, blocking the sword coming down at him. She shoved hard against the winged male who stood at least a head above her and drove him back toward the broken window.

"They're coming over the railing!" Tif shrieked.

Hooks with ropes latched onto the metal railing that led to the greater library below. Valeen kicked her opponent hard in the gut and he stumbled, catching himself on the window's ledge before falling out into the pouring rain. His dark eyes were rimmed in silver, a distinctive trait they were half-god and half-mortal, and could die by any blade, though they healed fast and moved even faster.

He jumped and flipped easily over her head and landed gracefully behind her. With a whirl, he struck out. Their blades hit and Valeen let her vines free. They curled around his neck and took hold of his wrists, dragging him back into the bookcase. She drove her sword through his chest. He let out a strangled cry then she whipped around, bloodied blade at the ready. There were seven more, all wearing a soft pink sash around their arms. Pink was *Pricilla's* color. Everything in her territory was infected with various shades of it.

Presco slashed his talons at one of the other dragon shifters. He ducked and tackled him over the edge of the railing. The loud crash of them hitting the bookshelves and the wood breaking below followed. Dust and debris billowed up in a cloud.

Cornered against the bookshelves by three of the assassins, Varlett growled. Black scales covered her body, and her talons doubled in size. "It's pathetic it takes three of you to face little old me."

"Don't toy with them. Kill them," Valeen snapped.

Her heart lurched into her throat seeing Katana curled up in the corner with Tif in her arms and an assassin closing in on them. "Katana run!"

Valeen's vine shot at the assailant cornering Katana and speared him through the gut and pinned him to the wall.

With great leather-like wings, the other two came for her. One launched himself over Presco's desk while the second charged around it. One's shimmering scales a deep blue, the other a fiery-red, fully covered their skin. Dragons' scales were naturally resistant to magic, and her vines wouldn't be able to pierce them. She brought her sword at the ready position and curled her fingers, taunting them to come for her.

"KILL THOSE BASTARDS!" Tif hollered like a maniac.

"Get out of here, Katana!"

Her eyes watered as she slowly rose up and limped toward the stairs.

The two dragons backed her toward the broken window. "We hear you're mortal now, goddess of night," the one on the left said. "It's a pity really."

"Mmmhmm," his partner agreed. "You were always one we worshipped for your greatness and prowess in battle, but the Council of the Gods pays *well*."

"Well enough to die? You can't take treasure to the afterlife."

Talons slashed down at her, *sidestep, swing*. Zythara seemed to sing in her hand, vibrating with a power of its own as she cut across the dragon's forearm and blood oozed between the scales. He hissed and with the other arm swung to backhand her. She ducked and pushed up, punching her goddess blade into his gut. He roared, half-beast half-human, and his friend charged. She became shadow; his wicked talons passed through her. Like a midnight wave, she curled behind him and reformed, shoving her sword through his back. She pushed harder to drive through the bones and muscles until the tip of her golden blade protruded out of his chest. "You chose the wrong side, dragon," she said close to his ear. "There was a reason you worshipped me."

Jerking the blade out, she turned just in time to duck under the slashing attack of another. His silver-rimmed brown eyes with the signature reptilian slit, told her he was both dragon and god, and other than a full-blooded immortal, he was the deadliest race in the realms. He was seven feet at least and corded with muscle. Long black hair was tied back, and a matching beard reached his collarbones.

"Where are your lover boys to save you now?" He drew a sword. "My mother sends her regards and hopes you will not be reborn again."

Chapter 20

VALEEN

This half dragon, half god must be Pricilla's offspring, and he was likely her most powerful heir sent to get the job done.

It was going to upset her when Valeen killed him.

He held a god blade in his hand; she knew by the particular shade of the golden color. It wasn't made of gold, however, gold broke too easily. This metal, known as *luthria,* was found in the heart of the winter goddess's mountain, or a deep cave in her own House of Night, and did not bend or break and would kill just about anything. Since he'd rather use a sword over scales and talons, he would lean into his god abilities more and depend less on his beast. That was how gods and goddesses usually raised their heirs.

"I am the goddess of night. It's you that's in need of a savior."

He didn't smile or show any signs of arrogance like his companions before him who now lay dead near her feet. His face hardened, eyes narrowing on her. He grabbed Presco's desk with one hand and threw it over the balcony's edge behind him like it weighed no more than a book.

Damn, he's strong. "I might be impressed if you weren't here to kill me."

Pain suddenly ripped into her shoulder, and she clamped her jaw to keep from screaming. Reaching up, she pressed her hand against the pain, and it came away bloodied. She snapped her head toward Varlett and one of her attackers had lodged a knife into her shoulder. It must be made from one of the special metals on Runevale to be able to penetrate her scales, the same as her goddess blade.

She took a throwing star from her belt and launched it at the temple of the man and dropped him like a sack of potatoes.

Varlett gave her a quick nod, jerked the knife free and slashed her talons across the neck of one of the others. A great spray of blood arched out and hit her across the cheek. The other slammed her into the bookshelf and she bit down on his forearm. He screamed and she shoved her black-scaled talons straight through his chest.

Blood and bits of flesh covered her hand as she punched through his spine. Flashbacks of her doing that to Thane, made her stomach roil. Valeen had nearly watched him die because of that witch, and even if they were fighting on the same side, Varlett was still her enemy.

"All your friends are dead," Valeen narrowed her eyes at him. Varlett stepped over her dead opponents and stood at Valeen's side. "Now you're the one outnumbered." She was more than certain the two of them could take him down.

And he knew it. One step back, two, he started to retreat. The giant of a male before them shifted his gaze back and forth, eyeing the identical wounds. "That's interesting."

"Valeen!" Piper's voice carried up from somewhere in the library below. "Where are you?"

"Up here!"

"We're coming!" Leif hollered.

A loud crash startled her and a moment later Presco flew over the railing and onto the balcony. The stairs rattled as Piper, Leif, and Fennan charged into the study.

The assassin glanced behind him, shifting from a fighting stance to letting his sword drop to his side. His dark eyes darted from her to the broken window behind her. He threw out his palm and Valeen shielded, bracing for whatever magic he would unleash. A blast hit like an explosion, knocking everyone back. Bookshelves crashed and books clattered, papers scattered through the air, and Presco's baubles of potions spilled and shattered. Even Valeen's shield took a hard hit. Her boots scraped across the wooden floor, driving her and Varlett back several feet.

The assassin's boots hit the ground rapidly, *thud, thud thud*. She dropped her shield and swung Zythara at him, cutting into his thigh but he leapt for the window, shifting mid-air and was in dragon form as soon as he hit the outside.

"He CANNOT get away! He knows about the link!" Valeen scrambled over to Presco and jerked at his arm to help him off the ground. The others were still groaning but if they were making noise, they were alive. Leif was buried under a pile of books, with Piper lying next to him. Fennan dripped with the colorful liquids from the potions and slowly got to his knees. Next to the railing, her sister held a hand to her bleeding head, but the cut looked small. And Tif scurried out from under her arm to inspect it.

Presco shook his head, clearing whatever confusion that blast caused. "I'm getting up." Together they ran for the broken window; he jumped and shifted to his great pearl dragon. Valeen braced herself at the edge of the window's threshold, a gust of cold wind nearly knocking her back. She gripped the wood, judging the distance to get to Presco and then leapt onto his back.

"Hold on tight! The rain will make my scales slick!"

She put her sword in the scabbard on her hip and wrapped her arms around Presco's spike. "Go!"

Icy drops pelted her skin, and a chilly wind ripped through her hair like claws. The dark clouds covered the sun and made it difficult to see the navy-blue dragon ahead. Flashes of lightning lit up the sky, cracks of thunder vibrated the very air.

Another flash and suddenly the dragon was gone. A cold dread trickled through her veins. Valeen whipped her head around, searching left, right, behind. "Where did he go?!"

"Impossible!" Presco kept his speed, and his great nostrils inhaled deeply. "I smell him close, but the weather is making it harder to follow."

Her heart crashed against her ribs. She stood slowly, trying to get a better view. *How could he just vanish? Where is he?!*

Whoosh, whoosh. There was a second set of wings.

Why couldn't they see him? "He must have invisibility as a power!"

SMACK!

The impact on Presco's right side knocked him sideways, and she was falling backward. Her stomach pitched and she waved her arms wildly trying to grab hold but there was nothing.

The enemy dragon became visible once again; his massive teeth were sunk into the side of Presco's neck. His roar was as loud as the thunder that followed it.

"PRESCO!" Valeen screamed, falling away with her hand stretched toward him.

Presco's back legs clawed at the enemy's underbelly, raking across his scales and leaving great red lines. They whirled and snapped, clawing, biting as they tumbled toward the ground.

Wind rushed by as she fell, her heart felt like it was still on Presco's back. *Shit, shit.* She flailed, and managed to flip over to face the ground, plummeting faster and faster. A scream ripped from her as the tops of the trees came closer and closer. She'd hit in seconds. *Get yourself together!* She shifted to shadow and slowed until she hovered above the dark tree line. *All Mother, this is the unnamed forest.*

She looked up; Presco and the other dragon crashed through the trees, snapping them like toothpicks, then a great *boom* followed. Dropping to the ground, she drew her goddess blade and sprinted toward the sound of snarls and growls.

"Presco!" She leapt over a fallen tree, weaved around trunks, and ducked under branches, breaths coming faster. "Presco, I'm almost there!"

She broke into the clearing of downed trees to see

the enemy dragon tear into Presco's wing and drag him to the ground. Shadow ripped from her like an ink cloud, and she pointed Zythara at the dragon's chest, then threw it. It arched through the air, flipping end over end. He shifted to his human form and disappeared from sight. With a thud, her blade embedded into the tree behind him. *Damn it all!*

Then it hit her, he was invisible, not gone and it was pouring rain. It was nearly impossible to hear over the drumming of the rain and thunder but there was still a chance. Scanning the woods, she searched for drops splattering where they shouldn't and found it. A hint of an outline of a head and shoulders as he sprinted away. She ran for her sword, gripped the handle, and jerked it free.

But Presco's groan halted her. Rivers of red ran over his light scales, the great slashes and punctures opened to his pink muscle underneath. *Presco.* The mud squashed around her boots, and she slid to a stop next to his head. "Where are you hurt the most?" *All Mother,* his wing was bent in ways it shouldn't, the leather torn and shredded in places. The teeth marks looked deepest at his neck, where he took the initial hit.

His deep heaving breaths that moved his belly up and down began to slow. "Presco!" She darted to the wound on his neck and gently placed a hand on him. "Don't you dare die on me! That is a command from your queen! I need you to shift into your human form."

"Can't," he groaned.

HEL! she screamed through their bond and drove her sword point into her palm to draw her own blood. *HEL!*

She couldn't find words. She just needed him.

She dipped her fingertip into the crimson in her hand and drew the healing rune on Presco's scales near the wounds. The healing spell quickly left her lips. She kept repeating it over and over, as she pressed the blade point into her own flesh. The spell required her own pain and the more she felt the faster it would work. "Come on!" she snarled. The wound barely moved. She pressed harder until the pain was so much, she started to feel nauseous, and blackness began to encroach at the edges of her vision. She'd shove this blade straight through her hand if it healed him fast enough to save him.

It was his dragon scales. They repelled magic, even healing magic.

Footsteps fast approaching forced her to pull the blade point from her flesh and face the intruder breaking through the dark tree line. Lightning flashed, illuminating Hel's face, all shadows and fury, as he took her and Presco in. He vanished in a puff of gray smoke then reappeared at her side and ran his hand over Presco's neck wound. "Was this another dragon?"

Valeen nodded, letting her sword fall to her side. The wound on her hand was already crusting over, but Presco's wasn't. "Help him," she pleaded.

"You need to shift, Presco. I can't heal you otherwise." His voice was husky.

"He's too weak." His breathing was shallow and slow now. Hot tears burned her eyes.

"Shift now!" Hel pressed both palms flat on his neck, and a warm amber light illuminated beneath them.

Presco let out a throaty cough and Valeen ran to his

face and gently rubbed the smooth scales between his huge nostrils. "Presco, you can do this. I am here for you. I will protect you." Dragons didn't shift during an injury because they didn't feel safe to do so. It was a natural reaction. He let out a puff through his nostrils and slowly nodded.

A shimmer worked across him and then he was a man again, lying on his side. Hel dropped to his knees and touched each of his wounds, while she took one of his huge hands in both of hers. After a few moments there was no trace of the attack on his body, but he was paler than usual. "How do you feel?" she asked.

He slowly blinked at her but couldn't seem to lift his head off the mossy ground. "I'll survive." His voice was hoarse but strong. "Forgive me for failing you, my queen. I should never have let you fall."

The tears she'd held back slipped out and she threw herself across him and cried in relief. "You're alive, that's all that matters. I should have protected you."

"A dragon protects his rider, my queen." He managed to lift an arm and sling it across her back.

"Who did this?" Hel's voice was eerily low, it made goosebumps rise across her skin. He was standing now. Darkness shadowed his face, hardened anything that was soft.

"I don't know who he is but he's a half-god, half-dragon. Likely the heir of Pricilla. We killed the others but..." her heart sank when she remembered what he witnessed. "He knows about Varlett and me."

"How the fuck does he know that?" Hel growled.

She grimaced and rose up. "He saw her get injured and watched the same happen to me."

Hel turned on his heel and marched in the direction the enemy dragon had gone. Toward the stone portal. She stepped to follow him but then glanced down at Presco. She couldn't leave him like this. What if someone else came? There was no way Presco could defend himself. "Hel, wait!"

His march turned into a run until he disappeared.

Chapter 21

VALEEN

"Go, Valeen," Presco said, rolling onto his knees.

"There could be more of them nearby. I can't leave you."

"You must make sure Hel stops that man from telling anyone about you and Varlett. That's more important than me."

She grabbed under his arm and heaved to help him to his feet. Worry gnawed at her gut, twisting her insides. "No, it's not. You're not some disposable piece of trash."

The roar of a dragon above made every muscle in her body seem to light with fire. She gripped Zythara and looked up to the breaks in the trees above. Raindrops burned her eyes, but she spotted the black dragon and a rider. They dropped in, shaking the ground as they landed. Onyx scales glistened with water; it was Varlett, then Thane dropped to the ground, landing in a crouch.

He rushed to close the distance between them and immediately took hold of her hand, running his fingertips across her palm where she'd stabbed herself. The scab looked like a little pink scar now. His green eyes lifted to her face. "Are you hurt? Varlett's hand..."

"I'm alright. I was trying to heal Presco. He went down hard."

He gave Presco a once over then with an accusatory glare, he said, "What happened?"

"The other dragon had the power of invisibility and caught us off guard. It's not his fault." Valeen stepped away from Presco's side and started toward the portal. The moss and mud squashed loudly under their boots. "But he knows about Varlett and me. Take Presco home. Make sure he gets rest and something to eat."

Thane stepped along with her. "Where are you going?"

"To stop him before he can spill my secret. Hel went after him."

"I'll go."

"I know you want to keep me safe but—"

"Val..."

"Thane." Her eyes softened and she lifted her chin in the direction of the castle. "There could be more of them back there, and what if they found Synick? They need you here. Make sure Katana and the others are safe. I'll be fine. Hel is there."

He grimaced at that. It wasn't how she meant it but saying she didn't need him anymore because she had Hel clearly hurt his ego... or his heart.

NIGHT MEETS THE ELF QUEEN

When she arrived at the portal and commanded it to take her to where Hel went, she came out in a small, wooded area with massively tall trees that reminded her of Briar Hollow where she grew up. The trunks were soft pink unlike the redwoods, but they had similar bark and leaves. The sun was bright and there wasn't a gray cloud in the blue sky. Her clothes still dripped from the rainstorm she just left.

A significant amount of blood was splattered across a fern frond just to the left of the portal. Several broken and flattened vegetation led north too. Her stomach coiled; was it Hel's blood or the bastard who hurt Presco? She drew Zythara and followed the trail.

Hel, where are you?

No answer. She quickened her pace.

Hel, he can turn invisible. Be careful.

A white butterfly fluttered before her as if leading the way. Peach-colored birds sang in the trees and bushy-tailed squirrels chittered above. The peace was deceiving. *All Mother, keep him safe. You gave me back my mate, don't take him again.*

Off the trail ahead, the tips of black boots peeking out from the thick ground foliage dropped her stomach. Her heart pounded along with her feet as she raced over the dirt trail. She skidded to a halt, frantically shoving aside the ferns and other vegetation uncovering the body lying beneath. It was the half dragon... missing his head.

Relief washed through her, and she finally took a deep breath. "Hel?" she kept her voice low, searching the immediate area. There could be any number of guards or hunters looking for her in Pricilla's territory. She knew it was hers because of the pink-trunked trees and even the grass seemed to have a hint of rose color at the tips. The goddess had an obsession.

If Hel had turned back, she would have run into him. With no other choice, she followed the trail further into Pricilla's land. Had someone else been here and taken him? Why wouldn't he have returned to the portal after he killed him?

The trail ahead opened up into a wide, sunny clearing and to a white castle tinted the lightest shade of blush. A twenty-foot-high wall surrounded it. Sliding between a set of trees, she peeked out, counting the guards on the top. At least ten in each of the many turrets and several more pacing in between. With the portals open and enemies like her, Hel, and the god of war, Pricilla no doubt had upped her security.

Hel, where are you? I'm in Pricilla's territory. I can see her castle, she hissed into his mind. Could he not hear? Maybe he was back in Adalon. They couldn't hear each other in different realms.

She scanned the many blooming, pale-pink trees alongside the road that led to the castle and rows of bright fuchsia flowers growing at the base of the wall.

Then you should be able to see me, he finally answered.

Her brows pinched and she shifted to the other side of the tree trunk to search for him again. She noted the guards on the walls had stopped pacing and were looking out.

There.

The breeze picked up and his black cloak waved behind him. He stood maybe a hundred yards from the wall with something in his grasp... a black-bearded head. In the other he held a pike. *All Mother have mercy.*

He shoved the wooden end of the weapon into the grass and then spiked the head onto the metal tip. "Is this what you wanted?" He shouted. "Is this your best? Keep sending your heirs as sacrificial lambs, Pricilla! There will be a line of heads outside your walls."

A lady dressed in fuchsia emerged from the shadows of a turret and stared down at him, gripping the edge of the stone. The very same who'd sentenced them.

No one shot at him. No enemy magic sought him out. The eerie silence was interrupted only by a soft rustle of wind fluttering the leaves.

No other mortal would dare stand alone in the wide open before an army who wished him dead. Not even an immortal would do that. Her heart felt like it was lodged in her throat. Her mate was a free target for anyone.

Slowly, she crept out from the cover of trees. If he was brave enough to do that, she could at least stand by his side.

In a cloud of gray smoke, he vanished, then a large, warm hand pressed into her low back. She jumped and turned right into Hel's arms. "Hel," she breathed and melted into his chest. "You reckless fool."

"It's time to go." His deep voice penetrated to her very bones, and then they were moving briskly down the path back to the portal. He didn't push her into a run, nor did he teleport them to get there faster. It was almost as if he was taunting Pricilla to do something.

"That was stupid to stand out in the open," she snapped, angry that he put himself in danger like that. "Anyone could have taken a shot at you. No, hundreds could have. *Shit*, thousands. We don't know how many archers she has, how many dragons she could have sent. We don't know anything!"

"I'm a little disappointed they didn't. But that tells me they're afraid."

"Did you stop him before he could tell?"

He looked down at her with an arched brow. "His head is outside the wall, not inside it, love."

Something warm and wet smeared across her palm. She pulled her hand from Hel's to find it smeared with a deep crimson. "Are you bleeding? Or is it... his?" She quickly checked herself to make sure it wasn't hers somehow.

"A bit of both, no doubt." His cheeks were flushed a light pink, and sweat glistened on his brow but otherwise he appeared normal. His black cloak could easily hide an injury though. The stone portal surrounded by bright pink and white peonies and a waist-height picket fence came into view. "You first." He gestured as it hummed to life. She pressed her hand against the iridescent white and pink marble stone and silently told it where to send her.

A moment later she stood in the quiet unnamed forest and whirled on Hel. The swirling pool snapped shut behind him. "Let me look at you."

"I'm fine. I can heal myself, remember?"

"He hurt you? Where?"

"He *nicked* me," Hel drawled, and strutted past her. "The bastard was fast and invisible. I just so happen to be able to be those things too."

She quickly matched his long strides, though she had to take twice as many steps to keep up. "We need to take care of this Varlett problem."

"Oh, I'm well aware of that. I'm going to gut that

bitch as soon as I get the chance, but for now, she and I are going to have a little chat."

"She'll probably enjoy getting a rise out of you knowing you can't do anything about it. We should spend our time looking for a way to break the link, not arguing with her."

He took her hand and pulled her into him. Dark-red eyes, so dark they were almost black seemed to penetrate her thoughts. Maybe he was sliding into her mind. She was wide open to him. He pressed his forehead to hers and let out a long breath. "I shouldn't have left you," he said softly. "I'm sorry."

She laid her head against his chest and listened to the steady *drum drum drum* of his heart. "There is nothing to apologize for. I'm fine."

He slid his hand up her neck and into the back of her hair. The feel of his fingers gliding along her skin raised goosebumps. "It was too close. That scared me. Gods, you terrify me."

"*I* terrify you?" she asked, puzzled.

"Yes. You're as strong as the ancient mountains and as delicate as a flower. You could destroy an army if you wanted but it would only take one little dagger in the right spot to lose you. So yes, you terrify me, Valeen." His fingers caressed along her spine. "After today's events I won't be leaving your side for a while."

"I'll be fine. I don't need a bodyguard anymore."

"It's not that I think you're incapable, Val, but do you agree you're safer with me?"

"Well, yes, but—"

"Just 'yes'." He brought her knuckles to his lips.

She pulled her hand out of his grasp and started walking. "You know I don't like to be told what to do."

"Which is exactly why I said I wouldn't be leaving your side, not that you wouldn't be leaving mine."

She glared over at him. He stared back. *Remember when I threw you over my shoulder and put you in your room?* he said.

Don't even think about trying that again.

He slowly smiled, then laughed. "You should see the look on your face right now."

"I swear to the All Mother, Hel. I will—"

"Run? You know I like hide and seek," he winked.

"I will beat your ass."

"If that's what turns you on." He shrugged and slipped his arm around her shoulders. She elbowed him in the side. He winced and sucked in a sharp breath then coughed trying to cover it up.

"I thought you healed yourself?" she didn't nudge him hard enough to hurt.

"I'm fine. It's nothing."

Rolling her eyes, she grabbed his cloak and pulled him to a stop. His thick leather vest made it impossible to lift his shirt, so she started with the top buttons.

"I didn't know you were so eager to get me naked."

"Shhh."

"Fine, fine, your majesty."

Once the vest was open, she pulled his tucked undershirt from his pants and pushed it up. The left side of his ribcage was dark-purple from his armpit to nearly his hip bone. Her stomach sank. "Hel, what is this?"

"He hit really fucking hard."

"And? I stabbed you and you healed in seconds."

"Like I said, I'll be fine." He took a step back and tucked his shirt back in. He started on the buttons of his vest and briefly met her gaze. His eyes were too dark. "Why are you staring at me like that?"

"You need my blood again, don't you?"

Why hadn't she noticed before that the tremors in his hands were back? He finished buttoning his vest and quickly pulled a civar out of the air and put it to his lips. "No, but I could use a sponge bath." He raised his bloody palms to her. "I'm filthy. If you're willing."

"Hel, don't lie to me."

"I'm not."

"It's been weeks since you had my blood in Presco's apartment."

"A night I won't soon forget. Your moans are music to my ears." The smoke rolled from his mouth into a heavy cloud until it drifted away on the breeze.

She pulled a knife from her belt and his hand flashed out, grabbing her wrist. "We're not doing that."

"Yes, we are."

"If," he said, holding up a finger, "we do that again, it won't be here or now. We need to be somewhere safe, where I can enjoy tasting you." His gaze trailed down to her collarbone and to the cleavage peeking out from her shirt. "And like I said, I need a bath."

Chapter 22

KATANA

Glass shards and splinters from the window were still embedded in Katana's back. She'd tried to reach around and pull some out herself, but many were too small to pinch, or she couldn't reach. After sipping on some brandy wine, the sting of it all was only a low ache.

With her legs slung over the side of a table in a room with shelves and cupboards of medical supplies, she kicked her feet waiting for someone to come help her. Several tables down, Piper, Leif, and Fennan had the house healer fussing over them. The healer kept smacking Leif on the shoulder for moving too much while she cut away his top. One of Fennan's hands was wrapped in a white cloth. He also had a few scrapes along the left side of his face. He wasn't worried about himself though. He held a thick bandage to Piper's head. She complained of feeling dizzy and he forced her to lie back.

Beside Katana was a table that held a bronze tin

labeled healing balm, a silver basin of water, a dry cloth, scissors, tweezers, and a small knife. She hoped no one planned to use the latter on her.

Little feet scurried across the wood floor then Tif appeared. "Thane is coming. I told him no one was helping you and you have the worst injuries."

"That is not true, Tif. Piper has a significant cut on her head and Leif may have broken his arm when the bookshelf fell on him, and Fennan is of course worried about them. I think I got the least of it."

She'd have sat closer to the others, but this was where the healer had steered her and told her to wait. It wasn't that she thought they were ignoring her on purpose. She simply wasn't part of their close group. She was the new outsider, *and* Valeen's sister. Although they'd been cordial to her, she was still not one of them. And from what she had seen since she'd arrived, the three of them had a grudge of sorts against Valeen. Sure, they'd fight to protect her but otherwise, they didn't interact with her much. If the gossip was correct, it was because Valeen chose Hel over their beloved king. Leif was the only one of the trio that didn't ignore Valeen.

Tif put a hand on her hip and pushed her bottom lip out. "Well, you haven't seen your back. It's covered in big red blood spots. And that cut above your eyebrow may be mostly healed but it's still there. And since you heal faster than the average person, I'm a little worried that if we don't hurry, your skin will heal around the pieces, and we'll have to cut them out. If we leave them there is the risk of infection. I can start picking out the glass shards and splinters if you want. I'll be gentle."

The sooner the better. She took another gulp of her rich, purple-berry wine. "That would be helpful, thank you, Tifapine."

"We need to take off your dress, at least the top half. I'll close the curtain." She dragged the white sheet in a half-circle around them, blocking anyone's view. Katana carefully raised her arms to gather her hair. The movement exacerbated the sting from the small cuts on her sides, but she pushed all her hair forward to get it out of the way. With her hands at her sides, she gripped the table and leaned slightly forward. A moment later Tif was on the table behind her with scissors in hand. "I have to cut the fabric. If I start untying it, it will probably hurt."

"Do what you need to. Just be careful not to cut my hair."

"I'll be careful." *Snip, snip, snip.* Tif set the scissors aside and gently peeled the fabric away from Katana's sticky skin. It hurt but she gripped the table harder and slammed her eyes shut. Once the fabric was free and fell to her waist, Tif let out a low whistle. "Ouch, this has to hurt. Thanks for protecting me by the way. You shielded me from all this. Some of these pieces might have killed me. I am small, you know. A big one came out when I pulled the dress off, but it could have pierced straight through my wee little heart."

Katana giggled, then hissed at the pain the movement caused. Her ribs seemed to be bruised on the left as well. Now that she thought about it, a large book had crashed into her side.

"Don't laugh if it's going to hurt," Tif chided. Cold metal from the tweezers touched her back then Tif pulled the first one. Katana flinched. "Hold completely still."

She was a fiery girl for being so small. "I will try."

"There is no try, only do. That's what mama always said... or was that papa? No, that was definitely papa. He said that when I said I would try to cut wood for the stove."

The others were already laughing and joking about the attack. Piper was going into detail about seeing Presco take out half the bookshelves in the library when he fell. "I wish we could have gotten there sooner," Leif joked. "Valeen, Presco, and Varlett got to have all the fun."

It was a strange way of thinking especially since they didn't know if Presco or Valeen were alright. Did they even care? Her stomach was still in knots from watching her sister fall from dragonback. Oh, she knew Valeen could use her shadow form to halt herself, but it didn't make her worry less. She'd disappeared into the forest, and they hadn't seen her since.

Quick footsteps approached and the curtain was suddenly whipped aside. With a gasp, she threw an arm across her naked breasts, although her hair covered her almost completely. "Thane," she squeaked. "*All Mother above*, I thought you were going to be Fennan or something."

He looked absolutely furious. "Katana, I'm so sorry. My healers won't be working here any longer—" He took her in then quickly jerked the curtain back into place. "Sorry, I should have asked for permission to enter and gave you time to... cover yourself." He stepped behind her where Tif stood, and for some reason, him being so close but out of sight sent a shiver through her and goosebumps trailed along her skin.

"The healer is busy. There is no reason to punish her. I am fine."

"Then she should have called for the other on duty. Your back is covered in blood. You don't look fine."

The chatter from Leif, Fennan, Piper, and the healer suddenly went silent.

"Thank you for coming," Katana said softly. She dropped her arm and settled into a comfortable position.

"Fortunately, it looks like your body is pushing out some of the larger pieces, which is good, but some smaller ones we'll have to manually pull." He still sounded grouchy. "I can take it from here, Tif."

"Ugh, fine." She hopped down. "Oh, I know, I'll get some snacks for you. Food always helps me feel better. Cookies, cupcakes, pastries? Or maybe something salty? Which do you prefer? Never mind, I'll get it all." She was already under the curtain and out of sight.

She turned her head slightly; he picked up the tweezers. "Did you find Valeen? Is she alright? What about Presco? We saw him go down and she fell..."

"She's fine and so is Presco. Hel healed his injuries, but he's fatigued." His tone began to have less of an edge to it now, and he carefully rested one hand on her bare shoulder. "Is it alright if I hold here?"

"Yes."

"I'm going to start pulling them out now."

"I am ready."

He plucked a splinter from her back, but it didn't seem to sting as much when he did it.

"Where is my sister?"

"On her way, I'm sure." His breath brushed against her skin, distracting her from the next pull. "They had to stop the last attacker."

She nodded, but worry made her suddenly nauseous. "Is Hel with her?"

"He is."

"Oh, good. That makes me feel better. I do not want her alone out there. She worries me. I know she is a formidable warrior, but we are mortal now." She licked her bottom lip. It was still strange for her to say that. She had never feared death before, or even worried about Valeen one day being taken. It made each day more precious.

"I'm sorry this happened." His voice was softer now. Gentle and repentant. "I told you you'd be safe here and then I let this happen."

"You cannot control everything, Thane."

"I know but you're in my house. Security is my responsibility."

"All anyone can do is their best. The rest is up to fate."

"Well, sometimes you have to make your own. Do you still have that dagger I gave you?"

She nodded. It was strapped to her thigh.

"Would you be willing to train more with me? If you have to run rather than fight... we need to get your endurance up." He pulled another few pieces quickly. "I'm almost finished."

This new mortal body of hers did need it. Sometimes her thighs burned, and she felt out of breath just climbing the many stairs in this castle. She peeked over her shoulder at him and curled one corner of her mouth, "What sort of *endurance* training did you have in mind?"

He paused, lifting his emerald eyes to her face. He then let out a deep chuckle and went back to plucking. "Running, Katana."

"That sounds rigorous and sweaty."

"It usually is."

"Will you be shirtless at least? It might take my mind off the actual running part."

He laughed again. "I could be... so could you."

"I am certain if I was running around topless, even with a bralette, the gossip would put you into an early grave. You threw your tunic over me the last time."

"I don't mind if it's just you and I."

She smiled at him. "So you *can* flirt. You are so serious all the time, I began to wonder."

He set the tweezers on the metal tray, picked up the cloth and dipped it into the water basin. Water splashed as he wrung it out. Then he gently started dabbing her scraped and bruised ribs. "I wasn't always."

He was heartbroken. She could see it in his aura at times, a gray-blue swirling around his chest, usually when her sister was around. "So tomorrow morning we go for a run, tops optional."

He worked the cloth slowly across her skin with the care a lover might use. "At least wear one until we get off the castle grounds."

"What if I just wore a cloak and nothing else?"

His cheeks lightly flushed, and he smiled. "You, Katana, are trouble."

"At least you are smiling again. And do not worry, I will be fully clothed."

"A shame really."

Now she was the one with a little flush to her cheeks. A few words like that made her stomach flutter like she was a young maiden once again.

He cleared his throat. "Does this still hurt?"

"It stopped hurting when I started drinking the wine. It is not that bad."

"Really? There are so many cuts and bruises."

"I have had worse," she said, then bit down on her bottom lip. She hadn't meant to say that.

He stopped wiping the blood from her skin, and she *felt* his stare on the back of her head. "From Atlanta?" His voice was so low it was almost a whisper but sounded more like a threat.

Her mouth was suddenly dry and all she could do was nod.

He continued wiping in silence. He went quiet for so long it made her nervous. What was he thinking? That she should have fought back? That she shouldn't have let it happen? "Are you... angry with me?" she asked.

He tossed the cloth into the bowl, the pink-tinted water sloshing over the side, and stepped in front of her. She couldn't bring herself to look at him, fearing the judgment she'd find there. He dropped into a squat, almost kneeling before her, so she had no choice but to see him. Fury made his aura a more fiery color, reds and oranges rather than his usual green and gold. She grimaced, waiting for his response.

"I'm never going to be angry with you for what he did to you, Katana. I'm angry that he did that to you." He dropped to one knee and undid the clasp on her heeled shoe. It was only then she realized she had a long red scrape going up the outside of her ankle to her mid calf.

Unbidden tears welled in her eyes as he removed her shoe. She hadn't been shown kindness like this in a long time. Atlanta gave her injuries; Thane mended them. He grabbed the damp cloth once again and wiped her wound. Then he took up the tin and rubbed the yellow salve across her broken skin.

"I'm seriously debating on finding that asshole."

"Oh, you must not do that," Katana breathed. As a primordial immortal, Atlanta could kill Thane.

"Why not?"

"I want to forget about him. I want nothing to do with him. It is in the past. He is the past."

He sighed and took off her other shoe. "If he ever comes here..."

A lump formed in her throat. That fear was always at the back of her mind.

Thane stood and lifted his black and green tunic over his head and handed it to her. "You can wear this until we get you back to your room. Tif cut your dress into pieces. It's not going back on."

She held the soft fabric against her chest. It was warm and smelled like him. "Thank you."

Chapter 23

VALEEN

The sunlight had dipped behind the mountains bathing the land in starlight. Even though the attack happened a couple hours before, her mind was still whirling with what could have happened. Namely almost losing Presco. The others had gotten hurt but nowhere as bad as him. Thankfully she was able to talk Hel into healing Leif's broken arm so he could fight if and when he needed to.

The candelabra on the bathroom counter gave off a warm cozy light. Hel's head rested on the edge of the copper bathtub with steam curling around him. With a sponge in hand, Valeen sat on a stool behind him, and dipped it into the hot water. Little green herbs and oils floated along the surface giving off the smell of citrus and thyme. She squeezed out the sponge on his chest and slowly moved it across his skin. He let out a pleased moan.

With her fingers, she brushed his black hair back away from his face but couldn't stop staring at the bruising on his ribs. His tattoos and runes did a decent job of hiding it and even though it was much smaller and yellow-hued signaling healing, it proved to her that he wasn't as invincible as he put on. The fact he hadn't used his magic and was letting his body heal on its own, meant that without her blood to revive his strength, he was weaker than he would admit.

He was scared of losing her, but he was vulnerable too. As much as they hated being mortal, there was something strangely beautiful in it. This moment, running a sponge across her mate's skin, just being here with him, meant more than if she knew there was a guarantee she could do this tomorrow and for eternity. And having lost him before, she wouldn't take these small, quiet moments for granted.

"Feel better?" she asked quietly.

"Mmhmm," he murmured with his eyes closed. "So, when are you going to marry me again?" His voice was huskier than usual.

She smiled and pulled the sponge across the matching lily mark on his chest and up his neck. It was here in her bedroom he'd asked her to marry him again. "I thought we could do that at House of Night, when it's rebuilt."

He frowned. "That's... a long way off."

The disappointment in his tone sent a tingle down her spine. This meant more to him than she originally thought.

He looked up at her through thick, dark lashes. "You left me and died several times and were with my cousin. It's been so long since we were married... it almost feels like it never happened." He caught her wrist and brought it to his lips, pressing kisses up to the bend in her elbow. "Don't forget, I want all of you, Miss Lightbringer."

Her breath hitched at the tenderness in his voice, the soft kisses adding to it. "I'll marry you wherever and whenever you want. I'd do it right now."

He smiled, bringing out the dimple on his cheek and closed his eyes once again. "It needs to be proper, and in front of your friends and aunt."

Oh, Aunt Evalyn...Valeen's heart ticked up speed. She had yet to tell Aunt Evalyn about Hel, let alone introduce them. Even as a primordial goddess, the thought terrified her. Evalyn was the only mother figure she'd ever known.

"That makes you nervous?"

How does he always know these things? "Uh, no," she said, aloud.

The corner of his mouth curled up. "Why?" he asked. She dunked the sponge again and slid it down his chest and across his abdomen. He caught her wrist before she could venture further. "You're trying to distract me."

"Fine." She dropped the sponge in the water and curled her arms around his neck and rested her cheek on the crown of his head. His hair faintly smelled of lemon. "The thought of introducing you to Aunt Evalyn makes me nervous because you're the Black Mage."

"And not the noble High King," Hel murmured.

"I'm sure she knows that's over. It's just convincing her that you're not a terrifying, frightening villain... will be difficult."

"But I am a frightening villain."

She giggled and leaned down to kiss his damp

cheek. "Not to me. Let's plan to have you meet Aunt Evalyn in the next few days." It had to be done some time, the sooner the better.

Her hair fell forward, and the ends dipped into the tub. Hel caught a lock of it between his fingers. "Why aren't you in here with me yet?"

"Because I'm still dressed."

"I know, it's rather disappointing."

She pulled away from him and went into the other room. "Where are you going?" he called after her.

Her weapons belt hung on the wall. She only needed the small knife. Pulling it from the sheath she set it on the bed then stripped her clothes. When she entered the bathing chambers again, Hel sat up straighter and his gaze trailed down her body, lingering a little longer on her breasts then on the knife in her hand.

"I'm slightly confused but strangely intrigued," he said with a smirk. "New foreplay idea? Or perhaps my mate wishes to try to kill me again. You do have a temper."

Biting her lower lip, she stepped behind him and pressed the dagger's blade to his throat. Then she grabbed his hair and pulled his head back. He was completely vulnerable and in her hands. "Does it turn you on?"

"Fuck," he hissed and gripped the sides of the tub. "I'm a little frightened of you sometimes, and I love it."

She pulled the blade away. His eyes sparkled with curiosity as she climbed into the tub with him. The hot water rose around her hips, and she leaned forward, kissing him, sliding her tongue against his. He gripped her hips and jerked her onto his lap. The kisses continued hot and wet until she pulled back and she slid the tip of the blade carefully across the top swell of her breast and cut open about an inch. Blood started to seep, and his dark eyes fell to the crimson staining her flesh. If she had to make taking her blood more appealing, so be it.

He let out a low growl, pressing his thumb to her mouth and tugging on her lower lip. "Gods, you truly are my undoing." Slowly, he lowered his mouth to drag his tongue over the blood. He closed his eyes, letting out a low hum of delight. Then he began sucking on it and Valeen arched her back, quietly gasping. Sensual magic seemed to be in his tongue as it swept over her skin. She wrapped her arms around the back of his neck and let him pull her onto his lap. He suddenly stood up, and she hooked her legs around his hips. Dripping wet, he carried her into the bedroom and to the oversized armchair. "I've been thinking about having you on this chair for days."

She pulled his lips to hers. "Days? Why wait?"

"I have a list. This was only one of them." Cupping her behind with one hand, he used the other to push a lock of wet hair off her forehead.

"Where else?"

"Remember that flat by the waterfall where you tried to push me to my death? And in your chariot while Starborn and Night fly us through the night sky."

"I remember. And I don't have... Starborn or Night or my chariot anymore." For a moment she let herself wonder what happened to her winged horses. Were they lost to the stars? Were they roaming the green hills in her old territory?

"You will. We'll find them." His lips roamed

hungrily over her throat until he set her on her knees in the chair. "Now be a good girl and turn around for me." Heat pooled between her thighs, and she whimpered as she turned and gripped the back of the headrest. "That's it. For once you do what you're told." He nipped her neck, and she closed her eyes. Arguing was the last thing she had in mind at the moment. His calloused fingers pushed her hair aside, and her breath caught as he kissed down her spine. Never had she wanted anything more than him, than this. He took her breasts in his hands and pulled her back flush against his front. "Do you want me, love?"

"Yes," she breathed.

He pushed her knees further apart. "I didn't hear you."

"Yes, I want you Hel," she panted.

"Good because I will always want more of you," he whispered.

Lying on the balcony of Thane's old bedroom next to her own gave the perfect view for the winking stars above Valeen. The soft silk nightgown she wore fit snugly against her and was perfect for the warm night. There were many nights she spent just like this at her old home, watching the stars on a blanket of sheepskin. The moon was half-full and partially covered by dark clouds. Crickets chirped in the bushes below, and the murmur of soft voices drifted up from the guards on patrol. Thane had doubled them the day after the attack.

Most of the past few days Katana and Valeen

helped Presco get his study back into order and tried to save as many of the books as possible. His desk was in shambles and pages scattered all over. After the initial cleanup it took them days to sort out which pages went to which books. But they used the time to talk about what she could use as an anchor for the magical shield to protect Palenor. What happened to House of Night couldn't happen here, and none of them wanted more random attacks. The last one almost killed Presco and hurt Katana and her friends. Thank the All Mother no one died.

And of course, they needed a way to break the spell between her and Varlett. Hel told Varlett if she didn't find a room in the castle where he could keep an eye on her, he'd put her in the dungeons. She must have believed him because she was here, a few doors down.

They all agreed the anchor had to be something connected to Valeen. Something strong and powerful. As a test they went out during the night and tried using her celestial crown Hel had pulled from the aether when she first woke him up. While her magic connected to the moon, the crown snapped in half before her shield could take any form, and Hel had to repair it.

Katana suggested using Soulender given that it was the most powerful weapon in the realms, but it wasn't exclusively Valeen's, and she didn't want to risk changing it from its original form. It was too precious of an item.

In Runevale it had taken a full castle and three moons to cover her entire territory. Here, at least, she only planned on shielding the Valley of the Sun. She, or any object she could use, simply wasn't powerful enough to protect all of Palenor.

She'd be lucky to even shield Castle Dredwich right now. Hel could place protective enchantments with runes as he'd done to her bedroom, but he had his own tasks to do, like finding their immortality. That also wouldn't shield the people outside these walls.

A quick wind brushed across her. Magic drifted in the air tingling the hairs on her arms and with it came the smell of the... sea. With her heart jumping into her throat, she shot up from the sheepskin, sensing the presence of someone powerful.

In half-shadow form, Valeen was on her feet and whirled to the doors. "Atlanta."

He was taller than she remembered but his presence was unmistakable. He stepped out from the umbra of the doorway into the moonlight. His aquamarine robe cut off at the shoulders and reached the back of his knees, trimmed in gold and white. Atop his head rested a golden crown with accents of pearls and seashells. Even the sandals on his feet were decorated with shells. His dirty-blond hair brushing against his shoulders was clumpy with the texture of dried salt water.

"Valeen," he whispered, not as surprised as he should be.

"What are you doing here?" She didn't return to her solid form. For all she knew sometime in the last two thousand years he could have taken the council's side. He'd remained neutral during the time of her trial and execution and that didn't sit right with her even now. And if Katana wanted nothing to do with him, that was reason enough not to trust him. She'd asked her why but without giving an explanation Katana said she would never go back to her old home—or to him. It had something to do with his many mistresses and wives no doubt. Katana had allowed it before despite Valeen telling her she deserved to be a sun, the center of someone's world, not a seashell among many. She was proud of her for not going back.

His brows furrowed. "I sensed... *her* a couple weeks ago and I've been having dreams about her ever since. At first, I thought it was nothing but that feeling led me here—to you. Were you in Runevale?"

"Are you alone?"

"It's only me. I haven't come to hurt you. You can relax."

"Forgive me if I don't."

"I don't agree with what the council is doing."

"And yet you do nothing about it."

He tilted his head. "What should I have done? You made mistakes. You were out of line."

"I lost *everything*, Atlanta. I saw the ruin that was left of House of Night, while you and the rest of the primordials stood by and allowed it to happen."

"You killed Synick and took Soulender for yourself. Many see you as a dangerous liability."

"Is that how *you* see me?"

"I'm a protector of the realms, Valeen, as were you at one time. You have gone off course. I don't know if it's because you crave more power or—"

"I did it because Synick *murdered* Katana. *All Mother*, we went over this countless times." She clenched her jaw tighter. "But what I do now is more than that."

Atlanta scoffed and ran his palm down his chest,

rattling his shell necklace. "You still believe it was him? He wouldn't have done that to her. He was a dear friend to us. You couldn't even prove it with evidence."

"I *know* he did. I'm not having this argument with you again. And I'm not 'off course'. I'm settling a wrong. Once I get my immortality and my home back, there will be peace."

"And the weapon?"

"Will remain with me until I believe there is a better solution."

"You aren't supposed to be the single judge. There is a council for a reason."

"A change of leadership is coming. A revolution one might say." Valeen tucked her hands behind her back and raised her chin slightly. "I'd call it a civil war, but I haven't been welcomed there in thousands of years."

Atlanta shook his head. "You won't succeed. You'll be doomed to die and be reborn again until you see reason."

"Not this time. Go back to Runevale and sit on your throne surrounded by your concubines while you ignore the injustices happening right before you."

His face hardened. "I am not commanded by anyone, least of all a disgraced goddess who is *mortal*. You're an elf now. Nothing more."

A deep voice cut through the dark. "I have this thing about people talking down to my wife." Hel prowled through the room behind Atlanta, his red eyes lit with disdain. "The next words out of your fucking mouth better be apologies."

Atlanta turned. "Hel." He stepped back against the balcony doorframe, putting both Valeen and Hel in his view.

Did he hurt you? Hel's question came into her mind.
No.

"That didn't sound like an apology. No, in fact, I'm sure it wasn't. Now I require begging for forgiveness."

Atlanta's eyes flicked back and forth; he was cornered, and gods were dangerous when cornered. *Be careful, Hel.*

"I am a primordial! You're nothing more than a dog who needs to be whipped and put on a leash—" Atlanta gasped reaching for his throat.

"A dog, am I?" Hel gave him a wicked smile and tsked. "Oh, I think someone has forgotten I'm a serpent, not a hound. You didn't even see my bite coming."

Atlanta's face went a deep shade of red. "How—dare—you."

Shit. Valeen called Soulender to her palm and readied herself to use it. No matter what Hel did, she was at his side. The golden blade glinted in the moonlight, catching Atlanta's eye. "I'd be careful of your next move, Atlanta," Valeen said. His jaw muscles twitched with his gaze locked onto the golden weapon in her hand.

"You're lucky she's the one holding that sword," Hel snarled. "If it were me, you'd already be dead. Set foot here again and you will be."

Atlanta suddenly gasped in air and his face began to return to its natural color.

"You and your husband are on your own in this conflict. You won't win." A swirl of water circled around him, and he vanished, leaving behind a puddle.

"How did he find you?" Hel demanded.

Valeen hurried inside and closed the balcony doors

behind her. "He said he thought he *felt* Katana and followed that feeling here, but he found me first."

"He doesn't know Katana is alive?"

"I don't know what he thinks." She glanced out the window. "Katana is leaving with Thane up north soon." Valeen nibbled her lower lip, worry churning her gut. "He could follow her there."

Chapter 24

KATANA

Katana made her way to the hot springs to soothe her achy, tired knees and ankles. She'd gone running to condition her mortal body with Thane and Leif the last couple days. They went easy on her, but she felt like a baby deer on new legs. For someone who healed fast, it wasn't nearly fast enough.

The steam rose off the water under the light of the half-moon. The dark clouds left openings to the sparkling sky. She stripped her dress and dipped her toes in, testing the water, and finding it perfectly hot. She moved down the stone steps leading in. The water reached her hips when she spotted male clothing hanging from a branch. Her eyes drifted to the grass below where a pair of boots, two shiny swords and a weapons belt waited. Those swords were familiar...

Someone cleared their throat, and she whipped her head to the shadows on the far side. Long dark hair draped over fair skin, green eyes, bright even at night. Katana gasped and quickly sank into the water to cover her nakedness. Last time she'd been in this pool she at least had on her bralette and underwear. Now she was completely nude.

"Um, hello. I did not see you, Thane. I thought I was alone."

He pressed his lips together to keep from smiling. "I figured. Although, you looked right in this direction when you arrived."

"I guess I need to be more observant."

"You do," he agreed. "I could have been someone who'd want to hurt you."

"But you are not."

He chuckled. "No. Are you sore?"

"We ran five miles just today. Half of it was uphill. I have a new appreciation for mortals." Before she could run and dance endlessly and not tire.

"I used to run ten miles every day when I was younger. Still do from time to time."

"Do you want a prize?" she teased, settling in on the opposite side of the pool, making sure there was plenty of space between them.

"I have a crown. That's better."

Katana smiled and they fell into silence. An owl quietly cooed in the canopy of trees above. Crickets chirped in the grass around them. The heat of the water warmed her face, and was it that or him that made the air feel charged? "You have not said anything about me being naked," she mused.

He tried not to smile. "Should I have?"

"Many males would at least try to peer through the

water or make lewd comments about me so casually disrobing in front of them."

"Ah, well, the water looks black from here so it's not as if I could see anything if I wanted to." He lifted a shoulder. "I doubt you'd appreciate lewd comments or me leering. I do have morals and manners, goddess."

"But you did watch me walk down the steps."

He smiled now. "I did. I'm afraid I have weaknesses. Admiring beauty like yours when it's on display is one of them."

She suddenly had the burning desire to know if he had any undergarments on. Not that it would matter, she wouldn't be moving from her spot, and he looked content to stay where he was at.

A strange tingling sensation ran through her, recognizing a familiar presence. She swore she even smelled the sea in the air. Her stomach plummeted and her heart raced. If he saw her naked in a pool with another male...

"I should probably head back inside," Katana whispered. "I did not realize the hour."

"You can stay. I'll go." His hand splashed through the water as he gestured toward the steps.

"No," she said, panic rising. Atlanta could be near watching them even now. He would kill Thane. It was better that she get out and face him... Or, All Mother above, maybe she was paranoid and allowed the demons of her past to get to her head again. How would he find her here? How could he even know she was alive?

He slowly waded through the water, drawing closer to her. "What's wrong?"

The shadows around them seemed to take form. The creak of the trees above made her jump. The crickets and rattling in the bushes sounded louder. She pressed her hands to the sides of her head and slammed her eyes shut. The moving shadows were only in her mind. There was nothing out there to get her. Synick was locked up. Atlanta was in another realm—and yet she felt him close.

"Hey." Thane's voice was gentle. A soft hand touched her shoulder, and she flinched curling her arms in on herself. "Katana, I won't hurt you. Open your eyes."

His face was close, and the soft expression eased the tension coiled in her body. Gently, he wrapped his hands around her wrists and slowly lowered them down into the water. "It's alright. You're here in Palenor, and no one is going to hurt you."

She slipped her hands into his and squeezed like he was her anchor to this world. "Alright," she whispered. She leaned forward and pressed her cheek against his wet, bare chest. She had a difficult time trusting people, males especially, but there was something about him that was different. She hoped her instinct didn't betray her. "I think he is here."

"Who?"

"Atlanta."

Thane tensed and placed a hand on her upper back and looked over the landscape. "He's never going to raise a hand to you again."

"He is a primordial. He could hurt you if you try to stop him." Her heart still raced. It felt like beating drums in her chest.

"I'm not afraid. You don't need to worry about me."

"What if he tries to take me?"

"He can try, but he won't. He not only has me standing in the way but your sister too, and when she's angry, she's—frightening." He chuckled and the sound and vibration of it seemed to magically slow her rapid heart. Even her breathing came easier.

"She really is." And that made her smile. She only wished she was as brave as her. Assassins attacked the castle, and all Katana did was cower in the corner while her sister killed them all and saved everyone.

As suddenly as the presence of her old husband appeared like a hand clenching her heart, it vanished. The weight of his briny sea magic lifted. She listened to the leaves flutter in the wind and peered out into the darkness. Maybe he was never even here, and it was her paranoia. There was only she and Thane, and she became acutely aware of her nakedness and his, and how close they stood together.

She lifted her chin. "Thank you for not judging me."

"We all have our demons, Katana. Some of us are just better at hiding them."

Slowly pushing backward, she said, "I think clothes would be a good idea. Unless you want to go to your side of the pool, where I can continue to admire you from afar." Atlanta would not ruin her new chance at life, even the fear of him.

"Admiring, were you?" he teased.

"Certainly. You are a work of art. I think your soul is beautiful too."

"You don't know some of the things I've done or

the violence that I am capable of. My soul isn't beautiful."

Her brows tugged. "Oh, but it is." She had only known him a short while, but he was good. She could see it in his aura even if he could not. Thane's aura was bright and warm, a very light shade of green intermixing with amber and gold. The green would mean he was connected to nature and had high empathy for those around him. The bright gold was usually a sign of responsibility, compassion, and harmony. It made her smile, harmony for someone who'd been named War. There were some faint swirls of red which showed that side, and of course the deep gray around his heart when Valeen was near. But that wasn't there tonight.

The reason why she was so surprised by Fennan and Piper's dislike of Hel was because she had seen his aura, and it was not dark or black. Hel had flecks of gold about him, but was mostly a cool blue with shades of gray. Blue was a sign of loyalty, passion, thoughtfulness, and an even temper. Someone with his color would not lash out without thinking. He was also a planner. The gray in him was different from Thane's. It wasn't sadness, it represented some less-than-moral things, but it wasn't his dominant color.

Her sister was the most complex she'd ever come across. She had a warm brightness overall with a mixture of purples that melted into maroon and red. The purple would be courageous, sensitive, confident, and creative; the red shades were for a fiery temper and strong will and often stubbornness.

"How could you know that?" Thane said, interrupting her from her thoughts.

"It is a gift. You are beautiful inside, but I see you can have the potential for a brutal side in battle."

He chuckled. "I am the god of war."

"Yes, but you are much more than that. And I can see how deeply you care because you loved my sister, but you are not angry with her for choosing someone else. Hurt maybe but not angry."

He dipped his hands into the water and splashed his face. "You see too much."

"You would prefer I did not?"

"I don't know." His throat bobbed as he watched her carefully. "And I mean this in the most respectful way, but could you please get lower under the water?"

She didn't realize she had stood taller, and half her breasts were out in the open. Rather than do as he asked, she smiled and arched a brow. "Do you ask that because my immodesty bothers you or because you like what you see?"

He groaned and scrubbed his hand down his face. "Katana, you know why. I may be composed but I'm not a saint. I'm very much a male who is very much attracted to you, and it's been *a while* since..."

"Since what?"

"I'm getting out." His voice was husky. "It's much too hot in here."

He slowly waded through the water, drawing closer to her. Was he going to turn toward the steps and get out or... Her heart beat faster when he kept his eyes on her, not taking the turn she expected. Warmth pooled between her thighs and her stomach tightened. She swallowed hard, and watched the tenseness on his face soften to something more sensual.

It would be so easy to explore the god of war's

body. But she wasn't ready to give her heart to anyone yet and neither was he. Unless this could be something casual without heartstrings attached.

She'd been with a few others before she married Atlanta, but those relationships happened from courtship and commitment. She'd never had sex with someone she wasn't in an exclusive relationship with, but the flutter in her belly made her want to try. It would be so freeing, a defiance to the caged bird she'd been.

No, it was the night air, the hot water on bare skin that was making them both heady. Add their mutual loneliness and it was a recipe for trouble. Time and sunlight would prove if it was something she wanted. Would Valeen even be fine with this? Her sister didn't want Thane in a romantic way anymore, but she'd still loved him once. Was it a betrayal?

"I'll get out," he whispered as if he had to talk himself into it.

Breathless, she nodded. "Yes, you said that."

Reading his expression was impossible. It was as if he was waiting for her permission to touch her, and yet begging her not to give it.

"I'll see you in the morning," she said, knowing that's what he truly wanted her to say. Even if he was tempting and her body craved intimacy she hadn't had in too long.

Without another word he made his way up the steps, water cascaded down his muscular back, over his firm, round, bare buttocks. He turned slightly, making his desire for her quite evident. To say he was well-endowed was almost an understatement.

With a towel that had hung on the tree branch, he

dried off and dressed while she stayed in the steamy water, waiting for him to leave. But he didn't go anywhere. He leaned against the tree and said, "I'm going to walk you back and make sure you get inside safely. Because even if I want to do ungentlemanly things to you right now, I am still a gentleman."

Chapter 25

VALEEN

The sun crested over the horizon while Valeen rolled the metal throwing star between her fingers, and Piper drew back an arrow. Valeen thought if they did something they used to do together, Piper might warm up to her again. Ever since she'd returned with her memories her friend avoided her. They hadn't even had a conversation other than a few words shared here or there when necessary.

The arrow cut through the air with a whistle and embedded into the center of the red target. "Nice shot," Valeen said.

"Thanks." Piper pulled another arrow and knocked it back. Her irritation was obvious simply by the way she jerked on the bow.

"Are you nervous to go to Ryvengaard again and see Prince Ronan?"

"Not really." The arrow hit its mark again. "Did you ask me out here for small talk or was there an actual reason?"

Valeen pressed her lips together and threw her star into the target dummy. It was painted white to look like a pale one and even had a tuft of white horsehair sticking out the top of the head. "I can't ask my friend to do something with me? We used to do this all the time and didn't need a *reason*."

"That was before." She dropped the bow to her side.

"Before what? I want to make sure we're good before you leave. I don't know when I'll see you again."

"It would have been nice if you had given *me* that courtesy before you left with Hel months ago."

"Thane told me to go, Piper. I was—heartbroken."

"Well, that got cured rather quickly."

"Don't do that. It's not fair."

"What isn't fair? That after everything Hel did to us and to Palenor, you chose him over Thane! I can't even fathom it. You broke Thane in a way no one ever could have. Sure, he puts on a good face, but you didn't see him after you left, and you haven't been there for him like I have after you *crushed* him."

"I never wanted to do that, Piper." She could see Thane's hurt. The way they interacted changed immensely but she didn't know how to make him feel better. It wasn't as if she could console him when she was the reason he was hurting. And she didn't dare risk getting too close or she'd hurt Hel. "It wasn't a decision you could ever understand. You don't know Hel like I do."

"I know enough about him to know he is a terrible person." Piper pinned her with a glare. "And I know Thane. I know how much he adored you and how much he sacrificed for you even when you were awful to him. And nothing that happened in the past could excuse Hel creating the pale one curse and not to mention the way he treated you. I was there during your training, and he was even worse to Thane."

She had points. Valeen would give her that. But Hel thought he'd been betrayed by the people he loved most. Thane had sacrificed more than she deserved, and a part of her was broken for walking away from him. He was good and frankly deserved better than her. Even as Layala they'd been at odds in one way or another. First about being forced into a mate bond and arranged marriage, then discrepancies over what to do about his father. One thing she knew for sure was that Hel wouldn't have had an inner conflict over what to do with Tenebris after the things he'd done to Layala: killing her parents, trapping her in a tower to starve. He wouldn't have even hesitated to take him down, father or not.

And someone better than her wouldn't have asked Thane to kill his own father...

"He didn't create the pale one curse on purpose. Yes, he made loyalty to him a clause in his spells, but the curse was an unforeseen consequence of magic."

"And that makes it better? You fought them. You almost turned into one! The white streak still in your hair is proof of that, and it's all his fault."

Valeen tried to understand where she was coming from by putting herself in Piper's place. Hating Hel was reasonable and warranted. She couldn't begrudge her for it. "I know that, but do *you* know why he did it in the first place? He did it for me. *And* Thane. He did it so he would have an army on his side to fight when we need them. If the person you loved was killed over and over and you were doomed to keep forgetting each other, wouldn't you be a little unhinged? And if you thought your own cousin, your *brother* took your wife from you, would you not be bitter? No, Hel is not Thane. Hel is not perfect, nor does he share all our morals, but he will do anything for those he loves, and I do mean *anything*."

With a heavy sigh, Piper tore her gaze away. "I wish I could understand but I just don't."

"You don't need to understand because he is the love of *my* life. He is *my* soulmate, not yours."

Piper turned to her with glittering eyes. "You were supposed to be our queen. You are Lady Lightbringer... You were supposed to be Queen of Palenor. Once you get what you want you will forget all about this place for your new home and leave us... forever."

Valeen's chest tightened. That struck her harder than she thought it would. She let out a slow breath, forcing her own tears back, swallowing the lump in her throat. "I am Queen of Villhara, goddess of night, but I am Lady Lightbringer too. I will always be your friend, Piper. I will *never* forget this place or you."

Piper suddenly threw her arms around Valeen. It felt completely out of character, and at first Valeen stiffened but then she wrapped her arms around her friend. Her quiet sobs brought more tears to Valeen's eyes. "I thought you were gone," Piper whispered. "I thought we lost *you*. I thought the part of you that I knew, the part of you that is Layala was gone. When I first met you, I never thought we'd be friends but you're one of the people I care most about."

"You didn't lose me, Piper." A tear slipped down

her cheek. "I'm still the stubborn elf you know and love."

"The stubborn part I don't love so much." They both laughed and Piper pulled back, wiping under her eyes. "And I lied. I'm so nervous about going back to Ryvengaard I want to throw up. Especially with Fennan going." She shoved her hands into her hair. "What am I going to do?"

"I think you're going to have to make the choice on who you want to try a relationship with."

"But what if Ronan just wants a fun roll in the sack and that's all? Fennan said he wants to marry me."

Valeen grinned. "When did he say he wanted to marry you? Did he get down on a knee and propose?"

Piper giggled and slowly shook her head. "It was while you were gone with Hel. He got ahold of one of my letters from Ronan and read it. Don't get me started because I was so angry with him for it. But no, it wasn't an official proposal. He said 'you can't be serious about this dragon bastard. I want to be the one to marry you, Piper. You're supposed to be with me.'"

"And what did you say?"

"I told him he was an asshole for going through my personal things and to stay out of my business or get out of my life."

Valeen bit down on her lip to try and not laugh but it burst out. "Holy All Mother, Piper. You're ruthless. And you thought I was mean."

"It's not mean after he snuck into my room and went through my drawers!"

"The elf you loved for years said he wanted to marry you!"

"I thought we solved this dilemma months ago,"

Hel said, popping in. He plucked up one of the arrows and with the snap of his fingers had Piper's bow in his hands. "The dragon prince, obviously." He had the arrow knocked and released in mere seconds. He hadn't even taken the time to set up the shot and still hit dead center.

"Well, I didn't ask for your opinion, did I?" Piper snapped. "You're the last person I'd get relationship advice from."

Hel smirked. "Oh Red, it's alright to admit you have feelings for me. I am the darkness that tickles most females' fantasies whether they admit it or not." He cupped the side of his mouth and leaned closer and hooked his thumb toward Valeen, "Just be careful, this one gets jealous easily."

"I'd rather stab my eye with a hot poker than have feelings for you other than loathing, you sick bastar—"

Hel snapped his fingers, and no sound came out of her mouth. "There's only one person in existence I've ever allowed to call me names and get away with it and that's not you. I'd rethink what you want to say next." He snapped his fingers again. "Maybe we should call a truce for Val's sake."

Piper narrowed her eyes at him. "Fine. But I'm never going to trust you."

"I wouldn't trust me if I was you either. I really don't have the best record." He took out a civar and put it to his lips. "I hope you're prepared to do what you need to to secure this alliance with the dragons."

Valeen crossed her arms. "What does that mean?"

"It means don't give him the goods until he's begging for it, then still deny him but tease. Tease the idea of it until that's all he thinks about. Assuming his parents approve that is. You'll get a ring, and we'll get our alliance. You realize that's what needs to happen right?"

Piper rolled her eyes.

"I'm serious. Marriages have been used to tether and secure alliances throughout history. Thane should offer his sister, but you seem to be the one the dragon wants. We *need* them."

Even if his delivery was crass, he was right. They needed the dragons for this war. "There are other ways if that's not what you want, Piper. You would likely have to live among the dragons, and it wouldn't be temporary."

Piper tapped her boot. "No, he's right. There might not be a Palenor left if we don't get the dragons with us. If I need to marry him, I will. I'll do what I need to do."

"That's the spirit," Hel said, with a slow clap, civar dangling between his lips. "I'd say play with little Ronan between his legs to get the ring but that might get you a wee dragon bab—"

"Hel." Valeen scowled. "Can you not be a prick today."

He laughed, dimpling his cheek. "I'm just razzing her a bit. Gods, you two need to loosen the corsets."

"Shut up," they said in unison.

"Oh, two mouthy, fire breathers. No wonder you're friends."

"I swear, Hel if you don't—"

"You'll threaten me with a wonderful time? Tie me up and whip me, love. I'm tingling just thinking about it."

"First of all, you don't even like being whipped. You're a closet, sweet romantic."

He pressed his palm to his chest looking exaggeratingly appalled. "Well, I never, how dare you try to ruin my bad reputation. Besides, I like tying *you* up. That little red number with your arms tied over your head is permanently ingrained in my mind."

Valeen flushed, recalling the night he'd used soft ribbons to pin her down on the bed under the night sky in Ryvengaard. She couldn't believe he said that in front of Piper... on second thought it wasn't surprising at all.

Laughter burst out of Piper, but she quickly covered her mouth as if she was shocked it came out.

"You secretly like me, Red, admit it."

Piper scowled at him then turned to Valeen. "I'm sorry it was inappropriate of me to laugh. You two are just a funny pair. Very... unexpected."

"I know my particular brand of transparency is hard to swallow sometimes but on a serious note, remember, Prince Ronan is a dragon, not an elf. They're unpredictable and territorial and once they find their heart's mate, it's for life. If that's you, Fennan better be careful." Hel blew out smoke. "And another thing. The gods and their spies will be watching and may try to stop this alliance." He turned to Valeen. "Speaking of gods, did you talk to Katana about who showed up last night?"

"She was asleep by the time I got to her room after we searched the castle to make sure he was gone, and still asleep this morning before we came out here."

"Who showed up?" Piper asked.

"Her former husband," Valeen answered.

"Oh." Piper blinked in surprise. "Thane said he could be a problem."

"I need to go find her and let her know."

"Yes, you do. I saw her at breakfast with Thane when I passed by a few minutes ago," Hel said. "Meanwhile, I need to pay our friend in the basement a visit."

STANDING OUTSIDE THE DINING ROOM, Valeen peeked through the crack in the door. Inside waited Thane, Katana, Fennan, and Leif. They all laughed, likely about something inappropriate Fen or Leif had said. Katana seemed to be adapting quite well to this place, and she was happy to see it.

Her stomach growled smelling the breakfast on the table, rich pastries, eggs, and potatoes. On her way out this morning, she only grabbed a roll that Tifapine had left behind.

The doors lightly creaked as she pushed through. Everyone turned to her, Katana with a bright smile, Leif's goofy grin, and Fennan stared at her apathetic. No doubt in his mind she'd betrayed Thane. He was his best friend after all, and she didn't expect him to understand.

Thane gave her a quick smile. "Come eat with us."

"Valeen," Katana said excitedly. "I am so glad you are here this morning."

She made her way over to the table and took the seat next to Katana. "How is everyone?"

"We're making preparations and need to go to the wall again," Fennan answered. "Are you busy or could you join us?"

"I can't today. I need to make headway on building my magical barrier around the city."

"I think I have an idea," said Katana. "We may not be able to use Soulender but what about Zythara? It is your sword, made specifically for you and has magical properties and it will not break like your crown."

"It might work. Except I need to use it to fight, and the item will need to be anchored."

"You have Soulender," Thane said, lifting his chin. "You don't need Zythara."

Katana added, "Anchored how?"

"Embedded in the ground. Probably within solid rock."

She didn't want to give up Zythara. That blade had been with her most of her life as the goddess of night. She'd missed it. And Soulender was used sparingly, only when needed. It didn't feel like her sword either. It couldn't be *owned* by anyone.

But if that was the answer to this dilemma, she would sacrifice Zythara for the time being. "I suppose I will give it a try. Katana, there is something I wanted to talk to you about." Leif and Fennan immediately started to get up from the table. "Something that could affect us all so stay."

Everyone shifted nervously, changing the mood. Leif picked up his fork and shoveled potatoes into his mouth.

"Last night Atlanta came to my room. He said he followed what he thought was you, Katana, but found me first. I believe he knows you're alive and it won't be the last time we see him. He also made it clear he is not on our side."

Katana was frozen in place staring, not at her but

passed her, with what she could only describe as terror. "Katana, are you alright?" she asked. Her sister never explicitly said why she did not want to see Atlanta again, but why was she afraid of him? Had she always feared him and Valeen never noticed before?

A fire lit in her chest; Atlanta must have done something to her. Her mind flipped through the possibilities, and each made her skin burn hotter. He'd always been a jerk, self-righteous and selfish, but she'd never suspected he was hurting her sister. That prick was going to get more than an earful the next time she saw him. "All of you need to be prepared for Atlanta to show up when you go north," Valeen said. "And after last night, I would expect hostility. He's an entitled asshole and I don't think he'll take 'no' for an answer."

Thane nodded. "We are prepared. She and I have discussed this already."

Her brows rose in surprise. "You have?" She leaned forward, resting her forearms against the table.

"She told me about Atlanta, and what happened," he said, but was almost hesitant to confess this, like he wasn't sure if he had permission to do so.

"I'm going to go check on the trainees." Fennan's chair scraped loudly against the floor. He grabbed Leif's shirt and tugged him up. "You're coming with me."

"Ugh, I'm still eating." He shoved one more bite of potato in his mouth and then was dragged out of the room. Valeen glanced between Katana and Thane, trying to decipher what she was missing.

Clearly, they had grown closer than she expected them to. Even though Katana was often with her in the library, much of her time was rumored to be spent with Thane going for runs and eating meals together.

"Katana, is there something I should know?"

"You don't know?" Thane asked.

Her sister still seemed to be... somewhere else in her mind. Was Atlanta involved in her death?

"Katana."

Finally, she snapped out of the trance and grabbed Valeen's hand on top of the table. "He did not hurt you, did he? Please tell me he did not."

"No, Hel came into the room, which only escalated tensions, but he knows I have Soulender and I'm not afraid to use it. He wouldn't dare touch me." But it became very clear to her that Atlanta had hurt *Katana* before and more than just emotionally. "Did he hurt you? Was he there with Synick that day?"

"Not with Synick, but—" Tears welled in her eyes. She quickly blinked them away and cleared her throat. "He had a bad temper."

Valeen closed her hand around Katana's. "How bad?"

"It did not happen all the time. Usually when he was upset about something else or if I questioned what he was doing or who he was with. I stopped asking, you know, after a while."

"Don't diminish it. If he frightens you, it was more than just one or two times." Valeen thought of that asshole putting his hands on her sweet innocent sister and it made her blood simmer. Then her breath hitched. "And you were an immortal goddess. We don't break or bruise easily." Angry heat burned her cheeks. "If he hurt you, it would have taken considerable effort."

"Please, just let it be. It was a long time ago."

"I should have just killed him last night. If I had known, I would have. Why didn't you ever tell me before? I could have helped you."

"*Valeen*," Katana pleaded, "I want a new life. He does not matter anymore. Revenge is not in me. I do not want you taking on my burdens as well. You have enough of your own."

"What's one more enemy at the end of the day?" She was going to send a message to Atlanta making it clear she would use the immortal weapon to defend her sister too. All Mother, he'd always rubbed her the wrong way. Katana was just so bright and lovely. She never let on that he was physically hurting her, and being an immortal, wounds would have healed almost instantly. There were never any marks...

Katana's bright lavender eyes burned into hers. "I am asking you to let it go."

"Only if he stays away," Valeen replied. "But if he comes to Adalon again... I won't make any promises."

"Deal," Katana said, and finally smiled.

Chapter 26

HEL

Down the steps to the dungeon Hel went into the damp darkness. Torches lit before he approached, chasing the shadows back. He found Synick right where he'd left him, chained to the floor and bound to the chair. The bastard lifted his head and managed to smirk, making the rotten muscles tense and bits of crepey, patchy skin twitch. It almost made his stomach turn.

Hel nodded at the guard on shift to watch Synick and tasked with dosing him with katagas serum every six hours. "You may go for now."

Probably desperate to get fresh air, he didn't even hesitate to leave out the door. It smelled like shit and piss down here. Hel lit up a civar just to mask the stench.

Synick watched him put the smoke to his mouth longingly. He was practically licking his lips and drooling.

"You're back," Synick croaked.

Hel leaned a shoulder against the bars. "Things are getting a bit dicey."

"What do you mean by that?"

"I killed Rogue, his wife, and Pricilla's heir. The retaliation will be soon." He tapped a finger against the cold bars of Synick's cell and took another inhale. "Which means you and I are at a crossroads. Do I send you back to the underrealm before they find out you're alive and get to you or keep you alive so you can help me? I'm leaning more toward killing you."

"Then do it," he sneered. "Kill me. What does it matter if I sit in a dark prison here or there?"

"You don't have to be here. We could find something more..." he glanced around at the terrible conditions, "appealing." He snapped his fingers and a civar appeared on Synick's lap. The chain clinked as he grabbed it and put it to the good side of his mouth.

"What do you want?"

"You know what I want. Give me the Sword of Truth, and I'll give you what they never offered. Your freedom. Along with riches. I'm sure we could even find you a nice castle across the seas."

A low laugh rumbled out of Synick's throat. "You think I haven't been offered the world for that thing?"

"Not by your favorite pupil." With a whisper of magic, the civar lit for Synick and he breathed it in deeply, closing his eyes.

"War was always my favorite."

Hel laughed and shook his head. "Oh, so it's jokes now. He has too many morals for you to favor him."

"Give me your wife and it's a deal."

Hel slid his nail against one of the bars. "That's the thing that's always been wrong with you, and why she never wanted you. You treat the fairer sex like objects. I can't give her away. She has a mind and will of her own. And even if I could, I'd rather cut my own throat than give her to you."

"Nothing will convince me to give up the weapon. You're wasting your breath but thank you for the civar. It's been a very long time since I had one."

"I believe you." Hel opened the cell door and stepped inside, tossing his civar to the ground. Opening his suit coat, he reached in and pulled out a twelve-inch dagger, silver with obsidian folded into the handle. "Goodbye, Synick."

"Hel, wait! Wait, don't send me back there. I know what I did was wrong. I learned my lesson, trust me. I'm not going to touch Katana or Valeen again."

"I know you won't." There were no more words to be minced. Synick was too much of a liability to keep around if he wasn't going to be useful. He wiggled like a worm in the chair, growing more frantic with each of Hel's steps. The blade's point aimed at Synick's heart.

"I know where your immortality is!"

It was more likely that it was a lie to save his skin but on the off chance that it wasn't... He rested the blade against Synick's chest but didn't push. "Where?"

"The demons deal in secrets." The chains holding his hands rattled as he trembled. "And when people die, they give useful secrets for favors."

Hel narrowed his eyes and slowly twisted the blade, putting more pressure behind it. "Go on."

"There was talk of the council giving your immortality to someone."

"What does that mean?"

"They used magic to put your immortality inside

someone else, to make them stronger and to keep it safe."

Hel growled at the thought. "Just mine?"

"All three."

He eased the blade off Synick's chest. Was it possible for his immortality to be given to another? He assumed it was a part of him, and could only be restored to him, but the note in Rogue's pocket had said their immortality wasn't hidden. He took that to mean their immortality was out in plain sight or being worn. Originally, the light essence was funneled into a small bottle made of manalus crystal. He'd watched Valeen's stripped from her. "You're lying."

"No." He slowly shook his head.

"It's not even possible. My immortality is a part of me, a part of my soul."

"It is possible, Hel. In my lifetime we only stripped one other of his immortality."

"Who?"

"His mother was half-siren half-goddess. His father was a full god. Offspring with that ratio can be mortal or immortal. He happened to be immortal. His immortality was transferred into another. There was a tournament. The champion won it. It was long before your time, but you must have been taught about it in your lessons."

A cold sweat broke out across Hel's body. An itch started at the back of his mind. He did vaguely remember learning about a tournament to become a god. If his own, if Val's had been placed into another, then how would they get it back? "Who are the three rumored to have our immortality?"

"Come now, Hel. You're intelligent. If you were on

the council and wanted to give immortality to three someones, who would they be?" Synick asked.

Someone he loved. A child. A lover. If memory served, the tournament they held long ago was for those *the council* nominated; not just anyone could participate.

Hel felt the blood drain from his face. Pricilla's heir. He'd used Soulender to cut off his head. Pricilla hadn't attacked him when he shoved her son's head on a pike. Had he destroyed his own immortality or Valeen's or Thane's? *Fuck*, had she sacrificed her own child and checkmated him?

There was the potential for taking someone else's but he didn't want someone else's immortal strength. He wanted his own. It was a part of him. Anything different would feel wrong.

"Give me names," Hel snarled.

"I said I knew where they were. By that I meant inside someone else. I don't know who." The decaying side of his face twitched as something skittered inside it.

"Why didn't you tell me this before?"

"When have I ever given you a completed puzzle? I give you pieces. That's the way it's always been. I gave you Rogue and you killed him. I gave you this. It's up to you to find out more."

There was more he knew. As much as Hel wanted to drive his dagger through the fucking bastard, he might need him.

When he was young, Synick intimidated him, scared him. There had been a small measure of respect for the primordial, even if he hated him. Now looking at his sickly, dirty state, Hel wondered what there ever was to be afraid of. Though caged beasts were dangerous when trapped and cornered. He turned on his heel and left the cell, slamming it closed without ever touching it. He faced his former mentor; the sad state of someone he once thought was untouchable reminded him of his own vulnerability. Anyone could be a step away from freedom to being chained in the dark like an unwanted animal.

"I want food, Hel. I want a bed and a fire. It's colder than the winter goddess's tits down here. I've given you two valuable pieces of information. You owe me."

With a snap of Hel's fingers, a bed made of straw and covered with burlap appeared. "A bed and a blanket for two pieces of information. But I don't owe you anything. It shows my utter benevolence just keeping you alive. After what you did to my wife and her sister, you owe an eternity of favors."

After making certain the lock was secure, and the guard waiting went back to his position, Hel found a bench outside. He laid on his back and stared up at the white puffy clouds, letting the sun bathe across his face. He should have seen this coming. Should have known they'd give the most precious gift of all, becoming a god, to others. "Fuck, I need a drink."

"Me too. We could go to Nerium Oleander and meet dear sweet Evalyn."

Gods, why does the Maker insist on torturing me? Hel took in a slow controlled breath before he sat up and faced the dragon wench he wanted dead. Varlett stood with her arms crossed, one hip popped out. No horns or talons out today. Which only made him more suspicious of her. And was she wearing... face powder? The pink cheeks weren't usual. Was she trying to make herself look less threatening?

He deadpanned, waiting for her to explain her unwanted presence.

"No?" she dropped her hands to her sides. "It will be fun. We can drink until we forget all the terrible things we've done."

He continued staring. Hopefully making her uncomfortable. He might growl and hiss if he thought it would make her go away. Just looking at her made him want to set fire to something, preferably her. Her hair in bright orange flames, her skin melting away, it would be glorious... if a dragon could burn. "There isn't enough alcohol in all the realms to make me forget what you did. I could be passed out, nearly dead, and I'd still fucking remember."

She huffed as if he was being absurd. "And you're so perfect? You are without a blemish on your record? We've all done terrible things. Even your precious Valeen."

"Name one thing that Valeen has done that's even comparable to you?"

"She stole Soulender and started the war of the realms."

"Gods, you're siding with the council now, aren't you? You're going to betray us in the end. I can already see it." She was like a plague that slowly ate away at everything good until it finally claimed life.

"I made my bet on who is going to win. I gambled my life on Valeen, otherwise, I'd have never tied myself to her."

Hel grumbled and stood, shoving his shoulder into her as he passed. "It's not wise to remind me of that fact." He kept his eyes on the gravel path ahead, willing her to just disappear behind him. A soldier leading a white horse came toward him. The clop of the hooves only brought on fantasies of jumping on and running her down. *Crunch. Crack.*

"If you can be forgiven for all that you've done, I should get that chance too. I was young, jealous, and stupid. You can understand that at least."

Hel whirled on her and shoved a finger into her chest. "I can understand that you lied to me. I can understand that you played us all against each other up until a few weeks ago when you were found out. You aren't stupid or young, Varlett. Jealous, certainly, but you knew what you were doing."

"There was no point I could have ever confessed without you immediately killing me. I wanted the truth to come out, but you haven't exactly been stable or forgiving."

Heat crawled up his spine. His hand trembled with the urge to wring her neck. "Get out of my sight."

"You're the one who told me to be here. I was fine in the woods alone."

"There will come a time when the only consequence of killing you will be regret that I didn't do it sooner." It took restraint not to drag her down to the dungeons. The only reason he hadn't was because he didn't want to risk Synick and her scheming together. That was what nightmares were made of.

"I want Valeen to get her immortality as much as you do for my own selfish reasons. So let me help. What do we know?"

His left eye began to twitch. In the back of his mind, he knew he could use her to help move this along, but his pride wouldn't let it happen. The soldier smiled, leading the horse until the steed looked at Varlett, and started retreating and reared up.

"Sorry, Lord," the soldier began, trying to regain control. "She doesn't usually spook like this."

"Mares can sense backstabbing whores." His eyes flicked to Varlett and then he was off again.

Varlett was quickly in step beside him. "Hel, please. Let me help."

"Do you hear that buzzing? It's a fly that just won't go away."

She halted and sneered at him. "When you come *needing* my help, be prepared to beg."

Magic cooled along his fingertips and slowly crept out. An invisible cord slid around her throat, and she gasped, reaching up. "If I need your help, the only thing I will hear from you is 'Yes, Hel, whatever you want, Hel'. Is that understood?"

The corner of her mouth twitched but she nodded. "Yes, Hel."

VALEEN

The library was quiet, the flipping pages of a book the only sound. Katana and Valeen found Presco at the top of the spiral stairs behind his new desk. Compared to the week before, this room was nearly brand-new again. Some of the shelves were still broken and there were stacks of books in the corners on the floor. He had beakers of colorful liquids boiling on a table in the corner and at least three books open in front of him.

Valeen set a plate of food in front of him. "You need to eat."

"Oh, I'm fine."

"No, you're not. You've been up here for days, and I know you haven't been hunting. You can eat some eggs at least."

Without further prompting, he took up the fork and shoveled in the eggs, clearing the entire plate in less than thirty seconds then pushed it aside.

Katana snickered. "Maybe we should have brought you more."

"I am just eager to get back to work, is all."

"Katana had an idea to use Zythara as the anchor."

Leaning back in his chair, it creaked under his considerable weight, and he folded his hands on his belly. "That could work. It did cross my mind, but I didn't think you would want to part with it."

"I don't want to, but I can't think of anything else and we're short on time. It's been over a week since the last attack. They'll make another move soon, and let's just pray it isn't an entire army."

"Well, we should give it a try then. It will need to be in a secure place not easily found."

"I was thinking on top of the waterfall. There is a stone platform." The very same platform she pushed Hel from and sent him tumbling off the cliff. It wasn't easily accessible, and the mountain's stone would be secure enough and might even be a good conductor for the shield.

"Let's go for a ride then. I could use a break to stretch my wings."

River water spilled over the edge of the slate rock, spraying mist all around them, dampening Valeen's hair and skin. A pixie fluttered around Katana's head then landed on her shoulder. The colorful little things didn't usually fly this high and avoided people, but leave it to her sister to be the one to attract them.

It pawed at her blonde hair and chittered something in her ear. She laughed and held out her finger. It hopped over to the end and danced for her, spinning around in a circle before the tiny wings fluttered and it flew away.

"What was that about?" Valeen asked.

"Nothing," she practically sang, "she just wanted to say 'hello'."

"Those things don't say 'hello'. They're mean."

"How could you say that? She was sweet."

"Why is it that animals and creatures always like you?" She could settle even the wildest of beasts.

"It is my aura. They are drawn to it and sense I will not hurt them."

"Well, I wouldn't hurt it."

"No, of course not, but you are a predator."

One thing Katana was not, was a predator. "Got it."

She took out her golden sword, longingly staring at the careful inscriptions along the blade. *Zythara—Darkbringer*. "I need your help," she whispered in the primordial language. It warmed in her hands in response. "We must protect the people of this city."

She turned it over, blade point down and drove it as hard as she could into a crack in the slate rock. It hit with a spark and a repelling force, throwing her back. She stumbled toward the water, waving her arms wildly to catch her balance. Presco lurched and hooked her arm before she fell over. With her mouth open in shock, she stared at it. This sword had never fought against her before.

"Perhaps it needs a little more coaxing," Presco mused.

Coaxing? It was her damn sword. It existed because she made it. Taking in a calming breath, she wrapped both of her hands around the hilt, and stared at it. It warmed again, sending a tingle through her. It liked being held by her. Of course it did. She was its creator. "I need you now for a shield."

It whispered back, *not a shield.*

"I know you're not a shield. You are a sword, and you belong to me."

To command and wield in combat, it answered. *To cut down our enemies.*

"I need you for a different purpose."

No.

Valeen balked. "Can you believe this?" she said to Presco.

"Is it speaking to you?"

"Yes. It won't let me use it as a shield."

"Well, it was forged by your hand and has likely inherited your stubbornness." He was on the verge of laughing about it.

"Exactly, it was forged by me and should do what I say." It was made of the rarest and strongest metal in the realms, found only in two places: the deep heart of the Black Mountain in House of Night, and in Mount Aeofi in the winter goddess's territory. It had taken her dwarven friends a decade to find enough to craft this blade, and she spent months forging it and getting it to bend to her will.

"You could try saying 'please'," Katana said with a wink.

She gritted her teeth and then huffed. "Please, Zythara allow me to use you as a shield."

No no no no no, it hissed. *Not my purpose.*

She shoved it back into the scabbard at her hip and crossed her arms. "We don't have anything else. Zythara was our only plan?"

Presco adjusted his glasses and tilted his head. "You could try reforging Lightbringer. It still lies broken in a tower, correct? Hel told me about it."

"Lightbringer didn't belong to the goddess of night. It was made by my elven father."

"Yes, it did. You have always been the goddess of night even before you remembered. And part of you is still the elf, Layala Lightbringer."

"And what if I take the time and effort to reforge it and it won't act as a shield conductor either? I don't remember Lightbringer having a mind of its own, but if I imbue it with my magic..."

Katana smiled brightly and her eyes widened. "Maybe Zythara cannot be a shield because this is not House of Night, it was not born here. But what if you and I imbued *our* magic into Lightbringer to shield day and night? We can instruct it that it is made for this purpose. To protect the elves. It was originally made here and for that purpose."

It might just work, and at this point, what other choice did they have? She shuddered at the thought of going back to the Void, surrounded by the pale ones. It made her uneasy to consider what memories and feelings it might bring up. The last time she was there, hundreds died, she'd been dragged against her will into that tower, terrified, and yet it had brought her... him.

"I'll get the sword, and we can start the reforging when you get back from the dragon court. If we want it to have both our magic in it, you'll need to help me. Have you ever worked in a forge or with weapons?" It had been an age or two since she had done it herself but hopefully the skill would come back to her. Presco was good at it if she was rusty.

Katana grinned. "I have never made a sword, but I have made rings and other pieces of jewelry."

And that told anyone everything they would need to know about how different they were.

Chapter 27

THANE

The afternoon sun peeked out from behind stark gray clouds, threatening rain. Thunder rumbled in the distance, but despite a coming storm, it was relatively warm, and the bees and birds fluttered about. Thane peered up at the top of the colossal wall that surrounded the dragon territory, waiting for one of the beasts to soar across it. It wouldn't be long before they noticed intruders on their land.

Thane sat on the grassy knoll under the cover of a bundle of redwood trees. He ran a whetstone along the edge of one of his swords and watched Katana move from one wildflower patch to another gathering her favorites along the way. The sway of her hips in her fitted peach dress did things to him he didn't care to admit.

"Why are we still stuck out here?" Fennan put his hands on his hips and lifted his chin up at the wall. His black curls bobbed against his forehead as he shook his head. "I thought they knew we were coming."

"They do." Thane continued sharpening his sword.

"This time they know who you are. They shouldn't keep the High Elf King waiting."

"We can't send a magical message without Hel here, so we wait for them to notice the smoke." He pointed the tip of his sword at the small fire they made. "Toss a few pieces of wetter wood on if you want them to see it faster."

Leif scratched at his scalp, tugging on a knot, then went back to digging under his dirty fingernails with the tip of a dagger. "It won't be long now, Fen. Have a bit of patience."

"As if you're one to talk."

"As your elder, I've got plenty of patience."

"You're not that much older than me."

"Thirty years, ya wee lad."

Fennan rolled his eyes. "In elven time, that is nothing."

"Still something."

Thane smiled and shook his head. It was nice to be away from the pressures of his duties and surrounded by his friends again. Being away from Valeen allowed him to simply be, without annoying thoughts of *what if* wandering through his head. If Ronan took more time, he wouldn't mind. There was something calming about being in the woods doing a mind-numbing task like sharpening his blades.

On his other side, Katana settled on the ground with her legs crossed and began braiding her long blonde hair, weaving in some of the blossoms she'd picked. He typically prided himself on being able to read people, but unlike her sister who always made certain everyone knew when she was pissed off, Katana was more of a mystery. A darkness plagued her and yet she was sweet and thoughtful. The violence of her past didn't make her bitter like many others. She lifted her chin and smiled at him, as if she knew he was thinking about her at that moment.

After being naked with her in the hot springs, it was hard to focus on anything else but what might have happened. That night was an accident. She hadn't known he was there when she stepped into the pool with nothing on. They seemed to keep running into each other in innocent ways that could be... more. And every time she was around, he felt almost an electric current that seemed to flow between them. Like if she moved, he would know it. It had to be her magic; what else could it be?

Piper dropped into a squat in front of Thane and offered her silver flask. "I don't know if you need this, but I do."

Thane took the flask and smelled it. A strong brandy. Today was not a day to risk drinking anything that dulled the senses. "What are you worried about? I'm not leaving until I get this alliance."

She frowned and let out a breath that puffed her freckled cheeks. "A lot of this rides on me."

"Who says?"

She deadpanned. "Thane. Let's not pretend what happens or doesn't happen with Ronan and I could sway the outcome of this alliance. If he wants to break it off with me, it could ruin our chances."

With his hands still on his hips, Fennan turned. The golden hoop in his ear caught the sunlight. "What are you talking about?"

Piper snatched back the brandy flask, and after a generous few gulps, she lifted a shoulder. He knew exactly what she was talking about. Thane hadn't pushed her to decide, but a betrothal to Ronan would likely help, if the King Drake Drakonan allowed it. Dragon royals were particular about who they married. Although, Piper wasn't his bargaining chip. He could give the dragon shifters the one thing they wanted most. A way back to their homeworld of Ryvengaard.

Leif put his dagger away and stood. "You're not thinking of marrying him, are you?"

"I've thought about it."

"You're going to marry him, not because you love him, but because you think it's your duty? Piper," Fennan ran his hand over his hair, "we don't need you to do that. What made you think so?"

"That isn't the only reason."

Fennan turned a sharp eye on Thane. "Did you push for this?"

Thane shoved one sword in the scabbard on his back. "No. It's her decision."

"You can't leave your home or the elves for these strangers," Fennan said angrily.

"I can do whatever I want!" she fired back.

Leif got in between them and brushed a stray lock of red hair off her cheek. He softened his voice when he spoke, "Listen, Red. We care about you, that's all."

"I know."

"It's not safe," Fennan snarled.

"He will keep me safe," she shouted around Leif.

"For how angry you are with Valeen you sure are a hypocrite. You're going to leave us for someone else."

"What!" Piper went to charge around Leif, but he caught her around the waist.

"Settle down, little fire."

Fennan sneered at them both. "Let go of her. Let her come at me."

"This is not even close to the same thing! You and I were never engaged to be married. You and I were never even more than friends. And Hel was her *husband*."

"Speaking of Hel, did he put you up to this?"

"Ugh! I'm capable of making my own decisions. I do have a mind!"

"Lay off, Fen," Leif snapped. Leif wrapped her up tighter and whispered something in her ear that calmed her down some. He was usually the one razzing her but not today. Thane didn't like to involve himself in these sorts of squabbles but if it went much further, he'd have to.

"What right do you have to even be involved in this discussion, Leif?"

"Well, I'm the only one of the two of us who has slept with her, so I have as much right as any."

Thane's arm froze, stopping the scrape of sharpening his sword. *When was that?* He wanted to ask but carefully set the whetstone down. Everyone went quiet while Piper looked absolutely mortified.

She whirled around in his arms and glared. "I can't believe you just said that."

"I must have heard that wrong." Fennan slowly shook his head.

"You didn't," Leif said.

Thane made his way over and pulled Piper from between them and walked her over behind a group of close trees. Tears rimmed her eyes, and she gripped the front of his shirt and buried her face in his chest. "It's fine, Piper. You don't need to be ashamed."

"It was a long time ago."

He tensed. "*How* long?" Leif was several years her senior, so it better not have been *that* long.

"I was sad about Fennan slinking off with some random girl in Doonafel, and we'd all just fought in a long battle against the pale ones. Leif was flirting, like usual. Osric had just died, and you were a mess, and I thought maybe I could be next. Any of us could die at any time. I didn't want to die having never experienced... Anyway, we decided not to talk about it again, so I wasn't treated differently by any Ravens. He swore he wouldn't say anything."

"I hope he was at least good to you."

She pulled away and covered her face with her hands. "Please don't embarrass me, Thane."

He laughed and gently patted her shoulder. "I don't want any details, Piper. I just know Leif is kind of a... brute. And I'll kick his ass if he was less than a gentleman."

She lifted her face. It was nearly as red as her hair. "Yes, he was good and gentle. He's a brute but not with me."

"Was it just the once—"

"*Thane.*"

He held up his hands in surrender. "Fine, fine. It's not my business." If he were a female and not her king, she might open up, but in all honesty, he didn't want to know details as much as she didn't want to tell them. If there wasn't a problem, he didn't care what they did. He glanced back. "I better get over there before they start fighting."

"Yeah." Piper turned on her heel and went for a walk in the opposite direction.

He wasn't surprised when Katana set her bouquet of flowers aside and followed after her. It seemed to be in her nature to comfort people, and even if she and Piper weren't close friends, it didn't matter.

"Good job, both of you." Thane shook his head at Fennan and Leif. They stood with their backs to each other but not far apart. "You've upset her, and she doesn't deserve that."

Fennan threw out his arms in exasperation. "I just don't understand where I went wrong. We were close. I knew she cared for me for years, loved me even, but I wasn't ready for a long-term commitment."

"Which is exactly why you don't deserve her now," Leif said, and stomped off.

"And you are ready now? Or is it just the thought of her being with someone else?" Thane asked.

"I love Piper. The harder I fight for her the more she pushes away. I thought that's what she wanted. She wanted me to want her back and I do."

Thane looked up to the top of the massive wall. It's what she wanted *before* Ronan came into the picture. "I had to let Layala go and hoped she would come back to me. She didn't. But you have to do the same, and if she comes back to you then it was meant to be. If she doesn't then there is someone else for you. It hurts, Fen, it hurts worse than you can imagine, but then one day you wake up and go about your morning and find you forgot to think about her. And slowly days go by where the 'what could have been' hurts less and you find joy in things you used to like again, and soon you can think about her without a pit in your stomach. Then you get to the point where you just want her to be happy even if it's not with you, and a while after that you really don't think about her at all. Then you get hope. Hope that you won't be alone forever."

"Shit, Thane." Fen groaned and ran his palm down his face. "But I don't want you to be right."

"You can keep fighting with her, Fen, but it's not getting you anywhere, and it will destroy any friendship you have."

He was quiet for a moment. "You won't be alone forever, Thane. You could be with anyone. You're a literal god-king." He let out a short laugh. "It's ridiculous how much of an advantage you have over the rest of us."

Thane smiled. "It does sort of make me an asshole, doesn't it?"

"Yeah," Fen said, and they both laughed until the shadow of a dragon blocked out the sun. "I guess the smoke worked. Now all I have to worry about is Ronan burning me to death with dragon's fire."

A branch snapped and the silver-haired Prince Ronan emerged out of the woods with his mute friend Dax. "I'd only do that if I thought you were an actual threat, Fennan." He smiled. "Welcome back to dragon territory, boys." Dax made a few hand gestures to Ronan, and he laughed. "Dax said I should make you tonight's dinner. Roasted elf is a delicacy." He turned in a half circle and found Piper and Katana walking their way. "There she is. I've been waiting a long time to see that pretty face."

Flushing, Piper picked up her pace and, in a few strides, Ronan closed the distance between them and wrapped his arms around her thighs and lifted her. She giggled and held onto his shoulder. "Hi, dragon prince."

"Hi, beautiful elf."

Chapter 28

THANE

The first place Ronan brought them to was the huge arena where he and Layala had fought Ronan's brother, Yoren, the eldest dragon prince, for the Scepter of Knowing. The memory of the red rose petals floating all around them as they stepped onto the sandy circle came to mind. He could almost hear them chanting now. This time they sat in a special walled-off area, mid-level as spectators. He was glad not to be a part of the show this time.

A table filled with refreshments, raw and cooked meat, piles of fresh fruit, and a small tabletop gold fountain of white wine made his empty stomach grumble. Ronan hadn't said why they were here, only that there would be entertainment while they talked.

A breeze came through the balcony to the arena, along with the stamping of thousands of feet as dragon shifters filed into the rows. The chortle of a crimson, horn-tailed wyvern sat perched on a wooden platform in the center. It raised its large head and sniffed through wide nostrils. Someone from the stands tossed a large bird leg at it. With a *snap*, it caught it in its teeth and swallowed it down, bones and all. It flapped its wings and let out a roar. A chain hooked around its ankle kept it from coming for the crowd.

Katana's hands wrapped around the stone railing that overlooked the arena. A breeze gently blew her long blonde hair blanketing her back, and the sun gave her tanned skin a glow. He'd seen her in whites or blues but today she wore a coral, thin-strapped dress that complemented her features. He noticed himself watching her too closely but couldn't seem to stop. He caught his thoughts drifting to places they shouldn't go, like if she wore any underwear under that silk dress. There were no lines anywhere on her curves. The back of the dress revealed enough that he knew she wasn't wearing a bralette.

"Why do you keep wyverns?" Piper asked, thankfully pulling him out of his inspection of Katana. What was wrong with him? She was Valeen's sister and off-limits. "Are they your pets?"

"I suppose you could call them that." Ronan stood at her side with his back to the wyvern. "Kane is the reigning champ. There's a match soon so the place will be packed."

Leif and Fennan were at the table dishing up their plates. His redheaded brute of a Raven stacked his higher than was appropriate for a royal setting. Not that he could really blame him. Leif was from a smaller village in Palenor, and he hadn't been raised in court to know proper etiquette. But at least they'd been given the time to change and wash. His long hair was even combed and half-tied back.

"You... make them fight? For entertainment?" Katana balked, pressing a hand to her chest and frowned. "That is barbaric."

"I mean, we *are* dragons," Ronan said with a shrug. "Barbarism is sort of our nature." He slipped his arm around Piper's shoulders. "Like when a male finds his heart mate for example, we mark her with our teeth." He clacked them together playfully, and Piper stared up at him both looking simultaneously curious and nervous.

"Like you bite her and leave... scars?" Katana blinked.

"Not scars. There's a venom produced when a male dragon is... aroused. And if he bites her it goes into her blood and that scent will stay with her and let other males know. It doesn't hurt. From everything I've heard, she likes it."

Thane knew this about dragons, but Piper certainly hadn't by the expression on her face. Fennan cleared his throat loudly from the banquet table. "Elves don't bite our females. We treat them with kindness and respect."

"There is no higher sign of respect than a dragon who bites his heart mate. He will never be with another again as long as he lives. He would die for her, kill for her, do anything."

"In a way it sounds romantic," Katana added with a smile.

"Oh, and as far as the wyverns go, we don't *make* them fight. They see another wyvern, they attack, unless it's a male and female during mating season. We only put a pair of wyverns in close proximity to each other and let nature take its course." He brushed his straight, silvery-blond hair over his shoulder. "Katana, I know Thane thinks I'm an idiot, but I'm not, so what are you the goddess of? Piper never mentioned you in her letters."

It was unnerving how perceptive Ronan was. He guessed that he and *Layala* were gods before they even knew. Thane always suspected he had the blood of the gods in his veins, but he never would have considered thinking more before his memories returned. The memories that changed *everything*. Sometimes he caught himself wishing that he could have lived the rest of his days blissfully unaware of his past life as War, but then the guilt came. That meant forgetting Hel. That meant him staying asleep in that tower forever, and even if his return took Valeen away, he wouldn't change it.

Katana combed her hair behind her ear. "How did you know?"

"I can smell it in your blood."

"Truly?" She smiled even brighter. "Well, I am the goddess of day."

"Good gods, are you really?"

"Yes," she said proudly. "I was born in a flash of bright light, lying in a bed of blossomed clovers. I first noticed my hands and brought them in front of my face," she curled them at her waist now, "and then I heard sound, wind moving in the trees and birds singing." She caught a lock of her hair and toyed with the end of it. "Then I saw Valeen next to me. She sat back on her knees, staring at me with such deep blue eyes. I didn't know what she was, what anything was then but I knew I was the same thing as her. She smiled and said, 'Hello' in the primordial language. I could never forget her voice. It was the first I ever heard. Our creators made us knowing the language, you see, and we were fully grown just as we are now, never children." She trailed off and looked back out over the arena as if she'd spoken too much.

Everyone stared. Leif even stopped eating. Fennan had set down his fork, enraptured.

It was the first time he'd ever heard this creation story. Valeen had never told him what it was like in those first moments. The way Katana spoke about it, made it feel... almost sacred.

She was sacred.

"Fascinating," Ronan said reverently. "We only have a vague history of the gods, but I always assumed if there was a goddess of night, there was also a goddess of day."

"Your assumption was correct."

"So are you eager to get back to your homeworld? Piper mentioned the portals going off-world being open."

"Not really. I like it here well enough."

"Wait." He blinked several times. "So if Layala is the goddess of night then is she the goddess you woke up next to?"

"I know Layala as Valeen, but yes, she is my sister. We are two sides of the same coin."

"Oh." His crystalline blue eyes widened then darted to Thane then back to her. "Interesting that you should both be connected with Thane."

She faced him, lavender eyes falling on him as if she was looking for an answer to a question. "It is curious. Though I suppose I am connected to Thane because of her."

Ronan put a hand in his pocket. "I heard about the engagement being called off, Thane. I was sorry to learn that."

"Are the King and Queen coming?" Thane got up from the seat he'd taken. He did *not* feel like talking about it. He wandered over to the table and pretended to be interested in the food.

"They should be here sooner or later. Mother's always fashionably late. She doesn't know you're coming, by the way." Ronan came up beside him and ripped off a leg from the massive raw bird in the center. It looked to be seasoned but not cooked.

"*By the way?*" Thane ground his teeth. "You know why we've come, and you couldn't at least tell them we'd be here?"

"Well, now that the Black Mage is back, it's going to be nearly impossible for them to agree to an alliance. They wouldn't when he was gone."

"The Black Mage is the god of mischief and magic and is with us now. The gods will come here and destroy Adalon. If you think hiding behind these walls will spare you, you're wrong."

"It's not me you need to argue with, Thane." Ronan bit into the meat. "I'm with you and so is Dax. We will fight with you."

Two dragons would not be enough. And Thane had almost forgotten Dax was even there. The dark-haired, muscular dragon stood silently in the corner with his arms crossed in front of him. "Daxy misses Layala. He was hoping to see her. They rode into battle together."

"She's not coming."

Thankfully everyone else had gone back to chatting so no one was focused on them. He seemed to pick up on Thane's emotion and plucked a strawberry and bit it in half. "Go ahead and eat while we wait for the festivities to begin. I made sure to have it stocked with food you elves like too. Rabbit food mostly."

Piper wandered over. "The fruit looks great."

He smiled and winked at her. "There's dessert as well. That's the chocolate cake we served last time. The same one you said you liked."

"Oh," Piper said, blushing as she picked up a white plate. "How did you remember?"

"I remember everything you say." He tapped the side of his head. "Dragons rarely forget especially when the one saying it has captured his every thought."

A flush spread under Piper's freckled cheeks and for once she looked speechless. Maybe it was because Fennan was here, or she hadn't ultimately made her decision yet. Months passed where their only interaction was communication through letters to each other. If Ronan was going to forget and move on from her, he would have already. Even if he thought she was his heart mate, which seemed implied based on what he saw earlier, he wouldn't bite her until she gave him permission to.

Cutting a piece of the cake, Piper slid it onto her plate. "You're very sweet for a barbaric dragon."

"Only when I'm around you."

Thane filled a plate with fruit, a couple slices of bread with butter and jam, and a few of the desserts, and made his way over to where Katana now sat. He skipped over the meat since she'd been offered it several times but had always politely declined. With her legs crossed, she bounced her foot watching the wyvern clack its talons on the wood platform it sat on.

"Are you hungry?" he asked, offering the plate.

"I am starved, actually. Thank you, Thane." She set the plate on her lap and started with the greens. With the others distracted, she leaned over. "I feel like going out there and setting the poor thing free."

"It would try to eat you. I don't know if I'd call it a 'poor thing'."

"I have a way with animals. Even predators."

"I'll have to see that in action, just not today. You wanted to experience other cultures, right?"

"Yes, I suppose I did. The scenery and architecture are gorgeous and the nests with the eggs were a fun surprise. I suppose I should have expected something like this given they are dragon shifters. It is only that the ones back home in my former territory were much more... how do I say this without being offensive..."

"Less beastly?"

"Yes." She bit into a crunchy, green stalk.

"In Ryvengaard there are different clans. Some of the dragons like to embrace their humane side more than others. They enjoy things like the arts and operas and have laws against murder. While others will kill another just for saying the wrong thing, without consequences. Here there is a bit of both."

"A true survival of the strong and ruthless then. I fear I would not make it as a dragon. I do not know if I could take a life even to save my own."

"You would survive if I was one too. I would be your darkness." Thane winked.

She smiled. "I know you are a warrior, but it is difficult for me to imagine you killing. You are kind, Thane."

"I've taken more life than anyone ever should. There is a reason I am the god of war, Katana." He wanted her to know his true nature. Even if she said she could see his soul, she was mistaken. He was a killer.

"But you do it to protect others."

"How do you know I haven't murdered just to murder?"

Her lavender eyes stared straight into his. It was as if she rifled through his mind, pulling memories, and he had the urge to look away; it was too intimate, too invasive and yet, he didn't. "Because I know."

"How?"

"I can see your heart through your eyes. You have a lovely aura."

That made him finally look away. His heart was too broken for him to want anyone to see.

"So, Thane." Ronan plopped down in the seat next to him. "Will this new enemy bring other dragons?"

"Many."

He nodded. "What else?"

"Frost giants, trolls, halfgods, goblins, monstrous creatures from other realms you've never heard of. Gods and goddesses who can't be killed by any mortal weapon."

"Mmmm sounds perilous, I like. These little squabbles with other dragon clans don't get me all riled up anymore and a dragon craves battle. When will this happen?"

Thane lifted a shoulder. "It's already been a few

weeks since the portals opened. They've sent smaller-scale attacks. Soon they will have gathered enough fighters to invade. They won't come here without certainty of victory."

"And what of your elven curse? If the Black Mage is on your side, has he ended it?"

"He will use them to fight."

Ronan shook his head. "Thane..."

"I know." He had the same hesitancy after spending years fighting against them. "But they are loyal to him. He created this army for this purpose. The curse just went further than he thought it would."

"Piper told me what he is to you. It's all sort of mind-boggling if you ask me, but can he be trusted? If they turn on us..." He folded his arms and they both looked out as another wyvern in a cage rose up out of the ground. This one was both taller and broader, and forest green. The extra-long spikes along its spine made it a barbed-backed wyvern. Thane had seen many wyvern fights in his previous life. Size didn't always matter, but barbed-backs were notoriously vicious. The two wyverns began to hiss and snarl at one another from across the arena.

"If the pale ones turn on us, then we all die, but he wants this revenge. He's obsessed with it. He won't let that happen."

"What if he turns them against us on purpose so he adds more to his army to control? We've dealt with him in the past. We know his nature."

"If he did, he would lose Valeen, and he won't risk that, because there is one thing he wants more than he wants revenge, and that's her."

He took in a deep inhale through his nose. "Males do insane things for a female, don't they?" He patted Thane's back. "Enjoy the show." He got up and went back to Piper at the railing. She barely reached his shoulder in height, and was petite in comparison, but somehow, they fit. He ran his fingertips across her shoulder blades then leaned down to whisper something in her ear. She looked up at him with an expression that said she was both scandalized and intrigued. After being around all the Ravens for so many years, she heard too much to be naive to the ways of males, but she was different with Ronan—more demure, like he tamed her warrior and brought out the feminine side in her. Maybe because with him she could simply be Piper rather than trying to prove her strength.

It was another hour before the stands filled and the cage around the green, barbed-backed wyvern dropped. Katana sat forward, chewing on one of her nails as the two beasts collided midair. The hit sounded like a crack of thunder, and the snarls like the terrifying sounds of a nightmare.

"All Mother above," she whispered as the red bit into the arm of the green and drove it to the sandy ground. They wrestled and rolled, snapping and clawing. "Is this to the death?"

"I'm not getting in there to stop it," Ronan said over his shoulder. "No one else is either."

The fight went on for a good twenty minutes before the red got ahold of the green's throat and tore it out. The crowd erupted into cheers, chanting, "Kane! Kane! Kane!" The red pressed his massive paw on the dead green's belly and roared.

Three dragon shifters in their beast form came out of doors that opened in the arena walls. The main difference between the shifters' dragons and the wyverns was size; the dragons were twice as large and had four legs with their wings out of their backs. The wyverns' wings were part of their front legs.

A cobalt-blue dragon snapped at the red wyvern, a warning bark. It backed up with a hiss, but didn't challenge him. Then two dragon shifters picked up the dead wyvern and carried him off, while the third raked the sand with its talons to spread the blood and clear the guts. The champion walked over to a door in the wall, scratched at it, and it opened to allow him inside.

"Is there more?" Katana sounded afraid of the answer.

"Oh, yes," Ronan said with a grin. "It's only getting started. A new pair will be out shortly."

A door behind them clicked open and heels tapped on the stone. "Ronan, what is this surprise?"

Thane turned to find the Queen of the Dragons, Nyrovia, striding into the room. Her silver-blonde hair was a shade lighter than Ronan's. They resembled each other, down to the icy-blue eyes and pale skin, like two winter storms. Her crimson, strapless gown hugged her bodice and flared at the hips.

"Hello, Mother. I invited friends."

Thane made his way over to greet her, and she dipped into a curtsy. "Hello, again, High King Thane."

Thane took her outstretched hand and kissed her knuckles. "Good afternoon, Queen Nyrovia. I hope you have been well."

She smiled and her gaze drifted to Piper and the

smile turned into something more pinched. "Always. What brings the High King of the elves and his companions to our home?"

"We can discuss that later, Mother," Ronan said. "Another match is about to start."

Chapter 29

VALEEN

Ebony mist rose up before her, shifting and moving like the surface of a dark ocean. It smelled of sulfur and burnt vegetation. If there were fires inside, she couldn't see yet. Deep within waited her broken sword right where she left it.

Low growls and gurgling noises coming from beyond the darkness made the hair on the back of her neck stand. It wasn't that she was afraid of the pale ones the way she'd been before. The thought of them attacking her wasn't the problem. What had always scared her more was that they were drawn to her and that she could command them.

"Afraid, love?" Hel's demeanor changed the moment they materialized here. His black cloak seemed to float around him on its own, his raven hair had fallen more on his face, partially covering his eyes. Playfulness danced at the corner of his mouth as he watched her, but he was the Black Mage now. Ready to command his legion of cursed monsters. "You know I won't let them hurt you."

"Afraid of your creatures who will kneel at my feet? They'll be calling me master over you soon."

He chuckled. "Really? And you'd like that?"

Damn, he called her out. "If it gets me what I want."

"You sound like me."

"Look, I just want this to be over, and if we must command these... things to win a war, then so be it. I'd rather have them under our control than have them fighting against us."

"Now you're thinking like a queen. True leaders don't think in black and white. There are many shades of gray. Some people die so others can live. Do you remember who told me that?"

She smiled. "I did."

"Yes. If all these elves had to turn and countless others die just so that you can live, I'll take that. And if that makes me terrible, then I'll take that too." He held out his rune-covered hand and for the briefest moment she hesitated to take it. Watching Aldrich turn was still fresh in her mind. The old bite mark on her thigh tingled. His waiting stare met hers and he leaned closer, brushing his lips across her ear. *You aren't afraid of my serpent's bite now, are you?*

Never. This was Hel, her soulmate. Her hand closed around his and together they stepped through the wall of darkness. Bones scattered across the mushy, black ground. The acrid smell of sulfur intensified, making her stomach turn. Pools of tar bubbled in small puddles here and there. But more repulsive than the landscape were the thousands of pale ones. A group to the left fought over a deer carcass.

Growls and metal clinking against metal pulled her attention to the right. Ten or so fought each other with rusted weapons. Their white skin and hair were a stark contrast to the black armor they wore. The detail of their pointed ears had never stood out to her before, but these were elves once. Elves who'd been cursed. Could they turn back to what they once were when this was over?

Wind picked up, billowing her loose hair around her face.

Heads snapped in her direction. One of them lifted his nose in the air and inhaled.

Feeling more and more of their creepy stares, she leaned closer, pressing her shoulder against Hel's side. There were so many...

"Master." One of them stood from a crouch, a rabbit's limp body in hand. Blood from the poor creature streaked down his chin. Valeen itched to pull out her sword. Her magic rose to the surface heating her skin beyond what was comfortable. It wanted to be unleashed, to destroy.

"Have you brought us a gift?" He licked his lips, trailing his gaze down her form.

Oh, she thought. *That was a mistake.*

"We're getting hungry waitin' in here." Another stepped closer. Soon they would be surrounded. "Just a finger." He reached for Valeen and faster than her eyes could track, Hel cut off the pale one's arm at the elbow. It hit the ground with a thud. Black blood gushed. A gurgled scream tore from the monster's throat as he held the stump. "Master, why?"

Then He cut off his head. It plopped and rolled to the toe of her boots. The waiting horde looked amongst one another, terrified and yet in awe.

"No one touches my wife." He pulled Valeen in front of him and pressed his hand onto her shoulder. "This is your queen. She is not to be touched or harmed. You will defend her against anyone." He pushed her directly in front of one of them and said softly in her ear, "Tell him to do something."

"Hel, I—"

"Do it." This was the Hel from her lessons, relentless and cold.

"Step back."

He did.

She turned to another. "Stand on one foot." Then another, "Kneel." Every command was followed, and she hadn't used her power of persuasion. Another pale one drew her attention, the most menacing of the group, with a hunched back and shoulders, and a scar over one eye that left it permanently closed. "You. What is your name?"

He cocked his head. "Name?" His voice was gravelly.

"Yes, you must have had a name once. You do realize you were once elves, who loved and cared for others?" She took a step closer. "So what was your name?"

"Not an elf," he mumbled, but she saw a spark behind his onyx eyes. He was... thinking. At least it seemed he was considering what she said.

Don't try to see compassion where there is none, love. They are lost to the abyss.

Everything about them would say so but it was still

a question lingering in her mind. Mathekis proved that they could reason and think critically. He didn't run on pure instinct. He remembered being a beautiful elf once; he even knew his previous name. *Can you... change them back? They could still fight for us.*

He slid his hand along her throat then to her jaw and tilted her chin upward to his. With his eyes locked onto hers he made sure she understood. *I told you before, I can't. I don't know how. This curse is beyond my control.*

But the goddess of wisdom and knowledge said that in order for the curse to be broken, Hel had to live once again, and the key was his heart... maybe there was another meaning behind it. Or maybe the goddess lied so she'd wake him up. She knew who Layala truly was, and Hel said she'd helped him. The goddess who only bore a set of twins, Hel's mother and Thane's father, would have had a motive to help him. Maybe Hel was right and there was no turning them back or ending it.

"Now," he turned to the waiting horde, "Where is Mathekis?"

"I am here, Lord." The pale ones parted for their other commander. He pushed through the crowd, shoving one of them over, ramming his shoulder into another. When he stood before Hel and Valeen, he bowed his head.

Of all the pale ones, he was the least monstrous in appearance. Although frightening with the black lips and eyes, he spoke with elegance the others lacked. "They are growing restless, Lord. They want to fight." He looked over at her with curiosity, almost smiling. It wasn't an expression she thought he was capable of.

He had told her once that she would stand beside the Black Mage, and that she had no reason to fear him. If only she'd known then.

"Don't worry, the battles will soon come," Hel said.

A pale one from the left blurted out, "Elves will come here? High King wants some more? I want his head." The deep chuckles and cackles flitting among them made her skin pebble.

"No, not the elves," Hel said, without the bite she expected. He spoke to him more like a father to a child. "We will be fighting alongside them against a new enemy. One more formidable and ruthless."

Murmurs and questions slithered across the sea of pale faces, but this news excited them. They didn't care who they would fight. They just wanted to slake their bloodlust. "What enemy?" Mathekis asked.

Hel tilted his head in the direction of the tower. "Come. We will talk."

THE TOWER STOOD amongst the jungle of red-leafed trees and dark vines sweeping among the trunks like serpents. But unlike a natural wood, there were no birds calling or fluttering from tree to tree. Only the hum of insects disturbed the quiet. The butterflies that once covered the door to the tower were no longer there, but the jasmine still grew untamed and beautiful, the smell of it drifted toward her. Whereas before it had been a mystery to her, now she knew why he'd put it there, even if he'd done it subconsciously. It had been her favorite flower after Katana died, because it was Katana's favorite. Jasmine was everywhere in and around her home in House of Night and it was everywhere here. And she hadn't noticed them before but bushes of deep purple lilies so dark they looked black grew at the base of the tower.

"The sword should be inside," Mathekis said, striding forward to open the door. "I haven't touched it and none of the others will have either."

Up the steep winding steps they went. Torches along the walls lit as Hel approached. The door at the top was left wide open and dangling from its hinges. After Hel and Mathekis had disappeared, Thane had angrily jerked on it, nearly ripping it off. The stone table Hel had spent four hundred years lying on made her uncomfortable.

Four hundred years he'd spent in this room waiting for her to wake him. Four hundred years lost in a plane of existence connected to her. Even if he said he didn't remember feeling awake until her mate bond to Thane was broken, what if he had? What if he'd spent all that time alone trapped in his own mind? Or had they been there together while they waited for her to be reborn? It was strange to contemplate where one's soul lingered in between lives. As an immortal, she'd never thought about it.

She watched him scoop up the pieces of Lightbringer and carry them to her. "It's only broken in one place."

Two pieces, snapped the moment her life fractured into Layala *and* Valeen. She couldn't go back to being Layala or even Valeen, the two had come together. This sword represented her elven side, represented the parents who sacrificed their lives for her, and the world that she needed to shield from her past mistakes.

The weight of the jade handle felt good in her palm. She held it to her chest and closed her eyes, vowing silently to restore what her elven father had made, vowing to fulfill the name she had been given. When she opened her eyes again, Hel was staring at her, the harshness in his face softened and his full lips parted. "Miss Layala Lightbringer," he said and smiled. "I think you will be their savior after all."

Valeen stood in front of an old red brick building with boarded-up windows, broken glass, and a rusted flat metal door handle. A few of the other buildings around it looked run down but just down the street was a bakery, a smithy with smoke rolling out of the chimney and elves walking about. Above the door were two old chains dangling from a metal post that once held a sign. The slabs of old weathered wood across the entrance with crooked nails came apart easily when she began tearing at them.

Hel joined in, pulling them off with his bare hands and gently setting the wood aside. He could have snapped his fingers, and it would all fall away but there was something reverent about hard work, and this place deserved that.

Her father's old forge was sacred ground now.

The handle squealed and ground as she pushed it down. She shoved her shoulder into the door, and it gave way, billowing up dust, creaking open to a dark room. Light spilled in from behind her, flooding across the brick floor at her feet. It smelled of old ash and soot in here.

A table on the right had an old silver vase at the center. A barrel full of tarnished weapons sat in the corner. She stilled, sweeping her gaze around to the large forge and tongs and other tools hanging near it but they looked in bad shape. This was where her father worked. This was where he created Lightbringer. She could hear the roaring fire, the pinging sound of a hammer hitting metal in her mind and it made her smile.

With a hand over her heart, she took a deep breath. *I'm so sorry.* She thought of the forget-me-nots she used to bring to the memorial in Briar Hollow and tears prickled. *I have not forgotten you.* She stepped over to the window and pulled down the wood boards covering them. More sunlight filled the smithy.

Hel sauntered over to a shelf lining the wall, ceiling to floor. He slid his finger over the dust then picked up a dagger with a gold and silver handle. "Why was this place abandoned?"

Valeen made her way over to the stone furnace that had long been extinguished and placed her hand on top of it. "Aunt Evalyn told me that after my father was executed the townsfolk closed it up rather than sell it. Out of respect." She didn't remember him, but it felt right being here to reforge Lightbringer. Almost as if his spirit was happy.

"I am sorry," he said softly and set the dagger down. The bump in his throat bobbed. "It's my fault this happened."

She shook her head. "No, you never told him to kill my parents. It was Tenebris's doing. It was his own greed for more power and magic that caused this."

He sat on one of the window ledges and crossed his

ankles, looking around the meager beginnings of her father with... sadness. Even if he hadn't lifted the blade or ordered her father's execution, Tenebris did it to take her for the Black Mage. For him. "Do you remember how to work a forge?"

"I think it will come back to me once I start. I planned to get the forge running first, then I'll wait for Katana to return. We decided she should imbue her magic in the blade along with mine." She took the end of the bellow and gave it a push, sending ash fluttering about. "Thane said they'd only be gone for a few days. We can get everything ready for when she returns. This place could use a good dusting and sweeping. The bellow is broken. And the forge stone has a crack in it."

"Not that I'm opposed to your idea, but waiting could be a mistake. They could be here tomorrow... tonight even. An army could be on the way at this very moment."

"If I want this shield to work for certain during the day, I need her."

"Then she should have stayed. I promised Thane I'd do my best to protect his city. Although I don't care all that much what happens to it, I gave him my word."

"Well, she's not. And I don't even know if I have the power to create a shield anymore. Prepare not to have one when they come."

"I'm prepared." He stood and walked over to the forge and touched the crack with his fingertip. It lit up like a candle at first, then the light traveled across the split and repaired the damage.

"I wish I had that talent," she muttered.

"You have many talents. Combat, leadership, seduction... even blacksmithing."

"Well, when you live thousands of years, you learn things just to pass the time. I wanted to make my own sword and so I learned from the dwarves. They were all too happy to teach me." She winked at him. "The *seduction* comes naturally."

He chuckled. "Ah, of course, who wouldn't want a beautiful goddess around? I bet you had their bushy beards in a tizzy."

"Back then I could get pretty much whatever I wanted."

He laughed again, his grin wrinkling the corners of his eyes. She loved seeing him happy. "I think you could now. *I'll* give you anything you want."

She started around the room, her boots lightly tapping on the stone. "Anything?"

"Anything."

"I want a castle of our own again. With a flower garden, so Katana will want to come over often."

"I'm working on it."

"And I want Starborn and Night back, if..." if her winged horses were still alive. They were born of the same stardust she was and had been with her for thousands of years.

"I'll find them."

She paused, touching the handle of a dusty sword sticking out from the barrel. Nervous butterflies and a flush worked up her body. She glanced over her shoulder at him. Two nights ago, she had a dream, and it had stuck in her head ever since. Two tiny, beautiful faces. "I want... two babies. A boy and a girl."

His smile slowly fell away, and he stared as if she'd said something sinister. He looked almost afraid. Maybe he no longer wanted children. His throat bobbed and his gaze fell to his boots. "Two? I wasn't aware you even wanted one."

This subject no doubt brought back old... feelings. She *did* leave him after Varlett's illusion of him saying he only wanted to be with Valeen for a powerful heir. "I do with you. I mean that. I had a dream... I have this feeling they're waiting."

Through thick, dark lashes, he peered at her. The intensity grew between them with each passing moment. A crease formed between his brows. All Mother, was he going to say anything?

She wished she could feel what he was feeling or hear his thoughts. Had he changed his mind about wanting children? She always assumed he did want them, but he never brought it up, not after he found out Synick desired to use her for a baby and killed Katana when she turned him down. She felt like she might vomit waiting for his response. She hadn't realized her hands were balled into fists until the ache set in.

If you don't want children—

"I would love to give you as many babies as you want, Val." His voice was husky and raw. "If it's truly what you want, and not because you feel you need to for any other reason."

That nervous energy slowly faded, and she smiled. "It was fear that stopped us from having children before. I'm not afraid anymore. It's what I want."

"The process is quite enjoyable. We can start practicing right now. Although I won't remove the prevention rune on me until the war is over. Pregnancy would make you too vulnerable and a child of ours would be hunted mercilessly. I won't do that to you or our child."

She stopped in front of him, and his big hands closed around her waist. It was his devotion that made her fall into him, scars and wickedness and all.

There was beauty in loving another so much you'd give them anything if they only asked. He opened his thighs and pulled her flush against him. He brushed his fingertips over her mouth, staring at it longingly. Like he was a desperate man in a blazing desert starving for a drink. "Is there anything else you want?" he asked.

"Life with you forever."

"Forever."

Chapter 30

THANE

The wyvern fights lasted well into nightfall. Leif and Fennan both had more to drink than they should have, and went to stew in their rooms while Ronan and Piper went for a stroll on the royal grounds. Why her relationship bothered them more this time than the last was a mystery. Maybe now they believed it was a real possibility Piper could leave, before that wasn't even a thought in anyone's mind.

Queen Nyrovia retired early from the fights but promised Thane an audience with her husband the following day.

"So, what did you think of the event?" Thane walked Katana to the guest wing and stopped at the door next to his where she would be staying. He wanted her close, not for any reason other than to make sure she was safe, he told himself. It was in case Atlanta showed up.

Lifting a shoulder, her brows rose. "It was interesting. I hate to admit it but the more fights I watched, the more I could not look away. Not that I enjoyed it. I detest violence, especially with animals."

Thane rubbed the back of his neck. She would detest *him* if she hated violence. "Well, um... sleep well, Katana." He groaned. "I said 'well' twice."

"Three times now," she teased.

He half smiled. "Yeah. Goodnight. If you need anything, I'll be right here."

Still facing him, she reached back, opened the door and stepped onto the threshold and... waited. "Goodnight, Thane."

His eyes fell to her lips and the sudden urge to kiss her was like a burning fire. "Katana," he breathed, leaning forward and gripping each side of the doorframe.

It was lust, pure lust, and had absolutely nothing to do with love. He didn't want love, but he wanted her. The intensity of the feeling sent his pulse racing. The breeze from the open window in her room trickled through the doorway, swirling with her scent all around him.

Her bright lavender eyes locked onto his and she took a small step inside the room, then another.

"Yes, Thane?"

As if he had no control, he found himself following her inside. "I—should let you get some sleep."

"I am not tired. You can stay for a while, if you would like. We can... talk." The lit candelabra on the bedside table was the only light in the room. The amber glow somehow enhanced her curves. The V-cut of her silk neckline showed off the roundness of her breasts.

"Yes, talk," he whispered, eyes traveling to the large

four-poster bed. He hurried to the only chair in the room and gripped the armrests.

Facing him, Katana leaned her back against the bedpost with one leg extended forward. It opened the slit in her dress to her upper thigh, almost where it creased at her hip. He didn't remember it being that high before. While watching him, she slowly began unwinding the small plaits in her braided hair. A few of the flowers she'd weaved in fell to the floor. Her fingers ran through her loose locks with a coy smile. Gods, he felt like he was going to catch fire at any moment. "Do you really think we have a chance?"

Thane gulped. "A chance?" Them? In a romantic way? He hadn't thought past wanting to bed her, past the sounds she would make with him inside her or the way he'd make her moan in ecstasy. He didn't want to think past that. Thinking about giving his heart away again made him want to vomit. Especially to her. He shouldn't want her at all. He promised Valeen he wouldn't hurt her, she was too good for him to do that, and right now, he couldn't give her all of him.

"At convincing the dragons to join us. Even Ronan seems reluctant."

"Oh, right, the dragons." Thane took a deep breath. "I must convince them. I won't leave until I do."

"You do seem like the type to get what he wants."

"Usually."

She smiled and laid herself across the bed, propping herself up on her side. The position of her thighs, one crossed over the other, hiked her dress up even higher, exposing the side of her ass. Just like he thought, she had no underwear on. *Shit*.

Thane tore his gaze away, trying to find something

else to focus on, but then he drifted right back to her. "Do you need a drink or anything?" He might have to get out of this room to catch some cool air. "Water perhaps?" He needed water, splashed in his face.

She propped herself up on her hand and draped the other over her waist. The V in her dress fell more to one side, and he was sure if she shifted a little, her nipple would show. She didn't seem to notice or care. "No, but thank you. Unless you do."

What was it about her he was so drawn to? "No."

"If you could be any other race, what would it be?" Katana asked. She always said things he wasn't expecting.

"I've never thought about it before."

"Well, think about it now." She flashed him a bright smile and with that he'd probably give her any answer she wanted.

"A dragon."

"Why?"

"They're ferocious. Good hunters. The second most lethal race in the realms."

She giggled. "I should have guessed that since you are the god of war. I think I would be a forest nymph."

"Why is that?" They were said to be gorgeous maidens, rarely sighted by men but could capture their hearts with nothing more than a look. She may very well be one already.

"So I could wander the woods singing and collecting flowers, and I would be beautiful of course."

"You're already very beautiful," he countered. "More so than any nymph."

"Have you ever seen one?"

"Once, long ago."

"But I could turn into a tree if a random male wanted to hunt me. I would never be found if I did not want to be. They are mysterious, and I should like to be that."

He'd never met anyone like Katana before. Even after being abused and traumatized, she was still bright—it was cliché to say it, but she reminded him of the sun. He was so used to death, violence and war, as was everyone around him, but she hadn't been tarnished by it. "I think you're mysterious."

"Do you?" Her lavender eyes sparkled.

"Yes. I can't understand how you are so—happy. You haven't let what happened change you for the worse."

"I will not lie and say there were not periods of my life that were gloomy and dark, or that I do not still struggle at times. You have seen me struggle, but one thing about the sun, Thane, is that it always rises."

The weight of the silence that followed and her stare made Thane's body buzz even more. He gripped the chair harder as if it was the anchor holding him down. He was a rock. He had immeasurable control. He'd resisted every single maiden who'd thrown themselves at him and even waited months for Layala to give into him. He could resist her. But gods above, it was like she was pulling him in with a chain, a hot chain that would not break.

"Can I ask you something personal?" Katana licked her bottom lip.

"Yes."

"Does it still hurt?"

He knew exactly what she was asking. "Yes, but not

as much as it did a few months ago. Can I ask you something?"

"It is only fair." She brushed her bright hair behind her shoulder and slowly ran her fingertips over her collarbone. Did she have any idea that her touch drew his attention there? Did she have any idea he was on the verge of igniting, and she was ten feet away?

"What are you thinking about?" he asked.

"I was thinking that I like the way you are looking at me right now."

He nearly choked on the saliva he swallowed down and swore under his breath.

She giggled, throwing herself back on the bed. She stared up at the ceiling for a moment then turned her head. "And I was thinking that maybe you do not simply want to just look."

Heat flooded his body, and he pressed himself harder into the seat cushion. "What are we doing, Katana? What are *you* doing?"

She sat up, dangling her feet off the bed. "I am not sure what you mean?" The bottom lip tucked between her teeth told him she knew exactly what he meant.

"Yes, you do."

She smiled again. "I call it flirting."

"You said you hadn't been pleased by a male in too long." He finally let go of the armrests and stood. One foot slowly stepped in front of the other. "Is that something you want or was that *flirting*?"

The room seemed to feel heavier, coated with desire. She looked down and gripped the bedding on either side of her hips. "A little of both. But I do not think your heart is ready."

"No," he said, putting his fingers under her chin

and lifting her face. "But it doesn't need to be. What happens in this room tonight can end here. It doesn't need to have anything to do with our hearts."

Her breathing quickened. "And tomorrow night?"

"We can worry about tomorrow night, tomorrow." He'd pushed Layala away when she wanted him because he loved her. He wanted to make certain she knew exactly who she was choosing. This was different. It had nothing to do with love. Anything else would be complicated and he didn't want that.

"I think we should take some time to mull this... arrangement over first. And if you feel the same way in the morning light, then..."

"You're the only thing I've thought about for days," he whispered. "It won't go away in the morning."

She blew out a breath. "Can I tell you the truth?"

His hands were trembling now. He had to know what her lips tasted like. "I only ever want the truth."

As she searched his face, her lavender eyes glittered in the candlelight. "You might be able to keep your heart out of it, Thane, but I do not know if I can with mine."

He smiled both relieved and disappointed. "Then I guess I'll say goodnight, once again. Sleep well." He quickly made his way into his own bedroom. Katana deserved someone who could give her more than he could now. She was already fragile, and he wouldn't break her further.

THANE WOKE UP IN A SWEAT, even his hair was dampened by it. Screaming. Someone was screaming. He threw his blankets aside and sprinted out of the room. Frozen in the hallway, he tried to figure out where the scream came from.

A chill ran down his back.

Katana.

He quickly pushed down the handle, locked. Her screaming stopped and the silence that followed made his stomach drop. He rammed his shoulder into the door, snapping the wood frame and shoved through. The room was dark except for the meager light coming in through the window. It was enough to know the bed was empty.

"Katana?" he panted.

A small whimper made him turn. In the corner of the room, he found her curled into herself, crying. He didn't smell blood, didn't see any sign of a struggle. He dropped into a crouch beside her and gently touched her bare shoulder.

"Please do not hurt me." She kept her face buried into her bent knees with her arms circled around her head. "Please."

"Katana," he said softly. "It's Thane. Was there someone here?"

"I did not do anything wrong."

He carefully pulled one of her arms away from her face, then the other. She turned her face away, and angry heat flooded his chest. This wasn't because of someone hurting her now. She was having another battle with the past. Either it was Synick or Atlanta that had made her this way and he wanted to kill both of them for it.

"Katana, I won't hurt you."

She shook her head and wrapped her arms around

herself again. "I did not even look at him, Atlanta. I promise." She turned to angle her back toward him. Her body shook with sobs, and he was almost sure she wasn't fully awake. "You are scaring them! Stop!"

Thane gritted his teeth. Oh, he was going to kill him. He swore it. He'd convince Valeen to give him Soulender just for a day.

"No! I do not want to die."

He gripped her shoulder and turned her. "Katana." She shielded her face, and he gently pushed her hands down. "Open your eyes. Look at me. It's me, Thane. Thane, the Elf King, the god of war. I am not Atlanta. You're safe. No one will hurt you."

A moment later, she lifted her chin and her eyes fluttered open. Her breathing was still entirely too fast, and she looked bewildered. "Thane?" she reached forward and cupped his cheeks. "Thane," she breathed. Then she pressed her hand over her stomach. She brought her palm up in front of her as if she expected to find something there. After blinking a few times, she dropped her hands as if reality rushed in. She pushed herself up and leaned back against the wall. "What are you doing in here?"

"You were screaming."

Her mouth fell open, mortified. "I was?"

"Yes."

Piper peeked in the door, as did Leif and Fennan. Thane quickly waved them off.

"I am sorry." She pushed her hands into her hair and then sank down the wall onto the floor again. "I did not mean to wake you." She forced a smile. "It was a nightmare. You can go back to your room."

He dropped down in front of her once more. "I'm

not leaving you like this. Do you want to tell me about it?"

A tear slid down her cheek and her smile faltered. "Please go. I do not want you to see me like this."

He shook his head.

She choked out a sob and pressed her face into her hands. "Thane, please leave me be. My issues are not yours. You do not want to get involved, remember?"

As if her pain seeped into him, his chest started to ache. "Come here." He took her arms and wrapped them around his neck, then picked her up, cradling both her legs to one side. Curling around him, she buried her face into the nape of his neck and quietly sobbed. He carried her over to her bed and climbed on, sitting against the stack of pillows with her on his lap. He stroked her hair and kept his other arm wrapped around her lower back. "Will you tell me about it?"

She sniffled and he felt the wetness of her tears against the skin on his neck. "It is silly. It is not even real."

"It's not silly if it does this."

"I dreamed Atlanta would not stop hitting me. The children were crying..." she sniffled again and went quiet.

"Did that happen?"

She nodded. "And then he stabbed me, and blood was pouring down my body. That did not happen."

"It did. He was just not the one who did it." Thane held her a little tighter. If he could take her pain and anguish away, he would.

"Yes." She paused, then whispered, "Thank you." They fell into a comfortable silence until her steady breathing told him she was asleep. But he didn't push her off his chest, didn't let go. He held her until the sun rose and peeked through the windows.

With the birds singing outside she lifted her head and smiled with sleepy eyes. Even with messy hair she was radiant. "Good morning."

He smiled back. "Hi."

So much for not getting his heart involved.

Chapter 31

HEL

The dust alone in the forge took hours to clear. Then there was the task of finding a few hammers and other tools she would need. Even if the neighboring elves boarded the old smithy, robbers or young reckless teens had come in and taken what was worth the most. Valeen would have to replace them before she repaired Lightbringer. The anvil was missing and the stone pot to melt the metal in was gone too.

As much as he wanted to help Valeen get this place up and running, he'd already put too much precious time into this when he had pressing questions that needed answering.

Presco walked about the open room scratching a quill across a page in a silver notebook. "I think I have listed all the things we'll need," he announced. "Some will be harder to find than others. Are you sure we can't just use the forge at the castle?"

"I need to do it here," Valeen said, running a frustrated hand across the top of her raven hair. A smudge of dirt smeared over her cheek and strands of her hair were coming loose from her braid. Dark circles were starting to form under her eyes. She insisted on staying up all night to work on her father's old smithy. But what she needed was rest. "This is where Lightbringer was made. I won't risk this not working. Everything has to be perfect, or the shield will fall."

Tifapine took a bunch of her gathered flowers and placed them in a blue vase on the old rickety table. "Well, I got something to spruce up the smell in here. It's a little musty and I've sneezed at least ten times. The flowers were out back. I wonder who planted them." She rubbed her hands together then rearranged the yellow and purple blooms. "And I borrowed the vase from Aunt Evalyn's place. It's only a few blocks from here. I hope she doesn't mind because I didn't ask. The place was busy. Nearly every table was full, and this guy kept yelling about the dice game they played, and it hurt my ears. I had to get out quick."

As annoying as the little creature could be, there was something about her that grew on him. She talked too much and ate too much but was good for occasional entertainment.

"That's great, Tif," Valeen said absently. She was bent over the table looking at the two pieces of Lightbringer. Her tongue slipped over her lips as she concentrated. "I think I'm going to have to melt down the whole blade."

Hel rubbed his chin. "Then it would be nearly a new sword. Are you sure you want to do that?"

"If I just meld the two pieces together it won't be

perfect and will weaken the blade. There would be bubbles and thin spots."

"You're only using it for a shield. It won't fall apart."

She huffed, stood tall, and crossed her arms. "Only? Lightbringer will need more strength to be a conductor than it would to strike, block, and kill."

Hel held up his hands in surrender and slowly backed toward the exit door. "Fine. What do I know? I have something I need to go do."

Her sleek brow arched. "What?"

He hadn't told her yet that he might have killed the person with one of their immortalities inside him... losing it forever. It wasn't a sure thing and there was no need to alarm her over it. Because that would mean one of the three of them would have to stay mortal. He already knew he and Thane would give up theirs for her but as for the two of them? He didn't want to think about having to fight Thane for it, and he didn't want her to go all self-sacrificing and give hers to one of them.

"Synick. I check on him every day. We can't be too careful with him."

"Did Katana's idea work? Being nicer to him, I mean. You never did tell me." She left her sword and stepped beside Presco and looked over his list. "Add another hammer in case one breaks."

"He didn't say anything worthwhile," Hel answered with a shrug. Just a hint that Hel might have destroyed one of their immortalities.

"Alright." She lifted her blue eyes to his. "Thank you for your help. We'll be here until we get hungry. Then I think we're going to Aunt Evalyn's to eat."

"I'm hungry now," Tif interjected. Hel only looked at her, and she blushed, and scurried off the table.

"I'll meet you there if I can so I can finally meet the mysterious Aunt Evalyn. I'll be on my best behavior of course." He took another step toward the door.

Something akin to fear flashed across her face. As far as he knew, she hadn't been in to see Evalyn since they'd returned, and her aunt had no idea she was with him... the Black Mage. He smiled watching her changing emotions.

"Well, um. Maybe..." In typical Valeen fashion—when she wasn't in a pissy mood, that was—she didn't want to tell him not to go and risk hurting him but explaining to her human aunt who he was and why she was with him would be a task he couldn't wait to witness.

"It will be a wonderful evening no doubt, Miss Lightbringer. It's probably best if you tell her about us before the coming wedding, don't you think?" He winked and slipped out the door.

The sun peeked out from behind the clouds and the heat from it instantly warmed his black suit. He quietly shut the smithy door and pulled out a civar. The sweet smell curled around him before he put it to his lips and inhaled.

There were two moves he could make next. He could find another god or goddess on the council to question about the flesh bags who stole their immortality, they'd have their security at an all-time high, and it would be difficult and dangerous to get to any of them, but not impossible... Or he could play on his hunch and go directly to question Pricilla's dead heir. That was assuming the bastard was in the underrealm.

If he worked for Pricilla, he'd no doubt done things to earn his spot there. But the worst place imaginable wasn't exactly on his list of places to visit, and the demon princes wanted him dead after he and Valeen killed their brother.

He stepped onto the brick road, his overcoat billowing out behind him in the breeze.

Out of the corner of his eye, he caught bright blonde hair and paused. Across the street in the shadows of the alleyway, Varlett leaned up against the brick, picking her teeth with a bone. This particular part of the city wasn't busy. The buildings were old and several of the establishments didn't appear to be open any longer. A bakery a few buildings down had a few patrons coming and going but heading in the other direction.

"Unless you have something monumentally important to say, make yourself disappear." Hel paused in the center of the road, taking another puff off his civar.

Varlett strutted to the edge of the building, boots clacking loudly. Staying just in the shadows, she tossed her bone aside. "I need your help. I wouldn't ask if you weren't my last resort."

"Oh, this ought to be good."

"I... I don't know what to do. I've tried everything I know."

He narrowed his gaze on her, a hood shadowing most of her face. "What are you talking about?" he said, irritated.

She came out into the sunlight and pulled her hood back. It had only been two days since he'd last seen her, but the change was significant. Her hands and cheeks were bony, her skin almost gray, rather than the vibrant bronze it always was. Her hair was nearly white... and those bloodshot eyes.

The smell of fear seeped from her as she carefully stepped closer. She was even thinner than the last time he saw her. Too thin. Her collarbones protruded in the extreme.

And Valeen's survival was connected to her...
"What did you do?"

"It's—I don't know what's wrong with me, Hel." Real fear filled her watery eyes. "I've tried all the healing potions, the runes, antidotes, everything I can think of, but it's getting worse."

"What. Did. You. Do?" he growled.

She twisted the hulking, silver, demon prince's ring on her finger. "I used demon magic to bring Thane back. He was dead, Hel. I didn't *heal* him."

Hel shot forward, grabbed her hand, pinched the ring, and pulled. This stupid fucking thing was what she used to blackmail Valeen in the first place. It didn't move. He twisted and pulled harder, and it didn't budge.

She grimaced the more he twisted. "It won't come off! Not since that day."

Hel conjured a knife, pressed it to her skin. She squealed, but he stopped himself. If he cut off her finger, he'd cut off Valeen's. *Fuck, fuck, fuck*! He shoved her arm away. Her back hit the brick building, and she hissed in pain. Gods, he knew there would be consequences of her using that ring but what did this mean? "Is this another one of your tricks?"

"I wouldn't do this to myself!" she snarled. She rubbed her elbow and nodded toward the old forge. "How is she?"

He glanced over his shoulder at the wooden door. His heart started pounding. Valeen *did* have dark circles under her eyes and generally looked tired. She wasn't losing weight like Varlett, but what if it was only affecting her slower? If Varlett brought Thane back from the dead, was the cost... a life for a life? "End the link. End it right fucking now. I know you can."

"So you can kill me the moment I do?"

"I won't kill you. I'll even help you if you break the connection and let her go." He tried to keep the desperation out of his voice, tried to sound cold but if Varlett was dying, so was his mate.

Varlett tore her gaze away. "And you think you could stop this?"

"I will try."

"That's not good enough!" she shouted. "I won't end it. You'll be a thousand times more motivated to help me while I'm still connected to her. So do something!"

His mind whirled. Sweat slid down the back of his neck. Gods when did the sun get so hot? The person he loved more than anything in any world could be taken from him again.

He could save her from someone's blade.

He could protect her from an attack but this... He was powerless, and he hated it even more because he was the god of magic.

He should be able to snap his fingers and end their link, but he knew Varlett would have set precautions for that. He would have. It would likely kill them both if he tried to end it. Varlett's one last "Fuck you". "I've created runes to stop magic from progressing—"

"I've done it," she snapped, peeling up the sleeve of

her left arm. A rune mark was just below the bend in her elbow. "It did nothing."

"Then we have to give the demon princes the ring back."

"That was my first thought, but it won't come off! I tried to cut it off, Hel. I can't even puncture the skin around it."

He growled at the thought of Valeen losing her finger. "Trade for me instead. End it with Valeen and bind yourself to me. I will become immortal. It's the same deal." And if the demon magic took him through the connection, he'd be reborn. He would find Valeen again.

Varlett rolled her eyes, then glared. "You really would do anything for her."

"Do it." A door creaked open. Fuck, it was her.

Hel turned on his heel to find Valeen marching toward them. She looked worried which meant she'd heard at least a little of what was said. "Hello, love."

She shot Varlett an icy glare, then the coldness turned to careful inspection. Even a fool would see the changes in her, and Valeen was no fool. Her brows rose in surprise. "So, you brought Thane back from the dead and now it's come to haunt you."

"Haunt *us*," Varlett added, clicking her talons together.

Hel gritted his teeth. *I'm going to kill that bitch.*

"No, this is your fault, Varlett," Valeen said angrily.

"I'm not denying that. But I don't know what to do. You know about demons, don't you Valeen? You're the oldest of us."

She crossed her arms. "I know what that ring can

do for a demon prince, but I don't know what it does to a mortal. It looks like it's draining your life."

"Our lives." She scowled. "This wouldn't matter if you found your immortality. Why isn't that your primary focus? What are you even doing in that old smithy?"

"None of your damn business."

"I'm looking for her immortality, and I'll find it," Hel said.

"In two days? Because at this rate, that's all I have left." She snarled at the both of them, baring her teeth. "When you two want to stop messing around, come find me. I'll be at the castle." All he imagined as she walked away was strangling her.

As soon as she was out of sight, Valeen rubbed her hands over her face. "All Mother, how could this happen *right now*? I wasn't so worried about her because she wasn't in any more danger than I was, but she looks like death walking."

It scared him to think about Valeen just dropping in his arms mid conversation. His heart began to pound his body heated with fury and terror. Would it happen that fast? With no warning? "I'll find a way today."

"Shit," she hissed. "Presco has been looking and without knowing what kind of magic she used we don't know how to counteract it."

"Presco is not me. You know what you are to me, Valeen." He ran the back of his fingers down the side of her face. She closed her eyes and leaned into him. He memorized her face for the thousandth time—the outline of her lips just slightly darker than the fullness, her thick lashes longer on the outer corners, her elegant regal nose etched into his mind. She was so lovely, it made him ache sometimes. But even if she looked different, even if she was scarred, he would still love her soul. In every life he'd been drawn to her. "I will do anything for you, and I will figure out how to save you no matter what it takes."

THE DOOR in front of him exploded off the hinges, spraying wood flying in all directions, and then crashed to the floor. Dust billowed up into the rays of sunshine filtering in through the window. Hel sauntered over the rubble and paused, spotting Varlett sipping from a steaming white cup in the corner.

Gods, I hate her. I think I despise her even more than Synick.

"Really? Blasting your way in here? You could have knocked."

"Get up."

"When is Thane coming back? I want to at least see him before I die. I loved him. You? You were someone who could teach me magic."

Her stupid comments didn't even get a rise out of him. "Give me your hand with the ring. I'm going to try something."

"Like what?" she growled, all throaty, like she was on the verge of shifting to her beast. She curled her hand against herself and held the other over it protectively.

Oh, no, we're not doing this. He jerked her arm and grabbed the ring. His magic hummed. If he could destroy it then it should stop what was happening.

Heat from the metal started to burn his skin. Shadows seeped out from between her fingers... not his. Shadows darkened the entire room. The walls creaked and groaned. An unnatural wind swirled while demonic whispers in their evil tongue seemed to come from everywhere. It wasn't a language he knew but he got the feeling of the threats, nonetheless.

Varlett squirmed and tried to tear away from him. "Stop it. Hel, stop! They're demanding you stop."

He worked to get inside the metal, to break it from within. Whatever magic protected it pushed back. *I am the god of magic. You will obey me.*

Not the god of our world, it hissed.

A powerful shock sent him stumbling backward. He ran his sleeve across his forehead, wiping away sweat. Varlett stared down at the ring, her entire body shaking. Tears slid down her ashen cheeks, and she sunk to the ground, folding her arms around her knees. "I'm going to die," she whispered.

If the ring wouldn't come off, and it couldn't be destroyed, there was only one way to fix this. He grabbed Varlett's arm, and in an instant, they were pulled through intense darkness and pressure and stood in the unnamed forest.

After realization set in, Varlett tried to jerk out of his grasp, but he held tighter. The stone portal a few feet away hummed to life with his presence. Her black scales attempted to surface, flickering here and there, then fading. His magic held hers at bay. No, she would not be getting away this time.

Varlett stared at the portal with horror. "Where are you taking me?"

He pictured Valeen's smiling face, the brightness in

her blue eyes, he could not watch her fade. He couldn't watch her become frail and wither away. He would not hold her in his arms and watch her soul leave this world again.

Fortune favored the bold, they said.

"Fuck it." With his clammy palm flat against the portal, it hummed and swirled at its center. His gut twisted into knots and his heart felt like it was in his throat. *Do not open this specific doorway for the goddess of night.*

With her brows tugged down, Varlett peered up at him. "Hel, where are we going?"

"To meet the brothers of the previous owner of that ring." He shoved Varlett through the darkness, then stepped in after her.

Chapter 32

THANE

Katana stayed in the bedroom while Thane wandered down the hall to get breakfast and bring it back. He found himself smiling as he descended the stairs and rounded a corner. A pair of guards nodded to him as he passed, and he grinned at them. It had been a while since his mood felt so... light.

He remembered this place well enough to know that the dining room was on the main floor and breakfast would probably already be out in a buffet. It wasn't until he heard hushed voices and Piper's name among them that he slowed his pace.

It was rude to eavesdrop, but he still hovered a few steps from the cracked doorway.

"We do not mix races, Ronan. You cannot marry this elf girl. I forbid it." It was the dragon king's voice, Ronan's father.

Thane glanced back to make sure no one was around. This was not something he'd anticipated. He thought Piper's relationship with Ronan would be an asset, a potential line for an alliance, but knowing the Drakonans from Ryvengaard, he should have realized.

"I love her."

"What do you know of love?" King Drake snapped. "You care for nothing but yourself. You don't do anything I ask. You brought shame upon our family for years acting like a buffoon in the local taverns. You went against my wishes to fight with the elves, thinking only of yourself. You could have brought that curse back here to our people."

"I'm not convinced the curse can affect any race but elves. And I will be the reason we get to go back to our home realm, if we do this right. Thane is the god of war."

"It's a myth! Nothing but a legend," King Drake bemoaned. "You live in a dream world, Ronan. There is no other realm. I don't even believe in the gods. Thane is nothing more than a mage. A powerful one but a mage nonetheless."

"You smelled it in his blood!"

"What I smelled was magic in him *and* Layala. I went along with this belief they are descendants of the gods because the people believe in the gods. I let them have their faith, but it is a story to give people hope."

"I know Ryvengaard is real, and so is Runevale. Piper has been there."

"Ryvengaard? Runevale? This elf girl has poisoned your mind. These places don't exist! She is a seductress trying to gain our favor for an alliance with the elves and their plight."

"Ryvengaard is our homeworld of the legend you speak so poorly of."

"Ronan, you've been fooled. They are using your

dreams and aspirations as leverage. You should know better."

"It is real, and we will go there, and when we do, I will bring Piper as my wife."

"No, you will end your relationship with her. She is not one of us. What would your children be? We are Drakonan dragons from a long line of the strongest and fiercest. Our mates are chosen for the future of our family name."

"Father."

"I will not allow it!" he boomed. "You've already ruined three betrothals in the last two hundred years. It is a disgrace on the Drakonan name. You will marry Sensa, as I arranged for you *five* years ago, and you will not purposefully break her heart like you did the others."

"You know I don't follow orders well, father."

"You will do it or so help me, boy."

"You'll deny me the throne? I'm the second-born son, father, and your firstborn already has two sons of his own. I'll never see it."

"No, but I will make sure that this elf girl is no longer a problem."

Silence fell a few beats and Ronan said, "You wouldn't dare."

"Don't test me."

Heavy footsteps from inside the room had Thane scrambling for somewhere to hide but in the long hall there were no alcoves or exits. The door flew open and crashed into the wall. Ronan stepped out and turned in Thane's direction. His crystal blue eyes widened and then he shut the door on his father.

"Thane. How much of that did you hear?"

"Enough." Thane put his hands in his pockets. Enough to know Piper was going to be heartbroken. The bigger problem was Thane planned to use a promise of going back to their homeworld of Ryvengaard as his leverage to get them to fight. King Drake didn't even believe it was possible to leave Adalon. Myth and legend he called it. But in all honesty, he didn't blame the king. There had been no sign of the gods or portals to other realms in over two thousand years. It was going to be more difficult to convince Drake than he thought.

"He's a stubborn old fool." Ronan tilted his head as a gesture to move on. They started down the hallway, putting distance between them and the king.

"Your father is skeptical, and not to blame."

"It is real, though, isn't it?" Ronan hadn't directly asked him before.

"It is."

"You've seen it? You've seen it with your own eyes? It's not a story that was passed down?"

"Before I was reborn as Thane, I lived there for a very long time. Both Ryvengaard and Runevale. I know the Drakonans from the other world. They own the treasury and are probably even more influential than the kings in Ryvengaard."

He nodded and crossed his arms behind his back. "I don't know how we can convince him."

Thane lifted a shoulder. "I'll just have to show him."

"What do you mean?"

"I can open a portal to Ryvengaard through the stones."

"You'd do that without an agreement?"

"I would do it to show him it's there and give him a taste of the world, but no one else goes."

Ronan smiled. "Not even me? I've dreamed about this since I was old enough to read the tales, Thane."

"You won't go running off once you're there, will you?"

"No, I don't want to make enemies with the god of war, and I don't plan to leave Piper behind, despite what my father said. What is it like?"

"Everything is bigger there. The trees, the boulders, the mountains. Even the birds and rodents. You will live longer there in your homeworld. There are other shifters like felines and wolves, but dragons rule."

"No doubt," he grinned.

Thane cleared his throat. "About Piper... I can't pretend I didn't hear him make a threat against her. She's a commander in my army, as well as one of my closest friends."

"He won't touch her."

"I'm not convinced of that. If you do marry Piper, it will have to wait until the war is over, and even then, your father isn't going to change his mind about her. Are you willing to be disowned over her?"

Ronan's usually playful expression turned into a frown.

"And *have* you thought of all the things your father said? They are legitimate concerns. What would your children be? Shifter or elf or something in between?" Dragons and other shifters usually didn't mate outside their race. He'd seen it a few times in Ryvengaard. The children usually did not have the ability to fully shift into dragon form, rather a half-shifter, only able to grow the dragon wings and talons, and scale up if they were lucky. Which for Piper wouldn't be an issue, but he could imagine Ronan being disappointed. They were usually not accepted by either parent's society and became outcasts. At least that was what he'd witnessed in Ryvengaard.

He nudged Thane with his elbow. "I'm not thinking about children, Thane. We haven't even become a mated pair yet."

"I highly doubt you haven't thought about it, Ronan. In fact, you can't convince me you haven't done extensive research. Even if you have everyone else fooled into thinking you're the half-wit family disgrace, you're not."

Ronan raised a brow and smirked. "What makes you so sure?"

"You're a student of history. You're a reader. You were able to sniff out our god heritage right away, to name a few."

"I've done my research on the topic and found a few instances. Our children would be carried in her womb, not hatched from an egg, be beautiful like the elves and be able to shift into half-beast form."

"It would be one in a million that they'd be able to fully shift into dragons."

"More like one in ten million." They came to the end of the hall and paused before entering a grand foyer. "You think she should be with Fennan, don't you?"

"I think she should be with whoever makes her happiest." Although he'd love for his two good friends to end up together, he understood why Piper felt the way she did. Fennan took too long to notice her. "And someone who will protect her from anyone, even his own family."

"*No one* will touch her."

WITH BREAKFAST IN BOTH HANDS, Thane pushed through Katana's broken door, his boots crunching over the wood splinters still on the floor. Katana sat in front of the open window before a mirror, running a comb through her long blonde hair. She hummed as she watched her reflection. Her demeanor was such a stark contrast to the way she was the night before, it caught him off guard. Wouldn't there be sadness in her eyes, or a trace of the fear she felt? But the sunbeams on her skin and hair made her light up. Maybe the sun gave her strength to overcome it. Maybe for her, the sun chased away any trace of gloom. She caught his eye in the mirror, and with a smile, turned to face him. He set her platter of fruits and nuts on the vanity top.

"You brought me breakfast? You are always so thoughtful."

"I heard your stomach growling."

She giggled. "Oh, right. It is such a strange thing for a body to do. I am still not used to it."

A growling stomach was completely normal to him, but he'd been in this elven body for almost thirty years. It was being immortal that would feel strange now. Without asking, he took hold of her hand and flipped it over. A little pink scar where she dragged the blade over her palm remained. He ran his thumb over it and goosebumps rose along her arm.

"Thane?" she whispered.

He let her hand go. "Yes?"

"I think I keep dreaming about Atlanta because he is still looking for me. Even if Valeen did not tell him I am here."

He nodded. "She said he might."

"He will want me to go back with him. I know he will."

"I'm not afraid of him."

"I am," she whispered. "I told you before I would speak to him if he came but... I am terrified."

"I'll be with you."

"I do not want him to hurt you."

"He won't."

"You do not know him like I do. When he sees you with me, even if we are not *together*, he will lose his temper. He is powerful—so powerful. The things I have seen him do are incredible. He can drown entire legions of soldiers in one fell swoop."

As the god of the seas and a primordial, he expected nothing less. Thane lowered into a crouch before her; he didn't want to be looking down at her when he said this. Her brows rose in curiosity, and she slid her hands over her knees. "You know who else is powerful? You, Katana. You have the power of the sun. You can stand up to him, and I will be with you. You won't face him alone." He took her hand, the one with the scar and held it. "I promise."

She blew out a long, slow breath, curling her fingers around his, and gave a quick squeeze. "Thank you."

"I have that meeting with the dragon king and queen. Would you like to join me?"

"I would love to. You might need my help

convincing them, although you could always use your persuasion gift that comes with being a god."

Not since his previous life as War had he used that gift. Although, he knew the ability was there and he had considered that. But nothing loses trust faster than taking someone's will. "That is temporary. It would take constant control, and I don't want to do that. It will make them hate me. No one likes being controlled like that."

"I rarely use my gift either. You do have a good heart, Thane, whether you believe it or not. You can do this."

Chapter 33

KATANA

The dragon shifters were ruthless, brutal, and yet there was beauty. Beauty among the architecture, the gold and precious jewels, and the way they treated their young with a balance of softness and ferocity that came with being partially beast. Five half-shifted children with great wings flew above playing a game of tag, their giggles making her smile. Two of them were the eldest dragon prince's children, and the others, she assumed, were cousins of the family.

The dragon king and queen were supposed to meet Thane to discuss his proposed alliance in this lovely courtyard. Piper, Leif, and Fennan sat on a stone bench talking quietly. She sensed some underlying tension between them but after their argument outside the wall a couple days before, she hoped they were working through their problems. Piper felt betrayed by Leif for telling their secret, and Fennan seemed to hold a grudge that it happened. And Leif, well, he was still flirty, but more subdued.

Worry lined Thane's forehead as he slowly paced back and forth. She wished she could take his anxiety away the way he could for her. It was as if his touch alone chased the monsters back into the shadows. His voice pulled her to the present when her own mind played tricks on her, dragging her into the past and to places that weren't real, but felt so.

He wasn't just Valeen's former lover in her eyes anymore. He was *her* protector. The type of friend she needed. The night of passion he offered, as tempting as it was, made her realize that she felt more for him than she should in just a few short weeks. But from the first words they shared, she knew he would be special to her, even if it seemed irrational at the time.

The children raced away, chasing after the oldest boy, and left the courtyard quiet. Leaving only the soft patter of Thane's boots, and the gentle wind in the treetops.

"They said they'd be here at noon." Fennan looked up at the sky. "I'd say we still have a half hour before then." He stood and pushed his hands into his pockets. "Want to go on a walk around the grounds with me?" he asked Piper.

She lifted a shoulder. "Sure. Are you alright with that, Thane?"

He waved a hand. "Go ahead, and no rush."

"I'm coming, too," Leif said.

After they were gone, Thane stopped his pacing and sat beside her on the bench. "Things changed this morning. I'm going to have to show King Drake Ryvengaard."

"Oh." Katana's eyes widened. "We're leaving Adalon?"

"I only want to show him it exists. It's been so long, the king—and I'm sure many others—don't believe in the gods and realms anymore."

She nodded. "I suppose that would happen. It would almost be preferable to be like them and not have to live with such long memories."

Thane reached over and placed his hand over hers. Until then, she hadn't realized she was digging her nails into her thighs, scrunching up the fabric of her silk dress.

"You don't need to be nervous," he said gently.

But for a reason she couldn't place, a pit in her stomach had been growing all morning. Maybe it was the thought of this negotiation. Maybe it was that last night could have changed her relationship with Thane. If they had slept together, would he treat her differently today? She didn't want it to change. She didn't want to lose the simplicity and friendship that had blossomed.

Katana closed her eyes and lifted her chin toward the sun to warm her face. She thought of her former home, the smell of the sea, and the waves crashing against the rocks. She missed the beach and the ocean.

Thane suddenly jerked his hand away and she felt him stand up. Her eyes flashed open, and her heart thundered in her chest.

An all too familiar male with a broad back and shoulder-length, dirty-blond hair stood in the courtyard. An aquamarine robe cut off at the shoulders, reached the back of his knees. Atop his head rested a golden crown with accents of pearls and seashells.

"Atlanta," Katana whispered, sinking further into the bench. She wanted to be brave, but her muscles froze.

Thane took a small step, angling himself in front of her. That triggered her to get up and stand beside him. One thing she would not do was allow Thane to be killed for her, no matter how much she feared her ex-husband.

"Katana," Thane breathed.

She held up her palm to him and strode forward. "It is alright. I will speak to him."

"Just say the word," he said with a quick nod.

She was more terrified of losing Thane than her own safety. She would not involve him in this.

"Is it you?" Atlanta took a step forward with a big smile. "How can this be?"

She slowly moved toward him, until they were within reaching distance. "Valeen brought me back. We do not quite understand either."

"Valeen? I saw her. She didn't tell me you were alive. Where is she?" He looked around, eyes flicking to Thane then back to her.

"She is—here." She gulped, hoping he wouldn't sniff out her lie. Her sister had the weapon that could kill him and might be the only person he'd fear. "I have to ask, Atlanta, did you do anything to help her when the council came for her? You know she is important to me."

His eyes narrowed slightly. "That sounded accusatory."

"It was a simple question," she said, softening her voice.

"Of course I did, but she dug her own grave by

siding with the Primevarr and marrying that prick. There wasn't anything I could do once she crossed certain lines."

Katana glanced over at Thane. "No one deserves what happened to them."

He let out a chuff and rolled his eyes. "She trapped us all in Runevale for thousands of years. As far as I'm concerned, she does deserve it."

"She did it to protect herself from the council, but it does not matter now. We could help her make peace."

He let out a short humorless laugh. "You always were a dreamer. There will be no peace as long as she keeps the immortal dagger."

"Why should she not have it? She is a primordial, and she is fair and just."

"It wasn't decided for her to be a keeper. She stole it."

Katana pressed her lips together, but didn't argue with him. It was pointless. They rarely saw eye to eye.

"Let's go home." He shot a glare at Thane.

She took in a deep breath, heart pounding. "I am staying."

"You're my first wife. You belong with me in Runevale. You can have your palace back. We will have a celebration, and the entire territory will worship you."

It wasn't even a temptation. She'd rather live in a small hut in the middle of nowhere than go back to that palace that was nothing more than a gilded cage. "I do not want to go."

"Why?" he narrowed his eyes at Thane. "Because of him?"

Her heart lurched into her throat. He could not

think Thane had anything to do with this or he'd kill him. "I am not one of your wives any longer." Katana was surprised at the strength in her own voice. "Things are going to be different now."

"You were always much more than one of my wives. You're my first," he said sharply. "And things may be different, but it doesn't change that you are my wife. We're leaving."

"I said, I am not going. Valeen needs me."

"What could you do to help her? You're even weaker now than you were before. I can sense you are mortal, like a delicate flower that could be crushed with little force. You need me to keep you safe."

"I will be fine on my own."

His posture visibly straightened, and he pushed his shoulders back, puffing up his chest. "According to the laws of Runevale, as my first wife, you belong to me."

"Death freed me from those chains. We are no longer married, and besides, I do not *belong* to you."

Atlanta sighed and took her hands. Her skin crawled with his touch, and she pulled, but he clamped down harder. "Katana, I missed you. You were the most important person in my life, and then you were just gone. I didn't know what to do. Our children miss you. Please come home. Yes, I took lovers to fill the void, but they mean nothing."

"You took lovers long before I died."

"It's only natural for gods. But you'll always be my number one, my first love, you know that." Atlanta's jaw muscles flickered. "You're the goddess of day, a primordial. They mean nothing compared to you. If you come with me, I'm sure I can help with Valeen's situation. I have sway with the council. Pricilla can be... persuaded."

"You will only help her if I go?" she asked, face scrunching in confusion. "You do not even care that I am alive, do you? This is about how you will look if I do not go back to your side when everyone finds out I am here."

"Enough." He turned and began to pull her with him. "Come. We're leaving."

She finally tugged out of his grasp. Atlanta looked at Thane again, gaze raking over him, assessing a threat.

"Time has not made me forget, Atlanta."

"Where are you getting these ideas?" Atlanta demanded.

"I am not going. I do not want to be with *you*," she snapped, showing her fire for the first time. Fire that had been stamped out long ago. Maybe a spark of it was still there.

She didn't even see his hand coming, only felt the crack of it against her face. Pain exploded in her cheek, far worse than any blow he'd delivered to her before. This fragile body couldn't take hits like this. Everything around her tilted, she felt herself falling and then hit the stone. Scared to get back up, fearing what he'd do if she did, she stayed down and brought her hand to her mouth. Blood streamed into her cupped palm.

"Do not speak to me in that tone again," Atlanta said so calmly it was eerie.

The low growl and footsteps made her push up slightly, just in time to see Thane smack Atlanta hard across the face, then again with the back of his hand. A red welt appeared on both cheeks. Atlanta took the hits, then lifted his chin with a snarl. His crown was misaligned but held on. A bead of blood welled crimson.

No.

Panic shot through her, and on wobbly legs and with a throbbing head, she pushed herself up. "Thane, no."

"You won't lift that hand when it's someone your own size?" Thane snapped. "Are you going to do something or just stand there?" He reached back and pulled out his sword.

A scream caught in her throat. Her heart crashed wildly as she staggered closer.

Atlanta dragged the back of his hand across his mouth, wiping the blood away. It was difficult to make an immortal bleed. "I could crush you, mortal. Easily drown you in my sea." Water suddenly whirled around his legs.

"And I could peel your skin from your bones. Maybe you can't die, but you'll wish you could." He pulled out his other sword. "Choose your weapon."

Katana stepped between them and held up one palm to Thane and the other to Atlanta. "*Please,* do not fight on my account. Please, I beg you. *Please.*" Atlanta would end him, and she couldn't live with it. It would break her. She would want to die.

"Do you not see you are worth this fight?"

"Thane," she choked out, warm tears sliding down her face. They weren't from the pain. She looked back at Atlanta, water swirling faster around his lower half, a blue trident in his hand. "If you attack him, Valeen will come for you, and she has Soulender. They have an alliance. If you leave now, I won't tell her what you did to me. What you did to me for years."

Atlanta narrowed his eyes. "I will leave but don't think this is over, whoever you are."

Thane pressed forward, pushing his chest into her waiting palm. "You know exactly who I am, and I hope this isn't over. Say when and where. It isn't Valeen you need to be afraid of."

Atlanta looked him over again, scrutinizing every inch. "Ah, I see. War, the fallen god. Mortal and vulnerable. I remember now. If it weren't for the trouble you caused Valeen, I wouldn't even know you at all. You're nothing, and not worth my time." He lowered his chin and said to Katana, "We'll speak again soon."

He waved his arm down his torso, water moved around him in a great whirl, and then he was gone, with nothing left but a puddle. Katana's shoulders sagged, and she nearly crumbled to the ground in relief. The tightness in her chest was like a wound-up ball of twine, until Thane put his swords away and took hold of both of her arms to inspect her face.

"Are you alright?" Thane asked. "That must hurt. I can heal it."

Katana crumbled into his chest, gripping the front of his tunic, and sobbed. "I wish I was strong like Valeen. I wish I could fight him, but I never could. When it comes to him, I am... pathetic. Even after all this time." Her body shook with sadness, frustration, and relief that Atlanta didn't hurt Thane. She wrapped her arms tighter around him. All Mother Above, he could have died. She could be holding his lifeless body right now. Atlanta had killed for less.

"You shouldn't have to fight him, but Katana, you

are strong. You stood your ground. You should be proud of yourself."

She lifted her face to look up at him. "Thank you... but you should not have done that. He is dangerous. You scared me."

"I don't want you to be afraid for me. I will protect you. You don't have to protect me."

"Promise me you will not fight him again."

He shook his head, then wiped a tear with his thumb. "That is a promise I won't make, Katana."

Chapter 34

VALEEN

Valeen felt the connection she always had with Hel vanish, leaving her cold. Her skin pebbled and the hair on the nape of her neck stood on end. The glass of water in her hand slipped and shattered over the table at Nerium Oleander. The pieces exploded upward and cut into the flesh on her hands and forearms. She barely noticed the sting or the blood dripping onto the wood.

Hel said if he or Thane died, I'd feel it. But he couldn't be. It wasn't even an hour before she spoke to him outside her father's old smithy. After a few deep breaths, she searched for him through their bond. His end was cold and empty. Like a hollowed-out tree.

Panic clawed its way through her, and she opened her mind to him, *Hel, where are you?*

Silence. Long painful silence.

"What's wrong?" Presco stood beside her. His voice

sounded far away like he was at the other end of a long tunnel. "Valeen."

She focused again, he wasn't gone, he couldn't be. If he'd been in mortal danger he would have told her, she would have felt it. If he was dying, he would have at least said goodbye in her mind.

But what if it happened too quickly?

Tears blurred her vision, while blood slid down her hands, *drip drip drip*, onto the floor.

"Val," Tifapine wailed. "You're bleeding. Oh, no, no, no." The sound of her little feet scampered away.

Presco's large hands cupped her face and forced her to look at him. "Valeen, what is wrong?"

She blinked, bringing him into focus. "It's Hel," she breathed. "I can't feel him." Maybe he just wasn't answering. Maybe he was in Runevale and couldn't hear her. She closed her eyes and searched for him again. *Hel, where are you?* The silence that answered caused a sharp pain in her chest. He was as much a part of her as her own beating heart, and she'd certainly know it was missing.

With fear written all over his face, Presco dropped his hold and took a step away. "As in... he's gone?"

Tears spilled down her cheeks. "I don't know. All Mother, it can't be." She swiped at her face. She wouldn't accept it. There had to be an explanation. "He said he needed to look at an old book that was left in the Mages Tower down south and that he'd return this evening."

Tif was suddenly on the tabletop with a cloth. "For the bleeding." She pushed it into Valeen's hand. "Although it already looks like it's stopped."

The front door to Nerium Oleander opened with a

click and Aunt Evalyn came through, carrying an envelope in her hand. "This was in the door. It's addressed to Valeen." Her brown eyes lifted to her. "This is what they call you now, isn't it?" She dashed across the room and snatched it from her aunt's hand. "What has gotten into you, Laya? What did I miss? I was outside for five minutes."

She tore open the red serpent seal and before she even read a word, she recognized his perfect elegant handwriting.

Val,
I had to do something to save you. Don't follow me.
~Hel

The words, *"Don't follow me"* made the hairs on her neck prickle. Raising her chin, the fear of his death vanished, and she was suddenly furious with him. The only way she wouldn't be able to feel him was if he was no longer in the realm of the *living*. Hel wasn't dead but he was among them in the underrealm.

Why would he go there? To return the ring? She pushed the letter into Presco's chest and shoved her fingers into her hair. All Mother, she'd killed their brother.

The demons were natural enemies to the gods but now the feud was personal. They'd kill Hel before he even had a chance to explain why he was there. And if they happened to listen long enough for the ring to be returned, they'd kill him out of spite or trap him there as they'd done once before.

"Varlett isn't well because of the demon prince's

ring, and since we haven't found a way to break the connection, he must be trying to stop Varlett from dying. For me."

Presco's throat bobbed as he peered down at the letter. "That would be the logical solution, but you don't think he went to the underrealm?"

"That stupid, reckless bastard," she hissed. "That's exactly what he did!"

"Am I missing something?" Aunt Evalyn had a hand on her hip. "Who are Hel and Varlett, and are you talking about the land of the dead? I heard about the supposed sightings of demons a few months ago but... what does this have to do with you?"

There wasn't time to catch her up on everything that had happened. She'd planned to introduce Hel to her and explain everything when he was present. It wasn't exactly easy to tell her that she was married to the elf Aunt Evalyn knew as the Black Mage. Explaining Presco was her dragon friend from her previous life had been difficult enough. "I have to go."

"Go where?" Aunt Evalyn whirled as Valeen rushed past her.

VALEEN PULLED open the lid of her large brown trunk. Inside gleamed her Raven armor, cleaned and polished from the last time she'd worn it into battle against the goblins.

The trunk scraped loudly as she dragged it past Presco, setting it in front of her dresser. Jerking open drawers, she pulled out her thick, black, battle-ready pants and the long-sleeved top that went underneath the armor.

"You can't seriously be considering going after him."

"I'm not considering it. I am going after him."

"Valeen," Presco's voice lowered. His jaw muscles feathered, and he pushed up his glasses. "It's too dangerous. He—"

"Is everything to me!" She pulled off her top with the bloodstains, and Presco immediately turned his back to her. "This is the underrealm! You've never been there. It is dark and evil and death. We barely made it out with our full power, and that was when War was with us."

"All the more reason you must stay here."

"He would come for me."

Presco sat in silence with that.

"Besides, if Varlett dies down there, so do I. I can't wait here hoping for the best."

She quickly dressed and slid on her armored chest piece, then her greaves and vambraces, then raised her right arm so Presco could access the buckles. "Secure this for me."

With a frown, Presco turned and worked on the buckles. "If you're going, I'm going."

"I will not ask this of you."

"You don't have to ask."

"Let me rephrase, you're not going," she said. He finished the last tie, and she secured her weapons belt on her hips, then summoned Soulender to her palm. She didn't know if she'd be able to pull it from the aether in the underrealm and slid it into her dagger holster. With her Raven-winged helmet under her arm, she was out the door. Presco was right beside her.

"You are my queen. I go where you go."

Guards at the bottom of the stairs turned toward them as they descended. "Lady Lightbringer." The soldier sounded concerned. "Should we be preparing for an attack?"

"Always be prepared for an attack," she said, and slipped her helmet on. "I will be gone for a day or two. Thane is not here. Be prepared for anything. Listen to your commanders."

"Lady," he breathed, and the other guards all looked at each other. "That would leave Princess Talon as the head of command."

"No." She shook her head. "Presco is head of command. He knows more about war and defense than anyone else here." She patted his shoulder.

"Lady *Lightbringer*," Presco hissed with a glare. "We have more to discuss."

She strode ahead and quickly pushed through the front doors. Once she hit the bottom of the stairs, she hurried down the pathway to the stables. Presco grabbed her arm and jerked her to a stop. He'd *never* touched her like this before. Her gaze dropped to his big hand gripping her arm. His talons were out, then lifted to his face.

"Listen to me," he pleaded. "If you and Hel don't make it, it could be thousands of years before... you can't leave. You must stay. If at least you live, you'll be able to help him remember when he's reborn."

After all this time, she barely got him back. Even talking about him dying and being reborn was out of the question. There was no telling when or who he'd be reborn to. It could be hundreds of years. Then even if she found who he was born to, she wouldn't want to see him until he was an adult.

"You have the rune to travel through the portal back to Ryvengaard should neither of us make it out."

"*Valeen.*" It was a cry.

"I'm not going to die. I refuse, and you know how stubborn I am." Valeen lifted a shoulder. "Besides, I should be the one to return that ring. I was the one who stole it to begin with. I will see you soon, Presco." It was best if this goodbye wasn't dragged out. She didn't wait for him to respond.

Midnight trotted over to the fence, and she popped open the gate. Using her magic for a boost, she hopped onto his bare back and without looking at her closest advisor and friend, she nudged his sides. Grass and clods of dirt flew up behind him as they made for the bridge. Mist from the waterfall moistened her skin. Hooves clopped loudly over the stone as they raced across the ravine.

A shadow above blocked out the sun. Valeen looked up to see Presco in dragon form flying with them.

MIDNIGHT REARED up as they approached the stone portal in the unnamed forest. The sun still shined high in the afternoon sky, so she didn't have to worry about the monsters that lurked in there. She slid down and stroked the sleek black hair on his neck. "Go home, Midnight. The underrealm is no place for a horse."

He tossed his head side to side and snorted.

"I said, go. *Ekatha.*" She shooed him in the primordial language, and he stomped his front hoof. "Stubborn beast." She grabbed his face and pressed her forehead to his. He whinnied and pushed harder into her. The scent of hay and horse sweat was strong. "You can't go where I'm going but I promise I will come back. We'll go ride wherever you want." He nibbled at the fabric on her shoulder as she rubbed along his forehead, then gently pushed him toward home. With big brown eyes, he looked at her one more time, then trotted out of sight.

At the sound of rustling branches and heavy footfalls, she sighed. He couldn't just leave her be. Presco came into view, dark blond hair disheveled, glasses crooked. She thought he would turn back at the edge of the wood. "Presco, please don't make this harder."

"I had to see you here at least."

Her hard outer shell was beginning to soften and that couldn't happen. It was too dangerous for Presco to go, and someone needed to be here to watch over Palenor. She quickly turned and pressed her hand to the stone. The portal hissed and cooed. "The dark queen returns," the voices said.

"I am not the dark queen. For the moon and stars are light, and I have always stood for what is good and fought for what I love. Open the door to the underrealm."

"*He* said not to," the voices whispered.

"I don't give a damn what he said. I am the goddess of night, and I command you to open it. You cannot deny me."

"As you wish, goddess."

The center swirled into a dark mass. Presco was suddenly beside her and pulled her into a hug. His large frame made her feel almost like a child in his arms. Saying goodbye to her oldest and most loyal friend tightened her throat with emotion. "It will be alright," she whispered. "Have dinner ready for me, will you?" She wouldn't say goodbye. It felt too final.

"Of course, my queen," he murmured.

After a moment, she pulled away and decided it was best to run in.

Light seemed to be sucked out of existence. Everything warm and good gone with it as she stumbled out of a doorway onto the mushy ground beneath her feet. She glanced down to find her boot stuck in the body cavity of a dead demon hound. Its bright green blood covered the leather. Jerking her foot out, she sidestepped it and kicked some of the muck off. "Yuck."

A strange, deep blue-gray glow illuminated the sky in this realm, almost a perpetual twilight, not quite day or night. Everything was black, from the top of the tree's leaves to their twisting roots jutting out of the dark, damp ground. She forgot how *heavy* the air felt.

Thick bubbling tar popped and gurgled nearby. The rotten smell of it almost made her gag. Distant wailing and moaning made her stomach turn. There was also a strange clicking sound, like hundreds of insect pincers clacking together.

Something grunted behind her. She jerked Soulender and whirled. The point of her blade was at the tall, blond male's chest in an instant. "*Presco*," she growled. "I told you to stay!"

The door back to the living realms snapped shut, the light around the edges going dark. It was the only way out.

"I'm sorry I disobeyed you, my queen, but I

couldn't let you go and live with myself if you died. I am a dragon, and battle is what we thrive on."

Valeen sighed and shook her head. As upset as she was that he did not listen, a small part of her was glad to have him. This place was unsettling, and he made it less so. "You should not be here... Come on. Let's find them." The warm spark of the line she had to Hel buzzed to life once again.

I guess the note I left wasn't clear enough, Hel's voice came to her mind, and she smiled. *Get that pretty ass back out that door.*

I am the goddess of night, one of the most powerful beings in all the realms. I fear no one and I am never commanded by anyone.

Using my own words against me, I see. The laughter in his voice made her heart flutter. He'd told her that exact thing during their training to get her to remember who she was. "What is Presco doing here?" he said, very much aloud.

Valeen turned and there he stood, with a grip on Varlett's arm. His face had smears of black and green across it, as did Varlett's hair. "You didn't get very far," Valeen teased.

"Yeah, well, we were attacked almost as soon as we stepped through the door. How did you know I was gone so fast?"

She swallowed hard, giving another look to the dead demon hounds scattered around. There were at least five of them, and they were only the first of the types of beasts they'd encounter down here. "I couldn't feel you anymore. I thought—for a moment I thought you died. But no, you're just infuriating and didn't bother to tell me you'd be coming to this shithole."

He let go of Varlett and held his arms open, "I'm still alive, love." She ran and jumped into his arms and wrapped herself around his body, hooking her legs around his hips.

"Ugh," Varlett groaned, rolling her eyes.

Hel pulled her in by the back of her head and kissed her hard, sliding his tongue against hers. If one thing was true it was that he knew how to kiss.

As much as I wish you had listened, I'm glad you're here, he said into her mind. He set her down and pulled out a shiny, black-bladed sword. It was made of obsidian, a demon's weakness.

"Can we hurry up so we can return this damn thing and get out of this place?" Varlett held up her hand with the big silver ring. "And I'd like to get my beauty back. I look like shit."

"Yeah, you do," Valeen said.

Varlett scowled at her. "You look a little run down yourself. I think that white in your hair is spreading, goddess."

Hel ran his fingers through the hair around her face. "We need to hurry."

Chapter 35

HEL

Hel tapped the tip of his blade against the toe of his boot. "Presco, you need to go back while you still can."

"You want to make sure she's safe, don't you? Then accept that I will stay and see this through with my queen."

"It wasn't a request. I don't need to accept anything."

Valeen flinched but didn't intervene. Hel flicked his wrist and Presco was shoved to the door by an invisible force. "Presco, just go please. I want you to be safe, and Palenor needs you."

"My queen needs me."

"You've gotten into a bad habit of not listening to your *queen*," Hel snapped. He gripped the flat gold door handle and said low, "I won't see her break because you die down here, and you would die like a sacrificial lamb, make no mistake. Besides, I need someone to be there to tell Thane where we are in case we can't get back." He opened the door to the unnamed forest on the other side. "Goodbye, Presco."

"Hel, don't do this!" He roared right before he was forced through.

Even if his methods were brutal, they were effective and necessary. Presco had grown too comfortable not following orders lately. He'd directly disobeyed him when he told him not to interfere at the Drakonan's treasury back on Ryvengaard and almost got himself killed then. This was as much for his own safety as it was to show Presco Hel was still in charge. And he saw the relief in Valeen's face as much as he knew she'd feel guilt for allowing him to throw Presco out.

Hel brushed some muck from the demon hounds off his shoulder. "Now, there are three levels, and we're on the top, one for each of the princes and their own personal domains. This level was Morv's and well, he's gone. The next is Lavix. His land could be a frozen wasteland or a scorching desert depending on mood. And Servante is the bottom level, which is where we need to go. Unless they figure out we're here and make their way up, which is likely."

"What is Servante's domain like?" Valeen asked. She hadn't been to the lower levels. The one time Valeen had been here, they never left Morv's domain.

Servante's domain was utterly wretched, smelled like death and decay, and was hot and humid. The hideous architecture with twisted faces of pain etched into gray stone sometimes still haunted his dreams. It was devoid of color. Everything from the structures to the caverns and jagged mountains were a flat gray.

There were no trees or plant life to speak of. Nothing that could potentially bring joy. The endless screaming and the dim half-light made even his skin crawl. "The souls there fight each other for his entertainment. If wrath was a place, his domain would be it."

"Did you have to fight?"

"No, he wouldn't risk me getting the better of him," Hel said. "I was in a small cage, drugged, and surrounded by the hounds." In a way it was a blessing he was half delirious.

Varlett snapped her head toward him. "You were kept in a cage down here? When? How?"

In the many years Varlett was his... accomplice, he didn't speak to her about his past. He didn't share parts of him she could use one day. She knew what was public knowledge and what he planned to do in the future, but he'd never confided in her about his personal feelings. "As if you cared."

Varlett sneered. "We were friends for a long time, Hel."

"I don't think you know what friendship is." Friends didn't use each other for mutual gain. Friends trusted each other. Friends cared about the well-being of each other. He didn't care for her at all. He never really had. She was... useful. Part of him hated that it was true, that he was capable of being so unfeeling. But she wasn't Valeen, no one compared once he'd had her. Every other female he'd been involved with was a cold, burnt wick of a candle while Valeen was an eternal flame.

He glanced at Valeen, looking for signs of the death that stalked Varlett. The midnight-violet light down here saturated her ink-black hair and made her skin a different shade, but she hadn't lost weight. Her face was full of life, unlike the dragon shifter. It didn't make sense.

"If the next level is cold or hot and the other is wrath, what is *this* level?" Varlett asked.

"There is no purpose here." He glanced about at the skeletal black trees and the bubbling tar pits. Somewhere in the underbrush, he heard the slithering of a snake. "The souls wander in this half-darkness, listening to the wailing and suffering of others in the lower levels. And the beasts keep them apart from each other so there is no companionship." It was strange that more monsters hadn't sought them out yet. They didn't experience fear, per se. From what he'd witnessed they only had a need to fulfill their master's wishes even if it put them at risk. So to smell the fallen hounds scattered about wouldn't stave them off.

"This sounds like the worst," Varlett whispered. "To be alone forever."

One day, she was going to find out exactly what that felt like. He started ahead, swatting Valeen's ass on the way by. "Have that sword at the ready, love. There will be illusions, don't be fooled. There will be monsters, don't hold back." He hated and loved that she was here. Hated that he was scared to lose her to this wretched place, loved that she came down to the underrealm for him.

"How do we move through the levels?" the dragon wench asked, trailing slightly behind them. "I'm guessing there's no stairs or signs pointing the way."

"We must find the key to the next door," Hel said, over his shoulder. Shadows of some terrible creature moved between the ebony tree trunks in the corners of

Hel's vision. They moved so fast he never could get a lock on one, but red eyes glowed in bushes, watching them as they passed.

Fortunately, and unfortunately, Hel knew exactly where the key was and what he must do to get it. Hel pulled a silver compass with two needles from his pocket. It was one he acquired some centuries ago after several deals with unreputable people. The shorter hand pointed in the direction of the demonic keys, and the longer was a guide to the doors. He didn't ask where or how it was made, or how the human man from a remote realm acquired it. It was best not to know these things.

They walked for what felt like hours, being stalked but never attacked. There was no telling time down here, nothing to indicate change. The sound of fizzling water told him they were close. He slipped between two pillars of stalagmites and stopped at the edge of a tar-like shore. The lake's surface was placid even with the shadows of souls and skeletons floating below the surface.

Valeen peered into the water. "Why are we stopping?"

Hel ground his teeth and placed the compass back in his pocket. "The key is down there." He slipped off his cloak and hung it on the nearby stalagmite.

Her eyes widened. "In the water?"

"Unfortunately."

"Wait." She slid in front of him and put her hands on his chest. "You're not going in there."

"It's the only way to get the key."

Her brows furrowed and her pretty eyes pleaded. "You hate swimming, and that is," once more she glanced down at the murky waters, "Hel, what's in there?" He did indeed hate swimming, and she knew it was because Synick tortured him in it, drowning him over and over when he was young. He didn't die; he was an immortal god, but it didn't stop the panic, the passing out, the choking, the hatred of getting into bodies of water that reached over his head. But he didn't like having a weakness or fear.

Valeen pushed Soulender into the sheath on her hip and reached for the buckle on her armor. "I'll get it. I'm a good swimmer."

Hel growled and grabbed her chin, forcing her to look at him. As if he'd send his wife into putrid waters infested with the dead while he waited on the shore. "You're not going in that fucking water. I am. Wait here, and when I surface be prepared to help pull me out." He dropped his hand and looked across the placid black surface. "The water turns the extraordinary, ordinary."

"What does that mean?"

"It washes away magic so I will lose mine for a time. Which means you cannot get in. We'll need your power to survive this place."

She frowned. "How long?"

"I don't know. It could be hours, days, or until we leave this realm."

"Alright." She held his gaze and gave his hand a squeeze. "You can do this."

He smiled and kicked off his boots. "Of course, love. I've done it once before. Whatever happens, do not come in this water." Before he could think about it further, he took in a deep breath and dove headfirst. The cold was shocking, but worse, the power that hummed through his veins left like a whiff of smoke caught on the wind.

He opened his eyes, and the burn was instant. Clenching his fists he fought through the pain. He had to see to find the key. It only took a few moments to get used to the burn, and he searched for the blue-green glow the key gave off. It was faint but there, much deeper down. He kicked and drove his arms as hard as he could. The skeletons and decaying bodies floating around in a circular motion didn't seem to notice or care he was there.

The pressure on his body, that ache in his lungs, brought a slow anxiety creeping up his chest. It was his body remembering, holding onto the past of drowning. *Don't be a little bitch,* he said to himself and kicked harder. A few feet more and he'd have it. The key was rusted metal, about the size of his forearm, with a skull at the top end.

With his fingers within reach he hesitated, knowing what would come next. He remembered this moment like it happened yesterday. But his lungs were already screaming for air, he could not wait.

Fuck. If he could use his magic, this would be easy. He'd annihilate anything that moved, he'd materialize on the shore in a flash, but right now all he had was his fists and an obsidian sword. Even they were slow in water.

One, two… three, he snatched the key from the rock and shoved it inside the hidden pocket of his vest and pushed off the rocky bottom. The skeletons and undead rushed him. Boney fingers outstretched, teeth bared. He shoved them away as he pushed hard upward. Something hooked around his foot, and he kicked with his other, snapping the skull backward.

I need air. I need to breathe. That anxious feeling in his chest started to shift to panic. He swam harder toward the surface, driving his arms, kicking as hard as he could. The dead swarmed, holding onto his shoulders, around his torso, trying to make him one of them. Something sharp sunk into the soft flesh on the back of his neck, the only part of him that wasn't covered in battle leather. He clenched his jaw, holding in a roar. He couldn't lose the air. His elbow swung back hard on the thing that bit him. He kicked and punched, throwing off the monsters.

He snapped off an arm that wouldn't let go and broke free of the swarm. The blue glow of the surface was finally there. He burst through and sucked in glorious air, choking on the remnants that had gotten into his mouth. He swiped his face to clear the burning water from his eyes. Valeen was blurry but she knelt at the edge, reaching toward him. "Hel, grab the vine!"

The black vine hovered above the water next to him and he reached for it, but his hand went through. He grabbed for it a second time and it swirled away like smoke, then reformed. Her vines were magic, and the waters of the underrealm he was soaked in dispelled it. "I can't grab hold. I'll make it without." With a few hard kicks and strokes of his arms, he was close to the edge now.

Valeen leaned over the water, reaching for him, while Varlett held onto her, keeping her from falling in. It was the first time he'd ever seen them actually work together. "That's something I never thought I'd see," he muttered, reaching for Valeen's hand.

Their fingers were inches apart.

A sharp, bony hand wrapped around his calf, and he plunged back under.

"Hel!" Her scream echoed across the waters.

Several of the monsters had created a chain to pull him down. The skeleton that held him now was wrapped around both his legs, and he plummeted fast. He jerked the obsidian sword from its sheath and hacked at the bones, but they didn't break.

A splash hit the water; Valeen swam toward him. *Get out!* he screamed into her mind. *Get out of the water! Get out!*

The golden blade in her hand glinted in the little light there was down here.

Shut up, you stubborn prick! she yelled back.

Soulender came down hard on the skeleton, breaking its arm, then she sliced through the other like it was not even there. Another swam at her and the blade began to glow so bright that the monsters screeched and shielded their faces. She gripped his hand, and they kicked to the surface.

Varlett stood on the edge waving at them. "Hurry!"

She grabbed Valeen's hand first but slid on the muddy bank and fell in herself, slipping under the black surface. Valeen was the first to drag herself out, then Hel flopped onto dry land, gasping and choking. "I fucking"—he sucked in a breath—"hate water."

Stumbling out of the lake, Varlett slipped again but finally crawled out. "Stupid mud. Now none of us have any magic down here." She found a rock to sit on and inspected the ring on her hand. "Although I can't imagine the lake water dismantling the magic of a demon prince's ring."

Valeen was on her hands and knees beside him, dripping with the foul black lake. "Are you alright? Did you get hurt?"

"Fine." He coughed out more of the salty water. "You?"

"Good. Did you get the key?"

He reached inside his vest and grabbed hold of it then held it up. He rolled onto his elbows and knees and slowly rose. His muscles were weak from fighting off the creatures that tried to drown him. Gods, he hated being mortal, and he hated even more that he needed his wife's blood to stay strong. He'd need it soon. It seemed the time between needing doses of her was shortening.

"Hel, the back of your neck is bleeding." Varlett's voice was like nails scraping glass. He couldn't wait to get rid of her.

"It's a scratch. Let's go."

"Hold on." Valeen grabbed his arm before he could march off and stepped behind him. He heard her heartbeat quicken. "This is a bite."

"It wasn't a demon. No venom. I'll be fine."

"I can heal you," Varlett said.

Hel sneered. "I don't want anything from you. You've done enough."

"I'm offering to *help* you even though you've dragged me to this wretched place."

"Dragged you? You think I want to be here? I'm doing you a favor by saving your life."

"Only because of her."

"Oh, you can be damn sure that's true."

"Whatever, Hel." Varlett shoved past him. "But when that bite starts affecting you, don't ask for help."

Valeen handed him his cloak. *Look, I don't want her help either, but we don't know what that bite could do. Will you please let her heal it?*

He slipped his cloak back on and shook the water from his hair. *It doesn't hurt. I'll heal.*

You said the water made you ordinary. Ordinary beings don't heal quickly.

I don't trust her, and I won't let that demon magic anywhere near me. You shouldn't either. Hel took out his compass once more. "Come on."

The three of them didn't have to go far to find the door to the next level. It was a massive black thing standing between a black rickety tree with twisted gnarled branches and a mucky bog with shallow dark puddles. The door itself was covered in ghastly faces of people being tortured. Were they real souls or was it a carving? The thought of them being actual people being trapped inside there made his skin crawl.

"Let's hope he's in a hot mood today because with no magic and being damp, we'll freeze to death in a matter of minutes." He pushed the key in the lock, and it clicked.

Chapter 36

THANE

Ronan came around the corner and stopped, taking in the two of them. Dried blood covered Katana's chin and deep red spots stained the front of her light blue dress. Thane still buzzed with rage and fought to keep his inner monster at bay. The side of him that took hold during battle, that saw only red, hovered near the surface. It was only her desperate pleas that stopped him and Atlanta from tearing into each other and turning this prestigious courtyard into rubble. If she had not stepped into harm's way he would have swung his sword, and there was no telling what would have happened after that.

"I'd hate to jump to conclusions, so what happened?" Ronan asked.

Katana shielded her mouth with her hand, fruitlessly trying to cover the bruising and blood. "It was not him."

"I've been around many battered ladies in my day.

They always say something like that." He shifted his light blue eyes to Thane and waited.

Thane knew what this must look like, but he was disappointed Ronan thought this low of him. There were very few instances Thane would strike a female, and they all went under the category of her trying to kill him or in battle. Never like this. "Her ex-husband, Atlanta, the god of the seas, came here and wanted her to leave with him. She didn't want to, and he hit her. I know it must sound unbelievable, but the portals are open now. This is only the beginning of what will come."

"The god of the seas," Ronan deadpanned. "Well, I hope you drew blood for that." He nodded toward Katana's lip.

"I smacked him hard. I'd have done more but..." He glanced down at Katana to find her eyes still watery, and even though her cut had crusted over and the bleeding stopped, her bottom lip was still swollen and purple. "Let me heal that for you."

Shaking her head, she took a step back. "I will be fine. I am going to change and clean up." Katana hurried away without pausing. Why wouldn't she accept his help?

"Excuse me, Ronan. I'll be right back." Thane chased after her. Several servants passed by him, entering the courtyard carrying gold-encrusted chairs with red velvet cushions. A wooden archway followed close behind.

"Why is this floor wet?" one of the servants complained. "Grab something to clean this up before the King and Queen arrive," she said to another.

Thane stepped out of the way as another pair

rolled out a red carpet leading from the courtyard entrance to the new setup. Katana disappeared around the corner, and he swore under his breath. He slipped between servants bringing in tables and baskets full of food. He finally caught sight of the tips of Katana's disappearing hair as she entered the castle through a side door. He held the door before it closed and fell into step beside her up a set of stairs.

"Thane," she gasped. "You need to be in the courtyard for the negotiation. They will not appreciate you making them wait."

"They don't care about making *me* wait," he said. "Besides, I want to help you. Why did you run off?"

She paused halfway up the stairs. "It is embarrassing to be seen like this. You saw the pity in Ronan's eyes. You do not know how many times I saw that before. I think I hate the pitying looks the most."

"You didn't do anything wrong, Katana."

"You cannot understand. I fought back in the beginning," she whispered. "I hit him back the first time he struck me, and then he hit harder. And he was trained in combat while I... I was a dancer. I never stood a chance, and the people who knew had this look on their faces like they felt sorry but did not dare speak up, or worse, judged me for not leaving, but how could I have *then* when he hunts me even *now*? He would not *let* me leave."

Thane softened his voice. "Next time he comes for you, he'll be dealing with me. I can promise you that." He decided right then in that moment that he was going to kill Atlanta. Before he only *wanted* to; now he was convinced. He took out his dagger and pressed the tip of it to his palm.

"What are you doing?" she demanded, grabbing his wrist and twisting the blade away.

"I need my blood to heal your lip. It's rune magic."

"No." She shook her head. "No, I will not let you hurt yourself to heal me."

"Katana."

"No." Her lavender eyes flicked across his face. That was the firmest he'd ever heard her. "I will heal in a couple of hours. Please, go to your negotiations. I do not want this deal to fall through because of me."

He sighed and shoved his dagger back in his weapons belt. "That can wait. What if Atlanta isn't gone and he's waiting to catch you alone?" Her breathing hitched and he could see in her face she hadn't thought of that. "I will take you to the room so you can change, and you can come back with me. They will understand our lateness."

"Alright," she said softly. "And Thane?"

"Yes?"

"Thank you."

Thane was used to being the one seated on the throne, on the dais above those he negotiated with. People from all over Adalon came to him for deals, and when he lived as War, they also came to him for alliances and bargains. He didn't like being the one who needed something.

Fennan and Leif sat on his left, Piper and Katana on the right. Ronan claimed he would remain neutral and didn't choose to be seated across from them like the rest of his family. Instead, he sat at the far left, his seat angled center between the two parties. To separate himself further he didn't wear royal red like his parents and brother but rather a rich blue and there was no crown on his head. In fact, Thane wasn't sure he'd ever seen him wear one.

The queen's gown was the color of rubies, and her wrists dripped in diamonds. The gaudy necklace of diamonds and sapphires was as extravagant as any crown. Each finger was adorned with a ring of precious jewels. Bright red lips stood out on her wintery pale skin. The glacial eyes that Ronan inherited watched him with dismay.

Yoren, the dragon prince Thane fought in the arena not long ago, stared him down. His crown was smaller than the king's towering one, but its peaks and valleys were still larger than Thane's. Dragons loved their treasure and battle. It had to eat at this Prince that he was bested by a pair of elves in front of his entire kingdom.

Thane stood and placed his hands behind his back. "I think you all know why I'm here, and this time I'm not leaving without an alliance. Soon it won't just be Palenor under attack."

"Yes, we've heard the Black Mage is back," Queen Nyrovia said, raising her icy head slightly. "And, therefore, you know what our answer will be. We will not risk being infected by your curse. It's why we stay in our mountains. The Black Mage and his pale ones do not come here."

"There is an enemy more powerful than the Black Mage coming."

"So, says you, the Elf King desperate for an ally," King Drake stated. His golden crown full of rubies sparkled upon his sleek black hair. The sunlight brought out a warmth in his golden-brown eyes, almost softening the harshness in his tone. "Who is this mysterious enemy?"

Thane pressed his lips together. After overhearing the king's opinion on other realms and the gods, the truth would sound insane to him. "You will believe it when you see it. And you'll see it when I call you into battle. I am not going to try to strong-arm you with fear but with an offer, it is not gold or silver, treasure, you have. Nor is it trade or food, you clearly have an abundance of what you need here. I will take you and your people to your homeworld. Dragons hail from a place not of this realm, but a world called Ryvengaard."

The king and queen exchanged a glance. Prince Yoren narrowed his eyes. "You come offering the one thing our people have always wanted, but have no proof," King Drake said.

Queen Nyrovia added, "And I suppose you will only take us there *after* we fight with you."

"That is typically how negotiations work, Mother," Ronan said.

"I do not offer charity," Thane replied. "You get something you want, and I get something I want."

King Drake stood, shaking his head. "We will not be played for fools by your lavish tales, King Thane." He stepped out from his chair, threw his crimson cloak behind him and turned to leave.

"Do not turn your back on me," Thane snarled, his voice carrying with it the persuasion of the gods. It had been a long time since he'd used it, but the power rushed out, nonetheless. "Turn around and face me."

The king stopped and followed the command. His

expression twisted into confusion. "What is this magic?"

Thane strode forward and shoved his finger into the king's chest. "I will no longer tolerate your disrespect, *dragon king*. The gods do not pay homage to beasts. You *will* come with me to the northern stone portal without protest, and I will show you the truth." Thane softened his voice. "I'm not fooling you. I'm opening your eyes."

ON DRAGON BACK, they flew over the tall evergreen forest of the north until Thane felt the portal's call, like a warm wind swirling around him, pulling him closer. He directed King Drake to take a downward turn, his sleek, bronze dragon tucked his wings and dived. Thane held on tighter as his stomach seemed to leave his body. Wind tore through his hair and whistled in his ears. Ronan followed after with Piper. The silver queen carried Katana, Prince Yoren with Fennan, and Leif took up the rear with Dax.

The stone portal waited in a clearing surrounded by thorn bushes of wild berries and white flowers shaped like tiny bells. Thane slid down the colossal dragon's body and hit the ground. As commanded, King Drake shifted back into his human form and followed without protest.

Thane pressed his hand to the mossy surface of the stone circle. "Hello, old friend." These portals were created all over the realms by the gods, and they'd been abandoned for thousands of years.

Creeping vines and other weeds curled around the

weathered gray stone, but it hummed to life, warming under his palm. He grabbed some of the most obnoxious weeds and jerked them down. This area had not been touched by people in ages. "Hello," it hissed, sounding like several voices coming together as one. "Too long, it has been."

"I know," Thane said, patting the stone affectionately.

"Who is talking?" Ronan and the rest of his family had taken several steps back.

"The portal," Piper answered. "It startled me the first time too."

"It's sentient?" he asked.

"In a way," Thane replied. "They were created by the combined powers of the primordials long, long ago."

"The primordials?" King Drake asked.

"The original seven gods and goddesses of Runevale. We don't have time for a history lesson." Thane reached back and pulled out a sword. One thing he wished he had was his axe, it was his god blade and was infused with magic, making it much stronger than any weapon the elves could make. "Are you ready? I don't know what we'll be met with on the other side so be prepared for anything."

Thane's Ravens took out their swords and the dragons all looked at each other nervously. Katana grinned with excitement, practically bouncing on her toes. In preparation for this, he'd asked her to change into something she could move in, and that meant swapping her usual pretty dresses for plain brown trousers, boots and a long-sleeved, cream-colored top. The top still had lace and puffed sleeves, which made him smile. The dagger he'd given her was secured on her belt, but she carried no other weapons.

The center of the circle swirled with an array of colors and then stilled. The other side showed a vast, extravagant hall painted white and gold, not a forest or island as he'd seen before. The painted mural on the right side of the ceiling was of full dragons flying among clouds and intermixed with them were males and females both in their nude human forms but with wings. The left section of the mural showed the primordial gods and goddesses. The first to catch his eye was a golden depiction of Katana, with flowing bright hair all around her holding a sun between her palms, and Valeen with black hair that glittered like the night sky at her back, a crescent moon in each hand. It was truly spectacular and must have taken many, many years.

He'd silently asked the portal to take him to the dragon capital's portal where he knew the Drakonan treasury was. If Ronan and his family saw it, he'd have their allegiance.

Thane took a step forward and a tall male in a deep-purple robe with sleeves that covered his hands and a hood covering half his head stepped into view. He and Thane stared at one another.

"Who's that?" Ronan asked.

"I have no idea."

"He doesn't look hostile. Can we go forward?"

If Thane had to guess, those were celestial robes, and this portal had been deemed sacred ground. Thane glanced back at the dragon king and queen. "I had not planned for anyone to see us enter. Was it enough to see this?" Thane gestured toward the portal. "It's there. There is no room like that anywhere in Adalon."

"For all we know this could be an illusion," Prince Yoren said. "A magic trick. Or even somewhere in Palenor you staged for this very reason. This doesn't prove anything."

"I'm not a liar," Thane said, keeping his voice even. But Fennan gave him a quick nod, a subtle way of telling him he thought they needed to go.

What none of them understood was that this portal had not been used for thousands of years and stepping through with witnesses would mean there would be questions. They could be detained.

"We cannot come across as hostile. Are we clear?" Thane said, making sure to look at each of them. "They could very well see us as a threat. We will be as new to them as that world is to you."

Queen Nyrovia's eyes had doubled in size, and she slowly moved toward it. She'd drabbed down for this, putting on pants but still wore plenty of jewelry on her fingers. "We must see it. There will be no hostility from us."

"If I say it's time to go, you move your asses back here. No questions. No hesitation."

"Agreed," King Drake said.

Thane went through first. The difference in the sweet incense filling the room hit him instantly. Then the heat from a roaring hearth, opposite of the cool forest he'd left behind. The robed male took several hurried steps backward, knocking over a tall candelabra. Thane held out his palm, stopping it from hitting the ground with his magic, and curled his fingers to set it back upright.

The male pulled his hood back, baffled at Thane. "Who are you?" he said in a language Thane had not heard in a long time, but one he knew well. Ronan stepped up beside him, looking about the room in awe. The others quickly followed and without even acknowledging the male in the robe, the king and queen started picking up chalices and talismans and books left on tables surrounding the stone portal; this one was coated in gold and decorated in jewels.

"Don't touch that," the robed male rushed forward, and blocked Queen Nyrovia from touching the old pages of a thick tome. "It is too old and must be treated with delicacy."

"He said to stop touching things," Thane translated to the others.

"Murelien tongue." The male furrowed his thick black brows at Thane. He reached up as if he wanted to touch Thane's pointed ear but then pulled his hand back, thinking better of it. "Where do you hail from, Elf?" he switched with ease to Murelien. It wasn't uncommon for educated societies to know the main languages of each realm.

"Adalon."

"How were you able to use the portal? It has not been active in over two thousand years. We of the Elgotta have guarded this portal for many millennia."

Thane knew that name, Elgotta. He remembered this guild from when he lived here. They were the ones who kept and preached the stories of the gods and realms.

"He is the god of war," Ronan said, stepping up beside him with a hand on his hip. Thane turned with a low growl in his throat. That was not the introduction he wanted. He planned to lay low, show them around and leave.

The male gasped and nearly lost his footing. He caught hold of the back of the bench next to him and steadied himself. Then with a slow hand he turned and gestured toward a statue that was roped off and must be twenty feet tall, carved out of a gray and white marble. With an axe in one hand, a sword in the other, he was dressed in battle armor.

"The god of war," the male said.

Thane slowly moved toward it, taking in the details of the face, *his* face. He glanced back at the Elgotta and noticed the tears lining his eyes. "I remember you. My village was burning, and we were under attack. I was but a child, barely eight years old. My father was dead, and my mother was bleeding out on the floor, unable to shift due to a poison. I'd picked up my father's spear to fight off the attacker before he could kill my mother. The soldier laughed at me and would have easily killed me, but you were suddenly there. Your axe stopped his blade from coming down on me and you cut his head off. And you said to me, 'go boy, take your mother and hide. Do not come out no matter what you hear. War is no place for children and their mothers'."

Dragons had long memories.

Chapter 37

THANE

The streets of Pearl Avenue were filled with extravagantly dressed dragon shifters and the scent of the many florals growing alongside the establishments. It was well known for wealth and prestige, and it appeared that hadn't changed in the two thousand years since he'd been here. Many of the ladies had parasols to shield the hot sun beaming down. It was much warmer than Palenor at the moment.

The dragon from the Elgotta guild led the way down the street, pointing out various shops. "Down about a half mile from here is the Drakonan Treasury and not far from that is the main Drakonan estate with the famous opera house that caught fire months back. It's still under repair."

Thane shielded his eyes to peer down the street. The golden domed peaks of the treasury could be seen from here.

"How did it catch fire?" Piper asked. "I mean, you're

dragons, I thought you'd have that sort of thing under control."

"It's not public knowledge but rumor has it, it was the same couple who killed the young lad Caliban Drakonan."

A slow trickle of dread worked its way through Thane. He'd forgotten Hel killed a Drakonan.

"Who has the balls to kill a Drakonan?" Ronan asked.

"They haven't been caught yet. I hear it was a couple who befriended the family looking to get a shop on Pearl Avenue. No one knows the motivation behind the murder." He pointed across the pearl brick street. A white carriage adorned in gold pulled by hippogriffs tottered by. Piper, Leif, and Fennan stared at the half horse-half bird in awe.

"What is that?" Fennan balked. "And can I have one?"

Leif nodded vigorously. "Can it fly?"

"Yes, a hippogriff flies," Thane said with a grin. "But no, we won't be getting one today."

"Come on, sire." Fennan's face lit up with excitement. "We need them in Palenor. Sure, we have horses, but a horse doesn't fly."

"We're not staying long enough for that, but after the war we'll buy some to bring home."

Grinning, Leif and Fennan nudged each other.

The Elgotta continued with his tour, "That there is Presco's Potions, a favorite of the ladies of our city. He's the reason you see so many vibrant hair colors."

Katana leaned closer to Thane and whispered, "Presco, as in our *Presco*?"

"He did mention owning a shop in Ryvengaard," he answered.

"Let's go in." Queen Nyrovia was already starting across the street.

Thane pressed his lips together. If one person recognized him, it was only a matter of time before someone else did and that someone could be hostile. War may have been the god the dragons worshiped but time changed things. He was the reason the council attacked Ryvengaard, and many dragons died, and then he disappeared. "It's not a good idea. We should go back—"

"Just for a few minutes? It will be fun. What could go wrong in a potion shop?" Katana's smile was hard to refuse. And he had promised to show her other realms. If only they weren't pressed for time, but he had a feeling they needed to get back to Adalon. Palenor needed its king.

"Ten minutes and then we're leaving. I've held my end of the bargain."

The doorbell chimed as the others filed in, but Thane stopped just outside and stared at the WANTED poster on the wall to the right of the entry. It was Hel and Valeen.

Mr. & Mrs. Black also known as Zar and Layala. Suspects in the murder of Caliban Drakonan. Any information leading to the capture of Mr. & Mrs. Black will be rewarded by the Drakonan Family handsomely.

"Maker above, Hel..." Thane groaned.

"That looks an awful lot like you," a voice came from his left. Thane turned to find a male in a black uniform trimmed in green. He was nearing seven foot tall and had a thick brown braided beard that reached his chest with matching bushy eyebrows.

"What does?"

The guard pointed at the sketch of Hel.

"Oh." Thane cleared his throat and silently cursed Hel and their creator for making them look alike. "That's not me."

"I'd say that too if I were a wanted criminal connected to the murder of a Drakonan."

"If I were this Mr. Black, why would I still be in town? I'm sure he's long gone."

"Maybe you thought growing out your hair with one of Presco's potions would change you enough to go unnoticed." Another guard stepped up beside him, this one with his weapon drawn. "Lowlifes always return to the scene of the crime."

"I'm not Mr. Black, I assure you."

"We'll let the Drakonans decide that. If you come without a fuss, and we do have the wrong elf—who happens to look like Mr. Black and definitely has the blood of the gods, just as he did—then you'll go and carry on about your life."

"But if you want to make a fuss," the other said, pointing the tip of his sword at Thane's throat. "We'll just bring your body, and they can decide if we got the wrong person."

Katana stepped back out the door, eyes flicking between Thane and the two guards. "What is going on?"

"Then maybe we'll get to have some fun with that beautiful thing." The guards stared at Katana, mesmerized.

Heat flooded Thane's body, and his magic flared in

his veins, furious and ready to be unleashed. "You're making a mistake."

Katana lifted her chin. "Why do you have your sword pointed at him? Leave him alone. He has not done anything wrong."

"Give me a couple hours with her and we might just let you go." The guard's disgusting smile sent a shock of fury through Thane.

The other guard twisted Katana around, then gripped her arms from behind. She squealed and tried to jerk away from him. "Cuff him. I'll bring the girl. The Drakonans can throw her in as part of the reward. Never seen a prettier thing in my life."

"Get your hands off her," Thane growled. His blood seemed to boil.

"You best just shut your mouth and turn around, elf."

"You have three seconds to let her go."

Two more guards came up, claws out. "What's going on here?"

"One," Thane said.

"This idiot wants to fight," the guard replied. "We think he's the one who killed Caliban."

"Two."

"Thane," Katana pleaded. "We can talk to them and clear up this misunderstanding. You do not have to do this. Please."

Thane hit the sword up, grabbed the dragon by the wrist and twisted the blade out of his hand then shoved it through the base of his throat. In three quick movements, he jerked it out, slashed another across the throat and cut down the third, then pointed the bloody sword at the male still holding Katana. His eyes had gone wide, and his body was now covered in navy dragon scales.

But it was her face, those big doe eyes that scared him. She finally saw him for what he truly was. "I told you to get your hands off her. You want to die next, dragon?"

The doorbell chimed again, and this time Ronan and Piper came out with Fennan right behind. "Woah." Ronan's bright eyes swept over the dead bodies. "I saw him rip out a dragon's heart once. Shoved his hand right through the fool's chest. I'd let her go."

The guard's gaze shifted between Thane and his companions and finally released Katana. She wrapped her arms around herself, rushing toward Thane.

"You won't get away with this," the dragon guard said.

"Yeah," Thane pulled Katana behind him. "I will. Send a message to the Drakonans for me. Tell them the god of war was here, and the last thing they want to do is start a fight with my cousin, Mr. Black, also known as the god of magic. My condolences for Caliban but it isn't worth it. The realm gates are open once again."

"The god—the god of war?" The dragon stared at him for another beat, then turned and ran.

People all around stopped and stared at the blood running into the streets. Watched as Thane threw down the sword and it clattered to the ground next to the bodies. Droplets of crimson had smattered across Katana's cheek. She reached up and swiped at her face only smearing the blood across her golden tan skin. When she looked at her palm she began to tremble. With the horror in her eyes, he knew she was drifting somewhere else in her mind. To the dark place he would have to pull her out of.

He turned on Ronan and shoved him into the wall with a snarl. "We're leaving. Now!"

BACK IN HIS guest room at Ronan's, Thane dipped his hands into a water basin and watched the clear liquid turn pink from dried blood. He scrubbed at his wrists and arms to clean off his crimes. Once all trace of blood was gone from his skin he tossed his stained shirt onto the floor. He didn't feel bad about killing them. The only thing that haunted him now was that he was the reason for the horrified look on Katana's face, and *that* devastated him. She wanted to see the good in him and now she knew the truth.

But they'd touched her, threatened her, and that was all it took for him to justify their deaths. And there was no time to be detained and questioned for Maker knows how long. The Drakonans on Ryvengaard could have imprisoned him along with everyone else and then demanded proof he was who he claimed to be. Once they believed him, they'd want to know where Hel and Valeen were. Either way, he wasn't going to get out of there quickly unless he did what he did.

He was done proving himself to dragons, and if the king and queen still refused this alliance, he'd kill them along with the crown prince and make Ronan their ruler. The time for diplomacy was over. Maybe Hel was right. Sometimes it took rolling heads to get somewhere.

He dried his hands off on a towel and his bare feet

quietly slapped on the cool stone floor of his room. An envelope sat on the dresser with a red wax seal of a serpent wrapped around a lily. Thane tossed the towel beside it and tore it open.

> *Hello cousin,*
> *If you're reading this, that means I went to the underrealm. It's likely Valeen will follow me if she finds where I've gone. Varlett's ring became a problem. It was life or death for Val. I'll return to the land of the living as quickly as I can, but I thought the High King would want to know his Palenor is vulnerable.*
> *~Hel*
> *P.S. If I die, you better not touch my wife again. I'll come back to haunt you and this time I won't be so nice.*

Thane growled, crumpled the letter and tossed the note into the roaring fire. That bastard was always doing something reckless and dragging Valeen along with him. Surprisingly, he didn't have the overwhelming urge to go after her, to save her like he used to. Before this would have consumed his every thought. But she wasn't his responsibility. It really wasn't his duty to protect her anymore. It was Hel's.

His jaw ached from clenching it so tight, and every muscle in his body seemed wound up, but that was from many things.

And how in the realms would taking Varlett to the underrealm rid them of the problem? And when did it become so urgent he had to go now?

A quiet knock on the door irritated him even more. "What?" he snapped. If it was Ronan with any other news than good, he was going to knock him out. Then when he came to, they could talk. Huffing and puffing, he stalked to the door and threw it open.

Katana blinked several times and seemed to shrink in on herself. "I can come back." Her voice was soft and timid.

He felt his own face fall and the stiffness in his shoulders loosened. "Katana," he said, surprised to see her. He didn't think she'd want to see him for a while after what he did. He didn't want to have to kill those shifters in front of her. He didn't want to subject her to violence like that. She'd been through enough of it. "Is everything alright?"

"I... uh... I was worried about you."

His brows furrowed and he leaned his bare shoulder against the doorframe. "Worried about me?"

"I should have listened to you when you said it was a bad idea. I sided with the queen to go into the shop and then you had to... I hope you are not angry with me."

He rubbed his chin, confused by her reaction. Why would she blame herself? Then it hit him, she was probably used to taking the blame from Atlanta. "I'm not angry with you at all. What happened wasn't your fault. It just happened."

"But I should have listened to you. We should have gone back and those dragon guards would not have approached you and you would not have had to kill them."

"I will never blame you for anything. I killed those dragon shifters because I needed to. It's the way of this wretched world."

"How do you not feel bad about it?"

"I just don't. They would have hurt you. They put their disgusting hands on you. That's all the reason I needed."

"Oh." She pulled her gaze away and he thought he saw the beginning of a smile.

He pushed off the frame and opened his door further. "Would you like to come in?"

Without a word, she whisked past him then turned. She took in several deep breaths, making her chest heave up and down in a distracting way. "I changed my mind."

He scratched the side of his head. "About wanting to come in? You're free to go whenever."

"No," she said softly. "About your... offer." She pushed the shoulder straps of her dress off and it fell in a heap around her ankles, leaving her completely bare in front of him. "One night and no promises."

His heart seemed to jump into his throat, and he quickly closed the door so no one passing by in the hallway might see her. He pressed his back against it and slowly drank her in. The fire from the hearth and the candelabra on the dresser next to her lit her up enough to see every curve. It felt wrong and positively right. At the thought of touching her, he shivered.

"No promises for tomorrow?"

She sauntered forward. "The only promise I want is that you will forget about everything outside this room and focus on me tonight and promise you will not regret it in the morning."

He swallowed hard. He wanted this. Wanted her. "Katana, I..."

"No one has ever stood up for me the way you do, and you do not ask for anything in return." She pressed her hand to his bare chest and looked up at him. "I do not need your heart, Thane."

He picked her up by the back of her thighs and wrapped her legs around his hips. "Alright, Katana, I'll make you those promises. Tonight, there is only you."

Her lips crashed into his and he set her on the silk-covered bed.

THE MORNING LIGHT peeked through the window and the heat of the sun wasn't the only thing warming Thane this morning. A soft, luscious body lay draped across his torso, blonde hair spread across his chest. Her quiet breath brushed across his skin, making him think of how she breathed his name while trembling the previous night.

She giggled when he kissed above her navel and gasped, gripping his shoulders when his lips traveled below it. The sound of her quiet moans haunted him now. The way she arched into him, wrapping her thighs tighter around his waist and how surprised she was that her pleasure started to peak. She asked him not to stop until she cried out, and he didn't. If anyone deserved to be pleased, to be cherished and worshiped, it was her. This goddess who'd been beaten and disparaged and treated the way no one should ever be. It amazed him still that she kept that light in her, and even if the darkness took her sometimes, she came back with a smile.

With a blush and a soft kiss, she'd confessed it was rare that she ever felt that and always thought something was wrong with her. After she said that, he made sure she hit that pleasure point three times more. The sound of her losing herself, and that he was the reason for it, was enough to make him climb into ecstasy with her. There wasn't anything wrong with her. It was her asshole of a partner.

Thane found his fingers absently running along her back as he stared up at the ceiling. One night of passion. That was all.

No promises for a relationship.

No love.

No more.

She pushed her hair out of her face, then lifted her head, blinking slowly and smiling. She turned to the window, shielding her eyes from the light. "It's morning already?"

He smiled. "You said, 'it's'."

"I suppose *I'm* picking up on how you all speak." Pushing herself up to her knees, she sat back and stretched her arms overhead, showing off her lovely body with a level of comfort that made him smile wider. "I'm so hungry. You left me famished."

He chuckled, desperately wanting to pull her back onto his chest. She slid off the bed and he stared at her perfect bare ass as she walked across the room to pick up her silk dress. Maker, just looking at her seemed to set him aflame.

"Thank you, Thane. I needed to feel... desired. I needed someone to show me what lovemaking could be and," she grinned, "you are very good."

His cheeks warmed, and he slipped out of the blankets and wrapped the sheet around his waist. "I needed that too. To feel wanted." After being crushed months ago by the elf he thought he'd spend forever with, it was everything he could have wanted. She wasn't just a quick lay to fill a void. He could have found that with just about any female.

"Why do you hide yourself from me?" she asked and seemed to be purely curious. "I've seen all that you are. Even had you in my mouth."

Gods, and how good her mouth felt too. Lifting a shoulder, he leaned against the bedpost. "I guess I'm just not as comfortable as you are with my own nakedness. Although I could look at yours all day."

She giggled. "Every bit of you is lovely, and I'm glad I was able to experience it." She winked then quickly made her way to the door and gripped the handle.

"You're leaving already?"

"It is morning, is it not? We said one night. And we are going back to Palenor today. I need to gather my things." Everything came out rushed, even her breath, and he couldn't help but think she wanted to get away from him. A slow sinking weight in his chest made him rub the spot, as if it could make it go away.

"Yes," he said, and swallowed to wet his dry throat.

She pulled the door open, and he nearly choked. "Katana, you're not dressed. Someone could see you." He hurried over and pulled the sheet from his waist and draped it around her. "And I don't want anyone seeing you like that but me." With her gaze lifted to his, his heart beat faster. That was not part of their agreement. Anyone could see her naked if she wanted. They weren't in a relationship. There was no commitment.

"I was not thinking. I do not normally walk around other people's homes undressed." She tugged the sheet off and pushed it back into his arms, then slipped her dress overhead. "See you at breakfast?"

"I'll stop by your room when I'm dressed."

"Alright."

When the door closed behind her, he wanted to vomit. He did not regret their night, but did she? She couldn't have run out of here faster. He dressed quicker than he ever had before and tied his hair back without bothering to run a comb through it. But as he raised his fist to knock on the door, he paused. Was he being too overbearing? She probably wasn't ready yet.

"Thane," Piper called, stepping out of her room down the hall.

"Hi, Piper."

"Are we leaving?"

"After I finalize this alliance."

She pressed her lips together nervously and sighed. "Thane..."

"What?" He really did not want to have to kill the royal family to get this done, but his duty was to his people, and to make sure the council did not kill Valeen again. He wouldn't let it happen, and it didn't matter who had to die as long as she and his brother did not. "Did Ronan say something? They're not going to agree, are they? *Shit*."

Piper suddenly broke into a huge grin and lightly punched his shoulder. "Got you! No, they definitely agreed. Ronan told me last night. We have our alliance with the dragons, Thane. Taking them to their homeworld did it! They will come when they're called. We're going to win this war. We're going to save Palenor."

"Truly?"

"Yes!"

"And what about you and Ronan?"

She lifted her shoulder, and he could tell she was trying to hide disappointment. "I don't know, Thane. He's been different than I thought. I thought he would want to move forward, but in a way, I think he's lost interest. I know you wanted me to help with the alliance, but I don't know if he will marry me."

"That's not it."

"Did he say something to you?"

"I told him he couldn't be with you until the war was over."

She scowled. "Why would you do that?"

"King Drake threatened your life if he married you... dragons don't typically mate outside their race, and he is a prince. They are particular about their bloodline, especially the Drakonans."

"Oh," she breathed, and looked away, a flush staining her cheeks. "I didn't... I don't know why I didn't think about that."

"But Ronan wants to be with you. In fact, he wants to marry you. It just can't be now, otherwise, it could jeopardize the alliance. If the king tries to hurt you, I'll have to kill him."

"He told you he wants to marry me?" she started to smile. "Even if... I can't let him give up anything for me. If his parents don't approve, they could cut him off."

"Worry about that later. For now, I need to make a binding pact with the king and queen so they can't back out." He pointed at Katana's door. "Will you wait for her and go with her to breakfast? Tell her I'm sorry but I had to leave."

"Of course." Piper suddenly began to study him

from the top of his head to his boots and leaned in a little closer. "You smell like her."

Thane glanced down as if he could see her scent. "I do?"

Piper chuckled. "Yeah, Thane, you do."

He turned on his heel. "I better hurry. The king and queen are probably waiting."

"Thane." Piper narrowed her eyes and lowered her voice, "Did you... Maker, you did," she accused. "You slept with her, didn't you?"

Thane kept walking and couldn't help but smile. "Find me downstairs." Now all he needed was the dragons to sign a magic-binding contract. Things were finally looking up.

Chapter 38

VALEEN

Standing in front of the door in the middle of this eerie dark wood made her skin feel like spiders crawled all over her. There was no mistaking that they were followed. By what? She wasn't sure. Pairs of red eyes glowed among the blackened foliage all around them. Popping up out of the bog were yellow eyes connected to any manner of creatures below the surface. Serpents slithered in the branches of the trees above their heads. The door was anchored to the ground but nothing else supported it. On the other side was more of this seemingly endless dark realm. The sooner they got out of here, the better.

Distant wailing came from inside of the horrible door with terrifying faces in it. It was essentially a portal to the next realm of the dead. Something behind it screamed. Valeen gripped Soulender tighter. The golden blade gave her comfort. It had shined with a light she'd never seen before when those creatures attacked them under the water.

The skin along the nape of her neck prickled. It felt wrong here, heavy, dark, and even if she was queen of the night, there weren't stars in the sky and no moons to speak of. This wasn't a peaceful night where she could marvel at the heavens. Even the goddess of night wished for sunshine sometimes.

"Don't you think it's strange we haven't been attacked again?" Varlett whispered, glancing behind her. "I can feel their presence, and I know we're being hunted, but why don't they move in?"

"Maybe *you* haven't been attacked," Hel grumbled.

"Aside from when you took the key."

"It's probably the ring you wear." Valeen nodded toward it. "Or they're afraid of a weapon created by the gods." She tapped her golden sword against her opposite shoulder. They should be terrified of it, and if they tried anything, they'd find out why.

"They no longer have a prince on this level to command them." Hel keenly watched the inky darkness around them. "Demon creatures need a master. It's what they were created for."

"I'm surprised one of the other princes hasn't come then," Varlett said.

The door to the next demon prince's realm was unlocked but Hel hadn't pushed it open yet. With his palm pressed against it, he glanced back, garnet eyes flicking between them. "They don't know we're here, but they will soon enough."

A few beats passed and Varlett cleared her throat. "Are you going to open it?"

"The door feels cold. Very cold."

"So we have to wait until you're dry." Varlett turned away and started walking into the shadowy forest. "I'll find some branches and make a fire." Her figure disappeared into the umbra.

Valeen lowered her voice. "There's something she isn't telling us. I can feel it. She doesn't move like someone who is ill even if she looks terrible."

"It could be a curse of some kind, like the pale one curse, and we can't risk something happening to you. I hate that we have to protect her, but we do, as if it was you."

"When you fought with her at Castle Dredwich, every strike, every cut affected me instantly. I felt her stub her toe the other day. Why isn't this?"

"I don't know."

Valeen shook her head and started pacing. "Maybe the link between us only responds to physical harm. Maybe whatever is happening to her, isn't *harming* her."

His brows furrowed and he stared into the darkness she'd disappeared into. "What if it's turning her into... something else."

One look was all it took to decide they were foolish to let her wander off. Together they ran. The creeping sounds in the bushes and the snapping and popping of hidden creatures seemed louder. Valeen ducked under a thick branch and weaved around protruding roots until she slid to a stop.

Varlett sauntered her way with a stack of branches in her arms. "What are you looking at?"

"You're... still here."

"Well, where else am I going to go?" she drawled. "I can't open the door out of the underrealm without one of you. I'm not a goddess."

Time seemed to pass slowly, with the wailing like

nails scraping on glass, the heavy breathing from unseen things, and the feeling of doom like a weight pressing in. Valeen took her boots off and placed them close to the fire. Her armor kept the moisture in her clothes but taking it off put her at risk, and yet without her magic, she didn't know if they'd survive this place. Reluctantly she removed her Raven armor and hung each piece on branches near the fire. Hel took his shirt off and stood only in his pants.

The strange light seemed to make Hel's tattoos shift and move. The lily mark on his chest almost appeared to bloom. It was eerie what tricks of the shadows could do. He rolled his neck side to side and then turned his backside to the fire, and that's when she noticed the dark streaks spreading out from the bite on his neck. *What is that?* Her stomach dropped and she grabbed his shoulder, forcing him to turn fully toward the firelight.

"What's wrong?" He glanced back at her.

"Kneel down so I can get a better look at this."

He dropped to one knee and rested his elbow on his thigh. "I can think of better things I'd like to do from my knees."

"So can I." The light hit his back fully, and she clenched her teeth. The ebony streaks like webbing on broken glass had spread almost to the middle of his shoulder blades. This was bad. She'd never seen anything like it. Obviously getting bitten by something that was dead was going to have consequences. Hel was just too stubborn to admit it. "How do you feel?"

"Like I'd rather be fucking you on a beach somewhere."

Now is not the time for your blasé attitude. "I'm serious."

Varlett choked out a laugh, and they both looked at her. "I'm surprised you're not blushing and berating him for his dirty mouth, Val."

She slowly rolled her eyes to Varlett and scowled at her. This dragon seriously needed to die. "You don't know me, Varlett, and you certainly don't know anything about our sex life."

"He told me all about you. How you lay like a dead fish, too proper to make a sound when he's railing you. How he wished you'd suck him off once in a while, but you never did."

Anger flushed her cheeks, and she accidentally dug her nails into Hel's shoulder, until he said, *Put the claws elsewhere. I never said that.*

Of course he didn't. It was just more of Varlett's lies and manipulation to try to drive a wedge between them again. She knew Hel wouldn't have said that even if he'd been angry with her. Mostly because it simply wasn't true. They had chemistry she'd never felt with anyone else, and it showed when they made love.

Hel pushed up and staggered slightly, shoving a finger at her. "First of all, I've never said a damn word about her to you."

Valeen held onto his arm. It was only her grip on him that kept him from falling over. The creatures around them, and Varlett shouldn't see him so weak. All Mother, if the princes showed up now... *You need to sit down and rest for a moment.*

"Second, if I did say anything, it would be that she is the sunrise after a long dark night, and the reason that I still wake up each day. She is my heart, the only one I have, and if you say another disrespectful thing about her, Varlett, I will invade your mind and turn you into my puppet on a string to dance for the demon princes forever."

Protective Hel certainly knew how to make her feel wanted.

"In your state you couldn't touch my mind," Varlett sneered.

"Want to find out?" He challenged.

Hel, now is not the time. You could hurt her more than you mean to and I don't know what that means for me. She stepped behind him and touched the outside of the bite mark; his skin was flaming hot. "Hel, how do you truly feel? Don't you dare lie to me."

"I'm a little dizzy," he murmured.

If he admitted that, he was more than a *little* dizzy. He'd downplay it.

"Are you ready to ask for my help?" Varlett twirled a lock of her silvery hair around her finger.

"I'd rather die," he snarled at her, then one of his knees buckled.

"Hel!" Valeen wrapped her arms around him from behind, but his weight pulled her with him to the ground.

He was on his hands and knees, breathing hard, heart pounding. *Promise me you will not let her anywhere near me with that demon's ring. You must not trust her. You understand? You don't know what she could truly do with that kind of magic.*

She knelt and took his face in between her palms. He was too warm. *I won't watch you die.*

I wouldn't ask this of you if it wasn't important.

His half-closed eyes and blown pupils sent her pulse racing. "Hel, we have to do *something*." She still couldn't feel her magic; it was like a spark between flint and rock that just wouldn't catch flame, and it made her sick. Did that pool shut off their powers until they left this realm? She'd racked her brain on what to do but came up with nothing. Without magic to heal him, all she could do was wait.

Hel's rough hands slid along her neck and up into her hair. "I am already prone to wickedness. I'm not a good person. If I'm touched by demon's magic—" he went back to speaking to her mind, *I don't know what it will do to me. I don't know who I could become... who she could turn me into.* His eyes were glassy, and his cheeks flushed from fever. "I will survive this bite. My body is pushing out the venom. I can feel it. Trust me. Please."

"You are better than you believe you are," she whispered.

"No, I am not."

She kissed him hard on the mouth. "Yes, you are." *Your serpent's bite doesn't scare me.*

He managed to half-smile. "Don't let her touch me no matter what happens. Promise me."

Gently, Valeen pushed away the sweat-damp hair stuck to his forehead. It wasn't a promise she wanted to make. She'd take a wicked Hel over a dead one. But she had to trust him. "She won't touch you. I promise."

Not long later, Hel laid on his side with his eyes shut, shallow breaths coming slower. Valeen nibbled on the edges of her nail, pacing next to him. Varlett sat at the edge of the fire, arms slung over her knees. It was difficult to tell if Varlett had any care at all for Hel as she stared at him. Would she save Hel the way she did

Thane? Did she ever love Hel? She wasn't certain Varlett knew what love actually was, other than love for herself.

"He would rather die than let me help him, huh?" Varlett picked up a stick and tossed it into the blue flame. "It wasn't always that way. He used to let me do many things to him."

It took every ounce of self-control not to react to that statement. This connection between them was going to drive her mad.

Dread and agony slowly increased with each passing moment he didn't get up. Valeen slipped her boots back on and trod down a trail in the black foliage while pacing next to Hel. *I could drag him to the door and take him back home, then I'd regain my powers, and he would recover faster on his own.*

"I healed Thane, and nothing bad has happened to him." Varlett tapped her talons together in a steady rhythm. "I promise I won't harm Hel."

"He said no, Varlett. I know you're used to manipulating everyone, but no."

"You'll let your mate die?"

"He won't die." Hel was strong and his will to live was as fiery as her temper.

"He's dying! Look at him!" Varlett shot to her feet. "I've never seen him like this. Never."

Valeen's stomach turned and she stared at his sheet-white face, the sweat beading on his brow and temples. His eyes fluttered and he let out a soft groan, curling in on himself. She dropped beside him, holding her hand against his forehead and then his cheek; his skin was on fire. "Hel, we have to go back."

"No," he panted. *We have to do this to save you.*

"I'm... I'm..." he groaned again and started shivering. "Fine. Just a little longer."

"Move." Varlett pushed her hip into Valeen, nearly knocking her off balance. "There's no more time."

"Don't touch him." She shoved Varlett and knocked her on her ass. It felt good to finally do *something*.

Varlett sprung to her feet once more. "Get out of the way. I'm not getting trapped down here if he dies."

Valeen pulled her blade, metal sliding against metal, and stood over Hel. "You will not touch him."

Her gut said not to trust her to use magic on him even under the guise of healing. Varlett had proven time and time again she was the enemy, and letting her touch Hel with that ring wasn't going to happen, she made a promise. Even if she hadn't promised Hel, Varlett was starting to look more like a demon by the minute.

A slow trickle of dread slid down her spine. Varlett *looked* like a demon... the ring wouldn't come off her finger, the third prince Morv was dead... her eyes were changing, *had* changed to red, and her skin was blue-gray like one of the princes. Even her hair was white.

All Mother above, she wasn't *dying at all*. She was turning into a demon, and not just any demon. She resembled the rulers of this realm.

"You can't use that blade on me. You'll hurt yourself," Varlett purred, starting to circle. She had her sights set on Hel with a possessiveness that had the hackles on Valeen's neck rising. "He should be mine, Val. We are much better suited for each other. We crave power, and he doesn't realize that with me, he could rule all of Runevale. You hold him back from what he could be. He wants power. He craves to be the ruler that all worship at his feet. Even his queen. I crawled on my knees for him, but you, you're too proud."

If she could claw out her eyes, she would. Gouge them out and feed them to the disgusting demon hounds. "You are so pathetic it's almost sad. He doesn't want power. He wants vengeance. He fights because he must."

"Are you so certain? He wasn't afraid to let me see who he truly is and it's as dark as this place. He even said himself he is not good. You're trying to turn him into something he is not. You're trying to turn him into Thane. You could go back to him, you know. He still loves you."

"Shut up." Valeen gripped the sword handle hard enough her hand ached. "I do know Hel's heart, and it belongs to me. He's *my* mate."

"Come on, Val. You're lying to yourself." She kept circling like a hawk, waiting for an opening. "You've seen the darkness in him, and it's blacker than mine."

"He only did those things to save me, to protect me."

"You think so? He does it because he enjoys being wicked. Is that what you truly want? You're supposed to be better than that, *Lightbringer*."

Valeen kept her sights on Varlett and slowly squatted down. "Get up, Hel. We have to go."

"I need just a few more minutes," he said through chattering teeth.

"You're not going anywhere with him." Varlett took a quick jump forward. Valeen jerked a throwing star from her belt and flicked it at Varlett. It cut through the air with a whistle; she turned her face, but it still grazed her cheek, leaving a two-inch gash.

Pain Valeen could handle.

Pain was temporary but letting Varlett get ahold of Hel might not be.

She waited for the sharp sting to mirror Varlett's, but it never came. She reached up and found no blood.

Something had changed...

Several pairs of glowing red eyes that had watched from afar drew closer. Low growls and hisses made the hair on her arms rise.

Reality flashed across Varlett's face, and her talons grew longer and sharper.

"You know what I think?" Valeen said, rising to her full height. "I think that all your past transgressions have come back to haunt you... *demon*. You've finally become what you always were inside."

"It doesn't change anything." Varlett's eyes glowed crimson now.

"Apparently it does. That spell you had over me is gone." Valeen threw another star, and it sliced into her other cheek, eliciting a hiss then a low growl from her nemesis. It was time to take sweet vengeance. This dragon had ruined her life. Had taken Hel from her and was the reason they were here in this shithole to begin with. Valeen raised Soulender and stood at the ready. "You know why I think that is? The connection is severed because the lake washed away the magic." She laughed, who could have ever guessed the underrealm would be the thing to end the spell between them? "You wanted to be immortal, it looks like you'll get your wish and live forever in the underrealm."

"Well, if it is true." Varlett crouched into a fighting position. "You're in my domain now."

Varlett sprang at her, talons cutting through the air

with blurred speed. She brought Soulender up to meet her strikes and sliced through the first talon. Varlett gasped and pulled back. "You're going to regret that!"

"I'll keep your talon for a trophy and wear it around my neck. And I'll carve 'the dragon who thought she could betray the goddess of night and live' on it" She kicked out, connecting the toe of her boot with Varlett's thigh, then swung her blade aiming for her chest. Varlett bent backward in an unnatural way to avoid the strike, kicked up, and slammed her boot into Valeen's forearm, nearly knocking Soulender from her grasp. *Shit.* The impact made her hand tingle, but the pain was nothing. It was a step closer to killing this wench.

Varlett squared her shoulders and jerked her own sword free. The next clash came in a fury of swings and blades cracking. This wasn't just about *now*; this was for the past, for the absolute devastation she'd put not only Valeen through, but Hel and Thane too. All her pent-up rage from being forced to hold back rippled through her movements, her swings came harder, faster, her kicks and parries that of a goddess as old as time. Her fist smashed into Varlett's nose, splitting open the bridge. She sliced into her thigh and opened a good five-inch gash.

A guttural growl ripped from her, like that of a beast. But Varlett too was a seasoned warrior, and it would take more than that to bring her down. That ring and this place gave her supernatural abilities she hadn't had before. She was faster, a match for Valeen in speed, and the hits vibrated her arms and hands. Varlett's elbow cracked her in the mouth, making her stumble back a step. If there was pain, she didn't feel it.

A coppery taste filled Valeen's mouth, and she spit. "That's all you've got, *bitch*?"

Roaring through her teeth, smoke billowing from her nostrils, she charged again. Valeen dipped and bobbed, anticipating the moves, learning her weaknesses. They hit swords and the black blade Varlett wielded shattered into a thousand splinters, sounding like glass breaking. Valeen swung at her throat, but she maneuvered just out of reach and stumbled over a protruding root and hit the ground.

"Get up, Varlett. When I kill you, I want you to be standing so I can watch you fall." She was waiting for her to shift into her beast form, for the wings to stretch and her mouth to turn into a vicious snout, but not even her scales made an appearance.

Varlett rolled backward, springing deftly to her feet. The amber of her eyes was completely taken over by crimson now. Her skin held no sign of ever being the bronze it once was, changing entirely to blue-gray. "You're not getting out of here alive. I will kill you and keep him. Together we will rule both the underrealm *and* the lands of the living."

She swore she heard Hel curse her, but it was drowned out by the rising growls and screeches surrounding them. The demons were getting restless and charged. As if the fighting and contention invigorated them.

Then it wasn't only their sounds anymore.

Several demon hounds came forth out of the shadows in low crouches. Three hounds moved in close behind Varlett, sniffing and becoming familiar. They weren't snarling or hostile... They were curious, almost as if greeting a new master.

Not almost... that's exactly what they were doing.
"Hel."

Can't take her down without me? He chuckled and then coughed.

There are demons everywhere. Do you want your wife to throw you over her shoulder and carry you out? Because I will if you don't get up.

He chuckled again. *Damn, I'm getting up.*

It was time to end this. Valeen went for her again, sword raised and hacked down—a hunch-backed hound jumped in front of Varlett and took the death blow.

Shit.

Ten other hounds crept in to surround and protect Varlett. Growling and snapping at Valeen.

Leaving her here with the dead would have to be as good as killing her and erasing her from existence. She'd never escape this place. Holding the point of her glowing blade at the beasts kept them back but wouldn't for long. Valeen backed up until she dropped to Hel's side and grabbed his arm. "Hel, now!"

"Alright." He groaned and pushed to his hands and knees. "I'm up." He got to one knee and rolled his neck from side to side. The black streaks from the bite had faded, and the teeth marks were now light pink scars. The tightness in her chest loosened some.

He bent over and scooped up his onyx sword, nails scraping the black soot it laid in. He raised his chin, eyes sweeping across the darkness before them. "What the fuck is going on?" He sounded exhausted as he staggered to his full height.

"I believe... she's become one of *them*. She was never dying. She was turning."

That tired look on his face turned to something darker. "I didn't anticipate this."

"I should have seen it before, but it doesn't matter, the link between her and I is gone, Hel. I'm free."

Hel took hold of her hand, eyes boring into her. "Are you absolutely certain?"

"It's done. I think it was the pool."

"Gods, you're right. It would have washed the magic away." He glared at Varlett who was still being sniffed and investigated by the hounds. She had a feeling it would only be moments before they turned on her and Hel at Varlett's command.

Valeen glanced at her armor hanging on the tree. It was too far away to grab. So were Hel's shirt and cloak. *It's time to go.*

Not until she's gone. I never want her to come back and haunt us. He took a step toward her, and Valeen jerked on his arm.

She is about to realize the demons will follow her command and neither of us have our magic. We need to leave before that happens. This place is death for her, Hel.

With a low frustrated growl, he hooked his arm around her waist; a coolness swept around her, and the pull to move through space tugged, but they went nowhere. His magic failed. "Fuck, this might be worse than if I couldn't get my dick up."

They would have to do this the old-fashioned way and run.

Her old enemy stroked the crown of the demon hound's head. It rubbed against her almost like a cat. "Mmm, my new pets." All the demons that had emerged seemed to be waiting.

NIGHT MEETS THE ELF QUEEN

Still holding Soulender at them, she took Hel's hand, and they slowly retreated. The hundreds of red eyes in the surrounding dark woods moved closer with each step she took back. Gangly skinny creatures with grotesquely large heads rose out of the bog waters dripping slime and muck.

Hel glanced over his shoulder and quick as a viper strike, he swung. She whirled to see a faceless, gangly creature right behind her squeal and sputter as it tipped backward. When it hit the ground small serpents swarmed it, burrowing into its flesh.

Even her nightmares couldn't have come up with this place. A wave of panic hit her. The darkness, the screams and growls, the evilness of this realm were getting to her head. This was worse than being trapped in the dragon treasury with the gargoyles.

Run, Valeen. Hel shoved her in the back, and she stumbled into a sprint. The exit door was far from here, across a plane of ghostly trees, murky bogs, and black lakes they'd crossed.

Everything looked the same. It would be easy to get lost. They'd traveled for what felt like hours to get to this point, but as she thought of leaving a light beam shot up into the sky. It was far, but it came from the door that led out of the underrealm.

"Hel, my dear," Varlett cooed. "Think of all we could do together now. With this ring, with this power." Valeen risked a peek and found Varlett marching after them with hundreds of demons in her wake. Even if she couldn't see what they were, their eyes glowed in the darkness. "Nothing could stop us. With your army of cursed elves and my demons, we could take down *anyone*. Immortality, it's yours.

Revenge—taken. Make me your queen and you will be king of all the realms."

"I already have my queen." *Don't look back. Keep running.*

A scream full of rage rippled across the land. "Kill them!"

The demons heard those words and rushed like a coming storm. Their feet beat against the black mushy ground. Valeen weaved around spindly trees and leapt over decaying men who screeched and tried to reach for her. Hounds with their massive, hunched shoulders, protruding ribs, and oversized snouts with jagged teeth raced up behind them.

Out of the shadows came several tall humanoid creatures with gangly limbs, pointy fingers as long as their forearms, no eyes, no nose, only an oversized mouth. Their skin was gray and sagging from their bones.

The ground shook from a gluttonous thing on two legs, carrying a club in each hand. Its black eyes looked like small pebbles in its two fat heads.

Venom-dripping jaws snapped. Roars and footsteps rumbled the ground with the charge. "I said not to look back." Hel took hold of her wrist and pushed them faster. His long legs covered twice the distance she could.

Valeen swung at the first demon hound to reach them, lopping off its head. Green blood spurted on the ground and the others roared. Soulender sliced into demon flesh and crushed through bones. Side by side, she and Hel fought, hacking, and screaming rage of their own.

Bodies were left in a trail behind them, hulking,

rotting things. Wails and screeches rang throughout the darkness. The demons kept coming, their numbers seemed endless, but the immortal blade shined brighter with each kill. It hummed with power that even the demon lake could not wash away.

Demons crept out in front of them to block their path. Valeen skid to a halt, catching Hel by the elbow. Hundreds more demons came from all directions until they were completely surrounded.

A cold wind ripped through the air, and the demons started to shake and backtrack. To the left the hounds backed off and parted for the two brothers who ruled this world.

Chapter 39

KATANA

Katana quickly bathed and changed into a pretty dress with bright florals and lace sleeves. Standing before the mirror she spent a little extra time on her hair, braiding half of it back into a crown, and applied a touch of blush to her cheeks and rose-colored balm to her lips. The night with Thane had been wonderful, the best night she'd had...maybe ever. Giving into Thane was everything she'd fantasized about and more.

She tried not to let the deal they made ruin her good mood. One time, nothing more. Already she felt the heartache creeping in. Why she thought she could get through it without feelings when she'd had them before last night was beyond her. *I literally call him my protector. Like he's mine. But he's not.*

A quiet knock on the door made her jump. She quickly slipped on her shoes. Maybe Thane would change his mind, and he'd come to confess he wanted more, not just lust. That last night made him realize he wanted to at least... try.

Taking in a deep breath, she pulled the door open, and her smile fell. "Piper."

"Hi, Katana. Thane had to go meet with King Drake, but he asked me to walk you to breakfast."

"Oh." She hated the sound of disappointment in her own voice. There went her dream of his confession of undying love. Well, she didn't want that yet. They'd only known each other a few weeks, she sounded naive even thinking he'd be in love with her already... or at all. "Will he be joining us?"

"I'm not sure."

This felt more like rejection than anything. Had she taken too long to get ready? She tried to hurry. Or had he rushed out of there, so he didn't have to face her? Maybe he thought talking with her would be awkward. *Damn it, this is not what I wanted.*

Breakfast felt like an eternity. The food was delicious and Piper, Fennan, and Leif were entertaining company but all she could think about was their High King's absence. Even the lovely music drifting through the open airy room full of sunlight, and the beautiful artwork of statues and paintings throughout the space couldn't take her mind off him. She was about to stand and return to her room until it was time to leave when she heard his voice in the outside hall.

A pit in her stomach deepened and yet the very sound of him sent a tingle down her spine. A moment later he walked through the archway with Prince Ronan at his side, and his emerald-green eyes went straight to her. His jaw muscles flickered and without a smile, he went directly to the banquet table. Her heart thrummed in her ears and heat rose in her cheeks.

She was going to be sick.

One night, nothing more. She chanted in her mind but got up from the table. She knew what she agreed to. There was no reason to be upset now.

"Would you like me to walk you back to your room?" Leif offered.

"Oh, no thank you. I can manage on my own. Enjoy your meal."

She hurried out of there as fast as she could and barely made it halfway down the corridor when she heard footsteps. Slowing, she turned and said, "Leif, I—oh." She blinked at Thane.

"Not Leif," he said.

"I can see that." She couldn't help but smile.

"Where are you going?"

"Just to pack my things." Never mind that she'd already done it.

"Did you get enough to eat?"

"I did. Thank you for asking."

With a sweep of his arm, he gestured for her to continue walking and fell into step beside her. "The contract is signed. They will come to our aid."

Beaming, she grabbed his wrist. "Really?"

"Yeah."

"That's wonderful news. I'm proud of you." She dropped her hold and tucked her hands behind her back.

He smiled at her. "Thank you."

An awkward silence fell. The sounds of birds chirping outside the windows and laughter from children drifted through the hall. Would it be appropriate to ask him how he felt about last night? Or should she just let it be?

He cleared his throat. "Ronan and Dax will take us to the portal, and we'll be back at the castle today."

They made their way up the stairs and down the hall to where their rooms were. "That's great." Ugh she hated that everything felt... stilted.

He stopped at her door and dipped his chin. "Well, I'll leave you to pack your things."

She tugged down on the door handle but turned back to him. "Thane?" He hadn't left yet.

"Yes?"

Tell him you want more than one night! "I really enjoyed last night, and I hope it does not change things between us."

He smiled and sighed in relief. "I liked last night too. I don't want it to change our friendship."

Friendship... "Right. Then we will not let it."

"I'll be packing my things as well and meet you downstairs."

"Alright."

THE RIDE to the portal was quick and the walk back was filled with banter and play between Leif, Piper, Fennan, and Thane.

Despite their conversation, the previous night had changed her friendship with Thane, for her part anyway. His laugh made her stomach seem to flip and do unnatural things. The way he smiled, even if it wasn't directed at her, heated her to the very core. His voice even sounded different to her ears, like he was a siren calling her to him. If he felt the same way, he didn't show it.

Once they stepped inside Castle Dredwich Leif, Piper, and Fennan went their separate ways, leaving her and Thane standing in the foyer. Thane turned to her to speak until Presco came around the corner. "I need to talk to you both about where Valeen and Hel are."

Sick to her stomach with the news, Katana found a large empty room at Castle Dredwich, with a harp that was enchanted to play on its own. As soon as she closed the double doors, the strings began to pluck. She couldn't break down and cry with worry. She had to believe they would make it back.

The All Mother hadn't brought them together again just for it all to end so swiftly. She pushed the heavy navy curtains to let in the sunlight and opened the windows for the warm summer breeze. Floral scents drifted inside, and the sun's rays filled her soul.

She took off her shoes and set them next to a high-backed velvet chair and pushed a table aside to clear a large open space. The rug beneath her feet was navy and white with florals and flourishes. Closing her eyes for a moment, she let the music flow into her, felt it in the very depths of her being, and then slowly moved her feet.

This was her offer to the All Mother to protect Valeen and Hel. She swept her arms, turned into a spin and leapt again. It had been a long time since she danced, and her ankles weren't used to the movements anymore, but it was coming back to her.

The harp seemed to move her, to lift her arms and bend her torso. She let her training take hold, not thinking of what would come next, but dipped and twirled and kicked. The flowy fabric of her sage-green dress whirled around her. Sweat beaded at her temples, and her breath came heavier than it did when she was a goddess, but she liked the way the movements worked on her muscles, the way it burned.

There was part of her that wanted to go to the underrealm to bring her sister back, but she knew she'd be more of a hindrance than anything. Valeen was strong, powerful, and determined, so she held out hope.

Katana lifted one leg high above her head then arched back until her hands touched the floor. She kicked back and flipped into a standing position again. Then she circled her arms and kicked her leg out and around her, spinning in place. Until she caught sight of something dark against the doors and stopped.

Her breath hitched and she nervously tucked her hair behind her ear. "Thane. I did not realize you came in." He was smiling. "How long have you been standing there?"

"I just walked in. You're a wonderful dancer."

"Thank you." She cleared her throat. "I used to dance in front of an audience of thousands, and yet for some reason you make me more nervous than they did."

His green eyes softened. She loved the color of them. It reminded her of a forest and the wilds and beauty of it. "Why?" he asked. "I'm not judging you. Admiring maybe."

"I know but one person is more intimate than many."

"Could anything be more intimate than last night?" He raised a brow.

She smiled and bit her lower lip. Her breath seemed to get away from her. "Well, last night wasn't a performance."

"It wasn't? It certainly felt like it."

Katana suddenly felt like she needed to drink cool water. "And how would you rate said performance?" She giggled while slowly moving her hips in a circle then winked at him.

He laughed. "One hundred out of ten."

All Mother, his voice and his gaze on her was making her stomach do things it shouldn't. *One night. One time. That's all.*

"You can keep dancing. I didn't mean to stop you."

"Oh, no, it's alright. I am glad you came. Have you heard anything more about Valeen and Hel?"

He strode forward to the table next to her and lifted the lid off a crystal bowl. He plucked out two of the silver-wrapped treats inside and rolled one between his fingers. "No. If they aren't back tonight... I'll go after them. I won't leave them down there."

Her heart seemed to clench in her chest. "You are very brave." She brushed her hands down her body to straighten the wrinkles in her ankle-length flowy dress. It was terrifying to think of him leaving for such a horrible, dangerous place and yet she adored him for it. It was how big his heart was, how much he cared for her sister and his brother, even if them being together broke him.

When she looked up, he was watching her. He

popped one of the chocolates in his mouth then held out the other to her. She carefully unwrapped it and bit it in half. It was sweet and gooey at the center. "Thank you."

"How are you feeling?"

"Scared." She ate the rest of the chocolate. "Would you like to help me finish my dance offering to the All Mother for Hel and Valeen's safety? I am so worried they will not come back. I wish I could do something. I wish I could go but—there is no sun there and I fear I would be even weaker than I already am. And it's not like I can fight well anyway."

Thane looked out the window. He took a few deep breaths as if trying to calm himself. "You truly believe the All Mother will help them? Because I think she left us a long time ago."

"Our creator's hands will be made known, even if in the smallest of ways, you simply have to look."

He held out his hand to her, palm up. "Either way, I would love to dance with you, Katana."

"Do you know how?" She felt herself smiling and placed her hand in his. Atlanta hated dancing with her. He thought it was a useless talent.

"Of course I do." He grinned and pulled them to the center of the soft rug and spun her in a circle.

"Show off." Her stomach fluttered as they stepped. She followed his lead to a dance she knew quite well. They started with the traditional steps, then he dipped her, gliding his hand up her spine to the back while the other slid down her thigh lifting it. Holding around his neck, she raised her pointed toe to the ceiling. When he pulled her back upright, he moved his hands to her waist and lifted her, turning in a circle.

The air felt charged now. The placement of his hands left her burning. The music changed to something more intimate, the slow plucking of strings and the soft melody of violins seemed to buzz in her veins.

Thane brought her down slowly, eyes holding hers, as if enchanted. Their lips were but a breath away. When her toes touched the ground, she spun away, and he caught her wrist, pulling her back in, caging her in his arms.

Her heart felt like it would pound out of her chest as those striking green eyes slowly rolled down to her lips. He waited inches away. She clutched the front of his tunic in her palms, trying to stop her body from trembling.

He wasn't ready for more. His *heart* wasn't ready. He'd said so himself, and yet it felt right to be in his arms. But she didn't want to be used to satisfy his loneliness until he was healed.

They said *once* for a reason, so there was no real hurt when it ended. And it would end. She hadn't loved Atlanta for a long time, and she was primed for something more than what he offered. She wanted love and romance. Heartfelt confessions and passionate nights, and a promise of more than a day.

"Thane..."

"Yes?" he breathed.

"Maybe dancing was not a good idea."

"Only if you don't desire me the way I desire you. I know we said once but...I can't stop thinking about you. Once was not enough. You've ignited a fire inside me." His voice was low and husky.

She pressed her forehead to his and closed her eyes. Truth was, she wanted him, craved him and the way he took her to a place of pleasure she hadn't known before. "Thane," she whispered, and cupped his face between her palms. "I want you, I do but..."

"But?"

As if she couldn't stop herself, she leaned in and kissed him. Warmth pulsed through her, and she gripped the back of his neck, his hands pulling her flush against him as his tongue caressed hers. He lifted her with ease, putting them eye to eye, and kissed her harder, faster until she had to pull back for air. They weren't immortals anymore, and any day could be their last. She started with the top button on his tunic, then went quickly to the next, exposing his soft ivory skin.

His throat bobbed as he stared down at her. "Katana," the way he said her name sent a chill down her spine. It was a plea. "Are you sure? I can't promise you more than today. Not yet."

"I know," she whispered, and finished with the last button. "And today, I want you."

He leaned down and kissed her, his hand glided up her thigh, pulling her dress with it. His lips moved to her throat, her collarbone, and he spent a lot of time simply kissing her skin, putting his hands all over her body, until every part of her was aflame. They ended up bare skin against bare skin, tangled on the soft rug, all hot kisses and bated breath.

The harp and violin still played a slow melody. The sun warmed her skin through the window, but then she realized the light wasn't only coming from outside. Her hair was alight in a messy halo on the floor around her.

Thane took a handful of the silky tresses and let it slide between his fingers. "Is this your magic?"

It wasn't something that had happened before. "It must be."

"You're beautiful, Katana. All of you." His lips and hands didn't leave her body after that. She didn't think of tomorrow or that next day, only of his soft sighs and whispers of her name.

Chapter 40

VALEEN

Hel angled himself in front of Valeen as the wicked brothers who ruled this realm came into view. With the presence of their masters, the remaining demon hounds and other nameless creatures pulled back.

"I thought I smelled the gods," said Servente, the tallest and most powerful of the pair. His tall black horns curled out of his pure white hair, red eyes glowed in the strange blue light of this place. His blue-gray skin had silver veins running up his bare arms. "We've had this discussion before. The gods do not belong in our realm, most especially the ones who killed our brother."

"I was returning Morv's ring." Valeen gestured toward Varlett. If they didn't notice her before, they did now. She stood half shadowed behind a rotting bush a few yards away. Several of the hounds still surrounded her. "As a peace offering. We want no more trouble with the lords of the underrealm."

Servante appeared beside Varlett and gripped her jaw between his long, spindly fingers, then leaned down and ran his nose along her neck, inhaling deeply. She held utterly still, her eyes going wide. Then he lifted her hand with the ring. "A dragon bearing my brother's ring," he mused.

Sweat beaded under her arms. There was no telling by the prince's body language if he was content with that or if he was angry. She inched backward, but Hel snatched her wrist. *Do not move yet,* he said.

The other demon prince, Lavix, went to Varlett's opposite side, inspecting her from crown to toe. He curled a lock of her hair around his finger and smelled it. "She's no longer a dragon, brother. She's one of us."

"So she is." He turned his attention back to Valeen. "You did more than return Morv's ring. You filled his place with a female."

"She was in possession of it when Morv died. What happened after was not our doing. We didn't even know that this was possible," Valeen said.

Lavix hissed, bearing his serrated teeth. "You mean when *you* killed him. We know it was you, goddess of night. Now we have a blood feud."

Servante nodded his agreement. "This cannot go unpunished." The demons all around started to make low gurgling noises. One of the hounds, the largest of them all, paced behind the brothers, waiting for the command to be let free and attack. Its spiny backbones protruded grotesquely. Its maw was full of rows of serrated teeth, dripping with green venom.

"Morv was there to *kill* my wife," Hel snapped.

"He's dead because he was weak." Squeals and howls from the hounds rose up all around them. They didn't like hearing their master degraded.

Servante's eyes narrowed at them both, and he clicked his forked tongue. "It is the way of things. Kill or be killed. I am disappointed my brother was bested by two half-gods. I can smell the mortal in you."

A quiet rustle in the bushes caught her ear. Valeen snapped her head left, and swung Soulender, cutting the head from a creeping dark-green serpent. "Keep your beasts back, demon, or your brother won't be the only prince of the underrealm to lose his life."

"You dare threaten us in *our* domain?" Servante boomed. "You are *foolish* to bring an immortal weapon to our world, where it could so easily fall into your enemies' hands, goddess."

"And yet you haven't tried to take it. You know that I may be part mortal, but my soul is as old as you are, and death will welcome you in his cold arms if you come near me."

"Your sword skill is impressive, but I have other powers, Valeen. You went into the lake of sorrows." He smiled, and it was hideous. "Your powers must be lacking."

Hel tensed and inched closer to her, using himself as a shield. "We've returned the ring. Your realm has a leader to fill the vacancy. There doesn't need to be a blood feud. End it now, and we will leave with no further killing."

Varlett looked more smug than ever. She knew she held the power here in the everdark. She may have wanted to leave when they walked into this place, but now, with her smile and proud stance between the brothers, she'd found her new home. Found new males to latch onto to give her power. It was always more, more, more, with her. She'd probably turn the two of them against each other eventually.

"You will leave when I say," Servante growled, crimson eyes flashing. "Didn't you learn that the last time, pet? It took your mother's begging to set you free all those years ago."

Hel went utterly still for a moment, then the muscles in his back tensed. "What did you say?"

"You think I let you go without a reason? You still have those scars on your face to remember that day." He gestured toward his own brow then chin, exactly where Hel was marked.

"My mother had nothing to do with it." He still held the worry that Servante was his father. *All Mother, what if it was true?*

"She offered to take your place."

"No." Hel shook his head in disbelief. "No, that can't be true."

That would mean his mother had been trapped in the underrealm for thousands of years...

"Why not?" Servante purred.

"My mother left me. She didn't love me enough to sacrifice her life for mine."

Servante laughed. "Oh, naive, selfish boy. She did. What a lovely whore she became."

Hel's jaw muscles twitched. "Show her to me."

"You're in my world. You don't get to make deman—"

"Show her to me now!" Hel roared. "Or I swear I will cut off your fucking head with that immortal sword even if it costs me my life after."

"Give me the immortal blade, and you can have her."

"No." Valeen gripped it tighter, bringing it closer to her body. As tragic of a story as it would be if Hel's mother Zaelia was here, no demon could ever possess this sword, even she would agree with that.

"You are dealing with a very different god now." Hel's face hardened. "If my mother is your prisoner, you will let her go."

He could be manipulating you.

You don't know that.

He's trying to get Soulender. He is the prince of deception. Even if he showed her to us, it could be an illusion.

How else would I have gone free, Valeen?

Valeen had no answer for that. *If she is here, we will come back for her. When we are immortal.*

Hel stared at her. A war was going on behind that beautiful face. His shoulders relaxed ever so slightly. "You will not get Soulender," Hel finally said. "And we're leaving now."

It wasn't even a moment later that light shined through the darkness, and a beautiful goddess with black hair and luminescent alabaster skin came from behind a wide tree. Valeen knew her, had seen her face on the wall of War's old estate. Her likeness had been in a portrait of her and her twin brother.

She wore a white gown, untouched by the darkness of this realm, but chains bound her ankles and wrists and connected around her neck.

"Zaelia, how lovely of you to join us," Servante said, holding out his hand. "Come." Her blue-green eyes darted between Hel and Servante. The chains clanked with each step, but she took his hand and held it. "Your son says you didn't love him."

"Zaurahel," she said softly. The corner of her mouth curled, and a dimple appeared. She was the female version of Hel. It was almost uncanny how much he resembled her. "It's good to see you... but you shouldn't be here."

This felt all wrong. If Hel's mother had spent so much time here, she wouldn't appear radiant and lovely. There would be signs of the evil of this place in her countenance. "Hel, we have to go," she breathed. Once, she'd been fooled by a perfect illusion, there wouldn't be a second time.

"Mother?"

"I will give my whore the choice to go free, if you will but give me the immortal weapon."

"Whore?" Hel's stance shifted. His bare shoulders tensed and tightened. "Whore?" his voice came out more disgusted this time. "You will let her go now."

Lavix made a move toward Hel, and Valeen pointed her sword. "Not another step."

Servante lifted his chin. "Give me Soulender and I will let all three of you go freely and unharmed."

Valeen hooked her arm around Hel's. "We can't do that." The demons behind them growled and snapped their jaws. Valeen jabbed the golden blade, backing them off as they hissed and spit. "Hel, we need to go now."

Zaelia raised a hand toward them, chains clanking. "Wait, don't leave me. Give them the weapon, please. I can't stand another moment in this place."

"We'll come back," she whispered.

"How could you leave your own mother?" Varlett

added, taking a step closer. "Me, I understand, but the goddess who gave you life? You've always wondered what happened to her."

She might not be real, Hel. There is magic swirling all around us. I can feel it. You said there would be illusions. Valeen pulled harder but he refused to move. *She wouldn't tell you to give them the sword. She would tell you to run.*

He turned on her. His eyes held such sorrow. *You've never been trapped here. You don't know how much you'd give to be free.*

Even Synick *didn't give them an immortal sword, Hel. Think about that.*

Turning toward his mother once more, he blinked away whatever emotion he had, and that mask returned. He was the Black Mage and did not care. He was the god of mischief who could fool all. "If it is true that you traded yourself for me, why did you abandon me in the first place?"

"Zaurahel, please." Tears ran down her face.

"You left me as a baby."

"I traded my life for yours! You don't know what happened." She started sobbing.

He stared Servante down. "The sword will never be yours. Keep her." It was cold. Unfeeling. Necessary.

Hel's white wings materialized, and he curled an arm around Valeen's waist.

"Sister," Servante said to Varlett. "Don't let them leave your new home. Take your revenge."

"With pleasure." She raised both arms upward. "Kill them." And the host of demons charged once again. The giant hound knocked others aside with its massive shoulders and howled. The fat twin-headed monster stomped toward them.

Hold onto me. Valeen wrapped her arms around Hel's neck, and they shot into the air. Beasts snapped at their heels, just out of reach. The giant hound ran up the fat monster and launched at them, latching onto Valeen's boot. She screamed and swung Soulender, slicing into the back of its neck, severing the spine. It dropped like a stone to the ground and green blood splattered all around its body. The others dove in and started eating it, tearing into the flesh, crunching bones and ripping limbs.

She moved her foot around to make sure she felt no sting and breathed a sigh of thanks that the teeth hadn't cut through the thick leather.

"Did the bite get through?" Hel sounded almost frantic.

"No, I'm alright... We'll come back for your mother."

"If that was truly her, we'll return."

Hel weaved between trees and rose above the black canopy of the forest into the deep blue-black sky. There was no sun or moon here to guide them, only an eerie glow that seemed to come from nowhere in particular.

"You're not the only thing that can fly down here, Hel!" Varlett let out a cackle that sent a chill down her back.

I hate that wench. And now she's a princess. A demon but still a princess.

A swarming dark cloud came up behind them. At first, she thought they were bees but there were at least a thousand bats. They twisted and turned as if they were one mind. The screeches and bellows grated on her sensitive ears.

The buzz of magic in her veins was but a whisper of what it could be. Not even enough to conjure a lily at this point. If hers was still this weak, it was a miracle Hel was even able to bring out his wings.

His muscles tensed as he held her tightly around her middle. Determination hardened his features. "I wanted to bring the ring back to save you, not make her a fucking princess of the underrealm," he muttered.

"I know."

"Hold on." His arms tightened around her, she hooked her heels behind his back, and he rolled left. Her stomach clenched, and she squeezed harder around his neck and hips. He twirled again and she held in a squeal. "Sorry. I had to get around that thing. Whatever it was."

Behind them, a giant gray monster with only a mouth on its misshapen head, chased after them, taking down trees in its way. It roared and jumped, massive three-fingered hands reaching for them. "UP! GO UP!"

His wings beat hard, taking them higher. The monster jumped again, propelling upward with an unnatural force. Valeen squealed through her teeth, leaned back, and swung down with Soulender, slicing through the monster's fingers. It roared, not in pain but in anger, barely missing Hel's boots.

The swarm of bats was gaining on them. Together, their wings sounded like a hive of bees, and the closer they came, the louder it was. She reached into her belt and threw a star at a fanged bat with a wingspan as wide as she was tall. The star lodged into its neck, and it went down with a screech. But she only had four more and there were too many to count.

Suddenly, Hel roared. There was a *snap*, and they were falling. The breath was pulled from her lungs at the rapid plummet.

Hel, what happened? Hel!

His face was twisted in agony, but he wrapped her tighter and angled his back toward the ground as they fell faster and faster. Tree branches broke and buckled beneath their combined weight. She tried to call on her vines to halt them, but nothing came—the spark of her magic wasn't there. *Shadows, vines, anything!* Branches whipped her face, cut into her cheeks and tore at her hair.

Hel hissed and grunted, taking the brunt of it all, until they smacked into the ground. He released his hold on her and rolled onto his side, coughing and gasping, trying to suck in shallow breaths.

"Hel!" *His wings, gods, his wings.* White feathers slowly fluttered from the trees and landed around them. The left one was broken in two places, half covered in black soot. The right side's feathers were smeared with blood. He cradled his right shoulder and repeated "fuck" at least ten times.

Horrified, she knelt helpless beside him. "Can you tuck your wings away?"

The sound of the swarm grew louder. The stomping of that giant creature shook the ground. The howling of the hounds echoed all around them.

"No," he wheezed. "They're not—*fuck*—I can't."

Tears burned. "We have to go. Take my hand."

Reaching out with his left, she pulled and draped

his arm around her shoulder. He outweighed her by about a hundred pounds with those wings, and she felt the pressure of it too. "We're almost to the door. We can make it."

Carrying the brunt of his weight slowed them down. The ground rumbled beneath their feet. The black muck and protruding roots slowed them even more. Her heart slammed in her chest, booming in her ears. *They're going to catch us,* she thought. "Faster, Hel."

"I'm trying, love."

She glanced back and clenched her teeth. Red eyes were all around and gaining. "They're almost to us. I'll have to fight them off." But she spotted light from the door through the forest of dark trees ahead.

"No, we're almost there. Keep going," Hel said, and seemed to regain some strength just seeing it.

The buzzing was above them now. She looked up, the bats dove like arrows, straight for them. "*Shit.*" The door was only a few feet in front away. "We can't let them out."

"Fuck that, if they get out, they get out." He took his arm from around her, wrapped his hand around the door handle and twisted.

She was right behind him, ready to push through the door—pain, searing, shocking pain through her center. A scream ripped from her throat. Hard metal stuck out from the center of her torso. *No no no no no no.*

"I hope you die and forget him again." Varlett's cold voice sent a chill down her back.

The sword was jerked free, and Valeen stumbled against the doorframe. Blood poured down her torso, warm and wet. *No, she isn't going to get away with that.* With a scream of rage, Valeen whirled and slashed her blade across Varlett's face, slicing open a wound across her eyes. From temple to temple a gaping gash opened up and streaks of blood ran down her face. Varlett reared back, grabbing her wound as she started screaming, screaming so loud it rang in Valeen's ears. "She took my eyes! I can't see! I can't see!"

"And you never will again." The world around her seemed to sway and the blood pouring down her body was colder now. Her feet slipped from beneath her and she fell back into Hel's arms. He was saying something, but she couldn't get words out of it. It was like she was under the surface of water where everything was muted.

Light burst across her vision, so bright she couldn't see. The heaviness of the underrealm vanished. Things came into focus. Sunlight filtered through the branches of the trees. The stone circle was close enough she could touch it. In the bright azure sky, a white puffy cloud shaped like a rabbit floated by. It was quiet. So quiet it was peaceful.

Was someone calling her name?

He sounded far away...

Hands gripped her face, and he was suddenly above her, as welcome as the sunrise. "Look at me, love." His voice was clear now. He was terrified and that confused her. Hel wasn't afraid of anything. "I'm so sorry. It should have been me. Hold on, alright? Hold on."

Everything seemed to rush in at once. The agonizing pain was fire consuming her flesh. The loss of blood made her cold body shake. The last words

Varlett said... Nausea rose up in her throat. "Don't let me forget you," she cried, reaching for her bloody stomach. "I don't want to leave you, please. I can't leave you again."

Hel pushed her hands away from the wound. "I won't let you die. You're not going to die," he said it like a command.

She reached up and touched his beautiful face, ran her fingertips over the scar on his brow, memorizing it. How could she ever forget someone she loved so much? It was cruel, after everything they'd been through. After how hard they fought, Varlett was going to be the one to tear them apart again.

The tremors intensified. "Hel, I want you to know, I always loved you. Even after—"

"Stop it. You're not going to die." He sounded agitated.

"I never stopped loving you. I will always love you."

He grabbed her face in both hands and pressed his forehead to hers. "My magic is coming back. You're going to be fine. You have to hold on. You *will* hold on. I forbid you to let go."

Her mouth started to fill with blood. "Alright," she whispered and felt warm liquid trickle out of the corner of her mouth. The sun warmed her face, and she thought of Katana. Katana was here. She couldn't leave her again.

Thick black boots, then long dark hair came into view. Thane stood over her and dropped to his knee, taking one of her hands. "Val, hold on. You'll be alright."

The pain was searing, and her body shook from it.

She gripped him so hard it was a wonder his bones didn't snap. "It hurts, Thane."

"Why aren't you healing her?" he snapped.

"I'm trying," Hel hissed.

In through the nose, out through the mouth, Hel chanted in her mind. *Breathe, love. I'm here with you. You're going to be fine.* Warmth trickled through her veins, chasing the iciness away. Pieces of black hair stuck to Hel's forehead, his brows were puckered, and his mouth pinched in concentration, and even when he was furious and scared, he was lovely.

How could someone be so beautiful it hurt?

The edges of her vision started to fade. *No, no, I can't forget him,* she thought. *Hel is your husband, your mate. Hel is your husband, your mate...* she chanted it over and over until everything went black.

Chapter 41

HEL

If he'd been furious going into the underrealm there wasn't a word to describe what he felt now. An insatiable heat was eating away at him. It wasn't just anger or dejection. It was the center of a sun ripping through him.

He marched with Valeen in his arms, his magic curled around them, casting shadows, curling like vipers ready to lash out.

With a snap of his fingers, her ripped and bloody clothes had been replaced. There wasn't a trace of dirt or black muck from the underrealm on her. Her thick raven hair flowed out in clean waves. She was radiant and lovely and good. Too good for him. Sometimes it was still a wonder that she was in love with him. There were times he thought she should be with Thane, that she might be better off, but he was too selfish to even consider it.

The wound Varlett had given her was healed as if it had never happened. Her heart beat steadily. A lovely song to his ears, but she had been on the edge of death. It had been within reach of her, beckoning her name. He'd felt the coldness all around them like frost on an autumn night as winter threatened. He'd seen death enough times to know what it looked like.

He curled her tighter to his chest and pressed his lips to the crown of her head. Sleep still claimed her. Before he'd picked her up, he'd pushed his way into her mind to make sure she was indeed there and found her dreaming in the gardens of what was once House of Night.

Even if he was on the verge of collapse, he should have been the one to push her through the door first, then Varlett would have stabbed him through the back and not her.

Pain and aching still throbbed in his shoulders and back. He hadn't used his magic to heal himself. He'd heal quick enough, but the pain was a punishment for what he allowed to happen. Even his wings were still out, bent and bloodied.

"What happened?" Thane's voice broke through his thoughts. Hel had nearly forgotten he was there. Slowly turning his head, he only looked at him and said nothing. He pulled Phantom along behind him. The sound of the hooves hitting the ground had become background noise.

"Hel."

"She almost fucking died, that's what happened."

"Where is Varlett?"

"She's a demon now, and the connection between them is severed," he said through clenched teeth. It was all he could manage. His magic was raging within him. He prided himself on control but right now he felt like he could explode. Part of him wanted to go back to make Varlett suffer. To inflict pain like she'd never felt before.

He glanced down at Valeen... but he had to think of her first. The only thing that mattered right now was getting her immortality. Varlett's sword wouldn't have gone through her if she had her immortal strength. No bite from a demon hound could kill her. Death couldn't steal her away. Except with the fucking sword Synick still had. He needed to get that too.

"Varlett is a demon? How?" Thane put a hand on Hel's shoulder and his magic flared on its own. Hissing, Thane jerked back and shook his palm. "You shocked me. What was that for?"

"Don't touch me right now, and she's a demon because of the ring."

"You could at least tell me if Val is going to be alright."

"She's fine until something else fucking happens. We're making a move. I'm done playing fucking footsy with the council. I'm going to invade Pricilla, and I need your help. Get your dragons and Ravens ready." Walking back to the castle was taking too long. As much as the sun was a welcome gift after the horrid underrealm, he wanted to sit in a dark room and contemplate killing every council member and how he was going to do it. In a flash, he stood outside Valeen's room and pushed through the door. His boots slammed on the stone floor, and he set her on the lavender quilt on the bed.

Pressing his palm to her forehead, he slipped into her mind again. Valeen was sitting cross-legged in a bed of moss, plucking the petals off a white daisy. Blossoming trees and blooming flowers were the backdrop behind her. The three moons in the sky were fully intact. It was their connected dreamworld. The place he'd spent all those years while he waited for her to wake him. It was almost comforting. There was nothing here that wanted them dead.

She lifted her chin and smiled at him. Gods, that smile could bring him to his knees. He would crawl to her right now if she asked.

I was waiting for you, she said softly.

It's time to wake up, love.

She frowned. *I had to come here so I wouldn't forget you. I felt myself...slipping away. I don't want to ever forget you again.*

I know. You won't. And I'm going to make sure of that. He held out his hand to her.

She tossed the flower aside and stood, brushing off bits of moss from her pants. The moment her hand clasped his, he was pushed out.

He stared down at her face in her bedroom at Castle Dredwich.

Moments passed.

Why wasn't she waking?

His heart started to pound and squeeze. As soon as he was pushed out, she should have woken.

"Val." He caressed her cheek. "Wake up."

She wasn't trapped there. It couldn't happen.

"Valeen."

Then her eyelids fluttered, and a wave of relief hit him in the chest. It took a moment, but her eyes flashed open, and his crashing heart slowed. "How are you feeling? Do you hurt anywhere?"

She reached up and touched his face, curling her

fingers against his cheek. "My Zaurahel." Goosebumps peppered his skin. Hearing his full name on her lips always sent a tingle down his spine. "I feel just fine. No pain. Thanks to you." She looked down at herself then inspected him. "Why are you still bloody and dirty?" She sat up against the headboard and tucked her legs to her chest.

"It doesn't matter."

"And your magic is... suffocating." Her blue eyes sparkled as she glanced around the room. He didn't even realize how dark it was here. His magic had taken the form of darkness to match his mood and shut out the sunlight from the windows. "You're still very angry. What happened after I blacked out?"

"Nothing." He'd only just about lost his mind at how close she came to dying.

"Well, you stink like the dead." She scrunched her nose, and that pulled a chuckle out of him.

That raging anger fueling his magic began to simmer and the sunlight filtered in. Frowning, she reached up and touched his broken wing. "Hel, why haven't you healed yourself? Do you need my blood again?"

The bones were almost back as they should be, but it was still obviously misaligned in a few places. "I deserve to suffer."

That frown turned into a scowl. "Are you out of your mind? Heal yourself or I will, and I know you don't want me cutting myself and driving a dagger to inflict pain to do it."

That was something he simply wouldn't allow her to do for him. With a snap of his fingers, his dirty clothes were replaced with a crisp black suit. His wings vanished and any injury he had was gone. He ran his hand through his clean hair, pushing it out of his eyes. "Better?"

She smiled and crawled over to softly kiss him on the lips. Then she straddled him and positioned herself nicely on his lap. "Yes." She surprised him by suddenly wrapping her arms tightly around the back of his neck. "I was so scared. Not even of death but of leaving you, forgetting you." She nuzzled her face below his ear and inhaled. "I just got you back and I never want to forget, not even your smell."

The tension coiled in his body relaxed and he rubbed his hands up and down her spine. His throat was uncomfortably tight. Only she could ever get him emotional like this. "I'm sorry I let that happen. It shouldn't have happened."

She started to breathe easier. "Remember the night you confessed you loved me?"

"The first or second time?"

She pulled back, smiling. "The first."

"Certainly." He brushed a stray piece of her raven hair off her forehead. He'd known long before he ever spoke it aloud, worried that if he said it, it would all slip away. He'd never really truly loved anything before her, and it scared him that she had such power over him. "I half said it the day at the restaurant when you grabbed Lily by the throat and threatened to turn her into an empty shell."

"Yes, but you said 'I *think* I'm in love with you'."

"I know what I said." He'd wanted to say he was in love with her, every part of her beautiful mind, soul, and body but he didn't just yet. "You looked stunning in that tight silver night dress. Your hair was up in a loose bun, and I'd thought about pulling the ribbon and letting it fall a hundred times. We'd stayed up all night playing cards on top of your bed. Every time one of us lost a game we had to confess something real. You'd confessed your dream of opening an art gallery with art from the best artists from every realm, but you weren't ready to open House of Night to the worlds yet. You were scared of what could happen. You'd never told me you were scared of anything before that. Then I lost the next... On purpose. Because I wanted to say it, but I needed a reason in my mind to confess. See, I was scared of that goddess, of the power she wielded to crush me in a moment with a few words."

He heard Valeen's heart skip. He'd never told her he lost on purpose.

Hel thought back to that exact moment. He had been sweating, his heart was beating so hard it was like he'd been sparring for hours. Every muscle had been taut, but he also felt like he could float into the sky.

"I leaned closer to you. I think I just couldn't help it. 'Come on, you lost, confess something', you teased. 'Fine, if I must confess something, it will be that... I'm in love with you, Valeen. I've been in love with you. And I can no longer picture my life without you in it.'" Hel chuckled to himself remembering the look of surprise on her face. Even now at this moment Valeen had that same expression. "And you said—"

"You love me? You're in love with me?" Valeen said and nuzzled her nose against his. "And you said," she lowered her voice trying to mimic him, "'yes, I love you. Why do you think I call you 'love'?"

"I never used that term for anyone else then."

"And you better not now."

He chuckled. "*Never*, love."

"And then what happened after? Remind me."

Hel smiled. "Well, you made me sweat. You stared at me for a good minute or so. I thought I was about to leave heartbroken until you climbed onto my lap, lips inches from mine and said, 'My heart has been closed for a long time, but you made me see that it was safe to love. I love you too, Zaurahel.' Things got hot and heavy after that. I wanted you so much I felt like I was on fire, but you said I had to wait to have you to test my devotion. Even though I know you wanted me." He squeezed her thighs and let out a low growl.

She giggled. "I did. It was hard to deny myself of you that night, and all the others until our wedding day. But you made it worth waiting for. These are the things I never want to forget again."

"You won't. I won't allow it."

A knock on the door, then it opened. Katana came through.

Valeen pulled back and twisted out of his arms. Her sister flew across the room and threw herself at Valeen. "Oh, thank the All Mother, you're safe. I've been worried. You aren't hurt, are you?"

Pulling back, Valeen shook her head. "I'm alright. *We're* alright."

He fell back on the bed, pulled out a civar and watched the silver smoke rise in little curling wisps.

"Where is Thane?" Katana asked, the worry clear in her voice. Hel glanced over at her. Something about her was different, her smell or maybe the shimmer in her hair.

"He found us at the portal. He's probably riding

back and almost here as we speak." The civar eased the burning fire in his chest a little more, though it didn't change his mind. He was going to make a move against the council. A monumental one that would shift the tide of this war.

"So he never went to the underrealm?" she nibbled on her lip.

"No." He blew out smoke and rose off the bed. He was going to need Thane for the plans his mind was working up. "But I do need to speak with him. Are you alright if I leave for a few minutes?" He brushed Valeen's arm and kissed her cheek.

"I'm fine, Hel. Take your time. I'm just going to bathe and then get something to eat."

With a finger to his temple, he said silently, *I'm right here if you need me.*

Chapter 42

KATANA

As soon as the door shut behind Hel, guilt started to eat away at her. While she was in the north with the dragons, she'd slept with the elf her sister was once going to marry, and again while Valeen was fighting for her life in the underrealm. She needed to talk to her before she found out another way.

"I'm going to hop into the bath really quick," Valeen said. "I look clean, but I don't feel it. I need to scrub that evil place off me. You can wait here if you don't mind."

"Oh, sure." Katana sat on the bench at the end of Valeen's bed.

Water splashed in the bathing chambers. It wasn't long later she heard her sister get in. "Ugh, it feels good to be back. I never want to go there again."

"I wouldn't either." Katana's stomach began to twist. "Are you hungry? I can go get you something to eat."

"No, stay and talk to me. My stomach can wait. What happened while you were gone?" Her voice sounded echoey from the other room.

"Um," she nervously pushed her hair behind her ears. The confession was on the tip of her tongue but then she remembered Atlanta and decided it was more important. "Well, Atlanta came. He and Thane got into a fight. Thane slapped him in the face. It was... actually amazing to see."

Water splashed and she imagined her sister bolting upright. "Did he try to take you?"

"He would have, yes."

"That prick. When this is over, I'm going after him."

She smiled even though she hated violence. It was nice to be loved and protected. "I told him you would. It's why he left. He fears you."

"As he should."

Katana giggled. "Thane wasn't afraid of him. I was surprised."

"No, he wouldn't be. Especially if he was protecting you. He would do anything for his friends."

"I gathered that." The word friend hit harder than it should. That was what she was to Thane, a friend, although she wished it was more. Did friends sleep together? Did friends think about each other all the time? No. "Val..."

"Yeah?"

"I need to tell you something and I don't know how you will feel about it." Sweat dampened her skin, and she suddenly found it harder to breathe.

"You can tell me anything."

"I..." she went quiet for a few beats. "I made love

with Thane. In Ryvengaard, and once when we got back."

Silence. Dead silence.

Shaking. Her hands were suddenly shaking.

"It didn't really mean anything. We agreed it was nothing. It was lust mostly, and I think I was just someone to help his loneliness."

More silence.

Katana wished she could see her sister's face to at least get some idea of what she was thinking, but she stayed seated on the bench and stared at the wall. "Are you angry?"

"No," Valeen answered finally. "I'm just... I don't know what I feel. Was it truly nothing?"

"For his part."

"Katana," Valeen sounded almost sad. "You're hurt?"

"No." That was the first lie she'd told. "I knew what I was getting myself into."

The smell of florals and perfume from the bath soap filled the air. "You care about him. I saw it even before you left. Of course, I don't blame you, Thane is... a beautiful person. I loved him too, and I want him to be happy."

A tear slipped down her cheek. "I don't know if I could say I *love* him. And he made it clear he doesn't want love."

"He needs time."

"You didn't."

The water splashed again and this time it sounded like she was getting out. A moment later she popped around the corner, wrapped in a white linen. "I had shed my fair share of tears for weeks. I had months to spend with Hel before I even remembered him. Months to get over Thane. And I fell in love with Hel when we were away and when I remembered everything, it entirely changed the way I thought about Thane. Thane has never loved someone the way I love Hel. Thane and I were forced into a relationship with each other through a spell that his parents ordered. We *had* to fall in love. I don't know if we would have otherwise."

"Maybe you wouldn't have." Katana sat taller. "Because he didn't just love you in this life. He loved you in the others too." Saying that out loud made her realize how much of a fool she was to have let herself feel anything for Thane, let alone be intimate with him.

Valeen's blue eyes glittered in the sunlight filtering in through the windows. She pushed her black hair back. "I'm not denying it was real, because it was... we just both changed."

"How can you be so... nonchalant about Thane and I sleeping together? Does it not bother you at all?" She flinched waiting for the inevitable confession her sister was upset about it.

But surprisingly, she chuckled and started going through her drawers. "It did sort of make my stomach drop when you first said it, but it wasn't feelings of jealousy. It's hard to explain, but I was a different person when I loved him." Glancing over her shoulder, she suddenly grinned. "It sounds a little strange given our past, but I know how good he is, and I know how good you are, and I think you are perfect for each other. And if you were together, we'd all stay close." She tugged out a black long-sleeved top. "Now, if you went after Hel, this conversation would be *very* different."

Katana was grinning. "Oh, I have no attraction to Hel," Katana said, then raised her palms in defense. "He's handsome, don't get me wrong, but he's—dark. And I'm—not. You know what I mean."

Valeen laughed. "I do. Oh, and I need to go talk to Presco. He's no doubt still upset that Hel threw him back out of the underrealm."

It was fun to think of her and Valeen in relationships with cousins who were as close as brothers, the only problem with that was she didn't want to forever live in Valeen's shadow. She didn't want to be Thane's second choice, always wondering in the back of her mind if he were given the chance, would he get back with Valeen. That was how she'd felt all her life with Atlanta.

"Let's go get Presco, eat our fill in the kitchen, and plan something fun tonight. After being in the underrealm I bet you need a stiff drink and some upbeat music. Dancing cures all." Katana wiggled her hips and stretched her arms overhead.

Valeen smiled. "I know just the place."

Chapter 43

VALEEN

The sign with a pink Nerium Oleander flower above the door came into view. Valeen intertwined her fingers with Hel's and paused in the alleyway. Tif scurried up beside her boot and grinned. "Good old Nerium O, but I fear that Katana is a little ritzy for this place."

"*Katana* will like it just fine," Katana said, and walked up on Valeen's other side. "It's charming already."

It was late afternoon, an hour before opening. The birds chirped in the blossoming trees and humans went about their day, coming in and out of the shops along the street. It was the human district in the city after all. Elves didn't venture here often. Did the people know that their king came here on occasion?

Thane crossed his arms and leaned up against the brick wall of the alley. "Have you spoken to Evalyn recently?"

"I have," Valeen answered. "I saw her a couple days ago."

"And you told her about... everything?" He glanced down at Hel and Valeen's clasped hands.

She cringed inside at the thought of telling her aunt she was with the elf she knew as the Black Mage. With a shrug, she tried to play it off nonchalantly. "I planned to do that today."

"Oh, this will be good." Leif laughed and strutted past them. "Better get the ale going now."

Piper hurried to catch up to him. "I can't wait to see her reaction."

Fennan bumped into Valeen and raised a brow. "You've never told her about Hel?"

"Not yet."

He started laughing too. "Who wants to take bets something gets thrown?"

Adjusting his golden glasses, Presco shook his head with a sigh. "Don't listen to them, my queen. I'm sure your aunt will understand." Good old Presco, he was always on her side, but he did shoot Hel a glare. "Even if your mate is difficult to get along with at times."

"I did it for your own good, Presco," Hel drawled. "You can thank me later."

"Wait, I want to bet! What are we betting? Chocolate? Wine?" Tif jumped up and down, holding her hand in the air.

Katana, Thane, and Presco were next to file into Nerium Oleander, leaving her and Hel alone in the alley.

Valeen wasn't sure she'd ever felt this nervous before. Fighting and battles, she knew, but as a goddess she never had parents to introduce her husband to, and Aunt Evalyn was the closest thing to a mother she ever had.

Aunt Evalyn also hated the Black Mage as much as anyone. It wasn't as if this was a simple introduction. But she wanted Hel to be fully a part of her life, and that meant meeting the woman who raised her.

"You're nervous." Hel's voice sent a tingle down her back.

"A little," she confessed.

He half smiled and ran his rough hand along her jaw. "Look, we can do this another time. I need to go anyway."

"No." She grabbed his hand. "No, I want you to meet her. You said three days before we march on Pricilla. I don't know when we'll get this chance again."

"Three days to get my army here. Not go get them in three days."

"Mathekis can lead them to the portal."

"Val, they need to see their true commander."

"Then give me one day. Just one day without talk of war and fighting. I need to forget about the under-realm. I can still feel the evilness of that place like a coating on my skin. The screams are still echoing in my mind. And your mother is weighing on me. I know we can't go there now but... I can't imagine how she must feel."

He frowned and pulled her in closer. "I don't even know if that was truly her. Like you said, it could have been an illusion."

"It's going to bother me until we know for sure."

He nodded. "But for tonight we don't talk about it. Or war or fighting."

She blew out a slow breath. "Alright, let's go in."

"I will be a perfect gentleman. I promise."

"You better be on your *best* behavior, Mr. Black."

He chuckled and happily followed behind her until she pushed through the door and the bell chimed. Valeen spotted her friends lined up at the bar top with Aunt Evalyn behind it pulling a bottle from the shelf.

Valeen took off her cloak and placed it on the hook next to the door. She adjusted her hair, left down in loose curls, and then pushed her shoulders back and trudged forward. She was a goddess as old as time, and yet around Aunt Evalyn she felt like a teenager again, about to be reprimanded.

"They're here," Leif sang. "How much silver you got?" He nudged Fennan's arm.

"What in the world are you two going on about?" Aunt Evalyn put a hand on her hip.

Her stern face cracked into a huge grin. "Layala! You're back. What has gotten into you lately? You ran off two days ago in a panic without even a goodbye."

"Sorry about that." She flushed.

"I was so worried. I know you're strong and powerful but you're still a daughter to me. And mothers never stop worrying, no matter how old you are." She came out from behind the bar and pulled her into a hug. Her cinnamon spice smell felt like home. A breath later, she went rigid and slowly pulled away. "Laya, who is this?"

Valeen turned. Hel had removed his overcoat and now wore a black top with red runes down the center button line. He'd rolled up his sleeves revealing his tattoos and runes. So much for being discreet. At least he didn't have on a black cloak with the hood pulled up. "Aunt Evalyn, I'd like you to meet... Hel."

"Hel...The one who left the letter in my door addressed to *Valeen*?" Her brown eyes narrowed on him like an insect that needed to be squashed. He stopped beside Valeen and put his arm around her shoulder, then kissed her temple. The lines between her eyebrows deepened. "I was hoping you got back with your betrothed *Thane*—although, strangely, they resemble one another a little too closely."

"No, he's not Thane but... they are related." Valeen rubbed her forehead, *as if that helps this situation?* She silently berated herself.

She glanced back at Thane, drinking a mug of ale. "Is this a long-lost brother?" she whisper-hissed. "Layala—you can't do that to Thane."

Leif and Piper snickered together. Tif sat on the bar top, kicking her feet over the edge, staring at them, no attempt at all to pretend like she wasn't eavesdropping.

"Brother only in my heart." Hel held out his hand and waited for her to take it. "It's a funny story, actually, but first I would like to say it's great to meet you, Evalyn. You raised a remarkable lady, and I thank you for all that you did to keep her safe."

Valeen flinched at Evalyn's disapproving glare sliding down his form then back up to his face. *Ugh, not the berries comment, please...* Aunt Evalyn reached up for her poison berry necklace and rubbed the twine. The comment was on the tip of her Aunt's tongue, she knew it, but as if thinking better of threatening to poison him, she hesitantly shook his hand. "She's remarkable on her own. This old gambler didn't have much to do with it. What did you say your name was again?"

Please don't say your full name, Valeen thought silently. She needed time to explain before he went and outed himself as the Black Mage. Aunt Evalyn knew his true name. Hel's garnet eyes flicked to her, she hadn't intended to send him her thoughts, but he must have heard it anyway. A mischievous smile tugged at the corner of his mouth, and she felt the heat rising in her neck.

"It's Hel. Black."

"Hel Black. And you're what, sleeping together? In love? What am I looking at here?"

Leif spit out his drink and laughed. All Mother above, it would be nice *not* to have an audience. She glared at them all. Katana was the only one who looked concerned. She grabbed Thane's hand. And waved at the others. "Let's take our drinks to the tables outside."

"Party pooper," Leif muttered, but everyone, including Tif, went out the back door.

Once it swung shut, Valeen relaxed a little. "He's..." Valeen swallowed hard.

"I'm her husband."

"Husband?" she balked. "Husband? You ran off and got married and didn't invite me to the wedding? When did you even meet him?"

"Oh, we met some time ago," Hel said, winking at Valeen. She let out a nervous laugh and tried to get her rapidly beating heart and erratic breath under control.

Aunt Evalyn still looked like she'd taken a swig of bad whisky, but there was nothing in her expression that said she suspected he was the villain of Adalon. She adjusted her colorful shawl and turned on her heel before either of them could answer. "I think I need a drink to finish this conversation." She made her way back behind the bar. "How long is 'some time' to you Mr. Black? I can guarantee she didn't know you from Briar Hollow." She waved at one of the empty tables. "Sit, I need the full story. Can I make either of you anything?"

How much does she know? Hel sent the question to her mind.

She knows I'm a goddess reborn. Not much else.

Hel nodded slowly, and the evening sun shining through the front windows made his eyes glitter with mischief. *This should be good then.* Hel pulled out a chair for Valeen and then took a seat of his own. "When did we meet, love? Before Evalyn was born of course but the number of years is evading me." Valeen's skin dampened with sweat. She laughed nervously.

Aunt Evalyn stopped what she was doing and tapped her fingers on a bottle of amber. "So, you met in her previous life?"

"Yes, exactly," Hel answered. He got up from the table and made his way over to Aunt Evalyn. "Allow me to make you a drink. Something special I can guarantee you've never had before."

"As long as it's strong." She fumbled through a stack of rolled up, yellowed papers from the corner cubby shelf, took one, then made her way over to the table Valeen sat at. The chair legs scraped loudly against the wood floor, as if she did it on purpose then she plopped into her seat, smugly. *Umm what is she holding?* Valeen chuckled nervously and started biting her nails. She wasn't even a nail-biter either.

Hel pulled a few different bottles from the shelves

and with a flick of his fingers three silver goblets appeared—one with rubies, one with amethyst, and the other with emeralds glittered on the outside. He poured a few different liquors he'd taken from the shelf into a separate glass, squeezed in fruit she had no idea where he'd gotten, then snapped his fingers and a silver flask appeared. She recognized the primordial letters across the center, revealing it was a light, sweet spirit used for adding flavor to drinks from Runevale. He must have had it stored in the aether.

He was not just dropping clues about who he was, he was practically spelling it out for her.

Valeen bounced her leg under the table. "So, Aunt Evalyn, how's business?"

"Booming."

"Has something changed?"

"Yeah, the pale ones aren't attacking. People are out spending their coin. I've even had a few elves in here say they wanted to come to see Layala Lightbringer's human caretaker."

"That's interesting. I wonder why they aren't attacking anymore?" Hel said, smirking.

"Yes, I *wonder*," Valeen said through her teeth.

"Maybe someone asked the Black Mage very politely to stop them."

"Or maybe someone did ask nicely, and the Black Mage was an asshole about it and told her she didn't look good *begging*."

He licked his lips while he poured the purple liquid into the large mixing cup, stirring the concoction with magic by rubbing his thumb and forefinger together. Then with a flick of his fingers ice balls tinkered into the goblets. "Maybe she wasn't being very nice to him at that time, but he stopped them anyway."

"We could go on about 'maybes' all day, but we don't really know." She gave Aunt Evalyn a nervous smile.

She scowled back.

"Oh, but don't we? Hypothetically, of course. Maybe it's because he is in love with this *someone* who made the request. Maybe he would do anything for her, even if they were enemies." With a careful hand, he poured the mixture over the ice, then carried them over. He set Aunt Evalyn's down first, then Valeen's, then his own.

Before Hel even sat down Aunt Evalyn slapped the rolled-up paper she had kept tucked away onto the table and pointed to the headline of the *Palenor Scroll:* **Is Layala Lightbringer's True Mate the Black Mage?**

It was an old article written by the now-handless and tongueless Telvian Botsberry. *Bloody All Mother above.* Valeen let out a long breath, picked up the goblet, brought it to her lips, and took a long drink.

"You think I didn't know exactly who he was the moment I saw him? As if you'd leave Thane for some random elf? I own a bar, Layala, I hear talk. You think I didn't figure out that the person you were training your magic with was him? Or that the mysterious masked stranger you danced with at the ball, that had everyone talking several months back, wasn't the man who has wanted you for your powers?" Aunt Evalyn threw her hand toward him. "As if any elf in Palenor has runes and tattoos everywhere besides the Black Mage." The runes showed clearly on his neck and his forearms. She turned to him with her wild eyes. "And if you were trying to hide it you did a terrible job, *Mr. Black*. And wasn't your surname *Everhath*?"

She's done her homework. "You're not frightened of me at all, are you?" Hel couldn't hold back his smile, bringing out the dimple on his cheek.

"My daughter is a reincarnated goddess. What would I be scared of?"

"Fair point. Well, I'm afraid you are right, Evalyn. And Everhath was the name of my elven blacksmith father. I really am just a humble elf from a modest upbringing."

Valeen let out a *ha*. *Says the elf with "KING" tattooed across his skin.*

Hel smiled and went on, "Although, you were wrong about one thing, Evalyn, I didn't want her for her powers."

"Well, I know that because she is no fool! If you only wanted to use her, she'd have figured that out, and the last thing she would have done is marry you!" Aunt Evalyn balked and snatched up the goblet. "Maker, help us." Then she tipped the goblet back and took a drink and kept drinking.

Hel grimaced. "I don't know if I'd do that. You said you wanted it strong."

Aunt Evalyn raised her brows, taking that as a challenge, she finished the drink in under five seconds flat. "I've been drinking booze for fifty years. Don't insult me thinking I can't handle my liquor, Mr. Black. In fact, I need another, and I'll get this one myself." She moved with a bit of a sway back to the bar.

"Gods, you two are more alike than I could have

ever guessed. Stubborn, mouthy, and rude. Not a single 'thank you' was uttered in there."

Valeen nearly choked on her own saliva and snapped her head in his direction. "Alright, let's not—"

Aunt Evalyn whirled just as she was about to step around the counter, pointing her finger right at him. "Don't think I won't toss you out of here like I'd do with any other chump giving me lip in my place."

Valeen rubbed her temples. Why did she think this would go any other way than terrible?

Hel bit down on his lower lip, obviously trying not to laugh. He tilted his head toward Valeen. "You give this one a run for her money with that audacity. Make my day, I'd love to see you try, Miss Evalyn. I won't even resist."

Well, now she had to defend her aunt. "She might not be able to toss you out of here, but I can."

"Oh, even better," Hel purred, picked up his goblet, and took a sip. "Let the fun begin. Bring out the shadows along with that temper, pretty please. It will make things interesting later tonight."

"If you think you're getting anything from me later without some *begging*, you're sorely mistaken."

"We'll see. I am quite irresistible. And I know you absolutely *love* my big, hard—"

"Do not finish that sentence," Valeen hissed. "And you say I'm rude. If anything, you're quite *annoying* right now."

"You're only proving my previous points; stubborn, mouthy, rud—" Hel ducked right before the goblet he'd given Aunt Evalyn flew over his head. It crashed to the floor and thumped several times before settling across the room. "Damn, woman. That would have hurt."

"That was the point!" Aunt Evalyn hollered.

"Maybe it's the drink. Alcohol does bring out the monster in some." He looked at Valeen. "You get a little more playful. Maybe you should drink up."

"Maybe you should shut *up* before I throw it in your face." She knew he was enjoying this. He liked to rile her.

"Ah, love, don't do that. It would be a waste. I saved that brandy wine for a special occasion, and here it is not even being appreciated. And when was the last time either of you had ice? And not even a mention of that, but of course I'm just the Black Mage. Just a big fucking asshole." He tsked and sipped his drink with a smile, as if this was the best time he'd had in a while.

"When did you marry this man?"

"I'm not a man," Hel said. "I'm a god trapped in an elf's body."

Aunt Evalyn scoffed at his claim, and snatched a whisky from the counter and drank a slug of booze straight from the bottle.

"We were married *before*," Valeen clarified. "In my first life, when I was just Valeen, the goddess of night. I know it's difficult to understand."

"Oh, I understand perfectly. This is a new life, so you're not actually married then? There's a chance to end this nonsense. No ceremony has taken place since you were born as Layala, correct?" Aunt Evalyn took another sip.

Valeen sighed. "Well, technically no, we haven't married since I was reborn but—"

Hel downed his own drink and set his goblet loudly

on the table. "Your aunt doesn't even think we're legitimate, and I get the impression your friends don't either. Why don't we have that wedding tonight—now?"

Valeen blinked at him. "*Now*?"

"Yes now, and right after I'll take you upstairs and consummate it so everyone will hear and no one else can say we're not actually married."

Aunt Evalyn choked on her drink and grabbed a napkin to pat her mouth. "Did you just say consummate upstairs in *my* place?"

Valeen stared at him trying to figure out if he was serious. *All Mother,* he was. A smile tugged at the corner of her mouth. "I don't have a dress—"

"He is the *Black Mage*," Aunt Evalyn crowed. "The Layala I know would never accept this. You can't marry the elf who created the pale one curse, the very same who is responsible for the deaths of thousands of elves!"

"I'm not just Layala anymore." Valeen had a bite in her tone for the first time. "If you took the time to get to know him, you'd like him. Hel is my soulmate. That is what my lily mark is from. He has the same, it happened thousands of years ago."

"And here I thought Thane was your mate."

"You know that bond was forced by magic. You used to hate that fact."

"Fine. Marry the mass murderer, what do I know? But there will be absolutely no consummation of this marriage in my place." She waved her hand dismissively and took another drink. "Stubborn as the day is long," she muttered to herself and went out the back door to join the others outside.

"Oh, there will be many hours of consummation." He smirked and kicked his feet up on the chair beside him. "If all you need is a dress," he snapped his fingers and three different gowns appeared and floated next to the table, "take your pick."

Chapter 44

VALEEN

Valeen hung all three of the dresses Hel had brought in one of Aunt Evalyn's rooms upstairs in Nerium Oleander. The first was a rich magenta with bell sleeves that draped to the floor and a fitted bodice sparkling with diamonds. It was beautiful but seemed a bit overstated for an intimate ceremony.

Then there was the dark-blue gown, almost black with a silver drape. The mermaid cut dress looked similar to her first wedding gown but didn't have the glitter and celestial details. The color was something she was drawn to, but she wanted something different. As much as she loved dark colors, she didn't feel it suited this ceremony.

The third, however, was an off-white gown that had a lavender undertone, floor length, fitted to the hips, and the sheer sleeves had strings of florals working up from the wrist to the shoulder. The lace on the bottom swirled into blooming lilies. It was a softer gown, for the part of her that wasn't a warrior out for vengeance. She wondered if he'd had this planned for some time and had snuck off to the dressmaker in town.

She pulled it off the hanger and turned to Piper, Katana, and Tif. Piper leaned up against the bedpost with her arms crossed. If it bothered her to help her pick a dress to marry Hel rather than Thane, she didn't voice it. Just being here rather than staying with the boys downstairs showed improvement with their friendship and Valeen's choice.

Aunt Evalyn was still bitter and drinking downstairs, probably on her fourth glass by now. If she was passed out by the time the ceremony ended it wouldn't surprise Valeen. Even if she had her qualms with this arrangement, she did agree to close the bar to the public. "You're going to do it either way, I may as well be there to see it happen," she'd said.

Valeen held the soft buttery fabric against herself. "What do you think of this one?"

Tif sat on the armrest of the sofa, bouncing her brown boots with a hole in each toe. She clapped her chubby hands then turned to Katana with a squeal. By the growing redness of her cheeks, she looked like she was trying very hard not to speak first.

Smiling, Piper nodded. "I think it's beautiful. Simple yet elegant. Although you always look great in ball gowns, I think this one suits you more."

"Yes, it's perfect," Katana said, in the seat beside Tif. "It's classy and understated, which is exactly what I'd expect you to wear. Especially since it's not a large ceremony."

"I love it!" Tif blurted out. She kicked her feet and pulled on her chocolate curls. "Try it on! We have to see it on you to decide for certain."

Using the dressing shade for privacy, she quickly changed. It was a perfect fit, the waist was snug but didn't affect her breathing, and the V-neck only hinted at cleavage. "I love the lily lace patterns. And the sleeves. It's so different from my last dress." She stepped out and turned in a slow circle. "I need help with the back."

Katana was the first to jump up and assist. "You are glowing in it! But do you want it to be different or would you rather something similar? Maybe you do want something more extravagant like the magenta dress? Or something else entirely. I'm sure we could arrange a fitting and postpone this for another day."

"I want it to be different, and I like that it's not yards of tulle like a ball gown actually."

"I'm just surprised you're getting married tonight. Did you have this secretly planned?" Piper asked.

"No, well, yes, we planned to marry but not tonight. We didn't have a date set." She glanced over at Piper. If anyone knew what Thane was feeling right now, it would be her. He hadn't looked at her quite the same since he'd returned from Ryvengaard. The pain behind his eyes seemed to have eased, like a dark storm cloud breaking away for sunlight to peek through. His smile toward her seemed genuine once again. Maybe he'd forgiven her for choosing Hel.

Through the mirror reflection she watched Katana work the buttons. Even if Katana thought Thane didn't want love, it wouldn't be surprising if she had everything to do with his mending heart. She pinched her lips together to keep from smiling.

"It's a fun surprise. Although I wish I could have planned this for you," Katana harrumphed with a pouty lip. Planning parties was one of Katana's favorite things to do, weddings made the top of the list. "I'd have a full tunnel of full blooming purple and white wisteria for you to walk down, and decadent food, rich wine, music. Yes, beautiful string music, and of course I'd spend hours styling your hair. Valeen, you're a goddess, and a queen, surely you want to have a big extravagant wedding? I'm sure Thane would let you have it at the castle. There's beautiful gardens and the waterfall as the backdrop would be magnificent."

"Oh, can I help plan?" Tif raised her hand. "I could help make the cake. Chocolate with a layer of strawberry filling or vanilla with chocolate cream drizzled with fudge."

"It would be beautiful, and the cake would be delicious no doubt, but I would rather not be married at Thane's castle," Valeen murmured. It was enough that she was there with another male, she didn't also need to marry there. "A small ceremony at my aunt's is perfect."

"Oh." Katana flushed, eyes going wide. "*Oh*, that is —I should have considered that. It's difficult enough with the servants gossiping behind his back, a wedding would be..." she trailed off with a grimace.

"Yeah. Besides, you know me, Katana, I'd much rather have a small gathering than something large, even if I am a queen and a goddess."

"Yes, you have always liked to slip among the shadows." She smiled. "I should not have even brought up marrying at Thane's castle. It was inconsiderate of me given the past. I apologize."

Lifting her shoulder, Piper said, "Well, if what I heard coming from one of the sitting rooms the other day was any indication, I think Thane will be just fine."

"*Piper*!" Katana cried, cheeks staining a rosy pink.

"What? I didn't stick around. I was walking by. She knows, doesn't she?"

"If you mean me, I know," Valeen said, trying to hide her smile. It was almost strange she felt no jealousy about it. Before Hel's return, she would have lost her mind to it. But she was so in love with Hel that he was all she could see. She almost felt like a young girl again, giddy to meet the boy she fancied.

Flustered, Katana pulled Valeen's hair out of the single braid and ran her fingers through it. "I told her. My sister was remarkably gracious about it."

"Well, she's getting laid by someone else." Piper plopped down on the bed. "And don't ever tell him this, or I will kill you, but I'd bet serious money Hel's good in bed."

Valeen whipped her head around in surprise. She rarely talked of Hel in a good light, let alone in a sexual manner. With her ankles crossed on the bed, Piper only smirked at her.

"I'd bet that too," Tif added with a sly grin. "Not that I know anything about that. I've never even kissed anyone. There was this boy in my village who tried once but I threw mud in his face."

Valeen burst out laughing. "Why would you do that?"

"I don't know. I feel bad about it now. Aren't we supposed to have dates for a wedding?"

"If you want one, why don't you ask Leif?"

"Um no." Tif rolled her eyes as if that were absurd. "But I do have someone in mind. I'll see you all soon!" She dropped to the floor and scampered out of the room.

"She's a strange little thing. Maker only knows who she'll ask to be her 'date'." Piper propped herself up on the headboard. "But come on, are you not going to tell us how Hel is?"

"That's not usually something I talk about openly. And you never asked about... well you know."

"Because he's my good friend, that would be weird. Hel is a mystery to me."

"It's just us," Katana added, and started combing her hair with a boar bristle brush she'd found in Aunt Evalyn's room. "It's not something to be ashamed of. Sex is completely natural, especially between mates. I can only imagine it's almost magical."

Letting out a sigh, Valeen nibbled on her lower lip. "Fine, yes, Hel is good. Remarkably good. And there *is* something magical about it. My skin starts to shimmer."

"Shimmer? Like your skin truly glitters?" Piper asked. "Is it his magic?"

Valeen's cheeks warmed. "I think it's my magic not his, but it's like tiny stars glowing on my skin. It fades quickly. It's never happened with anyone else."

"I wonder if it is a thing between mates. The glowing," Katana muttered and started a small braid above Valeen's ear. "Do we have a few pearl pins or a headdress? A veil? Anything?"

"I'll go ask Evalyn," Piper said.

"I think it probably is because we're mates," Valeen

answered, analyzing her sister's expression in the mirror. She was hiding something.

Deep breaths, deep breaths. Valeen closed her eyes for a moment. Katana and Piper had already gone through the door to the yard, leaving her alone. It wasn't that she was nervous to marry Hel again, it was more of a worry that Aunt Evalyn would say something regrettable and Hel would retort with something scathing, and this special moment would be ruined. Maybe they should have just married alone in the woods with Presco and Katana there as witnesses. *Too late now.*

She pushed through the door and froze. She might have paid more attention to the floral arches with ribbons dancing in the breeze, creating a tunnel of rich purple and white, or the fragrance of the flowers swirling around her. Even the luminor crickets and a few torches lit up the twilight evening. But past the white rose petals scattered over the grass, waited Hel.

He was magnificent.

Her breath caught a little as the corner of his mouth turned up and his dimple appeared. With his hair pushed back out of his face, it accentuated his beautiful bone structure and bright maroon eyes, more purple than red today. Tiny luminor crickets fluttered around him making his alabaster skin glow more golden.

She barely heard the muttering of Leif about her radiant beauty or the sniffle of her sister as she slowly walked toward *him*.

You are absolutely stunning, my love. If Serenity were a person, it would be you.

I was thinking the same thing about you.

She quickened her pace to the beat of the soft string music coming from somewhere unknown, either in the city or by Hel's doing. Placing one foot in front of the other, she padded over the grass and rose petals. She smiled at Thane next to Fennan and Leif. He nodded once and smiled at her graciously, as if he were truly happy. It was that moment she realized he'd fully let her go.

She pulled her gaze back to Hel, he waited with an outstretched hand. His fingers curled around hers, and they faced one another. With a gentle smile, and soft eyes, he rubbed his thumbs across the top of her knuckles.

"You're even more beautiful than last time." And this time around their vows meant more. It was hard won, after what felt like an eternity of a fight.

"Thank you," she whispered back.

Presco stood beside them holding open a book in his large hands. "I have known you both for longer than I have kept track and it brings me joy to see you come together once again. There is something enchanting about your love, and how you have fought your way back to each other after two thousand years and through all the things that would see you torn apart. It's a love for songs and stories that will live on through the ages."

With a white handkerchief, Aunt Evalyn dabbed at the corner of her eye. One day she would tell her the whole story.

Presco tapped his finger on the page. "The ceremony Hel has requested is not in your native tongue, apologies to those who don't understand the celestial language of Runevale, but I believe you'll feel the words, nonetheless." The words about being blessed to see the other as they truly were, to cherish and love, were a blur. Her focus was narrowed on him—on his touch, his magic that seemed to be swirling around her, wisps that caressed her skin creating chill bumps along her arms.

Presco pressed the ring she'd made in her father's forge days before into her palm. "I'm aware Valeen already has hers, but did you have another piece to add, Hel?"

"I do." Hel rubbed his forefinger and thumb together and then it appeared. A silver band with star and moon etchings around the outside. He took her hand and slid it on to sit against her original black diamond. "Let this ring be a reminder of my promises and devotion to only you."

Then she took Hel's hand and pushed on a simple black band made of onyx, repeating the same words. She leaned forward and whispered, "Our names *Zaurahel x Valeen* will appear across the band only under moonlight."

He smiled. "I like that very much."

A gold chain dangled from Presco's hand. First, he wrapped it around Valeen's wrist, then Hel's, to symbolize the joining. He took out a knife, cut their palms and they clasped hands. They'd done this before in their first life. It was how their blood was bound through all time, it was the reason she was able to wake him in the tower.

Her lily mate mark on her arm began to pulse and throb. Like it was trying to tell her this was right.

Presco said in the celestial tongue, "Keeper of my heart, bound by blood and by soul," and they repeated.

"Would either of you like to say anything further?" Presco said.

"I do," Hel said, and his dark lashes fluttered. He glanced down a moment then looked straight into her eyes. "Valeen, I vow to cherish you for all time in any life and in any realm, to give you everything my body and mind can provide. Everything that is mine, is yours. I promise my heart and soul to you. To always be your friend and your lover. I vow to make your enemies my enemies, and to end anyone who stands against you. I promise to forsake all others. I will give you anything your heart truly desires, and if I should ever go back on these vows, may the Maker and the All Mother strike me down."

A tear she hadn't even realized was there rolled down her cheek. His words were everything she could have wanted and more. Now anything she said would seem wholly inadequate. She hadn't prepared for this, so she went with what was in her heart. "Hel, our journey has not been easy, and fate has not been fair, but through this, I got to fall in love with you all over again. I vow to love you and only you with all my heart for all my days from now to the end of time. I promise to hold your heart and keep it safe, to love all that you are in the worst of times and the best. My soulmate, my heart, my husband, and my best friend."

His throat bobbed and the luminor crickets' light caught the glimmer in his eyes. Full of adoration and love.

NIGHT MEETS THE ELF QUEEN

"Now seal the marriage with a kiss."

Hel slid his arms around her waist, tugging her in closer. Their lips were a breath away, "I told you I'd always want more." Then their lips met, soft and gentle at first, then she threw her arms around his neck and their love spilled over into passion. He lifted her off the ground and the few chuckles only made Hel kiss her harder, his tongue sliding against hers. When he finally set her down and they pulled apart, his smile was gentle but full of true joy. This male who could be so cruel looked at her as if she were his whole world.

All mine. Forever, Hel whispered into her mind. *I'll never leave again, I'll never let you leave. It doesn't matter what happens. You'll always be mine, love.*

Chapter 45

VALEEN

Inside Nerium Oleander, bewitched wind and string instruments provided enchanting music. Aunt Evalyn's human waitresses and cook had filled a table with the food they'd meant for the patrons that night. All the tables that usually took up most of the room had been moved to the outside edges leaving space to dance and mingle.

Valeen wrapped her hand around Hel's elbow, smiling with a full heart. She was married to him again. He was all hers and no one could deny it. She leaned close to his ear. "You look good tonight. Very sexy, Mr. Black."

He smiled and gently took her earlobe between his teeth. "Thank you, Mrs. Black."

"Oh, look, someone made special seats for us," Valeen said, excitedly.

Aunt Evalyn nodded at her from behind the bar. She must have had her staff do this while they were outside.

"So we do." Hel led her to a seat decorated with flowers and ribbons, labeled "bride" and beside it was its counterpart labeled "groom". They weren't thrones or anything extravagant, but it was perfect, nonetheless. Once she took the seat, Hel kissed the top of her hand. A tingle started where his lips lingered on her skin, then his magic seemed to flow into her veins, heating her from the inside, sending a trill of desire rippling down her spine.

Her breath caught as he smiled, then she pulled her hand back. "What was that?"

"I was just letting you feel what I do for you."

With a flush, she stared into his eyes. "That was... intense."

"It is. But I have something for you before we sneak off. Wait here." He tilted his head in the direction of the door, and Thane rose up from the chair he'd taken. The two of them met near the exit and left.

She raised a brow and couldn't hold back her smile. *What are you up to?*

Be patient, he said back.

The mystery of what he might have in store had her feet bouncing. Tif was stuffing her face full at the banquet table. It struck her that Tif had claimed she was bringing a date, and she hadn't seen anyone new yet. Aunt Evalyn was sipping on a glass of whisky laughing at something Fennan said. Leif, Piper, and Katana started at the dessert table while Presco filled his plate with meat and vegetables.

Aunt Evalyn was the first to notice her sitting alone and rushed over, even though she'd already hugged and cried as soon as she finished kissing Hel at the end of the ceremony. "I hope you like the party we put together on short notice. The chairs were Katana's idea."

"It's all very lovely. Thank you."

"Lovely?" she laughed, crinkling the skin around her eyes. "You've gotten so proper lately. You even sit taller, as if you know nothing in this world could challenge you."

She smiled and winked. "There are not many things that *can* challenge me, Aunt Evalyn."

"Well, despite what I said earlier, I'm happy if you are. I'll do my best to get to know him rather than go off rumors."

Valeen crossed one leg over the other and drummed her fingernails on the wooden armrests. "I don't want you to get it wrong, Hel has done terrible things. I'm not going to tell you otherwise. But he has reasons, and it's namely because of the group of people who've been hunting and killing us for two thousand years now."

"This council you spoke of. Will they come here?" She twisted the poison berry necklace out of habit.

"They will. They've already sent their assassins. More will come. If things get bad in the city and I ask you to leave, I want you to go back to Briar Hollow. You should be safe there."

"I'm not one to run from a fight."

"I know, but this will be worse than anything Palenor has ever seen. The pale ones are insignificant compared to the army the council could gather. I don't ask much of you, but I would ask this."

"Fine, if you tell me to go, I will."

"Good."

Katana approached her with a drink in each hand.

"That was so sweet. I could see the love radiating off you both. Your aura is more pink and purple tonight, even Hel has some pink. Ugh." She did a dramatic dip backward of her head, pretending to faint. "I'm rather jealous of such a love. It's one of a kind." She pressed a glass into Valeen's hand.

Katana's ability to see auras was fascinating. She'd never met anyone else that could. "Thank you." She took the drink and glanced at the front entrance. "Do you know what they're doing?"

"I don't have the faintest idea."

Aunt Evalyn raised a fist at Leif behind the bar. "Hey! No one is allowed back there but me. I'll see you later." She hurried off just as Leif quickly poured himself a drink.

"I know what they're doing!" Tif tottered over carrying a white frosted cupcake with a shimmer of lavender on top.

"How?"

"I know everything," Tif said and bit into the cupcake. "One of the perks of being small is being able to sneak around and listen to conversations without anyone knowing. It's a wonderful surprise. I wondered where he snuck off to the other day, but I got my answer. I keep track of everyone."

Valeen crossed her arms. "Well, now I have to know."

"You'll find out in a few minutes. As hard as it is for me to keep my trap shut, I won't be the one to ruin the surprise. I know you said this wedding was spontaneous but maybe only to you. I think Hel has had this secretly planned for a while now."

Considering the gowns, flowers, and decor he'd managed to conjure up from the aether, Tif was right.

She turned around and waved at the food tables. At first, Valeen only saw the two-tiered vanilla poppy seed cake intended for the menu tonight, but caught a pair of tiny black boots poking out from under the white tablecloth.

"Tif, you actually brought someone?"

She stamped her foot then pointed at the ground beside her. The tablecloth lifted, then a small brown hat followed by a bushy copper beard and a pair of big eyes peeked out from under the linen. "He's being shy. I told him not to worry about the jumbos at this party."

"This is the date you decided to bring?" Valeen asked, smiling. The gnome boy pulled at his suspenders, snapped them against his chest, then winced.

"He is." She grinned and licked her cupcake. "The gnome colony isn't far from here if you know a quick hare to give you a ride."

Talking to birds and riding on hares, her small lady's maid kept surprising her. "You rode on the back of a hare?"

"Course. It's not as fast as a bird but my date won't ride birds. He thinks it's scary."

Katana and Valeen smiled at one another. "I remember when you wouldn't come near any jumbos besides me, Tifapine."

"He said he has liked me since we were fourteen. You reminded me of him earlier, he's the very same one I threw mud at for trying to kiss me. But if he likes me, he should do what I ask." She pointed at her side and stomped her boot.

Katana stooped down to her level. "Perhaps you should go take his hand and bring him over here. What is his name?"

"Tommy. Well, it's Tombuckle but I call him Tommy."

Katana stood and nudged Valeen's shoulder. "Tommy and Tifapine," she crooned. "That is the most adorable thing ever."

"Yes, Tif, help him be brave. I'm sure it's intimidating for him."

She rolled her eyes. "Oh, fine." A moment later she was dragging him across the wood floor. He was about an inch taller than her and quite slender in comparison. His crimson tunic had a couple brown and white striped patches, as did his matching pants. His boots had holes as well. Tif once told her it was fashionable.

Valeen squatted down as they approached. His cheeks went bright red, and he took off his hat and fidgeted with it.

"Val, this is Tommy. We grew up in the same gnome colony. Mama always told me he was a 'no good Dinglecopper', but," she turned and smiled at him, "he's my friend anyway."

"Hello, Tommy. How are you?"

"Quite well, thank you, your highness." His voice came out squeaky and he immediately looked down.

"What's a Dinglecopper?"

"That's his last name. Mama had a feud with his mama a while back over the possession of some razzleberry patches. They grow between our two gnome homes, you see. Mama said they were more on our side and were ours. His mama said they were theirs. I thought we should all share. But gnomes are very particular about sharing food."

"Well, I'm glad you could come, Tommy. Feel free to eat, drink, and dance."

Tif started dragging him along again. "Let's eat some of that poppy seed cake and then dance. You do know how to dance, don't you?"

"N-n-no, I don't know how to dance."

"Eh, you'll have to figure it out then, Tommy. It's not that hard."

Valeen laughed quietly. "He's going to have his hands full with her."

"Definitely," Katana agreed.

Piper and Leif made their way over. Leif was the first to wrap his arms around her and lift her off her feet. "I'm happy for you, Fightbringer, because you're happy. It's still a bit strange not seeing you with my High King but anyone can see how much you and Hel love each other."

"Thank you for being here. I hope you'll always be my friend."

"Always, Fightbringer. I wish you nothing but happiness in the future."

The next embrace came from Piper. Tonight, she smelled like brandy and her eyes were a bit glassy. It was a rare sight to see Piper give in to drink. As one of Thane's personal guards she liked to stay alert. It was good to see her relax. "I understand it better now, you and him. There is a past we weren't there to witness, and I realize we also weren't in Ryvengaard with you either. I'm sorry for judging you so harshly before. I hope you forgive me."

"Forgiven." The truth was she never even needed an apology from Piper.

Presco had given her his congratulations before she ever stepped away from Hel outside. It was rare but he'd even shed a tear and hugged her so tight she'd found it hard to breathe. He was currently locked into conversation near the bar with Fennan and Aunt Evalyn. The conversation was hard to hear over the music, but it had something to do with dragons and their appetites. She hadn't seen or spoken to Fennan much since she'd returned with Hel from Ryvengaard. It was no doubt on purpose on his end, given that Thane was his best friend and he never took a liking to Hel. Actually, she was surprised Fennan stayed for the ceremony.

Leif motioned behind her. "I think they're ready for you."

Hel stood at the entrance door, this time with a bundle of black cloth in his hand. In a few quick strides he was standing behind her. "I need to put this on you."

"A blindfold?"

Before she could say anything further, he was wrapping the silk around her eyes. When it was secure he leaned down to her ear, his warm breath whispering over her skin. "Can you see anything?"

The barest hint of light peeked through the bottom but that was it. "No."

"Good." He swept her into his arms, stealing a giggle from her. "I can't have you falling down the front steps on our wedding day." His boots clacked over the wood floor, her body bouncing lightly with his smooth gait. The whispers of the others put a permanent smile across her face. What could it be?

The smell of the outdoors along with the birds chirping told her they'd stepped onto the road. He gently set her on her feet and took hold of her hand, guiding her forward. "Hel, what is it? I don't like surprises."

"You'll like this one."

Her fingers suddenly bumped into something soft, not skin, not fluffy fur, but something almost as smooth as silk. Hel's quick fingers brushed the back of her head, and the blindfold fell away. She gasped and tears immediately blurred her vision. "Hel, you found them," she whispered.

Starborn and Night, her eternal winged horses, stood before her. Colossally tall, regal and muscular much like Phantom and Midnight. Their sleek black hair shined in the torchlight and the moonlight above. Starborn whinnied, fluttering his wings, and bumped his nose into her open palm. Night, whose full name was "Midnight" like her horse here in Palenor, nudged her shoulder with his muzzle. He inhaled, becoming familiar with her scent, remembering. The tears she'd tried to hold back slipped down her cheeks.

Her boys had returned home. Her boys she thought were gone forever.

"Technically, *we* found them," Hel said, and tilted his head to the right. Thane stepped from around Night's broad body, and she grinned.

"Thane, you helped too?"

"Well, I wasn't there but I remembered the song you used to sing to call them home." Thane patted

NIGHT MEETS THE ELF QUEEN

Night's thick neck. "Hel said they came quickly to the tune."

The click-clack of their hooves on the cobblestone was like music to her ears. She'd forgotten all about that song, though now she began to hum it. Starborn let out a puff of air and a quiet neigh. "Hi, babies. I've missed you." She scratched Starborn's forehead; it was his favorite, and gently pet Night's soft cheek. "When did you do this?"

"Yesterday, while you were having breakfast with Katana," Hel answered.

Starborn stretched his wings and tossed his head. That had been his signal he wanted to go for a ride. "You said you were checking on Synick."

He smirked. "I did for a few minutes."

Leif, Fennan, and Piper gathered near the door. "Do they truly have wings?" Fennan asked. "Or is it Hel's magic?"

"They are her horses of legend," Leif replied. "My Nana used to tell stories of them and how they'd fly her through the night sky in her golden chariot. On the winter solstice, the longest night of the year, they say she showered the sky with her stars. And every year if you watch the skies, you'll see the bundle of shooting stars following her chariot."

"Is that true?"

"Seen it myself many times. Not her, but the stars."

"What Fennan means, was Valeen actually the one who brings the star showers?" Piper added. "She's been gone for so long."

"I did start that, yes." Valeen smiled at them, resting her head against Night's shoulder. "Starborn and Night must have carried on the tradition without me."

Using her magic to lighten her weight, she sprung up onto his back and then laid against him. He smelled like the salty sea near her home in Runevale and the wild fields of House of Night. Oh, how she longed to go back there. Her throat tightened at the memory of the ruins. "I missed you." Starborn neighed and popped up on his hind legs, slamming back down, and pawing at the stone. "I missed you just as much." Her shadows slipped from her fingertips and slid along his back, brushing his hair from his eyes. "I promise we'll go riding later, but I can't right now. It's my wedding day." Starborn curled his top lip, baring his teeth, almost a smile, and Night bumped his muzzle into Hel and sniffed his hair. "They remember you."

"Of course they do." Hel chuckled and rubbed Night's neck. "They're intelligent."

Slipping off Night, she jumped back into Hel's arms and kissed him hard on the mouth. "Thank you so much. You don't know how much this means to me."

"I told you I'd find them." He set her down and turned her by the shoulders to face Thane.

He took her hand, lifting it to his mouth and his lips lightly touched her skin. "Congratulations, Val."

"Thank you for helping, Thane. Truly."

"Everyone head back inside for cake," Hel said, giving her and Thane a moment.

Thane's eyes followed the others as they moved away, watching Katana in particular, and then he turned back to her. "I wouldn't miss it. You're the two most important people in my life."

She frowned, looking down at his hand still holding hers. "Thane..."

"I truly am happy for you, Val, for both of you. You look beautiful. Even more than I imagined you would have."

"Thank you." In so many ways her romantic relationship with him felt like ending one of her journals and putting it on the shelf.

He wrapped her in a hug. There was no tension or unease, they were simply two friends who loved each other. He pulled back and adjusted the sleeves at his wrists. "I've kept you long enough." He smiled at Hel over her shoulder. "Your bride is waiting for a dance, Hel."

"I think there is another lovely goddess who is also waiting for a dance," Hel smirked at Thane.

"But first we need to get these two somewhere." Valeen made a clicking sound with her tongue. "Come on, Starborn, Night, let's take you around back." She couldn't very well leave them out in the street. Winged horses didn't exist in Adalon, and there were already a few onlookers down the road.

BACK INSIDE, romantic violin music played. Hel and Valeen shared their first dance while everyone watched. One of his hands rested low on her back, the other wrapped around her palm. The candles hovering above their heads gave off a subtle glow, bringing a moody ambiance. Valeen rested her cheek on his chest as they gently swayed to the tune.

"I hope this day is even more special than the last time," he murmured. The rumble of his voice made her skin tingle.

"It's more than I could have ever hoped for. Everyone I love is here." Although now that he'd given her his wedding gift hers seemed wholly inadequate. "There's something I wanted to give you but now that everyone has seen what you gave me..."

"You don't need to give me anything," Hel said. "My gift is you."

As much as she appreciated that sentiment, and she knew he meant it, she still wanted to give him something special. She paused and conjured the gift from the aether to her hand. It was a magenta, leather-bound book with gold-encrusted edges and a decorative heart with extravagant swirls at the center. "It's not much."

He smiled, bringing out his dimple and took it. "What is it?"

"It's the journal I started the day after our first kiss. It's the history of our time together, up through our wedding and about a year after."

"You started a heart journal after only one kiss? I'm flattered." He grinned even wider.

"We both knew our lives were going to change after that."

"I knew the moment I met you. It didn't take a kiss." He ran his fingertips over the heart of the journal. "You never let me read your journals."

"Well, I'm giving you this one to read. If you want to."

He tucked it inside his suit jacket. "Oh, I will be absolutely reading every word of it. Thank you, love.

You may not think it's a special gift but it's more than anything I'd ever ask for."

The song changed and Presco stepped in for a turn. "Do you mind if I dance with her for a moment, Hel?"

Hel patted his shoulder. "I suppose, but don't get too handsy or my threat about making your skull a decoration in my study still stands."

Presco laughed. "I'm always proper with her."

Valeen took his hand, and they began stepping to the music. "I appreciate you taking time away from your family and business to be here with me. I know it's a lot to ask. But we'll get our home back and rebuild."

"You don't even have to ask, Valeen. I'm at your side. I would bring my wife here, but I fear it's too dangerous right now. She understands."

"Ayva seems like a wonderful person."

"She is."

Valeen watched Hel pull Aunt Evalyn from behind the bar top, and to keep from laughing, she lightly sunk her teeth into her bottom lip. The look on Aunt Evalyn's face was a mixture of horror and curiosity as he dragged her onto the dance floor and spun her in a circle. Everyone joined in then; Fennan and Piper, Thane and Katana, Tif and Tommy, even Leif, pulling one of Aunt Evalyn's human waitresses.

Once the song changed Leif was next to tap her shoulder. He, of course, said inappropriate flirtatious things Valeen hoped Hel didn't hear. Thane held Tif for a dance. It was the most adorable thing she'd ever seen. Tif beamed too, like it was the greatest moment of her life.

Time seemed to fly by as they mingled, danced, and

ate. Before she knew it, Hel whispered in ear, "We have a night away to get to, and two horses out back who would love to take us there."

"Where are we going?"

"You'll see."

Chapter 46

THANE

Too much wine made Thane's body uncomfortably warm. He took off his jacket and undid a few buttons at the top of his tunic. Valeen danced with Hel in the center of Nerium Oleander. She giggled at something he said, and he leaned down and pressed a gentle kiss below her ear and then they were saying their goodbyes.

He might have been upset, wallowing in his wine, but someone else had him enraptured.

Katana. Even the sound of her name in his thoughts was like a song stuck on repeat.

The way her hips swayed moving around the room. How everything about her seemed to glow, from her bright hair to her golden skin. It had been a day since he'd caught her dancing, and they gave into each other once more on the rug.

They hadn't been alone together since, and it was eating him alive.

Was she avoiding him after she confessed to Valeen what happened? The only reason he even knew that she told Valeen was because Tif told him. She'd apparently been eavesdropping.

When he asked Katana to dance earlier, their conversation was very... stilted. Almost as if she was regretting sleeping with him again. He took another sip of wine. He shouldn't have given in a second time, even if he could hardly think of anything else.

The way her hair lit up like a candle... did it mean something? She said that had never happened before.

Gods, he cursed under his breath. *I should have left it to one time with no promises.* But even that thought made him almost sick. He didn't want to leave it with no promises at all. He wanted all the promises, and that scared him.

"You look glum." Fennan slid into the seat across from him. "Is it about the wedding?"

He drank more wine. "No. I'm not upset about her marrying Hel." Surprisingly, he wasn't. At one time he'd have been mad with jealousy, and sure there were some lingering feelings about her, but they were strangely platonic. The thought of even kissing her felt wrong, as if something deep inside him rejected the very idea of it.

"Alright." Fennan drummed his fingers on the glass mug in his hand. "Something else you want to talk about?"

"Not really." He watched Katana dancing with Leif, and the way she smiled up at him had his cheeks burning. Her laugh pierced his chest, sent a tingle down from the nape of his neck to his lower belly.

Fennan turned and followed his gaze. "Ah, Katana.

NIGHT MEETS THE ELF QUEEN

What is going on there? I see all the longing looks, you know. I think everyone can see them."

Thane leaned back, gazed locked onto her. He couldn't look away even if he wanted to. Her blonde hair tumbled down her back, almost reaching her plump cheeks. That gold dress hugged them too, not hiding a damn thing. "Nothing."

"You don't need to lie to me."

"There's nothing to lie about. We slept together and that was that. The end."

Fennan cocked a brow. "You slept with her? Thane, that's... she's Valeen's sister."

"I know."

"I didn't expect that from you."

"Why is that?" Thane brought the wine glass to his mouth, peering over the lip of it as Leif dipped her. He didn't like how low his hand was on her back. A few more inches and it would be inappropriate. A few more inches and he'd be out of this seat and across the room.

He let out a sharp breath and rubbed his temple. He shouldn't want her this much. She wasn't his. They weren't betrothed or committed.

"Well, I've slept with a handful of maidens in my day, and that was that, but that's not you, sire. And I know you all think I've gone through half the courtiers but it's not true. I flirt, sure, but I rarely take maidens to bed. It complicates things."

"Yeah," Thane agreed. "It does." Sleeping with Katana hadn't put out the fire of desire like he thought it would. If anything, it burned hotter.

"How about instead of staring at her, you go cut in?" Fennan said. "I'll go ask Piper."

Thane finished his glass of wine. "Good. You

should." Although he liked Ronan, he would rather see Fennan and Piper together. His best friend's happiness was important to him, and he didn't want to lose Piper. If she married Ronan, she'd leave them.

Before he even considered what he would say, he was standing beside Leif and Katana as the song ended. He simply took her hand and pulled her along with him as the next melody began.

They easily fell into step as if they'd been dancing together all their lives, as if she anticipated his moves.

Why wouldn't she look up at him?

They'd circled around the floor two times before she finally said, "Leif is a surprisingly good dancer."

"I noticed."

She lifted her chin. Her lavender eyes sparkled with mystery. "I noticed you noticing."

"I didn't like his hand placement. It was bordering inappropriate."

She tried to hold back her smile by pressing her lips together. "Yours is rather low."

He slid his hand down until he was full-on cupping her right cheek.

"Now who is inappropriate?"

"It's not when we're..." Friends who happened to know carnal knowledge of each other? Maker above, he couldn't even fool himself with that one. They were more than friends but less than a commitment.

Whatever it was, he didn't like it.

"What are we exactly?" She arched a brow. "This is a peculiar predicament we seem to have caught ourselves in."

"All I know is I don't like seeing other males touching you."

"Hmmm, well I suppose you will just have to learn not to look." Her tone wasn't playful, and she didn't smile and wink. She was serious. His jaw clenched and he gulped down his next comment about seeing if she said that the next time he took her to bed and her hair lit up. But there wouldn't be a next time. "And how are you feeling tonight about my sister?"

"I'm not feeling anything at all about your sister."

"Truly?"

"My feelings are somewhere else tonight."

She searched his face, his eyes, and then slowly smiled. "So, your heart is better."

"It is." He wouldn't admit she might have something to do with that. He cleared his throat. "Are you still having nightmares?" Piercing screams hadn't woken him in a few days but that didn't mean anything.

"Last night." Once more she lifted her gaze to his. "I dreamed that Synick escaped and... came into my room and tied me up. I hate how real the nightmares feel."

Was this a prophetic dream? In Ryvengaard their rooms were right next to each other, here she was in the same wing of the castle but on the floor below him.

That needed to change.

The possibility of Synick escaping was very real. He hadn't even checked on him since his return. Had Hel been keeping a close eye?

"Katana." He paused, waiting for her to meet his gaze again. "Remember when I promised to protect you?"

She smiled. "I do."

"I intend to keep that promise. If you are ever

afraid, you can stay with me. It wouldn't mean anything, and we don't even have to sleep in the same bed. It would be to keep you safe."

Her brows furrowed with hurt or confusion. She pulled away and they stood unmoving on the dance floor. "Did I say something wrong?"

"I just want to live without being afraid and... and the thing I'm even more afraid of than Atlanta or Synick is that... nothing we shared means anything to you."

His breath seemed to rush out all at once.

His heart stopped.

She pushed a hand through her hair and frowned. "You want to keep me close to keep me safe because I am *broken*. And I can see it's in your nature to protect and fix broken things but it's not because you..." She whirled and hurried for the bar top.

"You're not broken. Katana." His heart began to pound. His mouth went dry. "Katana, wait." He dashed after her.

She made a quick turn to hop onto a barstool in front of Evalyn. "I would love a glass of wine, Evalyn. That pink one looks delicious."

"Coming right up." She turned and reached for a tall-stemmed glass on the shelf.

Thane plopped down next to her and his leg began to bounce uncontrollably. "You're not broken."

"Yes, I am."

"No. You've had terrible things happen to you but that doesn't make you broken. What else were you going to say?"

"Nothing you want to hear," she said under her breath.

"'Not because I', what? Not because I care? I do care about you." More than a *friend* should.

She turned on her stool, and her knees bumped against his. "We cannot sleep in the same room. I won't."

"Why? Do you suddenly find me repulsive?"

She laughed and put a hand to her chest, drawing his gaze to her collarbones, then her cleavage. "Oh, Thane. I know you are not naive when it comes to ladies. You know exactly why I won't, and it has absolutely nothing to do with you being *repulsive*."

"I can control myself, if that's what you're worried about. I'll have a second bed brought in. Easy." He tapped his chin. "And we can put up a curtain, so you have privacy."

The strap of her dress fell from her shoulder, drooping the fabric and exposing the swell of her breast. He quickly lifted it back into place and let his fingers linger too long on her soft skin.

Her eyes fell to his hand sliding down her arm and the corners of her plump lips curled upward. "Well, I am glad it would be so easy for you to resist me, but no."

His fingers dug into his thigh. "I didn't mean it like that. I think it might be the hardest thing I'll ever do but I'll respect your wishes."

Evalyn set the wine in front of Katana with a raised eyebrow. She no doubt heard every word, even if they spoke quietly.

"Thank you so much, Evalyn." She took a sip and leaned in like she was going to tell her a secret. "Oh, it's as delicious as it looked. I do not think I've told you yet, but you have the most beautiful brown eyes. It was one of the first things I noticed about you. And Valeen told me all about you of course. I absolutely loved that you raised her in a cottage with a round door and taught her how to gamble."

Evalyn smiled. "Well, I probably shouldn't have taught her the gambling so young, but I did what I could with what I had."

"It's truly selfless to take on someone else's child without complaint."

"I'd do it again, if I had to."

Katana grinned and put her hand over Evalyn's. "I know. You have a splendid aura."

"A what?"

"I call it the color of your soul. Yours is mostly orange. It's the rarest. You like freedom and independence but are also selfless when it comes to helping others. You are a good multitasker and are not afraid to speak your mind."

"True," Thane added. "Especially the last part."

Evalyn laughed. "I don't know how you did that, but I'll just accept it. Can I get you anything, Thane?"

"No, but thank you. I've had more than enough for one night."

"Maybe you have, but I haven't. Not when Layala has married the Black Mage and I have to simply sit back and accept it."

"He's not as bad as you think he is."

"I can't believe you're standing up for him."

"It's complicated."

"So I see." Evalyn moved down the bar and started washing dishes in the sink.

Katana took a long drink of wine then turned back to him. "You know, those aren't only *my* wishes. You were the one who said, 'only once', then seduced me the second time."

His mouth dropped and his cheeks warmed. "Seduced you? Did you not want to?"

"No, I did. That is the problem, isn't it? Because I warned you my feelings would get involved." She pressed her palm over her heart and her eyes softened. "But truth be told, my feelings were involved before the first time. I am drawn to you far more than I should be. I shouldn't have come to you that night. It was a mistake." She took another gulp of wine like the confession pained her.

His heart was about to beat out of his chest. "A mistake?" That one bloody hurt. Felt like a damn knife to the chest. This—no strings attached—whatever it was, was all muddy now. He didn't sleep with his "friends". He didn't feel like he couldn't breathe without his "friends". If he didn't do something he was going to lose her, but he was terrified of what could happen to his fragile heart. Deep down he knew she already had the power to crush it. "You think I was a mistake?"

She cupped the side of his face and leaned closer. "I did not say that to hurt you. I'm sorry. You said not to involve our hearts, and I broke that on my end, but you've held up yours. So, it's done now." She dropped her hand and smiled sorrowfully at him. "I won't live in Valeen's shadow, Thane." She picked up her glass and walked over to sit beside Leif.

Shit, shit, shit. A storm of emotions ripped through him. He shoved his fingers into his hair, messing up the careful braids and tried to calm his erratic breathing.

Evalyn was suddenly there again and pushed a

shot glass of amber in front of him. "I think you do need this after all, High King."

He downed it and pushed it back. "Thanks."

"Tell ol' Aunt Evalyn what's going on."

Chapter 47

VALEEN

The disorientation of teleporting faded away and Valeen blinked, taking in the new surroundings. The air was balmy and warm, and smelled salty like the sea. The dew of it settled on her skin, curling a stray white lock of hair around her face. Crickets chirped and the sound of waves crashing somewhere nearby brought a smile to her lips. The stars twinkled above, and she looked up trying to get a read on where they were. He'd blindfolded her once again before this. If they were still in Adalon, she wasn't sure where. The dense vegetation with vines swinging from palm tree to palm tree, ferns, and colorful exotic blooms were out of place for Palenor.

At the edge of a cliff stood a cerulean-blue manor with white shutters and carefully tended florals around the base of the three-story building. "Where are we?"

They'd rode winged Night and Starborn back to the

castle and let them into the pasture with the others before they appeared here.

"It's an island off Palenor's southeast shore. The Isle of Mist."

She wasn't aware of any islands in the area. "Does someone live here?"

"It's an inn. There's a small village of elves here." He pointed down the roadway under a tunnel of sweeping trees. "About a fifteen-minute walk that way. By boat it would take a few hours or so to reach the shores of East Palenor."

Tugging her hand, they walked through the front entrance. Warm wood planks lined the inside from top to bottom. Potted green plants greeted them and an inviting smell of roasting meat. A few patrons sat at the round tables taking up the left side of the room. Directly ahead was a set of wide stairs and to the right a desk with a young elf behind it. Her big chestnut eyes widened, taking in both of them.

"Hello, can I help you?" she asked in a small voice.

"You can. We'd like the suite on the third floor, please," Hel said.

"The suite is reserved for Mr. Westover tonight, but—"

"The suite is reserved for me, take us there." His voice took on an entrancing tone, the poor girl had no chance of fighting.

"Of course it is, right this way."

She led them up the two sets of stairs and pushed a large silver key into the lock. A moment later she whisked into the room, making sure it was clear and then bowed her head and curtsied. "If you need room service or meals brought up all you have to do is ask."

"Thank you," Valeen said. The young elf left and Valeen ran her hand along the back of the tan leather chair. "I hope Mr. Westover doesn't come barging into our room at midnight."

Hel set her bag of personal items on the entry table. "That would be a regrettable choice for Mr. Westover if he does."

The suite had a charming set of turquoise couches and white painted walls with seashell decor throughout the room. An archway led to the large bed covered in crisp white linens with fresh lavender flower petals spread over the top.

In a few strides she pushed through the doors to the balcony. The moonlight shone brightly off the crested white waves rolling against the black sand beach below. "Wow, it's beautiful. It reminds me of home with the black sand." She turned, leaning her low back against the railing and folded her arms. "How long have you planned this?"

He rubbed his chin feigning deep thought, "If I'm being truthful, this has been on my mind since you woke me up."

She laughed and gripped the railing behind her. "Even though you were angry with me?"

His eyes smoldered as he prowled toward her. "Mmhmm. Even if you thought you were his then, you were mine." He took her face, and closing his eyes, pressed his forehead to hers. His shoulders lost some of their tenseness, as if a weight that had long fought against him lifted.

"We belong together. We always have," she breathed, gripping the front of his suit coat. She had to hold onto something; tonight, he made her feel particularly heady.

He softly kissed her cheek, then worked along her jaw, and finally her mouth. At first it was gentle, almost chaste, then her tongue swept against his, and he gripped her a little harder, the kiss intensifying. His deft fingers slid down her neck to her shoulders and along the fabric hem of her neckline.

"Wait," Valeen pulled back and pressed her fingertips to his mouth. "I want to freshen up."

He chuckled and curled a lock of her hair around his finger. "You look divine as you are now. Not even a hair out of place." He leaned in and kissed her again. His urgency was hard to resist. "Do you remember our first night together?" he asked between kisses.

He'd carefully removed her dress, his fingers trembled touching her bare skin, even his breath had been uneven. "Mmhmm. You were nervous."

"I was fucking terrified." His laugh sent a pleasant chill down her body. "You made me wait so long I was afraid I'd finish fast and leave you wanting, then you'd regret marrying me."

She laughed. "Six months isn't so long."

"Six wonderful and *agonizing* months."

She pushed off his suit jacket, then pulled at his top, popping several buttons to see his flesh. In the moonlight runes and tattoos stood out against his pale skin. "Besides, you didn't leave me wanting."

He kissed her neck, and she tilted her head back to give him more room. "No, I didn't." He reached around her back and tugged at the dress's fastens. It began to loosen so she ducked out of his grasp.

She walked backward toward the suite, leaving him looking confused. "Just, wait here a moment."

"Fine." He pulled his tunic over his head and dropped it next to his jacket.

She hurried through the room, grabbed her bag and dashed into the bathing chambers. Tearing the bag open, she rifled through it trying to remember what she had in there. It was a travel bag she had prepacked for a quick getaway, not for a wedding night. She pulled out a pair of plain white undergarments and a matching bralette. It paled in comparison to the racy red number he'd put her in their first night back together. She wanted something just as beautiful.

Sighing, she dropped the bag on the floor and started to pull the pins from her hair. It fell free from the braids and waved to her waist in thick black tresses. Checking herself in the small round mirror, she grabbed a balm for her lips and spread it over them. It was all she had. Without a fancy night dress, she only had one choice. She pushed the sleeves of the wedding gown off her shoulders, shimmied out of it, and let her undergarments drop to the floor with it.

With her fingers curled around the door handle, she took a few deep breaths. She wasn't nervous, it wasn't like this would be their first time, but it would be their first time as husband and wife in this life. A pleasurable trill tickled her stomach, and she pulled open the door. Hel waited on the sofa with his arms resting on the back of it, not a stitch of clothing on. His heated gaze started at her eyes and slowly trailed down.

"I didn't have a nightgown I thought was pretty

enough for tonight." She pushed her long hair behind herself revealing her nakedness to him fully.

"I prefer you in nothing. No need to hide some of my favorite parts, Mrs. Black." He curled his finger, beckoning her forward.

She sauntered to him and lowered onto his lap. Bare skin on bare skin. His warm hands slowly pressed into her waist and was about to take her breast into his mouth, but she lifted his face.

"I have a few rules now that we're officially married again."

He smiled, bringing out his irresistible dimple. "Rules?"

"You will never lie to me, nor I to you."

"Agreed."

"If something is bothering you, tell me. If you suspect something, say it. I never want there to be secrets between us, or a chance of one of us being deceived again. You trust me and I trust you."

"No secrets." His hands moved to her ass, and he lightly dug his fingertips into her flesh. "So, I must tell you then..."

Her heart seemed to skip a beat waiting for him to finish that sentence.

"Rumors in the underrealm made Synick believe that our immortalities were given to others. If it's true it would be people they care for. When I killed Pricilla's dragon heir with Soulender, I might have destroyed one of ours..."

Her breath caught. "But you don't know for sure."

"No. But my gut tells me it's true."

Valeen bit her lower lip. That would mean one of them wouldn't be able to become immortal again. The thought made her sick and she forced it away. "I don't want to worry about that tonight but thank you for telling me."

He buried his face between her breasts for a moment, drawing a giggle from her. "Are there any other rules I need to be aware of?"

"Only one." She slowly pushed her hips forward, a little more and he'd be inside her. "That even if one of us is angry at the other, we'll always be quick to forgive."

"I promise."

"Do you have anything you'd like to add?"

She wrapped her arms around his neck and his mouth swept over her skin, taking his time on the more sensitive areas. "You already know my rule, that you're mine, only mine. And I am yours."

HEL

He woke to the most beautiful sight there was in any realm—his wife naked, with her hair a mess, draped around her. It was too warm for a blanket, and he thanked the All Mother for that.

His fingers trailed along her spine, and he brushed her hair aside. This moment of blissful peace wouldn't last so he wanted to enjoy it.

She let out a small grunt and turned on her side away from him. "Grumpy this morning? I must not have done my duty last night, though I was convinced I had when you screamed like a wild cat."

Lifting her head, she groaned and shoved him. "I

did not sound like a wild cat." Then she rolled into him, wrapping her bare thigh around his hip. "I *just* woke up. I'm not grumpy."

"You've never been a morning person."

"Goddess of night, remember?"

He smiled, brushing stray hair off her cheek. She had a soft pink to her skin today. Her hand suddenly clamped around his hardened length and he sucked in a sharp breath. "Fuck," he murmured. Her slow movement along his tender flesh and a mischievous grin brought on a shudder. "Valeen."

They were soon a tangle of limbs, damp with sweat. Watching her come apart gave him a high he couldn't get enough of, so he kept going until she cried out again and again. He couldn't get enough of her, nor she him.

Scheming and war and troubles faded away. The outside world could wait while for one small moment it was just them, in love, mated and married once again. It was almost more special than the first time, at least it rivaled it.

"I don't know if I've ever craved you so much," she said in the late afternoon, sitting on the kitchen countertop in only his tunic. There was something about her in his clothes that made him almost feral. The apple crunched loudly between her teeth, and she leaned back on her hands and smiled at him. "I always want you but since the ceremony it's all I can think about."

He smiled, knowing the feeling, and pulled the scones he'd made out of the oven and set them on the stovetop. The smell of them filled the air making his mouth water. "It's quite the pull, isn't it?"

In a couple strides, he had his hands on her thighs and dragged her to the edge. The loose shirt fell to the side revealing her shoulder. He leaned in for a kiss then paused—the lily mark on her arm... "Your mate mark is different. There is a second flower on it. And it's darker, and more pronounced." The second flower was smaller on a stem to the right.

She glanced down at it then her fingertips ran over his and he shuddered at her touch. "So is yours. Mine was pulsing during the ceremony and while we *consummated*," she said the last word with a giggle. He loved her shy laughter.

"Interesting." He'd felt it too. "It makes sense it would change since we are reborn and renewed."

He snapped his fingers, and a scone appeared in his hand. He brought it to her mouth, and she bit into it. She moaned in delight and rolled her eyes back. He chuckled. "Good?"

"So good. I don't know what you do to make them taste better than anyone else. It's all the same ingredients."

"But it's made by the god of magic's hand. It's magic, love, that's the secret. I will it to taste divine."

She took it from his hand and devoured another bite. "You should bake more."

"When I don't have heads to roll, hearts to rip out, and a castle to build you, I will." The sound of the sea crashed, and the warm salt air fluttered in from the open windows. "Will you walk the beach with me?"

THE SAND WAS soft and squishy on his bare feet. They spent the day laughing and finding shells. The waves rolled over his ankles, but he didn't go in far. He was content to watch her swim from the shore. There were too many times he'd been forced to drown in it for training with Synick that he just couldn't enjoy swimming. And she knew that.

She dove underwater and came back up with a large white conch shell. "Look what I found," she said, grinning with almost childlike excitement. Even if he didn't care much for shells, it made him happy because she was. She rushed out of the water and set it in his hand. There was a pink iridescent shine to it.

"We'll keep it as a souvenir from our second honeymoon."

He couldn't remember a time in this life where he'd ever been this content. If she asked him to run away and give up their lives as gods, he would. He'd give up his revenge, he'd give it all up for her. Only the sad reality was eventually they'd be found. Assassins would come. Her life would always be in danger. So, for now, he'd cherish this day and tomorrow it was war.

Chapter 48

THANE

He'd spent the entire night pacing his room or the castle halls, going over every word Katana had said. *I won't live in Valeen's shadow.* She wasn't that, never that. He couldn't even compare them. They were so different.

Soon after she left him sitting at the bar with Evalyn, she asked her for a room, claiming she was too tired to walk back to the castle.

It's done now. It was a mistake.

The words kept ringing in his ears. *Mistake, mistake, mistake.*

She thought he was a mistake. It was as crushing as the day Valeen left with Hel—worse even. He felt like he was going insane, how could he love her already? The moment she walked away was when he realized losing her would break him in more ways than he could handle. Maker, he was a fool for telling her they could sleep in the same room and it didn't have to mean anything.

He stopped by her room to see if she'd returned this morning, to find it empty. Then he found himself at the stables and took Phantom out bareback. Waiting to have him saddled and readied was too long. Hooves pounded over the cobblestone streets of the city. He took the less-crowded route but there were still people who had to hurry out of his way.

He pulled Phantom to a stop and swung down. Evalyn's door was already open, letting in the warm morning air. The tables and chairs were set up for business once again. Leif was still passed out in the corner booth. He and Fennan decided to leave him rather than drag him back the night before.

Evalyn sat on a barstool with a white mug in hand and steam coming out the top. It smelled of fresh squeezed lemon and tea. "High King," Evalyn said with a small smile, then took a sip. "Took you long enough. She's upstairs. Second room on the right."

With the amount of wine he'd drunk the night before, he probably told her too much. It was strange he'd been so open with Valeen's aunt about everything, but she didn't judge him. She listened. He supposed being a bartender she was used to that. He even let a tear or two slip, but she said something that he wouldn't forget, "I know you loved my Layala, and it broke your heart to let her go, but are you going to let love walk away twice? Sometimes you have to fight for it, Thane, scared or not. I don't know Katana well, but even I can see she's in love with you and you might not know it yet, but you've fallen for her. Maybe you tried not to, but the eyes always give it away."

There was something deep inside him, driving him. He couldn't let Katana walk away even if he wanted to. If she'd gone to another realm, he'd find her. If Atlanta came and she said she was going with him, he'd fight, he'd kill him for her. Even if it wasn't what she wanted, he felt almost... savage thinking of her with someone else. The side of him that was War came raging to the surface.

With a deep calming breath, he tried to slow his hammering heart.

It didn't work.

He hurried across the big open room and swiftly made his way up the stairs. Second room on the right.

It was quiet. Not even a creak in the floorboards.

His own pulse thrummed in his ears. Clenching his teeth, he knocked three times and stood back.

Soft footsteps pattered behind the door. His heart felt like it was in his throat.

A moment later Katana was standing before him as radiant as the first blooms of spring. "Hello," he said, breathless.

She ran her hand through her messy hair and then crossed her arms, almost timidly. She wouldn't meet his eyes. There was something about her vulnerability that turned him into a primal beast ready to guard and protect her. "What are you doing here?" hugging her waist, she grabbed a handful of her golden silk dress.

"May I come in?" he asked. She stepped aside and opened the door wider. Once it clicked shut behind him, he turned. "I came because I had to see you."

With a sigh, she walked around him and sat on the rocking chair near the corner. She wasn't smiling and bright like she usually was, and he hated that it was because of him. "You don't have to worry about me. I'm not your problem, Thane."

His stomach dropped. It was time for the truth before it was too late. He strode to her and dropped to his knees, gripping the sides of the chair. There was a glisten in her eye as she stared down at him. "No, you're not my problem, Katana, you're my salvation."

She went utterly still. She even stopped breathing.

"I didn't want love. I didn't want to let someone into my already broken heart to crush it further. I'm scared, I'm terrified, but I am down on my knees begging you to forgive me for letting it get to this. I shouldn't have let you walk away last night. I," he gulped, "My heart *is* involved. It has been since I first saw you under that tree and that spider crawled under your dress. My heart was captured in the hot pool. It was yours the night I held you while you slept after your nightmare. I don't want to be your *friend*, Katana."

"You want me?" she leaned forward.

"Yes."

"Not just to warm your bed?"

He cringed at those words, that she ever believed that was all she was. It might have started out as lust, but he was fooling himself into thinking it was ever simply that. "You were never just that to me. I said it because I was afraid." He let out a trembling breath. "I want all of you, your beautiful heart and mind." They were not fire and ice, always battling for dominance, they were fire and fire, burning hotter, thriving off each other's flames.

He gulped when she stared. Maybe it was too late. Maybe she had changed her mind. No, it didn't matter.

NIGHT MEETS THE ELF QUEEN

If she said it was too late, he'd beg. He'd keep trying. He'd prove that it wasn't too late, it was just beginning.

She finally smiled and it was glorious and wonderful. She threw herself at him; he caught her in his arms and tipped, falling flat on his back. She giggled while lying on top of him. "Tell me again."

"I want to be with you." He laughed with her. "I want your good days and the bad. I want your laughter and smiles and to watch you dance and stay up all night talking to you and...other things all night. I want your heart. You already have mine."

She half laughed, half cried and started quickly kissing his neck and cheeks then she slowed and hovered over his mouth. "I knew you were going to change my world, Thane, and now... you *are* my world."

He pressed up to kiss her and brushed her hair behind her ear and lightly rubbed the soft roundness of it. "Will you come back with me to the castle then?"

"And for how long do you want me to stay?"

He swallowed hard. "Is it too soon to say I want you to stay with me always?"

She smiled and kissed him. "Do you love me?"

He nodded. "I do."

"Then it is not too soon. I've never felt drawn to someone the way I am to you. I think love is only part of what I feel for you, it was as if you were made for me and I for you. You understand me like no one else." She slowly lowered down and pressed her soft lips to his. "Maybe I wasn't brought back only to help my sister, maybe it was... for *us*, too."

In his soul he felt that it was true. That there was some force outside of them guiding and aiding them.

"When I go with Hel to fight Pricilla..." he didn't even want to think of parting from her, even for a day.

She groaned and laid her head on his chest. "I don't want you to go."

"I know."

"I just want to be with you. Whether we are lying like this or riding dragons or going for our runs. I just want to be near you."

"We will be together."

"I'm scared to lose you."

"It's why I must go. If I don't help Hel, they will destroy Palenor. If the council finds out what you mean to me, they could target you—as they do your sister. I won't have that. We have to attack. Hel has a plan to get our immortality..." a trickle of dread. Katana was not immortal.

"Valeen and I talked. She and I will stay and reforge Lightbringer to protect the city. If the battle should turn, they will come here."

"Yes, they will." His voice was low, almost angry. They would come to destroy his home and the maiden he loved. The thought of leaving her here, even with Valeen made him irrational. It went against every instinct firing inside him, but a battlefield on Runevale would be worse.

She lifted her head and propped her chin on her hands. "Promise you'll come back to me. Promise you will retreat if you must, just come back to me."

"I swear it."

Chapter 49

HEL

Hel pushed through the doors of Thane's study and found him leaning over a stack of papers. Ink and quill were by his right hand. The books on the shelves behind him were lined up perfectly. It wasn't that long ago he'd taken up this room for his own. The single bed that had once been in the corner was replaced with a chair and footstool and a potted ivy plant on a white stand.

He looked up from the page and set it down. "Hel," he sounded surprised.

Hel glided into the room with his hands behind his back. "Were you expecting someone else? Katana perhaps."

"Possibly."

Taking the seat across from Thane, Hel pulled out a civar and lit it. "I hope it works for you two. I called it weeks ago, she's perfect for you."

"I trust that it will," Thane said with a smile.

Something had happened while he and Valeen were gone but he wasn't one to pry with these sorts of things. Hel waved his hand, and a bottle of wine appeared along with two glasses. He poured one for Thane, then himself. "Now, to the reason I'm here. Are the dragons on their way? And what are their numbers?"

"The king has promised a hundred of his royal army. I sent for them while you were gone. They will be here in the morning."

"A hundred will do for this battle, but it wouldn't if they invaded. The combined army of the council will have a thousand dragons or more."

"He will send more when they come. But the population up north is smaller than Ryvengaard. Half of them are female and most of the males aren't soldiers, even if they're dragons. Anyway, I can't feed a thousand dragons for an unset amount of time while we wait to see if they invade Palenor."

Even a hundred dragons would go through Thane's food storage at the castle in a matter of days. And they preferred meat, which elves didn't have in abundance. "Mathekis is marching with my army as we speak. I made an appearance. They are eager for war."

Thane picked up his wine and rolled his eyes. 'They always are."

"Well, in this case it's to our advantage. Now, Pricilla's walls will be nearly impossible to break, and I think we should keep the dragons as a surprise."

"Then you need to draw her army out to fight," Thane mused. "How will you do that? It would be stupid of her to leave the walls."

"I'll piss her off."

"You killed her son and threw his head on a spike right in front of her and she did nothing."

"You let me worry about that while you do your part." Hel took a long inhale of the civar and slowly blew out smoke rings. "When I draw them out, I will need you to be there with the dragons and your Ravens. I need the god of war, my *brother,* with me."

"I will be there, Hel." Thane swirled his red wine around in his glass. "How are you going to get our immortality from her?"

"If negotiations don't work, I'll put Soulender to her throat."

Thane smiled behind his glass then held it up to Hel. "To battle."

"To the god of war."

Clink.

WAR DRUMS THUNDERED with the pounding of feet. Growls and cries for battle pierced the air. The pale ones were eager for this day. They'd been pent up in the Void for too long, and he promised them blood.

Blood they would have.

Pricilla's army was at her walls, archers ready. A dragon clung to each turret waiting to take flight. The mauve trees scattered blossoms into the air, creating a rich aroma, but it wouldn't cover the coming stench of death.

His pale ones already shouted for battle, their weapons raised high.

Hel sat on the back of Starborn at the front of his army. Mathekis waited beside him on a white horse with hooves the size of dinner plates and ebony armor cover its chest. "What are your orders, Lord?"

"We wait for Pricilla to meet with us." The saddle creaked under Hel as he adjusted the left stirrup. "There is a rule in Runevale. A meeting must take place before any battle between gods in case an agreement can be reached to prevent the loss of life."

"Would she give you the same right if we were still in Adalon, Lord?"

"We're not in Adalon." Truth was, he wanted to get her face-to-face to know if there were any other gods with her.

The gates opened and three riders on hippogriffs came out. Pricilla wore pink armor, and her hippogriff had a matching chest plate and helm. Everything in her territory had some shade of pink from fuchsia to salmon to a light blush. It was unsettling.

Hel nudged Starborn forward. Mathekis rode beside him, meeting them in the emptiness of the center field.

"Zaurahel." Pricilla raised her chin and touched her nose as if he had a stench. Across Pricilla's chest was a hot pink bow and on her back, a quiver of arrows. Her white corset with pink jewels and matching pants gave a false appearance of sweetness. Soft golden-brown curls tumbled in a half-up half-down style with little pops of baby's breath weaved in. Overly bright pink blush stained her cheeks and lips. There was something about her face that reminded him of a ferret with a small, upturned nose and pinched lips. "I would say it's good to see you, but, as always, it's a displeasure." Her voice was saccharine sweet and laced with poison.

"Likewise." But it wasn't Pricilla that had his attention now, it was Atlanta, god of the seas, primordial, and Katana's ex-husband. Atlanta wore full battle armor, his blue trident glittered in the sun, each point a threat. The fierceness in his eyes made him more than just an ally, he was here for personal reasons.

Any time primordials were involved it was personal. As the most powerful of the gods, they otherwise stayed neutral.

"Your disgusting creatures don't belong in my land. Remove them," Pricilla said.

"Gladly, if you give me what I want. If not, I am looking forward to seeing how far this curse will travel. It takes *one* bite to turn. Half your army could be mine by the end of this battle."

She waved a dismissive hand and giggled like a schoolgirl who'd just received flowers from her infatuation. "From what I hear it's a curse exclusive to the elves."

Hel smirked. "Are you absolutely certain of that?"

That stupid smile dropped, and her hawkish eyes narrowed. "So, you want your immortal strength back, is that it?" Pricilla sneered and petted the feathered neck of her hippogriff. The male to her left was Alehelm, god of vineyards. The golden helmet and armor with grapes and leaves etched into the metal was a giveaway. Perhaps the new member of the council to replace Rogue, or her lover. Either way he wasn't a threat.

"I wouldn't be here otherwise, wench."

Alehelm snorted in disgust. "Don't speak to the head of the council with such disrespect."

Her hippogriff was upset too, fluffing its feathers and snapping its beak. With slow methodical strokes, she calmed the animal. "Relax," she cooed. "His filthy words mean nothing."

"What are you even doing here, Alehelm?" Hel tsked.

"He's an ally."

"Rogue's replacement?"

She pursed her lips and scrutinized Hel from head to toe. "Rogue was an honorable god, and you, wicked savage, don't deserve to even say his name. His wife was innocent."

"So was mine."

"Ha," Pricilla guffawed. "Not only are you a murderer but a liar too. Valeen being innocent is the best joke I've heard in a long time. And where is your wife? She should be here for this negotiation."

"Far from here."

"Where is *mine*?" Atlanta snarled, slamming the hilt of his trident on the ground. "Give her to me and you'll get your immortality."

"Well, now, that is tempting." But no doubt a lie. Pricilla squirmed in her saddle at his words, ready to object to them. "Would that be only mine?"

"*One* in exchange for Katana," Pricilla added. "The other will not be given without Soulender in exchange."

"Other or *others*?"

Pricilla smiled, her bright pink lips spread wide over her too-white teeth. "You destroyed War's immortality when you murdered my son. And you have no one to blame but yourself."

A heavy stone seemed to drop into his gut. Hel gripped the reins until his hands ached. *Fuck*. "If immortality can be taken and given, then what's to stop me from taking yours."

"You don't have enough power to do that," she sneered.

"I have two primordial goddesses and the god of war on my side, I think we could pull it off."

"Give me my wife, now!" Atlanta jumped down from his hippogriff and marched toward Hel. His eyes were alight with an aquamarine flame. The ground beneath his feet turned watery.

This prick was truly starting to get on his nerves. First, he showed up in Palenor demanding things from Valeen and now he was stomping around like a great man child. Any god as old as Atlanta who couldn't control his temper was no one to fear. It made him easy to toy with. He gave away too much.

Starborn reared up, Hel tightened his thighs and gripped the saddle horn. Starborn's wings flared out, then he slammed down and snorted at Atlanta. "She's not here. Last I checked she was in bed... with my cousin."

"What?!" he boomed. "I will gut you where you stand."

"Why, that isn't very nice. I'm not the one humping her. War is. She has a sort of glow about her now. I'm certain she's never been happier." Hel couldn't help but smile. People simply were too easy to piss off.

"How dare you, you filthy little—"

"Atlanta," Pricilla chirped. "Don't fall for his games. You will get your wife back. Let us continue in a civilized manner."

"I will march right past you and go take her from the elven realm."

"You will not." Hel pulled the golden sword from his hip and pointed the tip of it at him. "You will not take another step forward until this negotiation is over. You can't start a battle until after. These are the rules of engagement *you* primordials set."

"Fine." He stared at the weapon all of them feared and backed up several paces.

"The immortal blade and Katana, for yours and Valeen's immortality," Pricilla said. "That's a simple request. Soulender doesn't belong to you. If Valeen had given us the sword two thousand years ago, as was required, none of this would have ever happened. You don't need to keep dying for this weapon."

Thunder cracked to the west drawing Hel's gaze to the dark clouds rolling in. It would rain soon. "I *will* see my immortality and Valeen's before any agreement is made."

"I thought you might say that. After you killed my son, I had to place them somewhere safer. I could have let you keep destroying your own chances of ever being a god again but—"

"You need the bargaining chips." And she knew Hel and Valeen would have nothing to lose and burn everything down if theirs were gone forever. Thunder rolled quietly. Birds took flight from the trees. Hel glanced back, searching among the woods for a sign of Thane and the dragons. They were well hidden if they were here.

His stomach began to knot. If Thane didn't show or the dragons refused because of the pale ones, he was on his own against three gods.

"I have the authority to give them to you, if you agree, but you must agree."

He glanced at Atlanta. The prick was practically foaming at the mouth. "Katana isn't mine to give—"

"Without your protection, she won't have a choice," Atlanta snapped. "Just don't interfere when I come for her."

"As I said, I won't agree to anything until I see my immortality."

"Yours and Valeen's immortality is safe, I give you my word," Pricilla said.

"Your *word* isn't enough."

"They are hidden inside my vault. I'd have to go inside."

"I'll wait." He held his arms out and glanced back at the pale ones. They raised swords, howled and jumped, ready to be unleashed. "But I would hurry. They're getting restless."

"Restless to die? My archers and dragons will destroy them."

"We'll see."

"So we are clear, I get your immortality, and you'll give us Soulender?" She grinned, eyes going wider with greed. Except for a few moments, she hadn't taken her gaze off of it since he'd taken it out.

"You will get this sword when mine and Valeen's immortality is in my hands." He held up the golden blade. "But I want my wife's land returned to her as well, and your oath that Soulender will not be used against Valeen, War, or myself."

"I never thought I'd see the day that you broke down and learned your lesson. Especially that stubborn wife of yours. A primordial really should know better. It isn't that hard, is it? To simply know when you're beaten."

Hel had to push down the fire boiling in his chest. "Enough of your gloating, do you agree or not?"

"I agree. I swear on my position as head of the council—neither you, nor Valeen, or War, will be harmed or killed by an immortal weapon as long as I—or a member of the council—hold it. And Valeen is entitled to House of Night. The other primordials would ensure that even if I didn't." The little smirk at the corner of her mouth almost drove him to madness.

"And Katana?" Atlanta asked.

He shrugged. "If you expect me to go fetch her for you, you're sorely mistaken. If you want her, get her yourself." He was betting on the hope that Valeen and Katana had their wall up before he could try.

"Does Valeen know you're here?" Pricilla eyed him suspiciously. "I hear you've reconciled, even after the betrayal that ruined you. But she always said she would never give up Soulender."

"I think my holding this sword is proof enough she changed her mind, and she's elsewhere because it would be stupid to have all three of us here for you to kill should things go sour." Hel tapped his temple. "Someone has to keep our memories."

Pricilla cackled. "A tragedy really, to forget each other over and over. But it had to be done. Two thousand years later and this can finally end. Marvelous." She clasped her hands tighter and let out a quiet squeal.

Hel didn't let his anger show, kept his expression bored. "My army is ready should you try anything."

Pricilla's lip curled in disgust at the pale ones lined up behind him. "You will wait here, and when the exchange is made, you will leave, but we will need to destroy these creatures. The council cannot allow them to exist any longer."

Hel nodded, glancing over at Mathekis, who shifted uncomfortably in his seat.

"He lives."

"Then more will be created."

"He won't turn anyone else, and if he does, I will personally kill them both."

"We cannot allow the risk."

"You will."

She sneered and turned her mount, while Atlanta and Alehelm stayed behind. *This will be an awkward few minutes. Might as well make it interesting.* "So, given that Katana is utterly in love with someone else, I think it's safe to say she is no longer interested in being married to you."

"That didn't stop you," Atlanta sneered.

"Well, I didn't beat my wife. In fact, I worship her, as a husband should. Usually with my tongue."

Atlanta's nose scrunched in distaste. "Gods don't worship their wives, even if they are primordial goddesses. You're pathetic, Zaurahel, and always have been."

"Must we resort to childish banter to pass the time? Because if we are, I'd bet money you stood by like a coward while Synick murdered Katana, too afraid to step in." Atlanta's aquamarine eyes flashed, brightening with his magic. "Oh, I've struck a nerve. Or maybe you were in on it with him. You grew tired of her complaints of you being unfaithful. She didn't like you fucking anything with tits and threatened to leave."

"You know nothing. Valeen has poisoned your mind with this lie about Synick."

"She didn't have to. Katana herself said he did it."

"I didn't even know an immortal weapon existed, no one did until she died."

"So you did stand by and watch."

"Synick is my friend. He swore he didn't do it."

A tingle of alarm slithered down Hel's spine. He'd checked on Synick before he left, the prick was still in the cell, still as pathetic as ever, dirty, rotting. "Is?"

"*Was*," Atlanta corrected, but his temperament cooled too quickly. "With Katana alive again it has put my mind back to that time."

He knows Synick is alive... he couldn't speak to Valeen's mind while they were in different realms; the connection was too far.

"Time is different as a god. It's meaningless," Alehelm added, lifting his chin proudly.

"Nobody invited you to join this conversation Alehelm."

"I am a second-generation god, I will not be told what to do by you, a disgraced elf who keeps monsters as company." He looked at Mathekis with disgust.

"Why don't you go crush some grapes with your feet and shove a few up your asshole while you're at it. You're no warrior, you shouldn't even be here." He gestured toward Mathekis. "He would best you in combat easily."

His face reddened with each passing moment. "I wouldn't be beaten by that *thing*," he retorted, pulling an axe from his back.

"Don't." Atlanta's hand shot toward his companion as he glared.

"This weasel deserves to die. He's a disgrace to the gods. We should not be making deals with him."

"You will hold your axe and do nothing, Alehelm. Pricilla has made an agreement."

"Go ahead and take a swing." Hel smiled, enraging Alehelm further. "Give me a reason to kill you."

"No!" Atlanta's voice deepened. "You will hold your ground, Alehelm, no matter what he says. Pricilla was right, we can't let his games get into our heads." He turned back to Hel. "When I come for Katana, you need to keep your wife and cousin in line too."

Hel chuckled. "I said if you wanted her to go get her. Not that I would help you. The god of war does what he pleases, and I never agreed to keep my wife out of anything, I can't speak for her."

"That's your problem. You have no control of her. It's the reason there was ever war in the first place, it's the reason she was fucking your cousin. If you'd kept your bitch in line, you wouldn't be here."

Heat boiled up from his core and he had to force his magic down. "Call her that again." He glared at him. "Go ahead. Do it." He gripped his weapon tighter and moved enough that Atlanta would see it as a threat. The prick's mouth stayed shut. "Like I said, you're a coward. Only a coward would be threatened enough by his wife to beat her and diminish her to *keep her in line*." He turned Starborn and tipped his chin to Atlanta. "As pleasant as your company is, I'll wait with my army for Pricilla's return."

He kicked him into a trot and searched the woods for a sign of Thane. He could send someone back to warn Valeen and Katana about Atlanta and his possible alliance with Synick. He couldn't figure out how

Atlanta knew, but he did... but why hadn't he set him free?

"Lord." Mathekis rode loyally beside him. "Is the plan the same? I'm surprised you didn't say 'no' about the other goddess since she is your wife's sister."

"I didn't expect Atlanta to be here. And I couldn't say 'no'. Had I said 'no' Atlanta would have stopped the negotiation. Once the exchange is made, we retreat to the woods and hold there. But right now, you need to go to Thane and tell him to have someone get a message to Valeen and Katana."

Hel stopped Starborn at the front of the line of pale ones and turned to find Atlanta was gone.

Chapter 50

VALEEN

Waiting on the shelf near the foundry was Lightbringer. In the dull light it didn't look remarkable, but it would be the thing that saved the elves of Palenor. She took the two pieces of Lightbringer off the shelf and held one in each hand.

To make it just as strong as before she'd have to melt down both pieces and reforge the entire blade, which would take weeks to smooth and perfect. And with Hel and Thane attacking Pricilla, they didn't have that kind of time.

She set the pieces on the anvil and turned to Katana. Her sister picked up the flower vase to toss out the old ones and replace them with the new bunch of daisies and poppies she'd plucked on their way here.

"I need you to heat the two broken ends so I can overlay them and meld them back together. It will save time."

Katana's brows puckered. "But it will be swollen on the spot."

"We don't have time to do it properly. It would take weeks at least to melt it down and remake it as it should be."

"Interesting. I had not heard that it takes that long." Her lavender eyes were hollow today and her smile was nowhere to be found. Valeen probably looked the same, if not worse. Both of the males they loved and cared for were off to war.

"How are things with Thane? Last we talked, you seemed unsure."

She broke into a smile and said, "He came to me yesterday." Her palms emitted a bright orange light, and it wasn't long before the two ends were glowing hot and ready to be molded.

Valeen smiled as she set the bottom piece slightly on top of the main and swung the hammer. The *ching* and clanking of metal hitting metal filled the room. Sparks flew, pelting against her thick blacksmith's apron; a few tiny holes burned into her sleeves. "And? You can't end it there."

She tucked her hair behind her ears and beamed. "Alright, fine. He told me he was just scared but that he does want to be with me. I–I love him, Val and he loves me. I don't even know how it happened. I just...I have to be near him."

Valeen's chest warmed and she swung the hammer again. There was something special about them together, she'd seen it with her own eyes. What she wanted more than anything was for both of them to be happy and now they were.

Katana walked over to the window and tugged the

old curtain aside. "It's too dreary in here. And hot. I'm sweating." She pushed open the window, letting in a breeze, then took her hair into her hands and tied it in a knot on her head. A sun tattoo was centered between her shoulder blades. It was a hollow circle, about the size of a small apple, in black ink with curling and twisting sun rays spreading out from it. A straight thin line came out from the center top and bottom, ending in three tiny dots.

"When did you get a tattoo? I don't remember you having one before." She turned Lightbringer over and struck again.

She turned around to face her with a hand on her hip. "What tattoo?"

With a chuckle, Valeen stopped hammering and let the tool fall to her side. "The *only* tattoo you have."

"I don't have a tattoo."

"You have a sun tattoo on your back. Did you forget about it?" Her hair was always down so she hadn't noticed it before.

"No..." she tried to look over her shoulder. "I can't see anything."

Valeen set the sword and hammer down. There was no mirror in here, but the shiny silver platter they'd brought with snacks would work. She pushed the fruit, nuts and cheeses onto a cloth and held up the platter.

Katana gasped when she saw it. "How did that get there! It wasn't there before..."

Valeen looked at her puzzled, and then it hit her. "You slept with Thane."

"Yeah." She narrowed her eyes in suspicion. "He didn't tattoo me if that's what you're saying."

"Does he have one?"

"I never saw one on him."

"You swear this wasn't here before?"

"It wasn't! I would remember getting a tattoo," Katana almost shrieked. Her voice always rose higher when she was nervous. "Why are you asking about Thane?"

"Long ago, when I searched for answers as to why my lily appeared on my arm, one of the things that Presco had found was that both mates would receive the same mark. Hel has the same one on his chest. For us, it was because I tried to kill him." Valeen paused when Katana raised her brows. "I know, it was a different time, anyway, most often soulmates are marked when they became... one."

"All Mother above... my hair glowed when we... but it can't be. I didn't see a tattoo on him." She started mumbling, "Of course I wasn't looking at every inch of him."

Valeen blew out a slow breath. If they were mates it might explain why Thane was drawn to her in Katana's absence...What were the chances that the sister goddesses of day and night were mated to cousins who were more like brothers?

It actually made her laugh. Of course, it should be that way. All along Thane had been perfect for Katana. All along Valeen and Hel and Thane were drawn together, until Katana could return.

"Will you heat this again?"

Still muttering Katana made her way over and the blade glowed hot.

She went back to hammering and only got in a handful of hard swings before a shadow moved past the front window. A chill ran through her and her gut said it was someone dangerous. An assassin sent by Pricilla while Hel and Thane were away?

"Katana, push that table in front of the door." She kept furiously swinging the hammer until sweat beaded on her brow.

"Why?" she asked but she quickly moved to the table and the legs scraped loudly across the stone. "What's wrong?"

"I think there's someone outside."

"It's the city. There are people everywhere." She shoved it against the door then brushed her palms together wiping away dust.

Pounding on the door startled her and she missed the sword, cracking the hammer into the anvil.

They went silent.

Valeen tried to see who was there from the window, but it was the wrong angle.

Fists slammed into the door again. Katana and Valeen exchanged a glance.

"Yes?" Valeen finally said. Maybe it was just someone looking for a blacksmith.

"Where are my two favorite goddesses?" cooed an eerily familiar voice.

Katana backed further into the room but didn't take her eyes off the door. "Val... it's... it's..." With a whimper she took out a dagger and moved closer to her sister.

Valeen stilled for only a moment then turned the sword over and started hammering on the other side. "I know," was all she said.

"How did he get out?"

The door handle jiggled then a moment later nails

scraped on the wood. "Goddess of night, goddess of day, please open the door. I want to play," Synick said in a sing-song voice.

"Heat this again. Hurry." It was still too thick and cooling too fast. With a glowing orange blade once again, she swung. Sweat slid down the back of her neck with the effort, but it was finally taking the form she needed. *I need you, Lightbringer. This city and the elves need you.*

Pounding started on the door again, this time harder, like a boot slamming against it rather than a fist.

"Valeen," Katana yelped. She almost tripped on the lip of a stone slab in retreat.

"Don't give him the satisfaction of being afraid. You're the goddess of day. Act like it." Now wasn't the time to be soft on Katana. She couldn't be the scared little lamb when there were wolves at the door. That was what got her killed before. Katana snapped her head toward Valeen as if she'd struck her. "Your problem isn't that you're incapable of being a terrifying threat, it's that you don't believe you are one. Be something to fear, Katana, and you won't be preyed upon. There is a time to be the soft petals of a rose and a time to be its thorns."

Katana's mouth hung open and she blinked in surprise, but she needed to hear it.

"It's almost ready." Valeen plunged the blade into the bucket of cold water. It sizzled and steamed. Pulling it free, she inspected it in the window's light. It was far from perfect, and she'd never want to show it off for craftsmanship, but it would have to do. "Now, mark it with your magic. Give it a piece of you."

With a firm nod, Katana's glowing fingertip etched a sun into the metal then she blew her breath over it. A tingle of her power fluttered across Valeen's skin like a summer breeze.

She didn't have a touch that could etch metal, so she pricked her finger on the point of the blade and wiped her blood across the already existing elvish runes that read "Lightbringer". "With this I give you a piece of me to connect with the moons' power and mine."

The door burst open, sending the table crashing into the wall, and a shadowy figure stepped into the frame.

Someone must have let him out. Someone must be with him to give him the confidence to come here and not run away. She swore under her breath, the guard tasked with dosing him every few hours must be dead too.

Valeen half stepped in front of Katana and pointed Lightbringer at Synick. The decayed half of his face was covered in a black mask. His sandy-blond hair was tied back into a sleek ponytail. She dropped her gaze to his hand and the weapon he held. A rose-gold sword with an amber stone in the pommel. Her stomach plummeted to her toes; that was the Sword of Truth. The very weapon he'd used to kill Katana...

"Well, well, we meet again." His voice made the hairs all over her body rise, a warning of the danger.

Valeen scanned behind him, looking for his accomplice. There was no way he was alone. She quickly passed Lightbringer to Katana. "Go out the back and find Night. Take the sword to the top of the ridge. I'll meet you there."

"I can't leave you."

"Go."

She slowly backed up, eyes darting from Valeen to Synick. "Val," she choked.

"Don't leave," Synick purred. "The party is only beginning. I always had a fantasy about having you both writhing under me at the same time."

Valeen conjured Zythara and the golden blade glinted. There was no one she hated more than this male. No one who deserved to be sent to the afterlife more than him. But she couldn't let anger and fury get in her head. Calm and calculated was the way.

"Oh, your goddess sword... not Soulender." He brought the rose-gold sword up and inspected its blade. "It's not a match for the Sword of Truth."

"I'm surprised you came alone, given how this went the last two times you and I met." Out of the corner of her eye, she caught Katana still standing in the same place.

"I'm not alone." He glanced over his shoulder and several of those undead creatures he'd conjured before stepped into the sunlight outside the door. "But they won't come in unless I want them to."

"How did you get out of your cell?"

"I have powerful friends in high places." His shit-brown eyes flicked to Katana for the briefest of moments. Then he took a step closer. If he expected her to retreat, he was wrong. She raised her chin.

Valeen suddenly felt ill. He'd looked at Katana for a reason, it was a tell. "What do you want? You should be running away, coward."

"Well, I did have to do something for my freedom. But I might be willing to forgo the bargain I made if you agree to give me what I've always wanted. An heir of pure primordial blood. The goddess of night's first child." His tongue flickered across his bottom lip. "A blood oath will do, one that will force you to comply. The council will be all too eager to welcome me back as the head member. Pricilla, goddess of the hunt, is my daughter, you know. There isn't anywhere she wouldn't find you, but I have the power to call this whole thing off. Even get you your immortality."

"I'd stab myself through the heart before I'd ever let you touch me."

He let out a dark chuckle. "Well, I'll just take her instead then." He lunged toward Katana and Valeen struck out. He brought his blade up to meet hers and they cracked with a spark, followed by a powerful blast that threw them apart. Valeen crashed into the anvil and Synick was thrown onto the table behind him.

"Stay away from her," Valeen growled. She turned her head ever so slightly to tell Katana to get out.

"Valeen!" Katana screeched.

She whipped her head back but a blast of cold hit her before she could shift to shadow. Ice rushed across her body, keeping her from being able to change forms. It stopped only when it got to her neck. Her arm was frozen, holding the sword raised high. Her vines were slow to grow, as if the ice affected them too... This was why Hel couldn't get out of the ice storm. It slowed magic.

He trampled her small vines under his boots and marched toward her.

The point of the Sword of Truth pressed against her throat. Her heart crashed wildly in her chest. Just a little push and she'd be gone forever. "Hmm, what to do with you, my sweet pet. Killing you would be a waste of such divine beauty. Besides, I can't kill the future mother of my heir." He stroked the side of her face, and she spat at him. He smiled and swiped the saliva off his cheek then licked it from his palm. "That's just the first taste."

"You're disgusting." Valeen's upper lip curled. The ice-cold temperature encasing her body finally set in and her teeth began to chatter.

"Once this is cleared up," he waved to the mask, "you won't say that."

Her sister was still here. "Katana, go get Presco!"

A line of ice cut across the floor and formed around her feet and ankles, locking her in place. "No, we're still waiting for my friend to show up. He's looking for you. I said I'd help."

Oh no no no no, Valeen's gut ached... a powerful friend in high places looking for Katana. This *friend* had to be Atlanta.

Synick dropped the sword point from her throat and leaned in, bringing his putrid face closer and closer. It didn't matter if he wore a mask to cover the rotten decay, she smelt it and knew what was there.

Ugh, gods, no, he is going to kiss me! She reared her head back then threw it forward and slammed her forehead into his mouth. The *crack* and his *hiss* were pure satisfaction. She didn't even mind that he struck her across the face after. The sting barely registered. Before he could do anything else, she fought harder to break free of his ice. Whispers of her shadows crept from her hair. The ice encasing her began to groan and splinter.

Heat abruptly flooded the room, and the ice began

to melt in rivers at her feet. Synick glanced behind Valeen, furrowing his brows. "Don't tell me you suddenly grew a backbone, Katana."

A ray of light as bright as the sun, burst and Valeen slammed her eyes shut.

Chapter 51

KATANA

A stream of powerful energy flowed through Katana's palms, heat and fire and light. She gritted her teeth, aiming all her anger at Synick. The window's glass shattered. Synick crashed through the door and was thrown across the wide cobblestone street and smacked into the opposite wall.

He didn't move.

Smoke rolled off the charred circle in the center of his chest armor. She couldn't tell if it burned a hole through to his flesh or not. Maybe he was dead. She never wanted to take a life, and hated violence, but this was necessary.

In two steps she was at Valeen's side and with radiant heat pulsing from her hands, she melted the rest of the ice encasing her. She lifted her chin to see her sister staring at her, jaw slack.

"Katana, that was… amazing."

She hugged Lightbringer closer to her chest and finally smiled. She'd done it.

A massive weight seemed to float off her shoulders.

For a moment, she'd frozen up, just like she always had, but as soon as he leaned in to kiss Valeen and then struck her, something in her snapped. "Thank you."

"I knew you had that in you!" Valeen stepped over broken glass and hurried toward the front door.

"Where are you going? We need to get Lightbringer to the cliff."

"We need that sword. That is the sword he used to kill you before."

But Synick began to move, and his creatures circled around him.

"We can take him, you and I." With her goddess blade in hand and shadows flowing out behind her like a cloak, Valeen started across the street. With a steadying breath, Katana steeled herself and followed.

A swirling tornado of water appeared directly in their path and panic froze her body. The water spilled to the ground and Atlanta stood with his trident in hand, battle armor on. Shock rooted her feet to the ground.

Now both her tormentors were here. She was ready to face one... but both?

"Get out of the way," Valeen snapped.

"You will leave him be." Atlanta puffed out his chest. "He is a primordial and with all of us alive again, the balance has finally been restored. Your husband made a deal to get your immortality back, and I will find a way to make Katana a full goddess once again as well." He turned to Katana and held out his hand. "It's time to come home. I've allowed you to have your time here, to have your fun with the god of war, but that ends now."

She shook her head. Her body recoiled on instinct, and she stepped back and curled her hands tighter around Lightbringer.

"Allowed?" Valeen balked. "She is not one of your slaves, Atlanta. She is a goddess and a primordial. She's free to do what she wishes, the same as you are."

Synick rose up, half leaning on the wall. His armor still smoked, and even pieces of the hair around his face were singed. Brushing the debris from his chest, he strode through his creatures and stood beside Atlanta. Apparently, the blast hadn't penetrated deep enough.

Valeen wrapped her hand around Katana's wrist and suddenly the world shifted. Her body became weightless and formless. She was shadow being pulled through space.

Their forms snapped back into place further down the street, and with Valeen pulling on her, they ran. They weaved through the streets. Rushing around crowds and cutting through back alleys when they could.

Somewhere behind them Atlanta roared, "KATANA!"

Her skin crawled and panic pushed her legs faster. She was thankful for the days she spent running with Thane and Leif to train for a moment like this.

"We place the shield as planned then we can force Atlanta out," Valeen said. "Once he's outside the wall he can't get back in, not unless one of us allows it. But we kill Synick and take that sword."

People behind them started screaming. "Monsters!" someone shouted. They'd encountered Synick's creatures.

NIGHT MEETS THE ELF QUEEN

"Watch it!" an elf spun out of the way to avoid being plowed over by Valeen and Katana.

Kids near a water fountain laughed and ran with them. As cute as they were, now wasn't the time. "Go! Run to your mothers!" Katana scolded. There was no telling what Synick would allow his undead creatures to do.

She glanced back to find water crept over the cobblestone street, it always preceded Atlanta.

Tears burned. Tears of anger, fear, hatred. Part of her didn't want to run, but to turn and put her power of the sun against his magic of the sea, proving exactly as Valeen said, she wasn't his slave. She was free. And sometimes freedom required a fight.

Valeen sang, half tuneless because of her heavy breathing but the words in the primordial language were clear. "On wings of shadow, fly as you might, come to me, Night take flight." It didn't matter where he was in the realm of Adalon, he'd hear the song and the magic in the words.

The last she'd seen him was behind the smithy grazing in a field, so he wasn't far. Her legs and lungs burned but it only fueled her to push harder. Wind ripped her hair free of the bun and sweat dripped down her temple.

They reached the end of the city, leaving behind buildings and crowds and sprinted over a grassy knoll toward Castle Dredwich. A winged shadow cast from above. With a *whoosh*, Night glided down and trotted to a stop. Valeen jumped onto his back then reached for her.

"KATANA!" Atlanta shouted again. "VALEEN! Stay where you are!"

Katana took her sister's waiting hand and she pulled her up. Once she had a grip on her, Valeen said, "Go Night. Fly high!"

He took off into a sprint and they lifted. Atlanta and Synick seemed to shrink as they rose. From here she had a perfect view of the city. Black smoke drifted from the center. Screams still echoed from the streets. The city guard rushed toward them.

"Is Synick attacking the city?" Katana whispered.

Valeen glanced back. "He's probably doing it to draw us there. He knows we'll want to help the people."

"Thane is not here to help them." She frowned. "We have to."

"Shield first, but we cannot place it near the waterfall anymore. They will see us, and I can't protect it there. We must place it inside the castle."

Night soared over the ravine that surrounded Castle Dredwich. Sprays of mist wrapped around them as they passed the waterfall. With a quick tug on the reins, Night dropped down at the base of the entrance steps.

"Where in the castle?" Katana hopped off first and dashed up the stairs.

"My room. It's protected by wards." Valeen was on her heels. The guards at the doors quickly pulled them open. They bounded up the next set of stairs and flew down the corridor to Valeen's room.

Once inside, Katana searched frantically for a place to hold it. There was nothing that looked stable enough. The bed wouldn't do, neither would a chair. It had to be something solid and near unmovable. "What do we use as an anchor?"

NIGHT MEETS THE ELF QUEEN

Valeen slammed her fist into the floor at the foot of her bed and cracked the stone. She hit it again and it opened enough to slide the blade into. "This will have to do."

Katana shoved it in until it wouldn't move further. "Now what?"

"Grab hold. We must give it our intention. Let your magic flow into it," her sister said.

Katana wrapped her hands around the pommel and pushed her magic into the sword. Light and shadow mixed as both of their powers circled around them. *Be a shield and protection for this city, for the elves. Draw from the sun, Lightbringer. I give you my power to do so. You are Lightbringer, give us your light.*

Valeen whispered, "Connect to the moon, shield and protect the Valley of the Sun. Save us from our enemies, let no one in or out unless I or the goddess of day wills it." A beam of white light shot straight into the ceiling. The sword began to shake, then the ground they stood on. A potted plant fell off the shelf and shattered on the floor, spilling soil. Valeen looked terrified. "I don't know if this floor will hold."

"It has to!" Katana kept her grip on the sword. "Finish it, Val!"

Valeen let go and ran to the windows, throwing a set of them open then raised her arms above her head. In one swift motion she dropped to her knee and touched the stone. The beam of light inside disappeared, but outside, it spread into a dome and began to shimmer into a thin veil dripping down around the city until it touched the grass below. The sword stopped shaking, giving off a subtle glow.

"We did it!" Katana clapped and jumped up and down. "It worked!"

Valeen sagged against the window's ledge and breathed out a long sigh. "We did it."

"Katana!" Atlanta's voice came from outside. He had to be just below the window.

Valeen slammed the windows shut and backed away. "He can't get in. No enemy of ours can pass the threshold."

"I will start killing your elven friends one by one until you come out." His voice was muffled through the glass, but she heard the threat loud and clear.

Katana peeked through the window. Atlanta held a guard by the throat, feet dangling off the ground.

"I have to go to him."

"No!" Valeen grabbed her. "No, you can't."

"I won't let him kill people for me."

"Then I will kill him. Stay here." Valeen was already running for the door before Katana could stop her.

"Valeen, no! You are not immortal yet. He could kill you." Panic made her chest heavy. She would not watch her sister die because she wanted to be free. She bolted after her but once she got to the hallway, Valeen vanished in a wisp of shadow. This couldn't be happening. She dashed back into the room and shoved open the window. "I'm coming out. Don't hurt him."

Atlanta tossed the guard aside. The poor elf hit the ground, coughing and sputtering for breath. Using her power, she became weightless and floated to the ground. Atlanta snatched her wrist and jerked her to his side.

Shadows preceded Valeen, swirling along the ground like a sea of her own as she appeared from around the bend of thick bushes. Black vines curled out of the ground a few feet from her and Atlanta, like serpents poised to strike. Soulender was in her grasp and murder filled her eyes. "Let her go, Atlanta."

Pain ripped across her scalp as he suddenly gripped her hair and jerked her in front of him. Then cold metal pressed to her throat. She went utterly still.

"Atlanta, no!" Valeen's eyes blew wide.

"Let us go or I'll kill her before you can take me down."

With a swipe of her hand over the blade, it vanished, and she raised her palms in surrender. "Don't hurt her, please."

"That sword," Atlanta growled. "Soulender is supposed to be with Hel right now and given to Pricilla."

There is a time to be the soft petals of a rose and a time to be its thorns. "It's alright, Val. I'll go and Atlanta will say nothing to Pricilla about Soulender. And there will be no fight here today. Do we have a deal?" With a blade to her throat, she had to be soft and bide her time until she could become the thorns.

Valeen's eyes glittered with tears.

Atlanta lowered the knife from her throat. "We do." Water swirled around their feet. Valeen stayed still, she threw no magic at Atlanta, no daggers, only watched helplessly as Atlanta's waters rose up and swallowed them.

Chapter 52

HEL

"Lord." Out of breath, Mathekis pushed through the line of pale ones, and rushed to his side.

Hel kept watch on Pricilla's fortress gate. It started to lift. His breath came quicker. All his careful planning, waiting in the Void for hundreds of years and creating the curse was going to finally pay off. He and Valeen would be fully god and goddess again. Immortality was within his reach and soon after that, vengeance. "What is it, Mathekis?"

"The elf king is not here."

A feverish heat burned through him, and he slowly turned. Mathekis took a step back, his pure black eyes in his pale face widened in fear. "Not here?" Hel snarled.

"There are no dragons, Lord. No elves. There is no one else."

Hel glanced at the woods behind him and his army. A slight breeze rustled the leaves but there was no other movement. He clenched his teeth so hard his jaw ached.

The gate lifted fully, and flanked by several guards, Pricilla rode out. A gust of wind fluttered past him, and thunder rolled in the distance. He had no idea how many soldiers she had hidden behind her fortress walls, and if Atlanta and Alehelm had brought even part of their forces with them, this would be a slaughter, not a battle.

"Fuck," he said through his teeth. Mathekis bowed and backed away. "This changes nothing. Wait for my command." Hel kicked Starborn's sides, he reared and took off.

How could Thane leave him to fight Pricilla alone? Had something happened or was this yet another betrayal? Pricilla and her group lined up and waited. Alone, he faced them.

"Where is Atlanta?" she demanded.

"Probably going after Katana." And that meant his own wife was in danger. This needed to happen fast.

With a frown, Pricilla shook her head. "Primordials always think they're above the rules that they themselves set." She took out a pink leather pouch from her satchel. Pulling the drawstrings, she opened it and pulled out two silvery crystals on golden chains. A slow, glowing pulse emanated from the one on the left. A warm tingle whirled around him, and then it was as if a tugging involuntarily pulled him forward. It was his immortality, he felt it. It wanted to be reunited.

"The sword." Pricilla dangled the thing he'd wanted for thousands of years just out of his reach. He pulled the weapon from the holster on his hip, and taking hold of the blade, angled the handle toward her.

At once, he grabbed the two chains, and she took the sword. Quickly, he placed the chains around his neck and tucked the precious items under the collar of his black armored chest plate. The power from each of them seeped into him, like trying to hold a star. It felt like a buzz of lightning waiting to strike.

"Pleasure doing business with you," Hel drawled.

Pricilla grinned as she ran her hand over the golden blade. Lifting it to the sky, the shiny metal glinted in the bit of sunlight that peeked through the dark thunderclouds. Then she swung it at Alehelm. The blade broke skin, but with that force his head should have been lopped off. If he'd given her the real Soulender his head would be on the ground.

He hadn't expected her to do that and unravel his deceit so quickly.

"You were going to kill me?" Alehelm's mouth hung open watching his blood drip down the blade.

Time to go. Hel turned Starborn and faced his army. Two thousand of them jumped and paced and clawed at the ground, waiting to be unleashed.

Pricilla screamed, the rage palpable, and thunder cracked. "Hel, we had a deal! Give me Soulender! This is not Soulender!"

From over his shoulder he said, "I made a deal to give you *that* sword. I never used the name Soulender, did I?" He kicked Starborn into a gallop. Hooves pounded, wind whistling in his ears.

"ATTACK!" Pricilla bellowed. "Stop him before he becomes immortal! Stop him!"

Foot soldiers poured out from the gate, dragons lifted from the turrets, and arrows cut through the air.

NIGHT MEETS THE ELF QUEEN

Hel shielded him and his mount with magic, arrows bounced off, thudding into the ground around him.

The earth began to shake. Minotaurs, trolls and giants, men and shifters thundered after him. Some of their weapons were larger than his horse.

A dragon swooped down at him, talons wide and ready to snap him in half. He jerked Starborn right and the dragon grabbed nothing but dirt.

"He cannot open the crystal! He will be more powerful than all of us!" Pricilla and Alehelm came up on either side of him. Their hippogriffs hovered just off the ground and snapped at Starborn. He screeched and bit back.

A pair of golden cuffs were in Pricilla's grasp, and just like katagas serum, they bound magic. It was what she'd used on him once before, the day he was captured. She'd used his want for Valeen against him, and said they had Valeen captured and that she wanted to talk to him. They did in fact have her at that time, but what he didn't know was that she planned to execute them all. He'd made the mistake of turning his back on Pricilla, where she slapped a cuff on him before he was taken down by her guards.

Now would be a good time for you to show up, Thane! he thought.

"To the woods!" Hel roared. Mathekis repeated and the pale ones turned and ran. It would look like a retreat. It wasn't.

Gritting his teeth, he flicked his wrist toward Pricilla and her mount's neck snapped. She went down hard. She hit the ground and rolled over and over. A sword whooshed over Hel's head. "Being god of the grapes doesn't make you well suited for a fight against the god of magic, you fucking prick." With another flick of his wrist, Alehelm was hit with a blast of sparking, crackling crimson energy that knocked him off. Without his rider, the hippogriff stopped and flew in the opposite direction.

Hel and Starborn raced to the edge of the woods before his army then he jerked the reins left, turning them. "Hold!"

Pricilla's army crashed toward them like a tidal wave coming to sweep away all in its path, thousands deep. More kept pouring out of the gates. Dragons flew in diamond formations of four, darkening the sky.

Hel's pulse pounded in his ears, his breath came slow and steady. He would not die this day. Not when he finally had what he wanted, his wife and his immortality. He took the silvery glowing crystal from inside his tunic and held it in his palm. Pain suddenly ripped through his hand. An arrow stuck through the center of his palm, and he dropped the crystal. "FUCK!" He snapped the back end of the arrow off and jerked it from his flesh.

Feet. Mere feet stood between them and the enemy. "Now! Kill them all! Feast on their blood, tear out their hearts!"

The pale ones surged around him like water over rock. Howls and battle cries ringing in his ears. They did not fear death. They only thought of doing what he commanded, and the collision was magnificent.

As they were once elves, the pale ones had elven swiftness and agility. Several of them ran up the trees and leapt onto the giants' backs. They cut into the trolls' legs, buckling them and stabbing wildly as they hit the ground. Blood poured from their lips as they tore into minotaurs and men. They would soon see if this curse would infect more than just elves.

But pale ones fell like any mortal. Clubs sent them flying. Spears impaled them to trees. Their bones crunched and their heads hit the ground. Through the breaks in the trees Hel spotted the dragons circling above. They'd either have to burn this forest down or change forms.

A group of half-shifted dragons hit the ground and charged straight through the battle lines for him. Hel dropped from Starborn, pulled his sword and thrust out his palm. Dragon scales didn't have many weaknesses, and they were nearly impervious to magic, but his percussion blast knocked them back. Pounding feet caught his ear, he whirled as a wildcat's cry pierced the air and shoved his sword into the chest of a feline shifter. And that was when he lost all sight of reason and let his training and instinct take over. His sword met flesh, his magic burned and maimed. Every time he paused to try to take out his immortality, another attack came; arrows, or dragon's fire, or an axe.

Hot blood splattered across his face. He slashed and hacked, sent hallucinations to the minds of his enemies so they would turn on each other or run. If he didn't stop this charge here, they would march straight through the portal to Palenor. To his wife.

Bodies piled up all around. The pale ones' numbers fell like leaves in autumn. Rain pounded the earth, making the ground muddy and slick. Screams and cries of agony filled his mind. The rain drenched his hair, blood ran into his eyes.

Mathekis cried, "We must retreat, Lord!"

"No! Keep fighting!"

A giant rumbled out from behind a tree and with an upward swing, his huge club hit Mathekis and sent him crashing into a tree. He struggled to rise. In a puff of smoke, Hel appeared in front of Mathekis and slashed the belly of the giant, spilling his insides. With a roar, he stumbled back and hit the ground with a earth-shaking *boom*.

"Now get up!" Hel jerked him to his feet. "Fight, Mathekis or there will be no one left."

"Save yourself, Lord. Go back to Palenor and live to fight another day."

"We are not losing this battle. I will not lose!"

"It is already lost!" Mathekis gripped the edges of Hel's chest armor and shook him. The screeches of Hel's dying army emphasized his words. "There are too many of them, even for you."

Alehelm, Pricilla, and three other gods he didn't know closed in around them. He only knew they were gods by the signature subtle glow to their skin. The sign of immortality. He didn't have any weapon that could kill them, Valeen did.

The golden cuffs dangling in Pricilla's grasp taunted him. "You can surrender, Hel. You don't have to die today."

Mathekis nodded at Hel. "Go, Lord." With his sword raised high, he charged. The god next to Pricilla threw out his palm and insects swarmed Mathekis, covering him in seconds. He screamed, clawing and batting to get them off. Then he fell to the ground and went still.

Fuck this.

"You must have forgotten who I am." He drove his

fist straight to the ground; the dirt, grass, and trees within a twenty-foot radius gave way and started falling into a pit. Hel's wings ripped out from his back, and he rose up. The gods who'd surrounded him scrambled to get away from the crumbling earth, crawling and clawing to grab hold of something solid.

"THANE! You gave me your word!" he shouted as he broke through the tops of the trees.

Swiftly unscrewing the top to the crystal, he marveled only a moment at the silver essence swirling inside. "You are mine," was all he whispered, and it pushed through the opening and hit him in the chest. A *thud, thud, thud,* pounded in his ears as the power flooded through his blood. A light burst across his vision like a blazing star then slowly faded. Everything was louder, brighter, and more colorful. A hot pulse poured out from his core to his fingertips, to the top of his head and down to his toes as if he was coated in warm honey.

He held his hand in front of himself— his skin had a new subtle glow to it. His magic hummed with a new intensity. He threw his head back and started laughing. He'd forgotten how it felt to be so powerful, unstoppable.

If the battle was lost, he was going to take out as many as he could, and no one could stop him.

THANE

PHANTOM SHIFTED and danced side to side nervously beneath Thane. He stomped and tossed his head, ready to charge into battle. On his right, Fennan twisted the reins in his hands. To his left, Piper kept looking at him. The screams and battle cries echoed through the forest and across the open plane between them. Swords clashed, metal rang on metal, beast fought beast. It was pure chaos the likes he hadn't seen in such a long time he'd forgotten the intensity of it.

He'd watched the exchange between Hel and Pricilla, watched the charge. Just like Hel said he would, he pissed her off enough to draw her army out. Beneath his Raven-winged helmet, sweat slid down the side of his face. Thunder clouds boomed to the east, rain poured but the sun still peeked through. The light reflecting off the pink-tinged trees created a red haze. That or all the blood being spilled.

"They are losing this battle," Piper finally said.

"We want the pale ones to die," Fennan said calmly.

"So you brought us here for what?" Piper growled. "To watch a slaughter and then have them march into Palenor?"

Thane remained silent. The pale ones fought as fiercely as he'd ever seen them. Teeth sunk into throats and guts hung from mouths. There wasn't any part of him that felt sorry to watch them die. Only that Hel was waiting. Having their master amongst them gave them a zealousness they didn't have before.

He watched several of Pricilla's army turn into a cursed creature, a minotaur, a handful of feline shifters, even a dragon. Even if they were killed, it was alarming.

"THANE! You gave me your word!" Hel's voice cut through the chaos, cut into his heart. He shot up above the trees, hovering on great white feathered wings, then a bolt of light burst out from him. An invisible wave rocked the ground...

"What was that?" Leif asked, leaning forward in his saddle. All the horses neighed and stomped at the disturbance.

"Hel just became a god again." Thane smiled slowly.

"Then he can't be killed." Fennan patted his horse's neck. "All the more reason we should wait until the pale ones die."

"But he could be captured," Piper added. "You said those cuffs the goddess has can bind his magic."

"If they can get them on him." Leif sounded proud of Hel.

"We wait." Thane gripped the saddle horn to keep his hands from trembling. He didn't want to wait. His mind said to charge in, but his gut said to hold. If Pricilla couldn't get to Hel, she'd go for Palenor and draw him away from her fortress, but the timing had to be right, or he'd lose more than half of his Ravens and he wasn't willing to do that.

From his position, hidden in the thick wood that circled Pricilla's fortress, he could see the fighting diagonal to him. Many dragons circled above but most of them had landed and marched into the fight on the ground.

"*Thane*. The portal is right where they are fighting." Piper had her sword in hand. "Palenor could be in danger."

"You hate the pale ones. We have wanted this curse gone all our lives. Now you'll watch it happen."

"I may not like Hel, but you told him we would be there to fight. They aren't the enemy right now."

"And we will attack when I say."

She threw her hand toward the battle. "We can attack the rear and box them in now."

"If you don't want to follow the commands of your *king* then go back home!"

Piper winced and turned away.

Prince Ronan, covered in silver dragon scales, stepped in front of Thane. "We don't have the numbers to fight her once his army is wiped out. If we wait much longer, she will overwhelm us too."

"I am the god of *war*," Thane barked. "I know what I'm doing. No one moves until I say!"

Foot soldiers still ran out from inside the fortress and if she had more than those five gods or demigods with her, he hadn't seen them yet. Gods and goddesses were worth ten of a good mortal soldier. They didn't tire and they didn't die, though they rarely fought. They'd rather have mortals do their bidding.

Time seemed to pass slowly. Minutes felt like hours. In the air, Hel shredded through a dragon like it was wet paper, straight through its chest and out its back. Once he hit the ground bodies flew up in the air by magic or his sword.

Pricilla and her ilk walked through the field, killing pale ones with ease. Though they kept their distance from Hel; they wanted to get him alone. But Thane would not leave him alone.

The moment he'd been waiting for finally happened; the flow of Pricilla's army from inside the gates stopped. Now he'd seen her final number. It was still twice what they had, but no matter. "Ronan, take her archers, burn down her catapults. Piper, Fennan, Leif, with me." He turned to Piper, "If we had not waited for all her army to come out, they would have boxed *us* in." Thane raised his sword high and turned around to his Ravens and the dragon army. "I know we have always fought against the pale ones but today they are our allies. They will not attack because a greater enemy threatens our land. This army of giants and minotaurs, of creatures you have never seen before, would come for our homes, for your children and your wives, and destroy everything. We stop them here. For Palenor!"

Their echoing cheers drew Pricilla's eye as they charged into the open. Phantom thundered over the grass. Armor clanked in a steady rhythm. Ronan took his beast form, followed by his dragon soldiers, and they soared for her fortress. Fire arched through the air, their talons slashed, breaking stone and sending bodies flying.

"Turn! Protect the rear!" Pricilla wailed. "Protect the fortress!"

Bones crunched under Phantom's hooves. Thane brought his sword down across a man, then the god of war lived up to his name. Everything in his path fell by blade or by magic. He boiled blood with his power. He hacked and stabbed, only seeing red. It didn't matter if Pricilla outnumbered them.

A half-shifted dragon covered in crimson scales ran up on Piper. He launched himself from Phantom and tackled him to the ground. Mud splattered across his face while they rolled and fought for dominance. Thane managed to gain top position and pushed the point of his blade closer and closer to the dragon's throat.

His enemy screamed, trying to dig talons into Thane's armored forearms. Dragon scales were nearly impossible to push through with an ordinary sword, but Ronan had brought weapons that could. All his Ravens had them, and so did he. The dragon's arms shook, so did Thane's, until the blade-point pierced his scales and he gurgled blood and went limp.

"Thane, behind you!" Piper smashed her shoulder into the minotaur coming up on him, then ducked under the axe and shoved her blade straight through his heart.

Thane nodded his thanks and rose up to fight. Leif and Piper fought back-to-back now. Screams of battle, cries for help, and roars from dragons became background noise.

Then he spotted Hel. Gore and blood smears covered him. He was nearly as good as Thane with a sword but favored his magic. The enemies dropped dead around him, legs breaking, necks snapping. With a stretch of Hel's hand, a bolt of lightning shot down from the sky and burnt a troll to ash. It had been millennia since they fought together like this. Thane fought his way to his side and Hel smiled over at him. "About time you showed up. I was beginning to think you'd abandoned me."

Hel's army was a quarter of what it was and dwindling. "I'm here, as I said."

They fought side by side after that. The cousins who were more like brothers. They'd betrayed and hated and fought each other, but in the end it didn't matter. Hel's enemies were Thane's enemies.

Momentum was on their side until horns blew all across the battlefield. Horns not of his or Hel's army but from another army coming over the horizon. Crimson flags with a white flame at the center rose high into the air. The goddess of fury.

"We cannot win this battle," Thane breathed. He whirled in a circle, finding his Ravens were too scattered. They'd lost all formation even if he could get them back into lines, Eliza brought another thousand or more.

A Raven right beside him took an ax to the chest and went down. Ronan and his dragons clashed with the enemy in the sky. Their numbers were even but Eliza had other winged fighters, riders on hippogriffs and griffins, and even men with feathered wings.

"Hel, we have to go back." He raised his sword and pointed it south toward the woods where the portal was. "Retreat!" Thane bellowed. "Raven's retreat! Ronan! Get your dragons back to the portal!"

Fennan carried the message, "Ravens retreat!" and soon others were shouting. The signal gave Pricilla's forces a boost in morale. They fought harder and chased his retreating soldiers.

Eliza ordered a charge, the incoming battalion roared, their feet thundering.

Hel jerked Thane by the collar of his armor. "I'll hold them off. Go!" He shoved him in the back.

Thane stumbled forward but turned and pointed at him, "You better come back, Brother!"

"I will," he smirked.

With a whistle, he ran. Phantom hopped over bodies and galloped to Thane. Mid stride, he leapt on. He glanced back as Hel swung his electric-blue sword furiously. "Keep fighting!" he commanded his army. "Fight to the very end! Bite them, turn them!"

The pale one's rage intensified. Entrails hung from mouths, blood oozed between their teeth and from their blades. They didn't touch any of Thane's Ravens or Ronan's dragons on the ground as they retreated.

Hel was sacrificing his army to save them...

With his Ravens riding and sprinting with him, and dragons landing all around them, they rushed into the woods. Thane smashed his hand to the portal, "Take us to Palenor," he commanded. It opened in a swirling pool and his soldiers sprinted through. "Get back inside the wall!"

Thane peered through the trees, his heart pounding, his breath rushing in and out. Hel raised his arms and called down a wall of lightning bolts that hit the ground and cut across the field, stopping Eliza's charge. Some of her fliers crashed into it and went down. He could only hold that for so long.

"Faster!" Thane waved his arm in a circle to get them moving.

The lightning wall dropped, and the charge resumed. The pale ones caught behind it rushed forward.

The last of his Ravens and dragons went through and the last pale ones fell. Hel was surrounded, bodies flew from magical blows, and he fought fiercely but he was alone. The enemy charged for the portal now, for him.

"HEL!" Thane hopped off Phantom and pushed him through the portal and sprinted for him. Starborn trotted up to the portal and went through. "HEL!" He swung at the first soldier to reach him, cutting up the belly and through the throat. One down...

He kept swinging, ten down.

Two giants standing twenty feet tall came up on either side; he dodged a blow and cut the back of the left's heels. The beast toppled with a screech. He narrowly missed the blow of a club and then hacked at the back of the giant's knee, buckling him.

He raised his sword to clash with a man when a hand gripped his arm, and he was suddenly pulled into darkness. Pressure crushed every inch of his body, then he stood outside the portal in the unnamed forest. It was quiet here. No charging enemies, no rain or thunder. Only the backs of the last of his soldiers marching toward home.

He bent over, grabbing the tops of his thighs, dragging in breath.

Hel let him go and placed both hands on the stone portal. "Don't let anyone else come through."

A moment passed. "There is a goddess requesting access," it hissed.

"No!" Hel growled. "Do not let her through."

"I cannot refuse her."

"You can't refuse me either!"

Thane pushed his palms against the rough surface. "Do not let her through."

"She will come through another way," the voices said.

"That will at least buy us some time," Hel said. "This is our land, not hers. Do not let her through here."

The portal went quiet, dormant. They both backed away and waited for movement, but it didn't come.

Worry gnawing at his gut, Thane turned to Hel. "The next closest portal is the Brightheart Forest. It gives us not even a few hours."

"Then we better hope Valeen and Katana finished that sword and that it worked." Hel grabbed Thane's collar and jerked him closer. "And you fucking idiot, I tried to send Mathekis to tell you that Atlanta wants Katana back. He asked for her in the negotiations. He's here."

Chapter 53

KATANA

The swirling waters fell away, and Atlanta loosened his grip on her. A meadow of tall green grass with patches of wildflowers surrounded them. In the distance the mountain peak behind Castle Dredwich was visible. The lip of the Valley of the Sun wasn't far off. She'd expected to be standing in the middle of the unnamed forest to be dragged through the portal to House of the Seas.

Atlanta strode away from her then suddenly halted as if he hit a wall. He pressed his hands flat against what appeared to be nothing. Then she remembered what Valeen said, "No one is allowed in *or out* unless I or the goddess of day wills it."

Atlanta was trapped inside unless she or Valeen allowed him to leave. She smiled and felt laughter bubbling up in her chest.

He whirled, ferocity taking over his features. "What magic is this?"

"I don't know."

His fists crashed into the invisible wall. Then he conjured his trident and stabbed wildly at it. He hit it with a blast of water, with a force that could cut through stone, and it only sprayed back at him. "Did you do this?"

She shook her head but the laughter that had been threatening broke free. Even with her hand over her mouth she couldn't stop.

Eyes blown wide with rage, Atlanta stalked toward her and backhanded her across the face. The blow knocked her off balance and she fell to one knee.

She rose back up and wiped the bead of blood at the corner of her mouth. "All you are is a boy who never learned to control his temper." He sneered and raised his hand, but she didn't flinch, didn't move. She pushed her shoulders back.

"You've been around your sister too long, but you'll remember your place. Now, let us pass."

"I can't. It's Valeen's magic. The same she had at House of Night." If he believed she had no control over it, he wouldn't try to force her to do it. If he found out she could open the way, it would be painful.

"It wasn't there before!" he shouted.

"Well, maybe it's because you took me. I don't know how her magic works. She knows I don't want to be with you, Atlanta. It's over. Just leave me alone and go live your life."

Her stomach dropped as rage twisted his face. Charging for her, he grabbed her arms, gripping hard enough to bruise. Water overtook them.

Moments later she stood outside a white manor with overgrown weeds around the front steps and along the walls. He dragged her along the trampled path and up the chipped stairs. The front door's blue paint peeled from harsh weather. Gold letters formed what she assumed was the name of the owners "Nerinhall".

Once they were through the door, he shoved her in the back. She stumbled into the entry table, knocking off the silver vase. It clattered loudly to the white marble floor.

Footsteps pounded. Someone else was here...

Synick came around the corner. Katana's gut seemed to twist, and she backed into Atlanta's arms. Of the two of them, she at least knew her former husband wouldn't kill her without reason.

He'd taken off the armor she'd burned a hole into and wore a sleeveless white top. Like his face hidden beneath the mask, there were signs of decay on his left arm, patches of scabbed skin, and divots where the muscles seemed to have been eaten away, although it wasn't as disgusting as before. It appeared being away from the underrealm was regenerating him, slowly.

"What are you doing here?" Synick asked. "I thought you'd be in House of the Seas by now."

"I would be, but we can't get out. Valeen has put up a wall."

"The bitch did that before."

"I know." Atlanta curled his arms around Katana's waist. Nausea rose up her throat and an involuntary shudder wracked her body. He must have mistaken it for a chill because he slipped off his cloak and put it around her shoulders. "I need to know, was it you that killed Katana before? Don't lie to me." His deep voice rumbled against her back.

If they started fighting, she could get away. "It was him," Katana said matter-of-factly.

"Of course it wasn't me." Synick stared right into Atlanta's eyes when he lied.

"She says it was you."

"Maybe it was a shapeshifter to look like me, but it was not me."

"And how would this shapeshifter have gotten an immortal weapon?" Atlanta gripped her tighter; his breath brushed the top of her head. His touch repulsed her, and she couldn't wait for an opening to get out of his grasp.

"You know as much as I. They were gifts from our creators meant to slay the demon princes and their kind if they should ever break free of the underrealm."

"It's rather convenient that you would blame a shapeshifter for something you did." Surprisingly, Katana no longer felt anger toward him. Fear didn't rise to the surface and make her want to cower either. All she felt was the urge to get away from both of them. "Why was your soul sent to the underrealm after your death if it were not true?" The half mask covering the decaying side of his face didn't hide the way he'd been punished for taking her life all those years ago.

He shifted his weight from one leg to the other, and looked away, focusing on the vase on the floor. "There were many things I am not proud of that I did to earn my place there, for which I was severely punished. Two thousand years of punishment, but it wasn't for what happened to you. And I plan to make amends for my past mistakes and retake my place on the council to set things right again in Runevale."

It was disgusting how easily he lied. The innocent

act was even worse after what she saw in the smithy. He would have forced himself on her sister right in front of her if he could have. She hated him more than Atlanta, despised him with every fiber of her being. Angry heat started to work its way through her body.

She looked up at Atlanta, and by the softening of his expression he either believed him or wanted to give him the chance to make amends as he said. Neither would be surprising, especially after he spoke of the balance being restored. He didn't *want* to believe it because then he'd be forced into killing or imprisoning Synick to avenge her.

"He stabbed me with the Sword of Truth. I laid there calling your name, Atlanta, and you never came," her voice broke on the last word. "He took me from you. He would do it again." She had to get them to fight.

"We are primordials, all of us are bonded. I would never kill you."

She turned and pressed her hands into Atlanta's chest. "He's lying. He wanted Valeen and when she wouldn't give herself to him, he killed me to punish her."

Atlanta's eyes smoldered with intensity. It was working.

Synick snorted as if it were ridiculous. "I don't even find Valeen attractive."

"No, you've told me many times you wanted her," Atlanta said, tone getting more menacing. "You watched her with lust in your eyes for too long."

"Be careful, Atlanta." Synick touched the bronze sword's hilt at his hip. "Believing your wife's lies won't end well."

"My wife doesn't lie. She never has. So, you want to kill me too? I thought primordials were bonded?" Atlanta boomed.

"We are. Which is why we need to band together to restore the balance. The way to Runevale is open again but unless this fight ends with the council, what's to stop Valeen from closing it again?"

The anger started slipping, and Katana clamped her hands into fists. *No, they can't find peace or come to an agreement.* "Look at him, Atlanta. He is cursed by demon magic. He shouldn't have the immortal sword."

"No, he shouldn't," Atlanta agreed. "I will take it to the council where it belongs." He held out his hand and Synick angled his hip away from him.

"I was head of the council."

"Long ago."

"The demons have gotten to his mind," Katana added. Holding Atlanta's waist, she slipped behind him. "I can see it. You know I see auras, Atlanta. His is as black as a raven's feather. He is wicked. He is more demon than god now. We must take the sword."

"Shut up, bitch," Synick snarled.

"Do not speak to my wife that way." Atlanta's trident appeared in his hand, and he slammed the end of it to the marble floor with a loud *crack*. "If you are trustworthy, give me the sword, and we shall go to the council together."

"Two thousand years of torture wouldn't make me give up this sword. I will go to the council myself."

"He will poison Pricilla's mind just as he has everyone else's," Katana whispered. "The aura doesn't lie, blackness oozes from him. You know I speak the truth, Atlanta." The truth was more powerful than all of his deception, and all she had to do was tell it.

Atlanta tilted his trident points at Synick, and Katana slowly backed away.

VALEEN

Paintings on the walls blurred as Valeen tore through the halls. She dashed past the guards and servants, down stairs and through twisting corridors. Talon and her group of friends quickly stepped aside when they saw her coming. Thane's sister had been unusually quiet and kept to herself since the death of her mother. Probably afraid she'd be next.

She hurried past the towering bookshelves and the smell of old paper, until she found her way up the metal spiraling stairwell to Presco's loft. He was pouring a deep-purple liquid into a larger beaker when she reached the top.

"My queen." His brow creased with worry. "What's wrong?"

She leaned back against the railing and took a few breaths. "He took her. Atlanta, took Katana, and Synick is with him. The wall is up so as long as she doesn't allow them through they won't be able to leave the city, but I have no idea where they are, and Hel and Thane are not back. We must go to them."

"Right away," he agreed and set down his vial.

They hurried down the steps, and marched side by side. Shelves of books towered above both their heads. A soft music played from enchanted strings in the musical section. "The only one who might be able to find her is Thane."

Presco nudged his gold glasses up higher on his nose. "Why is that?"

It was strange to say aloud but, "I think he is her mate. A sun tattoo appeared on her back after they slept together. He might not know it yet but if he accepts the bond, he might be able to communicate with her or at least be led to her."

With his brows practically hitting his hairline, he said, "I have been out of the loop. I wasn't aware they were intimate. Are you certain of this?"

"Not certain because Katana didn't see a mark on Thane."

"He might have noticed it, don't you think?"

"Unless it's somewhere he didn't see it. Or he didn't tell anyone."

Once they set foot out the front doors, one of the soldiers stopped her. "Lady, the king's Ravens are coming back. They say it was a retreat. What should we do?"

Valeen's heart skipped a beat, and she peered across the bridge and up the Valley's hill beyond the castle grounds. Dragons came into view followed by the first of the Ravens. She gritted her teeth and the ruler in her came forward. "Prepare for an attack. All available fighters in the city need to get to the wall and to their stations immediately."

STANDING at the entrance in the city wall, Presco and Valeen watched for Hel and Thane. Elves in Raven armor, many she'd fought beside before, marched past them. Ronan soared above, signaling for his dragons to land inside.

She approached one of the Ravens and held up a hand to stop him. "What happened?"

"Lady Lightbringer." He bowed his head then lifted his chin, face covered in mud and splatters of dried blood. "We thought we had victory in our grasp then their reinforcements came. A thousand or more. We had to retreat. There were... things we've never fought before. The High King has been warning us for months, but it was different seeing it." He had a far-off look on his face. For having only just learned there were other realms and marching through a portal to get to one, they had a remarkable amount of trust in Thane. Enough trust and adoration to follow their High King into a battle with pale ones and not against them. They would follow him anywhere.

"Well done soldier," she said, offering a smile. "It is an honor to have you as a Raven."

"Will they come here?"

She frowned but nodded. "Where is the High King?"

He twisted around. "He was right behind us...." he faced her once again. "The Ravens are saying the pale ones are all dead. The Black Mage held off the assault while we retreated."

Another soldier approached. "We recognized the king's cousin, Hel, was leading the pale ones, and we realized all along he's been the Black Mage. But he fought with us, not against us."

"Because of you, Lady Lightbringer." He smiled at her. "You changed his heart."

Taken aback, all she could do was stare at him. They understood that she was with the Black Mage and didn't hate her... or even him.

"Thank you, Lady." He moved on to rejoin the line filtering into the city.

Presco leaned in. "The elves really are a remarkable people. If war wasn't thrust upon them, I don't believe they would seek it."

"They wouldn't." She swallowed hard, holding back tears. She was still bewildered by their reaction. The Palenor Scroll had painted her as wicked, they knew her relationship was over with Thane, and now they knew she'd left him for the Black Mage, and they weren't angry. They still believed in her. The Ravens never wavered.

She felt for Hel and opened her mind to him. *Hel, are you here?*

"I'm here." She whirled and the smoke of his magic slowly dissipated around him and Thane, Phantom, and Starborn.

She threw herself at Hel and he chuckled as he caught her.

"Hello, love." He spoke softly in her ear.

"I was trying not to worry, but I couldn't help myself." She pressed her palms to the sides of his face, turning it to get a good look. "Your eyes..." The piercing cerulean blue-green of her memories replaced the maroon they'd been. They were such a striking color against his dark hair and lashes it was the first thing she noticed. Did this mean he wouldn't need her blood anymore? She twisted a lock of his hair around her finger, it was dirty with blood but there was still a luster to it that hadn't been there before. His ivory skin glowed the way all gods did.

Thane only glanced at her briefly and then started looking behind her and Presco.

You're immortal again. You did it.

He smiled, dimpled his cheek and kissed her hard. *I am.* "But we had to retreat. Eliza joined in and I don't know who else is coming. We managed to stop them from coming through the portal, but they'll be here soon." He lifted his eyes skyward. "Good, your wall is up. I was worried. Atlanta demanded Katana during the negotiations."

Valeen nibbled on her lower lip. The wall hadn't gone up in time.

"Where is Katana?" Thane looked worried now.

Her throat tightened with emotion. "Thane..."

"Where is she?" he demanded.

"You might be the only one who can find her."

"What does that mean?" Thane growled, the worried look in his eyes turned to fury.

"Atlanta got in before we could put up the wall and—"

He snatched her arm, gripping it hard. "How could you let that happen?"

"I tried to stop him, but he threatened to kill her. He had a knife to her throat. I had to let them go."

Hel peeled his grip from her then shoved him. "Don't ever grab her like that again. And don't blame Valeen for what Atlanta did. That is her sister, she cares for her as much or more than you."

"You don't know how much I care. I love her." With his hands curling and uncurling at his sides, Thane's chest heaved up and down with heavy breaths. He looked like he was about to lose control. "Why did you say I'm the only one who can find her?"

"There is a new mark on her. A sun. She said it wasn't there before you and her... were together."

"What does that mean?" His beautiful face started to twist from anger to agony.

"Oh, shit." Hel's brows rose. *That explains his reaction,* Hel said to her mind.

"What is it?" Thane demanded.

"I believe Katana is your soulmate, and," she had to take a steadying breath, "Atlanta wasn't alone when he attacked us... Synick escaped."

He stared at her, fury and agony and terror, warring for dominance. "No," his voice broke. Those emerald-green eyes watered and he tore his gaze away. "No. She's terrified of him, she's... I promised her I wouldn't let him hurt her again. I swore it."

Valeen held back tears. "Have you felt her? Can you speak to her?"

His hand ran down his face and he started pacing. "No, I don't know how. I haven't seen a mark on me... are you sure?"

"No, I'm not sure, but... it doesn't matter right now. We can spare some soldiers to go house to house until she is found."

He curled his hands into fists. "*I* will go house to house until she is found," he snapped. "I will find her and kill both Synick and Atlanta."

"We are about to be invaded." Hel crossed his arms. "The High King needs to prepare his people for battle. That is your duty."

"And that would stop you from finding Valeen?" Thane shook his head and marched inside the city.

Hel smirked, watching him walk away. "Well, she's definitely his mate. He just chose her over... everyone else."

"We need to go with him. My walls will hold until we find her."

Thane stopped and whirled on his heel. "How do you two speak to each other's minds?"

Chapter 54

KATANA

Atlanta turned and snatched Katana before she could back toward the door and shoved her into a small recess in the wall with a suit of black armor. To make it out the front entrance would mean she'd have to get around Atlanta, and Synick stood on the path of the back exit.

"Calm down, Atlanta. Put the trident away." Synick held up a palm and grasped the Sword of Truth in the other. "You don't want to do this. We can still work together."

"I don't work with demon cohorts."

"They tortured me for centuries. Believe me, I am not with the demon princes. But we are trapped here, and Valeen will eventually find her sister. What then? She has Hel, War, and an immortal weapon. We need each other."

There had to be a way out. She peered around the suit of armor's leg. There was a window in the wall directly across from her, but she'd have to run between them to get to it. There was a hallway around the corner to her right. Maybe she could slip unnoticed...

Katana.

She jumped, clutching her hands to her breast, startled by the male voice in her mind.

Katana, can you hear me?

Pressing herself against the wall behind the armor, she rubbed her temples. Surely, she was going mad. This wasn't another one of her panic attacks, was it? Her heart was beating hard, but that was because she was trapped in a house with the two males who'd tormented her.

Katana, I'm sorry I didn't keep my promise. Where are you? Please tell me. I will find you.

Thane? she thought. It was his voice certainly, she'd recognize it anywhere. He was in her dreams almost every night after all... the one respite between nightmares. The trauma of being taken must have broken her mind again, and of course she would think of him. She loved him.

She heard his sigh of relief. *Yes, Katana. Where are you?*

Are you truly talking to my mind? Are you real? She'd asked him that once before when he stood right in front of her. She'd felt as silly then as she did now.

I'm real, and I'm coming to get you. Is Synick there? Or just Atlanta?

Glass shattered, thuds and grunts filled the room. She hid further behind the suit of armor and slammed her eyes shut. *How are you talking to me? Is it Hel's magic?*

Atlanta started screaming and she pressed her hands over her ears.

There was only silence for a few breaths and then he said, *It's not Hel's magic. It's something else.*

She smiled and focused on him, picturing his beautiful face. *I'm in an abandoned white manor. Everything was overgrown outside. There is a name on the door, Nerinhall. That's all I know. We must still be in the Valley somewhere.*

"I'll kill her, Atlanta! I swear if you don't back off, I'll run her through, and you can watch her die."

She whimpered. *Hurry, Thane. Synick said he will kill me. He's fighting with Atlanta.*

I'm coming. The tone of his voice was different; he was afraid. *Can you get outside? Can you hide?*

I don't know. She peeked out from behind the armor. Feathers were scattered everywhere, the two sofas were torn to shreds. The wooden chairs at the table were broken.

Atlanta slammed Synick into the wall a few feet from her, cracking the stone.

A squeak escaped her throat, and she dashed for the entrance door.

"KATANA!" Atlanta bellowed. "Get back here!"

With tears sliding down her face, she threw the door open and leapt down the steps. Something crashed behind her. She pushed harder, driving her legs, pumping her arms. *Thane, I'm outside. I'm running!*

I'm coming.

There were no other homes close. There were only empty fields, not even woods to hide in. There was no one else here. How far away was Thane? She had only moments before—

Arms wrapped around her from behind, she

screamed, clawing and throwing her head back and slamming it into his jaw. The left hand was gloved... "No!" she shouted. "No!"

Brutally strong arms twisted her around and she came face-to-face with Synick. He pulled her against his chest and leaned down to her ear. "Going somewhere, goddess? The fun is just starting."

She shoved her burning, glowing palms to his face and dug in her nails. His scream rang in her ears, his skin melting under her touch. "Get off of me!"

Something hard cracked her in the side of the head. Pain came first, then darkness threatened, she stumbled back and fell down the dirt road. Blood dripped across her face, and she put one arm in front of the other, dragging herself along the ground. *Get up. Get up.* But the ringing in her ears was too loud, everything spun and tilted, she couldn't tell up from down.

"You didn't fight last time. This is much more entertaining." A shadow loomed above her.

She twisted to face him and scooted back. The blade of his sword was bloody. "You killed him," she whispered. Her vision was coming back into focus. The door to the manor was wide open. Atlanta was nowhere. "You *murdered* him?"

"He's not dead. Even if he's angry at the moment, he'll come round to my side. We've been best friends for too long for him not to. And when I bring you back to him, he'll see that." He smiled and took a step closer. She scrambled backward and, rising, she ran again.

"Thane!" she screamed. "Please come..." her voice cracked as she sobbed.

His footsteps thundered behind her. "Thane? So,

you are a whore like Atlanta said. Maybe I'll take my turn too."

He grabbed the back of her top, tearing the fabric. She twisted, pulling out of it, leaving her in a thin cream camisole and kept running.

Thump, thump, thump, he was right behind her. Her heart was going to beat out of her chest. He caught her hair and dragged her to a halt.

"Let go of me!" He threw her to the ground and was on top of her before she could move. "No! NO!" His rot smell filled her nose, and she gagged.

"Tell me how to dismantle Valeen's magic wall." He wrapped a hand around her throat and squeezed.

"I don't know."

"You're lying. What were you doing in the smithy?" She spit in his face, and he slapped her. It merely stung compared to what Atlanta had done. "Tell me how to get out of here."

"I do not know," she said through her bared teeth.

"Does it have something to do with that sword you had? She told you to take it to the cliff... but you didn't. I saw you go into the castle."

Her heart fluttered, but she didn't deny it. If she did, he might sense her lie.

"I can hear your heart beating oddly. That sword has something to do with it." His burnt skin was already healing.

The dagger. Thane had given her the weapon for a moment just like this. With one hand she pushed his face away, and with the other she pulled her dagger, angled it against his back where Thane had shown her, and shoved it in.

He reared back, wailing. "You bitch."

Wiggling free, she got up again. Her magic coiled through her, and her palms emanated a fiery heat. The sun beat down on her, warming her skin, intensifying her power.

He stood, frost curling around his palms. The skeleton creatures conjured out of nothing, five on each side of him. "You know what you fight fire with, don't you? You might have had a chance against me if you trained how to use that power of yours in combat, but you never did."

Angry tears burned. Her mind went to Thane, and how she wished she could see him one more time. *Thane. If I don't see you again—*

I'm almost there.

I just wanted to say—

Tell me when you see me.

Atlanta appeared in a cyclone of water, taking a stance between them. Whatever injuries he had were gone. "Enough, Synick." He held up his hands to both of them. "We have a bigger problem."

Distant hooves pounded in quick succession. Synick's smug expression fell away as he looked over her shoulder. "So, we do. How did they find us?"

She whirled to a black horse careening down the hillside, his rider with a glinting sword in hand... *Thane.*

Just behind him was another rider on a winged horse. Shadows rolled in waves all around her like a black thundercloud. Beside her Hel flew on white wings. She choked on a sob and ran for them. Before she could get five steps, Atlanta had her. He twisted her arm behind her back until she was sure it would break and gripped her around the neck. "You're hurting me," she whimpered.

"I know the little whore inside you wants to run to him, but you belong to me."

Phantom reared up as Thane pulled back on the reins and he leapt off, sword pointed at Atlanta. "Release her."

"That's not going to happen," Atlanta boomed in the same condescending tone he used when he spoke to the servants. "What you'll do is allow me and Katana a way through the barrier keeping us trapped here."

"And me," Synick added.

Full of fury, Valeen stepped up beside him, weapon in hand. "I swear I will tear off your limbs before I take off your head if you don't let her go." Hel landed on her other side and tucked his wings away. He didn't look angry but there was something frightening about his smirk.

"Katana for passage through the wall," Thane said.

"No." Atlanta tightened his grip.

"Take the deal," Synick said quietly. "They are immortal again. This is not a fight we will win right now. I know my nephews and I know her."

"I will not give her up."

"Fool, live to fight another day," Synick muttered.

"I'd rather see her dead than with him."

Katana gulped. She believed him.

"You're on your own then, Atlanta." He and his skeletons backed away slowly. By the sounds of their footsteps, they started running.

"He can't get out," Thane said. "We'll get him later." Then he glared at Atlanta. "Let her go."

Thane, Synick knows the Lightbringer sword has something to do with the magical barrier.

He didn't move, didn't tell the others to go after Synick. He stayed focused on her.

Atlanta's grip tightened around her throat, and she gasped. This couldn't happen. She wouldn't let him kill her in front of Thane and Valeen. It would haunt them forever.

With her hands burning, she reached back and shoved them into his eyes. He roared, slapping his hands over them. Then she was running. If she could make it into Thane's arms, she'd be safe. He caught her around the waist and held her for only a moment then pushed her behind him. "The sword."

Without hesitation, Valeen gave him a golden sword with a beautiful hilt and ancient script. Soulender.

Katana's heart lurched into her throat. As much as she hated Atlanta, she wasn't sure she could watch him die. Even if he would have killed her. "Wait," she breathed.

"Kill him," Hel said. "Kill him now while he's blind."

Screaming with rage, Atlanta started swinging his trident wildly.

Valeen grabbed Katana and turned her away. "This needs to happen."

"We can just lock him out." Her breaths came faster. "He has a territory. He's the father to my children. What happens to them if he dies?"

"If we just locked him out then you would be a prisoner to the valley and if the wall ever falls, he will be back for you. This must end."

Thane's jaw muscles feathered, and he said, "Don't hate me for what I'm about to do."

Valeen kept hold of Katana's head, covering her ears, not letting her turn. "Just keep looking at me."

Metal clashed, grunts and shouts made the hairs on her arms rise. The fight didn't last long. She slammed her eyes shut. The plop of something hitting the ground made her go very still. After a few breaths she pulled Valeen's hands down from her ears and turned. Atlanta was dead. His head lay beside his body.

As horrified as she was, she was also relieved. She ran to Thane and buried her face in his chest. It was his warm arms around her that stopped her from trembling. She couldn't be angry with him for what he'd done. He was her protector, as he'd promised. "Thank you for doing what I could not."

"I'm so sorry. I'm sorry," he muttered into her hair over and over. "I shouldn't have left you."

Her body shook with sobs. The rush of the fight slipped away, leaving her body weak, and her legs gave out. Thane caught her in his arms and held her to his chest. "Atlanta will never hurt you again."

She sniffled and lifted her chin. "I thought I might die again, and you were the last person I thought of." A tear fell from his brilliant green eyes. "I love you. You're everything I ever wanted and needed. I'm so happy you're mine."

Tears freely flowing now, he took her face in his hands. "I love you too, Katana. And you could hear me because you are my soulmate." He pushed aside his hair and on the back of his neck was a sun tattoo matching hers. "You are forever with me."

Her eyes widened at the sight of the mark, then she grinned and laughed. So, it was true after all. "My mate," she whispered.

Chapter 55

VALEEN

In the privacy of her rooms, Hel pressed a crystal on a golden chain into her hand. Standing close enough she felt the warmth of him, his beautiful blue-green eyes flicked back and forth between hers. His energy was electric, it waved off of him making her body tingle.

This was a triumphant male who had lived up to his promise, who'd gone through more than any sane person would to make certain his love wouldn't die yet again. "For you, love, as I promised. All you have to do is twist off the lid and you are a full goddess again."

The crystal pulsed with a silver luminescence. "Thank you, Zaurahel. You're an amazing person. Have I ever told you that?" she smiled, although this moment felt surreal. It had been so long since she died the first time, and all that happened in between.

He chuckled and rubbed his chin. "Am I?"

"No one would have gone through the lengths to

make this happen but you. Not only this fight against the council but going through everything, dealing with me hating you and wanting you dead while I didn't understand, watching and fighting through while I was with... Thane. Helping me remember you," she smiled, "making me fall in love with you again."

"It's partly madness," he smiled and licked his lower lip, "but there was no other choice for me. You are everything. Without you my life is *only* madness."

She smiled and kissed him softly. "I love your madness." She clutched the immortality to her chest and just let the power pulsing inside fill her with gratitude for a moment. "Did you give Thane his?"

Hel tore his gaze away and he quietly walked to the window to peer out. "I couldn't get his."

Every muscle in her body froze and a cold chill ran through her. "But you have it?"

With his arms crossed, he leaned against the window's ledge. "No. It was destroyed."

"You're certain of this?"

"No, but Pricilla said I destroyed it when I killed her heir."

"Is it possible to give him mine?"

He stalked across the room and pushed his finger under her chin. That madness he spoke of swirled at the edges of his eyes. His presence was all-consuming. "I didn't do all that I have done for you so you could give away the gift I fought so hard for. I will never watch you die again."

"But..." Thane had sacrificed so much.

"You will take the top off and you will become fully immortal. It's part of you, it belongs to no one else. The council may have been able to use magic to hold it inside others, but it's yours. You know Thane would never accept it."

No, he wouldn't. Her hand shook as she brought it up to twist off the top. Two thousand years she'd waited to be reunited with her immortal strength. Ordinary weapons wouldn't pierce her flesh, time would not age her, sickness would never haunt her. She would be faster and stronger than before.

One final turn and she lifted it off. Inside waited a swirling glittering essence. The memory of it being ripped from her with the combined magic of the council was vivid. The moment she was pushed to a cold stone block and turned her head at the last moment to look at Hel... not Thane. A tear rolled down his beautiful cheek. It was the first time she'd seen him cry. His last words to her in her mind were—*You are my mate and my wife. I will always love you. You don't need to be afraid. I will find you. One day we'll be together again, I promise.*

Tears filled her eyes even now. He kept that promise too.

It didn't matter that they had fought against each other. It didn't matter that he thought she'd left him. Those last moments made their true feelings come out. Tragedy did that. *I never stopped loving you, Zaurahel.* She'd whispered back just before the axe came down.

"What is it like when it becomes a part of you again?"

He grinned. "Not quite as good as making love to you but close."

"This should be interesting then." *Hello,* she thought. As if a bit shy, it slowly curled out and hovered before her. "It's beautiful, isn't it?" The glimmering silver was like misty water suspended in air. It twirled as if it was dancing for her, then almost like a serpent, it struck her chest. She nearly stumbled with the burst of power that rippled through her. It was like the day of her creation, when she'd awoken in the darkness and light flooded in.

Holding her hands out before her she inspected the new glow to her golden skin. She touched her ears, they were pointed at the tips, not rounded as they'd once been. So, she would always be an elf. That made her smile.

Hel grabbed her waist and lifted her in the air, spinning them in a circle. Then he pulled her against him and held her like if he didn't, she might disappear. "It worked. It really worked. We did it." He started laughing, genuine laughter full of joy. "You're safe now. We'll never be separated again."

ALL THAT WAS LEFT to do was wait for the battle. The warning bells would chime at the first sign of invasion. The army of elves and dragons were ready for the inevitable.

It was too quiet. The soldiers who usually patrolled the castle grounds were at the front. The maids and staff had gone home. Where there was usually chatter and music, there was only the wind and the sound of the waterfall crashing into the ravine.

With all of her friends present near the horse pasture, Valeen sat in the seat of her new white chariot. It looked almost identical to the one she'd had before. A wedding gift from Presco.

Starborn and Night were hooked to it. They happily swished their tails and grazed on the grass. If they knew battle was coming, they didn't care. They'd seen it all, and did not experience fear anymore.

With a civar between his lips, Hel leaned against the railing of the chariot. With a quick flick of his fingers, the smoke rolled into a heart, and he blew it at her.

She sent a letter to Aunt Evalyn and told her to hide with her wait staff in the hidden compartment beneath the floors of Nerium Oleander and not to come out until the battle was over. Part of her wanted to go there now and tell her to go back to Briar Hollow instead.

Not even a smile? Hel said.

His little heart trick was an attempt to get her mind off what was coming.

Using his finger, he started writing something with the smoke. When he finished, he flipped the message around to her. *Show me your boobs*, it read.

She rolled her eyes and laughed. He waved his hand through the message, and it dissipated. "That's better. The wall will hold, and the city will be safe because of you. We'll cut off Pricilla's head and Eliza's too. I'll kill the god of the grapes just because he annoys me while the rest of the council and their armies will fold and run."

"You make it sound so easy."

"Because I believe we will win."

"Who's the god of the grapes?"

"Alehelm."

"I don't remember him."

"He's not worth remembering." He took her hand and flipped her palm face up, the tip of his finger sliding across the lines.

"What about Synick? He's still running around only All Mother knows where."

"I'll gut him too." He shrugged and blew out a cloud of smoke. "I should have done it the moment he appeared."

"I want to be the one to kill him. And we should be looking for him." After all the disgusting, vile, putrid things he'd said and done, she wanted to be the one to end him again.

"By all means. Make it hurt. And he'll show up when the council does. There's no need to waste our efforts looking." He pressed his finger to a spot on her palm. "Two great loves. Three, maybe four lives, but one of them was fractured. Remember when I first told you that?"

"Yes."

"I couldn't figure out what the fractured line was that came back together. It's now, when your life as Layala joined with the first. You won't die again." He kissed her palm, and let it go.

"I thought you didn't believe in palm reading?"

He chuckled. "I didn't then."

She took hold of his hand and gently caressed the lines. Palm reading wasn't a skill she'd ever learned. "What do yours tell then?"

Curling his fingers, he smiled. "Mine tells me I have one love." He leaned forward and kissed her.

"And your life line?"

"Isn't clear. Not everyone's is."

The unknowing scared her. She bounced her leg nervously and got to her feet. She was too anxious to stay sitting. In the back of her mind, she couldn't shake the bad feeling that the council would break through somehow. If that happened, what of all the people here? Where would they go? Not to Calladira, the woodland elves wouldn't accept them. And the humans were afraid of elves; they wouldn't be welcomed there either. They'd be homeless, left to wander the wilderness, maybe north with the dragons. Although elves and dragons were such starkly different cultures, they could never coexist peacefully for long.

And her friends, where could they retreat to? And Tif and her gnome colony? The little gnome in her red hat sat on the bottom rung of the wood fence that surrounded the horse pasture. Humming merrily, she kicked her feet while plucking yellow flower petals from a dandelion. Katana sat in the grass beside her, showing Tif how to weave flowers into necklaces.

It was good to see her happy. She never smiled more brightly than she did with Thane. They were special people separately, but together, it was magical. He was the match to her bright sun. She didn't worry so much about Katana. Thane would protect her and take her far from here if he needed to.

Piper rocked side to side, keeping her gaze fixed on the skies. Ronan and Dax were up there somewhere. Fennan and Leif argued about where Princess Talon should be. At the moment, she was tucked away in her room.

"She should be at the Castle in Brightheart, not here." Fennan ran his hand through his short black curls.

"Brightheart is right where they'll be coming through the portal. They might destroy it on their way," Leif argued.

"Enough," Thane said, stopping his pacing. "It's too late to send her away."

To keep himself distracted, Presco took a brush from the stables and started combing Starborn. Her loyal right hand would be next to her in battle. It was how they'd always fought. She in her chariot, him flying beside her. If she landed, so did he. He'd been with her so long she couldn't even fathom him not making it through this fight. He was her oldest and most trusted friend.

Minutes seemed like hours. There was no sign of Synick, although Katana had warned them he might know of Lightbringer's significance to the wall.

Ronan and Dax flew in in their half-shifted forms and tucked their wings away. Their scales shifted to flesh, and they strutted side by side down the path. Ronan's silver hair was tied back, while Dax's dark-brown hair was left free. She hadn't seen either of them in a long time. Ronan was slightly taller than his friend but barely.

"What's with the pity party?" Ronan stopped before Piper and threw his arm around her shoulders. "The battle hasn't even started and you're all doom and gloom."

Dax hand-signed to Ronan, *Be right back,* then strutted right through Fennan, and Leif, and around Presco. Realizing who he was coming for, Valeen hopped out of her chariot, and he wrapped her in a bone-crushing hug. "Hi, Dax." The last time she'd seen him, she'd rode his beast into battle against King

Tenebris. Even if he couldn't speak, they had a special bond.

Hel flicked his civar and slowly blew out the last bit of smoke. "Who the fuck are you?"

Should she like it when he was jealous? No. Did she? Yes. She giggled and Dax let her go and grinned at Hel. With a bow, he took a step back. Facing Ronan, he signed, *This is her new man?* When she was Layala, she didn't know sign language, but as Valeen it was one of the many she knew.

"This is my husband," she said.

He turned to her, brows pinched. *You know sign?*

"I do."

He frowned. *Why didn't you tell me before?*

She signed back, *I do now. I didn't before.*

"Hel, this is Dax. He carried me into battle once before. He's Prince Ronan's closest friend."

He moved his hands quickly, *His only friend. Ronan is a dick. Anyone else is only his friend because he's royalty.*

"Hey!" Ronan crowed. "I saw that."

"Next time you approach my wife, don't touch her without her permission." Hel sneered.

Dax's brows rose. *I think Ronan and him would get along famously. They're both dicks.*

Valeen laughed, and Hel lifted his middle finger. "I know sign language too, asshole."

"Anyway." Ronan kissed the top of Piper's head. "The army from the council is three miles from here. The fight we just had in Runevale was nothing compared to what they have now. If I had to guess, fifteen thousand strong, and it looks like there is more coming."

The collective silence made the hairs on the back of

Valeen's neck rise. The quiet rustle in the trees and horses grazing in the pasture seemed loud. Hel's gaze darted to her then Thane. It was the first time she'd seen him show any indication of worry.

"Holy shit," Tif squeaked then slapped a chubby hand over her mouth.

"Fifteen thousand?" Valeen whispered. "How many of them are dragons?"

"There were at least a thousand in the air. There could be more on the ground, so we don't know their true number." He didn't sound particularly worried. In fact, he almost seemed excited. *Does he want to die?* she thought.

I think he might just be a little crazy, Hel said. She hadn't meant for him to hear that, and he smiled because he knew it too. "We knew this was coming," Hel said calmly, but quickly took out another civar.

Leif scratched his head, sweat beading on his brow. "Is the dragon king sending more of your fighters, Ronan?"

He dropped his arm from Piper and sighed. "I sent a dispatcher to my father, but I don't know if they'll be here in time."

"You don't seem worried," Hel mused.

He grinned. "If I die, I die fighting. It's what dragons love. This battle will be talked about for ages. If I go down, I will be the dragon prince who fought with the god of war, the goddesses of night and day, and the god of magic to save the elves. Greatness will be mine. Just remember to write songs about me, will you?"

Piper lightly punched him in the side. "Don't talk about dying before battle. It's bad luck."

Ronan tore his gaze from Hel and turned to her. "I'm talking about glory, darling." He lifted his chin. "The council you told us about, they think they are doing right, but they will be seen as the tyrants. Elves are known for their peaceful nature, and they've come to eradicate them. I wouldn't be surprised if your woodland elf neighbors joined us too."

"They won't." With a frown, Thane shook his head and folded his arms. "Not only have we killed their last three lords, they've never helped us before. Although as a last hope, I did send a messenger. I doubt they'll even believe what is about to happen unless they see it."

Ronan shrugged. "You never know. No one would have thought the pale ones would fight with you and not against you." He looked Hel up and down. "You're a remarkable warrior by the way, *Black Mage*. I had my doubts on what you were actually capable of but no wonder everyone was afraid of you. My parents wouldn't even leave the north because of you. Whispers of your return had them shitting their pants." He smirked. "And your cursed army went down, but it was magnificent. The history books will love this."

Hel chuckled and took a pull of smoke. "I have no quarrel with the dragons. Your parents don't need to fear me unless they give me a reason, like not showing up with reinforcements for example."

"Well, they did sign a contract that would kill them both if they don't, so they'll come, let's just hope it's in time."

"Ronan may want glory," Fennan said angrily, throwing his hand at him. "But this isn't about glory. We could easily lose this battle. We just lost all of Hel's army and at least two hundred Ravens, I don't know how many dragons you lost but that leaves us with maybe four thousand warriors." Fennan's voice came out scratchy. He looked like he might be sick. "The odds can't get much worse."

Valeen knew exactly how he felt but they had to believe they could win, or it was already lost. "I've seen battles won with worse odds. It's not hopeless."

"I haven't, and we have nowhere to retreat to this time."

Hel stepped forward. "That's right, so you better give this fight every fucking thing in you, or this city, your home, is gone. There will be no Palenor left. You are fighting for your land and your people. They will take the females as slaves, rape them and make them wish they were dead, and then kill every male here, including children. I have *seen* it. But they are only here on command of their god." Hel shoved his finger into Fennan's chest. "You are fighting with this." Just when she thought she couldn't love him more, he said that. She beamed at him, and he quickly added. "We show them no mercy."

Leif bobbed his head and grinned. "No mercy."

"None." Hel smiled back at him.

"No fucking mercy!" Ronan howled and threw his fist into the air. "I like this new curse word."

"No mercy!" Tif added to the chorus, and everyone laughed. Valeen blew out a slow breath and rolled her neck. It was time to kill as many people as possible. She took out Zythara and swung it around her hand.

Thane grabbed Fennan by the shoulder. "We have the magical barrier that gives us the advantage. We will send arrows and catapults at them, and we can retreat inside whenever we need to, and they can't get to us. We'll take out their leaders and they will leave. We can win this."

"Not only can we win, but we will," Valeen said. "You know why I named this sword Darkbringer? Because when I bring it out my enemies will not see light again. The god of war is your king and does not lose, and Hel wants revenge more than any of you truly know. We will win."

"It's time to get to our positions," Thane said. "They'll come from the west. Piper, you'll go with Ronan and help command aerial. Leif, Fennan, you're with me." He looked between Valeen, Hel, and Presco. "Where will you all be?"

"I'll be where I can take Pricilla's head," Hel said.

Worried, Valeen glanced at Katana. She was staying here at the castle with Tif and Talon. "Presco and I will fly with the dragons. You'll need us there."

"Damn, we get led into battle by the goddess of night." Ronan lightly punched Dax, and he grinned back.

Katana stood and brushed the grass off her tan pants. "If anything happens here, I can communicate with Thane," Katana assured. "Tif and I will wait in Valeen's room protected by the enchantments."

"Let's go." Thane held onto Phantom's reins and signaled everyone to move out, but he didn't mount him yet. He probably wanted a moment with Katana.

Valeen dropped into a crouch beside Katana and Tif. "Tif, stay in the room until I get back, alright?"

Tif put one of the flower necklaces over her own head. "I will, don't worry."

"Katana, nothing can happen to Lightbringer."

With a bright smile, she pressed her hand to Valeen's cheek and patted gently. "If Synick tries to sabotage it, I will tell Thane, and you'll come. Everything will work out. The All Mother is with us. I can feel it." She lifted her hand toward the sky. "There is not a cloud in the sky and the sun shines brightly upon us. You used to believe in miracles once. Believe again."

Chapter 56

VALEEN

The air was fresher up here. Wind whistled through the gaps in her winged helmet. Starborn and Night soared alongside Presco in his beast form and Hel with his wings. Ronan, Piper, and Dax flew just above, and behind them were Ronan's battalion of dragons.

It wasn't just the sheer number of the enemy on the ground surrounding the Valley's edge that took her breath away but the dragons circling above them. They looked like groups of dark clouds on the horizon. The roars and bellows rumbled through her chest. Not all of them were shifters either. There were wyverns among them.

The wall will hold, she chanted or prayed, she wasn't sure which.

Below, Thane, Fennan, and Leif were on the physical wall. "Archers ready!" his voice carried all the way up to where she was.

If this goes south, I won't let them take you again, Hel said. *Don't try to fight me if I tell you we're leaving.*

I'm not going to abandon everyone. This army is here because of us.

Or do fight me then, but you won't win.

She knew he meant it too. He would leave everyone to die and take her away kicking and screaming if he had to. *Then I won't let us lose.*

They flew through the shimmering magical barrier and her heart started hammering. Valeen raised her sword and turned to face the battalion behind her. "You are the bravest dragons there have ever been. I'd rather fight beside you than a thousand of them. If you want glory, this is where you get it! There is no surrender... for them! We kill them all."

The roars back filled her with a wild energy.

"We're with you, my queen," Presco said. "No matter the cost."

"It's an honor to fight beside you, Presco. Always."

She turned and gripped the reins, steering her winged horses straight into the first line of dragons. They dipped down under the swiping talons, and she shoved her blade upward and dragged it along the belly of a beast, spilling open his guts. Presco swung his giant paw, smacking another dragon's face aside and sunk his teeth deep into his neck. Hel dodged a stream of fire and cut the wings from the beast then the others clashed.

With wings tucked, a smaller navy-blue dragon bolted down, straight at her. Starborn and Night cut left, and evaded a hit. Valeen backflipped out of her chariot and dropped into a freefall. Bracing herself, she curled her legs as she landed on the dragon's back. It roared and twisted. Valeen's stomach dipped and she gripped the dragon's spike with both arms and held on through the barrel roll.

Once she evened out, Valeen drove Zythara straight into the back of its neck, severing the spine. There wasn't even a dying roar, the dragon's body went limp, and it plummeted. Starborn and Night came back around, and she leapt from the dragon's back to her chariot. She gripped the reins once again and caught her breath. *Whew. It's been a long time since I did something like that.*

"Up, up," she said in the primordial language. When her boots started to slide from the steep incline, she gripped the sides of the chariot. She needed to get a better view. A roar made her twist. Two dragons pursued her, one black, the other a charcoal. Both had massive gold horns at the tip of their snouts and riders on their back. The rider on the left wore no sleeves or pants and decorative gold armor; it wouldn't protect her from anything which meant she was a goddess, not afraid to die. Rich auburn hair and bronzed skin... Eliza, the goddess of fury.

The rider on the dragon next to her was her husband, the god of serenity. "I didn't think you were one for war, Lennox," she shouted at him.

"Only when war is necessary, Valeen. Attacking Pricilla forced my hand."

"Even out," she commanded her horses. She turned to Lennox. "And her killing me, Hel, and War, didn't?"

"You look alive to me," Eliza said and chucked a spear.

Valeen dipped and it whistled past her head and between Night's ears. Clenching her jaw, she pulled

Soulender and gripped Zythara in the other. Threatening her was one thing but her horses were another. They were eternal but they could be injured. Eliza and Lennox split and flew up on either side of her chariot. Her dragon snapped at Starborn, and he squealed and chomped back.

Lennox saluted and raised a pair of golden cuffs. "Surrender is an option. Our armies will leave if you come with us. The elves don't need to suffer."

"And you don't need to die, but you will. You chose the wrong side." She tapped the left side of the chariot, and her horses turned, forcing Eliza's dragon to tilt. Half-shadow, she launched herself over the side of her chariot and landed behind Eliza. The goddess of fury ducked under her swing and threw her leg back at Valeen's feet. She jumped and hacked downward, but Eliza turned and blocked the strike with her sword.

"She has Soulender!" Lennox bellowed.

They both swung, metal clashing against metal. Throwing a boot into Eliza's gut, she kicked her back and she stumbled over the saddle. She had to make this fast before Lennox got closer. Valeen jammed her blade into the dragon's side. He jerked in surprise and took a sharp downward turn, sending them both toppling.

"*Shit*, level out!" Eliza shouted at her dragon and grabbed hold of the stirrup of her saddle. Valeen managed to hook her elbow around Eliza's neck before she fell. Curling her thighs around the back of her hips, Valeen sent Zythara to the aether, switched Soulender to her other hand and shoved it into the side of Eliza's neck. She screamed and let go, dropping them both into a freefall.

"Eliza, no!" Lennox screamed.

Turning half-shadow slowed her down but she needed her chariot. The horses were still far above.

Below you, love.

A moment later, she slammed into Hel's arms. She circled her arms around his neck as he flew them rapidly upward straight to Lennox, whose dragon was careening down at them. He lifted her onto his shoulders, and she pressed her ankles tightly to his sides for balance.

"You got this?"

"Always," she said, and he turned left just in time to miss the dragon's jaws, and they flew straight at Lennox, and she gripped her weapon hard and shoved Soulender into his chest. With the momentum, it tore through him, cutting up through his shoulder and out.

"Fuck." Hel slowed to a hover and held onto her thighs beside his head. "You cut him in half."

She took several deep breaths, but it wasn't because of exertion. She felt more powerful than ever. Searching among the fight below, she watched several of Ronan's dragons get teamed up on and dragged down. Half of them were already dead on the ground or had dropped out of the sky. "We're going to have to send them back inside the wall or they're all dead."

"Look to the north."

Valeen turned and her heart leapt. "It's Drake Drakonan!" She knew by the red and gold collars they wore, matching Ronan's. And he had a thousand strong. She looked to find Ronan. Below and to the left, he and Dax still flew together, a team of their own. "Ronan! They're here!"

"Keep fighting! The king is here!" Ronan

commanded his dragons. Their viciousness intensified, harder strikes, spiked tails crashed, and more fire arched through the air.

Searching among the hundreds of dragons below for pearl scales and powder-blue horns was harder than she thought. They moved too fast and there were several light-colored dragons. The longer she looked the more her heart rose in her throat. "Where is Presco?"

"I was just with him..." Hel pointed right. "There."

He fought off three dragons, tearing into a wing with his back talons while biting the neck of another. The third hacked into his side, forcing him to release his bite. His back and neck were covered in thick red gashes. "Hel, go!"

She jumped from Hel and dove for Presco. The wind tore past, tears rolled up the side of her face into her hair. She screamed with rage, landing on one of his attackers and drove her sword into the back of his head. Then dragged herself down and sliced clean through, cutting his head off. Hel cut through the throat of the other, and Presco snapped the final dragon's neck. Hel swooped her up as the dragon she stood on started to fall.

Presco's eyes were unfocused. His snout horn was broken in half. His wings beat too slowly. "Hel, help him."

"You need to land and shift," Hel said.

He nodded but his body went limp.

"Presco!" Valeen screamed. "We have to stop him from hitting the ground!"

"I can't hold you and stop him." Valeen shoved herself out of Hel's arms and let herself fall. Hel dove for Presco and flew up under his chest and pushed. It slowed him but not enough. Panic that she'd held at bay this entire time fought its way free. Turning to shadow she drifted to Presco and reformed. "Wake up! Wake up!"

He groaned.

"Ronan! Help!" But where was he? The ground was coming too fast. "Presco! Wake up! Shift!"

"He's too heavy to stop!" Hel screamed with effort then he flew out from under Presco. The ground was feet away. All she could do was watch in horror as she took her half-shadow form to hover.

Boom.

Presco hit and dirt billowed up around him. She dropped beside his face and, with tears, pressed her hands to his snout. "Presco?"

Hel landed next to his chest and laid his ear against his pearl scales. "His heart is still beating."

With her chin trembling, she ran her hand over his smooth scales. "You're going to be alright." Smoke rolled out of his nostrils and a low rumble in his throat vibrated her hands. "I won't let anyone hurt you anymore." The wall was fifty yards away. If they could just get him inside...

"Hel, Valeen, watch out!"

Thane stood at the top of the stone wall, pointing. Valeen whirled to face the council's army running toward them. Thousands of boots and hooves stampeded. Weapons in both hands and shadows rolling off her, she stepped out in front of Presco with Hel at her side. "I won't leave him to be torn apart."

"They'll have to get through us first."

Valeen's shadows rolled out, her deadly vines curled out of the ground.

"Archers, fire!" Thane shouted.

The first enemy soldiers—giants, dragon shifters, feline shifters, men, even dwarves and elves, all on the front line—were a few yards away, wearing the colors of their god; greens and oranges, pinks and blues. Valeen took several sharp breaths and braced herself, her magic roaring in her veins. Throwing up her shield, she waited for the impact.

Then black armor glinted in the sunlight and the Ravens, with Thane at the front, rushed past her and met them.

Chapter 57

VALEEN

The killing, the death, the screams—it all seemed endless. Metal clanked and rang out as weapons clashed. There was so much screaming, whether for fury or sorrow, her ears could bleed from it.

There was a ferociousness amongst the elves she hadn't witnessed before. Their beautiful faces were twisted in rage. Their graceful moves suited for dancing were used to kill. Elves moved faster and were more agile than the other mortal races. This was their land, and they fought harder because of it. Their families were too close.

In her own mind she thought of Aunt Evalyn. If they got through, she could die hiding under the floor of Nerium Oleander. That couldn't happen.

The roars and crashes of the dragons were as loud as any thunderstorm. The flashes of color from their scales glimmered in the sunlight and might have been beautiful if this wasn't war, if blood and death didn't fill the skies too.

Win, we must win. All their lives, all the fighting to remember, Hel's sacrifice of four hundred years of sleep, the cursed pale ones who terrorized the land, all the consequences and hopes for the future came down to this one moment in time.

She swung Zythara and Soulender, only seeing ways to kill. She lost herself to it. Cutting through armor with ease, slicing open throats and arteries.

Blood. There was so much blood. Crimson splattered across her armor, her skin. The warm wetness became unnoticeable.

The minotaurs and giants hit hard but went down harder.

Catapults with giant boulders crashed into the magical wall. They broke against it, raining boulders and rocks below. Dragons took turns knocking their tails and blowing fire against it.

More than once the wall's iridescent rainbow shimmer faded in spots, and each time her heart stuttered.

But it held. Nothing had gotten through, not arrows nor beasts.

"Hit the wall harder!" one of the enemy commanders shouted. "Take it down! We must take out their archers!"

The gods and goddesses of the council and their allies were somewhere in the back of their armies, watching the battle. Maybe after Eliza and Lennox went down, they retreated or maybe they waited for another reason.

It didn't matter, she would get to them eventually.

Valeen moved like a night wind, going from shadow to her solid form in a breath. Her vines wreaked havoc, tearing through flesh, wrapping up monsters and men.

Explosions from Hel's magic went off all over the battlefield. Thane cut through enemies with precision and speed. Anything in his path went down.

Against anyone else it would've been over already.

The sun had moved halfway across the sky, but the enemy kept coming like waves crashing against a battered ship.

Valeen didn't tire, not with her immortality, but the elves did. Even with their valiant hearts and desperate desire for victory, they grew weary. Their swings were just a little slower, their groans more frequent.

At a faster rate they fell. It seemed like an endless number of enemy soldiers came from the back to replenish their dead.

We need to get the elves inside the wall, Valeen thought. They needed to rest.

An elf in silver armor beside her hit the ground, falling against her boot. His brown eyes stared up at her as he let out one last breath. A Raven in black went down on her other side. Spinning, she cut the throat of the green ogre who'd bludgeoned him. With a spray of dark-blue blood, it clutched at his neck and fell forward.

"Lady Lightbringer," one of the Ravens shouted. "The giant! Take the giant!"

A frost giant, blue as winter oceans and as tall as the tallest oak trees, stamped its thick ice-block feet. It spread ice over the grass and the fallen. Its long, thin arms became spears, jabbing and swinging. It laughed when it caught an elf and sent him flying.

It was lethal, but slow.

She took off, sprinting right at it, ducking under its swing and ran up its back. With a jump she hacked down and smashed Zythara into the crown of its head. Its ice body cracked and splintered then the entire giant shattered. Backflipping off, Valeen landed in a crouch behind it, letting the bits of ice roll around her toes.

The few Ravens who'd seen it, cheered and swung harder, cutting down the enemy faster.

"Back inside!" Thane's voice carried through the chaos. The elven archers rained arrows down, but it wasn't enough. There were too many of them.

Valeen slammed her fist to the ground and a wall of her black vines shot up, barbs grew to act like bars in between the stalks, and her dark-purple lilies sprayed a mist of poison. It gave the elves a moment to retreat inside the safety of the magic barrier.

But their axes hacked at her stalks, chipping away at them until they fell like trees. Enemy soldiers chased after them roaring and screaming.

Valeen whirled to find Presco. There were so many bodies on the ground in different armor, so many dragons and beasts laid dead left for the vultures to pick at, it was like looking for a seashell in a sea full of them.

"Presco!"

She finally managed to spot him in his human form, crawling toward the wall. Shoving her sword in the holster, she ran, jumping and hopping over bodies, both alive and dead and made it to him.

"Valeen," his voice was hoarse, but he sounded relieved. His tan tunic was stained with blossoms of blood and dirt, his shoulders still had deep gashes, but his scales were closing back together.

"Hold on, I'll get you inside." Presco was impossible to carry in his dragon form, but he was still heavy as a human. Using all her might, she dragged him. He grunted and hissed in pain, but it was better than dying. With her personal shield surrounding them, attacks and arrows bounced off. But they still jeered and stuck out their tongues.

"Come out, goddess, give us a taste." The ogre with big yellow tusks and a loin cloth licked the shield.

"Alright, have a taste." A black vine shot up out of the ground and pierced straight through his open mouth and out the back of his head. The others around him took a few steps back.

Once inside the magical dome, she moved Presco to sit up against the stone wall. Holding his side, he pressed himself against it. "Go. I'll recover." He reached into his pocket and pulled a small silver vial. "I have a healing potion I've been working on. It works for smaller injuries, we'll see what it does for me now."

"Are you sure? I can find Hel to heal you."

"No, I'll be alright." He winced, and took slow deep breaths. Biting the top of the cork he pulled it with his teeth and tipped the bottle back. He grimaced. "I need to work on the taste. And it only works on dragons at the moment but in the future..." Right before her eyes the gouges and cuts closed. "Win this battle, my queen. I know you can."

She nodded and lightly gripped his shoulder. "I will."

With a quick check she found Hel, Thane, Fennan, and Leif inside. All the living elves stood in the protected region, staring at the monsters that savagely fought against the magic wall. When the enemy got too close to the shield, Thane and others stabbed through it.

Some of the dragons on their side had flown back inside as well. But the battle raged on in the sky.

Ronan dropped in and shifted just before he hit the ground and caught Piper in his arms. "I need to fight with all I can, and I can't with her." He set her on her feet and silver scales rippled across his body.

"Ronan, wait!" Piper cried just as he shot back into the sky. "Come back!"

Fists beat against the invisible wall. Axes crashed into it. A frost giant hit it with a blast of ice, and it spread up and around but didn't get through.

"We need something big. Really big." Valeen glanced back, finding the peaks of Castle Dredwich. As long as the sword held, and as long as she and Katana lived, it wouldn't break... she hoped.

The few small but new black spots in the iridescent sheen made her stomach turn.

She watched Ronan fly higher and clash with another dragon, all teeth and claws and snarls. Ronan ferociously ripped a chunk out of the red dragon's shoulder. The scaled meat dropped to the fighters below. His back talons raked across the belly leaving long gaping lines. He thrust his head, driving the horn on his snout into the other dragon's eye. The beast let out a shrill throat noise and retreated backward. Ronan went in for the kill—but another came up behind him, with teeth bared and a sword for a tail.

"Ronan, behind you!" Piper wailed.

Dax shot up from below directly in between and the enemy dragon's sharp tail stuck right into Dax's chest.

"No," Valeen breathed. Her heart dropped and kept falling when Dax let out a half roar half cry and clutched at his chest.

"Dax!" Ronan whirled, leaving his back open and his opponent sunk his teeth in. He bellowed, swung his boulder tail, crashing it into both the attacking dragons, and hooked his paws around Dax's arm. The two of them tumbled into a downward spiral.

Piper screamed and bolted for him.

"No, Piper!" Fennan wrapped her up from behind. "You can't go out there! You'll never make it to him."

She smacked and bucked to get away from Fennan. "We can't leave him!"

With a *boom*, Dax and Ronan hit the ground. Without thinking about consequences, Valeen sprinted through the wall into the chaos. She held up her palm, conjuring her shield—its brilliant light shone. It had held against dragon fire, it had held against swords and demons, it would hold now.

The war drums beat with each step. The terrible screams of the monsters and enemy warriors sounded far off as she focused solely on getting to Ronan and Dax.

The shield shoved everything in her path aside. Red caught her eye, and she found Piper running beside her. Then Thane appeared on her other side. Hel flew above. She glanced back, Leif and Fennan were right there.

NIGHT MEETS THE ELF QUEEN

Fists and claws and weapons hit her shield, but they bounced off.

She pushed through until they found Ronan kneeling on the ground. Ronan held Dax in his arms, blood and dirt covered them both. Her knees wobbled and her throat constricted. The streaks of tears that cut through the mess on Ronan's stricken face made her blood seem to freeze.

KATANA

Katana chewed on the edges of her nails as she paced before the windows in Valeen's room. Smoke rose in the distance. Thunderous crashing from dragons and boulders hitting the magical shield echoed across the Valley. A few of the blows made her heart stop.

Even from here she could see the dark spots in the iridescent wall, and what looked like hairline cracks. *If that doesn't hold...* her throat tightened at the thought. The entire city would be overrun, all the innocent people sheltering here would be slaughtered.

Her body buzzed, her pace quickening. She *felt* the danger Thane was in, like his battle fueled racing heart was beating in her own ears. In her mind she could see flashes of what he saw through their bond; his blades cutting through armor, heads being separated from their bodies, and blood, so much blood. It made her ill.

He was severely outnumbered on the ground. He roared and shoved his sword through the chest of a man and then whirled and cut the throat of a squat green troll. The vision started to flicker—*no, no, no,* she slammed her eyes shut and rubbed her temples. She had to keep the connection open, she had to see him.

He'd held her and kissed her before he left but what if she lost him right when she found her mate? For the first time in her life she felt truly loved and appreciated by her partner. For the first time ever, she was truly in love.

Tif hung off one of the green vines draping across the windows and peered out. "I can't really see what's happening. Are they alright? Oh, I hate not knowing."

"Right now, I believe they're alright." Katana clutched at her chest as if it could calm her heart. "With King Drake's arrival we might have a chance of winning," but even as she said it her stomach seemed to coil as if knowing it was a lie.

"If that wall breaks," Princess Talon stared out the window on the opposite side of the room, "we must leave for the human lands. There are horses waiting just in case. Thane made arrangements for two guards to escort us."

Katana knew that he did, and that's what he wanted, he even made her promise she would go, but she didn't know if she could. What was life now without Thane? It was no life at all. "I don't know if I can leave Thane."

She shrugged. "Suit yourself, but the moment it goes down, I'm running. That's what my brother told me to do. The Ravens will protect their king if it breaks and they are overrun. They will get Thane out and he will meet us at the rendezvous point."

Pausing her pacing, she felt sick to her stomach. Would Thane leave to fight another day, or would he go down with his people?

A thud outside the door in the hallway made the hairs on her arms stand. "What was that?" Katana whispered.

"It sounded like someone fell." Tif swung down from the vine and landed on the stone floor. "I'll go check."

"No," Katana hissed and snatched the little gnome by the middle and held her against her chest.

She clutched at Katana's hand and with big brown eyes looked up at her. "What is it?"

Talon slowly stepped away from the window and moved toward the door. "What if someone got through the wall. We didn't lock it..."

The door handle clicked, and Talon froze in the center of the room. The hinges slowly creaked as the door crept open. Katana's heart plummeted to her toes, and she backed into the window.

Synick stood just outside the bedroom, hands poised on the threshold. The guard posted outside laid unmoving on the ground.

"I finally found the room with the sword and look what else there is. My favorite goddess to torture, along with friends." He stared at the softly illuminated sword, the very thing keeping this city from being destroyed.

"Anyone who wishes Valeen harm can't get in here," Katana reassured Talon and Tif as much as herself. It didn't stop Talon from backing away or even herself from pushing back against the window and reaching for a latch.

"I want out of this city." He tried to walk through the threshold of the door and slammed into an invisible wall. He pressed his hands to it and curled his upper lip baring his teeth. "More magic tricks, I see." She expected him to start screaming at them to let him in or cursing their names, but he didn't. He lifted his good eye to Talon. "Princess," his voice took on a melodic, resonant tone, one Katana knew well, "pull the sword free from the crack in the stone."

As if in a daze, Talon walked forward.

"NO!" Katana tossed Tif onto the bed and darted in front of Talon. The gift of persuasion was one she hadn't used in too long, but she grabbed Talon's shoulders and stared her in the face. Her blue eyes were unfocused. "Hold still," she commanded.

"I said, pull the sword. Pull it now. Push her out of the way if you must."

Talon shoved against Katana, knocking her off balance. Katana stumbled backward but regained her footing. The princess was stronger than she expected her to be. "Talon, you can't touch that sword. Everyone will die." Katana grabbed her arm and swung her backward until Talon hit the chest at the end of the bed and fell onto the mattress.

"Get up, Princess," Synick's voice seemed to echo through the room. "Get that sword and give it to me." His persuasion was much stronger than Katana's because he was used to doing it. Even before she died, she rarely ever used the gift. It had always felt wrong.

With her feet slightly wider than shoulder width and her hands out in front of her, she prepared to fight Talon off again. Under Synick's control she'd have no choice but to do as he told her to. "Talon, stay where you are."

"Kill her if you have to," Synick demanded.

Talon charged at her and slammed her shoulder

into Katana, taking her to the ground. Her breath whooshed out. Talon was suddenly on top of her with her hands around Katana's throat. The intense grip cut into her windpipe.

"Choke her until she doesn't move."

Katana screamed and bucked, slamming her fists into Talon's arms to break the hold. "Let go of me!" Katana felt her power in her own voice, and Talon released her. She would not kill Thane's sister no matter what happened. Shoving her hips up, she tossed Talon onto the ground. Talon scrambled up and dove for the sword's handle.

"No, don't!"

She grabbed hold of it and pulled. It moved an inch, and Katana wrapped her hands above Talon's and pushed down.

A flash of Thane slammed into her mind.

He was completely surrounded. Valeen knelt on the ground beside Dax and Prince Ronan, the pain in his face said more than words. Tears welled up.

Dax was gone... They were in trouble. So many, there were so many to fight, and she felt Thane's fear like it was wrapping around her. Doubt of victory crept into him, into her.

Choking on a sob, Katana pushed against Talon, her mind torn. *Thane, keep fighting!*

She wouldn't hurt Talon to stop her, but she had to do something. She glanced back at Synick and the triumph in his eyes. Talon growled and pulled harder. Katana's arms shook trying to keep the sword in place. She promised Valeen, she would protect it, protect the city.

Another flash of Thane—he screamed as he sunk

his sword into someone and then a dagger stuck into his forearm. *THANE!*

VALEEN

Valeen's breath caught seeing Dax's motionless body. His eyes were wide open, but his head hung lifeless to the side. Thane, Piper, Leif, and Fennan immediately started cutting down those closing in around them.

Hel slammed both fists into the ground and opened up a massive split. Wails and shrieks of those falling in followed.

The sound of her pulse hammering in her ears drowned out the battle. Valeen dropped to her knees and touched Dax's face. Already he felt colder. "Rest now in Serenity, Dax. You fought well." Her throat tightened and she lifted her gaze to his prince. "He's gone, Ronan."

Ronan screamed, gently laid him on the ground and brushed his fingers over his eyes to close them. With his face twisted in rage, he rose up and his talons shot out. He charged into the fight with a fury of swings.

A cry of pain took her from sadness to wrath in an instant. It was Leif, he stumbled back with a sword sticking through his right shoulder and fell to the ground. A battle cry tore from her throat, and she shoved her sword through the belly of his attacker. Then she went crazy, hacking and swinging. Her shadows rolled out, spreading like a fog on a cold day across the battlefield, sliding into ears and eyes, burning them from the inside. Screams of terror echoed all around. *All of you die, just fucking die.*

A man ran past her with blood pouring out of his eyes and mouth.

"Take her down! Get those cuffs on Valeen and Hel! Kill War!" Pricilla's shrill voice enraged her further. Someone jumped on her back, then two more. She shifted to shadow, the enemy soldiers fell through, and she let her vines finish the work.

A whoosh cut through the air. Something gold caught the light. A chain suddenly wrapped around Hel's neck.

Her heart shot into her throat. A furious heat rushed through her.

The pounding in her ears drummed harder. *That is my mate.*

"HEL!" Thane bellowed.

An explosion from a catapult rocked the ground ten feet from her, sending bodies flying into the air, knocking her off balance. She hit her knees, her hand falling into the squishy guts of a body. She might have been horrified if there was time for it.

But there wasn't.

She shoved to her feet and turned to shadow, drifting on the breeze until she stood between Hel and the god who held the golden chain. This was one of the gods on the council who'd voted to destroy her life, to take everything from her.

Corded with rippling muscular arms and as tall as any dragon, he smiled at her. He wore a halo of golden thorns for his crown. Bright green eyes shined against his black skin.

She raised Soulender. "You will not take my husband."

"Get her, Envar!" Pricilla yelled.

Hel fought to get the chain off his throat, but it must have been suppressing his magic.

With Soulender in hand, she ran at him.

"Cuff her!" Pricilla shrieked. "Cuff her now!"

The god, Envar, wearing all gold, pulled another chain from his hip, and with a whirl and a snap, he lassoed it around the wrist that held Soulender. Jerking it taught, he grinned. "Give me the dagger."

Her magic surged and tingled against her skin to turn to shadow, but nothing happened. It was as if her magic was in a cage while Envar's power fought against hers through the chain. His ability was a suppressor, and he could force his magic into precious metals. Her arm shook as she pulled against him. "Release me or I will kill you."

"Get Soulender!" Pricilla hopped off her hippogriff and charged with two others at her sides.

A second chain wrapped around Valeen's other wrist. Without her magic she couldn't send Soulender to the aether.

Pricilla reached for Soulender, and gritting her teeth, Valeen slammed her forehead into Pricilla's and sent her stumbling. "You can't have it!"

"Take her down!" Pricilla shouted.

Envar lassoed another chain around her torso, pinning her arms to her sides.

"Valeen, no!" Hel roared, sounding half mad. "I will fucking kill all of you!" He wrenched on the chain and jerked Envar off balance.

Thane slammed into Envar, tackling him to the

ground. The chains fell and her magic flooded out, shadows rolling all around her and she set her sights on Pricilla.

"YOU!" she pointed at her.

Pricilla started to backpedal. "Get her! I don't care if it takes a thousand of you, take her down!"

A loud cracking, like the splitting of a mountain, rent the air. Valeen skidded to a halt and turned toward the sound... toward the city.

"The wall is failing!" someone shouted.

"It's going to break!" another yelled with glee.

Black rippled across the sheen, and she shook her head in horror. If that wall went down everyone inside would die... Aunt Evalyn, the children, their mothers, everyone. "It can't break."

And then she watched it fall, the shimmer faded into nothing, leaving the city wide open.

"The wall is gone!" someone yelled.

Thane risked glancing back as he wrapped Envar's own chain around his throat. "No," he said in disbelief.

In a flash, Hel appeared and took Soulender from her grasp, vanished and reappeared beside Thane to shove it straight through Envar's eye, sinking it to the hilt.

Alehelm swung a golden chain around Hel's neck again and it hooked tight. He and two others started dragging him backward. "You're not as scary without your magic," Alehelm jeered.

"Help! We need help!" Fennan stood shoulder to shoulder with Piper and Ronan with Leif on the ground between them. Her mind whirled, pulled in so many directions. Hel, Katana, her friends, Pricilla... a huge, scaled arm hooked around her throat from behind and dragged her to the ground.

Golden cuffs clamped around both of her wrists, keeping her magic caged inside her. "AHHHHHH!" she wriggled and bucked. This was how they captured her before. The dragon slammed her to the ground and shoved a knee on her chest, pinning her in the dirt. Another grabbed her ankles. "HEL!" More of the gods and goddesses closed in with those golden chains and cuffs.

A chain curled around her throat, and they lifted her off the ground.

"HEL!" Her heart beat so hard it hurt. She kicked and fought but the dragons were too strong.

Through the chaos of the fight, she saw Hel roll with the chains and shove Soulender straight up under Alehelm's chin, blood ran down his hand and he jerked it free. But there were others surrounding him. Could he even see her now?

Thane was fighting off two ogres and three dragon shifters in their half-shifted forms. She wasn't even sure either of them had seen them take her.

"HEL!" she screamed again as they carried her further away.

"Shut her up before they find out we have her!" the dragon holding her torso said. The goddess with silver hair holding the chain around her neck tore off her sleeve and shoved it into Valeen's mouth.

Hel, I need you, I need you, I need you.

Bones cracked and a golden blade suddenly protruded from the dragon's chest. A tattooed hand wrapped around his throat and threw him. With one swing, Hel cut the head off the other. Valeen's back hit

NIGHT MEETS THE ELF QUEEN

the ground, and she spit out the gag and rolled to her knees.

Prowling for the goddess still holding the chain, Valeen felt the fury rolling off Hel. It was a white-hot heat, pulsing out from him. His magic couldn't be seen, but it could be felt—like a thick cloud wanting to choke the life from anything near. The enemy soldiers nearby backed away from him, terror filling their eyes. She couldn't see his face but theirs showed enough.

The goddess threw a man in front of her and Hel cut him down. She screamed, holding up her hands. "Wait, I was only following orders. I was forced to come here. I'm not a warrior, I'm a goddess of flora." Daisies bloomed around her feet. "See, I'm harmless."

"No mercy." The golden blade shoved through her heart. She gasped, then Hel pushed her to the ground. The daisies quickly closed around her making a strange cocoon.

Hel prowled back and lifted Valeen off her knees, put her over his shoulder and shot into the air. "I'm taking you away from here. We will not win this."

"No! No! You can't do this!" she beat against his back, then shoved at the golden cuffs on her wrists. If her bones could break, she would snap her thumbs to get them off, but she was immortal now. Nothing would break. "Thane and Piper and the others are still surrounded." She spotted them as they rose higher. "You can't leave him! He will die!" Tears blurred her vision. The booms of catapults launching boulders into the stone wall, the hammering of drums, the clashing of metal faded away.

The day she met Thane, the Elf King, at the pub in Briar Hollow came rushing back. Other memories too;

Piper painting runes on her forehead before a battle with the dragon Prince Yoren. Leif laughing and jeering that she had childbearing hips and she quickly threatened to break his hand. Fennan throwing a saddle on a horse for her when he said the task was below the High King's betrothed. The day *War* found her heartbroken and took her home... it all flashed across her mind in moments.

The Ravens fought to get to their king but there were too many standing between them.

Ronan changed into his beast form, scooped up Piper in one paw and Leif in the other. His tail slashed out, knocking down all the enemy fighters around Thane and Fennan then he lifted. Fire shot out of his mouth, burning down all those in its path.

But that left Thane and Fennan alone surrounded by thousands. Valeen pushed at her cuffs again. Her magic fought to break free, bits of shadow trailed from her fingertips, but it wasn't enough.

Thane looked up at them, and she reached toward him. How hurt and scared he must feel knowing that they were leaving him. "Hel, go back!"

His wings kept beating.

A minotaur stabbed Fennan through the chest and he fell. There wasn't even an opportunity for Thane to catch him or tell his best friend goodbye.

"No, Fennan!" she sobbed. She fought against Hel, hitting him and slapping his face but his grip only tightened. "Go back right now and get him or I'll never forgive you!"

Her shadows intensified and seeped through hairline cracks in the cuffs.

I'm sorry, but I won't let them take you. I won't let them strip you of your immortality again.

"Your *brother* is all alone!"

Thane broke free of the mob that surrounded him and was running toward the wall, fighting with all his might. But there were hundreds between him and safety. Their ascent slowed and Hel stretched his hand toward him. Fire erupted on both sides of Thane, acting as a momentary protective barrier. Then a bright light appeared.

Hel squinted and turned his face. "What is that?"

A brilliant light, as bright as the sun, hovered above the battlefield. Valeen shielded her eyes, everyone did. The enemy cowered in front of it and backed away.

But through the intense light, she saw a figure with flowing hair... Katana.

Something inside Valeen snapped.

"Let go of me, Hel," she said calmly now. Her hands trembled with the power raging inside her. The cuffs fractured more, darkness flowed through like steam coming up from fissures in the hot earth. She held her hands in front of her, in front of Hel. "Hel, let go. I can do this. They won't take me."

His brows pulled closer, and his mouth pinched but his eyes fixed on the cuffs. He looked furious and scared when he said, "Destroy them." As soon as he released her, the cuffs shattered, darkness flooded out of her like ink spilling over paper.

Becoming shadow, she vanished and reformed next to Katana. With a nod, Katana took Valeen's hand.

Valeen focused on the moon, on the stars in the sky and channeled their energy. The sky began to dim as if the sun was eclipsed, not from clouds but from the goddess of night's power. Katana's radiance shined even brighter.

Inside she was buzzing with a ferocity that made her tremble. Her power was the raging seas against a levee, and all she had to do was let go.

"Unleash hell." Light and darkness erupted, an invisible wave rolled forward across the battlefield knocking everything down, enemy dragons slammed into the ground throwing up chunks of earth. She tried to shield those dragons on their side but some of them fell too.

Behind that blast wave, a blazing yellow light razed one side and beside it a black wall pushed out consuming everything in its path. The center where light and dark met was like oil and water bouncing and swirling together. Heat and fire seared the air blowing her hair back.

In her mind she shielded Hel, Thane, and anyone she loved. The elves and the city were safe behind them.

She screamed as the power rushed through her veins, as all the stars in the heavens fueled her. It was almost too much—a dam against a violent river.

Katana whimpered and wailed, her body shaking—she was still mortal. There was no way she could hold this power. So Valeen channeled her magic too, taking the heat that seared her hand and ripped through her like lightning.

When every cell in her body felt like it was boiling and her limbs felt limp, she shut off the magic.

She dragged in deep breaths, waiting as the aftermath of what they'd done began to clear. Still hand in hand, the sisters lowered to the ground. Katana collapsed to her knees, her chest heaving up and down.

The light and darkness began to fade, and the smoke drifted. Her legs wobbled but sheer will kept her standing. She peered across the blackened and scorched battlefield. Smolder rose off the charred remains of thousands of bodies. More than half of the enemy army was wiped out in the wake of the sun and the moon.

It was terrible and glorious.

"Katana, are you alright?" Valeen glanced down.

"Yes," she breathed. "But I might vomit."

"Everyone does their first battle."

Well I'll be damned, Hel said in her mind, maybe in awe for the first time in his life. He dropped to the ground and immediately inspected her. "Are you hurt?"

"No, but that drained me."

"It may have but I've never seen anything more remarkable."

Thane was curled up on his knees a hundred yards from them. He lifted his head and slowly rose. There was nothing but dead burnt bodies within three hundred yards of him.

He spotted them and started running. On shaky legs Katana rose and he scooped her up. "Holy shit! Holy shit! When I saw you both hovering in the sky, I knew you were going to change the tides of this battle."

"It's not over yet," Hel said.

The voice of Pricilla shouting at what was left of her soldiers, echoed across the field. With the power of persuasion they couldn't resist, a few thousand strong surged forward. Their dragons rose off the ground, fire arcing in great blasts. Even if they were afraid, even if they didn't want to, they trampled over the scorched bodies or flew over the burnt landscape.

"Palenor!" Thane bellowed. "Push forward!"

King Drake's dragons swooped back into battle. Taking off from the ground or flying out from behind where Valeen and Katana had unleashed their power. The fight on the ground was terrible but it was the dragons that frightened her.

Some of them skirted around King Drake's force and went for the city.

"Stop them!" Thane roared. "Stop those dragons!"

King Drake himself slammed into the first and they smashed into the stone wall, taking out a massive chunk of it.

"Kill Pricilla and the persuasion from her commands will leave their minds," Thane said. "Find her!"

Deep horns blew from the east. Dread trickled through her. Just when they had a real chance of winning, the hope she'd gain slipped away.

Not more... she couldn't even muster the strength to turn and see what other army was coming for them.

She'd just given *everything* she had in her. *All Mother, please. We can't do this alone.*

A flock of blackbirds sailed overhead, ravens and crows cawing.

The blackbirds always seemed to come for Thane during battle...

"That's... *Valeen* look." Hel strangely sounded like he was in shock.

She slammed her eyes shut and reached deep down

to get the drive to keep fighting. *I have to fight. I have to finish this.* But even as a full goddess with all her strength, she wouldn't be able to channel power like that again for days.

Hel grabbed her chin and turned her face. "Open your eyes. That's Villhara's flag."

A tingle ran down her spine. She must not have heard him correctly.

"Val, that's *our* flag. And House of Night and House of Magic with it."

Finally, she dared to look, blinking several times. The black flag with a silver moon cycle around a starburst, rose high in the air. Hel's red flag with a serpent wrapped around a sword and a wreath of runes was beside it, and the purple sign of their combined territory, Villhara, a serpent wrapped around a lily on a vine.

It was a miracle. Nothing else could explain it... "But, it was gone. We saw it. House of Night was destroyed." And they'd heard that House of Magic had been taken over... and yet there were thousands of warriors marching with their flags. And at least a hundred more dragons in the sky.

In the front, on a white-winged horse, rode a goddess with flowing black hair. Even from this distance she knew that face. The beautiful face they'd left in the underrealm... or so she thought. "Hel, is that your mother?" she whispered in disbelief.

And beside her rode another; her twin, Balneir, Thane's father. And with them a god she'd known from the very beginning. She couldn't believe what she was seeing, but it was Era, a fellow primordial and the god of time. He *never* involved himself in wars.

Another still, a fourth horse carried Elora, the goddess of wisdom, the one who'd guided them through the stone.

"My mother *and* my grandmother." Hel's jaw had yet to close.

Thane stepped in front of them rubbing his eyes. "It can't be."

"It is," Hel breathed.

Hel's mother raised a gleaming spear and said, "For your King and Queen!"

Tears slipped down her cheeks. She lifted her eyes to the sky and smiled. *Thank you.*

Starborn and Night soared down just as their people rushed forward.

"Let's finish this." Valeen hopped into her chariot, and Hel stepped in with her.

Katana grabbed the edge of her chariot. "Don't leave Pricilla alive to do this again. Don't take her as a prisoner."

"I won't."

Katana let go and her legs gave way. Thane caught her before she hit the ground. "Lead them to victory for me," he said.

"We will." With a flick of Hel's fingers, her helmet vanished, and the weight of her crown settled there instead.

"For Villhara and for Palenor!" Valeen shouted.

Starborn and Night lifted into the air and Valeen and Hel raised their fists. The echoing cheers brought goosebumps across her skin.

An army of thousands raced down the valley hill behind them. She rode up beside the group of Ravens. The two forces clashed with the enemy in a fury of valor and vengeance.

The new force of dragons was enough to make the council's aerial force turn and flee or shift and drop to the ground.

Pricilla screamed, "Fight! Keep fighting!"

But even at her command some turned to run.

Palenor and Villhara overran them like a flood wave crashing down a mountainside.

Hel jumped out of the chariot and vanished before he hit the ground. Valeen pulled the reins and Starborn and Night landed at the back of the fighting.

The council's army fell like snow in winter. All that was left of the council was Pricilla. Hel had already killed the others. She had a few god allies but even they started to flee and commanded their legions to retreat.

"You cowards!" Pricilla shrieked. "Come back!"

When Hel reappeared, it was before Pricilla. Her usually perfectly sleek brown hair was a halo of frizz. Her pink armor was stained with blood. She squealed and stumbled backward into a soldier and threw him in front of her. "Stay away from me!"

Valeen stepped out of her chariot and slowly followed after him.

Hel cut down the soldier and shoved him aside. She grabbed yet another and another, in her retreat.

"You can't do this! I *am* the council!" She fell over a body and hit the ground. Holding up a sword to shield herself, she screamed.

Soulender hit, shattering her blade. Hel shoved his boot to her chest and squatted, putting the tip of Soulender to her throat. "Remember when I said I would come back and kill you? I always keep my promises. This is for my wife." He shoved the blade into her windpipe, and blood gurgled up out of her open mouth.

It was a moment she'd been waiting centuries for, and as she watched scarlet bubble out of Pricilla's mouth, she smiled. The ones who ordered the stripping of their immortality, who cursed them to die and be reborn were gone.

And that's when she saw *him*. Synick could have escaped with the wall down but instead he stood fifty yards away, staring at her with Sword of Truth in hand. "It was always supposed to come to this moment, Valeen! You, and me, the possessors of the immortal swords!"

Even if the armies of Villhara would overrun the council's fleeing fighters, it wasn't over yet. It wasn't over until Synick was dead and she had the other immortal sword in hand.

Chapter 58

VALEEN

With her goddess blade in hand and her magic flowing out in the form of shadows and vines all around her, she marched for Synick. Soldiers ran past her to chase down the enemy, weapons clashed further down the battlefield, and the elven archers on the wall cheered at the retreat of the invaders.

Synick didn't turn to run. He waited. They both knew this moment was coming and neither of them would back down.

He didn't have his skeleton creatures, and she didn't wait for anyone to help her either. This was one on one.

"It would be a shame for you to finally have everything you want, your immortality, your people, your mate, just for me to end you with this sword," Synick said as she approached.

"It would be, but that's not going to happen." She

swung and their blades hit with a spark. With a hard shove, she knocked him backward into the body of a dead dragon.

Now that she was immortal, she was physically stronger than him. With a downward hack, she went for his head. He dove to the side and her blade cut a streak in the dragon's flesh.

This was retribution. This was his judgment day, and he'd been found guilty.

She swung with the might of all the burning stars.

An ice storm began to swirl around them, tearing at her hair. Shards hit her skin but bounced off. Frost covered her armor but the drop in temperature didn't affect her. She fought back with her vines; they ripped out of the ground thick and strong, breaking up his winter fury.

She swung and he parried, knocking her blade aside, the Sword of Truth sliced through her armor like butter and cut into her lower right rib cage. The pain shocked her for a moment, and she whirled.

Her vine punched out of the ground, aiming straight for his chest. An ice shield formed to block it.

Out of the corner of her eye she spotted Hel moving in and shook her head. *I've got this.*

With a hard swing, she shattered his ice shield and cut off his decayed arm. He stammered backward, and held up the stump, then he gave a deranged smiled. "Doesn't hurt." He charged again.

She ducked under another slash and sidestepped a kick to her bleeding side. They went back and forth striking, magic whirling all around. His black mask fell revealing the decay, showing what he truly was inside.

They hit swords and pushed against each other. Then he made the mistake of puckering his lips, of losing focus to taunt her. She slammed her forehead into his mouth. With a hiss, he stumbled, and she kicked the Sword of Truth from his hand. It flipped end over end until it landed somewhere in the charred grass and amongst the dead.

Zythara hummed, warming her hand. *Let us end him*, it whispered to her.

Another kick to his gut and he backpedaled. She quickly followed with a stab straight to his heart and slowly shoved Zythara through his armor and bones. The crunch was as satisfying as his gasping. He clutched at her blade squirming as it sunk deeper. His mouth opened but nothing came out.

"I will never think of you again," she said. "I will even forget your name, but I'm certain you will never forget me. Say hello to the demon princes for me."

She jerked her sword free and watched him crumble to the ground. It was only moments later that his body decayed, and he was nothing but crusty old skin and bones wrapped in armor.

Over her shoulder she watched the flags of Villhara move toward the woods, chasing the last of the council's forces. The sounds of battle began to fade as the enemy soldiers died or surrendered.

With the Sword of Truth in hand, Hel walked toward her full of pride. "He will not haunt you or your sister anymore."

No, he wouldn't. A sob shook her body, and she slowly sank to her knees. It was done.

Hel dropped before her and wrapped her in his arms. "It's over, love. It's over."

Finally. After two thousand years and dying and being reborn too many times, it had come to an end.

She cried harder.

We are free, Hel said. *And vengeance is ours.*

I wish vengeance didn't have to cost so much. She peered over his shoulder at the death and destruction. The acrid smell of burning bodies and dead made her nauseous. The moaning sounds of those in pain and close to death was all around them.

With a sniffle, she wiped her cheeks with her palms then took his hand. "Let's find Katana, Thane, and the others." She hadn't seen Leif or Piper since Ronan took them during the commotion.

They didn't have to walk far to come upon Thane shuffling through the rubble of the dead. Katana stood next to him with a hand over her mouth, looking across the landscape with moisture lining her eyes.

It was always strange after something like this. There was the thrill of victory. Some of the archers on the wall cheered and celebrated, soldiers on the ground boasted about saving the city while others wondered who the army was that came to save them. Few had started looking amongst the dead or helped the injured.

A hundred yards or so away she spotted Piper, Leif, and Ronan marching toward them and relaxed a little. They were covered in soot and Leif's shoulder still bled but he was up and that meant he would be alright.

Valeen stopped beside her sister and tapped her arm. She whipped toward her and the frown at the corner of Katana's mouth threatened to turn upward. She threw her arms around her and quietly sobbed in Valeen's arms. "I'm so glad you're alright," Katana said softly. "I saw you fighting Synick and wished I could help but I can barely stand right now."

"You did enough. What you did saved us, and you saved Thane." Valeen pulled back and gently patted Katana's cheek. "You are remarkable, Katana. And Synick will no longer be a problem."

"What *we* did, Val." With a smile, Katana wiped the moisture from her cheeks. "Synick was there at the castle, and he persuaded Talon to pull the sword. I tried to stop her, but Thane needed me and I... I left. I left. I let the wall fall. I'm so sorry."

"You did the right thing. Is Tif alright?"

"She hid and Synick couldn't get into the room. I'm sure once Talon pulled Lightbringer free, he left. They must both be safe." With eyes wide with wonder, Katana peeked over her shoulder. "I saw your House of Night flag. How?"

She scanned the horizon for the gods and goddesses that came to their rescue. "I don't really know. I thought they were gone... but I saw Hel's mother and Thane's—well, *War's* father." She found them in the distance rounding up those who surrendered. Hel started helping Thane lift and push bodies, weapons, and armor. "What are they doing?"

Katana frowned. "He's trying to find... Fennan."

"Oh." The pit in her stomach sank. Just as she said that, Piper and Leif came up beside them.

Panting and swiping her brow, Piper asked, "Where's Fennan? He was with Thane."

She doesn't know... Valeen's heart was crushed a little more.

"They're looking for him," Katana said quickly and gave Valeen a sorrowful glance.

"Did he get knocked down by the blast?" Leif asked and immediately ran toward Thane to help. They must have had their back to him when he was stabbed through the chest. Piper stared at Valeen, searching her face.

Sorrow welled up in Valeen, gripping her throat. She pursed her lips and couldn't find her voice.

"Valeen, is he alright?" She took a step forward and grabbed hold of the collar of Valeen's armor. Her arm was trembling and her chin quivered. "Tell me he's alright." She glanced at Katana. "You didn't hurt him in the blast, did you?"

Katana quickly shook her head. "No."

Letting out a slow breath, Valeen said, "He didn't survive the battle, Piper."

Piper jerked her hand back as if Valeen had hit her. "No." She shoved her fingers into her hair and gripped it. "No. He's alive. I know he is."

Ronan put a hand on her shoulder, and she slapped it away. Her armor clanked with each step as she ran toward where Thane, Hel, and Leif were now gathered. Valeen caught up just as Piper pushed Leif and Thane aside and dropped to her knees. The horrified scream that rent the air sliced right into Valeen's heart.

"Wake up! Please, wake up!" She started shaking Fennan's lifeless body, and it took both Leif and Thane to pull her away. "I'm sorry. I'm so sorry I didn't mean what I said. I want you in my life."

Thane held her from behind while Leif took her flailing arms. "He's gone, Piper," Thane said, softly. "He's gone. You have to let him go."

"No, he has to come back. Come back to us, *please*! We need you—*I* need you."

NIGHT MEETS THE ELF QUEEN

"Piper, he knows you loved him." Leif's face twisted in sorrow.

She sagged in Thane's hold and gasped for air through her sobs. Valeen had to look away and found Hel. Even he was somber. There was a glimmer in his eye as he watched Piper.

Fennan's face merely looked like he was asleep. He must have been underneath others during the blast and been spared the burn. But the sword he'd been stabbed with still protruded from his chest.

The captain of the Ravens would long be remembered for his bravery, not only today but in many battles. Already others in Raven black were gathering, whispering Fennan's name. He died protecting his High King.

Ronan took Piper from Thane. She curled her arms around his neck, and he lifted her into his arms. "Come on, let's get you back to the castle." His dragon wings materialized. "Will you find Dax's body and make sure my father takes him? Dragons do not burn so his body will need to be taken north to be buried along with everyone else."

"I'll take care of it," Thane said.

With a frown, he nodded his thanks and carried Piper away.

A pair of elves brought over a stretcher. Thane and Leif put his body onto it. With a gentle hand, Thane pulled the sword from Fennan's body. This was the second close childhood friend Thane had lost to battle. But he didn't cry or scream, he placed a hand on Fennan's chest. "I will miss you, my friend. You are the bravest elf I know. You have been with me since we were boys, my best friend. I wish it didn't have to be this way, but you helped save Palenor, and I am proud of you. I always will be. I will never forget you."

Leif bent over and kissed his forehead. "You were a hero today, Fen. You saved my life and your king's. Already my life is worse without you in it. Go in peace, friend."

A rainbow appeared in the sky above Castle Dredwich. It arched beautifully across the Valley of the Sun as the pair of Ravens carried their captain back toward home. The sun shined brightly off the golden rooftops, lighting up the city. Every elf in their path dropped to a knee and bowed their head as he was carried away. It was a beautiful display of how much they respected and loved him.

Katana went to Thane and wrapped him in a hug again. He held her tightly to his chest and closed his eyes. It was wonderful to see they both had someone to love and comfort in hard times even if it didn't take away the pain of loss, it helped with the sting.

The four gods and goddesses who came to their rescue rode up beside them. Marching in a line behind them were the surrendered enemy soldiers with their hands bound behind their backs and warriors from Villhara guiding them in the direction of the portal in the unnamed forest.

Zaelia, Hel's mother, was the first to dismount. And the others followed. It was.... shocking to see them all here.

Firstly, she thought Hel's mother was trapped in the underrealm, and she hadn't seen the others in thousands of years. Thane's—or War's father, rather—hadn't helped them when the council sentenced them to die the first time; no one did. Era never involved himself in any conflicts. Elora was the only one of them that had previously aided them. She was the goddess who helped Hel get more powerful, and the same one who told Valeen how to wake him.

Zaelia stared at Hel more in surprise than in a loving way. As a mother who hadn't seen her child in so long, she supposed it would be surreal. "Zaurahel," she said softly as if his name was a prayer. Her gaze shifted to Thane. "And War. I am so happy to see you both."

"What are you all doing here?" Valeen blurted out. They all looked amongst each other. "I am eternally grateful, but I just don't understand. Where did our people come from? House of Night was destroyed."

"It was destroyed long ago." Elora nodded. It was strange seeing her now knowing who she truly was. This was the goddess who'd taught the primordials how to write and had opened the portals to the other worlds. She was there with Valeen and Katana at the beginning. "And it's a tragedy we shouldn't have allowed. Hel and War are also my blood." Elora's reddish-gold locks waved all around her. She patted her gray horse's neck. "I stood by last time and let this happen. I swore I wouldn't do it again. It was my daughter's idea to gather all that was left of your people. Many of them were under our care and we never let them forget."

"Well, thank you," Thane interjected. "One day we will repay you for this. You saved my people."

"You consider yourself an elf now?" Balneir looked confused. The twins had the same black hair and blue-green eyes against soft ivory skin.

"It is what I am, Father."

Balneir smiled. "Well, you're always my son and are welcome to come home to Runevale whenever you wish. I regret I couldn't do more to help you and Zaurahel sooner. With the portals closed, I was limited." He smiled at Hel now. "How is my nephew?"

"I am glad this is over." He walked over to Valeen's side and put his arm around her shoulder. "Thank you all for finding our people and bringing them here today. We would have lost otherwise."

Era hadn't taken his gaze off Hel since they'd stopped beside them. There was a curious look on his face as he inspected him, but he finally tore his eyes from him. "Katana, is it truly you? I did see you in a vision, but it didn't seem possible."

She beamed at him. "It is, Era. It's wonderful to see you. Thank you for helping us."

Hel cleared his throat. "I'm glad to see that you're not actually in the underrealm, Zaelia."

With pinched brows, Zaelia looked confused. "You know I was in the underrealm? It was long ago... how could you know that?"

"I had the unfortunate opportunity to go there recently—it's a story for another time. The demon said you'd traded yourself... for me."

She pursed her lips and glanced at Era. "I did once. Five hundred years in the underrealm was the price to set you free, which I agreed to. But thankfully Era was able to get me out in half the time."

Everyone was quiet for a moment. The things she must have gone through and seen... Hel rubbed the back of his neck. "You spent two hundred and fifty years in the underrealm? Because I was stupid and went there?"

With a deep inhale, she lifted her chin. "Even if I didn't raise you, I love you as a mother does. And yes, I did, and I would do it again for you. But once I got out, I wasn't myself for a long time."

"It took many years to recover her mind," Era added. "Or she would have wanted to be in your life sooner. You were already gone by the time she was ready."

"I know I wasn't a mother to you, and you don't owe me anything. I found myself scared and pregnant with someone I had only been with once at a party. Nothing was ever supposed to come of it... I regret to this day that I left you with my brother, even if he was good to you. I hope one day you can forgive me. And I don't need an answer here and now. I just want you to know I'd like to be in your life."

Hel ran his hand through his hair, breathed deeply and said nothing. She felt the unease coming off him. Like he wanted to be grateful but also didn't trust her.

"Who is Hel's father?" Valeen asked. If it was a brief encounter with a male at a party, and she did that sort of thing often, it was possible she didn't know.

She glanced at Era once again.

"I'm your father, Zaurahel." Era's voice was soft for how large of a male he was. At first glance they looked nothing alike. Era had short, wavy auburn hair and tanned, freckled skin. He had a wide jaw and thinner lips, but upon inspecting him closer, Valeen did see the resemblance; they had the same nose and eye shape, although in coloring and most other features Hel looked like his mother and uncle. "And like your mother said, you don't owe us anything, but we did owe you. The council is finished. The primordials will take back rule on Runevale, as we should have done long ago."

With his brows raised, Hel swallowed hard. He took hold of her hand and squeezed it. *My father is not a demon prince after all.*

Out of all their discussions of who they guessed his father was, Era was never a choice. They suspected it was someone powerful, given his gifts, but not Era. Valeen knew him; he was soft-spoken, quiet, kept to himself, and didn't like fighting or conflict. They were such polar opposites in personality, she never would have surmised. It was also strange that he'd never claimed him as his son before this. The gods, Era included, liked to have powerful children, and Hel was likely the strongest of all his heirs. Which made her suspect Zaelia hadn't told him for many years.

One day they would learn her story.

The sweet smell of his civar smoke drifted on the air. She looked up at him, his face was unreadable, something torn between relief and sadness. Dried blood was smattered across his cheek. He held the civar between his lips and let smoke roll out.

Seeing his estranged family and learning his father was Era was a lot to take in any time, but especially after a long battle.

Are you going to say anything?

Hel lifted a shoulder. *I don't know what to say. Nice to meet you, daddy, even if you haven't cared about my existence until now? He put a seed in my mother, nothing more.*

Thank the All mother they can't read minds. It was a typical Hel response, but warranted, nonetheless.

I'd say it out loud, but frankly, I'm tired and I'm not in the mood for bickering.

"Well, once things are settled, I'm sure we'll see you both more." Valeen leaned into Hel. "We'll invite you over once our home is rebuilt. All of you."

"We would like to help you rebuild." Zaelia glanced between the others, and they all nodded in agreement.

"Thank you."

Elora glanced over her shoulder. "The territory of House of Night and House of Magic are yours. No one will stand against you. Many of your people are eager to return to their old land."

"I will bring them home, once we help Thane here. This will take time to clean, and there are families who need to be told their sons are gone."

Hand in hand Valeen and Hel strode forward. They spent hours talking to the people who saved them. Helping to gather the dead while learning stories of where the people of Villhara had been. Some of them were descendants of those who'd lived in House of Night, but their parents told them stories. Others had lived in the time Valeen and Hel ruled; the undying waters of Runevale extended the lives of mortals. The excitement to go back and rebuild their land was clear in their bright eyes and smiles.

Many volunteered to stay and help the elves and dragons of the north clear the bodies, and the flames of the funeral pyres rose into the night sky.

King Drake Drakonan stayed to honor the fallen. He'd lost over a hundred dragons to the battle. One of them Valeen would never forget. She'd placed a midnight lily on Dax's chest and closed his hands over its stem. He was lined up with the others, ready to be taken home to the north and laid to rest.

There were tears of sorrow and joy. Songs of lament

and gratitude drifted throughout the city. People gathered around the battlefield with candles lit for those who'd passed. Even those from Villhara held candles for the dragons and elves who died. It was wonderous seeing her two worlds collide.

Six Weeks Later

Valeen stood in her chariot at the crest of the Valley of the Sun's hill overlooking the city. Starborn and Night grazed while they waited for her command. The sky was stained a bright salmon with the sun rising. White puffy clouds formed in the background behind Castle Dredwich. Palenor's flag waved in the breeze at its peak.

The once blackened and burned battlefield where freedom was won, was already green again with wildflowers blooming across it. Along the road people had planted trees in memory of those lost. A twenty-foot-tall statue of a regal dragon with its wings wide was being carved to be placed on the left side entrance in the wall. The stonemasons worked on another beside it, as tall as the dragon was an elf warrior in Raven armor—Fennan.

Her heart ached at the memories of this place. The good and the bad. It would always be a part of her.

But her time here had come to an end.

Hel sat on Midnight with Thane beside him on Phantom. They looked more alike than ever on their twin mounts and both wearing casual black attire. It was really Thane's lighter long hair that set them apart.

Katana had her own horse now, a beautiful dappled gray mare with a flowing white mane she'd named Calipso.

"We won because of you, Katana," Valeen said, pulling her gaze from the old battlegrounds.

"Oh, stop that. We won because of *you* and your people coming from Runevale."

Hel patted Midnight's neck. "Please, don't try to give me the glory, I'd be too humble to accept."

Valeen laughed. "Yes, Mr. Humble."

To her surprise, Piper trotted up on horseback with Ronan and Leif beside her. "So are we doing this?" Piper pulled back on the reins and grinned. Her horse whinnied as if feeling her excitement.

"I thought you two were going to Ryvengaard." Valeen couldn't hold back her grin. It was where Ronan's parents and many of the dragons had gone a couple weeks before. Prince Yoren stayed here in Adalon to guard their estate for now.

"At the moment my father and I aren't getting along so Piper and I decided to come with you for a while," Ronan said with a shrug. "You'll need some dragon muscle to rebuild a castle."

"And you need your best friend and bodyguard," Piper said. At least she was back to best-friend status.

The sound of whooshing wings drew her eyes to the sky. Presco dropped in from above in his half-shifted form with a black bag slung over his shoulder. He tucked his wings, but the tips rose well over his head. "Am I late?"

"Right on time." Valeen smiled at him. "And dragon muscle is always appreciated, Ronan."

Piper looked to Hel. "Remember when you offered to give me magic to be a better bodyguard for her?"

He chuckled. "Yeah, Red but she doesn't really need one anymore."

"Well, you never know. And I want to learn magic. What else am I going to do now that there are no pale ones to fight."

"If you start offering magic to the elves again, there may end up being pale ones once more," Valeen said and that was the last thing anyone wanted.

"No there won't because I will destroy that mate spell." Hel shifted in his saddle. "That's the one that started it."

"Do you want to learn potions, Piper? I could use an apprentice," Presco offered. "I'll need help with my new shop as well." Bottles clinked in his bag as he walked closer.

Her freckled smile broadened. "I would love that actually. I can't wait to start."

"I don't need a job. I'm just looking forward to seeing the beautiful goddesses and nymphs," Leif said, wiggling his brows. "Maybe I'll get at least a half goddess to fall for me. Fightbringer, you can vouch for me, right?"

Everyone laughed.

"I will certainly vouch for you, Leif," Valeen answered. "I shall introduce you as the mighty elf warrior, Leif, the goddess of night's favorite Raven."

"Oh, I like that," Leif slapped his leg and laughed.

"Hey, you can't pick a favorite Raven!" Piper scowled. "If you had one it should be me."

"It's just to help with the ladies, Pipe," Leif added.

"Thane's actually my favorite Raven," Valeen said with a wink.

"He doesn't count," Piper said.

All this talk of favorites is making me a little jealous, love.

Valeen laughed. *You are my number one, Hel.*

"Of course I count. I am the reason the Ravens exist," Thane said, smirking. "Are we missing anyone else?"

"Just one," Valeen answered.

Tif popped out of Hel's leather saddle bag, shoving the flap against Midnight. "Because I'm in here." She raised her hand. "Otherwise, we'd be missing two. Wherever my lady Queen goes, I go."

"Of course you do, Tif."

On a chestnut horse Aunt Evalyn rode up the hillside along the trail from the city.

Leif leaned over toward Thane and said, "I hope she packed some of that good whisky."

Cursing under her breath and wearing a broad-brimmed straw hat, and a colorful shall, Aunt Evalyn stopped her mount. "I'm really not meant for the wilderness and tent living. Are you sure you can't just come get me when the castle is done?"

Valeen laughed and shook her head. "No, I want you with me. Besides, we'll be staying in a few small cottages near the grounds. Some of the rebuilding has already begun thanks to Hel's mother."

She adjusted her hat and grumbled. "Fine, if you insist, but I'm opening a Nerium Oleander in this new place as soon as possible."

"I wouldn't expect any different from an old gambler."

Katana cleared her throat. "Now that everyone is here, I have an announcement." She pulled off her tan gloves and held up her left hand where a rose-gold diamond ring sparkled. "We have another wedding to plan!" She giggled and turned her hand so everyone could see it.

Her heart jumped in excitement. "When did this happen?"

"Last night!" she squealed.

"We plan to have the wedding next spring here in Palenor," Thane beamed. "We want to help you and Hel first, and I promised to take her traveling a few places."

"And it takes time to plan an event like this. I'm not like you, Val, no offense." She smiled at her. "I want the whole kingdom there."

Hel reached over and playfully shook Thane's shoulder. "Congratulations, brother." Everyone else followed to congratulate them. A spring wedding in Palenor would be beautiful. All the flowers and trees would be in bloom.

"I'm so happy for you both." Valeen made sure she held Thane's gaze when she said it. It wasn't long ago they talked in his bedroom about him finding his wife. *She better be damn near perfect*, Valeen had told him.

She was. More perfect than either of them could have imagined then.

NIGHT MEETS THE ELF QUEEN

Under a glittering colorful night sky, Valeen rode with Katana on her left and Hel on her right. Thane smiled at her from Katana's other side. Tif hung on Valeen's shoulder and kicked her little boots.

There was a wonder in Aunt Evalyn's face Valeen hadn't seen since she was young. Leif offered Aunt Evalyn a round silver flask. With a sly grin she took it, and they snickered together before taking sips.

There were tears in Presco's eyes as they made their way up the grassy knoll. It was his home too. And soon he'd bring his wife and children.

They rode across the green grass guided by the stars to the place below the constellation of the rearing horse Sargentos. The craggy black rocks came into view, and they stopped at the crest of the hill, looking over the old ruins of Valeen's castle.

This time seeing it didn't bring pain or sorrow. It didn't rip the air from her lungs.

It brought hope. A new beginning.

On the far hill toward the sea, a town was already being set up. Structures and frames of homes were being worked on. Small farms with wood fences dappled the area. Sheep bleated and cows mooed in the distance. It was going to be perfect.

"I can't wait to help you set up the gardens!" Katana practically squealed.

"Will I have my own room?" Tif asked, and climbed down Valeen. "I want a little nook with a tiny bed and a tiny door only I can fit through. And maybe another tiny bed for Tommy when he visits."

"You can have whatever you want." Valeen smiled. She pointed at the horizon. "Near the sea we will rebuild the magnificent city of Vesper. Presco's Potions will do nicely there with the ports as well."

Presco grinned. "It will."

People were already clearing the debris and the wilds that had taken over the ruins. What was salvageable from the rubble of the old moonstone was being stacked and cleaned.

On the far side of the castle, the row of six cottages with straw roofs and round front doors, made her laugh. They looked almost just like her home in Briar Hollow. She told Hel's mother Zaelia about it but didn't think she'd take it so literal when she asked her to prepare them a temporary place to stay.

The quaint white shutters were a nice touch too.

"Those look familiar," Aunt Evalyn said with a chuckle. "I like it already."

"It will do for now, but my queen deserves her throne." With a wave of Hel's hand, the rough black rocks near their feet began to roll and form into a high-backed chair with armrests and a smoothed-out seat.

He took her hand and guided her over to it. With tears blurring her vision, she sat and looked out over her land, her home. The stars and colorful waves in the sky seemed brighter than ever.

Suddenly her breath whooshed out. The broken silver moon Fennor slowly started to reform. While the sister moons Nuna and Luna shined with pride.

When she looked back at her friends—her family, Tif was the first to bow. Then Piper and Leif, followed by Thane and Katana, and Presco and Ronan. Finally, Hel inclined his head.

She almost broke down sobbing but sniffled and said softly, "Thank you."

It was a bliss she couldn't have even imagined, knowing all was as it should be, knowing they would never be hunted again. The people she loved were all finally safe.

The best part was that she'd have her soulmate, her husband that she loved so deeply at her side. There was a light in his eyes now. There was no reason for him to be consumed with vengeance and hatred. He smiled with joy that made him all the more beautiful.

She stood and pushed him onto the throne and sat on his lap. It was *their* land, their throne. He had fought harder than anyone to make this happen.

His hands threaded into her hair and he kissed her hard on the mouth. "Now I get to love you forever," Hel said tenderly.

"Forever."

Epilogue

The moonlight shone brightly through the glass dome at the center of the ballroom. The night sky sparkled with stars, and waves of greens, blues, and purples. Ball gowns swished and soft string music played. Vines of jasmine wrapped around the white pillars lining her new throne room.

Scarlet velvet curtains draped around the tall arched windows. A three-tiered golden fountain with red wine pouring over the sides waited off to the side. Tif was already there sipping on something she wasn't supposed to. Her little brown boots stuck out from under the white tablecloth, and her unique shadow with her red hat, round belly, wild curls, and a tea-length dress was outlined against it from inside.

Valeen laughed quietly to herself and searched among the crowd of dancers, a mixture of races from every realm, shifters of all kinds, elves, demigods, even humans.

Thane and Katana danced together. Of course, her sister wore the most beautiful golden ballgown and proved she was still the loveliest of all the goddesses.

Thane leaned down to her ear, and she threw her head back laughing. They were exquisite together.

Presco spun his wife Ayva in a circle and dipped her back. They'd moved *Presco's Potions* to Villhara, and it was thriving just as well as it had in Ryvengaard. Several of their guests had brilliantly colorful hair.

Near the drink tables Leif was sweet-talking a half-elf, half-goddess named Vivielle. He certainly had a thing for the redheads, and hers was as deep as a crimson rose.

Piper was playing some sort of drinking game with Ronan in the corner. They'd made House of Night their home the last seven years, but Ronan was itching for more. For land in Ryvengaard with the dragons he believed he was entitled to but would have to fight for. Piper pointed at him and pushed a shot glass into his hand. "You lost, drink it!"

"If you want to take advantage of me, it doesn't require alcohol." He winked at her and downed it.

Hel's mother and father were in attendance tonight as well. Even though they were all cordial, Hel was still not close to them. He cared enough to let them around and invite them to parties but there was still a part of him that just couldn't understand why they abandoned him.

It gave him some peace to know them though and know where he came from. But Zaelia was trying to make up for lost time and frequently visited. Valeen enjoyed her mother-in-law's company. Unlike Orlandia, she was kind and wanted to help where she could, funny too.

But where is Hel? This was *his* party really. He called it the Day of Reckoning. Tonight was the seventh anniversary of the day they became immortals again and defeated the council. It was a time of celebration, but it still reminded her of all the hurt and pain that came before.

Even if they were immortal now, she still woke up covered in sweat some nights, reaching for him to make sure he was there. There were moments she simply laid her head against his bare chest to listen to his heartbeat.

A wisp of cool air curled along the back of her neck, then warm hands closed around her waist. She smiled as he pulled her into the crowd of dancers. "Hello, love. How are you tonight?" He moved right into the steps with the other dancers, not missing a beat.

"I'm better now."

"You looked lost without me."

She traced one of the runes on his neck with her fingertip and smiled at the goosebumps that rose. "I would be lost without you."

"You don't have to worry about that, love. Didn't I do everything I promised?" His blue-green eyes sparkled in the starlight. "Or is there more?"

"You kept your promises, Hel." He always did. He'd given her revenge, immortality, his undying love. She peeked out the window at the beautiful garden she'd asked for. It was Katana's favorite place when she visited. They danced in the castle he said he would rebuild, and of course he'd found her winged horses Starborn and Night. Her throne wasn't made out of bones of their enemies, but she loved the shiny onyx stone.

"Then why do you look sad tonight? I don't like it."

She smiled at his hand on her low back pulling her

closer. "I'm not. I have everything I want. It's just," she blew out a slow breath, "sometimes I worry that you'll get bored with this peace. I mean, you *are* the god of mischief."

He laughed and spun her in a circle. Once he pulled her back in, he pressed her against him. "Mischief doesn't require war, love." In a few quick strides he whisked her over to the twin thrones. Once he was seated, he patted his lap, and she smiled as she sat. One arm circled around her waist and with the other hand he rubbed her back.

"Thane is the god of war, even if he says he is happy, even if he is High *Elf* King, he will crave it. I heard him talking to Ronan about war on Ryvengaard between the dragons. Prince Ronan wants to be *King* Ronan. And the Drakonans from Adalon aren't getting along with the Drakonans on Ryvengaard."

"You are worrying over nothing, Val." He smirked, revealing his dimple. "Or is it you that is bored? Do you want to go conquer a realm? We have both the immortal weapons, who would stand against us?"

Rolling her eyes, she shook her head. "It was agreed by the primordials that we could keep them because we *vowed* not to use them ever again."

"*You* vowed." He smirked. "We don't need them anyway. I will name these conquered lands after you."

She giggled and ran her hand through his hair. "You are terrible, Zaurahel."

"I am happy. I love you, and life with you is all I want. If Thane drags me into a war on Ryvengaard—"

"He is *not* immortal. He can't do the same things he did before."

"We're working on that." He nodded at something

across the room. "Besides, those two keep me plenty busy for now."

She twisted out of his grasp and smiled. Aunt Evalyn held the hands of two beautiful raven-haired children. With wide blue eyes, Sadira looked around the room. Aramis was wiggling to break free from Evalyn's hold.

"A boy and a girl, just like you wanted," Hel whispered against her ear. "Or do you want more?"

Their twins were five already. She couldn't believe how quickly time had passed. Sadira had a soft voice and was well-mannered until she was upset, then her fiery temper came out. She was showing signs of magic by making her toys float around her room, but they didn't know her specific affinity yet. Like her father, she had an ivory complexion, full pink lips and straight black hair that she liked to braid herself. She also loved to remind her brother she was technically the oldest of them.

Aramis was rambunctious, always on the move and liked to torment everyone by finding toads and small critters to hide in various places. His magic wasn't apparent yet, but he could already read books well beyond his age, books most children didn't read until they were in their teen years. With a splash of freckles across his nose and bright blue-green eyes against an olive-toned complexion, he was a good mix of his parents. His little cherub cheeks were perfectly kissable too.

"Two is perfect for me. Why, do you?"

"I'm exhausted just thinking about more." Hel chuckled. "Aramis is too much like his mother, wild and always getting into trouble."

NIGHT MEETS THE ELF QUEEN

Another eye roll was warranted. "You mean, he's exactly like you." Next to Sadira was their cousin, Alwyn, only three months younger than the twins. Her golden curls tumbled to her low back, and she had bright emerald-green eyes. She held the bottom hem of her dress and twirled in place. A dancer like her mother. "Evalyn spoils them. They're supposed to be asleep by now. She certainly didn't spoil me."

"She's older now. Let her spoil them a little. It makes her happy." He waved for them to come.

Aramis broke free first and ran at him giggling. Sadira's light-blue dress swished with each step. She stumbled on the hem of it, stopped, lifted it, and continued.

They quickly climbed the armrest and Sadira leaned forward and rubbed her nose against Hel's. It was their usual greeting and was the most precious thing she'd ever seen. Hel looked good as a father. The day the twins were born changed him. He joked that his black heart was now split three ways. It was funny sometimes to see this male who could be so ruthless, who would take life without remorse, covered in tattoos with a filthy mouth, and yet be so gentle and kind to their children.

Aramis stood on the armrest next to her and jumped onto her lap. "Mama!" He touched the tip of his little pointed ears poking out of his wavy, shaggy hair then hers. "How come Alwyn doesn't have ears like us? But Reed has ears like ours?"

"Well because she is only half elf."

"So is Reed. That's her brother."

Valeen chuckled. "She just has ears like Aunty Kat and Reed has ears more like Uncle Thane." When he first started talking, he couldn't say "Katana" without fumbling through the syllables and had settled on "Kat."

"But Aunt Kat is a goddess and so are you."

"Your mother is an elf *and* goddess," Hel said. "One day we will tell you the story."

Katana scooped Alwyn into her arms and carried her over with Thane right behind them. "The little gremlins snuck out of their beds," Katana teased.

"When is Reed going to be big enough to play sword fight?" Aramis pushed out his lower lip. "I hate playing with dolls and that's all the girls want to do."

"No, we play more than just dolls!" Alwyn crowed and stuck out her tongue.

"Don't do that, it's bad manners." Katana tapped her nose lightly. "Reed will play swords in a couple years, sweet boy. Be patient."

"Don't you play swords with Darrio? He's your age," Thane said, folding his arms. Piper and Ronan's son was over nearly every weekend.

Aramis folded his arms too. "He has wings, it's not fair. Even dad has wings. I want wings."

Hel laughed. "Maybe for your birthday."

Sadira grinned and clapped. "If he gets wings, I want them too!"

"Me too!" Alwyn squealed.

Thane nudged Hel's side. "You're on flying lessons then."

"Where's Tiffy? I want Tiffy. She's so squishy. I like to squeeze her." Sadira looked about the room. And as if on command Tif wandered up the steps of the dais.

"The cupcakes are phenomenal." Tif grinned with chocolate still smeared around her mouth. Sadira flew

NIGHT MEETS THE ELF QUEEN

at her, swooped her up and squeezed her so hard Tif's face turned bright red. "Can't breathe."

"For the last time, she's not a doll," Valeen said. "Be gentle!"

"Oh, sorry." Sadira set her down and then patted the top of Tif's hat.

Aunt Evalyn approached with a glass of wine. She had more energy here and even the gray in her hair had lessened. The undying waters of Runevale would give her a much longer life. "Sorry, I know I was on kid duty tonight, but Aramis was practically climbing the walls because he was so eager to see the party. Thankfully Reed and Darrio fell asleep. Darrio's nursemaid is with them."

"It's fine. Thank you for watching them tonight."

Thane took out his sword and Aramis's eyes lit up. "Who better to play sword fight with than your Uncle Thane."

Aramis jumped off her and took out his small wooden sword. "Yay!"

Sadira climbed onto Valeen's lap and started braiding a lock of her mother's hair. "Let's dance, mama."

"Alright, my love." She lifted Sadira on her hip and twirled to the music. Her little giggle filled Valeen with joy. Life was perfect.

Hours later, Valeen laid her head on Hel's chest. The crickets chirped outside the window and a cool breeze fluttered the curtains. The castle was quiet with everyone asleep in their rooms. She traced the lily tattoo on his chest while he played with her hair. Her skin tingled with his touch, that hadn't changed. She truly had everything she wanted, and it was even sweeter after how hard they had to fight to get it. "I love you, Zaurahel."

Lightly grabbing her chin, he lifted her face to his and kissed her. "I love you." She smiled and pulled back. With a low growl, he tugged on a lock of her hair and dragged her in. "Come back here. I want more. I will always want more."

The End

Acknowledgments

I must give a special thank you to Jessica Boaden, my story consultant, editor, PA, meme sharing Aussie friend I've never met in person but chat with all the time. This book was a challenge (a hot mess really) but you were there to help me make this ending great! You stuck through all the rewrites and never gave up on me! You're the best! This series wouldn't be what it is if you were here through each installment! You've been with me through so many of my books, and I love working with you on each and every book, and I appreciate how invested you get in the story and each character! Your comments make me laugh, give me a confidence boost, and also give great constructive criticism. Thank you!

Another special thanks to Brittany O'Barr, my sister! You've been with me since day one of writing books all those years ago and spend hours with every book I write, even with a new baby your pulled through to help with this one! You always take the time to talk with me and helping me work through plot issues, and brainstorm ideas. You give phenomenal feedback and I appreciate it. You're an amazing sister and great beta reader, and helped me make this book the best it could be! Thank you so much for being invested and helpful!

Thank you Tiffany Boland! Your excitement for this

series, great feedback and good eye for details is so helpful! I've loved working with you on the Elf Queen series. It's been such a joy, and you've been a great help in making this story what it is. It means a lot to me to have you read the books and love them like me! I was so happy to have you help on this last book in the Elf Queen series and make the ending even better!

Thank you Kathryn for being an early reader and joining in for the beta read! I appreciate your feedback and hyping up this series!

Thank you very much Charity Chimni, my amazing proofreader and assistant! I couldn't do this without you. You find errors that always surprise me and are a great help with all my book launches! I appreciate all the work you do with me and thank you so much for sticking with me all these years! You're always quick even with these long books and help in a pinch!

Thank you to my family for believing in me all these years. Thank you to my husband for being so supportive and taking care of our kiddos for hours each day so I am able to write and do what I love.

Thank you to all the readers who love my books, my characters, and help spread the word about this series. You've helped make my dreams come true! The Elf Queen has a special place in my heart and so do all of you!

About the Author

J.M. Kearl is a fantasy romance author. She writes feisty heroines to love and hunky heroes to fall in love with. She's also a mother of two and happily married to the love of her life. She lives in Idaho but is usually dreaming of somewhere tropical.

Sign up for J.M. Kearl's Newsletter: http://jmkearl.com/newsletter